Also available

THE MAMMOTH BOOK OF

VAMPIRES

Edited by
Stephen Jones

CARROLL & GRAF PUBLISHERS
New York

In memory of
Ronald Chetwynd-Hayes
(1919–2001)
a true gentleman and a
vampire's best friend

Carroll & Graf Publishers
An imprint of Avalon Publishing Group, Inc.
245 W. 17th Street
NY 10011–5300
www.carrollandgraf.com

First published in the UK by Robinson Publishing Ltd 1992

This revised edition by Carroll & Graf 2004

Special thanks to Hugh Lamb, Nick Austin, Val and
Les Edwards and Randy Broeckner for all their help
and support.

ISBN 0-7867-1372-0

Printed and bound in the EU

CONTENTS

ACKNOWLEDGMENTS

INTRODUCTION: THE CHILDREN OF THE NIGHT copyright © Stephen Jones 1992, 2004.

HUMAN REMAINS copyright © Clive Barker 1984. Originally published in *Books of Blood Volume 3*. Reprinted by permission of Sphere Books.

NECROS copyright © Brian Lumley 1986. Originally published in *The Second Book of After Midnight Stories*. Reprinted by permission of the author and the author's agent, The Dorian Literary Agency.

THE MAN WHO LOVED THE VAMPIRE LADY copyright © 1988 by Brian Stableford. Originally published in *The Magazine of Fantasy & Science Fiction*, August 1988. Reprinted by permission of the author.

A PLACE TO STAY copyright © Michael Marshall Smith 1998. Originally published in *Dark Terrors 4: The Gollancz Book of Horror*. Reprinted by permission of the author.

THE BROOD copyright © Ramsey Campbell 1980. Originally published in *Dark Forces*. Reprinted by permission of the author.

ROOT CELLAR copyright © Nancy Kilpatrick 1991. Originally published in *Vampire's Crypt* No.4, 1991. Reprinted by permission of the author.

HUNGARIAN RHAPSODY copyright © Ziff-Davis Publishing Co. 1958. Originally published in *Fantastic*, June 1958. Reprinted by permission of the author and the author's estate.

THE LEGEND OF DRACULA RECONSIDERED AS A PRIME-TIME TV SPECIAL copyright © Christopher Fowler 1992. Originally published in *Sharper Knives*. Reprinted by permission of the author.

VAMPIRE copyright © Richard Christian Matheson 1986. Originally published in *Cutting Edge*. Reprinted by permission of the author.

STRAGELLA copyright © The Clayton Magazines, Incorporated. Originally published in *Strange Tales*, June 1932. Reprinted by permission of the author.

A WEEK IN THE UNLIFE copyright © David J. Schow 1991. Originally published in *A Whisper of Blood*. Reprinted by permission of the author.

THE HOUSE AT EVENING copyright © Stuart David Schiff 1982. Originally published in *Whispers* No.15–16, March 1982. Reprinted by permission of the author and the author's estate.

VAMPYRRHIC OUTCAST copyright © Simon Clark 2003. Originally published on *Nailed by the Heart*, 17–31 July, 2003. Reprinted by permission of the author.

THE LABYRINTH copyright © Ronald Chetwynd-Hayes 1974. Originally published in *The Elemental*. Reprinted by permission of the author and the author's estate.

BEYOND ANY MEASURE copyright © Stuart David Schiff 1982. Originally published in *Whispers* No.15-16, March 1982. Reprinted by permission of the author and the author's estate.

DOCTOR PORTHOS copyright © Basil Copper 1968. Originally published in *The Midnight People*. Reprinted by permission of the author.

STRAIGHT TO HELL copyright © Paul McAuley 2000. Originally published in *The Third Alternative* Issue 24, 2000. Reprinted by permission of the author.

IT ONLY COMES OUT AT NIGHT copyright © Kirby McCauley 1976. Originally published in *Frights*. Copyright Dennis Etchison 1982. Reprinted by permission of the author.

INVESTIGATING JERICHO copyright © Chelsea Quinn Yarbro 1992. Originally published in *The Magazine of Fantasy & Science Fiction*, April 1992. Reprinted by permission of the author.

DRACULA'S CHAIR copyright © Peter Tremayne 1979. Originally published in *The Count Dracula Fan Club Book of Vampires*. Reprinted by permission of the author.

A TASTE FOR BLOOD copyright © Sydney J. Bounds 2004.

THE BETTER HALF copyright © Melanie Tem 1989. Originally published in *Isaac Asimov's Science Fiction Magazine*, mid-December 1989. Reprinted by permission of the author.

THE DEVIL'S TRITONE copyright © John Burke 2004.

CHASTEL copyright © Manly Wade Wellman 1979. Originally published in *The Year's Best Horror Stories: Series VII*. Reprinted by permission of the author and the author's estate.

DER UNTERGANG DES ABENDLANDESMENSCHEN copyright © Howard Waldrop 1976. Originally published in *Chacal* No.1, Winter 1976. Reprinted by permission of the author.

RED AS BLOOD copyright © Tanith Lee 1979. Originally published in *The Magazine of Fantasy & Science Fiction*, July 1979. Reprinted by permission of the author.

LAIRD OF DUNAIN copyright © Graham Masterton 1992.

A TRICK OF THE DARK copyright © Tina Rath 2004.

MIDNIGHT MASS copyright © F. Paul Wilson 1990. Originally published in *Midnight Mass*. Reprinted by permission of the author.

BLOOD GOTHIC copyright © Nancy Jones Holder 1985. Originally published in *Shadows 8*. Reprinted by permission of the author.

YELLOW FOG copyright © Les Daniels 1986. Originally published in *Yellow Fog*. Reprinted by permission of the author.

FIFTEEN CARDS FROM A VAMPIRE TAROT copyright © Neil Gaiman 1998. Originally published under the title 'Fifteen Painted Cards from a Vampire Tarot' in *The Art of Vampire: The Masquerade*. Reprinted by permission of the author.

VINTAGE DOMESTIC copyright © Steve Rasnic Tem 1992.

TRY A DULL KNIFE copyright © Harlan Ellison ® 1968. Renewed © The Kilimanjaro Corporation 1996. Originally published in *The Magazine of Fantasy & Science Fiction*, October 1968. Reprinted by arrangement with, and permission of, the author and the author's agent, Richard Curtis Associates, New York, USA. All rights reserved. Harlan Ellison is a registered trademark of The Kilimanjaro Corporation.

ANDY WARHOL'S DRACULA: ANNO DRACULA 1978-79 copyright © Kim Newman 1999. Originally published in *Andy Warhol's Dracula*. Reprinted by permission of the author.

INTRODUCTION

The Children of the Night

THE UNDEAD ... Nosferatu ... Children of the Night ... Call them what you will, what they all have in common is a need to suck the life-force from the living to prolong their own unnatural existence and propagate. For the classic vampire, the blood *is* the life.

However, in recent years many novels and short stories have elected to show the vampire in a somewhat different light – as a sympathetic, misunderstood character, a victim of its own affliction; or as a creature that feeds upon the human psyche or bodily fluids other than blood (thus enhancing the vampire's frequent identification with a dark sexuality). All these approaches are, of course, perfectly valid, and some have even produced modern classics of the genre.

Personally, I usually prefer a more traditional approach to vampire fiction.

This revised and expanded edition of *The Mammoth Book of Vampires* collects together thirty-five classic and contemporary stories of the undead by many of horror fiction's best-known names. As is to be expected in any representative collection, there are a number of the modern type of vampire stories I referred to above, but for the most part the bloodsuckers you will find within these pages are the real thing.

From Hugh B. Cave's memorable pulp thriller 'Stragella' through

Tanith Lee's twisted fairy tale 'Red as Blood' to Michael Marshall Smith's hallucinatory 'A Place to Stay', you will discover a modern mix of vampire fiction by such masters of the macabre as Clive Barker, Brian Lumley, Ramsey Campbell, Harlan Ellison, Neil Gaiman, Robert Bloch, Dennis Etchison and Karl Edward Wagner, amongst others.

There is original short fiction from Sydney J. Bounds, John Burke, Graham Masterton, Tina Rath and Steve Rasnic Tem; F. Paul Wilson, Les Daniels and Chelsea Quinn Yarbro are represented by three powerful novellas, and Kim Newman contributes another instalment in his popular and critically acclaimed *Anno Dracula* series.

As usual, all the stories in this volume were selected because they are particular favourites of mine. I have also attempted to put together an anthology that offers a relatively unfamiliar line-up of tales to even the most jaded vampire aficionado.

So before turning the page, make sure that the garlic is in place at window and door, the wooden stake is sharpened, and the holy water is close at hand. Just in case . . .

I bid you, welcome.

Stephen Jones
London, England

CLIVE BARKER

Human Remains

BEST-SELLING AUTHOR CLIVE BARKER was born in Liverpool, England, and began his literary career writing, directing and acting for the stage. Following the publication of his short stories in the *Books of Blood* in 1984, Barker went on to write numerous successful novels, including *The Great and Secret Show*, *Weaveworld*, *Imajica*, *The Thief of Always*, *Everville*, *Sacrament* and *Galilee*. More recently, he published a Hollywood ghost story, *Coldheart Canyon*, while *Abarat* was the first of a quartet of children's books profusely illustrated by the author. Douglas E. Winter's authorized biography, *Clive Barker: The Dark Fantastic*, appeared in 2001.

As a screenwriter, director and film producer, Barker created the *Hellraiser* and *Candyman* franchises, and his other film credits include *Nightbreed*, *Lord of Illusions*, *Saint Sinner* and the Oscar-winning *Gods and Monsters*.

An accomplished painter and visual artist, he has had exhibitions in New York and Los Angeles. He lives in Beverly Hills, California, with his partner, the photographer David Armstrong.

The story that follows is one of the author's earliest. It is also one of his most poignant. Prepare to meet a very different type of vampire . . .

SOME TRADES ARE BEST practised by daylight, some by night. Gavin was a professional in the latter category. In midwinter, in midsummer, leaning against a wall, or poised in a doorway, a fire-fly cigarette hovering at his lips, he sold what sweated in his jeans to all comers.

Sometimes to visiting widows with more money than love, who'd hire him for a weekend of illicit meetings, sour, insistent kisses and perhaps, if they could forget their dead partners, a dry hump on a lavender-scented bed. Sometimes to lost husbands, hungry for their own sex and desperate for an hour of coupling with a boy who wouldn't ask their name.

Gavin didn't much care which it was. Indifference was a trade-mark of his, even a part of his attraction. And it made leaving him, when the deed was done and the money exchanged, so much simpler. To say, "Ciao", or "Be seeing you", or nothing at all to a face that scarcely cared if you lived or died: that was an easy thing.

And for Gavin, the profession was not unpalatable, as professions went. One night out of four it even offered him a grain of physical pleasure. At worst it was a sexual abattoir, all steaming skins and lifeless eyes. But he'd got used to that over the years.

It was all profit. It kept him in good shoes.

By day he slept mostly, hollowing out a warm furrow in the bed, and mummifying himself in his sheets, head wrapped up in a tangle of arms to keep out the light. About three or so, he'd get up, shave and shower, then spend half an hour in front of the mirror, inspecting himself. He was meticulously self-critical, never allowing his weight to fluctuate more than a pound or two to either side of his self-elected ideal, careful to feed his skin if it was dry, or swab it if it was oily, hunting for any pimple that might flaw his cheek. Strict watch was kept for the smallest sign of venereal disease – the only type of lovesickness he ever suffered. The occasional dose of crabs was easily dispatched, but gonorrhoea, which he'd caught twice, would keep him out of service for three weeks, and that was bad for business; so he policed his body obsessively, hurrying to the clinic at the merest sign of a rash.

It seldom happened. Uninvited crabs aside there was little to do in that half-hour of self-appraisal but admire the collision of genes that had made him. He was wonderful. People told him that all the time. Wonderful. The face, oh the face, they would say, holding him tight as if they could steal a piece of his glamour.

Of course there were other beauties available, through the agencies, even on the streets if you knew where to search. But most of the hustlers Gavin knew had faces that seemed, beside his, unmade. Faces that looked like the first workings of a sculptor rather than the finished article: unrefined, experimental. Whereas he was made, entire. All that could be done had been; it was just a question of preserving the perfection.

Inspection over, Gavin would dress, maybe regard himself for another five minutes, then take the packaged wares out to sell.

He worked the street less and less these days. It was chancey; there was always the law to avoid, and the occasional psycho with an urge to clean up Sodom. If he was feeling really lazy he could pick up a client through the Escort Agency, but they always creamed off a fat portion of the fee.

He had regulars of course, clients who booked his favours month after month. A widow from Fort Lauderdale always hired him for a few days on her annual trip to Europe; another woman whose face he'd seen once in a glossy magazine called him now and then, wanting only to dine with him and confide her marital problems. There was a man Gavin called Rover, after his car, who would buy him once every few weeks for a night of kisses and confessions.

But on nights without a booked client he was out on his own finding a spec and hustling. It was a craft he had off perfectly. Nobody else working the street had caught the vocabulary of invitation better; the subtle blend of encouragement and detachment, of putto and wanton. The particular shift of weight from left foot to right that presented the groin at the best angle: so. Never too blatant: never whorish. Just casually promising.

He prided himself that there was seldom more than a few minutes between tricks, and never as much as an hour. If he made his play with his usual accuracy, eyeing the right disgruntled wife, the right regretful husband, he'd have them feed him (clothe him sometimes), bed him and bid him a satisfied goodnight all before the last tube had run on the Metropolitan Line to Hammersmith. The years of half-hour assignations, three blow-jobs and a fuck in one evening, were over. For one thing he simply didn't have the hunger for it any longer, for another he was preparing for his career to change course in the coming years: from street hustler to gigolo, from gigolo to kept boy, from kept boy to husband. One of these days, he knew it, he'd marry one of the widows; maybe the matron from Florida. She'd told him how she could picture him spread out beside her pool in Fort Lauderdale, and it was a fantasy he kept warm for her. Perhaps he hadn't got there yet, but he'd turn the trick of it sooner or later. The problem was that these rich blooms needed a lot of tending, and the pity of it was that so many of them perished before they came to fruit.

Still, this year. Oh yes, this year for certain, it had to be this year. Something good was coming with the autumn, he knew it for sure. Meanwhile he watched the lines deepen around his wonderful mouth (it was, without doubt, wonderful) and calculated the odds against him in the race between time and opportunity.

It was nine-fifteen at night. September 29th, and it was chilly, even in the foyer of the Imperial Hotel. No Indian summer to bless the streets this year: autumn had London in its jaws and was shaking the city bare.

The chill had got to his tooth, his wretched, crumbling tooth. If he'd gone to the dentist's, instead of turning over in his bed and sleeping another hour, he wouldn't be feeling this discomfort. Well, too late now, he'd go tomorrow. Plenty of time tomorrow. No need for an appointment. He'd just smile at the receptionist, she'd melt and tell him she could find a slot for him somewhere, he'd smile again, she'd blush and he'd see the dentist then and there instead of waiting two weeks like the poor nerds who didn't have wonderful faces.

For tonight he'd just have to put up with it. All he needed was one lousy punter – a husband who'd pay through the nose for taking it in the mouth – then he could retire to an all-night club in Soho and content himself with reflections. As long as he didn't find himself with a confession-freak on his hands, he could spit his stuff and be done by half ten.

But tonight wasn't his night. There was a new face on the reception desk of the Imperial, a thin, shot-at face with a mismatched rug perched (glued) on his pate, and he'd been squinting at Gavin for almost half an hour.

The usual receptionist, Madox, was a closet-case Gavin had seen prowling the bars once or twice, an easy touch if you could handle that kind. Madox was putty in Gavin's hand; he'd even bought his company for an hour a couple of months back. He'd got a cheap rate too – that was good politics. But this new man was straight, and vicious, and he was on to Gavin's game.

Idly, Gavin sauntered across to the cigarette machine, his walk catching the beat of the muzack as he trod the maroon carpet. Lousy fucking night.

The receptionist was waiting for him as he turned from the machine, packet of Winston in hand.

"Excuse me . . . Sir." It was a practised pronounciation that was clearly not natural. Gavin looked sweetly back at him.

"Yes?"

"Are you actually a resident at this hotel . . . Sir?"

"Actually—"

"If not, the management would be obliged if you'd vacate the premises immediately."

"I'm waiting for somebody."

"Oh?"

The receptionist didn't believe a word of it.

"Well just give me the name—"

"No need."

"Give me the name—", the man insisted, "and I'll gladly check to see if your . . . contact . . . is in the hotel."

The bastard was going to try and push it, which narrowed the options. Either Gavin could choose to play it cool, and leave the foyer, or play the outraged customer and stare the other man down. He chose, more to be bloodyminded than because it was good tactics, to do the latter.

"You don't have any right—" he began to bluster, but the receptionist wasn't moved.

"Look, sonny—" he said, "I know what you're up to, so don't try and get snotty with me or I'll fetch the police." He'd lost control of his elocution: it was getting further south of the river with every syllable. "We've got a nice clientele here, and they don't want no truck with the likes of you, see?"

"Fucker," said Gavin very quietly.

"Well that's one up from a cocksucker, isn't it?"

Touché.

"Now, sonny – you want to mince out of here under your own steam or be carried out in cuffs by the boys in blue?"

Gavin played his last card.

"Where's Mr Madox? I want to see Mr Madox: he knows me."

"I'm sure he does," the receptionist snorted, "I'm bloody sure he does. He was dismissed for improper conduct—" The artificial accent was re-establishing itself "—so I wouldn't try dropping his name here if I were you. OK? On your way."

Upper hand well and truly secured, the receptionist stood back like a matador and gestured for the bull to go by.

"The management thanks you for your patronage. Please don't call again."

Game, set and match to the man with the rug. What the hell; there were other hotels, other foyers, other receptionists. He didn't have to take all this shit.

As Gavin pushed the door open he threw a smiling "Be seeing you" over his shoulder. Perhaps that would make the tick sweat a little one of these nights when he was walking home and he heard a young man's step on the street behind him. It was a petty satisfaction, but it was something.

The door swung closed, sealing the warmth in and Gavin out. It was colder, substantially colder, than it had been when he'd stepped into the foyer. A thin drizzle had begun, which threatened to worsen as he hurried down Park Lane towards South Kensington. There were a couple of hotels on the High Street he could hole up in for a while; if nothing came of that he'd admit defeat.

The traffic surged around Hyde Park Corner, speeding to Knightsbridge or Victoria, purposeful, shining. He pictured himself standing on the concrete island between the two contrary streams of cars, his fingertips thrust into his jeans (they were too tight for him to get more than the first joint into the pockets), solitary, forlorn.

A wave of unhappiness came up from some buried place in him. He was twenty-four and five months. He had hustled, on and off and on again, since he was seventeen, promising himself that he'd find a marriageable widow (the gigolo's pension) or a legitimate occupation before he was twenty-five.

But time passed and nothing came of his ambitions. He just lost momentum and gained another line beneath the eye.

And the traffic still came in shining streams, lights signalling this imperative or that, cars full of people with ladders to climb and snakes to wrestle, their passage isolating him from the bank, from safety, with its hunger for destination.

He was not what he'd dreamed he'd be, or promised his secret self.

And youth was yesterday.

Where was he to go now? The flat would feel like a prison tonight, even if he smoked a little dope to take the edge off the room. He wanted, no, he *needed* to be with somebody tonight. Just to see his beauty through somebody else's eyes. Be told how perfect his proportions were, be wined and dined and flattered stupid, even if it was by Quasimodo's richer, uglier brother. Tonight he needed a fix of affection.

The pick-up was so damned easy it almost made him forget the episode in the foyer of the Imperial. A guy of fifty-five or so, well-heeled: Gucci shoes, a very classy overcoat. In a word: quality.

Gavin was standing in the doorway of a tiny art-house cinema, looking over the times of the Truffaut movie they were showing, when he became aware of the punter staring at him. He glanced at the guy to be certain there was a pick-up in the offing. The direct look seemed to unnerve the punter; he moved on; then he seemed to change his mind, muttered something to himself, and retraced his steps, showing patently false interest in the movie schedule. Obviously not too familiar with this game, Gavin thought; a novice.

Casually Gavin took out a Winston and lit it, the flare of the match in his cupped hands glossing his cheekbones golden. He'd done it a thousand times, as often as not in the mirror for his own pleasure. He had the glance up from the tiny fire off pat: it always did the trick.

This time when he met the nervous eyes of the punter, the other didn't back away.

He drew on the cigarette, flicking out the match and letting it drop. He hadn't made a pick-up like this in several months, but he was well satisfied that he still had the knack. The faultless recognition of a potential client, the implicit offer in eyes and lips, that could be construed as innocent friendliness if he'd made an error.

This was no error, however, this was the genuine article. The man's eyes were glued to Gavin, so enamoured of him he seemed to be hurting with it. His mouth was open, as though the words of introduction had failed him. Not much of a face, but far from ugly. Tanned too often, and too quickly: maybe he'd lived abroad. He was assuming the man was English: his prevarication suggested it.

Against habit, Gavin made the opening move.

"You like French movies?"

The punter seemed to deflate with relief that the silence between them had been broken.

"Yes," he said.

"You going in?"

The man pulled a face.

"I . . . I . . . don't think I will."

"Bit cold . . ."

"Yes. It is."

"Bit cold for standing around, I mean."

"Oh – yes."

The punter took the bait.

"Maybe . . . you'd like a drink?"

Gavin smiled.

"Sure, why not?"

"My flat's not far."

"Sure."

"I was getting a bit cheesed off, you know, at home."

"I know the feeling."

Now the other man smiled. "You are . . .?"

"Gavin."

The man offered his leather-gloved hand. Very formal, business-like. The grip as they shook was strong, no trace of his earlier hesitation remaining.

"I'm Kenneth," he said, "Ken Reynolds."

"Ken."

"Shall we get out of the cold?"

"Suits me."

"I'm only a short walk from here."

*   *   *

A wave of musty, centrally-heated air hit them as Reynolds opened the door of his apartment. Climbing the three flights of stairs had snatched Gavin's breath, but Reynolds wasn't slowed at all. Health freak maybe. Occupation? Something in the city. The handshake, the leather gloves. Maybe Civil Service.

"Come in, come in."

There was money here. Underfoot the pile of the carpet was lush, hushing their steps as they entered. The hallway was almost bare: a calendar hung on the wall, a small table with telephone, a heap of directories, a coat-stand.

"It's warmer in here."

Reynolds was shrugging off his coat and hanging it up. His gloves remained on as he led Gavin a few yards down the hallway and into a large room.

"Let's have your jacket," he said.

"Oh . . . sure."

Gavin took off his jacket, and Reynolds slipped out into the hall with it. When he came in again he was working off his gloves; a slick of sweat made it a difficult job. The guy was still nervous: even on his home ground. Usually they started to calm down once they were safe behind locked doors. Not this one: he was a catalogue of fidgets.

"Can I get you a drink?"

"Yeah; that would be good."

"What's your poison?"

"Vodka."

"Surely. Anything with it?"

"Just a drop of water."

"Purist, eh?"

Gavin didn't quite understand the remark.

"Yeah," he said.

"Man after my own heart. Will you give me a moment – I'll just fetch some ice."

"No problem."

Reynolds dropped the gloves on a chair by the door, and left Gavin to the room. It, like the hallway, was almost stiflingly warm, but there was nothing homely or welcoming about it. Whatever his profession, Reynolds was a collector. The room was dominated by displays of antiquities, mounted on the walls, and lined up on shelves. There was very little furniture, and what there was seemed odd: battered tubular frame chairs had no place in an apartment this expensive. Maybe the man was a university don, or a museum governor, something academic. This was no stockbroker's living room.

Gavin knew nothing about art, and even less about history, so the displays meant very little to him, but he went to have a closer look, just to show willing. The guy was bound to ask him what he thought of the stuff. The shelves were deadly dull. Bits and pieces of pottery and sculpture: nothing in its entirety, just fragments. On some of the shards there remained a glimpse of design, though age had almost washed the colours out. Some of the sculpture was recognisably human: part of a torso, or foot (all five toes in place), a face that was all but eaten away, no longer male or female. Gavin stifled a yawn. The heat, the exhibits and the thought of sex made him lethargic.

He turned his dulled attention to the wall-hung pieces. They were more impressive than the stuff on the shelves but they were still far from complete. He couldn't see why anyone would want to look at such broken things; what was the fascination? The stone reliefs mounted on the wall were pitted and eroded, so that the skins of the figures looked leprous, and the Latin inscriptions were almost wiped out. There was nothing beautiful about them: too spoiled for beauty. They made him feel dirty somehow, as though their condition was contagious.

Only one of the exhibits struck him as interesting: a tombstone, or what looked to him to be a tombstone, which was larger than the other reliefs and in slightly better condition. A man on a horse, carrying a sword, loomed over his headless enemy. Under the picture, a few words in Latin. The front legs of the horse had been broken off, and the pillars that bounded the design were badly defaced by age, otherwise the image made sense. There was even a trace of personality in the crudely made face: a long nose, a wide mouth; an individual.

Gavin reached to touch the inscription, but withdrew his fingers as he heard Reynolds enter.

"No, please touch it," said his host. "It's there to take pleasure in. Touch away."

Now that he'd been invited to touch the thing, the desire had melted away. He felt embarrassed; caught in the act.

"Go on," Reynolds insisted.

Gavin touched the carving. Cold stone, gritty under his finger-tips.

"It's Roman," said Reynolds.

"Tombstone?"

"Yes. Found near Newcastle."

"Who was he?"

"His name was Flavinus. He was a regimental standard-bearer."

What Gavin had assumed to be a sword was, on closer inspection, a standard. It ended in an almost erased motif: maybe a bee, a flower, a wheel.

"You an archaeologist, then?"

"That's part of my business. I research sites, occasionally oversee digs; but most of the time I restore artifacts."

"Like these?"

"Roman Britain's my personal obsession."

He put down the glasses he was carrying and crossed to the pottery-laden shelves.

"This is stuff I've collected over the years. I've never quite got over the thrill of handling objects that haven't seen the light of day for centuries. It's like plugging into history. You know what I mean?"

"Yeah."

Reynolds picked a fragment of pottery off the shelf.

"Of course all the best finds are claimed by the major collections. But if one's canny, one manages to keep a few pieces back. They were an incredible influence, the Romans. Civil engineers, road-layers, bridge builders."

Reynolds gave a sudden laugh at his burst of enthusiasm.

"Oh hell," he said, "Reynolds is lecturing again. Sorry. I get carried away."

Replacing the pottery-shard in its niche on the shelf, he returned to the glasses, and started pouring drinks. With his back to Gavin, he managed to say: "Are you expensive?"

Gavin hesitated. The man's nervousness was catching and the sudden tilt of the conversation from the Romans to the price of a blow-job took some adjustment.

"It depends," he flannelled.

"Ah . . ." said the other, still busying himself with the glasses, "you mean what is the precise nature of my – er – requirement?"

"Yeah."

"Of course."

He turned and handed Gavin a healthy-sized glass of vodka. No ice.

"I won't be demanding of you," he said.

"I don't come cheap."

"I'm sure you don't," Reynolds tried a smile, but it wouldn't stick to his face, "and I'm prepared to pay you well. Will you be able to stay the night?"

"Do you want me to?"

Reynolds frowned into his glass.

"I suppose I do."

"Then yes."

The host's mood seemed to change, suddenly: indecision was replaced by a spurt of conviction.

"Cheers," he said, clinking his whisky-filled glass against Gavin's. "To love and life and anything else that's worth paying for."

The double-edged remark didn't escape Gavin: the guy was obviously tied up in knots about what he was doing.

"I'll drink to that," said Gavin and took a gulp of the vodka.

The drinks came fast after that, and just about his third vodka Gavin began to feel mellower than he'd felt in a hell of a long time, content to listen to Reynolds' talk of excavations and the glories of Rome with only one ear. His mind was drifting, an easy feeling. Obviously he was going to be here for the night, or at least until the early hours of the morning, so why not drink the punter's vodka and enjoy the experience for what it offered? Later, probably much later to judge by the way the guy was rambling, there'd be some drink-slurred sex in a darkened room, and that would be that. He'd had customers like this before. They were lonely, perhaps between lovers, and usually simple to please. It wasn't sex this guy was buying, it was company, another body to share his space awhile; easy money.

And then, the noise.

At first Gavin thought the beating sound was in his head, until Reynolds stood up, a twitch at his mouth. The air of well-being had disappeared.

"What's that?" asked Gavin, also getting up, dizzy with drink.

"It's all right—" Reynolds, palms were pressing him down into his chair. "Stay here—"

The sound intensified. A drummer in an oven, beating as he burned.

"Please, please stay here a moment. It's just somebody upstairs."

Reynolds was lying, the racket wasn't coming from upstairs. It was from somewhere else in the flat, a rhythmical thumping, that speeded up and slowed and speeded again.

"Help yourself to a drink," said Reynolds at the door, face flushed. "Damn neighbours. . ."

The summons, for that was surely what it was, was already subsiding.

"A moment only," Reynolds promised, and closed the door behind him.

Gavin had experienced bad scenes before: tricks whose lovers appeared at inappropriate moments; guys who wanted to beat him up for a price – one who got bitten by guilt in a hotel room and smashed the place to smithereens. These things happened. But Reynolds was different: nothing about him said weird. At the back of his mind, at the very back, Gavin was quietly reminding himself that the other guys hadn't seemed bad at the beginning. Ah hell; he put the doubts away. If he started to get the jitters every time he went with a new face he'd soon stop working altogether. Somewhere along the line he had to trust to luck and his instinct, and his instinct told him that this punter was not given to throwing fits.

Taking a quick swipe from his glass, he refilled it, and waited.

The noise had stopped altogether, and it became increasingly

easier to rearrange the facts: maybe it had been an upstairs neighbour after all. Certainly there was no sound of Reynolds moving
around in the flat.

His attention wandered around the room looking for something to
occupy it awhile, and came back to the tombstone on the wall.

Flavinus the Standard-Bearer.

There was something satisfying about the idea of having your
likeness, however crude, carved in stone and put up on the spot
where your bones lay, even if some historian was going to separate
bones and stone in the fullness of time. Gavin's father had insisted on
burial rather than cremation: How else, he'd always said, was he
going to be remembered? Who'd ever go to an urn, in a wall, and cry?
The irony was that nobody ever went to his grave either: Gavin had
been perhaps twice in the years since his father's death. A plain stone
bearing a name, a date, and a platitude. He couldn't even remember
the year his father died.

People remembered Flavinus though; people who'd never known
him, or a life like his, knew him now. Gavin stood up and touched the
standard-bearer's name, the crudely chased "FLAVINVS" that was
the second word of the inscription.

Suddenly, the noise again, more frenzied than ever. Gavin turned
away from the tombstone and looked at the door, half-expecting
Reynolds to be standing there with a word of explanation. Nobody
appeared.

"Damn it."

The noise continued, a tattoo. Somebody, somewhere, was very
angry. And this time there could be no self-deception: the drummer
was here, on this floor, a few yards away. Curiosity nibbled Gavin, a
coaxing lover. He drained his glass and went out into the hall. The
noise stopped as he closed the door behind him.

"Ken?" he ventured. The word seemed to die at his lips.

The hallway was in darkness, except for a wash of light from the far
end. Perhaps an open door. Gavin found a switch to his right, but it
didn't work.

"Ken?" he said again.

This time the enquiry met with a response. A moan, and the sound
of a body rolling, or being rolled, over. Had Reynolds had an
accident? Jesus, he could be lying incapacitated within spitting
distance from where Gavin stood: he must help. Why were his feet
so reluctant to move? He had the tingling in his balls that always came
with nervous anticipation; it reminded him of childhood hide-and-
seek: the thrill of the chase. It was almost pleasurable.

And pleasure apart, could he really leave now, without knowing
what had become of the punter? He had to go down the corridor.

The first door was ajar; he pushed it open and the room beyond was a book-lined bedroom/study. Street lights through the curtain-less window fell on a jumbled desk. No Reynolds, no thrasher. More confident now he'd made the first move Gavin explored further down the hallway. The next door – the kitchen – was also open. There was no light from inside. Gavin's hands had begun to sweat: he thought of Reynolds trying to pull his gloves off, though they stuck to his palm. What had he been afraid of? It was more than the pick-up: there was somebody else in the apartment: somebody with a violent temper.

Gavin's stomach turned as his eyes found the smeared hand-print on the door; it was blood.

He pushed the door, but it wouldn't open any further. There was something behind it. He slid through the available space, and into the kitchen. An unemptied waste bin, or a neglected vegetable rack, fouled the air. Gavin smoothed the wall with his palm to find the light switch, and the fluorescent tube spasmed into life.

Reynolds' Gucci shoes poked out from behind the door. Gavin pushed it to, and Reynolds rolled out of his hiding place. He'd obviously crawled behind the door to take refuge; there was some-thing of the beaten animal in his tucked up body. When Gavin touched him he shuddered.

"It's all right . . . it's me." Gavin prised a bloody hand from Reynolds' face. There was a deep gouge running from his temple to his chin, and another, parallel with it but not as deep, across the middle of his forehead and his nose, as though he'd been raked by a two pronged fork.

Reynolds opened his eyes. It took him a second only to focus on Gavin, before he said:

"Go away."

"You're hurt."

"Jesus' sake, go away. Quickly. I've changed my mind . . . You understand?"

"I'll fetch the police."

The man practically spat: "Get the fucking hell out of here, will you? Fucking bum-boy!"

Gavin stood up, trying to make sense out of all this. The guy was in pain, it made him aggressive. Ignore the insults and fetch something to cover the wound. That was it. Cover the wound, and then leave him to his own devices. If he didn't want the police that was his business. Probably he didn't want to explain the presence of a pretty-boy in his hot-house.

"Just let me get you a bandage—"

Gavin went back into the hallway.

Behind the kitchen door Reynolds said: "Don't," but the bum-boy didn't hear him. It wouldn't have made much difference if he had. Gavin liked disobedience. Don't was an invitation.

Reynolds put his back to the kitchen door, and tried to edge his way upright, using the door-handle as purchase. But his head was spinning: a carousel of horrors, round and round, each horse uglier than the last. His legs doubled up under him, and he fell down like the senile fool he was. Damn. Damn. Damn.

Gavin heard Reynolds fall, but he was too busy arming himself to hurry back into the kitchen. If the intruder who'd attacked Reynolds was still in the flat, he wanted to be ready to defend himself. He rummaged through the reports on the desk in the study and alighted on a paper knife which was lying beside a pile of unopened correspondence. Thanking God for it, he snatched it up. It was light, and the blade was thin and brittle, but properly placed it could surely kill.

Happier now, he went back into the hall and took a moment to work out his tactics. The first thing was to locate the bathroom, hopefully there he'd find a bandage for Reynolds. Even a clean towel would help. Maybe then he could get some sense out of the guy, even coax him into an explanation.

Beyond the kitchen the hallway made a sharp left. Gavin turned the corner, and dead ahead the door was ajar. A light burned inside: water shone on tiles. The bathroom.

Clamping his left hand over the right hand that held the knife, Gavin approached the door. The muscles of his arms had become rigid with fear: would that improve his strike if it was required? he wondered. He felt inept, graceless, slightly stupid.

There was blood on the door-jamb, a palm-print that was clearly Reynolds'. This was where it had happened – Reynolds had thrown out a hand to support himself as he reeled back from his assailant. If the attacker was still in the flat, he must be here. There was nowhere else for him to hide.

Later, if there was a later, he'd probably analyse this situation and call himself a fool for kicking the door open, for encouraging this confrontation. But even as he contemplated the idiocy of the action he was performing it, and the door was swinging open across tiles strewn with water-blood puddles, and any moment there'd be a figure there, hook-handed, screaming defiance.

No. Not at all. The assailant wasn't here; and if he wasn't here, he wasn't in the flat.

Gavin exhaled, long and slow. The knife sagged in his hand, denied its pricking. Now, despite the sweat, the terror, he was disappointed. Life had let him down, again – snuck his destiny out of the back door and left him with a mop in his hand not a medal. All he could do was play nurse to the old man and go on his way.

The bathroom was decorated in shades of lime; the blood and tiles clashed. The translucent shower curtain, sporting stylised fish and seaweed, was partially drawn. It looked like the scene of a movie murder: not quite real. Blood too bright: light too flat.

Gavin dropped the knife in the sink, and opened the mirrored cabinet. It was well-stocked with mouth-washes, vitamin supplements, and abandoned toothpaste tubes, but the only medication was a tin of Elastoplast. As he closed the cabinet door he met his own features in the mirror, a drained face. He turned on the cold tap full, and lowered his head to the sink; a splash of water would clear away the vodka and put some colour in his cheeks.

As he cupped the water to his face, something made a noise behind him. He stood up, his heart knocking against his ribs, and turned off the tap. Water dripped off his chin and his eyelashes, and gurgled down the waste pipe.

The knife was still in the sink, a hand's-length away. The sound was coming from the bath, from *in* the bath, the inoffensive slosh of water.

Alarm had triggered flows of adrenalin, and his senses distilled the air with new precision. The sharp scent of lemon soap, the brilliance of the turquoise angel-fish flitting through lavender kelp on the shower curtain, the cold droplets on his face, the warmth behind his eyes: all sudden experiences, details his mind had passed over 'til now, too lazy to see and smell and feel to the limits of its reach.

You're living in the real world, his head said (it was a revelation), and if you're not very careful you're going to die there.

Why hadn't he looked in the bath? Asshole. Why not the bath?

"Who's there?" he asked, hoping against hope that Reynolds had an otter that was taking a quiet swim. Ridiculous hope. There was blood here, for Christ's sake.

He turned from the mirror as the lapping subsided – do it! do it! – and slid back the shower curtain on its plastic hooks. In his haste to unveil the mystery he'd left the knife in the sink. Too late now: the turquoise angels concertinaed, and he was looking down into the water.

It was deep, coming up to within an inch or two of the top of the bath, and murky. A brown scum spiralled on the surface, and the smell off it was faintly animal, like the wet fur of a dog. Nothing broke the surface of the water.

Gavin peered in, trying to work out the form at the bottom, his reflection floating amid the scum. He bent closer, unable to puzzle out the relation of shapes in the silt, until he recognised the crudely-formed fingers of a hand and he realised he was looking at a human form curled up into itself like a foetus, lying absolutely still in the filthy water.

He passed his hand over the surface to clear away the muck, his reflection shattered, and the occupant of the bath came clear. It was a statue, carved in the shape of a sleeping figure, only its head, instead of being tucked up tight, was cranked round to stare up out of the blur of sediment towards the surface. Its eyes were painted open, two crude blobs on a roughly carved face; its mouth was a slash, its ears ridiculous handles on its bald head. It was naked: its anatomy no better realised than its features: the work of an apprentice sculptor. In places the paint had been corrupted, perhaps by the soaking, and was lifting off the torso in grey, globular strands. Underneath, a core of dark wood was uncovered.

There was nothing to be frightened of here. An *objet d'art* in a bath, immersed in water to remove a crass paint-job. The lapping he'd heard behind him had been some bubbles rising from the thing, caused by a chemical reaction. There: the fright was explained. Nothing to panic over. Keep beating my heart, as the barman at the Ambassador used to say when a new beauty appeared on the scene.

Gavin smiled at the irony; this was no Adonis.

"Forget you ever saw it."

Reynolds was at the door. The bleeding had stopped, staunched by an unsavoury rag of a handkerchief pressed to the side of his face. The light of the tiles made his skin bilious: his pallor would have shamed a corpse.

"Are you all right? You don't look it."

"I'll be fine . . . just go, please."

"What happened?"

"I slipped. Water on the floor. I slipped, that's all."

"But the noise . . ."

Gavin was looking back into the bath. Something about the statue fascinated him. Maybe its nakedness, and that second strip it was slowly performing underwater: the ultimate strip: off with the skin.

"Neighbours, that's all."

"What is this?" Gavin asked, still looking at the unfetching doll-face in the water.

"It's nothing to do with you."

"Why's it all curled up like that? Is he dying?"

Gavin looked back to Reynolds to see the response to that question, the sourest of smiles, fading.

"You'll want money."

"No."

"Damn you! You're in business aren't you? There's notes beside the bed; take whatever you feel you deserve for your wasted time—" He was appraising Gavin. "—and your silence."

Again the statue: Gavin couldn't keep his eyes off it, in all its crudity. His own face, puzzled, floated on the skin of the water, shaming the hand of the artist with its proportions.

"Don't wonder," said Reynolds.

"Can't help it."

"This is nothing to do with you."

"You stole it . . . is that right? This is worth a mint and you stole it."

Reynolds pondered the question and seemed, at last, too tired to start lying.

"Yes. I stole it."

"And tonight somebody came back for it—"

Reynolds shrugged.

"—Is that it? Somebody came back for it?"

"That's right. I stole it . . ." Reynolds was saying the lines by rote, ". . . and somebody came back for it."

"That's all I wanted to know."

"Don't come back here, Gavin whoever-you-are. And don't try anything clever, because I won't be here."

"You mean extortion?" said Gavin, "I'm no thief."

Reynolds' look of appraisal rotted into contempt.

"Thief or not, be thankful. If it's in you." Reynolds stepped away from the door to let Gavin pass. Gavin didn't move.

"Thankful for what?" he demanded. There was an itch of anger in him; he felt, absurdly, rejected, as though he was being foisted off with a half-truth because he wasn't worthy enough to share this secret.

Reynolds had no more strength left for explanation. He was slumped against the door-frame, exhausted.

"Go," he said.

Gavin nodded and left the guy at the door. As he passed from bathroom into hallway a glob of paint must have been loosened from the statue. He heard it break surface, heard the lapping at the edge of the bath, could see, in his head, the way the ripples made the body shimmer.

"Goodnight," said Reynolds, calling after him.

Gavin didn't reply, nor did he pick up any money on his way out. Let him have his tombstones and his secrets.

On his way to the front door he stepped into the main room to pick up his jacket. The face of Flavinus the Standard-Bearer looked down at him from the wall. The man must have been a hero, Gavin thought. Only a hero would have been commemorated in such a fashion. He'd get no remembrance like that; no stone face to mark his passage.

He closed the front door behind him, aware once more that his tooth was aching, and as he did so the noise began again, the beating of a fist against a wall.

Or worse, the sudden fury of a woken heart.

The toothache was really biting the following day, and he went to the dentist mid-morning, expecting to coax the girl on the desk into giving him an instant appointment. But his charm was at a low ebb, his eyes weren't sparkling quite as luxuriantly as usual. She told him he'd have to wait until the following Friday, unless it was an emergency. He told her it was: she told him it wasn't. It was going to be a bad day: an aching tooth, a lesbian dentist receptionist, ice on the puddles, nattering women on every street corner, ugly children, ugly sky.

That was the day the pursuit began.

Gavin had been chased by admirers before, but never quite like this. Never so subtle, so surreptitious. He'd had people follow him round for days, from bar to bar, from street to street, so dog-like it almost drove him mad. Seeing the same longing face night after night, screwing up the courage to buy him a drink, perhaps offering him a watch, cocaine, a week in Tunisia, whatever. He'd rapidly come to loathe that sticky adoration that went bad as quickly as milk, and stank to high Heaven once it had. One of his most ardent admirers, a knighted actor he'd been told, never actually came near him, just followed him around, looking and looking. At first the attention had been flattering, but the pleasure soon became irritation, and eventually he'd cornered the guy in a bar and threatened him with a broken head. He'd been so wound up that night, so sick of being devoured by looks, he'd have done some serious harm if the pitiful bastard hadn't taken the hint. He never saw the guy again; half thought he'd probably gone home and hanged himself.

But this pursuit was nowhere near as obvious, it was scarcely more than a feeling. There was no hard evidence that he had somebody on his tail. Just a prickly sense, every time he glanced round, that someone was slotting themselves into the shadows, or that on a night street a walker was keeping pace with him, matching every click of his heel, every hesitation in his step. It was like paranoia, except that he wasn't paranoid. If he was paranoid, he reasoned, somebody would tell him.

Besides, there were incidents. One morning the cat woman who lived on the landing below him idly enquired who his visitor was: the funny one who came in late at night and waited on the stairs hour after hour, watching his room. He'd had no such visitor: and knew no-one who fitted the description.

Another day, on a busy street, he'd ducked out of the throng into the doorway of an empty shop and was in the act of lighting a cigarette when somebody's reflection, distorted through the grime on the window, caught his eye. The match burned his finger, he looked down as he dropped it, and when he looked up again the crowd had closed round the watcher like an eager sea.

It was a bad, bad feeling: and there was more where that came from.

Gavin had never spoken with Preetorius, though they'd exchanged an occasional nod on the street, and each asked after the other in the company of mutual acquaintances as though they were dear friends. Preetorius was a black, somewhere between forty-five and assassination, a glorified pimp who claimed to be descended from Napoleon. He'd been running a circle of women, and three or four boys, for the best part of a decade, and doing well from the business. When he first began work, Gavin had been strongly advised to ask for Preetorius' patronage, but he'd always been too much of a maverick to want that kind of help. As a result he'd never been looked upon kindly by Preetorius or his clan. Nevertheless, once he became a fixture on the scene, no-one challenged his right to be his own man. The word was that Preetorius even admitted a grudging admiration for Gavin's greed.

Admiration or no, it was a chilly day in Hell when Preetorius actually broke the silence and spoke to him.

"White boy."

It was towards eleven, and Gavin was on his way from a bar off St Martin's Lane to a club in Covent Garden. The street still buzzed: there were potential punters amongst the theatre and movie-goers, but he hadn't got the appetite for it tonight. He had a hundred in his pocket, which he'd made the day before and hadn't bothered to bank. Plenty to keep him going.

His first thought when he saw Preetorius and his pie-bald goons blocking his path was: they want my money.

"White boy."

Then he recognised the flat, shining face. Preetorius was no street thief; never had been, never would be.

"White boy, I'd like a word with you."

Preetorius took a nut from his pocket, shelled it in his palm, and popped the kernel into his ample mouth.

"You don't mind do you?"

"What do you want?"

"Like I said, just a word. Not too much to ask, is it?"

"OK. What?"

"Not here."

Gavin looked at Preetorius' cohorts. They weren't gorillas, that wasn't the black's style at all, but nor were they ninety-eight pound weaklings. This scene didn't look, on the whole, too healthy.

"Thanks, but no thanks." Gavin said, and began to walk, with as even a pace as he could muster, away from the trio. They followed. He prayed they wouldn't, but they followed. Preetorius talked at his back.

"Listen. I hear bad things about you," he said.

"Oh yes?"

"I'm afraid so. I'm told you attacked one of my boys."

Gavin took six paces before he answered. "Not me. You've got the wrong man."

"He recognised you, trash. You did him some serious mischief."

"I told you: not me."

"You're a lunatic, you know that? You should be put behind fucking bars."

Preetorius was raising his voice. People were crossing the street to avoid the escalating argument.

Without thinking, Gavin turned off St Martin's Lane into Long Acre, and rapidly realised he'd made a tactical error. The crowds thinned substantially here, and it was a long trek through the streets of Covent Garden before he reached another centre of activity. He should have turned right instead of left, and he'd have stepped onto Charing Cross Road. There would have been some safety there. Damn it, he couldn't turn round, not and walk straight into them. All he could do was walk (not run; never run with a mad dog on your heels) and hope he could keep the conversation on an even keel.

Preetorius: "You've cost me a lot of money."

"I don't see—"

"You put some of my prime boy-meat out of commission. It's going to be a long time 'til I get that kid back on the market. He's shit scared, see?"

"Look . . . I didn't do anything to anybody."

"Why do you fucking lie to me, trash? What have I ever done to you, you treat me like this?"

Preetorius picked up his pace a little and came up level with Gavin, leaving his associates a few steps behind.

"Look . . ." he whispered to Gavin, "kids like that can be tempting, right? That's cool. I can get into that. You put a little boy-pussy on my plate I'm not going to turn my nose up at it. But you hurt him: and when you hurt one of my kids, I bleed too."

"If I'd done this like you say, you think I'd be walking the street?"

"Maybe you're not a well man, you know? We're not talking about a couple of bruises here, man. I'm talking about you taking a shower in a kid's blood, that's what I'm saying. Hanging him up and cutting him everywhere, then leaving him on my fuckin' stairs wearing a pair of fucking' socks. You getting my message now, white boy? You read my message?"

Genuine rage had flared as Preetorius described the alleged crimes, and Gavin wasn't sure how to handle it. He kept his silence, and walked on.

"That kid idolised you, you know? Thought you were essential reading for an aspirant bum-boy. How'd you like that?"

"Not much."

"You should be fuckin' flattered, man, 'cause that's about as much as you'll ever amount to."

"Thanks."

"You've had a good career. Pity it's over."

Gavin felt iced lead in his belly: he'd hoped Preetorius was going to be content with a warning. Apparently not. They were here to damage him: Jesus, they were going to hurt him, and for something he hadn't done, didn't even know anything about.

"We're going to take you off the street, white boy. Permanently."

"I did nothing."

"The kid knew you, even with a stocking over your head he knew you. The voice was the same, the clothes were the same. Face it, you were recognised. Now take the consequences."

"Fuck you."

Gavin broke into a run. As an eighteen year old he'd sprinted for his county: he needed that speed again now. Behind him Preetorius laughed (such sport!) and two sets of feet pounded the pavement in pursuit. They were close, closer – and Gavin was badly out of condition. His thighs were aching after a few dozen yards, and his jeans were too tight to run in easily. The chase was lost before it began.

"The man didn't tell you to leave," the white goon scolded, his bitten fingers digging into Gavin's biceps.

"Nice try." Preetorius smiled, sauntering towards the dogs and the panting hare. He nodded, almost imperceptibly, to the other goon.

"Christian?" he asked.

At the invitation Christian delivered a fist to Gavin's kidneys. The blow doubled him up, spitting curses.

Christian said: "Over there." Preetorius said: "Make it snappy," and suddenly they were dragging him out of the light into an alley. His shirt and his jacket tore, his expensive shoes were dragged through dirt, before he was pulled upright, groaning. The alley was dark and Preetorius' eyes hung in the air in front of him, dislocated.

"Here we are again," he said. "Happy as can be."

"I . . . didn't touch him," Gavin gasped.

The unnamed cohort, Not-Christian, put a ham hand in the middle of Gavin's chest, and pushed him back against the end wall of the alley. His heel slid in muck, and though he tried to stay upright his legs had turned to water. His ego too: this was no time to be courageous. He'd beg, he fall down on his knees and lick their soles if need be, anything to stop them doing a job on him. Anything to stop them spoiling his face.

That was Preetorius' favourite pastime, or so the street talk went: the spoiling of beauty. He had a rare way with him, could maim beyond hope of redemption in three strokes of his razor, and have the victim pocket his lips as a keepsake.

Gavin stumbled forward, palms slapping the wet ground. Something rotten-soft slid out of its skin beneath his hand.

Not-Christian exchanged a grin with Preetorius.

"Doesn't he look delightful?" he said.

Preetorius was crunching a nut. "Seems to me—" he said, "—the man's finally found his place in life."

"I didn't touch him," Gavin begged. There was nothing to do but deny and deny: and even then it was a lost cause.

"You're guilty as hell," said Not-Christian.

"*Please.*"

"I'd really like to get this over with as soon as possible," said Preetorius, glancing at his watch, "I've got appointments to keep, people to pleasure."

Gavin looked up at his tormentors. The sodium-lit street was a twenty-five-yard dash away, if he could break through the cordon of their bodies.

"Allow me to rearrange your face for you. A little crime of fashion."

Preetorius had a knife in his hand. Not-Christian had taken a rope from his pocket, with a ball on it. The ball goes in the mouth, the rope goes round the head – you couldn't scream if your life depended on it. This was it.

Go!

Gavin broke from his grovelling position like a sprinter from his block, but the slops greased his heels, and threw him off balance. Instead of making a clean dash for safety he stumbled sideways and fell against Christian, who in turn fell back.

There was a breathless scrambling before Preetorius stepped in, dirtying his hands on the white trash, and hauling him to his feet.

"No way out, fucker," he said, pressing the point of the blade against Gavin's chin. The jut of the bone was clearest there, and he began the cut without further debate – tracing the jawline, too hot for the act to care if the trash was gagged or not. Gavin howled as blood washed down his neck, but his cries were cut short as somebody's fat fingers grappled with his tongue, and held it fast.

His pulse began to thud in his temples, and windows, one behind the other, opened and opened in front of him, and he was falling through them into unconsciousness.

Better to die. Better to die. They'd destroy his face: better to die.

Then he was screaming again, except that he wasn't aware of making the sound in his throat. Through the slush in his ears he tried to focus on the voice, and realised it was Preetorius' scream he was hearing, not his own.

His tongue was released; and he was spontaneously sick. He staggered back, puking, from a mess of struggling figures in front of him. A person, or persons, unknown had stepped in, and prevented the completion of his spoiling. There was a body sprawled on the floor, face up. Not-Christian, eyes open, life shut. God: someone had killed for him. *For him.*

Gingerly, he put his hand up to his face to feel the damage. The flesh was deeply lacerated along his jawbone, from the middle of his chin to within an inch of his ear. It was bad, but Preetorius, ever organised, had left the best delights to the last, and had been interrupted before he'd slit Gavin's nostrils or taken off his lips. A scar along his jawbone wouldn't be pretty, but it wasn't disastrous.

Somebody was staggering out of the mêlée towards him – Preetorius, tears on his face, eyes like golf-balls.

Beyond him Christian, his arms useless, was staggering towards the street.

Preetorius wasn't following: why?

His mouth opened; an elastic filament of saliva, strung with pearls, depended from his lower lip.

"Help me," he appealed, as though his life was in Gavin's power. One large hand was raised to squeeze a drop of mercy out of the air, but instead came the swoop of another arm, reaching over his shoulder and thrusting a weapon, a crude blade, into the black's mouth. He gargled it a moment, his throat trying to accommodate its edge, its width, before his attacker dragged the blade up and back, holding Preetorius' neck to steady him against the force of the stroke. The startled face divided, and heat bloomed from Preetorius' interior, warming Gavin in a cloud.

The weapon hit the alley floor, a dull clank. Gavin glanced at it. A short, wide-bladed sword. He looked back at the dead man.

Preetorius stood upright in front of him, supported now only by his executioner's arm. His gushing head fell forward, and the executioner took the bow as a sign, neatly dropping Preetorius' body at Gavin's feet. No longer eclipsed by the corpse, Gavin met his saviour face to face.

It took him only a moment to place those crude features: the startled, lifeless eyes, the gash of a mouth, the jug-handle ears. It was Reynolds' statue. It grinned, its teeth too small for its head. Milk-teeth, still to be shed before the adult form. There was, however, some improvement in its appearance, he could see that even in the gloom. The brow seemed to have swelled; the face was altogether better proportioned. It remained a painted doll, but it was a doll with aspirations.

The statue gave a stiff bow, its joints unmistakably creaking, and the absurdity, the sheer absurdity of this situation welled up in Gavin. It bowed, damn it, it smiled, it murdered: and yet it couldn't possibly be alive, could it? Later, he would disbelieve, he promised himself. Later he'd find a thousand reasons not to accept the reality in front of him: blame his blood-starved brain, his confusion, his panic. One way or another he'd argue himself out of this fantastic vision, and it would be as though it had never happened.

If he could just live with it a few minutes longer.

The vision reached across and touched Gavin's jaw, lightly, running its crudely carved fingers along the lips of the wound Preetorius had made. A ring on its smallest finger caught the light: a ring identical to his own.

"We're going to have a scar," it said.

Gavin knew its voice.

"Dear me: pity," it said. It was speaking with *his* voice. "Still, it could be worse."

His voice. God, his, his, his.

Gavin shook his head.

"Yes," it said, understanding that he'd understood.

"Not me."

"Yes."

"Why?"

It transferred its touch from Gavin's jawbone to its own, marking out the place where the wound should be, and even as it made the gesture its surface opened, and it grew a scar on the spot. No blood welled up: it had no blood.

Yet wasn't that his own, even brow it was emulating, and the piercing eyes, weren't they becoming his, and the wonderful mouth?

"The boy?" said Gavin, fitting the pieces together.

"Oh the boy . . ." It threw its unfinished glance to Heaven. "What a treasure he was. And how he snarled."

"You washed in his blood?"

"I need it." It knelt to the body of Preetorius and put its fingers in the split head. "This blood's old, but it'll do. The boy was better."

It daubed Preetorius' blood on its cheek, like war-paint. Gavin couldn't hide his disgust.

"Is he such a loss?" the effigy demanded.

The answer was no, of course. It was no loss at all that Preetorius was dead, no loss that some drugged, cocksucking kid had given up some blood and sleep because this painted miracle needed to feed its growth. There were worse things than this every day, somewhere; huge horrors. And yet—

"You can't condone me," it prompted, "it's not in your nature is it? Soon it won't be in mine either. I'll reject my life as a tormentor of children, because I'll see through *your* eyes, share *your* humanity . . ."

It stood up, its movements still lacking flexibility.

"Meanwhile, I must behave as I think fit."

On its cheek, where Preetorius' blood had been smeared, the skin was already waxier, less like painted wood.

"I am a thing without a proper name," it pronounced. "I am a wound in the flank of the world. But I am also that perfect stranger you always prayed for as a child, to come and take you, call you beauty, lift you naked out of the street and through Heaven's window. Aren't I? Aren't I?"

How did it know the dreams of his childhood? How could it have guessed that particular emblem, of being hoisted out of a street full of plague into a house that was Heaven?

"Because I am yourself," it said, in reply to the unspoken question, "made perfectable."

Gavin gestured towards the corpses.

"You can't be me. I'd never have done this."

It seemed ungracious to condemn it for its intervention, but the point stood.

"Wouldn't you?" said the other. "I think you would."

Gavin heard Preetorius' voice in his ear. "A crime of fashion." Felt again the knife at his chin, the nausea, the helplessness. Of course he'd have done it, a dozen times over he'd have done it, and called it justice.

It didn't need to hear his accession, it was plain.

"I'll come and see you again," said the painted face. "Meanwhile – if I were you—" it laughed, "—I'd be going."

Gavin locked eyes with it a beat, probing it for doubt, then started towards the road.

"Not that way. This!"

It was pointing towards a door in the wall, almost hidden behind

festering bags of refuse. That was how it had come so quickly, so
quietly.

"Avoid the main streets, and keep yourself out of sight. I'll find you
again, when I'm ready."

Gavin needed no further encouragement to leave. Whatever the
explanations of the night's events, the deeds were done. Now wasn't
the time for questions.

He slipped through the doorway without looking behind him: but
he could hear enough to turn his stomach. The thud of fluid on the
ground, the pleasurable moan of the miscreant: the sounds were
enough for him to be able to picture its toilet.

Nothing of the night before made any more sense the morning after.
There was no sudden insight into the nature of the waking dream
he'd dreamt. There was just a series of stark facts.

In the mirror, the fact of the cut on his jaw, gummed up and
aching more badly than his rotted tooth.

In the newspapers, the reports of two bodies found in the Covent
Garden area, known criminals viciously murdered in what the police
described as a "gangland slaughter".

In his head, the inescapable knowledge that he would be found out
sooner or later. Somebody would surely have seen him with Preetorius, and spill the beans to the police. Maybe even Christian, if he
was so inclined, and they'd be there, on his step, with cuffs and
warrants. Then what could he tell them, in reply to their accusations?
That the man who did it was not a man at all, but an effigy of some
kind, that was by degrees becoming a replica of himself? The
question was not whether he'd be incarcerated, but which hole
they'd lock him in, prison or asylum?

Juggling despair with disbelief, he went to the casualty department
to have his face seen to, where he waited patiently for three and a half
hours with dozens of similar walking wounded.

The doctor was unsympathetic. There was no use in stitches now,
he said, the damage was done: the wound could and would be
cleaned and covered, but a bad scar was now unavoidable. Why
didn't you come last night, when it happened? the nurse asked. He
shrugged: what the hell did they care? Artificial compassion didn't
help him an iota.

As he turned the corner with his street, he saw the cars outside the
house, the blue light, the cluster of neighbours grinning their gossip.
Too late to claim anything of his previous life. By now they had
possession of his clothes, his combs, his perfumes, his letters – and
they'd be searching through them like apes after lice. He'd seen how
thorough-going these bastards could be when it suited them, how

completely they could seize and parcel up a man's identity. Eat it up, suck it up: they could erase you as surely as a shot, but leave you a living blank.

There was nothing to be done. His life was theirs now to sneer at and salivate over: even have a nervous moment, one or two of them, when they saw his photographs and wondered if perhaps they'd paid for this boy themselves, some horny night.

Let them have it all. They were welcome. From now on he would be lawless, because laws protect possessions and he had none. They'd wiped him clean, or as good as: he had no place to live, nor anything to call his own. He didn't even have fear: that was the strangest thing.

He turned his back on the street and the house he'd lived in for four years, and he felt something akin to relief, happy that his life had been stolen from him in its squalid entirety. He was the lighter for it.

Two hours later, and miles away, he took time to check his pockets. He was carrying a banker's card, almost a hundred pounds in cash, a small collection of photographs, some of his parents and sister, mostly of himself; a watch, a ring, and a gold chain round his neck. Using the card might be dangerous – they'd surely have warned his bank by now. The best thing might be to pawn the ring and the chain, then hitch North. He had friends in Aberdeen who'd hide him awhile.

But first – Reynolds.

It took Gavin an hour to find the house where Ken Reynolds lived. It was the best part of twenty-four hours since he'd eaten and his belly complained as he stood outside Livingstone Mansions. He told it to keep its peace, and slipped into the building. The interior looked less impressive by daylight. The tread of the stair carpet was worn, and the paint on the balustrade filthied with use.

Taking his time he climbed the three flights to Reynolds' apartment, and knocked.

Nobody answered, nor was there any sound of movement from inside. Reynolds had told him of course: don't come back – I won't be here. Had he somehow guessed the consequences of sicking that thing into the world?

Gavin rapped on the door again, and this time he was certain he heard somebody breathing on the other side of the door.

"Reynolds . . ." he said, pressing to the door, "I can hear you."

Nobody replied, but there was somebody in there, he was sure of it. Gavin slapped his palm on the door.

"Come on, open up. Open up, you bastard."

A short silence, then a muffled voice. "Go away."

"I want to speak to you."

"Go away, I told you, go away. I've nothing to say to you."

"You owe me an explanation, for God's sake. If you don't open this fucking door I'll fetch someone who will."

An empty threat, but Reynolds responded: "No! Wait. Wait."

There was the sound of a key in the lock, and the door was opened a few paltry inches. The flat was in darkness beyond the scabby face that peered out at Gavin. It was Reynolds sure enough, but unshaven and wretched. He smelt unwashed, even through the crack in the door, and he was wearing only a stained shirt and a pair of pants, hitched up with a knotted belt.

"I can't help you. Go away."

"If you'll let me explain—" Gavin pressed the door, and Reynolds was either too weak or too befuddled to stop him opening it. He stumbled back into the darkened hallway.

"What the fuck's going on in here?"

The place stank of rotten food. The air was evil with it. Reynolds let Gavin slam the door behind him before producing a knife from the pocket of his stained trousers.

"You don't fool me," Reynolds gleamed, "I know what you've done. Very fine. Very clever."

"You mean the murders? It wasn't me."

Reynolds poked the knife towards Gavin.

"How many blood-baths did it take?" he asked, tears in his eyes. "Six? Ten?"

"I didn't kill anybody."

". . . monster."

The knife in Reynolds' hand was the paper knife Gavin himself had wielded. He approached Gavin with it. There was no doubt: he had every intention of using it. Gavin flinched, and Reynolds seemed to take hope from his fear.

"Had you forgotten what it was like, being flesh and blood?"

The man had lost his marbles.

"Look . . . I just came here to talk."

"You came here to kill me. I could reveal you . . . so you came to kill me."

"Do you know who I am?" Gavin said.

Reynolds sneered: "You're not the queer boy. You look like him, but you're not."

"For pity's sake . . . I'm Gavin . . . Gavin—"

The words to explain, to prevent the knife pressing any closer, wouldn't come.

"Gavin, you remember?" was all he could say.

Reynolds faltered a moment, staring at Gavin's face.

"You're sweating," he said. The dangerous stare fading in his eyes.

Gavin's mouth had gone so dry he could only nod.

"I can see," said Reynolds, "you're sweating."

He dropped the point of the knife.

"It could never sweat," he said, "Never had, never would have, the knack of it. You're the boy . . . not it. The boy."

His face slackened, its flesh a sack which was almost emptied.

"I need help," said Gavin, his voice hoarse. "You've got to tell me what's going on."

"You want an explanation?" Reynolds replied, "you can have whatever you can find."

He led the way into the main room. The curtains were drawn, but even in the gloom Gavin could see that every antiquity it had contained had been smashed beyond repair. The pottery shards had been reduced to smaller shards, and those shards to dust. The stone reliefs were destroyed, the tombstone of Flavinus the Standard-Bearer was rubble.

"Who did this?"

"I did," said Reynolds.

"Why?"

Reynolds sluggishly picked his way through the destruction to the window, and peered through a slit in the velvet curtains.

"It'll come back, you see," he said, ignoring the question.

Gavin insisted: "Why destroy it all?"

"It's a sickness," Reynolds replied. "Needing to live in the past."

He turned from the window.

"I stole most of these pieces," he said, "over a period of many years. I was put in a position of trust, and I misused it."

He kicked over a sizeable chunk of rubble: dust rose.

"Flavinus lived and died. That's all there is to tell. Knowing his name means nothing, or next to nothing. It doesn't make Flavinus real again: he's dead and happy."

"The statue in the bath?"

Reynolds stopped breathing for a moment, his inner eye meeting the painted face.

"You I thought I was it, didn't you? When I came to the door."

"Yes. I thought it had finished its business."

"It imitates."

Reynolds nodded. "As far as I understand its nature," he said, "yes, it imitates."

"Where did you find it?"

"Near Carlisle. I was in charge of the excavation there. We found it lying in the bathhouse, a statue curled up into a ball beside the remains of an adult male. It was a riddle. A dead man and a statue, lying together in a bathhouse. Don't ask me what drew me to the thing, I don't know. Perhaps it works its will through the mind as well as the physique. I stole it, brought it back here."

"And you fed it?"

Reynolds stiffened.

"Don't ask."

"I *am* asking. You fed it?"

"Yes."

"You intended to bleed me, didn't you? That's why you brought me here: to kill me, and let it wash itself—"

Gavin remembered the noise of the creature's fists on the sides of the bath, that angry demand for food, like a child beating on its cot. He'd been so close to being taken by it, lamb-like.

"Why didn't it attack me the way it did you? Why didn't it just jump out of the bath and feed on me?"

Reynolds wiped his mouth with the palm of his hand.

"It saw your face, of course."

Of course: it saw my face, and wanted it for itself, and it couldn't steal the face of a dead man, so it let me be. The rationale for its behaviour was fascinating, now it was revealed: Gavin felt a taste of Reynolds' passion, unveiling mysteries.

"The man in the bathhouse. The one you uncovered—"

"Yes . . .?"

"He stopped it doing the same thing to him, is that right?"

"That's probably why his body was never moved, just sealed up. No-one understood that he'd died fighting a creature that was stealing his life."

The picture was near as damn it complete; just anger remaining to be answered.

This man had come close to murdering him to feed the effigy. Gavin's fury broke surface. He took hold of Reynolds by shirt and skin, and shook him. Was it his bones or teeth that rattled?

"It's almost got my face." He stared into Reynolds' bloodshot eyes. "What happens when it finally has the trick off pat?"

"I don't know."

"You tell me the worst – Tell me!"

"It's all guesswork," Reynolds replied.

"Guess then!"

"When it's perfected its physical imitation, I think it'll steal the one thing it can't imitate: your soul."

Reynolds was past fearing Gavin. His voice had sweetened, as though he was talking to a condemned man. He even smiled.

"Fucker!"

Gavin hauled Reynolds' face yet closer to his. White spittle dotted the old man's cheek.

"You don't care! You don't give a shit, do you?"

He hit Reynolds across the face, once, twice, then again and again, until he was breathless.

The old man took the beating in absolute silence, turning his face up from one blow to receive another, brushing the blood out of his swelling eyes only to have them fill again.

Finally, the punches faltered.

Reynolds, on his knees, picked pieces of tooth off his tongue.

"I deserved that," he murmured.

"How do I stop it?" said Gavin.

Reynolds shook his head.

"Impossible," he whispered, plucking at Gavin's hand. "Please," he said, and taking the fist, opened it and kissed the lines.

Gavin left Reynolds in the ruins of Rome, and went into the street. The interview with Reynolds had told him little he hadn't guessed. The only thing he could do now was find this beast that had his beauty, and best it. If he failed, he failed attempting to secure his only certain attribute: a face that was wonderful. Talk of souls and humanity was for him so much wasted air. He wanted his face.

There was rare purpose in his step as he crossed Kensington. After years of being the victim of circumstance he saw circumstance embodied at last. He would shake sense from it, or die trying.

In his flat Reynolds drew aside the curtain to watch a picture of evening fall on a picture of a city.

No night he would live through, no city he'd walk in again. Out of sighs, he let the curtain drop, and picked up the short stabbing sword. The point he put to his chest.

"Come on," he told himself and the sword, and pressed the hilt. But the pain as the blade entered his body a mere half inch was enough to make his head reel: he knew he'd faint before the job was half-done. So he crossed to the wall, steadied the hilt against it, and let his own body-weight impale him. That did the trick. He wasn't sure if the sword had skewered him through entirely, but by the amount of blood he'd surely killed himself. Though he tried to arrange to turn, and so drive the blade all the way home as he fell on it, he fluffed the gesture, and instead fell on his side. The impact made him aware of the sword in his body, a stiff, uncharitable presence transfixing him utterly.

It took him well over ten minutes to die, but in that time, pain apart, he was content. Whatever the flaws of his fifty-seven years, and they were many, he felt he was perishing in a way his beloved Flavinus would not have been ashamed of.

Towards the end it began to rain, and the noise on the roof made him believe God was burying the house, sealing him up forever. And as the moment came, so did a splendid delusion: a hand, carrying a light, and escorted by voices, seemed to break through the wall, ghosts of the future come to excavate his history. He smiled to greet them, and was about to ask what year this was when he realised he was dead.

The creature was far better at avoiding Gavin than he'd been at avoiding it. Three days passed without its pursuer snatching sight of hide or hair of it.

But the fact of its presence, close, but never too close, was indisputable. In a bar someone would say: "Saw you last night on the Edgware Road" when he'd not been near the place, or "How'd you make out with that Arab then?" or "Don't you speak to your friends any longer?"

And God, he soon got to like the feeling. The distress gave way to a pleasure he'd not known since the age of two: ease.

So what if someone else was working his patch, dodging the law and the street-wise alike; so what if his friends (what friends? Leeches) were being cut by this supercilious copy; so what if his life had been taken from him and was being worn to its length and its breadth in lieu of him? He could sleep, and know that he, or something so like him it made no difference, was awake in the night and being adored. He began to see the creature not as a monster terrorising him, but as his tool, his public persona almost. It was substance: he shadow.

He woke, dreaming.

It was four-fifteen in the afternoon, and the whine of traffic was loud from the street below. A twilight room; the air breathed and rebreathed and breathed again so it smelt of his lungs. It was over a week since he'd left Reynolds to the ruins, and in that time he'd only ventured out from his new digs (one tiny bedroom, kitchen, bathroom) three times. Sleep was more important now than food or exercise. He had enough dope to keep him happy when sleep wouldn't come, which was seldom, and he'd grown to like the staleness of the air, the flux of light through the curtainless window, the sense of a world elsewhere which he had no part of or place in.

Today he'd told himself he ought to go out and get some fresh air, but he hadn't been able to raise the enthusiasm. Maybe later, much later, when the bars were emptying and he wouldn't be noticed, then he'd slip out of his cocoon and see what could be seen. For now, there were dreams—

Water.

He'd dreamt water; sitting beside a pool in Fort Lauderdale, a pool full of fish. And the splash of their leaps and dives was continuing, an overflow from sleep. Or was it the other way round? Yes; he had been hearing running water in his sleep and his dreaming mind had made an illustration to accompany the sound. Now awake, the sound continued.

It was coming from the adjacent bathroom, no longer running, but lapping. Somebody had obviously broken in while he was asleep, and was now taking a bath. He ran down the short list of possible intruders: the few who knew he was here. There was Paul: a nascent hustler who'd bedded down on the floor two nights before; there was Chink, the dope dealer; and a girl from downstairs he thought was called Michelle. Who was he kidding? None of these people would have broken the lock on the door to get in. He knew very well who it must be. He was just playing a game with himself, enjoying the process of elimination, before he narrowed the options to one.

Keen for reunion, he slid out from his skin of sheet and duvet. His body turned to a column of gooseflesh as the cold air encased him, his sleep-erection hid its head. As he crossed the room to where his dressing gown hung on the back of the door he caught sight of himself in the mirror, a freeze frame from an atrocity film, a wisp of a man, shrunk by cold, and lit by a rainwater light. His reflection almost flickered, he was so insubstantial.

Wrapping the dressing gown, his only freshly purchased garment, around him, he went to the bathroom door. There was no noise of water now. He pushed the door open.

The warped linoleum was icy beneath his feet; and all he wanted to do was to see his friend, then crawl back into bed. But he owed the tatters of his curiosity more than that: he had questions.

The light through the frosted glass had deteriorated rapidly in the three minutes since he'd woken: the onset of night and a rain-storm congealing the gloom. In front of him the bath was almost filled to overflowing, the water was oil-slick calm, and dark. As before, nothing broke surface. It was lying deep, hidden.

How long was it since he'd approached a lime-green bath in a lime-green bathroom, and peered into the water? It could have been yesterday: his life between then and now had become one long night. He looked down. It was there, tucked up, as before, and asleep, still wearing all its clothes as though it had had no time to undress before it hid itself. Where it had been bald it now sprouted a luxuriant head of hair, and its features were quite complete. No trace of a painted face remained: it had a plastic beauty that was his own absolutely, down to the last mole. Its perfectly finished hands were crossed on its chest.

The night deepened. There was nothing to do but watch it sleep, and he became bored with that. It had traced him here, it wasn't likely to run away again, he could go back to bed. Outside the rain had slowed the commuters' homeward journey to a crawl, there were accidents, some fatal; engines overheated, hearts too. He listened to the chase; sleep came and went. It was the middle of the evening when thirst woke him again: he was dreaming water, and there was the sound as it had been before. The creature was hauling itself out of the bath, was putting its hand to the door, opening it.

There it stood. The only light in the bedroom was coming from the street below; it barely began to illuminate the visitor.

"Gavin? Are you awake?"

"Yes," he said.

"Will you help me?" it asked. There was no trace of threat in its voice, it asked as a man might ask his brother, for kinship's sake.

"What do you want?"

"Time to heal."

"Heal?"

"Put on the light."

Gavin switched on the lamp beside the bed and looked at the figure at the door. It no longer had its arms crossed on its chest, and Gavin saw that the position had been covering an appalling shotgun wound. The flesh of its chest had been blown open, exposing its colourless innards. There was, of course, no blood: that it would never have. Nor, from this distance, could Gavin see anything in its interior that faintly resembled human anatomy.

"God Almighty," he said.

"Preetorius had friends," said the other, and its fingers touched the edge of the wound. The gesture recalled a picture of the wall of his mother's house. Christ in Glory – the Sacred Heart floating inside the Saviour – while his fingers, pointing to the agony he'd suffered, said: "This was for you."

"Why aren't you dead?"

"Because I'm not yet alive," it said.

Not yet: remember that, Gavin thought. It has intimations of mortality.

"Are you in pain?"

"No," it said sadly, as though it craved the experience, "I feel nothing. All the signs of life are cosmetic. But I'm learning." It smiled. "I've got the knack of the yawn, and the fart." The idea was both absurd and touching; that it would aspire to farting, that a farcical failure in the digestive system was for it a precious sign of humanity.

"And the wound?"

"—is healing. Will heal completely in time."

Gavin said nothing.

"Do I disgust you?" it asked, without inflection.

"No."

It was staring at Gavin with perfect eyes, his perfect eyes.

"What did Reynolds tell you?" it asked.

Gavin shrugged.

"Very little."

"That I'm a monster? That I suck out the human spirit?"

"Not exactly."

"More or less."

"More or less," Gavin conceded.

It nodded. "He's right," it said. "In his way, he's right. I need blood: that makes me monstrous. In my youth, a month ago, I bathed in it. Its touch gave wood the appearance of flesh. But I don't need it now: the process is almost finished. All I need now—"

It faltered; not, Gavin thought, because it intended to lie, but because the words to describe its condition wouldn't come.

"What do you need?" Gavin pressed it.

It shook its head, looking down at the carpet. "I've lived several times, you know. Sometimes I've stolen lives and got away with it. Lived a natural span, then shrugged off that face and found another. Sometimes, like the last time, I've been challenged, and lost—"

"Are you some kind of machine?"

"No."

"What then?"

"I am what I am. I know of no others like me; though why should I be the only one? Perhaps there *are* others, many others: I simply don't know of them yet. So I live and die and live again, and learn nothing—" the word was bitterly pronounced, "—of myself. Understand? You know what you are because you see others like you. If you were alone on earth, what would you know? What the mirror told you, that's all. The rest would be myth and conjecture."

The summary was made without sentiment.

"May I lie down?" it asked.

It began to walk towards him, and Gavin could see more clearly the fluttering in its chest-cavity, the restless, incoherent forms that were mushrooming there in place of the heart. Sighing, it sank face-down on the bed, its clothes sodden, and closed its eyes.

"We'll heal," it said. "Just give us time."

Gavin went to the door of the flat and bolted it. Then he dragged a table over and wedged it under the handle. Nobody could get in and attack it in sleep: they would stay here together in safety, he and it, he and himself. The fortress secured, he brewed some coffee and sat in the chair across the room from the bed and watched the creature sleep.

The rain rushed against the window heavily one hour, lightly the next. Wind threw sodden leaves against the glass and they clung there like inquisitive moths; he watched them sometimes, when he tired of watching himself, but before long he'd want to look again, and he'd be back staring at the casual beauty of his outstretched arm, the light flicking the wrist-bone, the lashes. He fell asleep in the chair about midnight, with an ambulance complaining in the street outside, and the rain coming again.

It wasn't comfortable in the chair, and he'd surface from sleep every few minutes, his eyes opening a fraction. The creature was up: it was standing by the window, now in front of the mirror, now in the kitchen. Water ran: he dreamt water. The creature undressed: he dreamt sex. It stood over him, its chest whole, and he was reassured by its presence: he dreamt, it was for a moment only, himself lifted out of a street through a window into Heaven. It dressed in his clothes: he murmured his assent to the theft in his sleep. It was whistling: and there was a threat of day through the window, but he was too dozy to stir just yet, and quite content to have the whistling young man in his clothes live for him.

At last it leaned over the chair and kissed him on the lips, a brother's kiss, and left. He heard the door close behind it.

After that there were days, he wasn't sure how many, when he stayed in the room, and did nothing but drink water. This thirst had become unquenchable. Drinking and sleeping, drinking and sleeping, twin moons.

The bed he slept on was damp at the beginning from where the creature had laid, and he had no wish to change the sheets. On the contrary he enjoyed the wet linen, which his body dried out too soon. When it did he took a bath himself in the water the thing had lain in and returned to the bed dripping wet, his skin crawling with cold, and the scent of mildew all around. Later, too indifferent to move, he allowed his bladder free rein while he lay on the bed, and that water in time became cold, until he dried it with his dwindling body-heat.

But for some reason, despite the icy room, his nakedness, his hunger, he couldn't die.

He got up in the middle of the night of the sixth or seventh day, and sat on the edge of the bed to find the flaw in his resolve. When the solution didn't come he began to shamble around the room much as the creature had a week earlier, standing in front of the mirror to survey his pitifully changed body, watching the snow shimmer down and melt on the sill.

Eventually, by chance, he found a picture of his parents he remembered the creature staring at. Or had he dreamt that? He thought not: he had a distinct idea that it had picked up this picture and looked at it.

That was, of course, the bar to his suicide: that picture. There were respects to be paid. Until then how could he hope to die?

He walked to the Cemetery through the slush wearing only a pair of slacks and a tee-shirt. The remarks of middle-aged women and school-children went unheard. Whose business but his own was it if going barefoot was the death of him? The rain came and went, sometimes thickening towards snow, but never quite achieving its ambition.

There was a service going on at the church itself, a line of brittle coloured cars parked at the front. He slipped down the side into the churchyard. It boasted a good view, much spoiled today by the smoky veil of sleet, but he could see the trains and the high-rise flats; the endless rows of roofs. He ambled amongst the headstones, by no means certain of where to find his father's grave. It had been sixteen years: and the day hadn't been that memorable. Nobody had said anything illuminating about death in general, or his father's death specifically, there wasn't even a social gaff or two to mark the day: no aunt broke wind at the buffet table, no cousin took him aside to expose herself.

He wondered if the rest of the family ever came here: whether indeed they were still in the country. His sister had always threatened to move out: go to New Zealand, begin again. His mother was probably getting through her fourth husband by now, poor sod, though perhaps she was the pitiable one, with her endless chatter barely concealing the panic.

Here was the stone. And yes, there were fresh flowers in the marble urn that rested amongst the green marble chips. The old bugger had not lain here enjoying the view unnoticed. Obviously somebody, he guessed his sister, had come here seeking a little comfort from Father. Gavin ran his fingers over the name, the date, the platitude. Nothing exceptional: which was only right and proper, because there'd been nothing exceptional about him.

Staring at the stone, words came spilling out, as though Father was sitting on the edge of the grave, dangling his feet, raking his hair across his gleaming scalp, pretending, as he always pretended, to care.

"What do you think, eh?"

Father wasn't impressed.

"Not much, am I?" Gavin confessed.

You said it, son.

"Well I was always careful, like you told me. There aren't any bastards out there, going to come looking for me."

Damn pleased.

"I wouldn't be much to find, would I?"

Father blew his nose, wiped it three times. Once from left to right, again left to right, finishing right to left. Never failed. Then he slipped away.

"Old shithouse."

A toy train let out a long blast on its horn as it passed and Gavin looked up. There he was – himself – standing absolutely still a few yards away. He was wearing the same clothes he'd put on a week ago when he'd left the flat. They looked creased and shabby from constant wear. But the flesh! Oh, the flesh was more radiant than his own had ever been. It almost shone in the drizzling light; and the tears on the doppelganger's cheeks only made the features more exquisite.

"What's wrong?" said Gavin.

"It always makes me cry, coming here." It stepped over the graves towards him, its feet crunching on gravel, soft on grass. So real.

"You've been here before?"

"Oh yes. Many times, over the years—"

Over the years? What did it mean, over the years? Had it mourned here for people it had killed?

As if in answer:

"—I come to visit Father. Twice, maybe three times a year."

"This isn't your father," said Gavin, almost amused by the delusion. "It's mine."

"I don't see any tears on your face," said the other.

"I feel . . ."

"Nothing," his face told him. "You feel nothing at all, if you're honest."

That was the truth.

"Whereas I . . ." the tears began to flow again, its nose ran, "I will miss him until I die."

It was surely playacting, but if so why was there such grief in its eyes: and why were its features crumpled into ugliness as it wept. Gavin had seldom given in to tears: they'd always made him feel weak and ridiculous. But this thing was proud of tears, it gloried in them. They were its triumph.

And even then, knowing it had overtaken him, Gavin could find nothing in him that approximated grief.

"Have it," he said. "Have the snots. You're welcome."

The creature was hardly listening.

"Why is it all so painful?" it asked, after a pause. "Why is it loss that makes me human?"

Gavin shrugged. What did he know or care about the fine art of being human? The creature wiped its nose with its sleeve, sniffed, and tried to smile through its unhappiness.

"I'm sorry," it said, "I'm making a damn fool of myself. Please forgive me."

It inhaled deeply, trying to compose itself.

"That's all right," said Gavin. The display embarrassed him, and he was glad to be leaving.

"Your flowers?" he asked as he turned from the grave.

It nodded.

"He hated flowers."

The thing flinched.

"Ah."

"Still, what does he know?"

He didn't even look at the effigy again; just turned and started up the path that ran beside the church. A few yards on, the thing called after him:

"Can you recommend a dentist?"

Gavin grinned, and kept walking.

It was almost the commuter hour. The arterial road that ran by the church was already thick with speeding traffic: perhaps it was Friday, early escapees hurrying home. Lights blazed brilliantly, horns blared.

Gavin stepped into the middle of the flow without looking to right or left, ignoring the squeals of brakes, and the curses, and began to walk amongst the traffic as if he were idling in an open field.

The wing of a speeding car grazed his leg as it passed, another almost collided with him. Their eagerness to get somewhere, to arrive at a place they would presently be itching to depart from again, was comical. Let them rage at him, loathe him, let them glimpse his featureless face and go home haunted. If the circumstances were right, maybe one of them would panic, swerve, and run him down. Whatever. From now on he belonged to chance, whose Standard-Bearer he would surely be.

BRIAN LUMLEY

Necros

BRIAN LUMLEY IS THE AUTHOR of the popular series of *Necroscope* vampire books. Born on England's north-east coast, Lumley was serving as a sergeant in the Corps of Royal Military Police when he discovered the stories of H.P. Lovecraft while stationed in Berlin in the early 1960s.

After deciding to try his own hand at writing horror fiction, initially set in Lovecraft's influential Cthulhu Mythos, he sent his early efforts to editor August Derleth. The latter's famed Arkham House imprint published two collections of Lumley's short stories, *The Caller of the Black* and *The Horror at Oakdene and Others*, plus the short novel *Beneath the Moors*.

The author continued Lovecraft's themes in a series of novels before the publication of *Necroscope* in 1986 made him a best-seller all over the world. The initial volume was followed by *Necroscope II: Wamphyri!* (a.k.a. *Necroscope II: Vamphyri!*), *Necroscope III: The Source*, *Necroscope IV: Deadspeak* and *Necroscope V: Deadspawn*.

The *Vampire World* trilogy appeared in the early 1990s, and that was followed by the two-volume *Necroscope: The Lost Years* and the three-volume *E-Branch* series. The success of the *Necroscope* books has also spawned a worldwide marketing industry of comic books, statuettes and a role-playing game based on the concepts. An annual convention is held in Britain for dedicated enthusiasts.

Lumley's other books include the *Psychomech* trilogy, *Demogorgon, The House of Doors, Fruiting Bodies and Other Fungi* (which includes the British Fantasy Award-winning title story), *A Coven of Vampires, The Whisperer and Other Voices, Beneath the Moors and Darker Places* and *Harry Keogh: Necroscope and Other Weird Heroes!*

In 1998 he was named Grand Master at the World Horror Convention, and *The Brian Lumley Companion*, co-edited with Stanley Wiater, appeared from Tor Books in 2002.

Written two years before *Necroscope*, 'Necros' is one of Lumley's best – a clever twist on the vampire theme, with an ending that is guaranteed to come as a surprise. The story also became the basis for one of the first episodes of the 1997 Canadian TV series *The Hunger*.

I

AN OLD WOMAN IN a faded blue frock and black head-square paused in the shade of Mario's awning and nodded good-day. She smiled a gap-toothed smile. A bulky, slouch-shouldered youth in jeans and a stained yellow T-shirt – a slope-headed idiot, probably her grandson – held her hand, drooling vacantly and fidgeting beside her.

Mario nodded good-naturedly, smiled, wrapped a piece of stale *fucaccia* in greaseproof paper and came from behind the bar to give it to her. She clasped his hand, thanked him, turned to go.

Her attention was suddenly arrested by something she saw across the road. She started, cursed vividly, harshly, and despite my meager knowledge of Italian I picked up something of the hatred in her tone. "Devil's spawn!" She said it again. "Dog! Swine!" She pointed a shaking hand and finger, said yet again: "Devil's spawn!" before making the two-fingered, double-handed stabbing sign with which the Italians ward off evil. To do this it was first necessary that she drop her salted bread, which the idiot youth at once snatched up.

Then, still mouthing low, guttural imprecations, dragging the shuffling, *fucaccia*-munching cretin behind her, she hurried off along the street and disappeared into an alley. One word that she had repeated over and over again stayed in my mind: "*Necros! Necros!*" Though the word was new to me, I took it for a curse-word. The accent she put on it had been poisonous.

I sipped at my Negroni, remained seated at the small circular table beneath Mario's awning and stared at the object of the crone's distaste. It was a motorcar, a white convertible Rover and this year's model, inching slowly forward in a stream of holiday traffic. And it was worth looking at it only for the girl behind the wheel. The little man in the floppy white hat beside her – well, he was something else, too. But *she* was – just something else.

I caught just a glimpse, sufficient to feel stunned. That was good. I had thought it was something I could never know again: that feeling a man gets looking at a beautiful girl. Not after Linda. And yet—

She was young, say twenty-four or -five, some three or four years my junior. She sat tall at the wheel, slim, raven-haired under a white, wide-brimmed summer hat which just missed matching that of her companion, with a complexion cool and creamy enough to pour over peaches. I stood up – yes, to get a better look – and right then the traffic came to a momentary standstill. At that moment, too, she turned her head and looked at me. And if the profile had stunned me . . . well, the full frontal knocked me dead. The girl was simply, classically, beautiful.

Her eyes were of a dark green but very bright, slightly tilted and perfectly oval under straight, thin brows. Her cheeks were high, her lips a red Cupid's bow, her neck long and white against the glowing yellow of her blouse. And her smile—

—Oh, yes, she smiled.

Her glance, at first cool, became curious in a moment, then a little angry, until finally, seeing my confusion – that smile. And as she turned her attention back to the road and followed the stream of traffic out of sight, I saw a blush of color spreading on the creamy surface of her cheek. Then she was gone.

Then, too, I remembered the little man who sat beside her. Actually, I hadn't seen a great deal of him, but what I had seen had given me the creeps. He too had turned his head to stare at me, leaving in my mind's eye an impression of beady bird eyes, sharp and intelligent in the shade of his hat. He had stared at me for only a moment, and then his head had slowly turned away; but even when he no longer looked at me, when he stared straight ahead, it seemed to me I could feel those raven's eyes upon me, and that a query had been written in them.

I believed I could understand it, that look. He must have seen a good many young men staring at him like that – or rather, at the girl. His look had been a threat in answer to my threat – and because he was practiced in it I had certainly felt the more threatened!

I turned to Mario, whose English was excellent. "She has something against expensive cars and rich people?"

"Who?" he busied himself behind his bar.

"The old lady, the woman with the idiot boy."

"Ah!" he nodded. "Mainly against the little man, I suspect."

"Oh?"

"You want another Negroni?"

"OK – and one for yourself – but tell me about this other thing, won't you?"

"If you like – but you're only interested in the girl, yes?" He grinned.

I shrugged. "She's a good-looker . . ."

"Yes, I saw her." Now he shrugged. "That other thing – just old myths and legends, that's all. Like your English Dracula, eh?"

"Transylvanian Dracula," I corrected him.

"Whatever you like. And Necros: that's the name of the spook, see?"

"Necros is the name of a vampire?"

"A spook, yes."

"And this is a real legend? I mean, historical?"

He made a fifty-fifty face, his hands palms-up. "Local, I guess. Ligurian. I remember it from when I was a kid. If I was bad, old Necros sure to come and get me. Today," again the shrug, "it's forgotten."

"Like the bogeyman," I nodded.

"Eh?"

"Nothing. But why did the old girl go on like that?"

Again he shrugged. "Maybe she think that old man Necros, eh? She crazy, you know? Very backward. The whole family."

I was still interested. "How does the legend go?"

"The spook takes the life out of you. You grow old, spook grows young. It's a bargain you make: he gives you something you want, gets what he wants. What he wants is your youth. Except he uses it up quick and needs more. All the time, more youth."

"What kind of bargain is that?" I asked. "What does the victim get out of it?"

"Gets what he wants," said Mario, his brown face cracking into another grin. "In your case the girl, eh? *If* the little man was Necros . . ."

He got on with his work and I sat there sipping my Negroni. End of conversation. I thought no more about it – until later.

II

Of course, I should have been in Italy with Linda, but . . . I had kept her "Dear John" for a fortnight before shredding it, getting mindlessly drunk and starting in on the process of forgetting. That had been a month ago. The holiday had already been booked and I wasn't about to miss out on my trip to the sun. And so I had come out on my own. It was hot, the swimming was good, life was easy and the food superb. With just two days left to enjoy it, I told myself it hadn't been bad. But it would have been better with Linda.

Linda . . . She was still on my mind – at the back of it, anyway – later that night as I sat in the bar of my hotel beside an open bougainvillaea-decked balcony that looked down on the bay and the seafront lights of the town. And maybe she wasn't all that far back in my mind – maybe she was right there in front – or else I was just plain daydreaming. Whichever, I missed the entry of the lovely lady and her shriveled companion, failing to spot and recognize them until they were taking their seats at a little table just the other side of the balcony's sweep.

This was the closest I'd been to her, and—

Well, first impressions hadn't lied. This girl *was* beautiful. She didn't look quite as young as she'd first seemed – my own age, maybe – but beautiful she certainly was. And the old boy? He must be, could only be, her father. Maybe it sounds like I was little naive, but with her looks this lady really didn't need an old man. And if she did need one it didn't have to be *this* one.

By now she'd seen me and my fascination with her must have been obvious. Seeing it she smiled and blushed at one and the same time, and for a moment turned her eyes away – but only for a moment. Fortunately her companion had his back to me or he must have known my feelings at once; for as she looked at me again – fully upon me this time – I could have sworn I read an invitation in her eyes, and in that same moment any bitter vows I may have made melted away completely and were forgotten. God, *please* let him be her father!

For an hour I sat there, drinking a few too many cocktails, eating olives and potato crisps from little bowls on the bar, keeping my eyes off the girl as best I could, if only for common decency's sake. But . . . all the time I worried frantically at the problem of how to introduce myself, and as the minutes ticked by it seemed to me that the most obvious way must also be the best.

But how obvious would it be to the old boy?

And the damnable thing was that the girl hadn't given me another glance since her original – invitation? Had I mistaken that look of hers? – or was she simply waiting for me to make the first move? *God, let him be her father!*

She was sipping Martinis, slowly; he drank a rich red wine, in some quantity. I asked a waiter to replenish their glasses and charge it to me. I had already spoken to the bar steward, a swarthy, friendly little chap from the South called Francesco, but he hadn't been able to enlighten me. The pair were not resident, he assured me; but being resident myself I was already pretty sure of that.

Anyway, my drinks were delivered to their table; they looked surprised; the girl put on a perfectly innocent expression, questioned the waiter, nodded in my direction and gave me a cautious smile, and the old boy turned his head to stare at me. I found myself smiling in return but avoiding his eyes, which were like coals now, sunken deep in his brown-wrinkled face. Time seemed suspended – if only for a second – then the girl spoke again to the waiter and he came across to me.

"Mr Collins, sir, the gentleman and the young lady thank you and request that you join them." Which was everything I had dared hope for – for the moment.

Standing up I suddenly realized how much I'd had to drink. I willed sobriety on myself and walked across to their table. They didn't stand up but the little chap said, "Please sit." His voice was a rustle of dried grass. The waiter was behind me with a chair. I sat.

"Peter Collins," I said. "How do you do, Mr – er?—"

"Karpethes," he answered. "Nichos Karpethes. And this is my wife, Adrienne." Neither one of them had made the effort to extend their hands, but that didn't dismay me. Only the fact that they were married dismayed me. He must be very, very rich, this Nichos Karpethes.

"I'm delighted you invited me over," I said, forcing a smile, "but I see that I was mistaken. You see, I thought I heard you speaking English, and I—"

"Thought we were English?" she finished it for me. "A natural error. Originally I am Armenian, Nichos is Greek, of course. We do not speak each other's tongue, but we do both speak English. Are you staying here, Mr Collins?"

"Er, yes – for one more day and night. Then—" I shrugged and put on a sad look, "—back to England, I'm afraid."

"Afraid?" the old boy whispered. "There is something to fear in a return to your homeland?"

"Just an expression," I answered. "I meant I'm afraid that my holiday is coming to an end."

He smiled. It was a strange, wistful sort of smile, wrinkling his face up like a little walnut. "But your friends will be glad to see you again. Your loved ones—?"

I shook my head. "Only a handful of friends – none of them really close – and no loved ones. I'm a loner, Mr Karpethes."

"A loner?" His eyes glowed deep in their sockets and his hands began to tremble where they gripped the table's rim. "Mr Collins, you don't—"

"We understand," she cut him off. "For although we are together, we too, in our way, are loners. Money has made Nichos lonely, you see? Also, he is not a well man and time is short. He will not waste what time he has on frivolous friendships. As for myself – people do not understand our being together, Nichos and I. They pry, and I withdraw. And so I too am a loner."

There was no accusation in her voice, but still I felt obliged to say: "I certainly didn't intend to pry, Mrs—"

"Adrienne," she smiled. "Please. No, of course you didn't. I would not want you to think we thought that of you. Anyway I will *tell* you why we are together, and then it will be put aside."

Her husband coughed, seemed to choke, struggled to his feet. I stood up and took his arm. He at once shook me off – with some distaste, I thought – but Adrienne had already signaled to a waiter. "Assist Mr Karpethes to the gentleman's room," she quickly instructed in very good Italian. "And please help him back to the table when he has recovered."

As he went Karpethes gesticulated, probably tried to say something to me by way of an apology, choked again and reeled as he allowed the waiter to help him from the room.

"I'm . . . sorry," I said, not knowing what else to say.

"He has attacks." She was cool. "Do not concern yourself. I am used to it."

We sat in silence for a moment. Finally I began. "You were going to tell me—"

"Ah, yes! I had forgotten. It is a symbiosis."

"Oh?"

"Yes. I need the good life he can give me, and he needs . . . my youth? We supply each other's needs." And so, in a way, the old woman with the idiot boy hadn't been wrong after all. A sort of bargain had indeed been struck. Between Karpethes and his wife. As that thought crossed my mind I felt the short hairs at the back of my neck stiffen for a moment. Gooseflesh grawled on my arms. After all, "Nichos" was pretty close to "Necros," and now this youth thing again. Coincidence, of course. And after all, aren't all relationships bargains of sorts? Bargains struck for better or for worse.

"But for how long?" I asked. "I mean, how long will it work for you?"

She shrugged. "I have been provided for. And he will have me all the days of his life."

I coughed, cleared my throat, gave a strained, self-conscious laugh. "And here's me, the non-pryer!"

"No, not at all, I wanted you to know."

"Well," I shrugged, "—but it's been a pretty deep first conversation."

"First? Did you believe that buying me a drink would entitle you to more than one conversation?"

I almost winced. "Actually, I—"

But then she smiled and my world lit up. "You did not need to buy the drinks," she said. "There would have been some other way."

I looked at her inquiringly. "Some other way to—?"

"To find out if we were English or not."

"Oh!"

"Here comes Nichos now," she smiled across the room. "And we must be leaving. He's not well. Tell me, will you be on the beach tomorrow?"

"Oh – yes!" I answered after a moment's hesitation. "I like to swim."

"So do I. Perhaps we can swim out to the raft . . .?"

"I'd like that very much."

Her husband arrived back at the table under his own steam. He looked a little stronger now, not quite so shriveled somehow. He did not sit but gripped the back of his chair with parchment fingers, knuckles white where the skin stretched over old bones. "Mr Collins," he rustled, "—Adrienne, I'm sorry . . ."

"There's really no need," I said, rising.

"We really must be going." She also stood. "No, you stay here, er, Peter? It's kind of you, but we can manage. Perhaps we'll see you on the beach." And she helped him to the door of the bar and through it without once looking back.

III

They weren't staying at my hotel, had simply dropped in for a drink. That was understandable (though I would have preferred to think that she had been looking for me) for *my* hotel was middling tourist-class while theirs was something else. They were up on the hill, high on the crest of a Ligurian spur where a smaller, much more exclusive place nested in Mediterranean pines. A place whose lights spelled money when they shone up there at night, whose music came floating down from a tiny open-air disco like the laughter of high-living elementals of the air. If I was poetic it was because of her. I mean, that beautiful girl and that weary, wrinkled dried up walnut of an old man. If anything I was sorry for him. And yet in another way I wasn't.

And let's make no pretense about it – if I haven't said it already, let me say it right now – I wanted her. Moreover, there had been that about our conversation, her beach invitation, which told me that she was available.

The thought of it kept me awake half the night . . .

I was on the beach at 9:00 a.m. – they didn't show until 11:00. When they did, and when she came out of her tiny changing cubicle—

There wasn't a male head on the beach that didn't turn at least twice. Who could blame them? That girl, in *that* costume, would have turned the head of a sphynx. But – there was something, some little nagging thing different about her. A maturity beyond her years? She held herself like a model, a princess. But who was it for? Karpethes or me?

As for the old man: he was in a crumpled lightweight summer suit and sunshade hat as usual, but he seemed a bit more perky this morning. Unlike myself he'd doubtless had a good night's sleep. While his wife had been changing he had made his way unsteadily across the pebbly beach to my table and sun umbrella, taking the seat directly opposite me; and before his wife could appear he had opened with:

"Good morning, Mr Collins."

"Good morning," I answered. "Please call me Peter."

"Peter, then," he nodded. He seemed out of breath, either from his stumbling walk over the beach or a certain urgency which I could detect in his movements, his hurried, almost rude "let's get down to it" manner.

"Peter, you said you would be here for one more day?"

"That's right," I answered, for the first time studying him closely where he sat like some strange garden gnome half in the shade of the beach umbrella. "This is my last day."

He was a bundle of dry wood, a pallid prune, a small, umber scarecrow. And his voice, too, was of straw, or autumn leaves blown across a shady path. Only his eyes were alive. "And you said you have no family, few friends, no one to miss you back in England?"

Warning bells rang in my head. Maybe it wasn't so much urgency in him – which usually implies a goal or ambition still to be realized – but eagerness in that the goal was in sight. "That's correct. I am, was, a student doctor. When I get home I shall seek a position. Other than that there's nothing, no one, no ties."

He leaned forward, bird eyes very bright, claw hand reaching across the table, trembling, and—

Her shadow suddenly fell across us as she stood there in that costume. Karpethes jerked back in his chair. His face was working, strange emotions twisting the folds and wrinkles of his flesh into stranger contours. I could feel my heart thumping against my ribs . . . why I couldn't say. I calmed myself, looked up at her and smiled.

She stood with her back to the sun, which made a dark silhouette of her head and face. But in that blot of darkness her oval eyes were green jewels. "Shall we swim, Peter?"

She turned and ran down the beach, and of course I ran after her. She had a head start and beat me to the water, beat me to the raft, too. It wasn't until I hauled myself up beside her that I thought of Karpethes: how I hadn't even excused myself before plunging after her. But at least the water had cleared my head, bringing me completely awake and aware.

Aware of her incredible body where it stretched almost touching mine, on the fiber deck of the gently bobbing raft.

I mentioned her husband's line of inquiry, gasping a little for breath as I recovered from the frantic exercise of our race. She, on the other hand, already seemed completely recovered. She carefully arranged her hair about her shoulders like a fan, to dry in the sunlight, before answering.

"Nichos is not really my husband," she finally said, not looking at me. "I am his companion, that's all. I could have told you last night, but . . . there was the chance that you really were curious only about our nationality. As for any veiled threats he might have issued: that is not unusual. He might not have the vitality of younger men, but jealousy is ageless."

"No," I answered, "he didn't threaten – not that I noticed. But jealousy? Knowing I have only one more day to spend here, what has he to fear from me?"

Her shoulders twitched a little, a shrug. She turned her face to me, her lips inches away. Her eyelashes were like silken shutters over green pools, hiding whatever swam in the deeps. "I am young, Peter, and so are you. And you are very attractive, very . . . eager? Holiday romances are not uncommon."

My blood was on fire. "I have very little money," I said. "We are staying at different hotels. He already suspects me. It is impossible."

"What is?" she innocently asked, leaving me at a complete loss.

But then she laughed, tossed back her hair, already dry, dangled her hands and arms in the water. "Where there's a will . . ." she said.

"You know that I want you—" The words spilled out before I could control or change them.

"Oh, yes. And I want you." She said it so simply, and yet suddenly I felt seared. A moth brushing the magnet candle's flame.

I lifted my head, looked toward the beach. Across seventy-five yards of sparkling water the beach umbrellas looked very large and close. Karpethes sat in the shade just as I had last seen him, his face hidden in shadow. But I knew that he watched.

"You can do nothing here," she said, her voice languid – but I noticed now that she, too, seemed short of breath.

"This," I told her with a groan, "is going to kill me!"

She laughed, laughter that sparkled more than the sun on the sea. "I'm sorry," she sobered. "It's unfair of me to laugh. But – your case is not hopeless."

"Oh?"

"Tomorrow morning, early, Nichos has an appointment with a specialist in Genova. I am to drive him into the city tonight. We'll stay at a hotel overnight."

I groaned my misery. "Then my case *is* quite hopeless. I fly tomorrow."

"But if I sprained my wrist," she said, "and so could not drive . . . and if he went into Genova by taxi while I stayed behind with a headache – because of the pain from my wrist—" Like a flash she was on her feet, the raft tilting, her body diving, striking the water into a spray of diamonds.

Seconds for it all to sink in – and then I was following her, laboring through the water in her churning wake. And as she splashed from the sea, seeing her stumble, go to her hands and knees in Ligurian shingle – and the pained look on her face, the way she held her wrist as she came to her feet. As easy as that!

Karpethes, struggling to rise from his seat, stared at her with his mouth agape. Her face screwed up now as I followed her up the beach. And Adrienne holding her "sprained" wrist and shaking it, her mouth forming an elongated "O." The sinuous motion of her body and limbs, mobile marble with dew of ocean clinging saltily. . . .

If the tiny man had said to me: "I am Necros. I want ten years of your life for one night with her," at that moment I might have sealed the bargain. Gladly. But legends are legends and he wasn't Necros, and he didn't, and I didn't. After all, there was no need. . . .

IV

I suppose my greatest fear was that she might be "having me on," amusing herself at my expense. She was, of course, "safe" with me – insofar as I would be gone tomorrow and the "romance" forgotten, for her, anyway – and I could also see how she was starved for young companionship, a fact she had brought right out in the open from the word go.

But why me? Why should I be so lucky?

Attractive? Was I? I had never thought so. Perhaps it was because I *was* so safe: here today and gone tomorrow, with little or no chance of complications. Yes, that must be it. *If* she wasn't simply making a fool of me. She might be just a tease—

—But she wasn't.

At 8:30 that evening I was in the bar of my hotel – had been there for an hour, careful not to drink too much, unable to eat – when the waiter came to me and said there was a call for me on the reception telephone. I hurried out to reception where the clerk discreetly excused himself and left me alone.

"Peter?" Her voice was a deep well of promise. "He's gone. I've booked us a table, to dine at 9:00. Is that all right for you?"

"A table? Where?" my own voice breathless.

"Why, up here, of course! Oh, don't worry, it's perfectly safe. And anyway, Nichos knows."

"Knows?" I was taken aback, a little panicked. "What does he know?"

"That we're dining together. In fact he suggested it. He didn't want me to eat alone – and since this is your last night . . ."

"I'll get a taxi right away," I told her.

"Good. I look forward to . . . seeing you. I shall be in the bar."

I replaced the telephone in its cradle, wondering if she always took an *apéritif* before the main course. . . .

I had smartened myself up. That is to say, I was immaculate. Black bow tie, white evening jacket (courtesy of C & A), black trousers and a lightly-frilled white shirt, the only one I had ever owned. But I might have known that my appearance would never match up to hers. It seemed that everything she did was just perfectly right. I could only hope that that meant literally everything.

But in her black lace evening gown with its plunging neckline, short wide sleeves and delicate silver embroidery, she was stunning. Sitting with her in the bar, sipping our drinks – for me a large whiskey and for her a tall Cinzano – I couldn't take my eyes off her. Twice I reached out for her hand and twice she drew back from me.

"Discreet they may well be," she said, letting her oval green eyes flicker toward the bar, where guests stood and chatted, and back to me, "but there's really no need to give them occasion to gossip."

"I'm sorry, Adrienne," I told her, my voice husky and close to trembling, "but—"

"How is it," she demurely cut me off, "that a good-looking man like you is – how do you say it? – going short?"

I sat back, chuckled. "That's a rather unladylike expression," I told her.

"Oh? And what I've planned for tonight is ladylike?"

My voice went huskier still. "Just what is your plan?"

"While we eat," she answered, her voice low, "I shall tell you." At which point a waiter loomed, towel over his arm, inviting us to accompany him to the dining room.

Adrienne's portions were tiny, mine huge. She sipped a slender, light white wine, I gulped blocky rich red from a glass the waiter couldn't seem to leave alone. Mercifully I was hungry – I hadn't eaten all day – else that meal must surely have bloated me out. And all of it ordered in advance, the very best in quality cuisine.

"This," she eventually said, handling me her key, "fits the door of our suite." We were sitting back, enjoying liqueurs and cigarettes. "The rooms are on the ground floor. Tonight you enter through the door, tomorrow morning you leave via the window. A slow walk down to the seafront will refresh you. How is that for a plan?"

"Unbelievable!"

"You don't believe it?"

"Not my good fortune, no."

"Shall we say that we both have our needs?"

"I think," I said, "that I may be falling in love with you. What if I don't wish to leave in the morning?"

She shrugged, smiled, said: "Who knows what tomorrow may bring?"

How could I ever have thought of her simply as another girl? Or even an ordinary young woman? Girl she certainly was, woman, too, but so . . . *knowing*! Beautiful as a princess and knowing as a whore.

If Mario's old myths and legends were reality, and if Nichos Karpethes were really Necros, then he'd surely picked the right companion. No man born could ever have resisted Adrienne, of that I was quite certain. These thoughts were in my mind – but dimly, at the back of my mind – as I left her smoking in the dining room and followed her directions to the suite of rooms at the rear of the hotel. In the front of my mind were other thoughts, much more vivid and completely erotic.

I found the suite, entered, left the door slightly ajar behind me.

The thing about an Italian room is its size. An entire suite of rooms is vast. As it happened I was only interested in one room, and Adrienne had obligingly left the door to that one open.

I was sweating. And yet . . . I shivered.

Adrienne had said fifteen minutes, time enough for her to smoke another cigarette and finish her drink. Then she would come to me. By now the entire staff of the hotel probably knew I was in here, but this was Italy.

V

I shivered again. Excitement? Probably.

I threw off my clothes, found my way to the bathroom, took the quickest shower of my life. Drying myself off, I padded back to the bedroom.

Between the main bedroom and the bathroom a smaller door stood ajar. I froze as I reached it, my senses suddenly alert, my ears seeming to stretch themselves into vast receivers to pick up any slightest sound. For there had been a sound, I was sure of it, from that room. . . .

A scratching? A rustle? A whisper? I couldn't say. But a sound, anyway.

Adrienne would be coming soon. Standing outside that door I slowly recommenced toweling myself dry. My naked feet were still firmly rooted, but my hands automatically worked with the towel. It was nerves, only nerves. There had been no sound, or at worst only the night breeze off the sea, whispering in through an open window.

I stopped toweling, took another step toward the main bedroom, heard the sound again. A small, choking rasp. A tiny gasping for air.

Karpethes? What the hell was going on?

I shivered violently, my suddenly chill flesh shuddering in an uncontrollable spasm. But . . . I forced myself to action, returned to the main bedroom, quickly dressed (with the exceptions of my tie and jacket) and crept back to the small room.

Adrienne must be on her way to me even now. She mustn't find me poking my nose into things, like a suspicious kid. I must kill off this silly feeling that had my skin crawling. Not that an attack of nerves was unnatural in the circumstances, on the contrary, but I wasn't about to let it spoil the night. I pushed open the door of the room, entered into darkness, found the lightswitch. Then—

—I held my breath, flipped the switch.

The room was only half as big as the others. It contained a small single bed, a bedside table, a wardrobe. Nothing more, or at least nothing immediately apparent to my wildly darting eyes. My heart, which was racing, slowed and began to settle toward a steadier beat. The window was open, external shutters closed – but small night sounds were finding their way in through the louvers. The distant sounds of traffic, the toot of horns – holiday sounds from below.

I breathed deeply and gratefully, and saw something projecting from beneath the pillow on the bed. A corner of card or of dark leather, like a wallet or—

—Or a passport!

A Greek passport, Karpethes', when I opened it. But how could it be? The man in the photograph was young, no older than me. His birthdate proved it. And there was his name: Nichos Karpethes. Printed in Greek, of course, but still plain enough. His son?

Puzzling over the passport had served to distract me. My nerves had steadied up. I tossed the passport down, frowned at it where it lay upon the bed, breathed deeply once more . . . and froze solid!

A scratching, a hissing, a dry grunting – from the wardrobe.

Mice? Or did I in fact smell a rat?

Even as the short hairs bristled on the back of my neck I knew anger. There were too many unexplained things here. Too much I didn't understand. And what was it I feared? Old Mario's myths and legends? No, for in my experience the Italians are notorious for getting things wrong. Oh, yes, notorious . . .

I reached out, turned the wardrobe's doorknob, yanked the doors open.

At first I saw nothing of any importance or significance. My eyes didn't know what they sought. Shoes, patent leather, two pairs, stood side by side below. Tiny suits, no bigger than boys' sizes, hung above on steel hangers. And – my God, my God – a waistcoat!

I backed out of that little room on rubber legs, with the silence of the suite shrieking all about me, my eyes bugging, my jaw hanging slack—

"Peter?"

She came in through the suite's main door, came floating toward me, eager, smiling, her green eyes blazing. Then blazing their suspicion, their anger as they saw my condition. "Peter!"

I lurched away as her hands reached for me, those hands I had never yet touched, which had never touched me. Then I was into the main bedroom, snatching my tie and jacket from the bed, (don't ask me why!) and out of the window, yelling some inarticulate, choking thing at her and lashing out frenziedly with my foot as she reached after me. Her eyes were bubbling green hells. "*Peter!*"

Her fingers closed on my forearm, bands of steel containing a fierce, hungry heat. And strong as two men she began to lift me back into her lair!

I put my feet against the wall, kicked, came free and crashed backward into shrubbery. Then up on my feet, gasping for air, running, tumbling, crashing into the night, down madly tilting slopes, through black chasms of mountain pine with the Mediterranean stars winking overhead, and the beckoning, friendly lights of the village seen occasionally below . . .

In the morning, looking up at the way I had descended and remembering the nightmare of my panic-flight, I counted myself lucky to have survived it. The place was precipitous. In the end I *had* fallen, but only for a short distance. All in utter darkness, and my head striking something hard. But . . .

I did survive. Survived both Adrienne and my flight from her.

And waking with the dawn, and gently fingering my bruises and the massive bump on my forehead, I made my staggering way back to my still slumbering hotel, let myself in and *locked* myself in my room – then sat there trembling and moaning until it was time for the coach.

Weak? Maybe I was, maybe I am.

But on my way into Genova, with people round me and the sun hot through the coach's windows, I could think again. I could roll up my sleeve and examine that claw mark of four slim fingers and a thumb, branded white into my suntanned flesh, where hair would never more grow on skin sore and wrinkled.

And seeing those marks I could also remember the wardrobe and the waistcoat – and what the waistcoat contained.

That tiny puppet of a man, alive still but barely, his stick-arms dangling through the waistcoat's armholes, his baby's head projecting, its chin supported by the tightly buttoned waistcoat's breast. And the large bull-dog clip over the hanger's bar, its teeth fastened in the loose, wrinkled skin of his walnut head, holding it up. And his skinny little legs dangling, twig-things twitching there; and his pleading, pleading eyes!

But eyes are something I mustn't dwell upon.

And green is a color I can no longer bear . . .

BRIAN STABLEFORD

The Man Who Loved the Vampire Lady

BRIAN STABLEFORD HAS PUBLISHED more than fifty novels and two hundred short stories, as well as several non-fiction books, thousands of articles for periodicals and reference books, several volumes of translations from the French, and a number of anthologies. He is a part-time Lecturer in Creative Writing at King Alfred's College, Winchester.

His novels include *The Empire of Fear, Young Blood, Werewolves of London* and a future history series comprising *Inherit the Earth, Architects of Emortality, The Fountains of Youth, The Cassandra Complex, Dark Ararat* and *The Omega Expedition. Complications and Other Stories* is a new collection, and other recent titles include *Kiss the Goat: A Twenty-first Century Ghost Story, Claire Lenoir and Other Stories* (a collection of translations of stories by Villiers de l'Isle Adam from Tartarus Press), and a set of translations of vampire novels by Paul Féval, comprising *The Vampire Countess, Knightshade* and *Vampire City*. His current projects include the compilation of a *Historical Dictionary of Science Fiction Literature* for Scarecrow Press.

" 'The Man Who Loved the Vampire Lady' was written in 1986," recalls Stableford, "when I was fascinated by the way that the then-nascent boom in revisionist vampire stories was putting a new spin on the sexual subtexts of the Victorian classics. (I was particularly impressed by Pierre Kast's *Vampires of Alfama*.) Having read critical accounts which suggested that Dracula's vampirism is a metaphorical transfiguration of syphilis, I figured that revisionist vampirism might equally well take some metaphorical inspiration from AIDS."

The following story is a touchingly romantic evocation of the vampire that also sets the scene for the author's longer work.

> *A man who loves a vampire lady may not die young,*
> *but cannot live forever.* WALACHIAN PROVERB

IT WAS THE THIRTEENTH of June in the Year of Our Lord 1623. Grand Normandy was in the grip of an early spell of warm weather, and the streets of London bathed in sunlight. There were crowds everywhere, and the port was busy with ships, three having docked that very day. One of the ships, the *Freemartin*, was from the Moorish enclave and had produce from the heart of Africa, including ivory and the skins of exotic animals. There were rumors, too, of secret and more precious goods: jewels and magical charms; but such rumors always attended the docking of any vessel from remote parts of the world. Beggars and street urchins had flocked to the dockland, responsive as ever to such whisperings, and were plaguing every sailor in the streets, as anxious for gossip as for copper coins. It seemed that the only faces not animated by excitement were those worn by the severed heads that dressed the spikes atop the Southwark Gate. The Tower of London, though, stood quite aloof from the hubbub, its tall and forbidding turrets so remote from the streets that they belonged to a different world.

Edmund Cordery, mechanician to the court of the Archduke Girard, tilted the small concave mirror on the brass device that rested on his workbench, catching the rays of the afternoon sun and deflecting the light through the system of lenses.

He turned away and directed his son, Noell, to take his place. "Tell me if all is well," he said tiredly. "I can hardly focus my eyes, let alone the instrument."

Noell closed his left eye and put his other to the microscope. He turned the wheel that adjusted the height of the stage. "It's perfect," he said. "What is it?"

"The wing of a moth." Edmund scanned the polished tabletop, checking that the other slides were in readiness for the demonstration. The prospect of Lady Carmilla's visit filled him with a complex anxiety that he resented in himself. Even in the old days, she had not come to his laboratory often, but to see her here – on his own territory, as it were – would be bound to awaken memories that were untouched by the glimpses that he caught of her in the public parts of the Tower and on ceremonial occasions.

"The water slide isn't ready," Noell pointed out.

Edmund shook his head. "I'll make a fresh one when the time comes," he said. "Living things are fragile, and the world that is in a water drop is all too easily destroyed."

He looked farther along the bench-top, and moved a crucible, placing it out of sight behind a row of jars. It was impossible – and unnecessary – to make the place tidy, but he felt it important to conserve some sense of order and control. To discourage himself from fidgeting, he went to the window and looked out at the sparkling Thames and the strange gray sheen on the slate roofs of the houses beyond. From this high vantage point, the people were tiny; he was higher even than the cross on the steeple of the church beside the Leathermarket. Edmund was not a devout man, but such was the agitation within him, yearning for expression in action, that the sight of the cross on the church made him cross himself, murmuring the ritual devotion. As soon as he had done it, he cursed himself for childishness.

I am forty-four years old, he thought, *and a mechanician. I am no longer the boy who was favored with the love of the lady, and there is no need for this stupid trepidation.*

He was being deliberately unfair to himself in this private scolding. It was not simply the fact that he had once been Carmilla's lover that made him anxious. There was the microscope, and the ship from the Moorish country. He hoped that he would be able to judge by the lady's reaction how much cause there really was for fear.

The door opened then, and the lady entered. She half turned to indicate by a flutter of her hand that her attendant need not come in with her, and he withdrew, closing the door behind him. She was alone, with no friend or favorite in tow. She came across the room carefully, lifting the hem of her skirt a little, though the floor was not dusty. Her gaze flicked from side to side, to take note of the shelves, the beakers, the furnace, and the numerous tools of the mechanician's craft. To a commoner, it would have seemed a threatening environment, redolent with unholiness, but her attitude was cool and controlled. She arrived to stand before the brass instrument that Edmund had recently completed, but did not look long at it before raising her eyes to look fully into Edmund's face.

"You look well, Master Cordery," she said calmly. "But you are pale. You should not shut yourself in your rooms now that summer is come to Normandy."

Edmund bowed slightly, but met her gaze. She had not changed in the slightest degree, of course, since the days when he had been intimate with her. She was six hundred years old – hardly younger than the archduke – and the years were impotent as far as her appearance was concerned. Her complexion was much darker than his, her eyes a deep liquid brown, and her hair jet black. He had not stood so close to her for several years, and he could not help the tide of memories rising in his mind. For her, it would be different: his hair was gray now, his skin creased; he must seem an altogether different person. As he met her gaze, though, it seemed to him that she, too, was remembering, and not without fondness.

"My lady," he said, his voice quite steady, "may I present my son and apprentice, Noell."

Noell bowed more deeply than his father, blushing with embarrassment.

The Lady Carmilla favored the youth with a smile. "He has the look of you, Master Cordery," she said – a casual compliment. She returned her attention then to the instrument.

"The designer was correct?" she asked.

"Yes, indeed," he replied. "The device is most ingenious. I would dearly like to meet the man who thought of it. A fine discovery – though it taxed the talents of my lens grinder severely. I think we might make a better one, with much care and skill; this is but a poor example, as one must expect from a first attempt."

The Lady Carmilla seated herself at the bench, and Edmund showed her how to apply her eye to the instrument, and how to adjust the focusing wheel and the mirror. She expressed surprise at the appearance of the magnified moth's wing, and Edmund took her through the series of prepared slides, which included other parts of insects' bodies, and sections through the stems and seeds of plants.

"I need a sharper knife and a steadier hand, my lady," he told her. "The device exposes the clumsiness of my cutting."

"Oh no, Master Cordery," she assured him politely. "These are quite pretty enough. But we were told that more interesting things might be seen. Living things too small for ordinary sight."

Edmund bowed in apology and explained about the preparation of water slides. He made a new one, using a pipette to take a drop from a jar full of dirty river water. Patiently, he helped the lady search the slide for the tiny creatures that human eyes were not equipped to perceive. He showed her one that flowed as if it were semiliquid itself, and tinier ones that moved by means of cilia. She was quite captivated, and watched for some time, moving the slide very gently with her painted fingernails.

Eventually she asked: "Have you looked at other fluids?"

"What kind of fluids?" he asked, though the question was quite clear to him and disturbed him.

She was not prepared to mince words with him. "Blood, Master Cordery," she said very softly. Her past acquaintance with him had taught her respect for his intelligence, and he half regretted it.

"Blood clots very quickly," he told her. "I could not produce a satisfactory slide. It would take unusual skill."

"I'm sure that it would," she replied.

"Noell has made drawings of many of the things we *have* looked at," said Edmund. "Would you like to see them?"

She accepted the change of subject, and indicated that she would. She moved to Noell's station and began sorting through the drawings, occasionally looking up at the boy to compliment him on his work. Edmund stood by, remembering how sensitive he once had been to her moods and desires, trying hard to work out now exactly what she was thinking. Something in one of her contemplative glances at Noell sent an icy pang of dread into Edmund's gut, and he found his more important fears momentarily displaced by what might have been anxiety for his son, or simply jealousy. He cursed himself again for his weakness.

"May I take these to show the archduke?" asked the Lady Carmilla, addressing the question to Noell rather than to his father. The boy nodded, still too embarrassed to construct a proper reply. She took a selection of the drawings and rolled them into a scroll. She stood and faced Edmund again.

"We are most interested in this apparatus," she informed him. "We must consider carefully whether to provide you with new assistants, to encourage development of the appropriate skills. In the meantime, you may return to your ordinary work. I will send someone for the instrument, so that the archduke can inspect it at his leisure. Your son draws very well, and must be encouraged. You and he may visit me in my chambers on Monday next; we will dine at seven o'clock, and you may tell me about all your recent work."

Edmund bowed to signal his acquiescence – it was, of course, a command rather than an invitation. He moved before her to the door in order to hold it open for her. The two exchanged another brief glance as she went past him.

When she had gone, it was as though something taut unwound inside him, leaving him relaxed and emptied. He felt strangely cool and distant as he considered the possibility – stronger now – that his life was in peril.

When the twilight had faded, Edmund lit a single candle on the bench and sat staring into the flame while he drank dark wine from a flask. He did not look up when Noell came into the room, but when the boy brought another stool close to his and sat down upon it, he offered the flask. Noell took it, but sipped rather gingerly.

"I'm old enough to drink now?" he commented dryly.

"You're old enough," Edmund assured him. "But beware of excess, and never drink alone. Conventional fatherly advice, I believe."

Noell reached across the bench so that he could stroke the barrel of the microscope with slender fingers.

"What are you afraid of" he asked.

Edmund sighed. "You're old enough for that, too, I suppose?"

"I think you ought to tell me."

Edmund looked at the brass instrument and said: "It were better to keep things like this dark secret. Some human mechanician, I daresay, eager to please the vampire lords and ladies, showed off his cleverness as proud as a peacock. Thoughtless. Inevitable, though, now that all this play with lenses has become fashionable."

"You'll be glad of eyeglasses when your sight begins to fail," Noell told him. "In any case, I can't see the danger in this new toy."

Edmund smiled. "New toys," he mused. "Clocks to tell the time, mills to grind the corn, lenses to aid human sight. Produced by human craftsmen for the delight of their masters. I think we've finally succeeded in proving to the vampires just how very clever we are — and how much more there is to know than we know already."

"You think the vampires are beginning to fear us?"

Edmund gulped wine from the flask and passed it again to his son. "Their rule is founded in fear and superstition," he said quietly. "They're long-lived, suffer only mild attacks of diseases that are fatal to us, and have marvelous powers of regeneration. But they're not immortal, and they're vastly outnumbered by humans. Terror keeps them safe, but terror is based in ignorance, and behind their haughtiness and arrogance, there's a gnawing fear of what might happen if humans ever lost their supernatural reverence for vampire-kind. It's very difficult for them to die, but they don't fear death any the less for that."

"There've been rebellions against vampire rule. They've always failed."

Edmund nodded to concede the point. "There are three million people in Grand Normandy," he said, "and less than five thousand vampires. There are only forty thousand vampires in the entire imperium of Gaul, and about the same number in the imperium of Byzantium – no telling how many there may be in the khanate of Walachia and Cathay, but not so very many more. In Africa the vampires must be outnumbered three or four thousand to one. If people no longer saw them as demons and demi-gods, as unconquerable forces of evil, their empire would be fragile. The centuries through which they live give them wisdom, but longevity seems to be inimical to creative thought – they learn, but they don't *invent*. Humans remain the true masters of art and science, which are forces of change. They've tried to control that – to turn it to their advantage – but it remains a thorn in their side."

"But they do have power," insisted Noell. "They *are* vampires."

Edmund shrugged. "Their longevity is real – their powers of regeneration, too. But is it really their magic that makes them so? I don't know for sure what merit there is in their incantations and rituals, and I don't think even *they* know – they cling to their rites because they dare not abandon them, but where the power that makes humans into vampires really comes from, no one knows. From the devil? I think not. I don't believe in the devil – I think it's something in the blood. I think vampirism may be a kind of disease – but a disease that makes men stronger instead of weaker, insulates them against death instead of killing them. If that *is* the case – do you see now why the Lady Carmilla asked whether I had looked at blood beneath the microscope?"

Noell stared at the instrument for twenty seconds or so, mulling over the idea. Then he laughed.

"If we could *all* become vampires," he said lightly, "we'd have to suck one another's blood."

Edmund couldn't bring himself to look for such ironies. For him, the possibilities inherent in discovering the secrets of vampire nature were much more immediate, and utterly bleak.

"It's not true that they *need* to suck the blood of humans," he told the boy. "It's not nourishment. It gives them . . . a kind of pleasure that we can't understand. And it's part of the mystique that makes them so terrible . . . and hence so powerful." He stopped, feeling embarrassed. He did not know how much Noell knew about his sources of information. He and his wife never talked about the days of his affair with the Lady Carmilla, but there was no way to keep gossip and rumor from reaching the boy's ears.

Noell took the flask again, and this time took a deeper draft from it. "I've heard," he said distantly, "that humans find pleasure, too . . . in their blood being drunk."

"No," replied Edmund calmly. "That's untrue. Unless one counts the small pleasure of sacrifice. The pleasure that a human man takes from a vampire lady is the same pleasure that he takes from a human lover. It might be different for the girls who entertain vampire men, but I suspect it's just the excitement of hoping that they may become vampires themselves."

Noell hesitated, and would probably have dropped the subject, but

Edmund realized suddenly that he did not want the subject dropped. The boy had a right to know, and perhaps might one day *need* to know.

"That's not entirely true," Edmund corrected himself. "When the Lady Carmilla used to taste my blood, it did give me pleasure, in a way. It pleased me because it pleased *her*. There *is* an excitement in loving a vampire lady, which makes it different from loving an ordinary woman . . . even though the chance that a vampire lady's lover may himself become a vampire is so remote as to be inconsiderable."

Noell blushed, not knowing how to react to this acceptance into his father's confidence. Finally he decided that it was best to pretend a purely academic interest.

"Why are there so many more vampire women than men?" he asked.

"No one knows for sure," Edmund said. "No humans, at any rate. I can tell you what I believe, from hearsay and from reasoning, but you must understand that it is a dangerous thing to think about, let alone to speak about."

Noell nodded.

"The vampires keep their history secret," said Edmund, "and they try to control the writing of human history, but the following facts are probably true. Vampirism came to western Europe in the fifth century, with the vampire-led horde of Attila. Attila must have known well enough how to make more vampires – he converted both Aëtius, who became ruler of the imperium of Gaul, and Theodosius II, the emperor of the east who was later murdered. Of all the vampires that now exist, the vast majority must be converts. I have heard reports of vampire children born to vampire ladies, but it must be an extremely rare occurrence. Vampire men seem to be much less virile than human men – it is said that they couple very rarely. Nevertheless, they frequently take human consorts, and these consorts often become vampires. Vampires usually claim that this is a gift, bestowed deliberately by magic, but I am not so sure they can control the process. I think the semen of vampire men carries some kind of seed that communicates vampirism much as the semen of humans makes women pregnant – and just as haphazardly. That's why the male lovers of vampire ladies don't become vampires."

Noell considered this, and then asked: "Then where do vampire lords come from?"

"They're converted by other male vampires," Edmund said. "Just as Attila converted Aëtius and Theodosius." He did not elaborate, but waited to see whether Noell understood the implication. An expression of disgust crossed the boy's face and Edmund did not know whether to be glad or sorry that his son could follow the argument through.

"Because it doesn't always happen," Edmund went on, "it's easy for the vampires to pretend that they have some special magic. But some women never become pregnant, though they lie with their husbands for years. It is said, though, that a human may also become a vampire by drinking vampire's blood – if he knows the appropriate magic spell. That's a rumor the vampires don't like, and they exact terrible penalties if anyone is caught trying the experiment. The ladies of our own court, of course, are for the most part onetime lovers of the archduke or his cousins. It would be indelicate to speculate about the conversion of the archduke, though he is certainly acquainted with Aëtius."

Noell reached out a hand, palm downward, and made a few passes above the candle flame, making it flicker from side to side. He stared at the microscope.

"*Have* you looked at blood?" he asked.

"I have," replied Edmund. "And semen. Human blood, of course – and human semen."

"And?"

Edmund shook his head. "They're certainly not homogeneous fluids," he said, "but the instrument isn't good enough for really detailed inspection. There are small corpuscles – the ones in semen have long, writhing tails – but there's more . . . much more . . . to be seen, if I had the chance. By tomorrow this instrument will be gone – I don't think I'll be given the chance to build another."

"You're surely not in danger! You're an important man – and your loyalty has never been in question. People think of you as being almost a vampire yourself. A black magician. The kitchen girls are afraid of me because I'm your son – they cross themselves when they see me."

Edmund laughed, a little bitterly. "I've no doubt they suspect me of intercourse with demons, and avoid my gaze for fear of the spell of the evil eye. But none of that matters to the vampires. To them, I'm only a human, and for all that they value my skills, they'd kill me without a thought if they suspected that I might have dangerous knowledge."

Noell was clearly alarmed by this. "Wouldn't. . . ." He stopped, but saw Edmund waiting for him to ask, and carried on after only a brief pause. "The Lady Carmilla . . . wouldn't she . . .?"

"Protect me?" Edmund shook his head. "Not even if I were her favorite still. Vampire loyalty is to vampires."

"She was human once."

"It counts for nothing. She's been a vampire for nearly six

hundred years, but it wouldn't be any different if she were no older than I.''

"But . . . she did love you?"

"In her way," said Edmund sadly. "In her way." He stood up then, no longer feeling the urgent desire to help his son to understand. There were things the boy could find out only for himself and might never have to. He took up the candle tray and shielded the flame with his hand as he walked to the door. Noell followed him, leaving the empty flask behind.

Edmund left the citadel by the so-called Traitor's Gate, and crossed the Thames by the Tower Bridge. The houses on the bridge were in darkness now, but there was still a trickle of traffic; even at two in the morning, the business of the great city did not come to a standstill. The night had clouded over, and a light drizzle had begun to fall. Some of the oil lamps that were supposed to keep the thoroughfare lit at all times had gone out, and there was not a lamplighter in sight. Edmund did not mind the shadows, though.

He was aware before he reached the south bank that two men were dogging his footsteps, and he dawdled in order to give them the impression that he would be easy to track. Once he entered the network of streets surrounding the Leathermarket, though, he gave them the slip. He knew the maze of filthy streets well enough – he had lived here as a child. It was while he was apprenticed to a local clockmaker that he had learned the cleverness with tools that had eventually brought him to the notice of his predecessor, and had sent him on the road to fortune and celebrity. He had a brother and a sister still living and working in the district, though he saw them very rarely. Neither one of them was proud to have a reputed magician for a brother, and they had not forgiven him his association with the Lady Carmilla.

He picked his way carefully through the garbage in the dark alleys, unperturbed by the sound of scavenging rats. He kept his hands on the pommel of the dagger that was clasped to his belt, but he had no need to draw it. Because the stars were hidden, the night was pitch-dark, and few of the windows were lit from within by candlelight, but he was able to keep track of his progress by reaching out to touch familiar walls every now and again.

He came eventually to a tiny door set three steps down from a side street, and rapped upon it quickly, three times and then twice. There was a long pause before he felt the door yield beneath his fingers, and he stepped inside hurriedly. Until he relaxed when the door clicked shut again, he did not realize how tense he had been.

He waited for a candle to be lit.

The light, when it came, illuminated a thin face, crabbed and wrinkled, the eyes very pale and the wispy white hair gathered imperfectly behind a linen bonnet.

"The lord be with you," he whispered.

"And with you, Edmund Cordery," she croaked.

He frowned at the use of his name – it was a deliberate breach of etiquette, a feeble and meaningless gesture of independence. She did not like him, though he had never been less than kind to her. She did not fear him as so many others did, but she considered him tainted. They had been bound together in the business of the Fraternity for nearly twenty years, but she would never completely trust him.

She led him into an inner room, and left him there to take care of his business.

A stranger stepped from the shadows. He was short, stout, and bald, perhaps sixty years old. He made the special sign of the cross, and Edmund responded.

"I'm Cordery," he said.

"Were you followed?" The older man's tone was deferential and fearful.

"Not here. They followed me from the Tower, but it was easy to shake them loose."

"That's bad."

"Perhaps – but it has to do with another matter, not with our business. There's no danger to you. Do you have what I asked for?"

The stout man nodded uncertainly. "My masters are unhappy," he said. "I have been asked to tell you that they do not want you to take risks. You are too valuable to place yourself in peril."

"I am in peril already. Events are overtaking us. In any case, it is neither your concern nor that of your . . . masters. It is for me to decide."

The stout man shook his head, but it was a gesture of resignation rather than a denial. He pulled something from beneath the chair where he had waited in the shadows. It was a large box, clad in leather. A row of small holes was set in the longer side, and there was a sound of scratching from within that testified to the presence of living creatures.

"You did exactly as I instructed?" asked Edmund.

The small man nodded, then put his hand on the mechanician's arm, fearfully. "Don't open it, sir, I beg you. Not here."

"There's nothing to fear," Edmund assured him.

"You haven't been in Africa, sir, as I have. Believe me, *everyone* is afraid – and not merely humans. They say that vampires are dying, too."

"Yes, I know," said Edmund distractedly. He shook off the older man's restraining hand and undid the straps that sealed the box. He lifted the lid, but not far – just enough to let the light in, and to let him see what was inside.

The box contained two big gray rats. They cowered from the light. Edmund shut the lid again and fastened the straps.

"It's not my place, sir," said the little man hesitantly, "but I'm not sure that you really understand what you have there. I've seen the cities of West Africa – I've been in Corunna, too, and Marseilles. They remember other plagues in those cities, and all the horror stories are emerging again to haunt them. Sir, if any such thing ever came to London. . . ."

Edmund tested the weight of the box to see whether he could carry it comfortably. "It's not your concern," he said. "Forget everything that has happened. I will communicate with your masters. It is in my hands now."

"Forgive me," said the other, "but I must say this: there is naught to be gained from destroying vampires, if we destroy ourselves, too. It would be a pity to wipe out half of Europe in the cause of attacking our oppressors."

Edmund stared at the stout man coldly. "You talk too much," he said. "Indeed, you talk a *deal* too much."

"I beg your pardon, sire."

Edmund hesitated for a moment, wondering whether to reassure the messenger that his anxiety was understandable, but he had learned long ago that where the business of the Fraternity was concerned, it was best to say as little as possible. There was no way of knowing when this man would speak again of this affair, or to whom, or with what consequence.

The mechanician took up the box, making sure that he could carry it comfortably. The rats stirred inside, scrabbling with their small clawed feet. With his free hand, Edmund made the sign of the cross again.

"God go with you," said the messenger, with urgent sincerity.

"And with thy spirit," replied Edmund colorlessly.

Then he left, without pausing to exchange a ritual farewell with the crone. He had no difficulty in smuggling his burden back into the Tower, by means of a gate where the guard was long practiced in the art of turning a blind eye.

When Monday came, Edmund and Noell made their way to the Lady Carmilla's chambers. Noell had never been in such an apartment before, and it was a source of wonder to him. Edmund watched the boy's reactions to the carpets, the wall hangings, the mirrors and ornaments, and could not help but recall the first time *he* had entered these chambers. Nothing had changed here, and the rooms were full of provocations to stir and sharpen his faded memories.

Younger vampires tended to change their surroundings often, addicted to novelty, as if they feared the prospect of being changeless themselves. The Lady Carmilla had long since passed beyond this phase of her career. She had grown used to changelessness, had transcended the kind of attitude to the world that permitted boredom and ennui. She had adapted herself to a new aesthetic of existence, whereby her personal space became an extension of her own eternal sameness, and innovation was confined to tightly controlled areas of her life – including the irregular shifting of her erotic affections from one lover to another.

The sumptuousness of the lady's table was a further source of astonishment to Noell. Silver plates and forks he had imagined, and crystal goblets, and carved decanters of wine. But the lavishness of provision for just three diners – the casual waste – was something that obviously set him aback. He had always known that he was himself a member of a privileged elite, and that by the standards of the greater world, Master Cordery and his family ate well; the revelation that there was a further order of magnitude to distinguish the private world of the real aristocracy clearly made its impact upon him.

Edmund had been very careful in preparing his dress, fetching from his closet finery that he had not put on for many years. On official occasions he was always concerned to play the part of mechanician, and dressed in order to sustain that appearance. He never appeared as a courtier, always as a functionary. Now, though, he was reverting to a kind of performance that Noell had never seen him play, and though the boy had no idea of the subtleties of his father's performance, he clearly understood something of what was going on; he had complained acidly about the dull and plain way in which his father had made *him* dress.

Edmund ate and drank sparingly, and was pleased to note that Noell did likewise, obeying his father's instructions despite the obvious temptations of the lavish provision. For a while the lady was content to exchange routine courtesies, but she came quickly enough – by her standards – to the real business of the evening.

"My cousin Girard," she told Edmund, "is quite enraptured by your clever device. He finds it most interesting."

"Then I am pleased to make him a gift of it," Edmund replied. "And I would be pleased to make another, as a gift for Your Ladyship."

"That is not our desire," she said coolly. "In fact, we have other matters in mind. The archduke and his seneschal have discussed certain tasks that you might profitably carry out. Instructions will be communicated to you in due time, I have no doubt."

"Thank you, my lady," said Edmund.

"The ladies of the court were pleased with the drawings that I showed to them," said the Lady Carmilla, turning to look at Noell. "They marveled at the thought that a cupful of Thames water might contain thousands of tiny living creatures. Do you think that our bodies, too, might be the habitation of countless invisible insects?"

Noell opened his mouth to reply, because the question was addressed to him, but Edmund interrupted smoothly.

"There are creatures that may live upon our bodies," he said, "and worms that may live within. We are told that the macrocosm reproduces in essence the microcosm of human beings; perhaps there is a small microcosm within us, where our natures are reproduced again, incalculably small. I have read. . . ."

"I have read, Master Cordery," she cut in, "that the illnesses that afflict humankind might be carried from person to person by means of these tiny creatures."

"The idea that diseases were communicated from one person to another by tiny seeds was produced in antiquity," Edmund replied, "but I do not know how such seeds might be recognized, and I think it very unlikely that the creatures we have seen in river water could possibly be of that character."

"It is a disquieting thought," she insisted, "that our bodies might be inhabited by creatures of which we can know nothing, and that every breath we take might be carrying into us seeds of all kinds of change, too small to be seen or tasted. It makes me feel uneasy."

"But there is no need," Edmund protested. "Seeds of corruptibility take root in human flesh, but yours is inviolate."

"You know that is not so, Master Cordery," she said levelly. "You have seen me ill yourself."

"That was a pox that killed many humans, my lady – yet it gave to you no more than a mild fever."

"We have reports from the imperium of Byzantium, and from the Moorish enclave, too, that there is plague in Africa, and that it has now reached the southern regions of the imperium of Gaul. It is said that this plague makes little distinction between human and vampire."

"Rumors, my lady," said Edmund soothingly. "You know how news becomes blacker as it travels."

The Lady Carmilla turned again to Noell, and this time addressed him by name so that there could be no opportunity for Edmund to usurp the privilege of answering her. "Are you afraid of me, Noell?" she asked.

The boy was startled, and stumbled slightly over his reply, which was in the negative.

"You must not lie to me," she told him. "You *are* afraid of me, because I am a vampire. Master Cordery is a skeptic, and must have told you that vampires have less magic than is commonly credited to us, but he must also have told you that I can do you harm if I will. Would you like to be a vampire yourself, Noell?"

Noell was still confused by the correction, and hesitated over his reply, but he eventually said: "Yes, I would."

"Of course you would," she purred. "All humans would be vampires if they could, no matter how they might pretend when they bend the knee in church. And men *can* become vampires; immortality is within our gift. Because of this, we have always enjoyed the loyalty and devotion of the greater number of our human subjects. We have always rewarded that devotion in some measure. Few have joined our ranks, but the many have enjoyed centuries of order and stability. The vampires rescued Europe from a Dark Age, and as long as vampires rule, barbarism will always be held in check. Our rule has not always been kind, because we cannot tolerate defiance, but the alternative would have been far worse. Even so, there are men who would destroy us – did you know that?"

Noell did not know how to reply to this, so he simply stared, waiting for her to continue. She seemed a little impatient with his gracelessness, and Edmund deliberately let the awkward pause go on. He saw a certain advantage in allowing Noell to make a poor impression.

"There is an organization of rebels," the Lady Carmilla went on. "A secret society, ambitious to discover the secret way by which vampires are made. They put about the idea that they would make all men immortal, but this is a lie, and foolish. The members of this brotherhood seek power for themselves."

The vampire lady paused to direct the clearing of one set of dishes and the bringing of another. She asked for a new wine, too. Her gaze wandered back and forth between the gauche youth and his self-assured father.

"The loyalty of your family is, of course, beyond question," she eventually continued. "No one understands the workings of society like a mechanician, who knows well enough how forces must be balanced and how the different parts of a machine must interlock and support one another. Master Cordery knows well how the cleverness of rulers resembles the cleverness of clockmakers, do you not?"

"Indeed, I do, my lady," replied Edmund.

"There might be a way," she said, in a strangely distant tone, "that a good mechanician might earn a conversion to vampirism."

Edmund was wise enough not to interpret this as an offer or a promise. He accepted a measure of the new wine and said: "My lady, there are matters that it would be as well for us to discuss in private. May I send my son to his room?"

The Lady Carmilla's eyes narrowed just a little, but there was hardly any expression in her finely etched features. Edmund held his breath, knowing that he had forced a decision upon her that she had not intended to make so soon.

"The poor boy has not quite finished his meal," she said.

"I think he has had enough, my lady," Edmund countered. Noell did not disagree, and, after a brief hesitation, the lady bowed to signal her permission. Edmund asked Noell to leave, and, when he was gone, the Lady Carmilla rose from her seat and went from the dining room into an inner chamber. Edmund followed her.

"You were presumptuous, Master Cordery," she told him.

"I was carried away, my lady. There are too many memories here."

"The boy is mine," she said, "if I so choose. You do know that, do you not?"

Edmund bowed.

"I did not ask you here tonight to make you witness the seduction of your son. Nor do you think that I did. This matter that you would discuss with me – does it concern science or treason?"

"Science, my lady. As you have said yourself, my loyalty is not in question."

Carmilla laid herself upon a sofa and indicated that Edmund should take a chair nearby. This was the antechamber to her bedroom, and the air was sweet with the odor of cosmetics.

"Speak," she bade him.

"I believe that the archduke is afraid of what my little device might reveal," he said. "He fears that it will expose to the eye such seeds as carry vampirism from one person to another, just as it might expose the seeds that carry disease. I think that the man who devised the instrument may have been put to death already, but I think you know well enough that a discovery once made is likely to be made again and again. You are uncertain as to what course of action would best serve your ends, because you cannot tell whence the greater threat to your rule might come. There is the Fraternity, which is dedicated to your destruction; there is plague in Africa, from which even vampires may die; and there is the new sight, which renders visible what previously lurked unseen. Do you want my advice, Lady Carmilla?"

"Do you *have* any advice, Edmund?"

"Yes. Do not try to control by terror and persecution the things that are happening. Let your rule be unkind *now*, as it has been before, and it will open the way to destruction. Should you concede power gently, you might live for centuries yet, but if you strike out . . . your enemies will strike back.''

The vampire lady leaned back her head, looking at the ceiling. She contrived a small laugh.

"I cannot take advice such as that to the archduke," she told him flatly.

"I thought not, my lady," Edmund replied very calmly.

"You humans have your own immortality," she complained. "Your faith promises it, and you all affirm it. Your faith tells you that you must not covet the immortality that is ours, and we do no more than agree with you when we guard it so jealously. You should look to your Christ for fortune, not to us. I think you know well enough that we could not convert the world if we wanted to. Our magic is such that it can be used only sparingly. Are you distressed because it has never been offered to you? Are you bitter? Are you becoming our enemy because you cannot become our kin?"

"You have nothing to fear from me, my lady," he lied. Then he added, not quite sure whether it was a lie or not: "I loved you faithfully. I still do."

She sat up straight then, and reached out a hand as though to stroke his cheek, though he was too far away for her to reach.

"That is what I told the archduke," she said, "when he suggested to me that you might be a traitor. I promised him that I could test your loyalty more keenly in my chambers than his officers in theirs. I do not think you could delude me. Edmund. Do you?"

"No my lady," he replied.

"By morning," she told him gently, "I will know whether or not you are a traitor."

"That you will," he assured her. "That you will, my lady."

He woke before her, his mouth dry and his forehead burning. He was not sweating – indeed, he was possessed by a feeling of desiccation, as though the moisture were being squeezed out of his organs. His head was aching, and the light of the morning sun that streamed through the unshuttered window hurt his eyes.

He pulled himself up to a half-sitting position, pushing the coverlet back from his bare chest.

So soon! he thought. He had not expected to be consumed so quickly, but he was surprised to find that his reaction was one of relief rather than fear or regret. He had difficulty collecting his thoughts, and was perversely glad to accept that he did not need to.

He looked down at the cuts that she had made on his breast with her little silver knife; they were raw and red, and made a strange contrast with the faded scars whose crisscross pattern still engraved the story of unforgotten passions. He touched the new wounds gently with his fingers, and winced at the fiery pain.

She woke up then, and saw him inspecting the marks.

"Have you missed the knife?" she asked sleepily. "Were you hungry for its touch?"

There was no need to lie now, and there was a delicious sense of freedom in that knowledge. There was a joy in being able to face her, at last, quite naked in his thoughts as well as his flesh.

"Yes, my lady," he said with a slight croak in his voice. "I had missed the knife. Its touch . . . rekindled flames in my soul."

She had closed her eyes again, to allow herself to wake slowly. She laughed. "It is pleasant, sometimes, to return to forsaken pastures. You can have no notion how a particular *taste* may stir memories. I am glad to have seen you again, in this way. I had grown quite used to you as the gray mechanician. But now. . . ."

He laughed, as lightly as she, but the laugh turned to a cough, and something in the sound alerted her to the fact that all was not as it should be. She opened her eyes and raised her head, turning toward him.

"Why, Edmund," she said, "you're as pale as death!"

She reached out to touch his cheek, and snatched her hand away again as she found it unexpectedly hot and dry. A blush of confusion spread across her own features. He took her hand and held it, looking steadily into her eyes.

"Edmund," she said softly. "What have you done?"

"I can't be sure," he said, "and I will not live to find out, but I have tried to kill you, my lady."

He was pleased by the way her mouth gaped in astonishment. He watched disbelief and anxiety mingle in her expression, as though fighting for control. She did not call out for help.

"This is nonsense," she whispered.

"Perhaps," he admitted. "Perhaps it was also nonsense that we talked last evening. Nonsense about treason. Why did you ask me to make the microscope, my lady, when you knew that making me a party to such a secret was as good as signing my death warrant?"

"Oh Edmund," she said with a sigh. "You could not think that it was my own idea? I tried to protect you, Edmund, from Girard's fears and suspicions. It was because I was your protector that I was made to bear the message. What have you done, Edmund?"

He began to reply, but the words turned into a fit of coughing.

She sat upright, wrenching her hand away from his enfeebled grip, and looked down at him as he sank back upon the pillow.

"For the love of God!" she exclaimed, as fearfully as any true believer. "It is the plague – the plague out of Africa!"

He tried to confirm her suspicion, but could do so only with a nod of his head as he fought for breath.

"But they held the *Freemartin* by the Essex coast for a full fortnight's quarantine," she protested. "There was no trace of plague aboard."

"The disease kills men," said Edmund in a shallow whisper. "But animals can carry it, in their blood, without dying."

"You cannot know this!"

Edmund managed a small laugh. "My lady," he said, "I am a member of that Fraternity that interests itself in everything that might kill a vampire. The information came to me in good time for me to arrange delivery of the rats – though when I asked for them, I had not in mind the means of using them that I eventually employed. More recent events. . . ." Again he was forced to stop, unable to draw sufficient breath even to sustain the thin whisper.

The Lady Carmilla put her hand to her throat, swallowing as if she expected to feel evidence already of her infection.

"You would destroy me, Edmund?" she asked, as though she genuinely found it difficult to believe.

"I would destroy you all," he told her. "I would bring disaster, turn the world upside down, to end your rule. . . . We cannot allow you to stamp out learning itself to preserve your empire forever. Order must be fought with chaos, and chaos is come, my lady."

When she tried to rise from the bed, he reached out to restrain her, and though there was no power left in him, she allowed herself to be checked. The coverlet fell away from her, to expose her breasts as she sat upright.

"The boy will die for this, Master Cordery," she said. "His mother, too."

"They're gone," he told her. "Noell went from your table to the custody of the society that I serve. By now they're beyond your reach. The archduke will never catch them."

She stared at him, and now he could see the beginnings of hate and fear in her stare.

"You came here last night to bring me poisoned blood," she said. "In the hope that this new disease might kill even me, you condemned yourself to death. What did you do, Edmund?"

He reached out again to touch her arm, and was pleased to see her flinch and draw away: that he had become dreadful.

"Only vampires live forever," he told her hoarsely. "But anyone may drink blood, if they have the stomach for it. I took full measure from my two sick rats . . . and I pray to God that the seed of this fever is raging in my blood . . . and in my semen, too. You, too, have received full measure, my lady . . . and you are in God's hands now like any common mortal. I cannot know for sure whether you will catch the plague, or whether it will kill you, but I – an unbeliever – am not ashamed to pray. Perhaps you could pray, too, my lady, so that we may know how the Lord favors one unbeliever over another."

She looked down at him, her face gradually losing the expressions that had tugged at her features, becoming masklike in its steadiness.

"You could have taken our side, Edmund. I trusted you, and I could have made the archduke trust you, too. You could have become a vampire. We could have shared the centuries, you and I."

This was dissimulation, and they both knew it. He had been her lover, and had ceased to be, and had grown older for so many years that now she remembered him as much in his son as in himself. The promises were all too obviously hollow now, and she realized that she could not even taunt him with them.

From beside the bed she took up the small silver knife that she had used to let his blood. She held it now as if it were a dagger, not a delicate instrument to be used with care and love.

"I thought you still loved me," she told him. "I really did."

That, at least, he thought, might be true.

He actually put his head farther back, to expose his throat to the expected thrust. He wanted her to strike him – angrily, brutally, passionately. He had nothing more to say, and would not confirm or deny that he did still love her.

He admitted to himself now that his motives had been mixed, and that he really did not know whether it was loyalty to the Fraternity that had made him submit to this extraordinary experiment. It did not matter.

She cut his throat, and he watched her for a few long seconds while she stared at the blood gouting from the wound. When he saw her put stained fingers to her lips, knowing what she knew, he realized that after her own fashion, she still loved him.

MICHAEL MARSHALL SMITH

A Place to Stay

MICHAEL MARSHALL SMITH IS A NOVELIST and screenwriter who lives in North London with his wife Paula and two cats.

His first novel, *Only Forward*, won the Philip K. Dick and August Derleth Awards, while *Spares* was optioned by Stephen Spielberg's DreamWorks SKG and translated in seventeen countries around the world. His most recent novel was the *Sunday Times* best-seller *The Straw Men*. The author's short stories have appeared in numerous anthologies and magazines, and six are currently under option for television. A new collection, *More Tomorrow and Other Stories*, was published by Earthling Publications in 2003, and he has recently completed his fifth novel, *The Lonely Dead*.

As Smith explains: "'A Place To Stay' was one of those stories where the place came first, and the story afterwards, seeping into the environment like flood water into a cellar. Having spent a week in New Orleans myself a few years ago, I know I found it increasingly hard to summon up enthusiasm for leaving. I *still* fantasize about the *muffelettas* at the French Bar, in fact, and it's been about eight years now. I'd love to go back, but the Old Quarter is like a pitcher plant: it's all too possible that I might not be able to scramble out a second time.

"There would be worse places to spend eternity, I guess . . ."

As you would expect from a writer of Smith's talent, the following is definitely not your ordinary type of vampire tale.

"JOHN, DO YOU BELIEVE in vampires?"

I took a moment to light a cigarette. This wasn't to avoid the issue, but rather to prepare myself for the length and vitriol of the answer I intended to give – and to tone it down a little. I hardly knew the woman who'd asked the question, and had no idea of her tolerance for short, blunt words. I wanted to be gentle with her, but if there's one star in the pantheon of possible nightmares which I certainly *don't* believe in, then it has to be bloody vampires. I mean, really.

I was in New Orleans, and it was nearly Hallowe'en. Children of the Night have a tendency to crop up in such circumstances, like talk of rain in London. Now that I was here, I could see why. The French Quarter, with its narrow streets and looming balconies frozen in time, almost made the idea of vampires credible, especially in the lingering moist heat of the fall. It felt like a playground for suave monsters, a perpetual reinventing past, and if vampires lived anywhere, I supposed, then these dark streets and alleyways with their fetid, flamboyant cemeteries would be as good a place as any.

But they *didn't* live anywhere, and after another punishing swallow of my salty Margarita, I started to put Rita-May right on this fact. She shifted herself comfortably against my chest, and listened to me rant.

We were in Jimmy Buffet's bar on Decatur, and the evening was developing nicely. At nine o'clock I'd been there by myself, sitting at the bar and trying to work out how many Margaritas I'd drunk. The fact that I was counting shows what a sad individual I am. The further fact that I couldn't seem to count properly demonstrates that on that particular evening I was an extremely *drunk* sad individual too. And I mean, yes, Margaritaville is kind of a tourist trap, and I could have been sitting somewhere altogether heavier and more authentic across the street. But I'd done that the previous two nights, and besides, I liked Buffet's bar. I was, after all, a tourist. You didn't feel in any danger of being killed in his place, which I regard as a plus. They only played Jimmy Buffet on the jukebox, not surprisingly, so I didn't have to worry that my evening was suddenly going to be shattered by something horrible from the post-melodic school of popular music. Say what you like about Jimmy Buffet, he's seldom hard to listen to. Finally, the barman had this gloopy eye thing, which felt pleasingly disgusting and stuck to the wall when you threw it, so that was kind of neat.

I was having a perfectly good time, in other words. A group of people from the software convention that I was attending were due to be meeting somewhere on Bourbon at ten, but I was beginning to think I might skip it. After only two days my tolerance for jokes about Bill Gates was hovering around the zero mark. To me, as an Apple Macintosh developer, they weren't actually that funny anyway.

So. There I was, fairly confident that I'd had around eight Margaritas and beginning to get heartburn from all the salt, when a woman walked in. She was in her mid-thirties, I guessed, the age where things are just beginning to fade around the edges but don't look too bad for all that. I hope they don't, anyway: I'm approaching that age myself and my things are already fading fast. She sat on a stool at the corner of the bar, and signalled to the barman with a regular's upward nod of the head. A minute later a Margarita was set down in front of her, and I judged from the colour that it was the same variety I was drinking. It was called a Golden something or other, and had the effect of gradually replacing your brain with a sour-tasting sand that shifted sluggishly when you moved your head.

No big deal. I noticed her, then got back to desultory conversation with the other barman. He'd visited London at some point, or wanted to – I never really understood which. He was either asking me what London was like, or telling me; I was either listening, or telling him. I can't remember, and probably didn't know at the time. At that stage in the evening my responses would have been about the same either way. I eventually noticed that the band had stopped playing, apparently for the night. That meant I could leave the bar and go sit at one of the tables. The band had been okay, but very loud, and without wishing them any personal enmity I was glad they had gone. Now that I'd noticed, I realized they must have been gone for a while. An entire Jimmy Buffet CD had played in the interval.

I lurched sedately over to a table, humming 'The Great Filling Station Hold-up' quietly and inaccurately, and reminding myself that it was only about twenty after nine. If I wanted to meet up with the others without being the evening's comedy drunk, I needed to slow down. I needed to have not had about the last four drinks, in fact, but that would have involved tangling with the space-time continuum to a degree I felt unequal to. Slowing down would have to suffice.

It was as I was just starting the next drink that the evening took an interesting turn. Someone said something to me at fairly close range, and when I looked up to have another stab at comprehending it, I saw that it was the woman from the bar.

"Wuh?" I said, in the debonair way that I have. She was standing behind the table's other chair, and looked diffident but not very. The main thing she looked was good-natured, in a wary and toughened way. Her hair was fairly blonde and she was dressed in a pale blue dress and a dark blue denim jacket.

"I said – is that chair free?"

I considered my standard response, when I'm trying to be amusing, of asking in a soulful voice if *any* of us are truly free. I didn't feel up to it. I wasn't quite drunk enough, and I knew in my heart of hearts that it simply wasn't funny. Also, I was nervous. Women don't come up to me in bars and request the pleasure of sitting at my table. It's not something I'd had much practice with. In the end I settled for straightforwardness.

"Yes," I said. "And you may feel absolutely free to use it."

The woman smiled, sat down, and started talking. Her name, I discovered rapidly, was Rita-May. She'd lived in New Orleans for fifteen years, after moving there from some godforsaken hole called Houma, out in the Louisiana sticks. She worked in one of the stores further down Decatur near the Square, selling Cajun spice sets and cookbooks to tourists, which was a reasonable job and paid okay but wasn't very exciting. She had been married once and it had ended four years ago, amidst general apathy. She had no children, and considered it no great loss.

This information was laid out with remarkable economy and a satisfying lack of topic drift or extraneous detail. I then sat affably drinking my drink while she efficiently elicited a smaller quantity of similar information from me. I was thirty-two, she discovered, and unmarried. I owned a very small software company in London, England, and lived with a dozy cat named Spike. I was enjoying New Orleans's fine cuisine but had as yet no strong views on particular venues – with the exception of the muffelettas in the French Bar, which I liked inordinately, and the po-boys at Mama Sam's, which I thought were overrated.

After an hour and three more Margaritas our knees were resting companionably against each other, and by eleven-thirty my arm was laid across the back of her chair and she was settled comfortably against it. Maybe the fact that all the dull crap had been got out of the way so quickly was what made her easy to spend time with. Either way. I was having fun.

Rita-May seemed unperturbed by the vehemence of my feelings about vampires, and pleasingly willing to consider the possibility that it was all a load of toss. I was about to raise my hand to get more drinks when I noticed that the bar staff had all gone home, leaving a handwritten sign on the bar which said LOOK, WILL YOU TWO JUST *FUCK OFF*.

They hadn't really, but the well had obviously run dry. For a few moments I bent my not inconsiderable intelligence towards solving this problem, but all that came back was a row of question marks. Then suddenly I found myself out on the street, with no recollection of having even stood up. Rita-May's arm was wrapped around my back, and she was dragging me down Decatur towards the Square.

"It's this way," she said, giggling, and I asked her what the hell I had agreed to. It transpired that we were going to precisely the bar on Bourbon where I'd been due to meet people an hour and a half ago. I mused excitedly on this coincidence, until Rita-May got me to understand that we were going there because I'd suggested it.

"Want to buy some drugs?" Rita-May asked, and I turned to peer at her.

"I don't know," she said. "What have you got?" This confused me until I realized that a third party had asked the original question, and was indeed still standing in front of us. A thin black guy with elsewhere eyes.

"Dope, grass, coke, horse . . ." the man reeled off, in a bored monotone. As Rita-May negotiated for a bag of spliffs I tried to see where he was hiding the horse, until I realized I was being a moron. I turned away and opened my mouth and eyes wide to stretch my face. I sensed I was in a bit of a state, and that the night was as yet young.

It was only as we were lighting one of the joints five minutes later that it occurred to me to be nervous about meeting a gentleman who was a heroin dealer. Luckily he'd gone by then, and my attention span was insufficient to let me worry about it for long. Rita-May seemed very relaxed about the whole deal, and as she was a local presumably it was okay.

We hung a right at Jackson Square and walked across towards Bourbon, sucking on the joint and slowly carooming from one side of the sidewalk to the other. Rita-May's arm was still around my back, and one of mine was over her shoulders. It occurred to me that sooner or later I was going to have to ask myself what the hell I thought I was doing, but I didn't feel up to it just yet.

I wasn't really prepared for the idea that people from the convention would still be at the bar when we eventually arrived. By then it felt as if we had been walking for at least ten days, though not in any bad way. The joint had hit us both pretty hard, and my head felt as if it had been lovingly crafted out of warm brown smoke. Bourbon Street was still at full pitch, and we slowly made our way down it, weaving between half-dressed male couples, lean local blacks and pastel-clad pear-shaped tourists from Des Moines. A stringy blonde popped up from nowhere at one point, waggling a rose in my face and asking "Is she ready?" in a keening, nobody's-home kind of voice. I was still juggling responses to this when I noticed that Rita-May had bought the rose herself. She broke off all but the first four inches of stem in a businesslike way, and stuck the flower behind her ear.

Fair enough, I thought, admiring this behaviour in a way that I found difficult to define.

I couldn't actually remember, now we were in the area, whether it was the Absinthe Bar we were looking for, the *Old* Absinthe Bar, or the *Original Old* Absinthe Bar. I hope you can understand my confusion. In the end we made the decision on the basis of the bar from which the most acceptable music was pounding, and lurched into the sweaty gloom. Most of the crowd inside applauded immediately, but I suspect this was for the blues band rather than for us. I was very thirsty by then, partly because someone appeared to have put enough blotting paper in my mouth to leech all the moisture out of it, and I felt incapable of doing or saying anything until I was less arid. Luckily Rita-May sensed this, and immediately cut through the crowd to the bar.

I stood and waited patiently for her return, inclining slightly and variably from the vertical plane like some advanced form of children's top. "Ah ha," I was saying to myself. "Ah ha." I have no idea why.

When someone shouted my name, I experienced little more than a vague feeling of well-being. "They know me here," I muttered, nodding proudly to myself. Then I saw that Dave Trindle was standing on the other side of the room and waving his arm at me, a grin of outstanding stupidity on his face. My first thought was that he should sit down before someone in the band shot him. My second was a hope that he would continue standing, for the same reason. He was part, I saw, of a motley collection of second-rate shareware authors ranged around a table in the corner, a veritable rogues' gallery of dweebs and losers. My heart sank, with all hands, two cats and a mint copy of the Gutenberg Bible on deck.

"Are they the people?"

On hearing Rita-May's voice I turned thankfully, immediately feeling much better. She was standing close behind, a large drink in each hand and an affectionate half-smile on her face. I realized suddenly that I found her very attractive, and that she was nice, too. I looked at her for a moment longer, and then leant forward to kiss her softly on the cheek, just to the side of the mouth.

She smiled, pleased, and we came together for another kiss, again not quite on the mouth. I experienced a moment of peace, and then suddenly I was very drunk again.

"Yes and no," I said. "They're from the convention. But they're not the people I wanted to see."

"They're still waving at you."

"Christ."

"Come on. It'll be fun."

I found it hard to share her optimism, but followed Rita-May through the throng.

It turned out that the people I'd arranged to meet up with *had* been there, but I was told that they had left in the face of my continued failure to arrive. I judged it more likely that they'd gone because of the extraordinary collection of berks they had accidentally acquired on the way to the bar, but refrained from saying so.

The conventioneers were drunk, in a we've-had-two-beers-and-hey-aren't-we-bohemian sort of way, which I personally find offensive. Quite early on I realized that the only way of escaping the encounter with my sanity intact was pretending that they weren't there and talking to Rita-May instead. This wasn't allowed, apparently. I kept being asked my opinion on things so toe-curlingly dull that I can't bring myself to even remember them, and endured fifteen minutes of Davey wank-face telling me about some GUI junk he was developing. Luckily Rita-May entered the spirit of the event, and we managed to keep passing each other messages on how dreadful a time we were having. With that and a regular supply of drinks, we coped.

After about an hour we hit upon a new form of diversion, and while apparently listening avidly to the row of life-ectomy survivors in front of us, started – tentatively at first, then more deliciously – to stroke each other's hands under the table. The conventioneers were now all well over the limit, some of them having had as many as four beers, and were chattering nineteen to the dozen. So engrossed were they that after a while I felt able to turn my head towards Rita-May, look in her eyes, and say something.

"I like you."

I hadn't planned it that way. I'd intended something much more grown-up and crass. But as it came out I realized that it was true and that it communicated what I wanted to say with remarkable economy.

She smiled, skin dimpling at the corners of her mouth, wisps of her hair backlit into golden. "I like you too," she said, and squeezed my hand.

Wow, I thought foggily. How weird. You think you've got the measure of life, and then it throws you what I believe is known as a "curve-ball". It just went to show. "It just goes to show," I said, aloud. She probably didn't understand, but smiled again anyway.

The next thing that I noticed was that I was standing with my back against a wall, and that there wasn't any ground beneath my feet. Then that it was cold. Then that it was quiet.

"Yo, he's alive," someone said, and the world started to organize itself. I was lying on the floor of the bar, and my face was wet.

I tried to sit upright, but couldn't. The owner of the voice, a cheery black man who had served me earlier, grabbed my shoulder and helped. It was him, I discovered, who'd thrown water over me. About a gallon. It hadn't worked, so he'd checked my pulse to make sure I wasn't dead, and then just cleared up around me. Apart from him and a depressed-looking guy with a mop, the bar was completely empty.

"Where's Rita?" I asked, eventually. I had to repeat the question in order to make it audible.

The man grinned down at me. "Now I wouldn't know *that*, would I?" he said. "Most particularly 'cos I don't know who Rita *is*."

'What about the others?' I managed. The barman gestured eloquently around the empty bar. As my eyes followed his hand, I saw the clock. It was a little after five a.m.

I stood up, shakily thanked him for his good offices on my behalf, and walked very slowly out into the street.

I don't remember getting back to the hotel, but I guess I must have done. That, at any rate, was where I found myself at ten the next morning, after a few hours of molten sleep. As I stood pasty-faced and stricken under the harsh light of the bathroom, I waited in horror while wave after wave of The Fear washed over me. I'd passed out. Obviously. Though uncommon with me, it's not unknown. The conventioneers, ratfinks that they were, had pissed off and left me there, doubtless sniggering into their beards. Fair enough. I'd have done the same for them.

But what had happened to Rita-May?

While I endured an appalling ten minutes on the toilet, a soothing fifteen minutes under the shower, and a despairing, tearful battle with my trousers, I tried to work this out. On the one hand, I couldn't blame her for abandoning an unconscious tourist. But when I thought back to before the point where blackness and The Fear took over, I thought we'd been getting on very well. She didn't seem the type to abandon anyone.

When I was more or less dressed I hauled myself onto the bed and sat on the edge. I needed coffee, and needed it very urgently. I also had to smoke about seventy cigarettes, but seemed to have lost my packet. The way forward was clear. I had to leave the hotel room and sort these things out. But for that I needed shoes.

So where were they?

They weren't on the floor, or in the bathroom. They weren't out on the balcony, where the light hurt my eyes so badly that I retreated back into the gloom with a yelp. I shuffled around the room again, even getting down onto my hands and knees to look under the bed. They weren't there. They weren't even *in* the bed.

They were entirely absent, which was a disaster. I hate shoes, because they're boring, and consequently I own very few pairs. Apart from some elderly flip-flops which were left in the suitcase from a previous trip, the ones I'd been wearing were the only pair I had with me. I made another exhausting search, conducting as much of it as possible without leaving the bed, with no success. Instead of just getting to a café and sorting out my immediate needs, I was going to have to put on the flip-flops and go find a fucking shoe store. Once there I would have to spend money which I'd rather commit to

American-priced CDs and good food on a pair of fucking *shoes*. As a punishment from God for drunkenness this felt a bit harsh, and for a few minutes the walls of the hotel room rang with rasped profanities.

Eventually I hauled myself over to the suitcase and bad-temperedly dug through the archaeological layers of socks and shirts until I found something shoe-shaped. The flip-flop was, of course, right at the bottom of the case. I tugged irritably at it, unmindful of the damage I was doing to my carefully stacked shorts and ties. Up came two pairs of trousers I hadn't worn yet – one of which I'd forgotten I'd brought – along with a shirt, and then finally I had the flip-flop in my hand.

Except it wasn't a flip-flop. It was one of my shoes.

Luckily I was standing near the end of the bed, because my legs gave way. I sat down suddenly, staring at the shoe in my hand. It wasn't hard to recognise. It was a black lace-up, in reasonably good condition but wearing on the outside of the heel. As I turned it over slowly in my hands like some holy relic, I realized that it even smelled slightly of Margaritas. Salt had dried on the toe, where I'd spilt a mouthful laughing at something Rita-May had said in Jimmy Buffet's.

Still holding it in one hand, I reached tentatively into the bowels of my suitcase, rootling through the lower layers until I found the other one. It was underneath the towel I'd packed right at the bottom, on the reasoning that I was unlikely to need it because all hotels had towels. I pulled the shoe out, and stared at it.

Without a doubt, it was the other shoe. There was something inside. I carefully pulled it out, aware of little more than a rushing sound in my ears.

It was a red rose, attached to about four inches of stem.

The first thing that strikes you about the Café du Monde is that it isn't quite what you're expecting. It isn't nestled right in the heart of the old town, on Royal or Dauphin, but squats on Decatur opposite the Square. And it isn't some dinky little café, but a large awning-covered space where rows of tables are intermittently served by waiters of spectacular moroseness. On subsequent visits, however, you come to realize that the *café au lait* really is good and that the *beignets* are the best in New Orleans; that the café is about as bijou as it can be given that it's open twenty-four hours a day, every day of the year; and that anyone wandering through New Orleans is going to pass the Decatur corner of Jackson Square at some point, so it is actually pretty central.

Midday found me sitting at one of the tables at the edge, so I wasn't surrounded by other people and had a good view of the street. I was on my second coffee and third orange juice. My ashtray had been emptied twice already, and I had an order of *beignet* inside me. The only reason I hadn't had more was that I was saving myself for a muffeletta. I'd tell you what they are but this isn't a travel guide. Go and find out for yourself.

And, of course, I was wearing my shoes. I'd sat in the hotel for another ten minutes, until I'd completely stopped shaking. Then I'd shuffled straight to Café du Monde. I had a book with me, but I wasn't reading it. I was watching people as they passed, and trying to get my head in order. I couldn't remember what had happened, so the best I could do was try to find an explanation that worked, and stick with it. Unfortunately, that explanation was eluding me. I simply couldn't come up with a good reason for my shoes being in my suitcase, under stuff that I hadn't disturbed since leaving Roanoke.

About nine months before, at a convention in England, I rather over-indulged an interest in recreational pharmaceuticals in the dissolute company of an old college friend. I woke the next morning to find myself in my hotel bed, but dressed in different clothes to those I'd been wearing the night before. Patient reconstruction led me to believe that I could *just about* recall getting up in the small hours, showering, getting dressed – and then climbing back into bed. Odd behaviour, to be sure, but there were enough hints and shadows of memory for me to convince myself that was what I had done.

Not this time. I couldn't remember a thing between leaving the Old Original Authentic Genuine Absinthe Bar and waking up. But strangely, I didn't have The Fear about it.

And then, of course, there was the rose.

The Fear, for those unacquainted with it, is something you may get after very excessive intake of drugs or alcohol. It is, amongst other things, the panicky conviction that you have done something embarrassing or ill-advised that you can't quite remember. It can also be more generic than that, a simple belief that at some point in the previous evening something happened that was in some way not ideal. It usually passes off when your hangover does, or when an acquaintance reveals that yes, you did lightly stroke one of her breasts in public, without being requested to do so.

Then you can just get down to being hideously embarrassed, which is a much more containable emotion.

I had mild Fear about the period in Jimmy Buffet's, but probably only born of nervousness about talking to a woman I didn't really know. I had a slightly greater Fear concerning the Absinthe bar, where I suspected I might have referred to the new CEO of a company who was a client of mine as a "talentless fuckwit".

I felt fine about the journey back to the hotel, however, despite the fact that I couldn't remember it. I'd been alone, after all. Everyone, including Rita-May, had disappeared. The only person I could have offended was myself. But how had my shoes got into the suitcase?

Why would I have done that? And at what point had I acquired Rita-May's rose? The last time I could remember seeing it was when I'd told her that I liked her. Then it had still been behind her ear.

The coffee was beginning to turn on me, mingling with the hangover to make it feel as if points of light were slowly popping on and off in my head. A black guy with a trumpet was just settling down to play at one of the other sides of the café, and I knew this guy from previous experience. His key talent, which he demonstrated about every ten minutes, was that of playing a loud, high note for a very long time. Like most tourists, I'd applauded the first time I'd heard this. The second demonstration had been less appealing. By the third time I'd considered offering him my Visa card if he'd go away.

And if he did it now, I was likely to simply shatter and fall in shards upon the floor.

I needed to do something. I needed to move. I left the cafe and stood outside on Decatur.

After about two minutes I felt hot and under threat, buffeted by the passing throng. No one had yet filled the seat I'd vacated, and I was very tempted to just slink right back to it. I'd be quiet, no trouble to anyone: just sit there and drink a lot more fluids. I'd be a valuable addition, I felt, a show tourist provided by the town's Management to demonstrate to everyone else how wonderful a time there was to be had.

But then the guy with the trumpet started a rendition of "Smells Like Teen Spirit" and I really had to go.

I walked slowly up Decatur towards the market, trying to decide if I was really going to do what I had in mind. Rita-May worked at one of the stores along that stretch. I couldn't remember the name, but knew it had something to do with cooking. It wouldn't be that difficult to find. But should I be trying to find it? Perhaps I should just turn around, leave the Quarter and go to the Clarion, where the convention was happening. I could find the people I liked and hang for a while, listen to jokes about Steve Jobs. Forget about Rita-May, take things carefully for the remaining few days, and then go back home to London.

I didn't want to. The previous evening had left me with emotional tattoos, snapshots of desire that weren't fading in the morning sun. The creases round her eyes when she smiled; the easy Southern rhythm of her speech, the glissando changes in pitch; her tongue, as it lolled round the rim of her glass, licking off the salt. When I closed my eyes, in addition to a slightly alarming feeling of vertigo, I could feel the skin of her hand as if it was still there against my own. So what if I was an idiot tourist. I was a idiot tourist who was genuinely attracted to her. Maybe that would be enough.

The first couple of stores were easy to dismiss. One sold quilts made by American craftspeople; the next wooden children's toys for parents who didn't realize how much their kids wanted video games. The third had a few spice collections in the window, but was mainly full of other souvenirs. It didn't look like the place Rita-May had described, but I plucked up my courage and asked. No one of that name worked there. The next store was a bakery, and then there was a fifty-yard open stretch that provided table space for the restaurant which followed it.

The store after the restaurant was called The N'awlins Pantry, and tag-lined "The One-Stop Shop for all your Cajun Cooking Needs". It looked, I had to admit, like it was the place.

I wanted to see Rita-May, but I was scared shitless at the thought of just walking in. I retreated to the other side of the street, hoping to see her through the window first. I'm not sure how that would have helped, but it seemed like a good idea at the time. I smoked a cigarette and watched for a while, but the constant procession of cars and pedestrians made it impossible to see anything. Then I spent a few minutes wondering why I wasn't just attending the convention, listening to dull, safe panels like everybody else. It didn't work. When I was down to the butt I stubbed my cigarette out and crossed back over the road. I couldn't see much through the window even from there, because of the size and extravagance of the window display. So I grabbed the handle, opened the door and walked in.

It was fantastically noisy inside, and crowded with sweating people. The blues band seemed to have turned a second bank of amplifiers on, and virtually everyone sitting at the tables in front of them was clapping their hands and hooting. The air was smeared with red faces and meaty arms, and for a moment I considered just turning around and going back into the toilet. It had been quiet in there, and cool. I'd spent ten minutes splashing my face with cold water, trying to mitigate the effect of the joint we'd smoked. While I stood trying to remember where the table was, the idea of another few moments of water-splashing began to take on a nearly obsessive appeal.

But then I saw Rita-May, and realized I had to go on. Partly because she was marooned with the conventioneers, which wouldn't have been fair on anyone, but mainly because going back to her was even more appealing than the idea of water.

I carefully navigated my way through the crowd, pausing halfway to flag down a waitress and get some more drinks on the way. Because obviously we needed them. Obviously. No way were we drunk enough. Rita-May looked up gratefully when she saw me. I plonked myself down next to her, glared accidentally at Dave Trindle, and lit another cigarette. Then, in a clumsy but necessary attempt to rekindle the atmosphere that had been developing, I repeated the last thing I had said before setting off on my marathon journey to the gents. "It just goes to show," I said.

Rita-May smiled again, probably in recognition at the feat of memory I had pulled off. "Show what?" she asked, leaning towards me and shutting out the rest of the group. I winked, and then pulled off the most ambitious monologue of my life.

I said that it went to show that life took odd turns, and that you could suddenly meet someone you felt very at home with, who seemed to change all the rules. Someone who made stale, damaged parts of you fade away in an instant, who let you feel strange magic once again: the magic of being in the presence of a person you didn't know, and realizing that you wanted them more than anything else you could think of.

I spoke for about five minutes, and then stopped. It went down very well, not least because I was patently telling the truth. I meant it. For once my tongue got the words right, didn't trip up, and I said what I meant to say. In spite of the drink, the drugs, the hour, I said it.

At the same time I was realizing that something was terribly wrong. This wasn't, for example, a cookery store.

A quick glance towards the door showed it also wasn't early afternoon. The sky was dark and Bourbon Street was packed with night-time strollers. We were sitting with the conventioneers in the Absinthe Bar, I was wearing last night's clothes, and Rita-May's rose was still behind her ear.

It was last night, in other words.

As I continued to tell Rita-May that I was really very keen on her, she slipped her hand into mine. This time they weren't covered by the table, but I found I didn't care about that. I did, however, care about the fact that I could clearly remember standing outside the Café du Monde and wanting her to touch my hand again.

In the daylight of tomorrow.

The waitress appeared with our drinks. Trindle and his cohorts decided that they might as well be hung for a lamb as for an embryo, and ordered another round themselves. While this transaction was being laboriously conducted I stole a glance at the bar. In a gap between carousing fun-lovers I saw what I was looking for. The barman who'd woken me up.

He was making four Margaritas at once, his smooth face a picture of concentration. He would have made a good photograph, and I recognized him instantly. But he hadn't served me yet. I'd been to the bar once, and been served by a woman. The other drinks I'd bought from passing waitresses. Yet when I'd woken up, I'd recognized the barman *because he'd served me.* That meant I must have bought another drink before passing out and waking up in the bar by myself.

But I couldn't have woken up at all. The reality of what was going on around me was unquestionable, from the smell of fresh sweat drifting from the middle-aged men at the table next to us to the way Rita-May's skin looked cool and smooth despite the heat. One of the conventioneers had engaged Rita-May in conversation, and it didn't look as if she was having too bad a time, so I took the chance to try to sort my head out. I wasn't panicking, exactly, but I was very concerned indeed.

Okay, I *was* panicking. Either I'd spent my time in the toilet hallucinating about tomorrow, or something *really* strange was happening. Did the fact that I hadn't been served by the barman yet prove which was right? I didn't know. I couldn't work it out.

"What do you think of Dale Georgio, John? Looks like he's really gonna turn WriteRight around."

I didn't really internalize the question Trindle asked me until I'd answered it, and my reply had more to do with my state of mind than any desire to cause offence.

"He's a talentless fuckwit," I said.

Back outside on the pavement I hesitated for a moment, not really knowing what to do. The N'awlins Pantry was indeed where Rita-May worked, but she was out at lunch. This I had discovered by talking to a very helpful woman, who I assumed also worked there. Either that, or she was an unusually well-informed tourist.

I could either hang around and accost Rita-May on the street, or go and get some lunch. Talking to her outside the store would be preferable, but I couldn't stand hopping from foot to foot for what could be as long as an hour.

At that moment my stomach passed up an incomprehensible message of some kind, a strange liquid buzzing that I felt sure most people in the street could hear. It meant one of two things. Either I was hungry, or my mid-section was about to explode, taking the surrounding two blocks along with it. I elected to assume that I was hungry and turned to walk back towards the square, in search of a muffeletta.

At Café du Monde I noticed that the dreadful trumpet player was in residence, actually in the middle of one of his trademark long notes. As I passed him, willing my head not to implode, the penny dropped.

I shouldn't be noticing that he was there. I *knew* he was there. I'd just been at Café du Monde. He was one of the reasons I'd left.

I got far enough away that the trumpet wasn't hurting me any more, and then ground to a halt. For the first time I was actually scared. It should have been reassuring to be back in the right time again. Tomorrow I could understand. I could retrace my steps here. Most of them, anyway. But I couldn't remember a thing of what had happened in the cookery store. I'd come out believing that I'd had a conversation with someone and established that Rita-May worked there. But as to what the interior of the store had been like, I didn't have a clue. I couldn't remember. What I could actually *remember* was being in the Absinthe Bar.

I looked anxiously around at tourists dappled by bright sunshine, and felt the early-afternoon heat seeping in through my clothes. A hippy face-painter looked hopefully in my direction, judged correctly that I wasn't the type, and went back to juggling with his paints.

On impulse I lifted my right hand and sniffed my fingers. Cigarette smoke and icing sugar, from the *beignets* I'd eaten half an hour ago. This had to be real.

Maybe there had been something weird in the joint last night. That could explain the blackout on the trip back to the hotel, and the Technicolor flashback I'd just had. It couldn't have been acid, but some opium-based thing, possibly. But why would the man have sold us it? Presumably that kind of thing was more expensive. Dealers tended to want to rip you off, not give you little presents. Unless Rita-May had known, and had asked and paid for it – but that didn't seem very likely either.

More than that, I simply didn't believe it was a drug hangover. It didn't feel like one. I felt exactly as if I'd just had far too much to drink the night before, plus one strong joint – except for the fact that I couldn't work out where in time I actually was.

If you close one of your eyes you lose the ability to judge space. The view flattens out, like a painting. You know, or think you know, which objects are closer to you – but only because you've seen them before when both of your eyes have been open. Without that memory, you wouldn't have a clue. The same appeared to be happening with time. I couldn't seem to tell what order things should be in. The question almost felt inappropriate.

Suddenly thirsty, and hearing rather than feeling another anguished appeal from my stomach, I crossed the road to a place that sold po-boys and orange juice from a hatch in the wall. It was too far to the French Bar. I needed food immediately. I'd been okay all the time I was at Café du Monde – maybe food helped tether me in some way.

The ordering process went off okay, and I stood and munched my way through French bread and *sauce piquante* on the street, watching the door to the N'awlins Pantry. As much as anything else, the tang of lemon juice on the fried oysters convinced me that what I was experiencing was real. When I'd finished I took a sip of my drink, and winced. It was much sweeter than I'd been expecting. Then I realized that was because it was orange juice, rather than a Margarita. The taste left me unfulfilled, like those times when you know you've only eaten half a biscuit but can't find the other piece. I knew I'd bought orange juice, but also that less than a minute ago I had taken a mouthful of Margarita.

Trembling, I slugged the rest of the juice back. Maybe this was something to do with blood-sugar levels.

Or maybe I was slowly going off my head.

As I drank I stared fixedly at the other side of the street, watching out for Rita-May. I was beginning to feel that until I saw her again, until something happened that conclusively locked me into today, I wasn't going to be able to stabilize. Once I'd seen her the day after the night before, it had to be that next day. It really had to, or how could it be tomorrow?

Unless, of course, I was back in the toilet of the Absinthe Bar, projecting in eerie detail what might happen the next day. About the only thing I was sure of was that I wanted to see Rita-May. I realized that she probably wouldn't be wearing what I'd seen her in last night, but I knew I'd recognize her in an instant. Even with my eyes open, I could almost see her face. Eyes slightly hooded with drink, mouth parted, wisps of clean hair curling over her ears. And on her lips, as always, that beautiful half-smile.

"We're going," Trindle shouted, and I turned from Rita-May to look blearily at him. They hadn't abandoned me after all: they were leaving, and I was still conscious. My habitual irritation towards Trindle and his colleagues faded somewhat on seeing their faces. They'd clearly all had a lovely time. In a rare moment of maturity, I realized that they were rather sweet, really. I didn't want to piss on their fireworks.

I nodded and smiled and shook hands, and they trooped drunkenly off into the milling crowd. It had to be well after two o'clock by now, but the evening was still romping on. I turned back to Rita-May and realized that it hadn't been such a bad stroke of luck, running into the Trindle contingent. We'd been kept apart for a couple of hours, and passions had quietly simmered to a rolling boil. Rita-May was looking at me in a way I can only describe as frank, and I leant forward and kissed her liquidly on the mouth. My tongue felt like some glorious sea creature, lightly oiled, rolling for the first time with another of its species.

After a while we stopped, and disengaged far enough to look in each other's eyes. "It just goes to show," she whispered, and we rested our foreheads together and giggled. I remembered thinking much earlier in the evening that I needed to ask myself what I thought I was doing. I asked myself. The answer was "Having an exceptionally nice evening", which was good enough for me.

"Another drink?" It didn't feel time to leave yet. We needed some more of being there, and feeling the way we did.

"Yeah," she said, grinning with her head on one side, looking up at me as I stood. "And then come back and do that some more."

I couldn't see a waitress so I went to the bar. I'd realized by now that the time switch had happened again, and I wasn't surprised to find myself being served by the smooth-faced barman. He didn't look too surprised to see me either.

"Still going?" he asked, as he fixed the drinks I'd asked for. I knew I hadn't talked to him before, so I guessed he was just being friendly.

"Yeah," I said. "Do I look like I'm going to make it?"

"You look fine." He grinned. "Got another hour or so in you yet."

Only when I was walking unsteadily back towards our table did this strike me as a strange thing to have said. Almost as if he knew that in a little while I was going to pass out. I stopped, turned, and looked back at the bar. The barman was still looking at me. He winked, and then turned away.

He knew.

I frowned. That didn't make sense. That didn't work. Unless this was all some flashback, and I was putting words into his mouth. Which meant that it was really tomorrow. Didn't it? Then why couldn't I remember what was going to happen?

I turned back towards Rita-May, and it finally occurred to me to ask her about what was going on. If she didn't know what I was talking about, I could pass it off as a joke. If the same thing was happening to her, then we might have had a spiked joint. Either way I would have learned something. Galvanized by this plan, I tried to hurry back through the crowd. Unfortunately I didn't see a large drunken guy in a check shirt lurching into my path.

"Hey! Watch it," he said, but fairly good-humouredly. I grinned to show that I was harmless and then stepped back away from the kerb. The woman I'd thought was Rita-May hadn't been. Just some tourist walking quickly in the sunshine. I looked at my watch and saw that I'd been waiting opposite the store for only twenty minutes. It felt like I'd been there for ever. She had to come back soon. She had to.

Then:

Christ, back here again, I thought. The switches seemed to be coming on quicker as time wore on, assuming that was what it was doing. Eating the food hadn't worked.

By the time I reached the hotel I'd started to forget, but I'd had enough sense left in me to take Rita-May's rose from my pocket and slip it into one of my shoes. Then I buried the shoes as deeply in the suitcase as I could. "That'll fuck you up," I muttered to myself. "That'll make you remember". I seemed to know what I meant. It was six in the morning by then, and I took a random selection of my clothes off and fell onto the bed. My head was a mess, and my neck hurt. Neither stopped me from falling asleep instantly, to find myself on Decatur, still waiting opposite the N'awlins Pantry.

That one took me by surprise, I have to admit. I was beginning to get the hang of the back-and-forth thing, even if it was making me increasingly terrified. I couldn't stop it, or understand it, but at least it was following a pattern. But to flick back to being at the hotel earlier that morning, and find that I'd hidden the shoes myself, was unexpected.

It was all getting jumbled up, as if the order didn't really matter, only the sense.

The people at the po-boy counter were beginning to look at me strangely, so I crossed back over to stand outside the N'awlins Pantry itself. It felt like I had been going back and forth over the road for most of my life. There was a lamp-post directly outside the store and I grabbed hold of it with both hands, as if I believed that holding something solid and physical would keep me where I was. All I wanted in the whole wide world was for Rita-May to get back.

When she did, she walked right up to the table, straddled my knees and sat down on my lap facing me. She did this calmly, without flamboyance, and no one at the nearby tables seemed to feel that it was in any way worthy of note. I did, though. As I reached out to pull her closer to me, I felt like I was experiencing sexual attraction for the very first time. Every cell in my body shifted nervously against its neighbour, as if aware that something rather unusual and profound was afoot. The band was still pumping out twelve-bar at stadium-concert volume, which normally blasts all physical sensation out of me: I can't, to put it bluntly, usually do it to music. That didn't appear to be the case on this occasion. I nuzzled into Rita-May's face and kissed her ear. She wriggled a little closer to me, her hand around the back of my head, gently twisting in the roots of my hair. My entire skin felt as if it had been upgraded to some much more sensitive organ, and had I stood up too quickly, in those jeans, I suspect something in my trousers would have just snapped.

"Let's go," she said suddenly. I stood up, and we went.

It was about three a.m. by then, and Bourbon Street was much quieter. We went up it a little way, and then took a turn to head back down towards Jackson Square. We walked slowly, wrapped up in each other, watching with interest the things our hands seemed to want to do. I don't know what Rita-May was thinking, but I was hoping with all of my heart that we could stay this way for a while. I was also still girding myself up to asking her if she was having any problems keeping track of time.

We got to the corner of the Square, and she stopped. It looked very welcoming in the darkness, empty of people and noise. I found myself thinking that leaving New Orleans was going to be more difficult than I'd expected. I'd spent a lot of my life leaving places, taking a quick look and then moving on. Wasn't going to be so easy this time.

Rita-May turned to me, and took my hands. Then she nodded down Decatur, at a row of stores. "That's where I work," she said. I drew her closer. "Pay attention." She smiled. "It's going to be important."

I shook my head slightly, to clear it. It was going to be, I knew. I was going to need to know where she worked. I stared at the N'awlins Pantry for a moment, memorizing its location. I would always forget, as it turned out, but perhaps that was part of the deal.

Rita-May seemed satisfied that I'd done my best, and reached up with her hand to pull my face towards hers.

"It's not going to be easy," she said, when we'd kissed. "For you, I mean. But please stick with it. I want you to catch up with me some day."

"I will," I said, and I meant it. Slowly, I was beginning to understand. I let go of the lamp-post with my left hand, and looked at my watch. Only another minute had passed. There was still no sign of Rita-May, just the slowly swarming mass of tourists, their bright colours warm in the sun. From a little way down the road I could hear the peal of one long trumpet note, and it didn't sound so bad to me. I glanced down Decatur towards the sound, wondering how far away she was, how many times I would have to wait. I decided to ask.

"As long as it takes," she said. "Are you sure this is what you want?"

In a minute Rita-May would give me the rose, and I'd go back to the bar to pass out as I had so many times before. But for now I was still here, in the silent square, where the only sign of life was a couple of tired people sipping *café au lait* in darkness at the Café du Monde. The air was cool, and soft somehow, like the skin of the woman I held in my arms. I thought of my house, and London. I would remember them with affection, but not miss them very much. My sister would look after the cat. One day I would catch up with Rita-May, and when I did, I would hold on tight.

In the meantime the coffee was good, the *beignets* were excellent, and there would always be a muffeletta just around the corner. Sometimes it would be night, sometimes day, but I would be travelling in the right direction. I would be at home, one of the regulars, in the corner of all the photographs which showed what a fine place it was to stay. And always there would be Rita-May, and me inching ever closer every day.

"I'm sure," I said. She looked very happy, and that sealed my decision for ever. She kissed me once on the forehead, once on the lips, and then angled her head.

"I'll be waiting," she said, and then she bit me softly on the neck.

RAMSEY CAMPBELL

The Brood

RAMSEY CAMPBELL HAS RECEIVED more awards for horror fiction than any other writer. He has been named Grand Master by the World Horror Convention and received a Lifetime Achievement Award from the Horror Writers Association.

Latest projects include a film of his novel *Pact of the Fathers*, which was filmed in Spain as *El Segundo Nombre* (*Second Name*); *Told by the Dead* is his new collection of short stories; *The Overnight* is his latest novel, and he is currently working on another, *Secret Stories*.

The author's M.R. Jamesian anthology *Meddling With Ghosts* is published by The British Library, and he recently co-edited the anthology *Gathering the Bones* with Jack Dann and Dennis Etchison. S.T. Joshi's study *Ramsey Campbell and Modern Horror Fiction* is available from Liverpool University Press, while *Ramsey Campbell, Probably* is a multiple award-winning non-fiction collection from PS Publishing.

Campbell reveals that " 'The Brood' had its origins in the view of street lamps on Princes Avenue from the window of Jenny's and my first flat, which we later lent to the protagonists of *The Face That Must Die*. When my biographer David Mathew recently attempted to photograph me in front of the building, a tenant demanded what we were up to. This was one of the rare instances where I found myself assuaging someone's paranoia."

Although the following story uses all the traditional trappings of vampire fiction, it remains firmly rooted in the author's unique world-view of mental and urban disintegration.

HE'D HAD AN ALMOST unbearable day. As he walked home his self-control still oppressed him, like rusty armour. Climbing the stairs, he tore open his mail: a glossy pamphlet from a binoculars firm, a humbler folder from the Wild Life Preservation Society. Irritably he threw them on the bed and sat by the window, to relax.

It was autumn. Night had begun to cramp the days. Beneath golden trees, a procession of cars advanced along Princes Avenue, as though to a funeral; crowds hurried home. The incessant anonymous parade, dwarfed by three stories depressed him. Faces like these vague twilit miniatures – selfishly ingrown, convinced that nothing was their fault – brought their pets to his office.

But where were all the local characters? He enjoyed watching them, they fascinated him. Where was the man who ran about the avenue, chasing butterflies of litter and stuffing them into his satchel? Or the man who strode violently, head down in no gale, shouting at the air? Or the Rainbow Man, who appeared on the hottest days obese with sweaters, each of a different garish colour? Blackband hadn't seen any of these people for weeks.

The crowds thinned; cars straggled. Groups of streetlamps lit, tinting leaves sodium, unnaturally gold. Often that lighting had meant – Why, there she was, emerging from the side street almost on cue: the Lady of the Lamp.

Her gait was elderly. Her face was withered as an old blanched apple; the rest of her head was wrapped in a tattered grey scarf. Her voluminous ankle-length coat, patched with remnants of colour, swayed as she walked. She reached the central reservation of the avenue, and stood beneath a lamp.

Though there was a pedestrian crossing beside her, people deliberately crossed elsewhere. They would, Blackband thought sourly: just as they ignored the packs of stray dogs that were always someone else's responsibility – ignored them, or hoped someone would put them to sleep. Perhaps they felt the human strays should be put to sleep, perhaps that was where the Rainbow Man and the rest had gone!

The woman was pacing restlessly. She circled the lamp, as though the blurred disc of light at its foot were a stage. Her shadow resembled the elaborate hand of a clock.

Surely she was too old to be a prostitute. Might she have been one, who was now compelled to enact her memories? His binoculars drew her face closer: intent as a sleepwalker's, introverted as a foetus. Her head bobbed against gravel, foreshortened by the false perspective of the lenses. She moved offscreen.

Three months ago, when he'd moved to this flat, there had been two old women. One night he had seen them, circling adjacent lamps. The other woman had been slower, more sleepy. At last the Lady of the Lamp had led her home; they'd moved slowly as exhausted sleepers. For days he'd thought of the two women in their long faded coats, trudging around the lamps in the deserted avenue, as though afraid to go home in the growing dark.

The sight of the lone woman still unnerved him, a little. Darkness was crowding his flat. He drew the curtains, which the lamps stained orange. Watching had relaxed him somewhat. Time to make a salad.

The kitchen overlooked the old women's house. See The World from the Attics of Princes Avenue. All Human Life Is Here. Backyards penned in rubble and crumbling toilet sheds; on the far side of the back street, houses were lidless boxes of smoke. The house directly beneath his window was dark, as always. How could the two women – if both were still alive – survive in there? But at least they could look after themselves, or call for aid; they were human, after all. It was their pets that bothered him.

He had never seen the torpid woman again. Since she had vanished, her companion had begun to take animals home; he'd seen her coaxing them toward the house. No doubt they were company for her friend; but what life could animals enjoy in the lightless, probably condemnable house? And why so many? Did they escape to their homes, or stray again? He shook his head: the women's loneliness was no excuse. They cared as little for their pets as did those owners who came, whining like their dogs, to his office.

Perhaps the woman was waiting beneath the lamps for cats to drop from the trees, like fruit. He meant the thought as a joke. But when he'd finished preparing dinner, the idea troubled him sufficiently that he switched off the light in the main room and peered through the curtains.

The bright gravel was bare. Parting the curtains, he saw the woman hurrying unsteadily toward her street. She was carrying a kitten: her head bowed over the fur cradled in her arms; her whole body seemed to enfold it. As he emerged from the kitchen again, carrying plates, he heard her door creak open and shut. Another one, he thought uneasily.

By the end of the week she'd taken in a stray dog, and Blackband was wondering what should be done.

The women would have to move eventually. The houses adjoining theirs were empty, the windows shattered targets. But how could they take their menagerie with them? They'd set them loose to roam or, weeping, take them to be put to sleep.

Something ought to be done, but not by him. He came home to

rest. He was used to removing chicken bones from throats; it was suffering the excuses that exhausted him – Fido always had his bit of chicken, it had never happened before, they couldn't understand. He would nod curtly, with a slight pained smile. "Oh yes?" he would repeat tonelessly "Oh yes?"

Not that that would work with the Lady of the Lamp. But then, he didn't intend to confront her: what on earth could he have said? That he'd take all the animals off her hands? Hardly. Besides, the thought of confronting her made him uncomfortable.

She was growing more eccentric. Each day she appeared a little earlier. Often she would move away into the dark, then hurry back into the flat bright pool. It was as though light were her drug.

People stared at her, and fled. They disliked her because she was odd. All she had to do to please them, Blackband thought, was be normal: overfeed her pets until their stomachs scraped the ground, lock them in cars to suffocate in the heat, leave them alone in the house all day then beat them for chewing. Compared to most of the owners he met, she was Saint Francis.

He watched television. Insects were courting and mating. Their ritual dances engrossed and moved him: the play of colours, the elaborate racial patterns of the life-force which they instinctively decoded and enacted. Microphotography presented them to him. If only people were as beautiful and fascinating!

Even his fascination with the Lady of the Lamp was no longer unalloyed; he resented that. Was she falling ill? She walked painfully slowly, stooped over, and looked shrunken. Nevertheless, each night she kept her vigil, wandering sluggishly in the pools of light like a sleepwalker.

How could she cope with her animals now? How might she be treating them? Surely there were social workers in some of the cars nosing home, someone must notice how much she needed help. Once he made for the door to the stairs, but already his throat was parched of words. The thought of speaking to her wound him tight inside. It wasn't his job, he had enough to confront. The spring in his guts coiled tighter, until he moved away from the door.

One night an early policeman appeared. Usually the police emerged near midnight, disarming people of knives and broken glass, forcing them into the vans. Blackband watched eagerly. Surely the man must escort her home, see what the house hid. Blackband glanced back to the splash of light beneath the lamp. It was deserted.

How could she had moved so fast? He stared, baffled. A dim shape lurked at the corner of his eyes. Glancing nervously, he saw the woman standing on the bright disc several lamps away, considerably farther from the policeman than he'd thought. Why should he have been so mistaken?

Before he could ponder, sound distracted him: a loud fluttering, as though a bird were trapped and frantic in the kitchen. But the room was empty. Any bird must have escaped through the open window. Was that a flicker of movement below, in the dark house? Perhaps the bird had flown in there.

The policeman had moved on. The woman was trudging her island of light; her coat's hem dragged over the gravel. For a while Blackband watched, musing uneasily, trying to think what the fluttering had resembled more than the sound of a bird's wings.

Perhaps that was why, in the early hours, he saw a man stumbling through the derelict back streets. Jagged hurdles of rubble blocked the way; the man clambered, panting dryly, gulping dust as well as breath. He seemed only exhausted and uneasy, but Blackband could see what was pursuing him: a great wide shadow-colored stain, creeping vaguely over the rooftops. The stain was alive, for its face mouthed – though at first, from its color and texture, he thought the head was the moon. Its eyes gleamed hungrily. As the fluttering made the man turn and scream, the face sailed down on its stain toward him.

Next day was unusually trying: a dog with a broken leg and a suffering owner, you'll hurt his leg, can't you be more gentle, oh come here, baby, what did the nasty man do to you; a senile cat and its protector, isn't the usual vet here today, he never used to do that, are you sure you know what you're doing. But later, as he watched the woman's obsessive trudging, the dream of the stain returned to him. Suddenly he realized he had never seen her during daylight.

So that was it! he thought, sniggering. She'd been a vampire all the time! A difficult job to keep when you hadn't a tooth in your head. He reeled in her face with the focusing-screw. Yes, she was toothless. Perhaps she used false fangs, or sucked through her gums. But he couldn't sustain his joke for long. Her face peered out of the frame of her grey scarf, as though from a web. As she circled she was muttering incessantly. Her tongue worked as though her mouth were too small for it. Her eyes were fixed as the heads of grey nails impaling her skull.

He laid the binoculars aside, and was glad that she'd become more distant. But even the sight of her trudging in miniature troubled him. In her eyes he had seen that she didn't want to do what she was doing.

She was crossing the roadway, advancing toward his gate. For a moment, unreasonably and with a sour uprush of dread, he was sure she intended to come in. But she was staring at the hedge. Her hands fluttered, warding off a fear; her eyes and her mouth were stretched wide. She stood quivering, then she stumbled toward her street, almost running.

He made himself go down. Each leaf of the hedge held an orange-sodium glow, like wet paint. But there was nothing among the leaves, and nothing could have struggled out, for the twigs were intricately bound by spiderwebs, gleaming like gold wire.

The next day was Sunday. He rode a train beneath the Mersey and went tramping the Wirral Way nature trail. Red-faced men, and women who had paralyzed their hair with spray, stared as though he'd invaded their garden. A few butterflies perched on flowers; their wings settled together delicately, then they flickered away above the banks of the abandoned railway cutting. They were too quick for him to enjoy, even with his binoculars; he kept remembering how near death their species were. His moping had slowed him, he felt barred from his surroundings by his inability to confront the old woman. He couldn't speak to her, there were no words he could use, but meanwhile her animals might be suffering. He dreaded going home to another night of helpless watching.

Could he look into the house while she was wandering? She might leave the door unlocked. At some time he had become intuitively sure that her companion was dead. Twilight gained on him, urging him back to Liverpool.

He gazed nervously down at the lamps. Anything was preferable to his impotence. But his feelings had trapped him into committing himself before he was ready. Could he really go down when she emerged? Suppose the other woman was still alive, and screamed? Good God, he needn't go in if he didn't want to. On the gravel, light lay bare as a row of plates on a shelf. He found himself thinking, with a secret eagerness, that she might already have had her wander.

As he made dinner, he kept hurrying irritably to the front window. Television failed to engross him; he watched the avenue instead. Discs of light dwindled away, impaled by their lamps. Below the kitchen window stood a block of night and silence. Eventually he went to bed, but heard fluttering – flights of litter in the derelict streets, no doubt. His dreams gave the litter a human face.

Throughout Monday he was on edge, anxious to hurry home and be done; he was distracted. Oh poor Chubbles, is the man hurting you! He managed to leave early. Day was trailing down the sky as he reached the avenue. Swiftly he brewed coffee and sat sipping, watching.

The caravan of cars faltered, interrupted by gaps. The last home-comers hurried away, clearing the stage. But the woman failed to take her cue. His cooking of dinner was fragmented; he hurried repeatedly back to the window. Where was the bloody woman, was she on strike? Not until the following night, when she had still not appeared, did he begin to suspect he'd seen the last of her.

His intense relief was short-lived. If she had died of whatever had been shrinking her, what would happen to her animals? Should he find out what was wrong? But there was no reason to think she'd died.

Probably she, and her friend before her, had gone to stay with relatives. No doubt the animals had escaped long before – he'd never seen or heard any of them since she had taken them in. Darkness stood hushed and bulky beneath his kitchen window.

For several days the back streets were quiet, except for the flapping of litter or birds. It became easier to glance at the dark house. Soon they'd demolish it; already children had shattered all the windows. Now, when he lay awaiting sleep, the thought of the vague house soothed him, weighed his mind down gently.

That night he awoke twice. He'd left the kitchen window ajar, hoping to lose some of the unseasonable heat. Drifting through the window came a man's low moaning. Was he trying to form words? His voice was muffled, blurred as a dying radio. He must be drunk; perhaps he had fallen, for there was a faint scrape of rubble. Blackband hid within his eyelids, courting sleep. At last the shapeless moaning faded. There was silence, except for the feeble, stony scraping. Blackband lay and grumbled, until sleep led him to a face that crept over heaps of rubble.

Some hours later he woke again. The lifelessness of four o'clock surrounded him, the dim air seemed sluggish and ponderous. Had he dreamed the new sound? It returned, and made him flinch: a chorus of thin, piteous wailing, reaching weakly upward toward the kitchen. For a moment, on the edge of dream, it sounded like babies. How could babies be crying in an abandoned house? The voices were too thin. They were kittens.

He lay in the heavy dark, hemmed in by shapes that the night deformed. He willed the sounds to cease, and eventually they did. When he awoke again, belatedly, he had time only to hurry to work.

In the evening the house was silent as a draped cage. Someone must have rescued the kittens. But in the early hours the crying woke him: fretful, bewildered, famished. He couldn't go down now, he had no light. The crying was muffled, as though beneath stone. Again it kept him awake, again he was late for work.

His loss of sleep nagged him. His smile sagged impatiently, his nods were contemptuous twitches. "Yes," he agreed with a woman who said she'd been careless to slam her dog's paw in a door, and when she raised her eyebrows haughtily: "Yes, I can see that." He could see her deciding to find another vet. Let her, let someone else suffer her. He had problems of his own.

He borrowed the office flashlight, to placate his anxiety. Surely he wouldn't need to enter the house, surely someone else – He walked home, toward the darker sky. Night thickened like soot on the buildings.

He prepared dinner quickly. No need to dawdle in the kitchen, no point in staring down. He was hurrying; he dropped a spoon, which reverberated shrilly in his mind, nerve-racking. Slow down, slow down. A breeze piped incessantly outside, in the rubble. No, not a breeze. When he made himself raise the sash he heard the crying, thin as wind in crevices.

It seemed weaker now, dismal and desperate: intolerable. Could nobody else hear it, did nobody care? He gripped the windowsill; a breeze tried feebly to tug at his fingers. Suddenly, compelled by vague anger, he grabbed the flashlight and trudged reluctantly downstairs.

A pigeon hobbled on the avenue, dangling the stump of one leg, twitching clogged wings; cars brisked by. The back street was scattered with debris, as though a herd had moved on, leaving its refuse to manure the paving stones. His flashlight groped over the heaped pavement, trying to determine which house had been troubling him.

Only by standing back to align his own window with the house could he decide, and even then he was unsure. How could the old woman have clambered over the jagged pile that blocked the doorway? The front door sprawled splintered in the hall, on a heap of the fallen ceiling, amid peelings of wallpaper. He must be mistaken. But as his flashlight dodged about the hall, picking up debris then letting it drop back into the dark, he heard the crying, faint and muffled. It was somewhere within.

He ventured forward, treading carefully. He had to drag the door into the street before he could proceed. Beyond the door the floorboards were cobbled with rubble. Plaster swayed about him, glistening. His light wobbled ahead of him, then led him toward a gaping doorway on the right. The light spread into the room, dimming.

A door lay on its back. Boards poked like exposed ribs through the plaster of the ceiling; torn paper dangled. There was no carton full of starving kittens; in fact, the room was bare. Moist stains engulfed the walls.

He groped along the hall, to the kitchen. The stove was fat with grime. The wallpaper had collapsed entirely, draping indistinguishable shapes that stirred as the flashlight glanced at them. Through the furred window, he made out the light in his own kitchen, orange-shaded, blurred. How could two women have survived here?

At once he regretted that thought. The old woman's face loomed behind him: eyes still as metal, skin the colour of pale bone. He turned nervously; the light capered. Of course there was only the quivering mouth of the hall. But the face was present now, peering from behind the draped shapes around him.

He was about to give up – he was already full of the gasp of relief he would give when he reached the avenue – when he heard the crying. It was almost breathless, as though close to death: a shrill feeble wheezing. He couldn't bear it. He hurried into the hall.

Might the creatures be upstairs? His light showed splintered holes in most of the stairs; through them he glimpsed a huge symmetrical stain on the wall. Surely the woman could never have climbed up there – but that left only the cellar.

The door was beside him. The flashlight, followed by his hand, groped for the knob. The face was near him in the shadows; its fixed eyes gleamed. He dreaded finding her fallen on the cellar steps. But the crying pleaded. He dragged the door open; it scraped over rubble. He thrust the flashlight into the dank opening. He stood gaping, bewildered.

Beneath him lay a low stone room. Its walls glistened darkly. The place was full of debris: bricks, planks, broken lengths of wood. Draping the debris, or tangled beneath it, were numerous old clothes. Threads of a white substance were tethered to everything, and drifted feebly now the door was opened.

In one corner loomed a large pale bulk. His light twitched toward it. It was a white bag of some material, not cloth. It had been torn open; except for a sifting of rubble, and a tangle of what might have been fragments of dully painted cardboard, it was empty.

The crying wailed, somewhere beneath the planks. Several sweeps of the light showed that the cellar was otherwise deserted. Though the face mouthed behind him, he ventured down. For God's sake, get it over with; he knew he would never dare return. A swath had been cleared through the dust on the steps, as though something had dragged itself out of the cellar, or had been dragged in.

His movements disturbed the tethered threads; they rose like feelers, fluttering delicately. The white bag stirred, its torn mouth worked. Without knowing why, he stayed as far from that corner as he could.

The crying had come from the far end of the cellar. As he picked his way hurriedly over the rubble he caught sight of a group of clothes. They were violently coloured sweaters, which the Rainbow Man had worn. They slumped over planks; they nestled inside one another, as though the man had withered or had been sucked out.

Staring uneasily about, Blackband saw that all the clothes were stained. There was blood on all of them, though not a great deal on any. The ceiling hung close to him, oppressive and vague. Darkness had blotted out the steps and the door. He caught at them with the light, and stumbled toward them.

The crying made him falter. Surely there were fewer voices, and they seemed to sob. He was nearer the voices than the steps. If he could find the creatures at once, snatch them up and flee – He clambered over the treacherous debris, toward a gap in the rubble. The bag mouthed emptily; threads plucked at him, almost impalpably. As he thrust the flashlight's beam into the gap, darkness rushed to surround him.

Beneath the debris a pit had been dug. Parts of its earth walls had collapsed, but protruding from the fallen soil he could see bones. They looked too large for an animal's. In the centre of the pit, sprinkled with earth, lay a cat. Little of it remained, except for its skin and bones; its skin was covered with deep pock-marks. But its eyes seemed to move feebly.

Appalled, he stooped. He had no idea what to do. He never knew, for the walls of the pit were shifting. Soil trickled scattering as a face the size of his fist emerged. There were several; their limbless mouths, their sharp tongues flickered out toward the cat. As he fled they began wailing dreadfully.

He chased the light toward the steps. He fell, cutting his knees. He thought the face with its gleaming eyes would meet him in the hall. He ran from the cellar, flailing his flashlight at the air. As he stumbled down the street he could still see the faces that had crawled from the soil: rudimentary beneath translucent skin, but beginning to be human.

He leaned against his gatepost in the lamplight, retching. Images and memories tumbled disordered through his mind. The face crawling over the roofs. Only seen at night. Vampire. The fluttering at the window. Her terror at the hedge full of spiders. *Calyptra*, what was it, *Calyptra eustrigata*. Vampire moth.

Vague though they were, the implications terrified him. He fled into his building, but halted fearfully on the stairs. The things must be destroyed: to delay would be insane. Suppose their hunger brought them crawling out of the cellar tonight, toward his flat – Absurd though it must be, he couldn't forget that they might have seen his face.

He stood giggling, dismayed. Whom did you call in these circumstances? The police, an exterminator? Nothing would relieve his horror until he saw the brood destroyed, and the only way to see that was to do the job himself. Burn. Petrol. He dawdled on the stairs, delaying, thinking he knew none of the other tenants from whom to borrow the fuel.

He ran to the nearby garage. "Have you got any petrol?"

The man glared at him, suspecting a joke. "You'd be surprised. How much do you want?"

How much indeed! He restrained his giggling. Perhaps he should ask the man's advice! Excuse me, how much petrol do you need for – "A gallon," he stammered.

As soon as he reached the back street he switched on his flashlight. Crowds of rubble lined the pavements. Far above the dark house he saw his orange light. He stepped over the debris into the hall. The swaying light brought the face forward to meet him. Of course the hall was empty.

He forced himself forward. Plucked by the flashlight, the cellar door flapped soundlessly. Couldn't he just set fire to the house? But that might leave the brood untouched. Don't think, go down quickly. Above the stairs the stain loomed.

In the cellar nothing had changed. The bag gaped, the clothes lay emptied. Struggling to unscrew the cap of the petrol can, he almost dropped the flashlight. He kicked wood into the pit and began to pour the petrol. At once he heard the wailing beneath him. "Shut up!" he screamed, to drown out the sound. "Shut up! Shut up!"

The can took its time in gulping itself empty; the petrol seemed thick as oil. He hurled the can clattering away, and ran to the steps. He fumbled with matches, gripping the flashlight between his knees. As he threw them, the lit matches went out. Not until he ventured back to the pit, clutching a ball of paper from his pocket, did he succeed in making a flame that reached his goal. There was a whoof of fire, and a chorus of interminable feeble shrieking.

As he clambered sickened toward the hall, he heard a fluttering above him. Wallpaper, stirring in a wind: it sounded moist. But there was no wind, for the air clung clammily to him. He slithered over the rubble into the hall, darting his light about. Something white bulked at the top of the stairs.

It was another torn bag. He hadn't been able to see it before. It slumped emptily. Beside it the stain spread over the wall. That stain was too symmetrical; it resembled an inverted coat. Momentarily he thought the paper was drooping, tugged perhaps by his unsteady light, for the stain had begun to creep down toward him. Eyes glared at him from its dangling face. Though the face was upside down he knew it at once. From its gargoyle mouth a tongue reached for him.

He whirled to flee. But the darkness that filled the front door was more than night, for it was advancing audibly. He stumbled, panicking, and rubble slipped from beneath his feet. He fell from the cellar steps, onto piled stone. Though he felt almost no pain, he heard his spine break.

His mind writhed helplessly. His body refused to heed it in any way, and lay on the rubble, trapping him. He could hear cars on the avenue, radio sets and the sounds of cutlery in flats, distant and indifferent. The cries were petering out now. He tried to scream, but only his eyes could move. As they struggled, he glimpsed through a slit in the cellar wall the orange light in his kitchen.

His flashlight lay on the steps, dimmed by its fall. Before long a rustling darkness came slowly down the steps, blotting out the light. He heard sounds in the dark, and something that was not flesh nestled against him. His throat managed a choked shriek that was almost inaudible, even to him. Eventually the face crawled away toward the hall, and the light returned. From the corner of his eye he could see what surrounded him. They were round, still, practically featureless: as yet, hardly even alive.

NANCY KILPATRICK

Root Cellar

AWARD-WINNING AUTHOR NANCY KILPATRICK has published in the fantasy, horror and mystery genres. Her twenty-six books include fourteen novels (the popular "Power of the Blood" vampire series, amongst others), five collections of her more than 150 published short stories, and seven anthologies she has edited, including *In the Shadow of the Gargoyle* and *Graven Images*.

She has recently completed *The Goth Bible* for St. Martin's Press, a non-fiction book on the Gothic lifestyle, and is co-editing a new Goth anthology with Nancy Holder.

Kilpatrick lives in a Gothically decorated apartment in Montréal, Canada, with her black cat Bella. When not writing, her favourite activity is travelling the world and visiting cemeteries, ossuaries and mummies with her photographer companion, Hugues Leblanc.

"I once lived for almost a year in a farmhouse exactly like the one in 'Root Cellar'," explains the author. "It was located in the small town of Napannee, Ontario. Many of the oddities in the story were in that house. The items found in the basement were actually discovered in the attic, and the windowsills were indeed found as in the story.

"The old part of the house always felt creepy to me and, in fact, we ended up not using it much. It was small, dark, and led to the dirt-floor basement, with the jars along the walls of the stairway, and that door . . . Living there, especially in fall and winter, really gave me a clear understanding of how a place could be haunted, by ghosts, and by memories . . ."

The subtle tale that follows was deservedly reprinted by Karl Edward Wagner in the twentieth volume of his *Year's Best Horror Stories* series.

AS VADIM STRUGGLED TO get out of the Toyota, rain slammed him back. Nearby maple branches, bereft of leaves, clung to one another. The mid winter sky was dead-grey but he noticed black storm clouds rushing to squelch even that little light.

Five strides and Vadim hit the porch of the farmhouse, just as thunder broke. Lightning cracked a willow across the road, severing a branch. An omen, he thought, shivering, hating himself for even thinking that way. The way *she* had taught him to think. He hurried indoors.

The 'new' part of his grandmother's house, built seventy-five years ago, looked the same. Too-tall ceilings. Cavernous rooms. Sparsely patterned wallpaper. Under the dust covers, like stern guardians, lay furniture that Vadim had no intention of exposing. His memories were olfactory and reeked of blood and decay. He would not be here now if Lola had not gone out of the country. Lola, his younger sister, was still a baby at twenty. Lola desperately pleaded for specific memorabilia before he boarded up the property forever.

Vadim had no such desires. His memories of years spent in this house were of dead space, the weighted stillness as heavy as his grandmother's hand. He had distanced himself mentally and eventually physically from her insidiousness. And soon the disconnection would be permanent.

He glanced into the kitchen. The electricity had been shut off three months ago, but lightning flashed; it was frightening how nothing had changed. Except the corner. No willow switch stood ready for duty. Still, he would not have been surprised to see his grandmother's severe face in the doorway or hear her diseased rantings echo through the rooms.

Vadim went to the cupboard above and to the left of the sink. Second shelf at the back. He retrieved the empty sugar bowl with the butterfly on the lid that Lola wanted. He felt no sentimental feelings, just a sense of claustrophobia, as if the past were crushed against the present, intent on devouring the boundaries, desperate to consume it. He hurried upstairs.

The master bedroom his grandparents had shared sixteen years ago when Grandpa Bentz died was as silent as ever. The lifeless blue duvet had been flung across the foot of the bed. His grandmother ended her existence wrapped in that comforter, alone in a pool of foul-smelling excrement. Alone until her rotting flesh had been discovered. "Death only comforts the living," she had said with authority often enough. The clock in the corner no longer ticked and Vadim was grateful.

He crossed the short hallway and took the attic stairs to the cramped and airless rooms to which he and Lola had once been banished. In his: wall cracks, as familiar and permanent as the creases of disapproval in his grandmother's face. A small dresser, its mirror wavy with age, unable to offer a true reflection. Vadim's single bed – springs that creaked so easily he had been afraid to breathe. That had creaked too often in rhythm to willow switches imprinting the family's ancient beliefs beyond his bare skin and deep into his cells.

In Lola's room he found the glass-unicorn music box and carried it and the sugar bowl down the narrower back stairs leading to the old part. He entered a shabby room that dated back two hundred years. Back to the fierce great-great-grandparents whom he had heard so much about. The ancestors who had immigrated from the old country where they had been persecuted. He had never felt safe in this part of the house.

Vadim paused. Outside black clouds smothered all light. He trembled as he reached into his raincoat pocket to pull out the flashlight. The sugar bowl slipped from his fingers. It hit the sloped hardwood and, even before he dropped the beam into the pieces, Vadim knew that it had shattered. Fear gripped him, the old, suffocating terror. But no ghost bent on punishment materialized. He exhaled; his nerves were on edge.

A flicker of blue lightning showed him something peculiar and Vadim ran the flashlight beam over the sills of the three large windows. "Mother of . . ." he whispered. Each sill was littered with fly carcasses, an inch thick. And the floor below the windows. And by the door. Thousands. No, tens of thousands. Black and iridescent green. Crisp hollowed shells that crunched beneath his soles. They clustered near the routes of egress but for them there had been no escape from this place.

Vadim no longer worried about the sugar bowl, he just wanted out before this tomb-of-the-dead sealed him in. But Lola had only asked for one thing more. Another object to cement her fantasy of happy memories and relegate the reality to insubstantial phantoms. The two of them were all that was left now. He needed her to ground him in the present, a world cleansed of superstition. Take it easy, he thought. Grandma Bentz is gone. I'll be out of here in five minutes.

The door to the root cellar was locked, as it always had been, but he broke the rusted padlock easily. The hinges squeaked as the door, warped from age and the moisture embedded in this part of the house, scraped the floor.

Mouldy air wafted out. Vadim aimed his light like a weapon into the appalling darkness. Ashamed, he watched his hand shake and heard ragged breath.

I can't do it, he thought. Memories of nights spent in the root cellar, crouched beneath the stairs, the smell of earth and vegetation and rot clogging his nostrils. And the sounds. Like nothing he had heard since, except in dreams. Over time he had learned to hum softly, loud enough to cover the noise, low enough not to bring down Grandma Bentz.

The doll Lola needed had been buried in a storage trunk for a decade and a half. The trunk in the cellar. Now that he'd broken the sugar bowl, there was no way to avoid getting it.

He stepped down into the dark pit. Cobwebs attacked his face and he gasped. "Weakling!" he admonished, repeating the word hurled so often at him. A word that must have travelled through generations.

Along the left of the stairs was a wall of shelves stocked with pickles and preserves. He read the ageing labels from the lowest shelf up: chilli sauce; corn relish; pickled cauliflower; carrots and dills dating back to 1790. A jar of murky contents, the yellowed label smudged. Beets, maybe. These had been here when he was a child, since before his grandmother was a girl. Every generation added to the store and Grandma Bentz had contributed the row second from the top. She had not allowed any of the jars to be touched, calling them "Memories". Food uneaten. Life preserved forever.

The steps creaked in familiar spots as Vadim made his way to the dirt floor. He waved the light into each corner. The steamer trunk sat furthest from the stairs. In front of the metal door.

He placed the unicorn securely in his coat pocket and tucked the flashlight under one arm, ready to tackle this lock. But the latch was open, as if someone had expected him to come this way. Vadim glanced at the door and listened. Nothing.

He lifted the lid of the trunk. On the left, as if unaware of her surroundings, Lola's porcelain doll grinned up at him.

Only two other objects competed for his attention. A piece of barn board with postcards nailed to it. A small black coffin.

At the sight of the coffin, Vadim shook with fear and rage. Tears threatened to swell over his eyelids and he could not stop himself from yelling "Bitch!" She knew him so well. She had tricked him. Again.

He was startled by a noise behind the door. A rat. Or his imagination. He did not believe it had been either.

Vadim wanted to grab the doll and bolt but decades of anger solidified. And he was curious. He lifted the board and ran the light from left to right along both rows. Each Victorian card was a pastel sketch. Together the eight pictures told a story:

Woman alone, happily swinging on porch swing.

Man in cloak approaches.

Man kisses woman on neck.

Woman dead in coffin.

Woman rises to join man.

Man and woman kiss boy on neck.

Boy dead in coffin.

Boy rises to join woman and man.

A quaint Gothic record of family madness, he thought. To be handed down from generation to generation with the silver. But he had no intention of passing it further.

Vadim placed the board carefully back into the trunk. He snatched up the doll and stuffed it in his other pocket, ready to abandon this prison forever. Yet he felt compelled to look inside the coffin. She must have known he would. "You'll die of curiosity," Grandma Bentz had always predicted. He had believed she intended to fulfil that prophecy.

He picked up the crude wooden box and shook it but had no sense of what lay within. Less than a foot long, three inches at the widest part, shaped like an old-fashioned casket. A morbid miniature in flat black. The dead crawled from his memory: A nighthawk he had buried in a box he made, much like this one. His mother and father, killed in a barn fire. Grandpa Bentz — who knows how he died? It was only his grandmother's corpse that he had not viewed. Neither he nor Lola had attended the service. Nor gone to the cemetery. "If you don't witness the dead, how do you know they are?" Grandma Bentz had repeated at every demise, and the words haunted him now.

Vadim used his car key to pry between the lid and the box. The birch was hard and he was careful to wedge the metal in and lift the nails without damaging the wood. Images formed in his mind, gruesome pictures, parts severed from the living, stolen away from the light, drained of vitality, suspended in darkness forever to shrivel and emaciate slowly.

The lid was a quarter-inch above the box and he was sweating. Suddenly time and space expanded. Endless. Hopeless. The eternity he had always feared clawed at the edges of his consciousness.

There was no point in hesitating and Vadim no longer considered it. Instead he struggled to defend himself from his most recent ancestor's bequest. A gift that he would leave to rot in the belly of this house. That would end with him and Lola, the last of a tortured line.

He yanked the lid away. The root cellar became a frozen grave. "What did you expect?" he chided, his voice unfamiliar and cold in the hollowness.

A sharp wooden stake lay inside the casket. Who had she intended it for? She had forced him to this point just as she had meticulously nurtured every dark and savage impulse in him. He threw his head back and laughed until tears flowed and then he began to howl like the doomed animal he felt himself to be. Scratching behind the door brought him to his senses.

Vadim took the stake out and dropped the coffin back into the trunk, then slammed the lid. The sound was heavy and final in the stillness. But he was not sure what to do. Every possibility seemed annihilating. And he had no idea which act would be giving in to her iron will and which constituted resisting.

While he waited, thinking, listening, Vadim spun the stake in his fingers, the tip pointing toward him, and then away. Him. Away. But he did not hesitate long. All too soon the metal door opened inward.

ROBERT BLOCH

Hungarian Rhapsody

ROBERT BLOCH WAS BORN IN CHICAGO but lived in Los Angeles for many years. His interest in horror first blossomed when he originally saw Lon Chaney Sr's performance in the 1925 *The Phantom of the Opera*. After discovering the pulp magazine *Weird Tales*, he began corresponding with author H.P. Lovecraft, who advised him to try his own hand at writing fiction. The rest, as they say, is history.

After his first story was published in 1934, Bloch quickly established himself as a popular and prolific short-story writer, and by the 1940s he had begun to develop his own unique style of twisted psychological horror and grim graveyard humour. Although he wrote more than two dozen novels, over 400 short stories, and numerous scripts for TV and movies, he will always be identified with his 1959 novel *Psycho* and Alfred Hitchcock's subsequent film version. His wonderfully entertaining autobiography, *Once Around the Bloch*, was published in 1993, the year before he died.

Over the years the author wrote numerous stories about vampirism, and choosing one for this collection proved to be more difficult than I had expected. In the end I picked 'Hungarian Rhapsody' because it had not been anthologized quite so often as some of his other, more famous, tales. It is a fine example of 1950s paranoia and Bloch's renowned sense of black humour.

RIGHT AFTER LABOR DAY the weather turned cold and all the summer cottage people went home. By the time ice began to form on Lost Lake there was nobody around but Solly Vincent.

Vincent was a big fat man who had purchased a year-round home on the lake early that spring. He wore loud sports-shirts all summer long, and although nobody ever saw him hunting or fishing, he entertained a lot of weekend guests from the city at his place. The first thing he did when he bought the house was to put up a big sign in front which read SONOVA BEACH. Folks passing by got quite a bang out of it.

But it wasn't until fall that he took to coming into town and getting acquainted. Then he started dropping into Doc's Bar one or two evenings a week, playing cards with the regulars in the back room.

Even then, Vincent didn't exactly open up. He played a good game of poker and he smoked good cigars, but he never said anything about himself. Once, when Specs Hennessey asked him a direct question, he told the gang he came from Chicago, and that he was a retired business man. But he never mentioned what business he had retired from.

The only time he opened his mouth was to ask questions, and he didn't really do that until the evening Specs Hennessey brought out the gold coin and laid it on the table.

"Ever see anything like that before?" he asked the gang. Nobody said anything, but Vincent reached over and picked it up.

"German, isn't it?" he mumbled. "Who's the guy with the beard – the Kaiser?"

Specs Hennessey chuckled. "You're close," he said. "That's old Franz Joseph. He used to be boss of the Austro-Hungarian Empire, forty–fifty years ago. That's what they told me down at the bank."

"Where'd you get it, in a slot-machine?" Vincent wanted to know.

Specs shook his head. "It came in a bag, along with about a thousand others."

That's when Vincent really began to look interested. He picked up the coin again and turned it in his stubby fingers. "You gonna tell what happened?" he asked.

Specs didn't need any more encouragement. "Funniest damn thing," he said. "I was sitting in the office last Wednesday when this dame showed up and asked if I was the real-estate man and did I have any lake property for sale. So I said sure, the Schultz cottage over at Lost Lake. A mighty fine bargain, furnished and everything, for peanuts to settle the estate.

"I was all set to give her a real pitch but she said never mind that, could I show it to her? And I said, of course, how about tomorrow, and she said why not right now, tonight?

"So I drove her out and we went through the place and she said she'd take it, just like that. I should see the lawyer and get the papers ready and she'd come back Monday night and close the deal. Sure enough, she showed up, lugging this big bag of coins. I had to call Hank Felch over from the bank to find out what they were and if they were any good. Turns out they are, all right. Good as gold." Specs grinned. "That's how come I know about Franz Joseph." He took the coin from Vincent and put it back in his pocket. "Anyway, it looks like you're going to have a new neighbor out there. The Schultz place is only about a half-mile down the line from yours. And if I was you, I'd run over and borrow a cup of sugar."

Vincent blinked. "You figure she's loaded, huh?"

Specs shook his head. "Maybe she is, maybe she isn't. But the main thing is, she's stacked." He grinned again. "Name's Helene Ester-hazy. Helene, with an *e* on the end. I saw it when she signed. Talks like one of them Hungarian refugees – figure that's what she is, too. A countess, maybe, some kind of nobility. Probably busted out from behind the Iron Curtain and decided to hole up some place where the Commies couldn't find her. Of course I'm only guessing, because she didn't have much to say for herself."

Vincent nodded. "How was she dressed?" he asked.

"Like a million bucks." Specs grinned at him. "What's the idea, you figuring on marrying for money, or something? I tell you, one look at this dame and you'll forget all about dough. She talks something like this ZaZa Gabor. Looks something like her, too, only she has red hair. Boy, if I wasn't a married man, I'd—"

"When she say she was moving in?" Vincent interrupted.

"She didn't say. But I figure right away, in a day or so."

Vincent yawned and stood up.

"Hey, you're not quitting yet, are you? The game's young—"

"Tired," Vincent said. "Got to hit the sack."

And he went home, and he hit the sack, but not to sleep. He kept thinking about his new neighbor.

Actually, Vincent wasn't too pleased with the idea of having anyone for a neighbor, even if she turned out to be a beautiful redheaded refugee. For Vincent was something of a refugee himself, and he'd come up north to get away from people; everybody except the few special friends he invited up during summer weekends. Those people he could trust, because they were former business associates. But there was always the possibility of running into former business rivals – and he didn't want to see any of them. Not ever. Some of them might nurse grudges, and in Vincent's former business a grudge could lead to trouble.

That's why Vincent didn't sleep very well at night, and why he always kept a little souvenir of his old business right under the pillow. You never could tell.

Of course, this sounded legitimate enough; the dame probably was a Hungarian refugee, the way Specs Hennessey said. Still, the whole thing might be a very clever plant, a way of moving in on Vincent which wouldn't be suspected.

In any case, Vincent decided he'd keep his eye on the old Schultz cottage down the line and see what happened. So the next morning he went into town again and bought himself a very good pair of binoculars, and the day after that he used them when the moving van drove into the drive of the Schultz place half a mile away.

Most of the leaves had fallen from the trees and Vincent got a pretty clear view from his kitchen window. The moving van was a small one, and there was just the driver and a single helper, carrying in a bunch of boxes and crates. Vincent didn't see any furniture and that puzzled him until he remembered the Schultz cottage had been sold furnished. Still, he wondered about the boxes, which seemed to be quite heavy. Could the whole story be on the up-and-up and the boxes maybe filled with more gold coins? Vincent couldn't make up his mind. He kept waiting for the woman to drive in, but she didn't show, and after a while the men climbed into their van and left.

Vincent watched most of the afternoon and nothing happened. Then he fried himself a steak and ate it, looking out at the sunset over the lake. It was then that he noticed the light shining from the cottage window. She must have sneaked in while he was busy at the stove.

He got out his binoculars and adjusted them. Vincent was a big man, and he had a powerful grip, but what he saw nearly caused the binoculars to drop from his fingers.

The curtain was up in her bedroom, and the woman was lying on the bed. She was naked, except for a covering of gold coins.

Vincent steadied himself and propped both hands up on the sill as he squinted through the binoculars.

There was no mistake about it – he saw a naked woman, wallowing in a bed strewn with gold. The light reflected from the coins, it danced and dazzled across her bare body, it radiated redly from her long auburn hair. She was pale, wide-eyed, and voluptuously lovely, and her oval face with its high cheekbones and full lips seemed transformed into a mask of wanton ecstasy as she caressed her nakedness with handfuls of shimmering gold.

Then Vincent knew that it wasn't a plant, she wasn't a phoney. She was a genuine refugee, all right, but that wasn't important. What was important was the way the blood pounded in his temples, the way his throat tightened up until he almost choked as he stared at her, stared at all that long, lean loveliness and the white and the red and the gold.

He made himself put down the binoculars, then. He made himself pull the shade, and he made himself wait until the next morning even though he got no rest that night.

But bright and early he was up, shaving close with his electric razor, dressing in the double-breasted gab that hid his paunch, using the lotion left over from summer when he used to bring the tramps up from the city. And he put on his new tie and his big smile, and he walked very quickly over to the cottage and knocked on the door.

No answer.

He knocked a dozen times, but nothing happened. The shades were all down, and there wasn't a sound.

Of course he could have forced the lock. If he'd thought she was a plant, he'd have done so in a moment, because he carried the souvenir in his coat-pocket, ready for action. And if he'd had any idea of just getting at the coins he would have forced the lock, too. That would be the ideal time, when she was away.

Only he wasn't worried about plants, and he didn't give a damn about the money. What he wanted was the woman. Helene Esterhazy. Classy name. Real class. A countess, maybe. A writhing redhead on a bed of golden coins—

Vincent went away after a while, but all day long he sat in the window and watched. Watched and waited. She'd probably gone into town to stock up on supplies. Maybe she visited the beauty parlor, too. But she ought to be back. She had to come back. And when she did—

This time he missed her because he finally had to go to the bathroom, along about twilight. But when he returned to his post and saw the light in the front room, he didn't hesitate. He made the half-mile walk in about five minutes, flat, and he was puffing a little. Then he forced himself to wait on the doorstep for a moment before knocking. Finally his ham-fist rapped, and she opened the door.

She stood there, staring startled into the darkness, and the lamplight from behind shone through the filmy transparency of her long hostess-gown, then flamed through the long red hair that flowed loosely across her shoulders.

"Yes?" she murmured.

Vincent swallowed painfully. He couldn't help it. She looked like a hundred-a-night girl; hell, make it a thousand-a-night, make it a million. A million in gold coins, and her red hair like a veil. That was all he could think of, and he couldn't remember the words he'd rehearsed, the line he'd so carefully built up in advance.

"My name's Solly Vincent," he heard himself saying. "I'm your neighbor, just down the lake a ways. Heard about you moving in and I thought I ought to, well, introduce myself."

"So."

She stared at him, not smiling, not moving, and he got a sick hunch that she knew just what he'd been thinking.

"Your name's Esterhazy, isn't it? Tell me you're Hungarian, something like that. Well, I figured maybe you're a stranger here, haven't got settled yet, and—"

"I'm quite satisfied here." Still she didn't smile or move. Just stared like a statue; a cold, hard, goddam beautiful statue.

"Glad to hear it. But I just meant, maybe you'd like to stop in at my place, sort of get acquainted. I got some of that Tokay wine and a big record-player, you know, classic stuff. I think I even have that piece, that *Hungarian Rhapsody* thing, and—"

Now what had he said?

Because all at once she was laughing. Laughing with her lips, with her throat, with her whole body, laughing with everything except those ice-green eyes.

Then she stopped and spoke, and her voice was ice-green too. "No thank you," she said. "As I say, I am quite satisfied here. All I require is that I am not disturbed."

"Well, maybe some other time—"

"Let me repeat myself. I do not wish to be disturbed. Now or at any time. Good evening, Mr—" The door closed.

She didn't even remember his name. The stuckup bitch didn't even remember his name. Unless she'd pretended to forget on purpose. Just like she slammed the door in his face, to put him down.

Well, nobody put Solly Vincent down. Not in the old days, and not now, either.

He walked back to his place and by the time he got there he was himself again. Not the damfool square who'd come up to her doorstep like a brush salesman with his hat in his hand. And not the jerk who had looked at her through the binoculars like some kid with hot pants.

He was Solly Vincent, and she didn't have to remember his name if she didn't want to. He'd show her who he was. And damned soon.

In bed that night he figured everything out. Maybe he'd saved himself a lot of grief by not getting involved. Even if she was a real disheroo, she was nuttier'n a fruitcake. Crazy foreigner, rolling around in a pile of coins. All these Hunky types, these refugees, were nuts. God knows what might have happened if he'd gotten mixed up with her. He didn't need a woman, anyway. A guy could always have himself a woman, particularly if he had money.

Money. That was the important thing. She had money. He'd seen it. Probably those crates were full of dough. No wonder she was hiding out here; if the Commies knew about her haul, they'd be right on the spot. That's the way he figured it, that's the way Specs Hennessey, the real-estate man, had figured it.

So why not?

The whole plan came to him at once. Call a few contacts in the city – maybe Carney and Fromkin, they could fence anything, including gold coins. Why the setup was perfect! She was all alone, there was nobody else around for three miles, and when it was over there wouldn't be any questions. It would look like the Commies had showed up and knocked the joint over. Besides, he wanted to see the look on her face when he came busting in—

He could imagine it now.

He imagined it all the next day, when he called Carney and Fromkin and told them to come up about nine. "Got a little deal for you," he said. "Tell you when I see you."

And he was still imagining it when they arrived. So much so that both Fromkin and Carney noticed something was wrong.

"What's it all about?" Carney wanted to know.

He just laughed. "Hope you got good springs in your Caddy," he said. "You may be hauling quite a load back to town."

"Give," Fromkin urged.

"Don't ask any questions. I've got some loot to peddle."

"Where is it?"

"I'm calling for it now."

And that's all he would say. He told them to sit tight, wait there at the house until he came back. They could help themselves to drinks if they liked. He'd only be a half-hour or so.

Then he went out. He didn't tell them where he was going, and he deliberately circled around the house in case they peeked out. But he doubled back and headed for the cottage down the way. The light was shining in the bedroom window, and it was time for the wandering boy to come home.

Now he could really let himself go, imagining everything. The way she'd look when she answered the door, the way she'd look when he grabbed her gown and ripped it away, the way she'd look when—

But he was forgetting about the money. All right, might as well admit it. The hell with the money. He'd get that too, yes, but the most important thing was the other. He'd show her who he was. She'd know, before she died.

Vincent grinned. His grin broadened as he noticed the light in the bedroom flicker and expire. She was going to sleep now. She was going to sleep in her bed of gold. So much the better. Now he wouldn't even bother to knock. He'd merely force the door, force it very quietly, and surprise her.

As it turned out, he didn't even have to do that. Because the door was unlocked. He tiptoed in very softly, and there was moonlight shining in through the window to help him find his way, and now there was the thickness in the throat again but it didn't come from confusion. He knew just what he was doing, just what he was going to do. His throat was thick because he was excited, because he could imagine her lying in there, naked on the heap of coins.

Because he could *see* her.

He opened the bedroom door, and the shade was up now so that the moonlight fell upon the whiteness and the redness and the golden glinting, and it was even better than he'd imagined because it was real.

Then the ice-green eyes opened and for a moment they stared in the old way. Suddenly there was a change. The eyes were flame-green now, and she was smiling and holding out her arms. Nuts? Maybe so. Maybe making love to all that money warmed her up. It didn't matter. What mattered was her arms, and her hair like a red veil, and the warm mouth open and panting. What mattered was to know that the gold was here and she was here and he was going to have them both, first her and then the money. He tore at his clothes, and then he was panting and sinking down to tear at her. She writhed and wriggled and his hands slipped on the coins and then his nails sank into the dirt beneath.

The dirt beneath—

There was dirt in her bed. And he could feel it and he could smell it, for suddenly she was above and behind him, pressing him down so that his face was rubbing in the dirt, and she'd twisted his hands around behind his back. He heaved, but she was very strong, and her cold fingers were busy at his wrists, knotting something tightly. Too late he tried to sit up, and then she hit him with something. Something cold and hard, something she'd taken from his own pocket; *my own gun,* he thought.

Then he must have passed out for a minute, because when he came to he could feel the blood trickling down the side of his face, and her tongue, licking it.

She had him propped up in the corner now, and she had tied his hands and legs to the bedpost, very tightly. He couldn't move. He knew because he tried, God how he tried. The earth-smell was everywhere in the room. It came from the bed, and it came from her, too. She was naked, and she was licking his face. And she was laughing.

"You came anyway, eh?" she whispered. "You had to come, is that it? Well, here you are. And here you shall stay. I will keep you for a pet. You are big and fat. You will last a long, long time.''

Vincent tried to move his head away. She laughed again.

"It isn't what you planned, is it? I know why you came back. For the gold. The gold and the earth I brought with me to sleep upon, as I did in the old country. All day I sleep upon it, but at night I awake. And when I do, you shall be here. No one will ever find or disturb us. It is good that you are strong. It will take many nights before I finish.''

Vincent found his voice. "No," he croaked. "I never believed – you must be kidding, you're a refugee—''

She laughed again. "Yes. I am a refugee. But not a *political* refugee.'' Then she retracted her tongue and Vincent saw her teeth. Her long white teeth, moving against the side of his neck in the moonlight . . .

Back at the house Carney and Fromkin got ready to climb into the Cadillac.

"He's not showing up, that's for sure," Carney said. "We'll blow before there's any trouble. Whatever he had cooked up, the deal went sour. I knew it the minute I saw his face. He had a funny look, you know, like he'd flipped.''

"Yeah," Fromkin agreed. "Something wrong with old Vincent, all right. I wonder what's biting him lately.''

CHRISTOPHER FOWLER

The Legend of Dracula Reconsidered as a Prime-time TV Special

CHRISTOPHER FOWLER LIVES AND WORKS in central London, where he is a director of the Soho movie-marketing company The Creative Partnership, producing TV and radio scripts, documentaries, trailers and promotional shorts. He spends the remainder of his time writing short-stories and novels, and he contributes a regular column about the cinema to *The 3rd Alternative*.

His books include the novels *Roofworld, Rune, Red Bride, Darkest Day, Spanky, Psychoville, Disturbia, Soho Black, Calabash, Full Dark House, Plastic* and *The Water House,* and such short story collections as *The Bureau of Lost Souls, City Jitters, Sharper Knives, Flesh Wounds, Personal Demons, Uncut, The Devil in Me* and *Demonized*. His short story 'Wageslaves' won the 1998 British Fantasy Award, and 'Breathe' is a new novella due from Telos Publishing. Fowler also scripted the 1997 graphic novel *Menz Insana*, illustrated by John Bolton.

"I know what a grimly debilitating task it is trying to sell to television," admits the author. "You pursue a clueless commissioning editor for months, nearing a deal, only to find that they have been replaced by someone who knows even less. I have more respect for plumbers, carpenters and people who drive vans, because at least they know what they're doing.

"It struck me, as I waltzed through yet another meeting with Channel 4 editors about 'a new series like that one Roald Dahl used to do' (none of the executives could remember what it was called – nor had they read his original stories) that here was a parasitic relationship corresponding to that of a vampire and his victim. Voila – the story does what it says on the tin."

The cautionary tale that follows should serve as a warning to all aspiring scriptwriters . . .

Journal of J.H.

16 July–NYC

I figured with a name like mine it was the best thing to do, kind of like an omen, y'know? I started it while I was at school – just about the only thing I *did* start at school apart from a fuckin' fight. I got maybe seventy, seventy-five pages finished before they threw me out. Most of the guys in my year were taking advanced business studies, high-risk trading in non-government-approved chemicals, how to improve your yield by cutting your shit with powdered laxative. Lemme tell you, I stayed out of *that* stuff 'cause I'm a white boy and I just don't got the connections. So if I didn't live down to the neighborhood expectations, sue me – I walked outta school with bigger plans.

I wanted – I *want* – to write. I knew that much when I was five. Not classical stuff, 'cause let's face it a guy like me ain't ever gonna get to college given the fact that if my Ma ever got hold of enough money without turning tricks or robbing a bank, only the latter of which is unlikely, she'd blow it on a trip to Vegas to see Wayne Newton before she turned it over to me. So I figure I have to do it the other way around, which is write something first then sell it to the Big Boys. And hence the thing about my name, which is Harker, John Harker like the guy in *Dracula*, which gives me what to write about.

See, a guy with a pothole in his head can figure out the future is in media. You got more leisure time, you got more technological hoozis to play with, satellites and hi-definition and sixty-'leven channels, you're gonna need more programming to put out on the air. These network guys are strip-mining the past for black-and-white sitcoms no one watched the first time around 'cause they were so crummy, anything they can slam out into the ether, build themselves some ratings and get a station profile, get advertisers knocking at their door with thirty-second spots for haemorrhoid ointment, and a guy like me, written off in the third grade as one of the Future Losers of

America, stands a real chance of selling them something. First a pilot, then a series, then ninety-eight shows stripped weeknights coast to coast, bouncing off into space for the rest of eternity. Immortality, man. Immortality.

But first things first. I just finished writin' a sure-fire script, a new version of *The Legend of Dracula* told from my viewpoint, John Harker's angle on the battle with the Lord of the Undead, and let me explain here that this script cost me on account of I got caught writing it in the store and they threw me out, so as of today I got no job.

Which means, according to this Self-Help book I'm readin', it's time to take stock of myself.

I got my health, my height and my happiness (if a lifestyle scenario which excludes fun, sex and money can be called that). I got an apartment in Queens. I'm renting with these two guys who're never home, but findin' the rent keeps me working my butt off half the night at the store, only now I don't have that job.

So I'll get another, no big deal, and meanwhile it allows me the time to go through the phone book calling the networks to find out who's the big cheese in each organization that I can send my script to. The script's a second draft for a feature-length TV movie, but it's all there, they can make out what it's about, so I outlay a fucking grotesque amount of money on photocopying and postage and send off twenty-three separate envelopes in the Manhattan area.

And then I sit back and wait.

Which is what I'm doin' now.

9 August – NYC

A guy can die from waiting.

After sending those packets I'm really glad I didn't splash out on a radiopager 'cause to be absolutely frank my phone has not been ringing off the wall. At first I think maybe they don't like the subject matter, it's kind of ghoulish although there is what you'd call a subtext on the human condition, and the subtext is the reason for doing it.

I mean Dracula's been done to death, backwards, forwards, male, female, black, white, straight, gay, musical, comedy, soap, kid's stuff, and every version available on tape, CD, LP, VHS or Beta. See, I got this theory. Times have changed; we don't die in the bosom of the family no more, we die in the arms of efficient strangers. It's 'cause we've become scared of death. And the more scared we get, the more sanitized we make the process of decay, the more we sugar up the Dracula legend to give us a palatable handle on dying.

So Dracula's been turned into some kind of upscale Eurotrash salesman, and he's everywhere, soft drinks, breakfast cereal, you name it. New York has vampires up the wazoo, but the Undead have been totally emasculated. They're clowns now, an' that sure takes the sting out of death.

So my script, my own *Legend of Dracula*, puts that life-draining shock of mortality back where it should be. It returns physical gravity to the material, provides us with a fear of death so real and deep and strong that we have to embrace it, and through catharsis allow it to exist in our lives once more.

Listen to me, I'm sitting on the john thinking my script is gonna change the fucking world and the truth is I can't get a network executive to read it. Not one reply so far, can you *believe* that?

Time for me to shit or get off the pot. So I ring around, try and get to speak to these guys.

Now, I ain't so naïve to think I can just zip through the chain of command and reach Mr Key-Decision-Maker straight off the bat, but I figure that sending out the script gives me a talking point, an edge even, and out of twenty-three packages one must have eventually landed on the right desk. I start at the top of the list an' I call each one: NBC, ABC, CBS, HBO, Ted Turner, Cable, and not only can I not reach the busy-busy PA bitches with the English accents, I cannot get beyond the fucking switchboards of these places.

I presume my script reached one of your readers, I hear myself saying, to which some girl wearing a plastic headset asks me if it was a solicited manuscript, and if it wasn't can I come and collect it 'cause they don't get returned no more on account of so many being received and cluttering up the place.

I just thought I'd start at the top. Start with the Big Guns, y'know? I never really expected it to get picked up at that stage. Time to move down the list to the smaller independent companies, people who handle specialist material. No need for somethin' like this to have big names in; it's the idea that counts. I sit and compile a new list and do the same thing again with the photocopies and the mailings, 'cause if I give this up I sure as hell ain't got anything else to look forward to. Only it used up all my money, and I'm still lookin' for a job. So I go to see Frankie at the AcuPak Night Storage way down on 3rd, but it don't pan out. I thought you said you'd always have a job for me, Frankie, I say, but he grinds his cigarette on the floor of the stock-room and looks dumbly at me. Everywhere's cuttin' back, John, he replies. There's a recession on, ain't you heard?

Yeah, I heard all right. Which is why I just left Queens for this un-air-conditioned shithole apartment on Bleeker that's cheap on account of the guy who owns it is a total burned-out fuckup and his lover needs someone there to keep a watch on him and stop him from sticking stuff in his arms every chance he gets. So now each night I have to close the bedroom door to block out the sound of Tina Turner singing "Break Every Rule" for the four millionth time before I can concentrate on getting the script out. This time I will get it to the right people.

I have faith.

Probably 'cause that's all I have.

20 September – NYC

What is it about Robert De Niro's name? I cannot *believe* this shit. Once again, no replies through the mail but then I can't be sure if Mr Manic Depressive Disco-Dolly don't reach the mailbox before me and set fire to the post. (I empty uppers and downers out the bathroom cabinet as fast as he puts 'em in, but I can't always be sure what he's taking 'cause he lies about it. Right now he's dancing around in the next room to some old Diana Ross album. He's not happy – it's a high. It's 11:00 a.m. By my estimation he's peaking about twelve hours too early.)

This time I figure why wait longer and start calling around almost immediately, and now I get a new kind of standard reply. I mean, it's obvious that small TV companies can't afford a fancy Upper East Side address, but just because De Niro put TriBeCa Films in a street full of warehouses don't mean every two-bit TV exec in town should evoke his name like a fucking talisman. Well, they say, we're small but we're very selective, situated near Bobby (Get this, *Bobby* De Niro, as if the exec goes over his place for cocktails) De Niro's place.

I'm thinking listen, you could be workin' out of eastern Turkey for all I care so long as you read the goddamn script, and *this* is the crunch – for all the talk they give out, usually about themselves and the saintlike regard the industry has for them, for all the smooth dialogue it emerges that none of them, not one, has read the damned thing. There's too much stuff coming in all the time. Too much loose paper around. Every dickhead with a desktop and an hour on his hands thinks he's got a script inside.

An' you know, maybe that includes me, but I still have faith in the script. That's what I tell myself as I type out the "C" list and set about borrowing more postage money. My name is John Harker and I was born to battle the Prince of Darkness. And that's what I'm gonna do.

27 September – NYC

Well, the Disco Diva took a dive.

Yes, my room-mate managed to set fire to himself while enjoying the intoxicatin' effects of several noxious substances, which means he's in the hospital and I'm out of my watchdog job and out on the street. I think his lover was more pissed that the sound system got burned up than anything else. I don't even have the money to phone around the networks, 'cause these companies keep you on call-waiting systems for fuckin' hours, so I just did something I said I was never gonna do and that was, I sold a pint of blood. Under the circumstances, it seems appropriate.

It's hard conducting business from a call box, but it's paying dividends. I start early, catch 'em before they got a chance to think. And guess what, someone has read the script and likes it. Two people, in fact. Both of them say they're interested. I got me a pair of meetings to take. Oh, I *like* the sound of that. Priorities first, though. At the moment I got nowhere to sleep, and no good clothes. It's still hot at night, I can rough it for a couple of days until something turns up, take the meetings – after all, they're interested in the quality of writing, not whether I shop at Armani – and maybe get an advance.

Round Two to the Harker family.

Good shall prevail.

2 October – NYC
I should know better by now.

The first meeting's at a place called Primetime Product, situated, natch, near Bobby's building, and is taken in an office the size of a basketball court by a guy who's coping with premature baldness by growing a ponytail. He gives me the once-over, wrinkles his nose as he lets me sit down and hunts out the script. Then he asks me how I'd feel about turning it into a half-hour sitcom featuring Dracula as a funny superhero. I give the idea careful consideration, then tell him I don't think it'll work, and remember, I say this with an image of me sleepin' on a park bench in mind. But he wants the bones without the meat and it really *won't* work, a child of five could see that. End of meeting, shown to the door, thanks for comin' in – and I have to ask for the fuckin' script back because he's returning it to the shelf behind his desk even as he's talking me out.

Sleepin' in the park is okay because the cops don't run you in anymore – these days there's too many people an' nowhere to put us all. I could have done without some drunk puking his guts up on the next bench all night, but right now it don't pay to be fussy, and besides I'm already thinkin' of the next meeting. I got two shirts, one pair of sneakers and one pair of shoes, one T-shirt and a pair of ratty jeans, plus a nylon backsack containing a shave bag, a blanket and the scripts. There's other stuff at my Ma's but she's in Atlantic City underneath some loser and I don't got the keys to her apartment.

Next day's a real hot one, so I go for a swim an' use my last five bucks to get my shirt laundered so maybe I won't look like a total bum.

I get to PowerVision (I'd like to meet the guy who sits in a room thinkin' up these names) at twenty before the meeting, an' I'm still sittin' there at twenty after. The woman who sees me is dressed so severe that first of all I think she's wearin' a grey cardboard box. She looks at me funny even though I don't smell and my shirt looks great. Then she tells me she hasn't read the script but she's been instructed to buy it. Although I'm gettin' excited this alarm bell is goin' off inside me, and I ask what she would like to do with it.

And she says I want to give it to our writers to see what *they* can do. I ask her what she means. *I'm* the writer. I mean, if they like what I've written, why get someone else to fuck with it? I guess I'm not supposed to speak at this stage 'cause she looks at me as if I just took a shit in her fruitbowl. Well, she says, the piece is way too downbeat. It can be Gothic, but it's got to be fun. We could liven up Dracula by giving him a wacky sidekick. I point out that there's one in the book we can use, and I see her flinch at the word *we*. Renfield, I say. He's an interesting character. What's he like? she asks. He's insane, I explain, and he eats flies. Not on television, she replies, not if we want a family audience. Also, the title has to go. We've already got a new title. *Fangs A Million.*

You can figure out the rest. At least this meeting lasted longer than the first one, mainly 'cause she was late gettin' it started.

On the way back I gave blood again, which gives me some ready cash, but I gotta tell you this is depressing the hell out of me. Tomorrow I'll maybe try to tap some guys I know for a loan. Then I guess I'll start calling again.

It's a setback for the Harker family as the Lord of the Undead goes into the lead. Where the hell is Van Helsing when you need him?

19 October – NYC

In the last couple of days the weather has turned. Central Park never looks fresh at the best of times. Even in spring the greenery has a kind of dusty look about it, an' now it's just brown. There's nothing lyrical you can write about autumn in this city. New England maybe but not here. I can't believe I'm still sleeping rough. It's gettin' too cold to stay out all night. I did one smart thing while it was hot – I kept out of the sun. You get a tan in New York, you automatically look like a bum unless you're wearing good clothes.

Nobody I know has any money to spare, but I ain't going to panhandle for it. That's what I told CeeCee, you offer a service or no deal. I was always taught that nobody rides for free. He laughed an' said that's exactly what he believes. CeeCee used to work at the coffee shop on Bleeker, but he got canned and now he's started hustling again, which I figure you have to be pretty fuckin' desperate to do these days, and I ain't that desperate. Yet.

Trouble is I can't get welfare 'cause I ain't been out of work long enough, and in theory my Ma can still help. Of course, she's in a garter belt on her knees in some motel workin' off her blackjack bill at the Trump Casino, but try finding a sympathetic ear for that one. I been workin' on some revisions to the script, some improvements I think they'll go for. Trouble is I got no access to a typewriter. It's all written longhand, and the networks won't read longhand.

I got the blood thing down to a fine art by loaning out my card to a rota system. See, they won't let you give blood again until you've made it up fully, and they date-stamp your card, but a bunch of us go to different clinics with each others' cards. It shaves off a few days and don't harm you none so long as you keep eating.

I guess this is the low point of my life right now. It can only get better from here. I even called around to my Ma but there was no one home. I've walked my ass off going to every single goddamned company on my list tryin' to get to see someone, anyone who could help. That's it; I've tried them all except the pornos, and out of the whole shebang I got me one decent new lead: I read that some rich NoHo gallery just financed a new TV company to develop independent projects for the cable nets, so I dropped a script around to them, called them back a week later and they want to see me tomorrow. I'll go along, but I ain't expecting a miracle. It's starting to get dark out here, and the park is looking more and more like Transylvania to me.

23 October – NYC

Max Barclay has the same number of letters in his name as Van Helsing, and the same powers. I feel like he just jumped on the refectory table and pulled down the drapes, blasting pure morning light across the prostrate figure of the Count. And in a way, that's what he's done. He's saving my fuckin' life is what he's doing. Let me go back three days.

WorldView TV turns out to be a pretty snappy joint, located in an area where the only thing that separates power-dressed corporate executives from bums lying in doorways pissing their pants is a foot of concrete and a window. Their receptionist is hip enough to once me over without calling security, which is a relief as I am sporting that "just attacked in the park" look, then this beefy guy who may be a pro-football player comes up and shakes the bones outta my hand and tells me how he loves the script.

And how he wants to make it.
Just the way it is.

An' that's where we are right now. It's gonna take a while to sort out the contract, but it's gonna happen. The bad news is, no loan until it does, but hey, it's always darkest before the dawn. That script is my stake, and now I've found someone with a hammer. Together we'll nail the son of a bitch.

27 October – NYC
No news yet.
   Called Max today and we talked over problems with the script, all minor. He says he may be able to get some upfront money soon. I don't want him to know I'm still living in the park. It could fuck things up between us; he'll think I'm some kind of nut. I want this to be right. One day I'll be mixing drinks in my seventeen-bedroom adobe-style Bel-Air ranch house telling kids how tough it was to break into showbiz, and at least I won't be lying.
   My dawn will break.

11 November – NYC
I called Max and told him about my cash-flow problem. It took a certain amount of pride swallowing, but I can't live like this much longer. He breezily suggested meeting over a drink but I can't let him see me, it's just too fuckin' humiliating. I got no clean clothes and no money. It is so fucking cold that even the seasoned park bums have all moved on, God knows where. Maybe they just froze up an' got covered over with leaves. Maybe that's what'll happen to me if I don't get a few regular meals soon.
   Max says there's something he forgot to mention before, and that is he has to present the script to his board. There's no chance they'll turn it down so long as his recommendation stays, but it delays things. It ain't his fault, he doesn't know what I'm goin' through here. And I ain't about to tell him any more than I have to.

18 November – NYC
Just when I thought my "income" couldn't get any lower, some attitudinous dude at the clinic finally figured out what we've been doing with the donor cards. A few days back, the temperature went out the bottom end of the thermometer, so I moved down into the subway. The smells here are warm and bad. You can taste disease in the air. But the people are worse. Dangerous, like regular laws don't apply to them underground.
   CeeCee says I can stay with him, it's a nice place, he can get me

some duds an' a spending roll. All I have to do is take a couple of the extra johns from him. He says I got a good body, I could earn two, three hundred bucks a night. I told him things are bad but I'm just not ready for that kind of stuff.

I tell myself I'm the one with the moral strength. A Harker. A defender of the faith. So instead of waking in a soft bed, I look up at the city through a fucking grating.

30 November – NYC
I know the number so well I punch it out in my sleep: Wait. Give the extension. Wait. Max Barclay, please. Wait. Last Tuesday I spoke to the PA again, Stephanie from London. Very polite. Max is in Hawaii for two weeks, didn't he tell me he was taking a vacation?

No, he fucking didn't.

I try to explain I'm not badgering her, all I want is some reassurance, a sign of faith. I had – I *have* – faith in my script. Max says he has too but he don't ever prove it. It seems the board weren't entirely happy. There have to be a few small changes made. Okay, I'll wear the changes but let's get the contract through first, then we'll talk changes.

Changes. Dear God. I'm at CeeCee's apartment. When it started to snow an' the subway filled with crazies, the cops threw us back on the street an' I knew the time had finally come. I got no more blood to give. My weight was down to 120 pounds. I looked like a peeled stick. CeeCee's been good, at a price. I take no more than one john a night, and nothing too wild. If they won't wear a rubber they're out on their ass. I do it without thinking. I daren't let myself think. This is one part of my biography that's gonna stay in the drawer.

There's a new scene in the script.

By the dying light of the chamber's fire, the Count can be seen stepping forward. He stands a full head taller than the librarian. Gently, he takes Harker's face in his pale, tapered fingers and studies him, a spider examining a new kind of fly. The chill from his dead eyes sinks into Harker's bones. The young man is truly face to face with death. He feels the vampire's gaze killing off the cells in his body, and his brain starts to grow numb. He knows that if, at this moment, the Count chooses to let him die, he will indeed die. The numbness rapidly spreads. His will is drained away like blood leaking from a deep wound. Reason fades, to be replaced by a thrilling new sensation far beyond fear, an awakening ecstasy as Harker finally understands the night, the eternal night . . .

And the Count releases him, breaking off his gaze. He has granted his foe a steady, lingering look into the abyss. But the sight has made Harker stronger, because it has made death his friend. It has given him the power to free himself.

I hold on to that thought.

22 December – NYC

Max says I'm difficult, too idealistic, that nobody survives intact. I assume he's talking about the script. At least he's back from his vacation and we actually get to meet again now that I have some clothes. We drink red wine in a fashionable media joint on Amsterdam, surrounded by flickering TV monitors. Well, I say, this is the longest courtship I've had before somebody's fucked me, and he laughs. The contract's gonna be through after Christmas, he promises, when WorldView's legal department finally get to check everything out with the Bram Stoker estate, plus every other joker with a claim to the character who reckons they have exclusive copyright. It better come through, I say, 'cause right now what we have here is a failure to remunerate. He laughs again, tells me I'm really on form tonight.

If Max has noticed that I'm going quietly nuts waitin' for the green light, he ain't showing it. He wishes me a happy Christmas an' walks off into the snow with his scarf around his shoulders, that's how confident he is. Me, I don't wanna leave the bar. Leavin' the bar means leaving the warm an' going back to CeeCee's. Back to work. But at least I know now that I have the strength to get through it.

The Harker family will be avenged.

16 January – NYC

Why is it all the changes have to come from my side? He remains motionless, a silhouette on the ramparts, a shadow in the doorway. I adapt to survive. He lives on, unchanging, the eternal victor, the cape wrapped around his elegant form like a suit of armour. Impenetrable. Immovable.

It isn't fair.

CeeCee is dead. On Christmas Eve he went out to some fancy new club, and that was the last anyone saw of him. The cops say he got rolled by a john over at the Adonis around 2:00 a.m. Christmas morning. Ordinarily he wouldn't have died but he'd had a little booze and taken a few uppers, and the shock of hitting the ground did something to his neck. He never regained consciousness. The cops asked me if he had any family. It never occurred to me he even had a family.

Christmas morning. What a lonely time to die.

*   *   *

CeeCee always said I could stay on in the apartment. He knew I didn't like taking the johns. He wanted to help me so he said I could stay. He never told no one else. I went in his bedroom to pack up his stuff and it was like a little kid's. Teddy bears and movie-star posters. The next night I came home and found the locks had been changed. I wish he'd told someone else I could stay.

I called Max to ask about the contract, but he wasn't there and the English PA wouldn't give me his home number. I found myself crying on the phone. Fucking pathetic.

Goin' back on the street was a shock. When I get ahold of Max I'm gonna ask him to put up or shut up. Hell, I'm gonna ask him if I can stay at his place while I'm writing the script. I should retitle the fuckin' thing *Out for The Count*, 'cause that's what I'm gonna be soon if he says no.

I'll do anything to get out of this situation, man.

Anything.

24 January – NYC

I am undead. That's how I think of it. Trapped in limbo. This is living death. Darkness reigns and Harker loses. Now and forever.

Fuck Max. Wherever he is, fuck him. He could have told me, he must have known. You don't leave a job without a little preparation. You don't just up and blow. The PA says he's gone out to LA, she don't know his whereabouts. She couldn't tell the truth if her fuckin' life depended on it. Lying is part of her job description.

The new guy's name is Feinstein.

I spoke to him after calling so many times he finally had to speak to me. He told me the first thing he did when he took over the job was freeze all of Max's projects. He needs to determine a budget floor and ceiling for next season, and he won't be rushed. It'll take some time to establish market windows. That's not to say the door is closed on my script. By this time I figure either he used to be a builder or he's incapable of gettin' through a sentence without using media-speak.

I tell him I am experiencing a downturn in my fiscal well-being at the moment and may not be alive by the time he gets around to perusing my masterpiece. Perhaps I can call him in a day.

Taken aback, he agrees. But not to a day. A week.

One week. Days, hours, minutes.

Nights.

I don't work on the script no more. I can't 'cause some asshole lifted my bag on the subway, and the last copy I had was in there. It's 3:00 a.m., way below freezing, and I'm hustling for johns on 42nd St.

Man, this is so far below my dignity, it's horrifyin'. I got a cold that won't go away, an' a dream that won't die. Better if it did. Better to let it go.

Maybe I been fightin' on the wrong side all this time. After all, my namesake met his end in the book, but it was just the beginning of the Count's career.

They say people are attracted to him because of the darkness.

The dark never seemed attractive to me until now.

31 January – NYC
Another couple of days, he tells me.

There are so many scripts to go through, and he must be fair to every one. Call him back at the end of the week and he promises to have an answer, this way or that. The PA tells him mine's one of the best scripts she's ever read, an' she's been in the business a long time.

I am standing in the phone booth listenin' to this.

It's so cold I can't tell where my feet end and the side-walk starts. I have two dollars in my pocket, a cold sore on my lip, and there are no johns on the street. I stayed a couple of nights at this guy Randy's apartment but it turns out he really wanted to beat me with a studded strap, so I got out. It was worth good money, but hey, I have my pride. That's a joke, by the way. There's a sticker on the coin box in front of me, some broad offering guys an enema and I'm thinkin' well, at least it would warm me up. I feel weird, like I passed beyond some kind of barrier.

I can't give blood no more. They don't want it. They said it's gone bad. I got bad blood now. I told the doc I'd been bitten, but he didn't get it. Two more days. The dark before the dawn. This is gonna be an eleventh-hour rescue, I can tell you.

You should never have tried to fight him, Jonathan.

2 February – NYC
A foot of snow around the call box an' I got sweaty hands.

I got a pocket full of quarters which it turns out I need 'cause they leave me on call-wait for ten minutes, during which I get to listen to three songs from *South Pacific*. Then he's not at his desk. It takes them a couple more minutes to locate him. I'm thinking this is good, this is a build-up of tension, this makes the news stronger.

Well, it does do that, at least.

I really didn't like it, he says. Not *Sorry for fucking you around* or *Maybe you'd like to write something else for us*. Just I *really* didn't like it. But that's not the best part. He leaves a small silence while I'm supposed to make grateful noises for his opinion. Then he says I should remember the network buzzwords, which are *Feelgood* and *Reassurance*. The public don't want to see this kind of thing, he says, it's way too depressing. They need to be told that everything's okay. I should bear that in mind next time.

I guess I could have screamed and shouted at him, but I just said quietly, There isn't gonna be a next time, and hung up.

At least it's over. I kind of feel better now. Not knowing was more painful than I'd realized. Yeah, I feel better now. I'm a little shaky walkin' out of the box, but the sun is shining. I should of asked him to return the script, but somethin' in me didn't want it back. The battle's ended. Dawn's here.

I gotta get myself a new jacket. This one's too thin. I'm freezin' my ass off. Pockets are ripped. Gonna get myself cleaned up. That's how I'll start. First the jacket. Then the life.

At least I took the bastard on, right?
    Maybe I didn't win, but I sure as hell held him at bay once more. Isn't that all you can ever do?

J.H.

RICHARD CHRISTIAN MATHESON

Vampire

RICHARD CHRISTIAN MATHESON is the son of veteran science fiction and fantasy author Richard Matheson. A novelist, short-story writer and screenwriter/producer, he has scripted and executive produced more than five hundred episodes of prime-time network television and was the youngest writer ever put under contract by Universal Studios.

His debut novel *Created By* was published to great acclaim in 1993, and his short fiction has been collected in *Scars and Other Distinguishing Marks* and *Dystopia*. He has also completed his second novel and is writing a third.

As well as creating a new reality show for Fox TV, Matheson has recently scripted a number of feature films, a television pilot for Showtime Networks and two four-hour mini-series of Dean Koontz's *Sole Survivor* and Roger Zelazny's *The Chronicles of Amber*. He continues to play drums for the blues/rock band Smash-Cut, in which he performs along with Craig Spector and Preston Sturges Jr. The band is currently at work on their debut album and play clubs in Los Angeles.

"I've played drums my whole life," explains the author. "Like any creative form, its disciplines are multiple. But in time, as technique refines, rigors evolve into emotion; deeper rhythms of self.

"For beginners, a drum set is a daunting fascination; endless choices seduce and paralyze and, for a time, it seems *cool*, itself, sleeps under those skins; an elusive hipness only maple sticks could possibly stir.

"But with experience, what is inevitably discovered is that the beats and fills left out are the coolest thing of all; a mysterious effect, undeniable despite illogic.

"For me, this insight has been a chrysalis path of nearly four decades, almost perfectly paralleling my discovery, as a writer, that what's withheld has eloquence; transcendence.

"Which brings me to 'Vampire'.

"Its original draft was twelve pages long, but in rewriting it, I felt it too long, too detailed. I began its edit, in something of an unmerciful trance, and when done, what remained was a connection via minimal dots; a stream of consciousness set to a tempo; staccato. Fleshless.

"Though some detractors of the story may disagree, it is not a poem, bohemian dismissal of form, nor designed peculiarity. Rather, it is what was strong enough to survive my unsentimental pen.

"Considered as cadence and pulse, the story is a drum solo of sorts; percussive, propelled by unstated detail.

"Sometimes absence is presence."

'Vampire' is the shortest story in this book. It is also one of the most powerful.

Man.
Late. Rain.
Road.
Man.
Searching. Starved. Sick.
Driving.
Radio. News. Scanners. Police. Broadcast.
Accident. Town.
Near.
Speeding. Puddles.
Aching.
Minutes.
Arrive. Park. Watch.
Bodies. Blood. Crowd. Sirens.
Wait.
Hour. Sit. Pain. Cigarette. Thermos. Coffee.
Sweat. Nausea.
Streetlights. Eyes. Stretchers. Sheets.
Flesh.

Death.

Shaking. Chills.

Clock. Wait.

More. Wait.

Car. Stink. Cigarette.

Ambulance. Crying. Tow truck. Bodies. Taken.

Crowd. Police. Photographers. Drunks. Leave.

Gone.

Street. Quiet.

Rain. Dark. Humid.

Alone.

Door. Out. Stand. Walk. Pain. Stare. Closer.

Buildings. Silent. Street. Dead.

Blood. Chalk. Outlines. Closer.

Step. Inside. Outlines. Middle.

Inhale. Eyes. Closed.

Think. Inhale. Concentrate. Feel. Breathe.

Flow.

Death. Collision. Woman. Screaming. Windshield. Expression.

Moment. Death.

Energy. Concentrate. Images. Exploding.

Moment.

Woman. Car. Truck. Explosion.

Impact. Moment.

Rush.

Feeling. Feeding.

Metal. Burning. Screams. Blood. Death.

Moment. Collision. Images. Faster.

Strength. Medicine.

Stronger.

Concentrate. Better.

Images. Collision. Stronger. Seeing. Death.

Moment. Healing. Moment.

Addiction.

Drug. Rush. Body. Warmer.

Death. Concentrating. Healing. Addiction. Drug.

Warm. Calm.

Death. Medicine.

Death.

Life.

Medicine.

Addiction. Strong.

Leave.

Car. Engine. Drive. Rain. Streets. Freeway. Map.

Drive. Relax. Safe. Warm. Rush. Good.
Radio. Cigarette. Breeze.
Night.
Searching. Accidents. Death.
Life.
Dash. Clock. Waiting.
Soon.

HUGH B. CAVE

Stragella

HUGH B. CAVE WAS BORN in 1910 in Chester, England, but migrated to America with his family when he was almost five. While editing trade journals, he sold his first pulp-magazine story, 'Island Ordeal', to *Brief Stories* in 1929. Cave quickly established himself as an inventive and prolific writer and became a regular contributor to *Strange Tales*, *Weird Tales*, *Ghost Stories*, *Black Book Detective*, *Thrilling Mysteries*, *Spicy Mystery Stories*, and the so-called "shudder pulps", *Horror Stories* and *Terror Tales*.

He then began spending his winters in Haiti and Jamaica and after writing highly praised travel books and a number of mainstream novels about those two Caribbean countries, began contributing fiction regularly to *The Saturday Evening Post* (forty-six stories) and many other "slick-paper" magazines.

In 1977 Karl Edward Wagner's Carcosa imprint published a hefty volume of Cave's best horror tales, *Murgunstrumm and Others*, which won a World Fantasy Award for best collection, and Cave returned to the genre with stories in *Whispers* and *Fantasy Tales*, followed by a string of modern horror novels: *Legion of the Dead*, *The Nebulon Horror*, *The Evil*, *Shades of Evil*, *Disciples of Dread*, *The Lower Deep*, *Lucifer's Eye*, *Isle of the Whisperers*, *The Dawning*, *The Evil Returns* and *The Restless Dead*.

Cave's short fiction has been collected by a number of publishers, including Starmont House, Fedogan & Bremer, Tattered Pages

Press, Black Dog Books, Subterranean Press, Ash-Tree Press, The Sidecar Preservation Society, Necronomicon Press and Crippen & Landru. A new biography of the author by Milt Thomas, entitled *Cave of a Thousand Tales*, is published by Arkham House.

The author has been presented with several awards during his writing career. These include a Phoenix Award (1987), a Special Committee Award from the World Fantasy Convention (1997), and Lifetime Achievement Awards from The Horror Writers Association (1991), The International Horror Guild (1997) and the World Fantasy Convention (1999).

In a career that has spanned an incredible eight decades, it is perhaps not surprising that all the author can recall about 'Stragella' is that, "At the time, I suppose it was probably just another story aimed at *Strange Tales* and its editor, Harry Bates."

The following novella dates from Cave's most prolific period and is a classic vampire chiller written in the extravagant style of the pulp magazines of the 1930s.

NIGHT, BLACK AS PITCH and filled with the wailing of a dead wind, sank like a shapeless specter into the oily waters of the Indian Ocean, leaving a great gray expanse of sullen sea, empty except for a solitary speck that rose and dropped in the long swell.

The forlorn thing was a ship's boat. For seven days and seven nights it had drifted through the waste, bearing its ghastly burden. Now, groping to his knees, one of the two survivors peered away into the East, where the first glare of a red sun filtered over the rim of the world.

Within arm's reach, in the bottom of the boat, lay a second figure, face down. All night long he had lain there. Even the torrential shower, descending in the dark hours and flooding the dory with life-giving water, had failed to move him.

The first man crawled forward. Scooping water out of the tarpaulin with a battered tin cup, he turned his companion over and forced the stuff through receded lips.

"Miggs!" The voice was a cracked whisper. "Miggs! Good God, you ain't dead, Miggs? I ain't left all alone out here—"

John Miggs opened his eyes feebly.

"What – what's wrong?" he muttered.

"We got water, Miggs! Water!"

"You're dreamin' again, Yancy. It – it ain't water. It's nothin' but sea—"

"It rained!" Yancy screeched. "Last night it rained. I stretched the tarpaulin. All night long I been lyin' face up, lettin' it rain in my mouth!"

Miggs touched the tin cup to his tongue and lapped its contents suspiciously. With a mumbled cry he gulped the water down. Then, gibbering like a monkey, he was crawling toward the tarpaulin.

Yancy flung him back, snarling.

"No you won't!" Yancy rasped. "We got to save it, see? We got to get out of here."

Miggs glowered at him from the opposite end of the dory. Yancy sprawled down beside the tarpaulin and stared once again over the abandoned sea, struggling to reason things out.

They were somewhere in the Bay of Bengal. A week ago they had been on board the *Cardigan*, a tiny tramp freighter carrying its handful of passengers from Maulmain to Georgetown. The *Cardigan* had foundered in the typhoon off the Mergui Archipelago. For twelve hours she had heaved and groaned through an inferno of swirling seas. Then she had gone under.

Yancy's memory of the succeeding events was a twisted, unreal parade of horrors. At first there had been five men in the little boat. Four days of terrific heat, no water, no food, had driven the little Persian priest mad; and he had jumped overboard. The other two had drunk salt water and died in agony. Now he and Miggs were alone.

The sun was incandescent in a white hot sky. The sea was calm, greasy, unbroken except for the slow, patient black fins that had been following the boat for days. But something else, during the night, had joined the sharks in their hellish pursuit. Sea snakes, hydrophiinae, wriggling out of nowhere, had come to haunt the dory, gliding in circles round and round, venomous, vivid, vindictive. And overhead were gulls wheeling, swooping in erratic arcs, cackling fiendishly and watching the two men with relentless eyes.

Yancy glanced up at them. Gulls and snakes could mean only one thing – land! He supposed they had come from the Andamans, the prison isles of India. It didn't much matter. They were here. Hideous, menacing harbingers of hope!

His shirt, filthy and ragged, hung open to the belt, revealing a lean chest tattooed with grotesque figures. A long time ago – too long to remember – he had gone on a drunken binge in Goa. Jap rum had done it. In company with two others of the *Cardigan*'s crew he had shambled into a tattooing establishment and ordered the Jap, in a bloated voice, to "paint anything you damned well like, professor. Anything at all!" And the Jap, being of a religious mind and sentimental, had decorated Yancy's chest with a most beautiful Crucifix, large, ornate, and colorful.

It brought a grim smile to Yancy's lips as he peered down at it. But presently his attention was centered on something else – something unnatural, bewildering, on the horizon. The thing was a narrow bank of fog lying low on the water, as if a distorted cloud had sunk out of the sky and was floating heavily, half submerged in the sea. And the small boat was drifting toward it.

In a little while the fog bank hung dense on all sides. Yancy groped to his feet, gazing about him. John Miggs muttered something beneath his breath and crossed himself.

The thing was shapeless, grayish-white, clammy. It reeked – not with the dank smell of sea fog, but with the sickly, pungent stench of a buried jungle or a subterranean mushroom cellar. The sun seemed unable to penetrate it. Yancy could see the red ball above him, a feeble, smothered eye of crimson fire, blotted by swirling vapor.

"The gulls," mumbled Miggs. "They're gone."

"I know it. The sharks, too – and the snakes. We're all alone, Miggs."

An eternity passed, while the dory drifted deeper and deeper into the cone. And then there was something else – something that came like a moaning voice out of the fog. The muted, irregular, sing-song clangor of a ship's bell!

"Listen!" Miggs cackled. "You hear—"

But Yancy's trembling arm had come up abruptly, pointing ahead. "By God, Miggs! Look!"

Miggs scrambled up, rocking the boat beneath him. His bony fingers gripped Yancy's arm. They stood there, the two of them, staring at the massive black shape that loomed up, like an ethereal phantom of another world, a hundred feet before them.

"We're saved," Miggs said incoherently. "Thank God, Nels—"

Yancy called out shrilly. His voice rang through the fog with a hoarse jangle, like the scream of a caged tiger. It choked into silence. And there was no answer, no responsive outcry – nothing so much as a whisper.

The dory drifted closer. No sound came from the lips of the two men as they drew alongside. There was nothing – nothing but the intermittent tolling of that mysterious, muted bell.

Then they realized the truth – a truth that brought a moan from Miggs' lips. The thing was a derelict, frowning out of the water, inanimate, sullen, buried in its winding-sheet of unearthly fog. Its stern was high, exposing a propeller red with rust and matted with clinging weeds. Across the bow, nearly obliterated by age, appeared the words: *Golconda – Cardiff*.

"Yancy, it ain't no real ship! It ain't of this world—"

Yancy stooped with a snarl, and picked up the oar in the bottom of the dory. A rope dangled within reach, hanging like a black serpent over the scarred hull. With clumsy strokes he drove the small boat beneath it; then, reaching up, he seized the line and made the boat fast.

"You're – goin' aboard?" Miggs said fearfully.

Yancy hesitated, staring up with bleary eyes. He was afraid, without knowing why. The *Golconda* frightened him. The mist clung to her tenaciously. She rolled heavily, ponderously in the long swell; and the bell was still tolling softly somewhere within the lost vessel.

"Well, why not?" Yancy growled. "There may be food aboard. What's there to be afraid of?"

Miggs was silent. Grasping the ropes, Yancy clambered up them. His body swung like a gibbet-corpse against the side. Clutching the rail, he heaved himself over; then stood there, peering into the layers of thick fog, as Miggs climbed up and dropped down beside him.

"I – don't like it," Miggs whispered. "It ain't—"

Yancy groped forward. The deck planks creaked dismally under him. With Miggs clinging close, he led the way into the waist, then into the bow. The cold fog seemed to have accumulated here in a sluggish mass, as if some magnetic force had drawn it. Through it, with arms outheld in front of him, Yancy moved with shuffling steps, a blind man in a strange world.

Suddenly he stopped – stopped so abruptly that Miggs lurched headlong into him. Yancy's body stiffened. His eyes were wide, glaring at the deck before him. A hollow, unintelligible sound parted his lips.

Miggs cringed back with a livid screech, clawing at his shoulder. "What – what is it?" he said thickly.

At their feet were bones. Skeletons – lying there in the swirl of vapor. Yancy shuddered as he examined them. Dead things they were, dead and harmless, yet they were given new life by the motion of the mist. They seemed to crawl, to wriggle, to slither toward him and away from him.

He recognized some of them as portions of human frames. Others were weird, unshapely things. A tiger skull grinned up at him with jaws that seemed to widen hungrily. The vertebrae of a huge python lay in disjointed coils on the planks, twisted as if in agony. He discerned the skeletonic remains of tigers, tapirs, and jungle beasts of unknown identity. And human heads, many of them, scattered about like an assembly of mocking, dead-alive faces, leering at him, watching him with hellish anticipation. The place was a morgue – a charnel house!

Yancy fell back, stumbling. His terror had returned with triple intensity. He felt cold perspiration forming on his forehead, on his chest, trickling down the tattooed Crucifix.

Frantically he swung about in his tracks and made for the welcome solitude of the stern deck, only to have Miggs clutch feverishly at his arm.

"I'm goin' to get out of here, Nels! That damned bell – these here things—"

Yancy flung the groping hands away. He tried to control his terror. This ship – this *Golconda* – was nothing but a tramp trader. She'd been carrying a cargo of jungle animals for some expedition. The beasts had got loose, gone amuck, in a storm. There was nothing fantastic about it!

In answer, came the intermittent clang of the hidden bell below decks and the soft lapping sound of the water swishing through the thick weeds which clung to the ship's bottom.

"Come on," Yancy said grimly. "I'm goin' to have a look around. We need food."

He strode back through the waist of the ship, with Miggs shuffling behind. Feeling his way to the towering stern, he found the fog thinner, less pungent.

The hatch leading down into the stern hold was open. It hung before his face like an uplifted hand, scarred, bloated, as if in mute warning. And out of the aperture at its base straggled a spidery thing that was strangely out of place here on this abandoned derelict – a curious, menacing, crawling vine with mottled triangular leaves and immense orange-hued blossoms. Like a living snake, intertwined about itself, it coiled out of the hold and wormed over the deck.

Yancy stepped closer, hesitantly. Bending down, he reached to grasp one of the blooms, only to turn his face away and fall back with an involuntary mutter. The flowers were sickly sweet, nauseating. They repelled him with their savage odor.

"Somethin'—" Miggs whispered sibilantly, "is watchin' us, Nels! I can feel it."

Yancy peered all about him. He, too, felt a third presence close at hand. Something malignant, evil, unearthly. He could not name it.

"It's your imagination," he snapped. "Shut up, will you?"

"We ain't alone, Nels. This ain't no ship at all!"

"Shut *up*!"

"But the flowers there – they ain't right. Flowers don't grow aboard a Christian ship, Nels!"

"This hulk's been here long enough for trees to grow on it," Yancy said curtly. "The seeds probably took root in the filth below."

"Well, I don't like it."

"Go forward and see what you can find. I'm goin' below to look around."

Miggs shrugged helplessly and moved away. Alone, Yancy descended to the lower levels. It was dark down here, full of shadows and huge gaunt forms that lost their substance in the coils of thick, sinuous fog. He felt his way along the passage, pawing the wall with both hands. Deeper and deeper into the labyrinth he went, until he found the galley.

The galley was a dungeon, reeking of dead, decayed food, as if the stench had hung there for an eternity without being molested; as if the entire ship lay in an atmosphere of its own – an atmosphere of the grave – through which the clean outer air never broke.

But there was food here; canned food that stared down at him from the rotted shelves. The labels were blurred, illegible. Some of the cans crumbled in Yancy's fingers as he seized them – disintegrated into brown, dry dust and trickled to the floor. Others were in fair condition, air-tight. He stuffed four of them into his pockets and turned away.

Eagerly now, he stumbled back along the passage. The prospects of food took some of those other thoughts out of his mind, and he was in better humor when he finally found the captain's cabin.

Here, too, the evident age of the place gripped him. The walls were gray with mold, falling into a broken, warped floor. A single table stood on the far side near the bunk, a blackened, grimy table bearing an upright oil lamp and a single black book.

He picked the lamp up timidly and shook it. The circular base was yet half full of oil, and he set it down carefully. It would come in handy later. Frowning, he peered at the book beside it.

It was a seaman's Bible, a small one, lying there, coated with cracked dust, dismal with age. Around it, as if some crawling slug had examined it on all sides, leaving a trail of excretion, lay a peculiar line of black pitch, irregular but unbroken.

Yancy picked the book up and flipped it open. The pages slid under his fingers, allowing a scrap of loose paper to flutter to the floor. He stooped to retrieve it; then, seeing that it bore a line of penciled script, he peered closely at it.

The writing was an apparently irrelevant scrawl – a meaningless memorandum which said crudely:

It's the bats and the crates. I know it now, but it is too late. God help me!

With a shrug, he replaced it and thrust the Bible into his belt, where it pressed comfortingly against his body. Then he continued his exploration.

In the wall cupboard he found two full bottles of liquor, which proved to be brandy. Leaving them there, he groped out of the cabin and returned to the upper deck in search of Miggs.

Miggs was leaning on the rail, watching something below. Yancy trudged toward him, calling out shrilly:

"Say, I got food, Miggs! Food and brand—"

He did not finish. Mechanically his eyes followed the direction of Miggs' stare, and he recoiled involuntarily as his words clipped into stifled silence. On the surface of the oily water below, huge sea snakes paddled against the ship's side – enormous slithering shapes, banded with streaks of black and red and yellow, vicious and repulsive.

"They're back," Miggs said quickly. "They know this ain't no proper ship. They come here out of their hell-hole, to wait for us."

Yancy glanced at him curiously. The inflection of Miggs' voice was peculiar – not at all the phlegmatic, guttural tone that usually grumbled through the little man's lips. It was almost eager!

"What did you find?" Yancy faltered.

"Nothin'. All the ship's boats are hangin' in their davits. Never been touched."

"I found food," Yancy said abruptly, gripping his arm. "We'll eat; then we'll feel better. What the hell are we, anyhow – a couple of fools? Soon as we eat, we'll stock the dory and get off this blasted death ship and clear out of this stinkin' fog. We got water in the tarpaulin."

"We'll clear out? Will we, Nels?"

"Yah. Let's eat."

Once again, Yancy led the way below decks to the galley. There, after a twenty-minute effort in building a fire in the rusty stove, he and Miggs prepared a meal, carrying the food into the captain's cabin, where Yancy lighted the lamp.

They ate slowly, sucking the taste hungrily out of every mouthful, reluctant to finish. The lamplight, flickering in their faces, made gaunt masks of features that were already haggard and full of anticipation.

The brandy, which Yancy fetched out of the cupboard, brought back strength and reason – and confidence. It brought back, too, that unnatural sheen to Miggs' twitching eyes.

"We'd be damned fools to clear out of here right off," Miggs said suddenly. "The fog's got to lift sooner or later. I ain't trustin' myself to no small boat again, Nels – not when we don't know where we're at."

Yancy looked at him sharply. The little man turned away with a guilty shrug. Then hesitantly:

"I – I kinda like it here, Nels."

Yancy caught the odd gleam in those small eyes. He bent forward quickly.

"Where'd you go when I left you alone?" he demanded.

"Me? I didn't go nowhere. I – I just looked around a bit, and I picked a couple of them flowers. See."

Miggs groped in his shirt pocket and held up one of the livid, orange-colored blooms. His face took on an unholy brilliance as he held the thing close to his lips and inhaled its deadly aroma. His eyes, glittering across the table, were on fire with sudden fanatic lust.

For an instant Yancy did not move. Then, with a savage oath, he lurched up and snatched the flower out of Miggs' fingers. Whirling, he flung it to the floor and ground it under his boot.

"You damned thick-headed fool!" he screeched. "You – God help you!"

Then he went limp, muttering incoherently. With faltering steps he stumbled out of the cabin and along the black passageway, and up on the abandoned deck. He staggered to the rail and stood there, holding himself erect with nerveless hands.

"God!" he whispered hoarsely. "God – what did I do that for? Am I goin' crazy?"

No answer came out of the silence. But he knew the answer. The thing he had done down there in the skipper's cabin – those mad words that had spewed from his mouth – had been involuntary. Something inside him, some sense of danger that was all about him, had hurled the words out of his mouth before he could control them. And his nerves were on edge, too; they felt as though they were ready to crack.

But he knew instinctively that Miggs had made a terrible mistake. There was something unearthly and wicked about those sickly sweet flowers. Flowers didn't grow aboard ship. Not real flowers. Real flowers had to take root somewhere, and, besides, they didn't have that drunken, etherish odour. Miggs should have left the vine alone. Clinging at the rail there, Yancy *knew* it, without knowing why.

He stayed there for a long time, trying to think and get his nerves back again. In a little while he began to feel frightened, being alone, and he returned below-decks to the cabin.

He stopped in the doorway, and stared.

Miggs was still there, slumped grotesquely over the table. The bottle was empty. Miggs was drunk, unconscious, mercifully oblivious of his surroundings.

For a moment Yancy glared at him morosely. For a moment, too, a new fear tugged at Yancy's heart – fear of being left alone through the coming night. He yanked Miggs' arm and shook him savagely; but there was no response. It would be hours, long, dreary, sinister hours, before Miggs regained his senses.

Bitterly Yancy took the lamp and set about exploring the rest of the ship. If he could find the ship's papers, he considered, they might dispel his terror. He might learn the truth.

With this in mind, he sought the mate's quarters. The papers had not been in the captain's cabin where they belonged; therefore they might be here.

But they were not. There was nothing – nothing but a chronometer, sextant, and other nautical instruments lying in curious positions on the mate's table, rusted beyond repair. And there were flags, signal flags, thrown down as if they had been used at the last moment. And, lying in a distorted heap on the floor, was a human skeleton.

Avoiding this last horror, Yancy searched the room thoroughly. Evidently, he reasoned, the captain had died early in the *Golconda*'s unknown plague. The mate had brought these instruments, these flags, to his own cabin, only to succumb before he could use them.

Only one thing Yancy took with him when he went out: a lantern, rusty and brittle, but still serviceable. It was empty, but he poured oil into it from the lamp. Then, returning the lamp to the captain's quarters where Miggs lay unconscious, he went on deck.

He climbed the bridge and set the lantern beside him. Night was coming. Already the fog was lifting, allowing darkness to creep in beneath it. And so Yancy stood there, alone and helpless, while blackness settled with uncanny quickness over the entire ship.

He was being watched. He felt it. Invisible eyes, hungry and menacing, were keeping check on his movements. On the deck beneath him were those inexplicable flowers, trailing out of the unexplored hold, glowing like phosphorescent faces in the gloom.

"By God," Yancy mumbled, "I'm goin' to get out of here!"

His own voice startled him and caused him to stiffen and peer about him, as if someone else had uttered the words. And then, very suddenly, his eyes became fixed on the far horizon to starboard. His lips twitched open, spitting out a shrill cry.

"Miggs! Miggs! A light! Look, Miggs—"

Frantically he stumbled down from the bridge and clawed his way below decks to the mate's cabin. Feverishly he seized the signal flags. Then, clutching them in his hand, he moaned helplessly and let them fall. He realized that they were no good, no good in the dark. Gibbering to himself, he searched for rockets. There were none.

Suddenly he remembered the lantern. Back again he raced through the passage, on deck, up on the bridge. In another moment, with the lantern dangling from his arm, he was clambering higher and higher into the black spars of the mainmast. Again and again he slipped and caught himself with outflung hands. And at length he stood high above the deck, feet braced, swinging the lantern back and forth. . . .

Below him, the deck was no longer silent, no longer abandoned. From bow to stern it was trembling, creaking, whispering up at him.

He peered down fearfully. Blurred shadows seemed to be prowling through the darkness, coming out of nowhere, pacing dolefully back and forth through the gloom. They were watching him with a furtive interest.

He called out feebly. The muted echo of his own voice came back up to him. He was aware that the bell was tolling again, and the swish of the sea was louder, more persistent.

With an effort he caught a grip on himself.

"Damned fool," he rasped. "Drivin' yourself crazy—"

The moon was rising. It blurred the blinking light on the horizon and penetrated the darkness like a livid yellow finger. Yancy lowered the lantern with a sob. It was no good now. In the glare of the moonlight, this puny flame would be invisible to the men aboard that other ship. Slowly, cautiously, he climbed down to the deck.

He tried to think of something to do, to take his mind off the fear. Striding to the rail, he hauled up the water butts from the dory. Then he stretched the tarpaulin to catch the precipitation of the night dew. No telling how long he and Miggs would be forced to remain aboard the hulk.

He turned, then, to explore the forecastle. On his way across the deck, he stopped and held the light over the creeping vine. The curious flowers had become fragrant, heady, with the fumes of an intoxicating drug. He followed the coils to where they vanished into the hold, and he looked down. He saw only a tumbled pile of boxes and crates. Barred boxes which must have been cages at one time.

Again he turned away. The ship was trying to tell him something. He felt it – felt the movements of the deck planks beneath his feet. The moonlight, too, had made hideous white things of the scattered bones in the bow. Yancy stared at them with a shiver. He stared again, and grotesque thoughts obtruded into his consciousness. The bones were moving. Slithering, sliding over the deck, assembling themselves, gathering into definite shapes. He could have sworn it!

Cursing, he wrenched his eyes away. Damned fool, thinking such thoughts! With clenched fists he advanced to the forecastle; but before he reached it, he stopped again.

It was the sound of flapping wings that brought him about. Turning quickly, with a jerk, he was aware that the sound emanated from the open hold. Hesitantly he stepped forward – and stood rigid with an involuntary scream.

Out of the aperture came two horrible shapes – two inhuman things with immense, clapping wings and glittering eyes. Hideous; enormous. *Bats!*

Instinctively he flung his arm up to protect himself. But the creatures did not attack. They hung for an instant, poised over the hatch, eyeing him with something that was fiendishly like intelligence. Then they flapped over the deck, over the rail, and away into the night. As they sped away towards the west, where he had seen the light of that other ship twinkling, they clung together like witches hell-bent on some evil mission. And below them, in the bloated sea, huge snakes weaved smoky, golden patterns – waiting!. . .

He stood fast, squinting after the bats. Like two hellish black eyes they grew smaller and smaller, became pinpoints in the moon-glow, and finally vanished. Still he did not stir. His lips were dry, his body stiff and unnatural. He licked his mouth. Then he was conscious of something more. From somewhere behind him came a thin, throbbing thread of harmony – a lovely, utterly sweet musical note that fascinated him.

He turned slowly. His heart was hammering, surging. His eyes went suddenly wide.

There, not five feet from him, stood a human form. Not his imagination. Real!

But he had never seen a girl like her before. She was too beautiful. She was wild, almost savage, with her great dark eyes boring into him. Her skin was white, smooth as alabaster. Her hair was jet black; and a waving coil of it, like a broken cobweb of pitch strings, framed her face. Grotesque hoops of gold dangled from her ears. In her hair, above them, gleamed two of those sinister flowers from the straggling vine.

He did not speak; he simply gaped. The girl was bare-footed, bare-legged. A short, dark skirt covered her slender thighs. A ragged white waist, open at the throat, revealed the full curve of her breast. In one hand she held a long wooden reed, a flute-like instrument fashioned out of crude wood. And about her middle, dangling almost to the deck, twined a scarlet, silken sash, brilliant as the sun, but not so scarlet as her lips, which were parted in a faint, suggestive smile, showing teeth of marble whiteness!

"Who – who are you?" Yancy mumbled.

She shook her head. Yet she smiled with her eyes, and he felt, somehow, that she understood him. He tried again, in such tongues as he knew. Still she shook her head, and still he felt that she was mocking him. Not until he chanced upon a scattered, faltering greeting in Serbian, did she nod her head.

"Dobra!" she replied, in a husky rich voice which sounded, somehow, as if it were rarely used.

He stepped closer then. She was a gipsy evidently. A Tzany of the Serbian hills. She moved very close to him with a floating, almost ethereal movement of her slender body. Peering into his face, flashing her haunting smile at him, she lifted the flute-like instrument and, as if it were nothing at all unnatural or out of place, began to play again the song which had first attracted his attention.

He listened in silence until she had finished. Then, with a cunning smile, she touched her fingers to her lips and whispered softly:

"You – mine. Yes?"

He did not understand. She clutched his arm and glanced fearfully toward the west, out over the sea.

"You – mine!" she said again, fiercely. "Papa Bocito – Seraphino – they no have you. You – not go – to them!"

He thought he understood then. She turned away from him and went silently across the deck. He watched her disappear into the forecastle, and would have followed her, but once again the ship – the whole ship – seemed to be struggling to whisper a warning.

Presently she returned, holding in her white hand a battered silver goblet, very old and very tarnished, brimming with scarlet fluid. He took it silently. It was impossible to refuse her. Her eyes had grown into lakes of night, lit by the burning moon. Her lips were soft, searching, undeniable.

"Who are you?" he whispered.

"Stragella," she smiled.

"Stragella. . . . Stragella. . . ."

The name itself was compelling. He drank the liquid slowly, without taking his eyes from her lovely face. The stuff had the taste of wine – strong, sweet wine. It was intoxicating, with the same weird effect that was contained in the orange blooms which she wore in her hair and which groveled over the deck behind her.

Yancy's hands groped up weakly. He rubbed his eyes, feeling suddenly weak, powerless, as if the very blood had been drained from his veins. Struggling futilely, he staggered back, moaning half inaudibly.

Stragella's arms went about him, caressing him with sensuous touch. He felt them, and they were powerful, irresistible. The girl's smile maddened him. Her crimson lips hung before his face, drawing nearer, mocking him. Then, all at once, she was seeking his throat. Those warm, passionate, deliriously pleasant lips were searching to touch him.

He sensed his danger. Frantically he strove to lift his arms and push her away. Deep in his mind some struggling intuition, some half-alive idea, warned him that he was in terrible peril. This girl, Stregella, was not of his kind; she was a creature of the darkness, a denizen of a different, frightful world of her own! Those lips, wanting his flesh, were inhuman, too fervid—

Suddenly she shrank away from him, releasing him with a jerk. A snarling animal-like sound surged through her flaming mouth. Her hand lashed out, rigid, pointing to the thing that hung in his belt. Talonic fingers pointed to the Bible that defied her!

But the scarlet fluid had taken its full effect. Yancy slumped down, unable to cry out. In a heap he lay there, paralyzed, powerless to stir.

He knew that she was commanding him to rise. Her lips, moving in pantomime, formed soundless words. Her glittering eyes were fixed upon him, hypnotic. The Bible – she wanted him to cast it over the rail! She wanted him to stand up and go into her arms. Then her lips would find a hold. . . .

But he could not obey. He could not raise his arms to support himself. She, in turn, stood at bay and refused to advance. Then, whirling about, her lips drawn into a diabolical curve, beautiful but bestial, she retreated. He saw her dart back, saw her tapering body whip about, with the crimson sash outflung behind her as she raced across the deck.

Yancy closed his eyes to blot out the sight. When he opened them again, they opened to a new, more intense horror. On the *Golconda*'s deck, Stragella was darting erratically among those piles of gleaming bones. But they were bones no longer. They had gathered into shapes, taken on flesh, blood. Before his very eyes they assumed substance, men and beasts alike. And then began an orgy such as Nels Yancy had never before looked upon – an orgy of the undead.

Monkeys, giant apes, lunged about the deck. A huge python reared its sinuous head to glare. On the hatch cover a snow-leopard, snarling furiously, crouched to spring. Tigers, tapirs, crocodiles – fought together in the bow. A great brown bear, of the type found in the lofty plateaus of the Pamirs, clawed at the rail.

And the men! Most of them were dark-skinned – dark enough to have come from the same region, from Madras. With them crouched Chinamen, and some Anglo–Saxons. Starved, all of them. Lean, gaunt, mad!

Pandemonium raged then. Animals and men alike were insane with hunger. In a little struggling knot, the men were gathered about the number-two hatch, defending themselves. They were wielding firearms – firing pointblank with desperation into the writhing mass that confronted them. And always, between them and around them and among, darted the girl who called herself Stragella.

They cast no shadows, those ghost shapes. Not even the girl, whose arms he had felt about him only a moment ago. There was nothing real in the scene, nothing human. Even the sounds of the shots and the screams of the cornered men, even the roaring growls of the big cats, were smothered as if they came to him through heavy glass windows, from a sealed chamber.

He was powerless to move. He lay in a cataleptic condition, conscious of the entire pantomime, yet unable to flee from it. And his senses were horribly acute – so acute that he turned his eyes upward with an abrupt twitch, instinctively; and then shrank into himself with a new fear as he discerned the two huge bats which had winged their way across the sea. . . .

They were returning now. Circling above him, they flapped down one after the other and settled with heavy, sullen thuds upon the hatch, close to that weird vine of flowers. They seemed to have lost their shape, these nocturnal monstrosities, to have become fantastic blurs, enveloped in an unearthly bluish radiance. Even as he stared at them, they vanished altogether for a moment; and then the strange vapor cleared to reveal the two creatures who stood there!

Not bats! Humans! Inhumans! They were gipsies, attired in moldy, decayed garments which stamped them as Balkans. Man and woman. Lean, emaciated, ancient man with fierce white mustache; plump old woman with black, rat-like eyes that seemed unused to the light of day. And they spoke to Stragella – spoke to her eagerly. She, in turn, swung about with enraged face and pointed to the Bible in Yancy's belt.

But the pantomime was not finished. On the deck the men and animals lay moaning, sobbing. Stragella turned noiselessly, calling the old man and woman after her. Calling them by name.

"Come – Papa Bocito, Seraphino!"

The tragedy of the ghost-ship was being reenacted. Yancy knew it, and shuddered at the thought. Starvation, cholera had driven the *Golconda*'s crew mad. The jungle beasts, unfed, hideously savage, had escaped out of their confinement. And now – now that the final conflict was over – Stragella and Papa Bocito and Seraphino were proceeding about their ghastly work.

Stragella was leading them. Her charm, her beauty, gave her a hold on the men. They were in love with her. She had *made* them love her, madly and without reason. Now she was moving from one to another, loving them and holding them close to her. And as she stepped away from each man, he went limp, faint, while she laughed terribly and passed on to the next. Her lips were parted. She licked them hungrily – licked the blood from them with a sharp, crimson tongue.

How long it lasted, Yancy did not know. Hours, hours on end. He was aware, suddenly, that a high wind was screeching and wailing in the upper reaches of the ship; and, peering up, he saw that the spars were no longer bare and rotten with age. Great gray sails stood out against the black sky – fantastic things without any definite form or outline. And the moon above them had vanished utterly. The howling wind was bringing a storm with it, filling the sails to bulging proportions. Beneath the decks the ship was groaning like a creature in agony. The seas were lashing her, slashing her, carrying her forward with amazing speed.

Of a sudden came a mighty grinding sound. The *Golconda* hurtled back, as if a huge, jagged reef of submerged rock had bored into her bottom. She listed. Her stern rose high in the air. And Stragella with her two fellow fiends, was standing in the bow, screaming in mad laughter in the teeth of the wind. The other two laughed with her.

Yancy saw them turn toward him, but they did not stop. Somehow, he did not expect them to stop. This scene, this mad pantomime, was not the present; it was the past. He was not here at all. All this had happened years ago! Forgotten, buried in the past!

But he heard them talking, in a mongrel dialect full of Serbian words.

"It is done. Papa Bocito! We shall stay here forever now. There is land within an hour's flight, where fresh blood abounds and will always abound. And here, on this wretched hulk, they will never find our graves to destroy us!"

The horrible trio passed close. Stragella turned, to stare out across the water, and raised her hand in silent warning. Yancy, turning wearily to stare in the same direction, saw that the first streaks of daylight were beginning to filter over the sea.

With a curious floating, drifting movement the three undead creatures moved toward the open hatch. They descended out of sight. Yancy, jerking himself erect and surprised to find that the effects of the drug had worn off with the coming of dawn, crept to the hatch and peered down – in time to see those fiendish forms enter their coffins. He knew then what the crates were. In the dim light, now that he was staring directly into the aperture, he saw what he had not noticed before. Three of those oblong boxes were filled with dank grave-earth!

He knew then the secret of the unnatural flowers. They *had* roots! They were rooted in the soil which harbored those undead bodies!

Then, like a groping finger, the dawn came out of the sea. Yancy walked to the rail, dazed. It was over now – all over. The orgy was ended. The *Golconda* was once more an abandoned, rotted hulk.

For an hour he stood at the rail, sucking in the warmth and glory of the sunlight. Once again that wall of unsightly mist was rising out of the water on all sides. Presently it would bury the ship, and Yancy shuddered.

He thought of Miggs. With quick steps he paced to the companion-way and descended to the lower passage. Hesitantly he prowled through the thickening layers of dank fog. A queer sense of foreboding crept over him.

He called out even before he reached the door. There was no answer. Thrusting the barrier open, he stepped across the sill – and then he stood still while a sudden harsh cry broke from his lips.

Miggs was lying there, half across the table, his arms flung out, his head turned grotesquely on its side, staring up at the ceiling.

"Miggs! Miggs!" The sound came choking through Yancy's lips. "Oh, God, Miggs – what's happened?"

He reeled forward. Miggs was cold and stiff, and quite dead. All the blood was gone out of his face and arms. His eyes were glassy, wide open. He was as white as marble, shrunken horribly. In his throat were two parallel marks, as if a sharp-pointed staple had been hammered into the flesh and then withdrawn. The marks of the vampire.

For a long time Yancy did not retreat. The room swayed and lurched before him. He was alone. Alone! The whole ghastly thing was too sudden, too unexpected.

Then he stumbled forward and went down on his knees, clawing at Miggs' dangling arm.

"Oh God, Miggs," he mumbled incoherently. "You got to help me. I can't stand it!"

He clung there, white-faced, staring, sobbing thickly – and presently slumped in a pitiful heap, dragging Miggs over on top of him.

It was later afternoon when he regained consciousness. He stood up, fighting away the fear that overwhelmed him. He had to get away, get away! The thought hammered into his head with monotonous force. Get away!

He found his way to the upper deck. There was nothing he could do for Miggs. He would have to leave him here. Stumbling, he moved along the rail and reached down to draw the small boat closer, where he could provision it and make it ready for his departure.

His fingers clutched emptiness. The ropes were gone. The dory was gone. He hung limp, staring down at a flat expanse of oily sea.

For an hour he did not move. He fought to throw off his fear long enough to think of a way out. Then he stiffened with a sudden jerk and pushed himself away from the rail.

The ship's boats offered the only chance. He groped to the nearest one and labored feverishly over it.

But the task was hopeless. The life boats were of metal, rusted through and through, wedged in their davits. The wire cables were knotted and immovable. He tore his hands on them, wringing blood from his scarred fingers. Even while he worked, he knew that the boats would not float. They were rotten, through and through.

He had to stop, at last, from exhaustion.

After that, knowing that there was no escape, he had to do something, anything, to keep sane. First he would clear those horrible bones from the deck, then explore the rest of the ship. . . .

It was a repulsive task, but he drove himself to it. If he could get rid of the bones, perhaps Stragella and the other two creatures would not return. He did not know. It was merely a faint hope, something to cling to.

With grim, tight-pressed lips he dragged the bleached skeletons over the deck and kicked them over the side, and stood watching them as they sank from sight. Then he went to the hold, smothering his terror, and descended into the gloomy belly of the vessel. He avoided the crates with a shudder of revulsion. Ripping up that evil vine-thing by the roots, he carried it to the rail and flung it away, with the mold of grave-earth still clinging to it.

After that he went over the entire ship, end to end, but found nothing.

He slipped the anchor chains then, in the hopes that the ship would drift away from that vindictive bank of fog. Then he paced back and forth, muttering to himself and trying to force courage for the most hideous task of all.

The sea was growing dark, and with dusk came increasing terror. He knew the *Golconda* was drifting. Knew, too, that the undead inhabitants of the vessel were furious with him for allowing the boat to drift away from their source of food. Or they *would* be furious when they came alive again after their interim of forced sleep.

And there was only one method of defeating them. It was a horrible method, and he was already frightened. Nevertheless he searched the deck for a marlin spike and found one; and, turning sluggishly, he went back to the hold.

A stake, driven through the heart of each of the horrible trio. . . .

The rickety stairs were deep in shadow. Already the dying sun, buried behind its wreath of evil fog, was a ring of bloody mist. He glanced at it and realized that he must hurry. He cursed himself for having waited so long.

It was hard, lowering himself into the pitch-black hold when he could only feel his footing and trust to fate. His boots scraped ominously on the steps. He held his hands above him, gripping the deck timbers.

And suddenly he slipped.

His foot caught on the edge of a lower step, twisted abruptly, and pitched him forward. He cried out. The marlin spike dropped from his hand and clattered on one of the crates below. He tumbled in a heap, clawing for support. The impact knocked something out of his belt. And he realized, even as his head came in sharp contact with the foremost oblong box, that the Bible, which had heretofore protected him, was no longer a part of him.

He did not lose complete control of his senses. Frantically he sought to regain his knees and grope for the black book in the gloom of the hold. A sobbing, choking sound came pitifully from his lips.

A soft, triumphant laugh came out of the darkness close to him. He swung about heavily – so heavily that the movement sent him sprawling again in an inert heap.

He was too late. She was already there on her knees, glaring at him hungrily. A peculiar bluish glow welled about her face. She was ghastly beautiful as she reached behind her into the oblong crate and began to trace a circle about the Bible with a chunk of soft, tarry, pitch-like substance clutched in her white fingers.

Yancy stumbled toward her, finding strength in desperation. She straightened to meet him. Her lips, curled back, exposed white teeth. Her arms coiled out, enveloping him, stifling his struggles. God, they were strong. He could not resist them. The same languid, resigned feeling came over him. He would have fallen, but she held him erect.

She did not touch him with her lips. Behind her he saw two other shapes take form in the darkness. The savage features of Papa Bocito glowered at him; and Seraphino's ratty, smoldering eyes, full of hunger, bored into him. Stragella was obviously afraid of them.

Yancy was lifted from his feet. He was carried out on deck and borne swiftly, easily, down the companionway, along the lower passage, through a swirling blanket of hellish fog and darkness, to the cabin where Miggs lay dead. And he lost consciousness while they carried him.

He could not tell, when he opened his eyes, how long he had been asleep. It seemed a long, long interlude. Stragella was sitting beside him. He lay on the bunk in the cabin, and the lamp was burning on the table, revealing Miggs' limp body in full detail.

Yancy reached up fearfully to touch his throat. There were no marks there; not yet.

He was aware of voices, then. Papa Bocito and the ferret-faced woman were arguing with the girl beside him. The savage old man in particular was being angered by her cool, possessive smile.

"We are drifting away from the prison isles," Papa Bocito snarled, glancing at Yancy with unmasked hate. "It is his work, lifting the anchor. Unless you share him with us until we drift ashore, we shall perish!"

"He is mine," Stragella shrugged, modulating her voice to a persuasive whisper. "You had the other. This one is mine. I shall have him!"

"He belongs to us all!"

"Why?" Stragella smiled. "Because he has looked upon the resurrection night? Ah, he is the first to learn our secret."

Seraphino's eyes narrowed at that, almost to pinpoints. She jerked forward, clutching the girl's shoulder.

"We have quarreled enough," she hissed. "Soon it will be daylight. He belongs to us all because he has taken us away from the isles and learned our secrets."

The words drilled their way into Yancy's brain. "The resurrection night!" There was an ominous significance in it, and he thought he knew its meaning. His eyes, or his face, must have revealed his thoughts, for Papa Bocito drew near to him and pointed into his face with a long, bony forefinger, muttering triumphantly.

"You have seen what no other eyes have seen," the ancient man growled bitterly. "Now, for that, you shall become one of us. Stragella wants you. She shall have you for eternity – for a life without death. Do you know what that means?"

Yancy shook his head dumbly, fearfully.

"We are the undead," Bocito leered. "Our victims become creatures of the blood, like us. At night we are free. During the day we must return to our graves. That is why" – he cast his arm toward the upper deck in a hideous gesture – "those other victims of ours have not yet become like us. They were never buried; they have no graves to return to. Each night we give them life for our own amusement, but they are not of the brotherhood – yet."

Yancy licked his lips and said nothing. He understood then. Every night it happened. A nightly pantomime, when the dead become alive again, reenacting the events of the night when the *Golconda* had become a ship of hell.

"We are gipsies," the old man gloated. "Once we were human, living in our pleasant little camp in the shadow of Pobyezdin Potok's crusty peaks, in the Morava Valley of Serbia. That was in the time of Milutin, six hundreds of years ago. Then the vampires of the hills came for us and took us to them. We lived the undead life, until there was no more blood in the valley. So we went to the coast, we three, transporting our grave-earth with us. And we lived there, alive by night and dead by day, in the coastal villages of the Black Sea, until the time came when we wished to go to the far places."

Seraphino's guttural voice interrupted him, saying harshly:

"Hurry. It is nearly dawn!"

"And we obtained passage on this *Golconda*, arranging to have our crates of grave-earth carried secretly to the hold. And the ship fell into cholera and starvation and storm. She went aground. And – here we are. Ah, but there is blood upon the islands, my pretty one, and so we anchored the *Golconda* on the reef, where life was close at hand!''

Yancy closed his eyes with a shudder. He did not understand all of the words; they were in a jargon of gipsy tongue. But he knew enough to horrify him.

Then the old man ceased gloating. He fell back, glowering at Stragella. And the girl laughed, a mad, cackling, triumphant laugh of possession. She leaned forward, and the movement brought her out of the line of the lamplight, so that the feeble glow fell full over Yancy's prostrate body.

At that, with an angry snarl, she recoiled. Her eyes went wide with abhorrence. Upon his chest gleamed the Crucifix – the tattooed Cross and Savior which had been indelibly printed there. Stragella held her face away, shielding her eyes. She cursed him horribly. Backing away, she seized the arms of her companions and pointed with trembling finger to the thing which had repulsed her.

The fog seemed to seep deeper and deeper into the cabin during the ensuing silence. Yancy struggled to a sitting posture and cringed back against the wall, waiting for them to attack him. It would be finished in a moment, he knew. Then he would join Miggs, with those awful marks on his throat and Stragella's lips crimson with his sucked blood.

But they held their distance. The fog enveloped them, made them almost indistinct. He could see only three pairs of glaring, staring, phosphorescent eyes that grew larger and wider and more intensely terrible.

He buried his face in his hands, waiting. They did not come. He heard them mumbling, whispering. Vaguely he was conscious of another sound, far off and barely audible. The howl of wolves.

Beneath him the bunk was swaying from side to side with the movement of the ship. The *Golconda* was drifting swiftly. A storm had risen out of nowhere, and the wind was singing its dead dirge in the rotten spars high above decks. He could hear it moaning, wheezing, like a human being in torment.

Then the three pairs of glittering orbs moved nearer. The whispered voices ceased, and a cunning smile passed over Stragella's features. Yancy screamed, and flattened against the wall. He watched her in fascination as she crept upon him. One arm was flung across her eyes to protect them from the sight of the Crucifix. In the other hand, outstretched, groping ever nearer, she clutched that hellish chunk of pitch-like substance with which she had encircled the Bible!

He knew what she would do. The thought struck him like an icy blast, full of fear and madness. She would slink closer, closer, until her hand touched his flesh. Then she would place the black substance around the tattooed cross and kill its powers. His defense would be gone. Then – those cruel lips on his throat. . . .

There was no avenue of escape. Papa Bocito and the plump old woman, grinning malignantly, had slid to one side, between him and the doorway. And Stragella writhed forward with one alabaster arm feeling . . . feeling. . . .

He was conscious of the roar of surf, very close, very loud, outside the walls of the fog-filled enclosure. The ship was lurching, reeling heavily, pitching in the swell. Hours must have passed. Hours and hours of darkness and horror.

Then she touched him. The sticky stuff was hot on his chest, moving in a slow circle. He hurled himself back, stumbled, went down, and she fell upon him.

Under his tormented body the floor of the cabin split asunder. The ship buckled from top to bottom with a grinding, roaring impact. A terrific shock burst through the ancient hulk, shattering its rotted timbers.

The lamp caromed off the table, plunging the cabin in semi-darkness. Through the port-holes filtered a gray glare. Stragella's face, thrust into Yancy's, became a mask of beautiful fury. She whirled back. She stood rigid, screaming lividly to Papa Bocito and the old hag.

"Go back! Go back!" she railed. "We have waited too long! It is dawn!"

She ran across the floor, grappling with them. Her lips were distorted. Her body trembled. She hurled her companions to the door. Then, as she followed them into the gloom of the passage, she turned upon Yancy with a last unholy snarl of defeated rage. And she was gone.

Yancy lay limp. When he struggled to his feet at last and went on deck, the sun was high in the sky, bloated and crimson, struggling to penetrate the cone of fog which swirled about the ship.

The ship lay far over, careened on her side. A hundred yards distant over the port rail lay the heaven-sent sight of land – a bleak, vacant expanse of jungle-rimmed shore line.

He went deliberately to work – a task that had to be finished quickly, lest he be discovered by the inhabitants of the shore and be considered stark mad. Returning to the cabin, he took the oil lamp and carried it to the open hold. There, sprinkling the liquid over the ancient wood, he set fire to it.

Turning, he stepped to the rail. A scream of agony, unearthly and prolonged, rose up behind him. Then he was over the rail, battling in the surf.

When he staggered up on the beach, twenty minutes later, the *Golconda* was a roaring furnace. On all sides of her the flames snarled skyward, spewing through that hellish cone of vapor. Grimly Yancy turned away and trudged along the beach.

He looked back after an hour of steady plodding. The lagoon was empty. The fog had vanished. The sun gleamed down with warm brilliance on a broad, empty expanse of sea.

Hours later he reached a settlement. Men came and talked to him, and asked curious questions. They pointed to his hair which was stark white. They told him he had reached Port Blair, on the southern island of the Andamans. After that, noticing the peculiar gleam of his blood-shot eyes, they took him to the home of the governor.

There he told his story – told hesitantly, because he expected to be disbelieved, mocked.

The governor looked at him cryptically.

"You don't expect me to understand?" the governor said. "I am not so sure, sir. This is a penal colony, a prison isle. During the past few years, more than two hundred of our convicts have died in the most curious way. Two tiny punctures in the throat. Loss of blood."

"You – you must destroy the graves," Yancy muttered.

The governor nodded silently, significantly.

After that, Yancy returned to the world, alone. Always alone. Men peered into his face and shrank away from the haunted stare of his eyes. They saw the Crucifix upon his chest and wondered why, day and night, he wore his shirt flapping open, so that the brilliant design glared forth.

But their curiosity was never appeased. Only Yancy knew; and Yancy was silent.

DAVID J. SCHOW

A Week in the Unlife

DAVID J. SCHOW LIVES IN the Hollywood Hills and collects everything he can find connected with the Creature from the Black Lagoon.

His collection of essays from *Fangoria* magazine, *Wild Hairs*, won the 2001 International Horror Guild Award for Best Non-fiction. The author's more recent books include the final volume of the *Lost Bloch* trilogy (subtitled *Crimes and Punishments*), and *Elvisland*, a landmark collection of John Farris's short fiction (both of which he edited); a resurrected, polished and spiffed-up reissue of his first collection, *Seeing Red*; a trade paperback edition of his fourth collection, *Crypt Orchids*; a new collection of living-dead stories entitled *Zombie Jam*; a short novel, *Rock Breaks Scissors Cut*, and a new mainstream suspense novel, *Bullets of Rain*.

"'A Week in the Unlife'," explains Schow, "is a relic of the pre-Goth, post-Rice explosion in Vamp Lit, when fiction about bloodsuckers became so prolific that it nearly merited its own bookstore shelf, and suffered the streamlining fallout of genrefication. There were punk vampires, porn vampires, rave vampires, corporate vampires, gay vampires, and sperm vampires aplenty, overrunning book after book, each twist of little substance beyond a one-liner gimmick. They're vampires – but they have AIDS! They're vampires – and they hate biker werewolves! It was enough to make you puke blood, the way Udo Kier did in *Blood for Dracula* (a.k.a. *Andy Warhol's Dracula*).

"By and large, most of the flood damage resulting from this overflow was ultraconservative, derivative, demographic, super-dull, and already moribund. Beyond *Dracula*, (and, in modern times, *'Salem's Lot*), the seminal or breakout works remained largely unread (such as Lucius Shepard's *The Golden*). Vampire enthusiasts would do well to exhume and rediscover Richard Matheson's *I Am Legend,* and Leslie Whitten's *Progeny of the Adder.* Virtually 90% of the idiom of the modern, pop vampire story sprang or spun off from one, or both, of these fundamental novels.

"It was distaste for such an adulterated cliché as vampirism that played a big part in the creation of the above-mentioned books. It is the ultimate challenge for a writer, confronting something so worn out: *Transcend me if you can.*

"It is the over-saturation of vampire lore, and the trivialist's lust to accumulate ever more of it, that is itself a new form of vampirism. The vampire hunter of 'Unlife' is a creature who feeds off *your* need to believe in vampires."

Initially written as a reaction against the genre, the following story fits very nicely into this particular themed anthology . . .

I

WHEN YOU STAKE A bloodsucker, the heartblood pumps out thick and black, the consistency of honey. I saw it make bubbles as it glurped out. The creature thrashed and squirmed and tried to pull out the stake – they always do, if you leave on their arms for the kill – but by the third whack it was, as Stoker might say, dispatched well and duly.

I lost count a long time ago. Doesn't matter. I no longer think of them as being even *former* human beings, and feel no anthropomorphic sympathy. In their eyes I see no tragedy, no romance, no seductive pulp appeal. Merely lust, rage at being outfoxed, and debased appetite, focused and sanguine.

People usually commit journals as legacy. So be it. Call me sentry, vigilante if you like. When they sleep their comatose sleep, I stalk and terminate them. When they walk, I hide. Better than they do.

They're really not as smart as popular fiction and films would lead you to believe. They do have cunning, an animalistic savvy. But I'm an experienced tracker; I know their spoor, the traces they leave, the way their presence charges the air. Things invisible or ephemeral to ordinary citizens, blackly obvious to me.

The journal is so you'll know, just in case my luck runs out.

Sundown. Nap time.

II

Naturally the police think of me as some sort of homicidal crackpot. That's a given; always has been for my predecessors. More watchers to evade. Caution comes reflexively to me these days. Police are slow and rational; they deal in the minutiae of a day-to-day world, deadly enough without the inclusion of bloodsuckers.

The police love to stop and search people. Fortunately for me, mallets and stakes and crosses and such are not yet illegal in this country. Lots of raised eyebrows and jokes and nudging but no actual arrests. When the time comes for them to recognize the plague that has descended upon their city, they will remember me, perhaps with grace.

My lot is friendless, solo. I know and expect such. It's okay.

City by city. I'm good at ferreting out the nests. To me, their kill-patterns are like a flashing red light. The police only see presumed loonies, draw no linkages; they bust and imprison mortals and never see the light.

I am not foolhardy enough to leave bloodsuckers lying. Even though the mean corpus usually dissolves, the stakes might be discovered. Sometimes there is other residue. City dumpsters and sewers provide adequate and fitting disposal for the leftovers of my mission.

The enemy casualties.

I wish I could advise the authorities, work hand-in-hand with them. Too complicated. Too many variables. Not a good control situation. Bloodsuckers have a maddening knack for vanishing into crevices, even hairline splits in logic.

Rule: Trust no one.

III

A female one, today. Funny. There aren't as many of them as you might suppose.

She had courted a human lover, so she claimed, like Romeo and Juliet – she could only visit him at night, and only after feeding, because bloodsuckers too can get carried away by passion.

I think she was intimating that she was a physical lover of other-worldly skill; I think she was fighting hard to tempt me not to eliminate her by saying so.

She did not use her mouth to seduce mortal men. I drove the stake into her brain, through the mouth. She was of recent vintage and did not melt or vaporize. When I fucked her remains, I was surprised to find her warm inside, not cold, like a cadaver. Warm.

With some of them, the human warmth is longer in leaving. But it always goes.

IV

I never met one before that gave up its existence without a struggle, but today I did, one that acted like he had been expecting me to wander along and relieve him of the burden of unlife. He did not deny what he was, nor attempt to trick me. He asked if he could talk a bit, before.

In a third-floor loft, the windows of which had been spray-painted flat black, he talked. Said he had always hated the taste of blood; said he preferred pineapple juice, or even coffee. He actually brewed a pot of coffee while we talked.

I allowed him to finish his cup before I put the ashwood length to his chest and drove deep and let his blackness gush. It dribbled, thinned by the coffee he had consumed.

V

Was thinking this afternoon perhaps I should start packing a Polaroid or somesuch, to keep a visual body count, just in case this journal becomes public record someday. It'd be good to have illustrations, proof. I was thinking of that line you hear overused in the movies. I'm sure you know it: "*But there's no such THING as a vampire!*" What a howler; ranks right up there alongside "*It's crazy – but it just might work!*" and "*We can't stop now for a lot of silly native superstitions!*"

Right; shoot cozy little memory snaps, in case they whizz to mist or drop apart to smoking goo. That bull about how you're not supposed to be able to record their images is from the movies, too. There's so much misleading information running loose that the bloodsuckers – the real ones – have no trouble at all moving through any urban center, *with impunity*, as they say on cop shows.

Maybe it would be a good idea to tape record the sounds they make when they die. Videotape them begging not to be exterminated. That would bug the eyes of all those monster movie fans, you bet.

VI

So many of them beleaguering this city, it's easy to feel outnumbered. Like I said, I've lost count.

Tonight might be a good window for moving on. Like them, I become vulnerable if I remain too long, and it's prudent operating procedure not to leave patterns or become predictable.

It's easy. I don't own much. Most of what I carry, I carry inside.

VII

They pulled me over on Highway Ten, outbound, for a broken left tail-light. A datafax photo of me was clipped to the visor in the Highway Patrol car. The journal book itself has been taken as evidence, so for now it's a felt-tip and high school notebook paper, which notes I hope to append to the journal proper later.

I have a cell with four bunks all to myself. The door is solid gray, with a food slot, unlike the barred cage of the bullpen. On the way back I noticed they had caught themselves a bloodsucker. Probably an accident; they probably don't even know what they have. There is no sunrise or sunset in the block, so if he gets out at night, they'll never know what happened. But I already know. Right now I will not say anything. I am exposed and at a disadvantage. The one I let slip today I can eliminate tenfold, next week.

VIII

New week. And I am vindicated at last.

I relaxed as soon as they showed me the photographs. How they managed documentation on the last few bloodsuckers I trapped, I have no idea. But I was relieved. Now I don't have to explain the journal – which, as you can see, they returned to me immediately. They had thousands of questions. They needed to know about the mallets, the stakes, the preferred method of killstrike. I cautioned them not to attempt a sweep and clear at night, when the enemy is stronger.

They paid serious attention this time, which made me feel much better. Now the fight can be mounted en masse.

They also let me know I wouldn't have to stay in the cell. Just some paperwork to clear, and I'm out among them again. One of the officials – not a cop, but a doctor – congratulated me on a stout job well done. He shook my hand, on behalf of all of them, he said, and mentioned writing a book on my work. This is exciting!

As per my request, the bloodsucker in the adjacent solitary cell was moved. I told them that to be really sure, they should use one of my stakes. It was simple vanity, really, on my part. I turn my stakes out of ashwood on a lathe. I made sure they knew I'd permit my stakes to be used as working models for the proper manufacture of all they would soon need.

When the guards come back I really must ask how they managed such crisp 8×10s of so many bloodsuckers. All those names and dates. First class documentation.

I'm afraid I may be a bit envious.

FRANCES GARFIELD

The House at Evening

IN THE LATE 1930S and 1940s Frances Garfield had a number of stories published in the classic pulp magazines *Weird Tales* and *Amazing Stories*, although she was never prolific.

Born Frances Obrist in Texas in 1908, she was of course better known as Frances Wellman, for fifty-five years the wife of author Manly Wade Wellman. After she retired from her job as a secretary in a school of public health, she kept thinking up ideas for new stories and telling them to her husband. When he told her that they were ''women's stories'' and that she would have to write them herself, she returned to her typewriter and resumed her fiction career after four decades.

During the 1980s and early 1990s she was published in such magazines and anthologies as *Whispers*, *Fantasy Tales*, *Fantasy Book*, *Kadath*, *The Tome*, *Whispers IV* and *The Year's Best Horror Stories*.

Although Frances Garfield died in 2000, 'The House at Evening' is a wonderfully atmospheric vampire story that makes us all glad that she returned to the fold.

THE SUN HAD SET and another twilight had begun. The western sky took on a rosy tinge, but none of the soft color penetrated into the lofty bedroom.

Claudia leaned toward the bureau. Her stormy black locks curtained her face as she brushed and brushed them. It was a luxurious, sensuous brushing. Her hair glistened in the light of the oil lamp.

Across the room sat Garland. She quickly combed her short blonde hair into an elfish mop of curls. "Thank goodness I don't have to worry about a great banner like yours," she said.

"Never you mind," Claudia laughed back. "We both know it's impressive."

They both applied makeup generously. Claudia fringed her silvery eyes with deep blue mascara and Garland brushed her pale eyebrows with brown. Each painted her lips a rosy red and smiled tightly to smooth the lipstick.

They finished dressing and went down the squeaking staircase to the big parlor. Darkness crept in, stealthily but surely. They picked up jugs of oil and went about, filling and lighting all the ancient glass-domed lamps. Light flickered yellow from table and shelf and glistened on the wide hardwood floor boards. Claudia took pride in those old expanses, spending hours on her knees to rub them to a glow. Garland arranged a bowl filled with colorful gourds on the mahogany table that framed the back of a brocaded couch. She put two scented candles into holders and lighted them.

Then they stood together to admire the effect of the soft light, Claudia in her red satin, Garland in her dark, bright blue. They checked each other for flaws and found none.

"I'd like to go walking outside, the way we used to do," said Garland. She glanced down at her high-heeled slippers. They weren't too high. "I'll only be gone a little while."

"There's not much to see out there," said Claudia. "Nobody much walks here anymore. It's been a long time since we've had company."

"Maybe I'm just being sentimental," smiled Garland. Her eyes twinkled for a moment, as if with some secret delight. "But maybe I'll bring somebody back."

"I'll stay here in case anybody calls," Claudia assured her.

The big wooden front door creaked shut behind Garland. She crossed the gray-floored piazza and ran down the steps to the path of old flagstones. Periwinkle overflowed them and knotted its roots everywhere. Ivy and honeysuckle choked the trees, autumn leaves poured down from the oaks. An old dead dogwood leaned wearily at the lawn's edge. Garland picked her way carefully.

An owl shrieked a message in the distance. Garland smiled to herself. She had worn no wrap out in the warm evening, but she nestled into the soft collar of her silky dress to feel its closeness. She breathed deeply of the night air.

Falling leaves whispered like raindrops. But there were only vagrant clouds in the sky. A young moon shone upon the old sidewalk, upon old houses along they way. They were large, pretentious houses, the sort called Victorian. They were ramshackle. No light shone from any window. Garland might have been the only moving creature in the neighborhood. Once this had been an elegant area on the edge of the old town that existed mainly for Ellerby College, but people had moved out. Deterioration had set in. Urban renewal threatened the neighborhood.

All at once Garland heard something – voices, hushed, furtive. She saw two tall young men coming toward her. She looked at them in the moonlight. They were handsome, sprucely dressed, looked like muscular young athletes. She hadn't seen their like for a while, and she felt a surge of warmth through her body.

They were near now, she could hear what they said.

"My Uncle Whit used to come here when he was in college," one young voice declared. "He said this was called Pink Hill. Said you'd be mighty well entertained."

Now she passed them, and turned at once to go back toward her house. She quickened her steps. For a moment she didn't know whether to be sad or happy. If only she hadn't lost her touch – but she knew her body, firm, sweet-looking. As she passed them again, she spoke.

"Hey," she greeted them.

One, tall with a neat, dark beard, spoke shyly, "Nice evening, isn't it?"

Garland smiled. If she had had dimples, she would have flashed them. "Yes, but there's a chill in the air. I think I'll just go back home. Maybe make some hot chocolate – or tea."

Away she walked ahead, her hips swinging a trifle, not so fast as to lose touch with them.

They seemed to be following her, all right. The bearded one was speaking, and Garland strained her ears to hear.

"After all," he was saying, "we did sort of think we were looking for experience."

The other, the fair-haired athletic one, said something too soft for Garland to hear. But it sounded like agreement.

She walked on, watching her feet on the treacherous pavement. There were so many cracks in that old cement. Sure enough, the two boys were coming along with her. Again she felt a flood of internal warmth. She felt almost young again, almost as young as she must look. Carefully she timed the sway of her hips. There was the house. Along the flagstones she minced happily, and up the steps and in at the door.

"We're going to have company, Claudia," she said.

Claudia swept the room with an appraising glance, and smiled a cool smile. "Tell me," she said quickly.

"Two really lovely young men, coming along to follow me. One with bright hair and a football body. The other tall, bearded, neat, sophisticated looking. We'll have to do them credit."

"Well, there's a bottle of port out, and some of those cheese biscuits I made." Claudia studied the table in the lamplight. "We'll be all right."

From outside they heard footsteps on the porch, and hesitant whispering.

"They're beautiful," said Garland.

Silence for an instant. Then a guarded tattoo of knocks on the panel of the door. A knock, Garland guessed, taught them by good old Uncle Whit.

"Okay, here we go," said Claudia, and gave Garland a triumphant look. "Remember your company manners."

She glided to the door, her red gown hugging her opulent hips and her slim waist. Her dress was long. It swept the floor and it accentuated every curve and hollow of the well-used body. She could be proud of how she looked, how she moved. She graduated magna cum laude in every way.

She opened the door, and the lamplight touched the two young men.

Garland had appraised them accurately. They wore well-fitting suits and open shirts. The taller one had a close-clipped beard, dark and sleek. Promising and intelligent. The other, of medium height but with broad shoulders, looked powerfully muscled. Undoubtedly undergraduates at Ellerby College. Fine prospects, both of them.

"Good evening, gentlemen," Claudia gave them her personal, hospitable smile.

"Good evening, ma'am," said the dark one, like a spokesman. He would be for Garland, thought Claudia. For her the other, the sturdy one.

"Well," said the tall one. "Well, we thought—" He paused embarrassedly.

"We thought we'd come walking this way," spoke up the other. "My name's Guy and this is Larry. We – we're students."

"Freshmen," added Larry. "We go to Ellerby."

"I see," Claudia soothed them. "Well, won't you come in?"

"Yes, ma'am," said Guy gratefully. They entered together and stood side by side. Their smiles were diffident. Claudia closed the door behind them.

Larry studied the parlor with politely curious eyes. "This is a great place," he offered. "Wonderful. It's – well, it's nostalgic."

"Thank you," Garland smiled to him. "Come sit here and see if this couch wasn't more or less made for you."

He hesitated, but only for a moment. Then he paced toward the couch. He wore handsome shiny boots. He and Garland sat down together and Claudia held out her hand to Guy.

"You look like somebody I used to know," she said, slitting her silvery eyes at him. "He played football at State. Came visiting here."

"Maybe all football players look alike," Guy smiled back. "I came to Ellerby to play tight end, if I can make it."

Beside Larry on the couch, Garland turned on her personality. It was as if she pressed a button to set it free.

"Would you like a glass of this port?" she asked. "It's very good."

"Let me do it." He took the bottle and poured. His hand trembled just a trifle. "Here." And he held out the glass.

"No, it's for you," she said. "I'll wait until later."

Larry sipped. "Delicious."

"Yes, only the best for our friends."

"We surely appreciate this, ma'am," he said, sipping again.

"You may call me Garland."

Claudia had seated Guy in a heavily soft armchair and had perched herself on its arm. They were whispering and chuckling together.

"Larry," said Garland, "you look to me as if you've been around a lot."

"Maybe my looks are deceptive," he said, brown eyes upon her. "I – I've never been at a place like this before."

Garland edged closer to him. "Tell me a little about yourself."

"Oh, I'm just a freshman at Ellerby. Nothing very exciting about that."

"But it must be." She edged even closer. "Just being on campus must be exciting. Come on, tell me more."

She put her hand on his. He took it in his warm clasp.

"Well, freshman year is rough." He seemed to have difficulty talking. "There's no hazing at Ellerby any more, not exactly, but you have to take a lot of stuff to get ready to be a sophomore."

She pulled his young arm around her shoulder and began to count the fingers on his hand with delicate little taps. Across the room, Claudia was sitting on Guy's lap, pulling his ear. They seemed to have come to good terms.

"This is really a great house," Larry said slowly. "It's—" He gulped. "It's nice," he said.

And right here it would come, Garland thought, something about how she was too lovely a girl to be in such a sordid business. To her relief, he didn't say it. Again she must take the initiative. She pulled his hand to where it could envelop her soft breast and held it there.

"Like it?" she whispered.

He must know what was coming, but plainly he was drowned in all sorts of conflicting emotions. Uncle Whit hadn't coached him, not nearly enough. He looked around the lamplit room with his eyes that were somehow plaintive. His beard seemed to droop.

"All right, Larry," said Garland, "come with me."

She got up and tugged his hand to make him get to his feet. He smiled. Of course, get him somewhere away from Claudia and Guy, there so cozy in the armchair. She picked up a lamp and led him into the hall.

"Wow," he said. "That staircase. Spiral. Looks like something in a historical movie."

"Does it?"

The staircase wound up into dark reaches. Gently Garland guided him and he seemed glad to be guided. She shepherded him past the torn spots in the carpeting, away from the shaky stretch of the balustrade, up to the hall above. She held up the lamp. It showed the faded roses on the carpet.

"Here," she said, "this is my room."

She opened the heavy door and pushed it inward. They stepped across the threshold together. She set the lamp on a table near the oriel window.

"I swear, Garland," he muttered, "this is great. That old four-poster bed, the bench – they must be worth a lot. They're old."

"Older than I am," she smiled at him.

"You're not old, Garland. You're beautiful."

"So are you," she told him truthfully.

They sat down on the bed. It had a cover of deep blue velvet with dim gold tassels. Larry seemed overwhelmed.

"I can't tell you how lovely all this is," he stammered.

"Then don't try. Put your feet up. That's right. Now relax."

He sank back. She pulled the loose shirt collar wider. "What a beautiful neck you have."

"Oh," he said, "it's Guy who's got the neck. All those exercises, those weights he lifts."

"Let Claudia attend to Guy. You're here with me."

Outside the door, a soft rustling. Garland paid no attention. Larry was quiet now, his eyes closed. Garland bent to him, her tender fingers massaging his temples, his neck. He breathed rhythmically, as though he slept. Closer Garland bent to him, her hands on his neck. Her fingers crooked, their tips pressed.

The lamplight shone on her red lips. They parted. Her teeth showed long and sharp. She crooned to him. She stopped. Her mouth opened above his neck.

Outside, voices spoke, faint, inhuman.

Garland rose quickly and went to the door. She opened it a crack.

Shapes hung there, gaunt and in ragged clothes. "Well," she whispered fiercely, "can't you wait?"

"Let me in," said one of them. Eyes gleamed palely. "Let me in," said another. "Hungry, hungry—"

"Can't you wait?" asked Garland again. "After I'm finished, you can have him. Have what's left."

She closed the door on their pleas, and hurried back to where Larry lay ready, motionless, dreaming, on the bed.

SIMON CLARK

Vampyrrhic Outcast

SIMON CLARK LIVES IN DONCASTER, South Yorkshire. His early short stories were published in the small press and he made his first professional sale to BBC local radio. Since then his fiction has appeared in numerous anthologies and been broadcast nationwide.

Clark's debut novel, *Nailed by the Heart*, appeared in 1995 and was followed by several more titles, including *Blood Crazy, Darker, King Blood, Vampyrrhic, The Fall, Judas Tree, Stranger*, and the British Fantasy Award-winning *The Night of the Triffids*. 2003 saw the publication of *Vampyrrhic Rites*, the sequel to *Vampyrrhic*, an epic tale of Norse vampires plaguing a modern-day English town.

His short stories have been collected in *Blood and Grit* and *Salt Snake*, and he has also written prose material for the rock band U2.

"To celebrate the appearance of *Vampyrrhic Rites*," explains the author, "I published 'Vampyrrhic Outcast' exclusively on my website. It was only intended to loosely allude to the novel, but when I began writing it I realized that once more the themes and characters of both *Vampyrrhic* and its sequel had got a grip on me and I began to ask myself, was 'Vampyrrhic Outcast' a self-contained story, or was it really the opening of *Vampyrrhic* volume three?

"I hadn't consciously planned a third volume in the series. Now I'm not so sure."

In the following story, set in the Vampyrrhic outlands, a lonely soul searches for a place of safety . . .

'You are as the darkness of night touched by the pale light of the moon'
        – from *Skanda Purana* (India, circa 1,000 AD)

BY THE LIGHT OF a midnight moon the town of Leppington lay sleeping. Twenty hours of heavy July rain filled the streets with pools of water that glittered silver. Each one duplicated the image of the moon. A hard disc as white as bone that oh-so-faintly revealed dead lunar seas.

The girl walked barefoot down the deserted street, her toes sinking into puddles, annihilating those shimmering copies of a faraway world.

I'm late, she told herself. *I'm too late; they'll have left without me.*

Those urgent thoughts pulsed through her mind. She moved faster: a lonesome figure gliding through this remote Yorkshire town that was a desolate and eerie place at this time of night. Above still-glistening rooftops that burned with silver dashes of moonlight, she glimpsed the range of dark, forbidding hills that formed an unbroken wall as if to keep Leppington town an eternal prisoner.

Thoughts darted fiercely, prompting her to break into a run. *I'm going to leave here. You can't keep me for ever. Once I find them they'll take me with them. I need never return to this godforsaken graveyard of a place ever again.*

She turned a corner in the street, then paused. Standing there, dwarfing the surrounding buildings, looking for all the world like a huge tombstone thrusting up out of damp earth was the Station Hotel. No lights showed through the windows in its Gothic face. It was unlikely that there would be any hotel guests . . . after all, who would willingly stay in such a grim building with its morbid adornment of gargoyles and its glowering faces carved into lintels? If by some slim chance there were any guests, they had probably chosen to escape their surroundings in sleep.

A figure appeared in the shadows of an alleyway to her right. She could see palely gleaming arms. They were bare, she noted. Their skin showed as an icy blue colour patterned with thick, black veins. There was no face – at least none she could see as it was so deeply swathed in gloom.

Whoever the stranger was, he watched her. Cold waves of fear washed through her body. She backed away from the figure as it took a step forward.

The hotel was only a hundred paces away. *I could run for it. Perhaps he wouldn't have a chance to catch me . . .*

As she tensed, ready to flee for the hotel, she heard the man speak. The voice had a diseased quality to it, as if the vocal cords had been rotted by some necrotic infection. "Go back to where you came from. You don't belong here. Go back . . ."

The moment she turned, ready to run, she stumbled, falling to her hands and knees in a pool of water that covered half the road. For a moment she froze there, shocked by both the fall and the appearance of the loathsome stranger. Dazed, she looked down into the water. The hard, gleaming disc of the moon was reflected there. And, as she watched, another pale object appeared to float alongside it. She saw a face – a terrible face that made her gasp. Its skin had the appearance of candle wax; there were blue tints dappling its strangely broad forehead. While the eyes—

That stare made her blood creep, as if turning it to ice in her veins. Breaking free of the hypnotic gaze, she leapt to her feet and ran toward the Station Hotel. The abrasive road surface would be ripping the bare soles of her feet, but she could not stop now.

He's following me, she thought. *I know he is. I mustn't look back.* An access path led down the side of the looming Gothic structure to the rear yard. She took it, her feet either splashing puddles or slapping down on nineteenth-century cobblestones. *Please be there. Don't leave without me . . .* Only when she was round the corner of the hotel did she glance back. The courtyard was empty. Here, moonlight glinted on the cobbles. It put images in her mind of walking across the scaly back of some primeval monster. Even as she crossed the ground to a lighted window at the rear of the hotel it seemed to twitch beneath her feet, as if her imagined monster slept only fitfully and would soon wake to roar out its fury at her for disturbing it.

It will only be a moment before the man from the alley finds me here. Oh God, those eyes . . . Her stomach muscles writhed as if a fistful of worms slid through her intestines. Those evil-looking eyes. There had been no colour to them – only a glistening white like the boiled flesh of an egg. Worse, in the centre of each eye a tiny black pupil glared with such ferocity that her legs had nearly folded under her. She knew that if she looked into those eyes again she would never break free of their hold.

She glanced about the gloom-drenched courtyard. Still no sign of the figure that had frightened her so much. Yet shadows seeped along the ground, as if spreading stains of blood crept towards her. Irrationally she thought: *I can't let those shadows touch me. They are poison . . . No . . .* She swayed, dizzy. *No, that doesn't make sense. That's a mad thought. Only –*

She turned her back on the areas of darkness flowing across the cobbled surface, devouring the bright licks of reflected moonlight.

Even to look at those shadows made her uneasy. What was important was to get inside the hotel.

Now, that was a beautiful image. Of her standing in the brightly-lit hotel kitchen, the door locked solidly behind her, seeing familiar faces. Of *not* being alone. *Alone* she could not handle any more. *Alone* is a cancer of the spirit. *Alone* is debilitating . . . loneliness has the relentless, erosive power to grind away at confidence, at physical strength.

Just for a moment recollection of the loneliness that she had endured roared over her in a great black tide. Its grim currents carried a diffused but permanent cloud of terror. Every time she awoke she dreaded being engulfed by this awful feeling that soon something terrible would happen to her. Only she would be power-less to seek help . . . or even find anyone who could offer comfort and companionship if disaster struck.

Maybe this is what I've been dreading? Perhaps the sense of foreboding was a premonition of the stranger waiting for me in the alley? That I've always known that one day – one night! – I'd find myself alone here, and come face to face with the man who will take my life.

A sudden scraping sound made her flinch. She glanced back. Saw nothing but shadow and the gloom-filled void of the archway in the wall that led out onto the river bank. Now she could hear the hissing roar of the river itself. All this rain had swollen it, engorging the body of water into flood. Only now the sound of the river was like a voice calling her to it.

No. No! She pressed the palms of her hands against her ears. *It's this weird little town. It has that effect on you. The longer you stay the more it insinuates strange ideas into your head.* For some reason, when she closed her eyes she imagined that a labyrinth of tunnels ran beneath the houses. And in these tunnels swarmed pallid, maggot-like men and women that lusted for human blood – and the warmth of a human body, one they could wind their vein-knotted arms around. Blood and body heat – beneath the skin the pair are brother and sister. The tangible embodiment of this *intangible* thing we call Life . . .

Now her eyes were closed and she tottered forward until she leaned against the hotel wall, her face pressing cold brick that possessed the damp, clammy touch of a dead hand. Images flew through her mind of pallid, naked forms that swam through deep waters. The River Lepping roared beyond the yard wall. And she imagined a hundred faces floating up through the swirling flood to cry out to her. Angry voices that demanded she leave this place while she still could.

No. I will not let this town put those thoughts into my head. I am sane. I am rational. I will not think about vampires.

Vampires? Even to think the word made her eyes snap open. *Vampires? Why did I use that word?* She shuddered to the roots of her bones. If she did not find another human being to talk to right at this moment she realized she would lose her mind. Above her head, cloud drew cobweb strands across a ghosting moon. Even the little light it cast into the yard was dying now. She must get inside the hotel. She must find human company.

Feeling her way along the wall, she reached the window that formed a block of shining yellow in that unyielding membrane of brick. Once more, her mind spun out strange ideas: *Yes, the wall is a membrane. At one side are light, life, companionship and safety. While on this side . . .*

Then she had reached the window. For a second the brilliance of the electric light inside dazzled her. Screwing up her eyes, she brought her face close to the glass and peered in. A dresser full of blue plates. An antique-looking stove. A Yorkshire range in black-painted iron. Brass kettle. Belfast sink. A wall clock showing half-past midnight. But where was . . . ah, there!

Angling her head to one side, she made out the vast kitchen table that dominated the room. Around it sat five men and women. They were holding a conversation – an intense one. Those that were not speaking listened solemnly. Inside was full of light – a beautiful, brilliant, Pentecostal light. It suppressed shadows; it did not yield before things that creep out of the night. The air inside would be warm; it would smell pleasantly of soap and the lingering after-aroma of freshly cooked food. She saw bottles of wine. Every now and again the men and women would sip from their glasses.

It looked wonderful. She wished she was sitting in their company drinking that red wine – a delicious rouge colour. She could imagine how it would taste, its velvety softness. Her tongue ran across her top lip while her gaze roved over the people at the table. An elegant woman dressed in black: she had long hair that was a gunmetal blue. The way she held herself suggested an aristocratic ancestry. The man sitting beside her was in his thirties. His eyes were soulful, caring, yet touched with melancholy. Three other people, in their late teens or early twenties, she guessed, sat across the table from him.

Suddenly she realized she could hear the sound of approaching footsteps. It must be the stranger from the alleyway. *It has to be. He's followed me here.* She glanced to the corner of the building, expecting the loathsome figure to appear at any moment. Nothing yet. But the slow footfalls sounded louder. Quickly, she tapped on the window-pane with her fingernails. The group inside still talked. Some serious subject that involved them deeply. She tapped again.

Why don't they hear me?

She glanced to the corner of the building. The sound of footsteps grew louder. Oh no . . . she could see a strange, humped shadow looming across the cobblestones. Her pursuer must be walking along the access path to the yard now; the street lights were behind him, throwing the grotesque shadow forward.

Heart pounding, she rapped on the window. This time it was loud enough for the men and women to swing their heads around to look in her direction. She saw their eyes widen. One of the women screamed.

"Please, let me in. I'm being followed . . . please, he's nearly—"

Then from behind a pair of hands grasped her shoulders. She glanced fearfully down to see fingers that were bloated like raw sausages – the skin was a sickening mix of grey and blue tints, while the fingernails were ragged, purple things. So cold as well . . . the fingers had the feel of raw meat taken from a refrigerator. That cold seeped through her clothes into her own skin, chilling the blood that ran through her veins, oozing into every secret place of her.

She tried to cry out, but shock had locked her throat tight. All she could manage was a hoarse gasping sound. The powerful hands dragged her away from the kitchen window. In seconds she had been hauled through the gateway onto the river bank. Here there were no lights. It was merely a strip of muddy ground from which bulged malformed growths of bushes and willow trees that loomed over black river water.

Even though she struggled, the grip on her shoulders was so powerful that she could not turn around to see her attacker's face.

Oh, but she remembered it though. That dead white face. With colourless eyes centred by fierce black pupils that seemed to burn holes through her heart . . .

Despite her terror she realized that the door to the hotel had opened.

A voice called, "Who's there?"

Once more she tried to cry out, only she was too breathless from the violence of being dragged through the witch-tangle of branches to the water's edge. The River Lepping roared at her now. A full-blooded sound that vibrated through her body.

But even though the sound pounded at her awareness, she heard only too well what the man breathed into her ear with that toxic voice.

"Why didn't you listen to me? I said you don't belong here."

"Please," she choked out the word. "Don't kill me . . . please don't kill me."

"Listen carefully to what I'm about to tell you." The man held her so that her face almost touched the water's dark surface. She saw two

R. CHETWYND-HAYES

The Labyrinth

~~O~~ CHETWYND-HAYES was known as "Britain's Prince of
~~D~~uring a publishing career that lasted more than forty years,
~~pud~~uced eleven novels, more than 200 short stories, and edited
~~fi~~ve anthologies.

~~I~~n Isleworth, West London, he started writing fiction in the
~~5~~0s, and his first published book was the science fiction novel
~~ _from the Bomb_ in 1959. His second novel, _The Dark Man_ (a.k.a.
~~ Survived_), appeared five years later.

~~ ~~looking on a bookstall in the early 1970s, he noticed the
~~ ~~ of horror titles and submitted a collection of his own
~~w~~hich eventually appeared in paperback as _The Unbidden_.
~~ ~~g a full-time writer, he began producing a prolific number
~~ ~~ stories and sedate tales of terror, many tinged with his
~~ ~~ sense of humour.

~~ ~~ies were widely anthologized and collected in such volumes
~~T~~error, _Terror by Night_, _The Elemental_, _The Night Ghouls and Other_
~~ ~~s, _The Monster Club_, _Tales of Fear and Fantasy_, _The Cradle_
~~ ~~d _Other Stories of Fantasy and Horror_, _The Fantastic World of_
~~ ~~ _A Book of Vampires and Ghouls_, _Tales of Darkness_, _Tales from_
~~ ~~Quiver of Ghosts_, _Tales from the Dark Lands_, _Ghosts from the Mist_
~~ ~~ales from the Shadows_, _Tales from the Haunted House_, _Dracula's_
~~ ~~he House of Dracula_, _Shudders and Shivers_, _The Vampire Stories_

faces reflected there. Both blue-white, cheeks patterned with black
veins. Two faces with white staring eyes punctuated by fierce black
pupils. "Don't you understand?" he hissed. "You're already dead."

As the word _dead, dead, dead_ reverberated in her ears he threw her
into the river.

First of all she struggled to keep her head above the flood waters of
the Lepping, while trying to swim to the bank. Then the words of the
vampire sank deep enough into her mind for her to accept the truth.
"You're already dead."

Fierce currents rolled her onto her back. She floated downstream
looking up at the moon through overhanging willows. Silver-edged
clouds floated high in the sky. They moved with the flow of the night
winds, she moved with the flow of the night river. Just like those
clouds she had no control over her direction.

I'm already dead, she thought. _I don't need to swim._ Understanding
seeped coldly through her. _I don't need to breathe. Because I am dead_ . . . At
last she surrendered to the power of the river. It floated her past rocks,
rolled her over, spun her in its grave eddies, then its remorseless
undertow pulled her down under the black waters, down to the bottom
of the river bed that was an expanse of slick mud. Being unable to
breathe made no difference to her. She did not drown. Could not
drown. Pale shapes swam in front of her face. For a moment she thought
they were softly swollen fish, then she realized that they were her own
hands floating backward and forward in this cold body of water.

There's no point fighting this, she told herself. _I may as well let the river
carry me to the sea. I'm truly lost now. Even if I could climb out, I can never
return home._

Once more her face broke the surface. For mile after mile she
floated on her back, passing under bridges, beneath trees that
arched over the water, between meadows. Above her the moon
shone down. In her imagination it became a hard, round eye gazing
dispassionately at the woman in the water, knowing that she was
doomed and coolly observing what fate would eventually befall her.
She was nothing but a piece of driftwood now. Lost to her family, to
humanity, and to God.

Once the stream carried her past a house on the river bank. There
was a light burning in the upstairs window – a little block of yellow
radiance. Music ghosted from the house, too. A melancholy song that
eerily echoed her journey through a night-time countryside that
seemed haunted by the ghosts of all those tomorrows she would
never now experience.

Presently the flow carried her away from the house and the music.
Soon it was lost in the distance.

She closed her eyes. It only seemed for a moment, and then she realized that she lwas lying on solid ground. Opening her eyes, she sat up and looked around.

Moonlight revealed that she had been washed up on a beach. Oddly, it was tempting to lie there and not to even attempt to walk ever again. Only the water receded as a retreating ocean tide a dozen miles away reduced water levels upstream. As if walking in her sleep, she rose to her feet. There, on higher ground and almost engulfed by hawthorn, was a tumbledown cottage. Strangely, she felt herself drawn to it. *Maybe the river brought me here because I was meant to see it*, she thought. *Perhaps I'm here for a purpose.* The moon was bright enough to show her a path that ran through waist-high nettles and hemlock. It appeared to lead directly to the cottage that stood half-hidden from view alongside this remote stretch of river.

With her bare feet whispering through the plants, she glided almost dreamily to the gate that led into a garden grown wild – where roses ten feet high nodded huge heads of pink petals.

Seconds later, she approached one of the windows. The panes were cracked; some were partially covered by a green skin of moss. Slowly, slowly, as if she knew someone – or some *thing* – waited for her in the cottage, she leaned forward to look through one of the panes.

Inside was the kitchen of a long-since-abandoned house. Abandoned by human occupants, that was.

Sitting around a rotting table on decaying wooden chairs were five figures. Five beings that had once been men and women. Some wore ragged clothes; a pair were near-naked. The women possessed long manes of hair that poured in tangled coils of glossy black down their backs. Their skin was a deadly white with tints of blue. A cold, cold colour that sent a shiver down her spine. They sat at the table without moving. The males possessed powerfully muscular arms that were tracked with black veins. The faces of males and females alike were waxy mask-things that revealed no expression. It was their eyes that confirmed what they were.

Like those of the stranger who had thrown her in the river, their eyes possessed no iris, so they revealed no colour. What they had were tiny black pupils that lent them such an air of ferocity. All the time she watched the gathering in the derelict cottage, they did not move. They did not even blink or shift their gaze from the barren table top.

She realized that if she moved with enough stealth, she could leave this damned and desolate place without attracting their attention. Yet, just for a second, she saw herself sitting at that table with them . . . waiting with those festering dead-alive carcasses until the end of time. These were the abandoned scraps of their race, rejected by their

fellow vampires. They had no purpose. Perha[ps] lusts only burned dimly inside the stone-cold mu[scles] hearts. Pitiful, ugly, lonely creatures that had f[...]

Taking a step back, she glanced over her shoul[der] from here would be the river. Not that it could kil[l...] would it be a comfort to her either? All that wa[...] water was a drifting existence without compani[on...] Once more that great dark tide of loneliness sw[ept] tottered, almost losing her balance. Could she fac[e...] malignancy of solitude. How it corroded her sa[...] moment the most miserable, the most unbearably [...] And that moment of unyielding unhappiness woul[d...] another just as bad.

A mere thirty paces back to the river . . . then s[...] that gathering of animated death in the decaying c[ottage...] paces . . . she could cover that distance in twenty [...]

This time she did not hesitate when she move[d...] tapped on the window.

"Please," she whispered. "Please . . . let me in. I [...] alone."

The night-time breeze carried her words away int[o...] they died beneath a cold, cold moon.

RONA[...]
Chill" [...]
he pr[...]
twenty[...]
Born[...]
early 1[...]
The M[...]
And L[...]
Whi[...]
profus[...]
stories[...]
Becom[...]
of gho[...]
disarm[...]
His [...]
as *Cold[...]*
Grisly[...]
Demon[...]
Kamtell[...]
Beyond[...]
of Time[...]
Childre[...]

of R. Chetwynd-Hayes (a.k.a. *Looking for Something to Suck and Other Vampire Stories*), *Phantoms and Fiends* and *Frights and Fancies.*

The anthology movies *From Beyond the Grave* (1973) and *The Monster Club* (1980) were both adapted from his work. In the latter, based on probably his most successful book, the author himself was portrayed by veteran horror actor John Carradine. Chetwynd-Hayes's stories were also extensively adapted for radio, and his tale 'Housebound' became the basis for a 1973 episode of the TV series *Rod Serling's Night Gallery.*

In 1989 he was presented with Life Achievement Awards by both the Horror Writers of America and the British Fantasy Society, and he was the Special Guest of Honour at the 1997 World Fantasy Convention in London. R. Chetwynd-Hayes died in 2001.

"Me and vampires have always got on well together," explained the author, and to prove it here is a somewhat unusual twist on the theme . . .

THEY WERE LOST. Rosemary knew it and said so in forcible language. Brian also was well aware of their predicament but was unwilling to admit it.

"One cannot be lost in England," he stated. "We're bound to strike a main road if we walk in a straight line."

"But suppose we wander in a circle?" Rosemary asked, looking fearfully round at the Dartmoor landscape, "and finish up in a bog?"

"If we use our eyes there's no reason why bogs should bother us. Come on and stop moaning."

"We should never have left that track," Rosemary insisted. "Suppose we get caught out here when night falls?"

"Don't be daft," he snapped, "it's only mid-day. We'll be in Princetown long before nightfall."

"You hope." She refused to be convinced. "I'm hungry."

"So am I." They were walking up a steep incline. "But I don't keep on about it."

"I'm not keeping on. I'm hungry and I said so. Do you think we'll find a main road soon?"

"Over the next rise," he promised. "There's always a main road over the next rise."

But he was wrong. When they crested the next rise and looked down, there was only a narrow track which terminated at a tumbledown gate set in a low stone wall. Beyond, like an island girdled by a yellow lake, was a lawn-besieged house. It was built of grey stone and seemed to have been thrown up by the moors; a great, crouching monster that glared out across the countryside with multiple glass eyes. It had a strange look. The chimney stacks might have been jagged splinters of rock that had acquired a rough cylindrical shape after centuries of wind and rain. But the really odd aspect was that the sun appeared to ignore the house. It had baked the lawn to a pale yellow, cracked the paint on an adjacent summerhouse, but in some inexplicable way, it seemed to disavow the existence of the great, towering mass.

"Tea!" exclaimed Rosemary.

"What?"

"Tea." She pointed. "The old lady, she's drinking tea."

Sure enough, seated by a small table that nestled in the shade of a vast multi-coloured umbrella was a little white-haired old lady taking tea. Brian frowned, for he could not understand why he had not seen her, or at least the umbrella, before, but there she was, a tiny figure in a white dress and a floppy hat, sipping tea and munching sandwiches. He moistened dry lips.

"Do you suppose," he asked, "we dare intrude?"

"Watch me," Rosemary started running down the slope towards the gate. "I'd intrude on Dracula himself if he had a decent cup of tea handy."

Their feet moved on to a gravel path and it seemed whatever breeze stirred the sun-warm heather out on the moors did not dare intrude here. There was a strange stillness, a complete absence of sound, save for the crunch of feet on gravel, and this too ceased when they walked on to the parched lawn.

The old lady looked up and a slow smile gradually lit up a benign, wizened little face, while her tiny hands fluttered over the table, setting out two cups and saucers, then felt the teapot as though to make sure the contents were still hot.

"You poor children." Her voice had that harsh, slightly cracked quality peculiar to some cultured ladies of an advanced age, but the utterance was clear, every word pronounced with precision. "You look so hot and tired."

"We're lost," Rosemary announced cheerfully. "We've wandered for miles."

"I must apologise for intruding," Brian began, but the old lady waved a teaspoon at him as though to stress the impossibility of intrusion.

"My dear young man – please. You are most welcome. I cannot recall when I last entertained a visitor, although I have always hoped someone might pass this way again. The right kind of someone, of course."

She appeared to shiver momentarily, or perhaps tremble, for her hands and shoulders shook slightly, then an expression of polite distress puckered her forehead.

"But how thoughtless I am. You are tired having wandered so many miles and there are no chairs."

She turned her head and called out in a high-pitched, quivering voice. "Carlo! Carlo!"

A tall, lean man came out of the house and moved slowly towards them. He was dressed in a black satin tunic and matching trousers and, due possibly to some deformity, appeared to bound over the lawn, rather than walk. Brian thought of a wolf, or a large dog that has spotted intruders. He stopped a few feet from the old lady and stood waiting, his slate-coloured eyes watching Rosemary with a strange intensity.

"Carlo, you will fetch chairs," the old lady ordered, "then some more hot water."

Carlo made a guttural sound and departed in the direction of the summerhouse, leaping forward in a kind of loping run. He returned almost immediately carrying two little slatted chairs and presently Brian and Rosemary were seated under the vast umbrella, drinking tea from delicate china cups and listening to the harsh, cultivated voice.

"I must have lived alone here for such a long time. Gracious me, if I were to tell you how long, you would smile. Time is such an inexhaustible commodity, so long as one can tap the fountainhead. The secret is to break it down into small change. An hour does not seem to be long until you remember it has three thousand, six hundred seconds. And a week! My word, did you ever realise you have six hundred and four thousand, eight hundred seconds to spend every seven days? It's an enormous treasure. Do have another strawberry jam sandwich, child."

Rosemary accepted another triangular, pink-edged sandwich, then stared open-eyed at the house. At close quarters it looked even more grim than from a distance. There was the impression the walls had drawn their shadows above themselves like a ghostly cloak, and although the house stood stark and forbidding in broad daylight, it still seemed to be divorced from sunshine. Rosemary of course made the obvious statement.

"It must be very old."

"It has lived," the old lady said, "for millions upon millions of seconds. It has drunk deep from the barrel of time."

Rosemary giggled, then hastily assumed an extravagantly serious expression as Brian glared at her. He sipped his tea and said: "This is really most kind of you. We were fagged out – and rather scared too. The moors seemed to go on and on and I thought we would have to spend the night out there."

The old lady nodded, her gaze flickering from one young face to the other.

"It is not pleasant to be lost in a great, empty space. Doubtless, if you had not returned before nightfall, someone would have instigated a search for you."

"Not on your nelly," Rosemary stated with charming simplicity. "No one knows where we are. We're sort of taking a roaming holiday."

"How adventurous," the old lady murmured, then called back over one shoulder. "Carlo, the hot water, man. Do hurry."

Carlo came bounding out of the house carrying a silver jug in one hand and a plate of sandwiches in the other. When he reached the table his mouth was open and he was breathing heavily. The old lady shot him an anxious glance.

"Poor old boy," she consoled. "Does the heat get you down, then? Eh? Does the heat make you puff and pant? Never mind, you can go and lie down somewhere in the shade." She turned to her guests and smiled a most kindly, benign smile. "Carlo has mixed blood and he finds the heat most trying. I keep telling him to practise more self-control, but he will insist on running about." She sighed. "I suppose it is his nature."

Rosemary was staring intently at her lap and Brian saw an ominous shake of her shoulders, so he hurriedly exclaimed:

"You really live all alone in that vast house? It looks enormous."

"Only a small portion, child." She laughed softly, a little silvery sound. "You see the windows on the ground floor which have curtains? That is my little domain. All the rest is closed up. Miles upon miles of empty corridors."

Brian re-examined the house with renewed interest. Six lower windows looked more wholesome than the others; the frames had, in the not-too-distant past, been painted white and crisp white curtains gave them a lived-in look, but the panes still seemed reluctant to reflect the sunlight and he frowned before raising his eyes to the upper storeys.

Three rows of dirt-grimed glass: so many eyes from behind which life had long since departed, save possibly for rats and mice. Then he started and gripped his knees with hands that were not quite steady. On the topmost storey, at the window third from the left, a face suddenly emerged and pressed its nose flat against the glass. There was no way of telling if the face were young or old, or if it belonged to a man, woman or child. It was just a white blur equipped with a pair of blank eyes and a flattened nose.

"Madam . . ." Brian began.

"My name," the old lady said gently, "is Mrs Brown."

"Mrs Brown. There's a . . ."

"A nice homely name," Mrs Brown went on. "Do you not think so? I feel it goes with a blazing fire, a singing kettle and muffins for tea."

"Madam – Mrs Brown. The window up there . . ."

"What window, child?" Mrs Brown was examining the interior of the teapot with some concern. "There are so many windows."

"The third from the left." Brian was pointing at the face, which appeared to be opening and shutting its mouth. "There is someone up there and they seem to be in trouble."

"You are mistaken, my dear," Mrs Brown shook her head. "No one lives up there. And without life, there can be no face. That is logic."

The face disappeared. It was not so much withdrawn as blotted out, as though the window had suddenly clouded over and now it was just another dead man's eye staring out over the sun-drenched moors.

"I could swear there was a face," Brian insisted, and Mrs Brown smiled.

"A cloud reflection. It is so easy to see faces where none exist. A crack in the ceiling, a damp patch on a wall, a puddle in moonlight – all become faces when the brain is tired. Can I press you to another cup?"

"No, thank you." Brian rose and nudged Rosemary to do the same. She obeyed with ill grace. "If you would be so kind as to direct us to the nearest main road, we will be on our way."

"I could not possibly do that." Mrs Brown looked most distressed. "We are really miles from anywhere and you poor children would get hopelessly lost. Really, I must insist you stay here for the night."

"You are most kind and do not think us ungrateful," Brian said, "but there must be a village not too far away."

"Oh Brian," Rosemary clutched his arm. "I couldn't bear to wander about out there for hours. And suppose the sun sets . . .?"

"I've told you before, we'll be home and dry long before then," he snapped, and Mrs Brown rose, revealing herself as a figure of medium height, whose bowed shoulders made her shorter than she actually was. She shook a playful finger at the young man.

"How could you be so ungallant? Can you not see the poor girl is simply dropping from fatigue?" She took Rosemary's arm and began to propel her towards the house, still talking in her harsh, precise voice. "These big strong men have no thought for us poor, frail women. Have they, my dear?"

"He's a brute." Rosemary made a face at Brian over one shoulder. "We wouldn't have got lost if he hadn't made us leave the main track."

"It is the restless spirit that haunts the best of them," Mrs Brown confided. "They must wander into strange and forbidden places, then come crying home to us when they get hurt."

They moved in through the open french windows, leaving the hot summer afternoon behind them, for a soft, clinging coolness leapt to embrace their bodies like a slightly damp sheet. Brian shivered, but Rosemary exclaimed: "How sweet."

She was referring to the room. It was full of furniture: chairs, table, sideboard, from which the sheen of newness had long since departed; the patterned carpet had faded, so had the wallpaper; a vase of dried flowers stood on the mantelpiece and from all around – an essential part of the coolness – came a sweet, just perceptible aroma. It was the scent of extreme old age which is timidly approaching death on faltering feet. For a moment, Brian had a mental picture of an open coffin bedecked with dying flowers. Then Mrs Brown spoke.

"There are two sweet little rooms situated at the rear. You will rest well in them."

Carlo emerged from somewhere; he was standing by the open doorway, his slate-grey eyes watching Mrs Brown as she nodded gravely.

"Go with him, my dears. He will attend to your wants and presently, when you have rested, we will dine."

They followed their strange guide along a gloom-painted passage and he silently opened two doors, motioned Rosemary into one, then, after staring blankly at Brian, pointed to the other.

"You've been with Mrs Brown a long time?" Brian asked in a loud voice, assuming the man was deaf. "Must be rather lonely for you here."

Carlo did not answer, only turned on his heel and went back along the passage with that strange, loping walk. Rosemary giggled.

"Honestly, did you ever see anything like it?"

"Only in a horror film," Brian admitted. "Say, do you suppose he's deaf and dumb?"

"Fairly obviously," Rosemary shrugged. "Let's have a look at our rooms."

They were identical. Each held a four-poster bed, a Tudor-style chest of drawers and a bedside cupboard. The same faint odour prevailed here, but Rosemary did not seem to notice it.

"Do you suppose this place runs to a bath?" she asked, seating herself on Brian's bed.

Before he could answer, Carlo's lean form filled the doorway and he made a guttural sound while beckoning them to follow him. He led the way down the passage and at the very end opened a door and motioned them to enter the room beyond. It was empty save for a very ancient hip-bath and six leather buckets lined up against one wall.

They began to laugh, clinging to each other for support. Their silent guide watched them with an expressionless stare. Brian was the first to regain his powers of speech.

"Ask a silly question," he gasped, "and you'll get a ridiculous answer."

"I rarely eat."

Mrs Brown was sipping daintily from a glass of mineral water and watching the young people with lively interest as they each consumed a large steak and a generous helping of fresh salad.

"When you are my age," she went on, "one's fires need little fuel. A sip of water, an occasional nibble, the odd crumb."

"But you must eat," Rosemary looked at the old lady with some concern. "I mean – you have to."

"Child—" Mrs Brown beckoned to Carlo who started to collect the empty plates, "—food is not necessarily meat and vegetables. Passion will feed the soul and nourish the body. I recommend love as an *hors d'oeuvre*, hate as the *entrée* and fear as a chilly dessert."

Rosemary looked nervously at Brian, then took a long drink of water to hide her confusion. The young man decided to bring the conversation back to a more mundane plane.

"I am most interested in your house, Mrs Brown. It seems a shame that so little of it is used."

"I did not say it was not used, dear," Mrs Brown corrected gently. "I said no one lived in the region that lies outside this apartment. There is, as I am sure you will agree, a difference."

Carlo returned, carrying a dish of large, pink blancmange; this he deposited on the table after giving the girl and young man a long, expressionless stare.

"You must forgive Carlo," Mrs Brown said while she carved the blancmange into thin slices. "It is some time since we entertained guests and he is apt to stare at that which he is not allowed to touch."

Brian nudged Rosemary, who was watching the blancmange carving with undisguised astonishment. "Mrs Brown, you say the rest of the house is used, but not lived in. I'm sorry, but . . ."

"Does anyone live in your stomach?" Mrs Brown asked quietly.

He laughed, but seeing no smile on the wrinkled face opposite quickly assumed a serious expression.

"No, of course not."

"But it is used?" Mrs Brown persisted.

He nodded. "Yes indeed. Quite a lot."

"So with the house." She handed Rosemary a plate that contained three thin slices of pink blancmange and the girl said "Thank you" in a strangled voice. "You see, the house does not require people to live in it, for the simple reason that it is, in itself, a living organism."

Brian frowned as he accepted his plate of sliced blancmange.

"Why not?" The old lady appeared surprised that her word should be doubted. "Do you begrudge a house life?"

They both shook their heads violently and Mrs Brown appeared satisfied with their apparent acquiescence.

"After all, in ordinary houses, what are passages? I will tell you. Intestines. Bowels, if you wish. And the boiler which pumps hot water throughout the body of the house? A heart – what else could it be? In the same way, that mass of pipes and cisterns that reside up in the loft, what are they if not a brain?"

"You have a point," Brian agreed.

"Of course I have," Mrs Brown deposited another slice of blancmange on Rosemary's plate. "But of course I was referring to ordinary houses. This is not an ordinary house by any means. It really lives."

"I would certainly like to meet the builder," Brian said caustically. "He must have been a remarkable chap."

"Builder!" Mrs Brown chuckled. "When did I mention a builder? My dear young man, the house was not built. It grew."

"Nutty as a fruit cake." Rosemary spoke with strong conviction while she sat on Brian's bed.

"True," Brian nodded, "but the idea is rather fascinating."

"Oh, come off it. How can a house grow? And from what? A brick?"

"Wait a minute. In a way a house does grow. It is fathered by an architect and mothered by a builder."

"That's all very well," Rosemary complained, "but that old sausage meant the damned thing grew like a tree. Frankly, she gives me the willies. You know something? I think she's laughing at us. I mean to say, all that business of carving blancmange into thin slices."

"A house is an extension of a man's personality." Brian was thinking out loud. "In its early life it would be innocent, like a new-born baby, but after it had been lived in for a bit . . ." He paused, "then the house would take on an atmosphere . . . could even be haunted."

"Oh, shut up." Rosemary shivered. "I'm expected to sleep here tonight. In any case, as I keep saying, the old thing maintains the house grew."

"Even that makes a kind of mad logic." He grinned, mocking what he assumed to be her pretended fear. "We must reverse the process. The atmosphere came first, the house second."

"I'm going to bed." She got up and sauntered to the door. "If you hear me scream during the night, come a-running."

"Why bother to go?" Brian asked slyly. "If you stay here, I won't have to run anywhere."

"Ha, ha. Funny man. Not in this morgue." She smiled impishly from the doorway. "I'd be imagining all manner of things looking down at me from the ceiling."

Brian lay in his four-poster bed and listened to the house pre- paring for sleep. Woodwork contracted as the temperature dropped; floorboards creaked, window frames made little rattling noises, somewhere a door closed. Sleep began to dull his senses and he became only half-aware of his surroundings; he was poised on the brink of oblivion. Then, as though a bomb had exploded, he was blasted back into full consciousness. A long drawn-out moan had shattered the silence and was coming at him from all directions. He sat up and looked round the room. So far as he could see by the light of the rising moon that filtered through his lace curtains, the room was empty. Suddenly, the groan was repeated. He sprang out of bed, lit his candle, and looked wildly around him. The sound was everywhere – in the walls with their faded pink-rose wallpaper, in the cracked ceiling, the threadbare carpet. He covered his ears with shaking hands, but still the mournful groan continued, invading his brain, seeping down into his very being, until it seemed the entire universe was crying out in anguish. Then, as abruptly as it began, it ceased. A heavy, un- natural silence descended on the house like a great, enveloping blanket. Brian hastily scrambled into his clothes.

"Enough is enough." He spoke aloud. "We're getting out – fast."

Another sound came into being. It began a long way off. A slow, hesitant footstep, married to squeaking floorboards, a laborious picking up and putting down of naked feet, interspersed with a slow slithering which suggested the unseen walker was burdened with the tiredness of centuries. This time there was no doubt as to where the sound was coming from. It was up above. The soft, padding steps passed over the ceiling and once again the house groaned, but now it was a moan of ecstasy, a low cry of fulfilment. Brian opened the bedroom door and crept out into the corridor. The moaning cry and the slithering footsteps merged and became a nightmarish symph- ony, a two-toned serenade of horror. Then, again, all sound ceased and the silence was like a landmine that might explode at any moment. He found himself waiting for the moan, the slithering overhead footsteps to begin all over again – or perhaps something else, something that defied imagination.

He tapped on Rosemary's door, then turned the handle and entered, holding his candle high and calling her name.

"Rosemary, wake up. Rosemary, come on, we're getting out of here."

The flickering candle-flame made great shadows leap across the walls and dance over the ceiling; it cut ragged channels through the darkness until, at last, his questing eye saw the bed. It was empty. The sheets and blankets were twisted up into loose ropes and a pillow lay upon the floor.

"Rosemary!"

He whispered her name and the house chuckled. A low, harsh, gurgling laugh, which made him run from the room, race down the long corridor, until he lurched into the dining-room. An old-fashioned oil lamp stood on the table, illuminating the room with a pale orange light and revealing Mrs Brown, seated in an armchair, calmly darning a sock. She looked up as Brian entered and smiled like a mother whose small son has strayed from his warm bed on a winter's night.

"I would put the candle down, dear," she said, "otherwise you will spill grease all over the carpet."

"Rosemary!" he shouted. "Where is she?"

"There's really no need for you to shout. Despite my advanced years, I am not deaf." She broke the wool, then turned the sock and examined her work with a certain pride. "That's better. Carlo is so hard on his socks." She looked up with a sly smile. "It is only to be expected, of course. He has hard feet."

"Where is she?" Brian set down the candle and moved closer to the old woman, who was now closing her work-basket. "She's not in her room and there are signs of a struggle. What have you done with her?"

Mrs Brown shook her head sadly.

"Questions, questions. How hungry youth is for knowledge. You demand to know the truth and, should I gratify your desire, how distressed you would become. Ignorance is a gift freely offered by the gods and so often it is spurned by misguided mortals. Even I sometimes wish I knew less, but . . ." Her sigh was one of sad resignation. "Time reveals all to those who live long enough. I should go back to bed, dear. The young need their sleep."

Brian advanced a few steps, then spoke in a carefully controlled voice.

"I am going to ask you for the last time, Mrs Brown, or whatever your name is – what have you done with Rosemary?"

She looked up and shook her head in sad reproof.

"Threats! How unwise. A sparrow should never threaten an eagle. It is so futile and such a waste of time."

Mrs Brown carefully placed her work-basket on the floor, then snapped in a surprisingly firm voice: "Carlo!"

There came, from somewhere to Brian's rear, a low, deep growl. Such a menacing sound might have issued from the throat of a large dog whose mistress has been threatened, or a she-wolf protecting her young, but when the young man spun round, he saw Carlo standing a few feet away. The man had his head tilted to one side and his large, yellow teeth were bared as he growled again. His stance was grotesque. He was leaning forward slightly as though preparing to spring and his fingers were curved, so that with their long, pointed nails, they looked uncannily like talons; his cheeks seemed to have shrunk and his black hair lay back over his narrow skull like a sleek, ebony mane.

"Will you believe me?" Mrs Brown said, and her voice was less harsh – much younger. "I have only to say one word and your windpipe will be hanging down your shirt-front."

"You are mad." Brian backed slowly away and Carlo moved forward, matching him step for step. "You are both mad."

"You mean," Mrs Brown came round and joined Carlo, "we are not normal by your standards. That much I grant you. Sanity is only a form of madness favoured by the majority. But I think the time has come for you to meet truth, since you are so eager to make her acquaintance."

"I only want to find Rosemary, then get out of here," Brian said.

"Find your little friend? Perhaps. Leave here? Ah . . ." Mrs Brown looked thoughtful. "That is another matter. But come, there is much for you to see, and please, no heroics. Carlo is on the turn. He is apt to be a little touchy when the moon is full."

They filed out into the hall, Mrs Brown leading the way with Brian following and the grim Carlo bringing up the rear. To the right of a great staircase was a black door and this Mrs Brown unlocked, then entered the room beyond, where she proceeded to light a lamp from Brian's candle.

The light crept outwards in ever-increasing circles as she turned up the wick, revealing oak-panelled walls and a cobweb-festooned ceiling. The room was bare, except for the portrait hanging over a dirt-grimed marble fireplace. To this the young man's eyes were drawn like a pin to a magnet.

The background was jet-black and the face corpse-white; the large black eyes glared an intense hatred for all living things and the thin-lipped mouth was shut tight, but so cunningly had the portrait been painted that Brian had the feeling it might open at any moment.

"My late husband," Mrs Brown stated, "was a partaker of blood."

The statement did not invite comment and Brian made none.

"It must be the best part of five hundred years since they came down from the village," Mrs Brown continued. "Chanting priests looking like black ravens, mewing peasants huddled together like frightened sheep. I recall it was night and the mists shrouded the moors and swirled about their thrice-accursed cross as though it wished to protect us from the menace it represented."

She paused and Brian realised that she looked much younger. The face was filling out, the shoulders were no longer bowed.

"They did not consider I was of great importance," Mrs Brown went on, "so I was merely tied to a tree and flogged, thereby providing entertainment for the herd of human cattle who liked nothing better than to see a woman writhe under the lash. But him. . . . They dug a hole, and laid him flat, having bound his body in cords that were sealed with the dreaded sign. Then they drove a stake through his heart. . . . Fools."

She glared at Brian and clenched her small fists.

"They left him for dead. Dead! His brain still lived. The blood was only symbolic, it was the vital essence we needed – still need: the force that makes the soul reach out for the stars, the hammer that can create beauty out of black depravity."

She went over to the portrait and stroked the white, cruel face with hands that had become long and slender.

"When they buried his beautiful body they planted a seed, and from that seed grew the house. A projection of himself."

"I don't believe you." Brian shook his head. "I won't – can't believe you."

"No!" She laughed and Carlo howled. "Then feel the walls. They are warm, flesh of his flesh. Moist. The body fluids seep out when he is aroused. Look." She pointed to a great double door set in one wall. "Look, the mouth. When I open the lips, food pops in. Succulent, living food and we all benefit. I, Carlo, who sprang from the old people – I still let him roam the moors when the moon is full – and, of course, He. The House. He needs all the sweet essence he can get. He sleeps after meat and no longer moans. I do not like to hear him moan."

"Where is Rosemary?" Brian asked again and knew what must follow.

"She passed through the lips an hour since." Mrs Brown laughed very softly and Carlo made a whining sound. "Now, if you would find her, there is not really much alternative. You must follow her through the great intestines, down into the mighty bowels. Wander and cry out, trudge on and on, until at last your will is broken and He can take from you what he needs."

"You want me to go through those doors?" Brian asked, and there was a glimmer of hope. "Then go wandering through the corridors of an empty house? When I find Rosemary, we will break out."

The woman smiled as she motioned to Carlo.

"Part the lips, Carlo."

The man, if indeed that which crept forward was a man, silently obeyed; the great doors groaned as they swung inwards and Brian saw a murky passage, lined with green tinted walls. A warm, sweet, cloying odour made his stomach heave and he drew back.

"She's waiting for you," Mrs Brown said softly, "and she must be very frightened wandering through the labyrinth, not exactly alone, but I doubt if she will appreciate the company. Most of them will be well digested by now."

Carlo was waiting, his hand on the handle of one door; his eyes were those of a hungry wolf who sees his prey about to be devoured by a lion. Brian, without a sideways glance, passed through the entrance and the doors slammed to behind him.

There were no stairs. The corridors sometimes sloped upwards, at others they spiralled down; there were stretches when the floor was comparatively level, but the corridors were never straight for long. They twisted, crossed other passages, suddenly split, leaving the wanderer with a choice of three or more openings; occasionally they came to a blank end, forcing him to retrace his footsteps. Light was provided by an eerie greenish glow radiating from the walls and ceiling and sometimes this light pulsated, suggesting it originated from some form of decay.

Brian stumbled onwards, shouting Rosemary's name, and his echo mocked him, went racing on ahead until it became a faraway voice calling back along the avenues of time. Once he stumbled and fell against the wall. Instantly, the moist, green surface contracted under his weight and there was an obscene sucking sound when he pulled himself free. A portion of his shirt sleeve remained stuck to the wall and there was a red mark on his arm.

When he had been walking for some thirty minutes he came upon the window passage. There was no other word to describe it, for one wall was lined with windows, each one set about six feet apart, and he gave a little cry of joy, certain this was the place from which he and Rosemary could make their escape. Then he saw – them. Before each window stood one, occasionally two, forms – hideously thin, scarecrow figures that pawed at the window panes with claw-like fingers and emitted little animal whimpers.

Brian approached the first window and gave a quick glance through the grimy panes. He was two floors, if that was the right expression, up, and he saw the lawn then, further out, the moors, all bathed in brilliant moonlight. Even as he watched, a great hound went bounding across the lawn. It cleared the low wall in a single leap, then streaked out across the moor. Something touched Brian's arm and he spun round to face one of the creatures that had silently crept along from the next window. He saw at close quarters the skeleton face covered with brown, wrinkled skin, and the vacant blue eyes that stared up at him with mute, suffering appeal. He judged the man to have been a tramp, or possibly a gypsy, for he wore the remnants of a red shirt and brown corduroy trousers. The claw-hands plucked feebly at his arm, the mouth opened, revealing toothless gums, and a hoarse whisper seeped out.

"The old cow said come in."

"How long have you been here?" Brian asked, uncomfortably aware that a number of other grotesque bundles of rag and bones were leaving their posts by the windows and slithering on naked feet towards him. The whisper came again.

"The old cow said come in."

"Have you seen a young girl?" Brian shouted. "Have any of you seen a girl?"

The man tried to grip his arm, but there was no strength left in the wasted frame and he could only repeat the single phrase:

"The old cow said come in."

They were all clustered round him. Three bore some resemblance to women, although their hair had fallen out, and one, a tall, beanstalk of a creature, kept mumbling: "Pretty boy," while she tried unsuccessfully to fasten her gums into his neck.

"Break the windows!" Brian shouted, pushing them away as gently as he could. "Listen, break the windows, then I'll be able to climb down and fetch help."

"The old cow said come in." The man could only repeat over and over the six ominous words, and a wizened, awful thing, no higher than a child, kept muttering: "Meat," as it tried to fasten its mouth on Brian's right hand.

Unreasoning terror made him strike the creature full in the face and it went crashing back against the wall. Instantly, the green surface bent inwards and a deep sigh ran through the house, making the ghastly pack go slithering along the corridor, their remaining spark of intelligence having presumably warned them this sound was something to be feared. The small, child-size figure was left, stuck to the wall like a fly on gummed paper, and, as the green light pulsated, the creature jerked in unison.

Brian pulled off one of his shoes and smashed the heel against the nearest window-pane. He might just as well have struck a slab of solid rock for all the impression he made, and at last he gave up and continued his search for Rosemary. After an hour of trudging wearily along green-tinted passages, he had no idea how far he had travelled, or if indeed he was just going round in a perpetual circle. He found himself dragging his feet, making the same hesitant, slithering footsteps that had so alarmed him in his bedroom, centuries ago.

The corridors were never silent, for there were always cries, usually some way off, and a strange thudding sound which came into being when the green light pulsated, but these offstage noises became as a murmur when the scream rang out. It was a cry of despair, a call for help, a fear-born prayer, and at once Brian knew who had screamed. He shouted Rosemary's name as he broke into a run, terrified lest he be unable to reach her, at the same time in dread of what he might find. Had she not screamed again he would doubtlessly have taken the wrong passage, but when the second shriek rang out he ran towards the sound and presently came to a kind of circular hall. They were clinging to her like leeches to a drowning horse. Their skeleton hands were tearing her dress, their toothless mouths fouled her flesh, and all the while they squealed like a herd of hungry pigs. He pulled them away and the soulless bodies went hurtling back against vibrating walls; bones snapped like frost-crisp twigs and despairing whimpers rose to an unholy chorus.

He took Rosemary in his arms and she clung to him as though he were life itself, clutching his shoulders in a terrified grip while she cried like a lost child. He murmured soft, unintelligible words, trying to reassure himself as much as her, then screamed at the pack who were again slowly moving in.

"Don't you understand, this is not real. It's the projection of a mad brain. A crazy nightmare. Try to find a way out."

It is doubtful if they heard, let alone understood what he was saying, and those that could still move were edging their way forward like rats whose hunger is greater than their fear.

"Can you walk?" he asked Rosemary and the girl nodded. "Good, then we must make our way downwards. The woman's apartment is on the ground floor and our only hope is to batter those doors in and escape across the lawn."

"It's impossible." Rosemary was clinging to his arm and they were leaving the creatures behind. "This place is a labyrinth. We will wander round and round these corridors until we drop."

"Nonsense." He spoke sharply. "The house can't be all that big and we are young and fit. So long as we go down, we're bound to find the doors."

This was easier said than done. Many corridors sloped down, only to slant up again, but presently they came out into a window passage and found they were somewhere at the rear of the house, but only one floor up.

"Now," Brian kissed Rosemary. "Only one more slope to go and we're there."

"But we're the wrong side of the house," Rosemary complained, "and even if we find the doors, how are you going to break through them?"

"One step at a time. Let's find them first, then, maybe, I'll use you as a battering ram."

It took an hour to find the next downward slope and then only after they had retraced their steps several times, but at last they were moving downwards, Rosemary shivered.

"It's getting colder."

"Yes, and that damned stink is becoming more pronounced. But never mind, we'll soon be there."

They went steadily downwards for another five minutes and then Rosemary began to cry.

"Brian, I can't go on much longer. Surely we've passed the ground floor ages ago? And there's something awful down here. I can feel it."

"It can't be more awful than what's up above," he retorted grimly. "We must go on. There's no turning back unless you want to finish up a zombie."

"Zombie!" She repeated dully.

"What did you imagine those things were, back there? They died long ago and only keep going because the house gives them a sort of half life. Mrs Brown and Carlo appear to be better provided for, but they died centuries ago."

"I can't believe all this." Rosemary shuddered. "How can a place like this exist in the twentieth century?"

"It doesn't. I should imagine we stumbled across the house at the right, or in our case, the wrong time. I suppose you might call it a time-trap."

"I don't know what you are talking about," Rosemary said, then added, "I very rarely do."

The passage was becoming steeper, spiralling round and sloping down until they had difficulty in remaining upright. Then the floor levelled out and after a space of about six feet came to an end.

"Earth." Brian felt the termination wall. "Good, honest earth."

"Earth," Rosemary repeated. "So what?"

Brian raised his eyes ceilingwards and then spoke in a carefully controlled voice. "So far we have been walking on a floor and between walls that are constructed of something very nasty. Right? Now we are facing a wall built or shovelled into place – I don't care – of plain, down to earth – earth. Got it?"

Rosemary nodded. "Yes, so we have got down to the house foundations. But I thought we were looking for the doors."

Brian gripped her shoulders.

"Say that again."

"Say what again? Look, you're hurting me."

He shook her gently. "The first bit."

She thought for a moment. "So we have got down to the house foundations. What's so important about that?"

He released her and went up close to the wall, where he stood for a few minutes examining its surface, then he came back and tilted her chin up so she was looking directly into his eyes.

"Will you try to be very, very brave?"

Fear came rushing back and she shivered.

"Why?"

"Because I am going to break down that wall." He spoke very slowly. "And on the other side we may find something very nasty indeed."

She did not move her head, only continued to gaze up into his eyes.

"Isn't there any other way?" she whispered.

He shook his head.

"None. None whatsoever."

There was a minute of complete silence, then:

"What are you going to use as a shovel?"

He laughed and went back to the wall which he pounded with his fist.

"I could say you have a point there, but I won't. Let's take an inventory. What have we that is pick- and shovel-worthy? Our hands, of course. Shoes? Maybe." He felt in his pocket and produced a bunch of keys and a penknife. "This might start things going, then I can pull the loose stuff out with my hands."

He sank the penknife blade into the soft, moist earth and traced the rough outline of a door, then he began to deepen the edges, digging out little lumps of earth that fell to the ground like gobbets of chewed meat. Brian then removed his shoes and used the heels to claw out a jagged hole.

"If I can work my way through," he explained, "it should be an easy matter to pull the entire thing down."

He dug steadily for another five minutes, then a glimmer of light appeared and, after a final effort, he was able to look through an opening roughly six inches in diameter.

"What can you see?" Rosemary asked, her tone suggesting she would rather not know.

"It seems to be some kind of large cave and it's lit up with that green light, just like the passages. I can see hunks of rock lying about, but not much else. Well, here goes.''

He thrust his right hand through the aperture, curled his fingers round the inner wall and pulled. A large chunk came away, then he began to work with both hands, pulling, clawing, and the entire wall came tumbling down. He wiped his hands on already stained trousers, then put on his shoes.

"Now," he said, "for the moment of truth."

They were in a rough, circular cavern; it was perhaps twenty feet in diameter and an equal distance in height. Loose lumps of rock littered the floor, but there was no sign of anyone – alive or dead – and Brian gave a prolonged sigh of relief.

"I don't know what I expected to see, but thank heavens, I don't see it. Now, we must start looking for a way out. I'll go round the walls, you examine the floor. Never know, there might be a hole going down still further."

He turned his attention to the irregular walls, leaving Rosemary to wander miserably among the large rocks and boulders that formed a kind of fence round the centre of the cavern. He looked upwards and saw, some twenty feet from the ground, a fairly large hole. Deciding it would be worth investigating, he began to ascend the wall and found the task easier than he had supposed, for projecting rocks made excellent footholds. In a few minutes he had reached his objective. The hole was in fact a small cave that was about seven feet high and five across, but alas there was no exit.

He was about to descend and continue his search elsewhere when Rosemary screamed. Never before had he realised a human throat was capable of expressing such abject terror. Shriek after shriek rang out and re-echoed against the walls, until it seemed an army of banshees were forecasting a million deaths. He looked down and saw the girl standing just inside the fence of stones looking down at something he could not see; her eyes were dilated and seemed frozen into an expression of indescribable horror.

Brian scrambled down the wall and ran over to her; when he laid hands on her shoulders she flinched as though his touch were a branding iron, then her final shriek was cut off and she slid silently to the floor.

A few feet away there was a slight indentation, a shallow hole, and he experienced a terrifying urge not to look into it, but he knew he must, if for no other reason than a strange, compelling curiosity.

He dragged Rosemary well back and left her lying against one wall, then he returned, creeping forward very slowly, walking on tip-toe. At last he was on the brink of hell. He looked down.

Horror ran up his body in cold waves; it left an icy lump in his stomach and he wanted to be sick only he had not the strength. He had to stare down, concentrate all his senses and try to believe.

The head bore a resemblance to the portrait in Mrs Brown's ante-room; it was dead-white, bloated, suggesting an excess of nourish-ment consumed over a very long period. The hair was at least six feet in length and was spread out over the loose rock like a monstrous shroud. But the torso and arms grew out of the ground. The shoulders and part of the forearms were flesh, but further down the white skin assumed a greyish colour and, lower still, gradually merged into solid rock. Most horrifying of all was the profusion of fat, greenish, tubelike growths that sprouted out from under forearms and neck and, so far as Brian could see, the whole of the back. Obscene roots spreading out in every direction until they disap-peared into the black earth, writhing and pulsating, carrying the vital fluid that circulated round the house.

The eyes were closed, but the face moved. The thin lips grimaced, creating temporary furrows in the flabby fat. Brian withdrew from the hole – the grave – and at last his stomach had its way and allowed him to be violently sick. By the time he returned to Rosemary, he felt old and drained of strength. She was just returning to consciousness and he smoothed back her hair.

"Are you fit enough to talk?" he asked.

She gave a little strangled gasp.

"That . . . that thing . . ."

"Yes, I know. Now listen. I am going to take you up there," He pointed to the cave set high up on the opposite wall. "You'll be all right there while I do what must be done."

"I don't understand." She shook her head. "What must you do?"

"Mrs Brown told me her husband was a partaker of blood. In other words, a vampire, and centuries ago the local lads did the traditional things and drove a stake through his heart. She said something else. It wasn't his body they should have destroyed, but his brain. Don't you see? This house, the entire set-up, is a nightmare produced by a monstrous intelligence?"

"I'll believe anything." Rosemary got to her feet. "Just get me out of here. I'd rather walk the passages than spend another minute with that . . . thing."

"No." He shook his head. "I must destroy the brain. The only point is, when I do . . ." He looked round the cavern, then over to the entrance of the green-walled passage. ". . . anything may happen."

"What about you?" she asked.

"So soon as the job is finished, I'll join you."

He might have added, "If I can," but instead guided Rosemary to the wall and assisted her up to the cave.

"Now," he instructed, "stay well back and don't, in any circumstances, so much as put your nose outside. Understand?"

"God, I'm petrified," she said.

"Don't let it get around," he nodded grimly, "but so am I."

He came back to the hole like a released spirit returning to hell. As he drew nearer, the terror grew until it required a desperate effort to raise one foot and put it down before the other. Only the memory of Rosemary up there in the cave kept his spark of courage alive. At last he again gazed down at that horrible growth; it groaned and the sound raced round the cavern and up through the house. The face grimaced and twitched, while the green tubes writhed like a nest of gorged worms. Brian selected a rock which was a little larger than the bloated head and, gripping it in both hands, prepared to hurl it down. He had tensed his muscles, and was turning slightly to one side, when the eyelids flicked back and he was staring into two pools of black hate.

The shock was so intense he automatically slackened his grip and the rock slid from his fingers and went crashing down somewhere behind him. The mouth opened and a vibrant whisper went racing up through the house.

"Elizabeth . . . Carlo . . ."

The words came out slowly, rather like a series of intelligible sighs, but from all around, from the walls, the floor, the high roof – never from the moving lips.

"Would . . . you . . . destroy . . . that . . . which . . . you . . . do . . . not . . . understand?"

Brian was fumbling for the rock, but he paused and the whispering voice went on.

"I . . . must . . . continue . . . to . . . be . . . I . . . must . . . grow . . . fill . . . the . . . universe . . . consume . . . take . . . strength . . ."

A padding of fast-running paws came from the passage entrance and a woman's voice was calling out.

"Petros, drink of his essence . . . will him into walking death."

There was a hint of fear in the terrible eyes. The whispering voice again ran through the house.

"He . . . is . . . an . . . unbeliever . . . he . . . is . . . the . . . young . . . of . . . a . . . new . . . age . . . why . . . did . . . you . . . let . . . him . . . through . . .?"

The great dog leapt over the loose earth and emerged from the passageway; it was black as midnight, like a solid shadow newly escaped from a wall, and it padded round the cavern before jumping up on to a boulder and preparing to leap. Brian hurled a rock at it and struck the broad, black snout. The beast howled and fell back as Mrs Brown spoke from the entrance.

"You will not keep that up for long. Carlo cannot be killed by the likes of you."

She had been transformed. The once white hair was now a rich auburn, the face was as young as today, but the glorious eyes reflected the evil of a million yesterdays. She wore a black evening dress that left her arms and back bare and Brian could only stare at her, forgetting that which lay behind him and Rosemary, up in the cave. All he could see was white flesh and inviting eyes.

"Come away," the low, husky voice said. "Leave Petros to his dream. He cannot harm you and it would be such a waste if Carlo were to rip your nice body to shreds. Think of what I can offer. An eternity of bliss. A million lifetimes of pleasure. Come."

He took one step forward, then another, and it seemed he was walking into a forbidden dream; all the secret desires that up to that moment he had not realised existed flared up and became exciting possibilities. Then, just as he was about to surrender, go running to her like a child to a beautiful toy, her voice lashed across his consciousness.

"Carlo . . . now."

The dog came snarling over the rocks and Brian fell back, suddenly fully aware of the pending danger. He snatched up a piece of jagged rock and threw it at the oncoming beast. He hit it just above the right ear, then began to hurl stones as fast as he could pick them up. The dog leapt from side to side, snarling with pain and rage, but Brian realised it was coming forward more than it retreated and knew a few minutes, at the most, must elapse before he felt those fangs at his throat. By chance his hands closed round the original small boulder – and it was then he understood what must be done.

He raised the rock high above his head, made as though to hurl it at the dog, which momentarily recoiled, then threw it back – straight at the head of Petros.

The house shrieked. One long-drawn-out scream and the dog was no longer there; instead, Carlo ran towards his mistress, making plaintive, guttural cries, before sinking down before her, plucking frantically at the hem of her black dress.

Brian looked back and down into the hole and saw that the head was shattered and what remained of the flesh was turning black. The green tubes were now only streaks of deflated tissue and the life-giving fluid no longer flowed up into the body of the house. From up above came a deep rumbling sound and a great splintering, as though a mountain of rocks were grinding together. Brian ran towards the far wall and, quickly scrambling up into the cave, found Rosemary waiting to welcome him with outstretched arms.

"Keep down," he warned. "All hell is going to break loose at any moment."

They lay face down upon the floor, and Brian had to raise his head to see the final act. The green light was fading, but before it went he had a last glimpse of the woman staring blankly at the place where Petros had lain. She was patting Carlo's head. Then the ceiling came down and for a while there was only darkness filled with a mighty rumbling and crashing of falling rock. Fantasy tumbling down into the pit of reality. Time passed and the air cleared as the dust settled and presently, like a glimmer of hope in the valley of despair, a beam of light struck the entrance to the cave. Brian looked out, then up. Twenty feet above was a patch of blue sky.

They came up from the pit, bruised, clothes torn, but happy to be alive. They trudged hand-in-hand out across the moors and after a while looked back to see a pile of rocks that, at this distance, could have been mistaken for a ruined house.

"We will never talk about this to anyone," Brian said. "One does not talk about one's nightmares. They are so ridiculous in the light of day."

Rosemary nodded. "We slept. We dreamed. Now we are awake."

They walked on. Two figures that distance diminished until they became minute specks on a distant horizon. Then they were gone.

The early morning breeze caressed the summer grass, harebells smiled up at a benign sky and a pair of rabbits played hide and seek among the fallen rocks. To all outward appearances the moors were at peace.

Then a rabbit screamed and a stoat raised blood-dripping jaws.

KARL EDWARD WAGNER

Beyond Any Measure

KARL EDWARD WAGNER WAS ONE of the genre's finest practitioners of horror and dark fantasy, and his untimely death in 1994 robbed the field of one of its major talents.

Born in Knoxville, Tennessee, Wagner trained as a psychiatrist before becoming a multiple British Fantasy and World Fantasy Award-winning author, editor and publisher. His early writing included a series of fantasy novels and stories featuring Kane, the Mystic Swordsman. His first novel, *Darkness Weaves With Many Shades* (1970), introduced the unusually intelligent and brutal warrior-sorcerer, and Kane's adventures continued in *Death Angel's Shadow, Bloodstone, Dark Crusade* and the collections *Night Winds* and *The Book of Kane*. More recently, the complete Kane novels and stories have been collected in two volumes by Night Shade Books, *Gods in Darkness* and *The Midnight Sun*.

In the early 1970s Wagner started the acclaimed Carcosa small-press imprint with friends David Drake and Jim Groce. He also edited three volumes of Robert E. Howard's definitive Conan adventures and continued the exploits of two of Howard's characters, Conan and Bran Mak Morn respectively, in the novels *The Road of Kings* and *Legion from the Shadows*. He also edited three *Echoes of Valor* heroic-fantasy anthologies and a collection of medical horror stories, *Intensive Scare*. He took over the editing of *The Year's Best Horror*

Stories in 1980 from Gerald W. Page and for the next fourteen years turned it into one of the genre's finest showcases.

Wagner's own superior short horror tales were collected in *In a Lonely Place, Why Not You and I?* and *Unthreatened by the Morning Light.* A tribute collection entitled *Exorcisms and Ecstasies* was published in 1997.

As the author revealed: " 'Beyond Any Measure' explores the relationships of eroticism and horror – and the title is from Richard O'Brien's *The Rocky Horror Picture Show.* 'Erotic nightmares beyond any measure and sensual daydreams to treasure forever'.

"It was written as an intended screenplay, and the story contains cinematic references and homages beyond counting. Fans of *The Avengers* television series will be quick to recognize the play on the infamous 'A Touch of Brimstone' episode, shown only in later reruns on American TV . . ."

The sensual story which follows justifiably won a World Fantasy Award for Best Novella.

I

"IN THE DREAM I find myself alone in a room. I hear musical chimes – a sort of music-box tune – and I look around to see where the sound is coming from.

"I'm in a bedroom. Heavy curtains close off the windows, and it's quite dark, but I can sense that the furnishings are entirely antique – late Victorian, I think. There's a large four-poster bed, with its curtains drawn. Beside the bed is a small night table upon which a candle is burning. It is from here that the music seems to be coming.

"I walk across the room toward the bed, and as I stand beside it I see a gold watch resting on the night table next to the candlestick. The music-box tune is coming from the watch, I realize. It's one of those old pocket-watch affairs with a case that opens. The case is open now, and I see that the watch's hands are almost at midnight. I sense that on the inside of the watchcase there will be a picture, and I pick up the watch to see whose picture it is.

"The picture is obscured with a red smear. It's fresh blood.

"I look up in sudden fear. From the bed, a hand is pulling aside the curtain.

"That's when I wake up."

"Bravo!" applauded someone.

Lisette frowned momentarily, then realized that the comment was directed toward another of the chattering groups crowded into the gallery. She sipped her champagne; she must be a bit tight, or she'd never have started talking about the dreams.

"What do you think, Dr Magnus?"

It was the gala reopening of Covent Garden. The venerable fruit, flower and vegetable market, preserved from the demolition crew, had been renovated into an airy mall of expensive shops and galleries: "London's new shopping experience." Lisette thought it an unhappy hybrid of born-again Victorian exhibition hall and trendy "shoppes." Let the dead past bury its dead. She wondered what they might make of the old Billingsgate fish market, should SAVE win its fight to preserve that landmark, as now seemed unlikely.

"Is this dream, then, a recurrent one, Miss Seyrig?"

She tried to read interest or skepticism in Dr Magnus' pale blue eyes. They told her nothing.

"Recurrent enough."

To make me mention it to Danielle, she finished in her thoughts. Danielle Borland shared a flat – she'd stopped terming it an apartment even in her mind – with her in a row of terrace houses in Bloomsbury, within an easy walk of London University. The gallery was Maitland Reddin's project; Danielle was another. Whether Maitland really thought to make a business of it, or only intended to showcase his many friends' not always evident talents was not open to discussion. His gallery in Knightsbridge was certainly successful, if that meant anything.

"How often is that?" Dr Magnus touched his glass to his blonde-bearded lips. He was drinking only Perrier water, and, at that, was using his glass for little more than to gesture.

"I don't know. Maybe half a dozen times since I can remember. And then, that many again since I came to London."

"You're a student at London University, I believe Danielle said?"

"That's right. In art. I'm over here on fellowship."

Danielle had modelled for an occasional session – Lisette now was certain it was solely from a desire to display her body rather than due to any financial need – and when a muttered profanity at a dropped brush disclosed a common American heritage, the two *émigrés* had rallied at a pub afterward to exchange news and views. Lisette's bed-sit near the Museum was impossible, and Danielle's roommate had just skipped to the Continent with two months' owing. By closing time it was settled.

"How's your glass?"

Danielle, finding them in the crowd, shook her head in mock dismay and refilled Lisette's glass before she could cover it with her hand.

"And you, Dr Magnus?"

"Quite well, thank you."

"Danielle, let me give you a hand?" Maitland had charmed the two of them into acting as hostesses for his opening.

"Nonsense, darling. When you see me starting to pant with the heat, then call up the reserves. Until then, do keep Dr Magnus from straying away to the other parties."

Danielle swirled off with her champagne bottle and her smile. The gallery, christened "Such Things May Be" after Richard Burton (*not* Liz Taylor's ex, Danielle kept explaining, and got laughs each time), was ajostle with friends and well-wishers – as were most of the shops tonight: private parties with evening dress and champagne, only a scattering of displaced tourists, gaping and photographing. She and Danielle were both wearing slit-to-thigh crepe de Chine evening gowns and could have passed for sisters: Lisette blonde, green-eyed, with a dust of freckles; Danielle light brunette, hazel-eyed, acclimated to the extensive facial makeup London women favored; both tall without seeming coltish, and close enough of a size to wear each other's clothes.

"It must be distressing to have the same nightmare over and again," Dr Magnus prompted her.

"There have been others as well. Some recurrent, some not. Similar in that I wake up feeling like I've been through the sets of some old Hammer film."

"I gather you were not actually troubled with such nightmares until recently?"

"Not really. Being in London seems to have triggered them. I suppose it's repressed anxieties over being in a strange city." It was bad enough that she'd been taking some of Danielle's pills in order to seek dreamless sleep.

"Is this, then, your first time in London, Miss Seyrig?"

"It is." She added, to seem less the typical American student: "Although my family was English."

"Your parents?"

"My mother's parents were both from London. They emigrated to the States just after World War 1."

"Then this must have been rather a bit like coming home for you."

"Not really. I'm the first of our family to go overseas. And I have no memory of Mother's parents. Grandmother Keswicke died the morning I was born." Something Mother never was able to work through emotionally, Lisette added to herself.

"And have you consulted a physician concerning these nightmares?"

"I'm afraid your National Health Service is a bit more than I can cope with." Lisette grimaced at the memory of the night she had tried to explain to a Pakistani intern why she wanted sleeping medications.

She suddenly hoped her words hadn't offended Dr Magnus, but then, he scarcely looked the type who would approve of socialized medicine. Urbane, perfectly at ease in formal evening attire, he reminded her somewhat of a blonde-bearded Peter Cushing. Enter Christopher Lee, in black cape, she mused, glancing toward the door. For that matter, she wasn't at all certain just what sort of doctor Dr Magnus might be. Danielle had insisted she talk with him, very likely had insisted that Maitland invite him to the private opening: "The man has such *insight*! And he's written a number of books on dreams and the subconscious – and not just rehashes of Freudian silliness!"

"Are you going to be staying in London for some time, Miss Seyrig?"

"At least until the end of the year."

"Too long a time to wait to see whether these bad dreams will go away once you're back home in San Francisco, don't you agree? It can't be very pleasant for you, and you really should look after yourself."

Lisette made no answer. *She* hadn't told Dr Magnus she was from San Francisco. So then, Danielle had already talked to him about her.

Dr Magnus smoothly produced his card, discreetly offered it to her. "I should be most happy to explore this further with you on a professional level, should you so wish."

"I don't really think it's worth . . ."

"Of course it is, my dear. Why otherwise would we be talking? Perhaps next Tuesday afternoon? Is there a convenient time?"

Lisette slipped his card into her handbag. If nothing else, perhaps he could supply her with some barbs or something. "Three?"

"Three it is, then."

II

The passageway was poorly lighted, and Lisette felt a vague sense of dread as she hurried along it, holding the hem of her nightgown away from the gritty filth beneath her bare feet. Peeling scabs of wallpaper blotched the leprous plaster, and, when she held the candle close, the gouges and scratches that patterned the walls with insane graffiti seemed disquietingly nonrandom. Against the mottled plaster, her figure threw a double shadow: distorted, one crouching forward, the other following.

A full-length mirror panelled one segment of the passageway, and Lisette paused to study her reflection. Her face appeared frightened, her blonde hair in disorder. She wondered at her nightgown – pale, silken, billowing, of an antique mode – not remembering how she came to be wearing it. Nor could she think how it was that she had come to this place.

Her reflection puzzled her. Her hair seemed longer than it should be, trailing down across her breasts. Her finely chiselled features, prominent jawline, straight nose – her face, except the expression, was not hers: lips fuller, more sensual, redder than her lip-gloss, glinted; teeth fine and white. Her green eyes, intense beneath level brows, cat-cruel, yearning.

Lisette released the hem of her gown, raised her fingers to her reflection in wonder. Her fingers passed through the glass, touched the face beyond.

Not a mirror. A doorway. Of a crypt.

The mirror-image fingers that rose to her face twisted in her hair, pulled her face forward. Glass-cold lips bruised her own. The dank breath of the tomb flowed into her mouth.

Dragging herself from the embrace, Lisette felt a scream rip from her throat . . .

. . . And Danielle was shaking her awake.

III

The business card read *Dr Ingmar Magnus*, followed simply by *Consultations* and a Kensington address. Not Harley Street, at any rate. Lisette considered it for the hundredth time, watching for street names on the corners of buildings as she walked down Kensington Church Street from the Notting Hill Gate station. No clue as to what type of doctor, nor what sort of consultations; wonderfully vague, and just the thing to circumvent licensing laws, no doubt.

Danielle had lent her one of his books to read; *The Self Reborn*, put out by one of those minuscule scholarly publishers clustered about the British Museum. Lisette found it a bewildering *mélange* of occult philosophy and lunatic-fringe theory – all evidently having something to do with reincarnation – and gave it up after the first chapter. She had decided not to keep the appointment, until her nightmare Sunday night had given force to Danielle's insistence.

Lisette wore a loose silk blouse above French designer jeans and ankle-strap sandal-toe high heels. The early summer heat wave now threatened rain, and she would have to run for it if the grey skies made good. She turned into Holland Street, passed the recently closed Equinox bookshop, where Danielle had purchased various works by Aleister Crowley. A series of back streets – she consulted her map of Central London – brought her to a modestly respectable row of nineteenth-century brick houses, now done over into offices and flats. She checked the number on the brass plaque with her card, sucked in her breath and entered.

Lisette hadn't known what to expect. She wouldn't have been surprised, knowing some of Danielle's friends, to have been greeted with clouds of incense, Eastern music, robed initiates. Instead she found a disappointingly mundane waiting room, rather small but expensively furnished, where a pretty Eurasian receptionist took her name and spoke into an intercom. Lisette noted that there was no one else – patients? clients? – in the waiting room. She glanced at her watch and noticed she was several minutes late.

"Please do come in, Miss Seyrig." Dr Magnus stepped out of his office and ushered her inside. Lisette had seen a psychiatrist briefly a few years before, at her parents' demand, and Dr Magnus's office suggested the same – from the tasteful, relaxed decor, the shelves of scholarly books, down to the traditional psychoanalyst's couch. She took a chair beside the modern, rather carefully arranged desk, and Dr Magnus seated himself comfortably in the leather swivel chair behind it.

"I almost didn't come," Lisette began, somewhat aggressively.

"I'm very pleased that you did decide to come." Dr Magnus smiled reassuringly. "It doesn't require a trained eye to see that something is troubling you. When the unconscious tries to speak to us, it is foolhardy to attempt to ignore its message."

"Meaning that I may be cracking up?"

"I'm sure that must concern you, my dear. However, very often dreams such as yours are evidence of the emergence of a new level of self-awareness – sort of growing pains of the psyche, if you will – and not to be considered a negative experience by any means. They distress you only because you do not understand them – even as a child kept in ignorance through sexual repression is frightened by the changes of puberty. With your cooperation, I hope to help you come to understand the changes of your growing self-awareness, for it is only through a complete realization of one's self that one can achieve personal fulfillment and thereby true inner peace."

"I'm afraid I can't afford to undergo analysis just now."

"Let me begin by emphasizing to you that I am not suggesting psychoanalysis; I do not in the least consider you to be neurotic, Miss Seyrig. What I strongly urge is an *exploration* of your unconsciousness – a discovery of your whole self. My task is only to guide you along the course of your self-discovery, and for this privilege I charge no fee."

"I hadn't realized the National Health Service was this inclusive."

Dr Magnus laughed easily. "It isn't, of course. My work is supported by a private foundation. There are many others who wish to learn certain truths of our existence, to seek answers where mundane science has not yet so much as realized there are questions. In that regard I am simply another paid researcher, and the results of my investigations are made available to those who share with us this yearning to see beyond the stultifying boundaries of modern science."

He indicated the book-lined wall behind his desk. Much of one shelf appeared to contain books with his own name prominent upon their spines.

"Do you intend to write a book about me?" Lisette meant to put more of a note of protest in her voice.

"It is possible that I may wish to record some of what we discover together, my dear. But only with scrupulous discretion, and, needless to say, only with your complete permission."

"My dreams." Lisette remembered the book of his that she had tried to read. "Do you consider them to be evidence of some previous incarnation?"

"Perhaps. We can't be certain until we explore them further. Does the idea of reincarnation smack too much of the occult to your liking, Miss Seyrig? Perhaps we should speak in more fashionable terms of Jungian archetypes, genetic memory or mental telepathy. The fact that the phenomenon has so many designations is ample proof that dreams of a previous existence are a very real part of the unconscious mind. It is undeniable that many people have experienced, in dreams or under hypnosis, memories that cannot possibly arise from their personal experience. Whether you believe that the immortal soul leaves the physical body at death to be reborn in the living embryo, or prefer to attribute it to inherited memories engraved upon DNA, or whatever explanation – this is a very real phenomenon and has been observed throughout history.

"As a rule, these memories of past existence are entirely buried within the unconscious. Almost everyone has experienced *déjà vu*. Subjects under hypnosis have spoken in languages and archaic dialects of which their conscious mind has no knowledge, have recounted in detail memories of previous lives. In some cases these submerged memories burst forth as dreams; in these instances, the memory is usually one of some emotionally laden experience, something too potent to remain buried. I believe that this is the case with your nightmares – the fact that they are recurrent being evidence of some profound significance in the events they recall."

Lisette wished for a cigarette; she'd all but stopped buying cigarettes with British prices, and from the absence of ashtrays here, Dr Magnus was a nonsmoker.

"But why have these nightmares only lately become a problem?"

"I think I can explain that easily enough. Your forebears were from London. The dreams became a problem after you arrived in London. While it is usually difficult to define any relationship between the subject and the remembered existence, the timing and the force of your dream regressions would seem to indicate that you may be the reincarnation of someone – an ancestress, perhaps – who lived here in London during this past century."

"In that case, the nightmares should go away when I return to the States."

"Not necessarily. Once a doorway to the unconscious is opened, it is not so easily closed again. Moreover, you say that you had experienced these dreams on rare occasions prior to your coming here. I would suggest that what you are experiencing is a natural process – a submerged part of your self is seeking expression, and it would be unwise to deny this shadow stranger within you. I might further argue that your presence here in London is hardly coincidence – that your decision to study here was determined by that part of you who emerges in these dreams."

Lisette decided she wasn't ready to accept such implications just now. "What do you propose?"

Dr Magnus folded his hands as neatly as a bishop at prayer. "Have you ever undergone hypnosis?"

"No." She wished she hadn't made that sound like two syllables.

"It has proved to be extraordinarily efficacious in a great number of cases such as your own, my dear. Please do try to put from your mind the ridiculous trappings and absurd mumbo-jumbo with which the popular imagination connotes hypnotism. Hypnosis is no more than a technique through which we may release the entirety of the unconscious mind to free expression, unrestricted by the countless artificial barriers that make us strangers to ourselves."

"You want to hypnotize me?" The British inflection came to her, turning her statement into both question and protest.

"With your fullest cooperation, of course. I think it best. Through regressive hypnosis we can explore the significance of these dreams that trouble you, discover the shadow stranger within your self. Remember – this is a part of *you* that cries out for conscious expression. It is only through the full realization of one's identity, of one's total self, that true inner tranquillity may be achieved. Know thyself, and you will find peace."

"Know myself?"

"Precisely. You must put aside this false sense of guilt, Miss Seyrig. You are not possessed by some alien and hostile force. These dreams, these memories of another existence – this is *you*."

IV

"Some bloody weirdo made a pass at me this afternoon," Lisette confided.

"On the tube, was it?" Danielle stood on her toes, groping along the top of their bookshelf. Freshly showered, she was wearing only a lace-trimmed teddy – cami-knickers, they called them in the shops here – and her straining thigh muscles shaped her buttocks nicely.

"In Kensington, actually. After I had left Dr Magnus's office." Lisette was lounging in an old satin slip she'd found at a stall in Church Street. They were drinking Bristol Cream out of brandy snifters. It was an intimate sort of evening they loved to share together, when not in the company of Danielle's various friends.

"I was walking down Holland Street, and there was this seedy-looking creep all dressed out in punk regalia, pressing his face against the door where that Equinox bookshop used to be. I made the mistake of glancing at him as I passed, and he must have seen my reflection in the glass, because he spun right around, looked straight at me, and said: 'Darling! What a lovely surprise to see you!'"

Lisette sipped her sherry. "Well. I gave him my hardest stare, and would you believe the creep just stood there smiling like he knew me, and so I yelled, 'Piss off!' in my loudest American accent, and he just froze there with his mouth hanging open."

"Here it is," Danielle announced. "I'd shelved it beside Roland Franklyn's *We Pass from View* – that's another you ought to read. I must remember someday to return it to that cute Liverpool writer who lent it to me."

She settled cozily beside Lisette on the couch, handed her a somewhat smudged paperback, and resumed her glass of sherry. The book was entitled *More Stately Mansions: Evidences of the Infinite* by Dr Ingmar Magnus, and bore an affectionate inscription from the author to Danielle. "This is the first. The later printings had two of his studies deleted; I can't imagine why. But these are the sort of sessions he was describing to you."

"He wants to put *me* in one of his books," Lisette told her with an extravagant leer. "Can a woman trust a man who writes such ardent inscriptions to place her under hypnosis?"

"Dr Magnus is a perfect gentleman," Danielle assured her, somewhat huffily. "He's a distinguished scholar and is thoroughly dedicated to his research. And besides, I've let him hypnotize me on a few occasions."

"I didn't know that. Whatever for?"

"Dr Magnus is always seeking suitable subjects. I was fascinated by his work, and when I met him at a party I offered to undergo hypnosis."

"What happened?"

Danielle seemed envious. "Nothing worth writing about, I'm afraid. He said I was either too thoroughly integrated, or that my previous lives were too deeply buried. That's often the case, he says, which is why absolute proof of reincarnation is so difficult to demonstrate. After a few sessions I decided I couldn't spare the time to try further."

"But what was it like?"

"As adventurous as taking a nap. No caped Svengali staring into my eyes. No lambent girasol ring. No swirling lights. Quite dull, actually. Dr Magnus simply lulls you to sleep."

"Sounds safe enough. So long as I don't get molested walking back from his office."

Playfully, Danielle stroked her hair. "You hardly look the punk rock type. You haven't chopped off your hair with garden shears and dyed the stubble green. And not a single safety pin through your cheek."

"Actually I suppose he may not have been a punk rocker. Seemed a bit too old, and he wasn't garish enough. It's just that he was wearing a lot of black leather, and he had gold earrings and some sort of medallion."

"In front of the Equinox, did you say? How curious."

"Well, I think I gave him a good start. I glanced in a window to see whether he was trying to follow me, but he was just standing there looking stunned."

"*Might* have been an honest mistake. Remember the old fellow at Midge and Fiona's party who kept insisting he knew you?"

"And who was pissed out of his skull. Otherwise he might have been able to come up with a more original line."

Lisette paged through *More Stately Mansions* while Danielle selected a Tangerine Dream album from the stack and placed it on her stereo at low volume. The music seemed in keeping with the grey drizzle of the night outside and the coziness within their sitting room. Seeing she was busy reading, Danielle poured sherry for them both and stood studying the bookshelves – a hodgepodge of occult and metaphysical topics stuffed together with art books and recent paperbacks in no particular order. Wedged between Aleister Crowley's *Magick in Theory and Practice* and *How I Discovered My Infinite Self* by "An Initiate," was Dr Magnus's most recent book, *The Shadow Stranger*. She pulled it down, and Dr Magnus stared thoughtfully from the back of the dust jacket.

"Do you believe in reincarnation?" Lisette asked her.

"I do. Or rather, I do some of the time." Danielle stood behind the couch and bent over Lisette's shoulder to see where she was reading. "Midge Vaughn assures me that in a previous incarnation I was hanged for witchcraft."

"Midge should be grateful she's living in the twentieth century."

"Oh, Midge says we were sisters in the same coven and were hanged together; that's the reason for our close affinity."

"I'll bet Midge says that to all the girls."

"Oh, I like Midge." Danielle sipped her sherry and considered the rows of spines. "Did you say that man was wearing a medallion? Was it a swastika or that sort of thing?"

"No. It was something like a star in a circle. And he wore rings on every finger."

"Wait! Kind of greasy black hair slicked back from a widow's peak to straight over his collar in back? Eyebrows curled up into points like they've been waxed?"

"That's it."

"Ah, Mephisto!"

"Do you know him, then?"

"Not really. I've just seen him a time or two at the Equinox and a few other places. He reminds me of some ham actor playing Mephistopheles. Midge spoke to him once when we were by there, but I gather he's not part of her particular coven. Probably hadn't heard that the Equinox had closed. Never impressed me as a masher; very likely he actually did mistake you for someone."

"Well, they do say that everyone has a double. I wonder if mine is walking somewhere about London, being mistaken for me?"

"And no doubt giving some unsuspecting classmate of yours a resounding slap on the face."

"What if I met her suddenly?"

"Met your double – your *Doppelgänger*? Remember William Wilson? Disaster, darling – *disaster*!"

V

There really wasn't much to it; no production at all. Lisette felt nervous, a bit silly and perhaps a touch cheated.

"I want you to relax," Dr Magnus told her. "All you have to do is just relax."

That's what her gynecologist always said, too, Lisette thought with a sudden tenseness. She lay on her back on Dr Magnus's analyst's couch: her head on a comfortable cushion, legs stretched primly out on the leather upholstery (she'd deliberately worn jeans again), fingers clenched damply over her tummy. A white gown instead of jeans, and I'll be ready for my coffin, she mused uncomfortably.

"Fine. That's it. You're doing fine, Lisette. Very fine. Just relax. Yes, just relax, just like that. Fine, that's it. Relax."

Dr Magnus's voice was a quiet monotone, monotonously repeating soothing encouragements. He spoke to her tirelessly, patiently, slowly dissolving her anxiety.

"You feel sleepy, Lisette. Relaxed and sleepy. Your breathing is slow and relaxed, slow and relaxed. Think about your breathing now, Lisette. Think how slow and sleepy and deep each breath comes. You're breathing deeper, and you're feeling sleepier. Relax and sleep, Lisette, breathe and sleep. Breathe and sleep . . ."

She *was* thinking about her breathing. She counted the breaths; the slow monotonous syllables of Dr Magnus's voice seemed to blend into her breathing like a quiet, tuneless lullaby. She *was* sleepy, for that matter, and it was very pleasant to relax here, listening to that dim, droning murmur while he talked on and on. How much longer until the end of the lecture . . .

"You are asleep now, Lisette. You are asleep, yet you can still hear my voice. Now you are falling deeper, deeper, deeper into a pleasant, relaxed sleep, Lisette. Deeper and deeper asleep. Can you still hear my voice?"

"Yes."

"You are asleep, Lisette. In a deep, deep sleep. You will remain in this deep sleep until I shall count to three. As I count to three, you will slowly arise from your sleep until you are fully awake once again. Do you understand?"

"Yes."

"But when you hear me say the word *amber,* you will again fall into a deep, deep sleep, Lisette, just as you are asleep now. Do you understand?"

"Yes."

"Listen to me as I count, Lisette. One. Two. Three."

Lisette opened her eyes. For a moment her expression was blank, then a sudden confusion. She looked at Dr Magnus seated beside her, then smiled ruefully. "I was asleep, I'm afraid. Or was I . . .?"

"You did splendidly, Miss Seyrig." Dr Magnus beamed reassurance. "You passed into a simple hypnotic state, and as you can see now, there was no more cause for concern than in catching an afternoon nap."

"But I'm sure I just dropped off." Lisette glanced at her watch. Her appointment had been for three, and it was now almost four o'clock.

"Why not just settle back and rest some more, Miss Seyrig. That's it, relax again. All you need is to rest a bit, just a pleasant rest."

Her wrist fell back onto the cushions, as her eyes fell shut.

"Amber."

Dr Magnus studied her calm features for a moment. "You are asleep now, Lisette. Can you hear me?"

"Yes."

"I want you to relax, Lisette. I want you to fall deeper, deeper, deeper into sleep. Deep, deep sleep. Far, far, far into sleep."

He listened to her breathing, then suggested: "You are thinking of your childhood now, Lisette. You are a little girl, not even in school yet. Something is making you very happy. You remember how happy you are. Why are you so happy?"

Lisette made a childish giggle. "It's my birthday party, and Ollie the Clown came to play with us."

"And how old are you today?"

"I'm five." Her right hand twitched, extended fingers and thumb.

"Go deeper now, Lisette. I want you to reach farther back. Far, far back into your memories. Go back to a time before you were a child in San Francisco. Far, farther back, Lisette. I want you to go back to the time of your dreams."

He studied her face. She remained in a deep hypnotic trance, but her expression registered sudden anxiousness. It was as if she lay in normal sleep – reacting to some intense nightmare. She moaned.

"Deeper, Lisette. Don't be afraid to remember. Let your mind flow back to another time."

Her features still showed distress, but she seemed less agitated as his voice urged her deeper.

"Where are you?"

"I'm . . . I'm not certain." Her voice came in a well-bred English accent. "It's quite dark. Only a few candles are burning. I'm frightened."

"Go back to a happy moment," Dr Magnus urged her, as her tone grew sharp with fear. "You are happy now. Something very pleasant and wonderful is happening to you."

Anxiety drained from her features. Her cheeks flushed; she smiled pleasurably.

"Where are you now?"

"I'm dancing. It's a grand ball to celebrate Her Majesty's Diamond Jubilee, and I've never seen such a throng. I'm certain Charles means to propose to me tonight, but he's ever so shy, and now he's simply fuming that Captain Stapledon has the next two dances. He's so dashing in his uniform. Everyone is watching us together."

"What is your name?"

"Elisabeth Beresford."

"Where do you live, Miss Beresford?"

"We have a house in Chelsea. . . ."

Her expression abruptly changed. "It's dark again. I'm all alone. I can't see myself, although surely the candles shed sufficient light. There's something there in the candlelight. I'm moving closer."

"One."

"It's an open coffin." Fear edged her voice.

"Two."

"*God in Heaven!*"

"Three."

VI

"We," Danielle announced grandly, "are invited to a party."

She produced an engraved card from her bag, presented it to Lisette, then went to hang up her damp raincoat.

"Bloody English summer weather!" Lisette heard her from the kitchen. "Is there any more coffee made? Oh, fantastic!"

She reappeared with a cup of coffee and an opened box of cookies – Lisette couldn't get used to calling them biscuits. "Want some?"

"No, thanks. Bad for my figure."

"And coffee on an empty tummy is bad for the nerves," Danielle said pointedly.

"*Who* is Beth Garrington?" Lisette studied the invitation.

"Um." Danielle tried to wash down a mouthful of crumbs with too-hot coffee. "Some friend of Midge's. Midge dropped by the gallery this afternoon and gave me the invitation. A costume revel. Rock stars to royalty among the guests. Midge promises that it will be super fun; said the last party Beth threw was unbridled debauchery – there was cocaine being passed around in an antique snuff box for the guests. Can you imagine that much coke!"

"And how did Midge manage the invitation?"

"I gather the discerning Ms. Garrington had admired several of my drawings that Maitland has on display – yea, even unto so far as to purchase one. Midge told her that she knew me and that we two were ornaments for any debauchery."

"The invitation is in both our names."

"Midge *likes* you."

"Midge despises me. She's jealous as a cat."

"Then she must have told our depraved hostess what a lovely couple we make. Besides, Midge is jealous of everyone – even dear Maitland, whose interest in me very obviously is not of the flesh. But don't fret about Midge – English women are naturally bitchy toward 'foreign' women. They're oh-so proper and fashionable, but they never shave their legs. That's why I love mah fellow Americans."

Danielle kissed her chastely on top of her head, powdering Lisette's hair with biscuit crumbs. "And I'm cold and wet and dying for a shower. How about you?"

"A masquerade?" Lisette wondered. "What sort of costume? Not something that we'll have to trot off to one of those rental places for, surely?"

"From what Midge suggests, anything goes so long as it's wild. Just create something divinely decadent, and we're sure to knock them dead." Danielle had seen *Cabaret* half a dozen times. "It's to be in some back alley stately old home in Maida Vale, so there's no danger that the tenants downstairs will call the cops."

When Lisette remained silent, Danielle gave her a playful nudge. "Darling, it's a party we're invited to, not a funeral. What is it – didn't your session with Dr Magnus go well?"

"I suppose it did." Lisette smiled without conviction. "I really can't say; all I did was doze off. Dr Magnus seemed quite excited about it, though. I found it all . . . well, just a little bit scary."

"I thought you said you just dropped off. *What* was scary?"

"It's hard to put into words. It's like when you're starting to have a bad trip on acid: there's nothing wrong that you can explain, but somehow your mind is telling you to be afraid."

Danielle sat down beside her and squeezed her arm about her shoulders. "That sounds to me like Dr Magnus is getting somewhere. I felt just the same sort of free anxiety the first time I underwent analysis. It's a good sign, darling. It means you're beginning to understand all those troubled secrets the ego keeps locked away."

"Perhaps the ego keeps them locked away for some perfectly good reason."

"Meaning hidden sexual conflicts, I suppose." Danielle's fingers gently massaged Lisette's shoulders and neck. "Oh, Lisette. You mustn't be shy about getting to know yourself. *I* think it's exciting."

Lisette curled up against her, resting her cheek against Danielle's breast while the other girl's fingers soothed the tension from her muscles. She supposed she was overreacting. After all, the nightmares were what distressed her so; Dr Magnus seemed completely confident that he could free her from them.

"Which of your drawings did our prospective hostess buy?" Lisette asked, changing the subject.

"Oh, didn't I tell you?" Danielle lifted up her chin. "It was that charcoal study I did of you."

Lisette closed the shower curtains as she stepped into the tub. It was one of those long, narrow, deep tubs beloved of English bathrooms that always made her think of a coffin for two. A Rube Goldberg plumbing arrangement connected the hot and cold faucets, and from the common spout was affixed a rubber hose with a shower head which one might either hang from a hook on the wall or hold in hand. Danielle had replaced the ordinary shower head with a shower massage when she moved in, but she left the previous tenant's shaving mirror – a bevelled glass oval in a heavily enameled antique frame – hanging on the wall above the hook.

Lisette glanced at her face in the steamed-over mirror. "I shouldn't have let you display that at the gallery."

"But why not?" Danielle was shampooing, and lather blinded her as she turned about. "Maitland thinks it's one of my best."

Lisette reached around her for the shower attachment. "It seems a bit personal somehow. All those people looking at me. It's an invasion of privacy."

"But it's thoroughly modest, darling. Not like some topless billboard in Soho."

The drawing was a charcoal and pencil study of Lisette, done in what Danielle described as her David Hamilton phase. In sitting for it, Lisette had piled her hair in a high chignon and dressed in an antique cotton camisole and drawers with lace insertions that she'd found at a shop in Westbourne Grove. Danielle called it *Dark Rose*. Lisette had thought it made her look fat.

Danielle grasped blindly for the shower massage, and Lisette placed it in her hand. "It just seems a bit too personal to have some total stranger owning my picture." Shampoo coursed like seafoam over Danielle's breasts. Lisette kissed the foam.

"Ah, but soon she won't be a total stranger," Danielle reminded her, her voice muffled by the pulsing shower spray.

Lisette felt Danielle's nipples harden beneath her lips. The brunette still pressed her eyes tightly shut against the force of the shower, but the other hand cupped Lisette's head encouragingly. Lisette gently moved her kisses downward along the other girl's slippery belly, kneeling as she did so. Danielle murmured, and when Lisette's tongue probed her drenched curls, she shifted her legs to let her knees rest beneath the blonde girl's shoulders. The shower massage dropped from her fingers.

Lisette made love to her with a passion that surprised her – spontaneous, suddenly fierce, unlike their usual tenderness together. Her lips and tongue pressed into Danielle almost ravenously, her own ecstasy even more intense than that which she was drawing from Danielle. Danielle gasped and clung to the shower rail with one hand, her other fist clenched upon the curtain, sobbing as a long orgasm shuddered through her.

"Please, darling!" Danielle finally managed to beg. "My legs are too wobbly to hold me up any longer!"

She drew away. Lisette raised her face.

"Oh!"

Lisette rose to her feet with drugged movements. Her wide eyes at last registered Danielle's startled expression. She touched her lips and turned to look in the bathroom mirror.

"I'm sorry," Danielle put her arm about her shoulder. "I must have started my period. I didn't realize . . ."

Lisette stared at the blood-smeared face in the fogged shaving mirror.

Danielle caught her as she started to slump.

VII

She was conscious of the cold rain that pelted her face, washing from her nostrils the too-sweet smell of decaying flowers. Slowly she opened her eyes onto darkness and mist. Rain fell steadily, spiritlessly, glueing her white gown to her drenched flesh. She had been walking in her sleep again.

Wakefulness seemed forever in coming to her, so that only by slow degrees did she become aware of herself, of her surroundings. For a moment she felt as if she were a chess-piece arrayed upon a board in a darkened room. All about her, stone monuments crowded together, their weathered surfaces streaming with moisture. She felt neither fear nor surprise that she stood in a cemetery.

She pressed her bare arms together across her breasts. Water ran over her pale skin as smoothly as upon the marble tomb-stones, and though her flesh felt as cold as the drenched marble, she did not feel chilled. She stood barefoot, her hair clinging to her shoulders above the low-necked cotton gown that was all she wore.

Automatically, her steps carried her through the darkness, as if following a familiar path through the maze of glistening stone. She knew where she was: this was Highgate Cemetery. She could not recall how she knew that, since she had no memory of ever having been to this place before. No more could she think how she knew her steps were taking her deeper into the cemetery instead of toward the gate.

A splash of color trickled onto her breast, staining its paleness as the rain dissolved it into a red rose above her heart.

She opened her mouth to scream, and a great bubble of unswallowed blood spewed from her lips.

"Elisabeth! Elisabeth!"

"Lisette! Lisette!"

Whose voice called her?

"Lisette! You can wake up now, Lisette."

Dr Magnus's face peered into her own. Was there sudden concern behind that urbane mask?

"You're awake now, Miss Seyrig. Everything is all right."

Lisette stared back at him for a moment, uncertain of her reality, as if suddenly awakened from some profound nightmare.

"I . . . I thought I was dead." Her eyes still held her fear.

Dr Magnus smiled to reassure her. "Somnambulism, my dear. You remembered an episode of sleepwalking from a former life. Tell me, have you yourself ever walked in your sleep?"

Lisette pressed her hands to her face, abruptly examined her fingers. "I don't know. I mean, I don't think so."

She sat up, searched in her bag for her compact. She paused for a moment before opening the mirror.

"Dr Magnus, I don't think I care to continue these sessions." She stared at her reflection in fascination, not touching her makeup, and when she snapped the case shut, the frightened strain began to relax from her face. She wished she had a cigarette.

Dr Magnus sighed and pressed his fingertips together, leaning back in his chair; watched her fidget with her clothing as she sat nervously on the edge of the couch.

"Do you really wish to terminate our exploration? We have, after all, made excellent progress during these last few sessions."

"Have we?"

"We have, indeed. You have consistently remembered incidents from the life of one Elisabeth Beresford, a young English lady living in London at the close of the last century. To the best of your knowledge of your family history, she is not an ancestress."

Dr Magnus leaned forward, seeking to impart his enthusiasm. "Don't you see how important this is? If Elisabeth Beresford was not your ancestress, then there can be no question of genetic memory being involved. The only explanation must therefore be reincarnation – proof of the immortality of the soul. To establish this I must first confirm the existence of Elisabeth Beresford, and from that demonstrate that no familial bond exists between the two of you. We simply must explore this further."

"Must we? I meant, what progress have we made toward helping me, Dr Magnus? It's all very good for you to be able to confirm your theories of reincarnation, but that doesn't do anything for me. If anything, the nightmares have grown more disturbing since we began these sessions."

"Then perhaps we dare not stop."

"What do you mean?" Lisette wondered what he might do if she suddenly bolted from the room.

"I mean that the nightmares will grow worse regardless of whether you decide to terminate our sessions. Your unconscious self is struggling to tell you some significant message from a previous existence. It will continue to do so no matter how stubbornly you will yourself not to listen. My task is to help you listen to this voice, to understand the message it must impart to you – and with this understanding and self-awareness, you will experience inner peace. Without my help . . . Well, to be perfectly frank, Miss Seyrig, you are in some danger of a complete emotional breakdown.''

Lisette slumped back against the couch. She felt on the edge of panic and wished Danielle were here to support her.

''Why are my memories always nightmares?'' Her voice shook, and she spoke slowly to control it.

''But they aren't always frightening memories, my dear. It's just that the memory of some extremely traumatic experience often seeks to come to the fore. You would expect some tremendously emotional laden memory to be a potent one.''

''Is Elisabeth Beresford . . . dead?''

''Assuming she was approximately twenty years of age at the time of Queen Victoria's Diamond Jubilee, she would have been past one hundred today. Besides, Miss Seyrig, her soul has been born again as your own. It must therefore follow . . .''

''Dr Magnus. I don't *want* to know how Elisabeth Beresford died.''

''Of course,'' Dr Magnus told her gently. ''Isn't that quite obvious?''

VIII

''For a wonder, it's forgot to rain tonight.''

''Thank god for small favors,'' Lisette commented, thinking July in London had far more to do with monsoons than the romantic city of fogs celebrated in song. ''All we need is to get these rained on.''

She and Danielle bounced about on the back seat of the black Austin taxi, as their driver democratically seemed as willing to challenge lorries as pedestrians for right-of-way on the Edgeware Road. Feeling a bit self-conscious, Lisette tugged at the hem of her patent leather trench coat. They had decided to wear brightly embroidered Chinese silk lounging pyjamas that they'd found at one of the vintage clothing shops off the Portobello Road – gauzy enough for stares, but only a demure trouser-leg showing beneath their coats. ''We're going to a masquerade party,'' Lisette had felt obliged to explain to the driver. Her concern was needless, as he hadn't given them a second glance. Either he was used to the current Chinese look in fashion, or else a few seasons of picking up couples at discos and punk rock clubs had inured him to any sort of costume.

The taxi turned into a series of side streets off Maida Vale and eventually made a neat U-turn that seemed almost an automotive pirouette. The frenetic beat of a new wave rock group clattered past the gate of an enclosed courtyard: something Mews – the iron plaque on the brick wall was too rusted to decipher in the dark – but from the lights and noise it must be the right address. A number of expensive-looking cars – Lisette recognized a Rolls or two and at least one Ferrari – were among those crowded against the curb. They squeezed their way past them and made for the source of the revelry, a brick-fronted town-house of three or more storeys set at the back of the courtyard.

The door was opened by a girl in an abbreviated maid's costume. She checked their invitation while a similarly clad girl took their coats, and a third invited them to select from an assortment of masks and indicated where they might change. Lisette and Danielle chose sequined domino masks that matched the dangling scarves they wore tied low across their brows.

Danielle withdrew an ebony cigarette holder from her bag and considered their reflections with approval. "Divinely decadent," she drawled, gesturing with her black-lacquered nails. "All that time for my eyes, and just to cover them with a mask. Perhaps later – when it's cock's-crow and all unmask . . . Forward, darling."

Lisette kept at her side, feeling a bit lost and out of place. When they passed before a light, it was evident that they wore nothing beneath the silk pyjamas, and Lisette was grateful for the strategic brocade. As they came upon others of the newly arriving guests, she decided there was no danger of outraging anyone's modesty here. As Midge had promised, anything goes so long as it's wild, and while their costumes might pass for street wear, many of the guests needed avail themselves of the changing rooms upstairs.

A muscular young man clad only in a leather loincloth and a sword belt with broadsword descended the stairs leading a buxom girl by a chain affixed to her wrists; aside from her manacles, she wore a few scraps of leather. A couple in punk rock gear spat at them in passing; the girl was wearing a set of panties with dangling razor blades for tassels and a pair of black latex tights that might have been spray paint. Two girls in vintage Christian Dior New Look evening gowns ogled the seminude swordsman from the landing above; Lisette noted their pronounced shoulders and Adam's apples and felt a twinge of jealousy that hormones and surgery could let them show a better cleavage than she could.

A new wave group called the Needle was performing in a large first-floor room – Lisette supposed it was an actual ballroom, although the house's original tenants would have considered tonight's ball a *danse macabre*. Despite the fact that the decibel level was well past the threshold of pain, most of the guests were congregated here, with smaller, quieter parties gravitating into other rooms. Here, about half were dancing, the rest standing about trying to talk. Marijuana smoke was barely discernible within the harsh haze of British cigarettes.

"There's Midge and Fiona," Danielle shouted in Lisette's ear. She waved energetically and steered a course through the dancers.

Midge was wearing an elaborate medieval gown – a heavily brocaded affair that ran from the floor to midway across her nipples. Her blonde hair was piled high in some sort of conical headpiece, complete with flowing scarf. Fiona waited upon her in a page boy's costume.

"Are you just getting here?" Midge asked, running a deprecative glance down Lisette's costume. "There's champagne over on the sideboard. Wait, I'll summon one of the cute little French maids."

Lisette caught two glasses from a passing tray and presented one to Danielle. It was impossible to converse, but then she hadn't anything to talk about with Midge, and Fiona was no more than a shadow.

"Where's our hostess?" Danielle asked.

"Not down yet," Midge managed to shout. "Beth always waits to make a grand entrance at her little do's. You won't miss her."

"Speaking of entrances . . ." Lisette commented, nodding toward the couple who were just coming onto the dance floor. The woman wore a Nazi SS officer's hat, jackboots, black trousers and braces across her bare chest. She was astride the back of her male companion, who wore a saddle and bridle in addition to a few other bits of leather harness.

"I can't decide whether that's kinky or just tacky," Lisette said.

"Not like your little sorority teas back home, is it?" Midge smiled.

"Is there any coke about?" Danielle interposed quickly.

"There was a short while ago. Try the library – that's the room just down from where everyone's changing."

Lisette downed her champagne and grabbed a refill before following Danielle upstairs. A man in fish-net tights, motorcycle boots and a vest comprised mostly of chain and bits of Nazi medals caught at her arm and seemed to want to dance. Instead of a mask, he wore about a pound of eye shadow and black lipstick. She shouted an inaudible excuse, held a finger to her nostril and sniffed, and darted after Danielle.

"That was Eddie Teeth, lead singer for the Trepans, whom you just cut," Danielle told her. "Why didn't he grab *me*!"

"You'll get your chance," Lisette told her. "I think he's following us."

Danielle dragged her to a halt halfway up the stairs.

"Got toot right here, loves." Eddie Teeth flipped the silver spoon and phial that dangled amidst the chains on his vest.

"Couldn't take the noise in there any longer," Lisette explained.

"Needle's shit." Eddie Teeth wrapped an arm about either waist and propelled them up the stairs. "You gashes sisters? I can dig incest."

The library was pleasantly crowded – Lisette decided she didn't want to be cornered with Eddie Teeth. A dozen or more guests stood about, sniffing and conversing energetically. Seated at a table, two of the ubiquitous maids busily cut lines onto mirrors and set them out for the guests, whose number remained more or less constant as people wandered in and left. A cigarette box offered tightly rolled joints.

"That's Thai." Eddie Teeth groped for a handful of the joints, stuck one in each girl's mouth, the rest inside his vest. Danielle giggled and fitted hers to her cigarette holder. Unfastening a silver tube from his vest, he snorted two thick lines from one of the mirrors. "Toot your eyeballs out, loves," he invited them.

One of the maids collected the mirror when they had finished and replaced it with another – a dozen lines of cocaine neatly arranged across its surface. Industriously she began to work a chunk of rock through a sifter to replenish the empty mirror. Lisette watched in fascination. This finally brought home to her the wealth this party represented: all the rest simply seemed to her like something out of a movie, but dealing out coke to more than a hundred guests was an extravagance she could relate to.

"Danielle Borland, isn't it?"

A man dressed as Mephistopheles bowed before them. "Adrian Tregannet. We've met at one of Midge Vaughn's parties, you may recall."

Danielle stared at the face below the domino mask. "Oh, yes. Lisette, it's Mephisto himself."

"Then this is Miss Seyrig, the subject of your charcoal drawing that Beth so admires." Mephisto caught Lisette's hand and bent his lips to it. "Beth is so much looking forward to meeting you both."

Lisette retrieved her hand. "Aren't you the . . ."

"The rude fellow who accosted you in Kensington some days ago," Tregannet finished apologetically. "Yes, I'm afraid so. But you really must forgive me for my forwardness. I actually did mistake you for a very dear friend of mine, you see. Won't you let me make amends over a glass of champagne?"

"Certainly." Lisette decided that she had had quite enough of Eddie Teeth, and Danielle was quite capable of fending for herself if she grew tired of having her breasts squeezed by a famous pop star.

Tregannet quickly returned with two glasses of champagne. Lisette finished another two lines and smiled appreciatively as she accepted a glass. Danielle was trying to shotgun Eddie Teeth through her cigarette holder, and Lisette thought it a good chance to slip away.

"Your roommate is tremendously talented," Tregannet suggested. "Of course, she chose so charming a subject for her drawing."

Slick as snake oil, Lisette thought, letting him take her arm. "How very nice of you to say so. However, I really feel a bit embarrassed to think that some stranger owns a portrait of me in my underwear."

"Utterly chaste, my dear – as chaste as the *Dark Rose* of its title. Beth chose to hang it in her boudoir, so I hardly think it is on public display. I suspect from your garments in the drawing that you must share Beth's appreciation for the dress and manners of this past century."

Which is something I'd never suspect of our hostess, judging from this party, Lisette considered. "I'm quite looking forward to meeting her. I assume then that Ms. is a bit too modern for one of such quiet tastes. Is it Miss or Mrs Garrington?"

"Ah, I hadn't meant to suggest an impression of a genteel dowager. Beth is entirely of your generation – a few years older than yourself, perhaps. Although I find Ms. too suggestive of American slang, I'm sure Beth would not object. However, there's no occasion for such formality here."

"You seem to know her well, Mr Tregannet."

"It is an old family. I know her aunt, Julia Weatherford, quite well through our mutual interest in the occult. Perhaps you, too . . .?"

"Not really; Danielle is the one you should chat with about that. My field is art. I'm over here on fellowship at London University." She watched Danielle and Eddie Teeth toddle off for the ballroom and jealously decided that Danielle's taste in her acquaintances left much to be desired. "Could I have some more champagne?"

"To be sure. I won't be a moment."

Lisette snorted a few more lines while she waited. A young man dressed as an Edwardian dandy offered her his snuff box and gravely demonstrated its use. Lisette was struggling with a sneezing fit when Tregannet returned.

"You needn't have gone to all the bother," she told him. "These little French maids are dashing about with trays of champagne."

"But those glasses have lost the proper chill," Tregannet explained. "To your very good health."

"Cheers." Lisette felt lightheaded, and promised herself to go easy for a while. "Does Beth live here with her aunt, then?"

"Her aunt lives on the Continent; I don't believe she's visited London for several years. Beth moved in about ten years ago. Theirs is not a large family, but they are not without wealth, as you can observe. They travel a great deal as well, and it's fortunate that Beth happened to be in London during your stay here. Incidently, just how long will you be staying in London?"

"About a year is all." Lisette finished her champagne. "Then it's back to my dear, dull family in San Francisco."

"Then there's no one here in London . . .?"

"Decidedly not, Mr Tregannet. And now if you'll excuse me, I think I'll find the ladies'."

Cocaine might well be the champagne of drugs, but cocaine and champagne didn't seem to mix well, Lisette mused, turning the bathroom over to the next frantic guest. Her head felt really buzzy, and she thought she might do better if she found a bedroom somewhere and lay down for a moment. But then she'd most likely wake up and find some man on top of her, judging from this lot. She decided she'd lay off the champagne and have just a line or two to shake off the feeling of having been sandbagged.

The crowd in the study had changed during her absence. Just now it was dominated by a group of guests dressed in costumes from *The Rocky Horror Show*, now closing out its long run at the Comedy Theatre in Piccadilly. Lisette had grown bored with the fad the film version had generated in the States, and pushed her way past the group as they vigorously danced the Time Warp and bellowed out songs from the show.

"'Give yourself over to absolute pleasure,'" someone sang in her ear as she industriously snorted a line from the mirror. "'Erotic nightmares beyond any measure,'" the song continued.

Lisette finished a second line, and decided she had had enough. She straightened from the table and broke for the doorway. The tall transvestite dressed as Frankie barred her way with a dramatic gesture, singing ardently: "'Don't dream it – be it!'"

Lisette blew him a kiss and ducked around him. She wished she could find a quiet place to collect her thoughts. Maybe she should find Danielle first – if she could handle the ballroom that long.

The dance floor was far more crowded than when they'd come in. At least all these jostling bodies seemed to absorb some of the decibels from the blaring banks of amplifiers and speakers. Lisette looked in vain for Danielle amidst the dancers, succeeding only in getting champagne sloshed on her back. She caught sight of Midge, recognizable above the mob by her conical medieval headdress, and pushed her way toward her.

Midge was being fed caviar on bits of toast by Fiona while she talked with an older woman who looked like the pictures Lisette had seen of Marlene Dietrich dressed in men's formal evening wear.

"Have you seen Danielle?" Lisette asked her.

"Why, not recently, darling," Midge smiled, licking caviar from her lips with the tip of her tongue. "I believe she and that rock singer were headed upstairs for a bit more privacy. I'm sure she'll come collect you once they're finished."

"Midge, you're a cunt," Lisette told her through her sweetest smile. She turned away and made for the doorway, trying not to ruin her exit by staggering. Screw Danielle – she needed to have some fresh air.

A crowd had gathered at the foot of the stairway, and she had to push through the doorway to escape the ballroom. Behind her, the Needle mercifully took a break. "She's coming down!" Lisette heard someone whisper breathlessly. The inchoate babel of the party fell to a sudden lull that made Lisette shiver.

At the top of the stairway stood a tall woman, enveloped in a black velvet cloak from her throat to her ankles. Her blonde hair was piled high in a complex variation of the once-fashionable French twist. Strings of garnets entwined in her hair and edged the close-fitting black mask that covered the upper half of her face. For a hushed interval she stood there, gazing imperiously down upon her guests.

Adrian Tregannet leapt to the foot of the stairway. He signed to a pair of maids, who stepped forward to either side of their mistress.

"Milords and miladies!" he announced with a sweeping bow. "Let us pay honor to our bewitching mistress whose feast we celebrate tonight! I give you the lamia who haunted Adam's dreams – Lilith!"

The maids smoothly swept the cloak from their mistress' shoulders. From the multitude at her feet came an audible intake of breath. Beth Garrington was attired in a strapless corselette of gleaming black leather, laced tightly about her waist. The rest of her costume consisted only of knee-length, stiletto-heeled tight boots, above-the-elbow gloves, and a spiked collar around her throat – all of black leather that contrasted starkly against her white skin and blonde hair. At first Lisette thought she wore a bull-whip coiled about her body as well, but then the coils moved, and she realized that it was an enormous black snake.

"Lilith!" came the shout, chanted in a tone of awe. "Lilith!"

Acknowledging their worship with a sinuous gesture, Beth Garrington descended the staircase. The serpent coiled from gloved arm to gloved arm, entwining her cinched waist; its eyes considered the revellers imperturbably. Champagne glasses lifted in a toast to Lilith, and the chattering voice of the party once more began to fill the house.

Tregannet touched Beth's elbow as she greeted her guests at the foot of the stairway. He whispered into her ear, and she smiled graciously and moved away with him.

Lisette clung to the staircase newel, watching them approach. Her head was spinning, and she desperately needed to lie down in some fresh air, but she couldn't trust her legs to carry her outside. She stared into the eyes of the serpent, hypnotized by its flickering tongue.

The room seemed to surge in and out of focus. The masks of the guests seemed to leer and gloat with the awareness of some secret jest; the dancers in their fantastic costumes became a grotesque horde of satyrs and wanton demons, writhing about the ballroom in some witches' sabbat of obscene mass copulation. As in a nightmare, Lisette willed her legs to turn and run, realized that her body was no longer obedient to her will.

"Beth, here's someone you've been dying to meet," Lisette heard Tregannet say. "Beth Garrington, allow me to present Lisette Seyrig."

The lips beneath the black mask curved in a pleasurable smile. Lisette gazed into the eyes behind the mask, and discovered that she could no longer feel her body. She thought she heard Danielle cry out her name.

The eyes remained in her vision long after she slid down the newel and collapsed upon the floor.

IX

The Catherine Wheel was a pub on Kensington Church Street. They served good pub lunches there, and Lisette liked to stop in before walking down Holland Street for her sessions with Dr Magnus. Since today was her final such session, it seemed appropriate that they should end the evening here.

"While I dislike repeating myself," Dr Magnus spoke earnestly. "I really do think we should continue."

Lisette drew on a cigarette and shook her head decisively. "No way, Dr Magnus. My nerves are shot to hell. I mean, look – when I freak out at a costume party and have to be carted home to bed by my roommate! It was like when I was a kid and got hold of some bad acid: the whole world was some bizarre and sinister freak show for weeks. Once I got my head back on, I said: No more acid."

"That was rather a notorious circle you were travelling in. Further, you were, if I understand you correctly, overindulging a bit that evening."

"A few glasses of champagne and a little toot never did anything before but make me a bit giggly and talkative." Lisette sipped her half of lager; she'd never developed a taste for English bitter, and at least the lager was chilled. They sat across from each other at a table the size of a hubcap; she in the corner of a padded bench against the wall, he at a chair set out into the room, pressed in by a wall of standing bodies. A foot away from her on the padded bench, three young men huddled about a similar table, talking animatedly. For all that, she and Dr Magnus might have been all alone in the room. Lisette wondered if the psychologist who had coined the faddish concept of "space" had been inspired in a crowded English pub.

"It isn't just that I fainted at the party. It isn't just the nightmares." She paused to find words. "It's just that everything somehow seems to be drifting out of focus, out of control. It's . . . well, it's frightening."

"Precisely why we must continue."

"Precisely why we must not." Lisette sighed. They'd covered this ground already. It had been a moment of weakness when she agreed to allow Dr Magnus to buy her a drink afterward instead of heading back to the flat. Still, he had been so distressed when she told him she was terminating their sessions.

"I've tried to cooperate with you as best I could, and I'm certain you are entirely sincere in your desire to help me." Well, she wasn't all *that* certain, but no point in going into that. "However, the fact remains that since we began these sessions, my nerves have gone to hell. You say they'd be worse without the sessions. I say the sessions have made them worse, and maybe there's no connection at all – it's just that my nerves have gotten worse, so now I'm going to trust my intuition and try life without these sessions. Fair enough?"

Dr Magnus gazed uncomfortably at his barely tasted glass of sherry. "While I fully understand your rationale, I must in all conscience beg you to reconsider, Lisette. You are running risks that . . ."

"Look. If the nightmares go away, then terrific. If they don't, I can always pack up and head back to San Francisco. That way I'll be clear of whatever it is about London that disagrees with me, and if not, I'll see my psychiatrist back home."

"Very well, then." Dr Magnus squeezed her hand. "However, please bear in mind that I remain eager to continue our sessions at any time, should you change your mind."

"That's fair enough, too. And very kind of you."

Dr Magnus lifted his glass of sherry to the light. Pensively, he remarked: "Amber."

X

"Lisette?"

Danielle locked the front door behind her and hung up her inadequate umbrella in the hallway. She considered her face in the mirror and grimaced at the mess of her hair. "Lisette? Are you here?"

No answer, and her rain things were not in the hallway. Either she was having a late session with Dr Magnus, or else she'd wisely decided to duck under cover until this bloody rain let up. After she'd had to carry Lisette home in a taxi when she passed out at the party. Danielle was starting to feel real concern over her state of health.

Danielle kicked off her damp shoes as she entered the living room. The curtains were drawn against the greyness outside, and she switched on a lamp to brighten the flat a bit. Her dress clung to her like a clammy fish-skin; she shivered, and thought about a cup of coffee. If Lisette hadn't returned yet, there wouldn't be any brewed. She'd have a warm shower instead, and after that she'd see to the coffee – if Lisette hadn't returned to set a pot going in the meantime.

"Lisette?" Their bedroom was empty. Danielle turned on the overhead light. Christ, it was gloomy! So much for long English summer evenings – with all the rain, she couldn't remember when she'd last seen the sun. She struggled out of her damp dress, spread it flat across her bed with the vague hope that it might not wrinkle too badly, then tossed her bra and tights onto a chair.

Slipping into her bathrobe, Danielle padded back into the living room. Still no sign of Lisette, and it was past nine. Perhaps she'd stopped off at a pub. Crossing to the stereo, Danielle placed the new Blondie album on the turntable and turned up the volume. Let the neighbors complain – at least this would help dispel the evening's gloom.

She cursed the delay needed to adjust the shower temperature to satisfaction, then climbed into the tub. The hot spray felt good, and she stood under it contentedly for several minutes – initially revitalized, then lulled into a delicious sense of relaxation. Through the rush of the spray, she could hear the muffled beat of the stereo. As she reached for the shampoo, she began to move her body with the rhythm.

The shower curtain billowed as the bathroom door opened. Danielle risked a soapy squint around the curtain – she knew the flat was securely locked, but after seeing *Psycho* . . . It was only Lisette, already undressed, her long blonde hair falling over her breasts.

"Didn't hear you come in with the stereo going," Danielle greeted her. "Come on in before you catch cold."

Danielle resumed lathering her hair as the shower curtain parted and the other girl stepped into the tub behind her. Her eyes squeezed shut against the soap, she felt Lisette's breasts thrust against her back, her flat belly press against her buttocks. Lisette's hands came around her to cup her breasts gently.

At least Lisette had gotten over her silly tiff about Eddie Teeth. She'd explained to Lisette that she'd ditched that greasy slob when he'd tried to dry hump her on the dance floor, but how do you reason with a silly thing who faints at the sight of a snake?

"Jesus, you're chilled to the bone!" Danielle complained with a shiver. "Better stand under the shower and get warm. Did you get caught in the rain?"

The other girl's fingers continued to caress her breasts, and instead of answering, her lips teased the nape of Danielle's neck. Danielle made a delighted sound deep in her throat, letting the spray rinse the lather from her hair and over their embraced bodies. Languidly she turned about to face her lover, closing her arms about Lisette's shoulders for support.

Lisette's kisses held each taut nipple for a moment, teasing them almost painfully. Danielle pressed the other girl's face to her breasts, sighed as her kisses nibbled upward to her throat. She felt weak with arousal, and only Lisette's strength held her upright in the tub. Her lover's lips upon her throat tormented her beyond enduring; Danielle gasped and lifted Lisette's face to meet her own.

Her mouth was open to receive Lisette's red-lipped kiss, and it opened wider as Danielle stared into the eyes of her lover. Her first emotion was one of wonder.

"You're not Lisette!"

It was nearly midnight when Lisette unlocked the door to their flat and quietly let herself in. Only a few lights were on, and there was no sign of Danielle – either she had gone out, or, more likely, had gone to bed.

Lisette hung up her raincoat and wearily pulled off her shoes. She'd barely caught the last train. She must have been crazy to let Dr Magnus talk her into returning to his office for another session that late, but then he was quite right: as serious as her problems were, she really did need all the help he could give her. She felt a warm sense of gratitude to Dr Magnus for being there when she so needed his help.

The turntable had stopped, but a light on the amplifier indicated that the power was still on. Lisette cut it off and closed the lid over the turntable. She felt too tired to listen to an album just now.

She became aware that the shower was running. In that case, Danielle hadn't gone to bed. She supposed she really ought to apologize to her for letting Midge's bitch lies get under her skin. After all, she had ruined the party for Danielle; poor Danielle had had to get her to bed and had left the party without ever getting to meet Beth Garrington, and she was the one Beth had invited in the first place.

"Danielle? I'm back." Lisette called through the bathroom door. "Do you want anything?"

No answer. Lisette looked into their bedroom, just in case Danielle had invited a friend over. No, the beds were still made up; Danielle's clothes were spread out by themselves.

"Danielle?" Lisette raised her voice. Perhaps she couldn't hear over the noise of the shower. "Danielle?" Surely she was all right.

Lisette's feet felt damp. She looked down. A puddle of water was seeping beneath the door. Danielle must not have the shower curtains closed properly.

"Danielle! You're flooding us!"

Lisette opened the door and peered cautiously within. The curtain was closed, right enough. A thin spray still reached through a gap, and the shower had been running long enough for the puddle to spread. It occurred to Lisette that she should see Danielle's silhouette against the translucent shower curtain.

"Danielle!" She began to grow alarmed. "Danielle! Are you all right?"

She pattered across the wet tiles and drew aside the curtain. Danielle lay in the bottom of the tub, the spray falling on her upturned smile, her flesh paler than the porcelain of the tub.

XI

It was early afternoon when they finally allowed her to return to the flat. Had she been able to think of another place to go, she probably would have gone there. Instead, Lisette wearily slumped onto the couch, too spent to pour herself the drink she desperately wanted.

Somehow she had managed to phone the police, through her hysteria make them understand where she was. Once the squad car arrived, she had no further need to act out of her own initiative; she simply was carried along in the rush of police investigation. It wasn't until they were questioning her at New Scotland Yard that she realized she herself was not entirely free from suspicion.

The victim had bled to death, the medical examiner ruled, her blood washed down the tub drain. A safety razor used for shaving legs had been opened, its blade removed. There were razor incisions along both wrists, directed lengthwise, into the radial artery, as opposed to the shallow, crosswise cuts utilized by suicides unfamiliar with human anatomy. There was, in addition, an incision in the left side of the throat. It was either a very determined suicide, or a skillfully concealed murder. In view of the absence of any signs of forced entry or of a struggle, more likely the former. The victim's roommate did admit to a recent quarrel. Laboratory tests would indicate whether the victim might have been drugged or rendered unconscious through a blow. After that, the inquest would decide.

Lisette had explained that she had spent the evening with Dr Magnus. The fact that she was receiving emotional therapy, as they interpreted it, caused several mental notes to be made. Efforts to reach Dr Magnus by telephone proved unsuccessful, but his secretary did confirm that Miss Seyrig had shown up for her appointment the previous afternoon. Dr Magnus would get in touch with them as soon as he returned to his office. No, she did not know why he had cancelled today's appointments, but it was not unusual for Dr Magnus to dash off suddenly when essential research demanded immediate attention.

After a while they let Lisette make phone calls. She phoned her parents, then wished she hadn't. It was still the night before in California, and it was like turning back the hands of time to no avail. They urged her to take the next flight home, but of course it wasn't all that simple, and it just wasn't feasible for either of them to fly over on a second's notice, since after all there really was nothing they could do. She phoned Maitland Reddin, who was stunned at the news and offered to help in any way he could, but Lisette couldn't think of any way. She phoned Midge Vaughn, who hung up on her. She phoned Dr Magnus, who still couldn't be reached. Mercifully, the police took care of phoning Danielle's next of kin.

A physician at New Scotland Yard had spoken with her briefly and had given her some pills – a sedative to ease her into sleep after her ordeal. They had driven her back to the flat after impressing upon her the need to be present at the inquest. She must not be concerned should any hypothetical assailant yet be lurking about, inasmuch as the flat would be under surveillance.

Lisette stared dully about the flat, still unable to comprehend what had happened. The police had been thorough – measuring, dusting for fingerprints, leaving things in a mess. Bleakly, Lisette tried to convince herself that this was only another nightmare, that in a moment Danielle would pop in and find her asleep on the couch. Christ, what was she going to do with all of Danielle's things? Danielle's mother was remarried and living in Colorado; her father was an executive in a New York investment corporation. Evidently he had made arrangements to have the body shipped back to the States.

"Oh, Danielle." Lisette was too stunned for tears. Perhaps she should check into a hotel for now. No, she couldn't bear being all alone with her thoughts in a strange place. How strange to realize now that she really had no close friends in London other than Danielle – and what friends she did have were mostly people she'd met through Danielle.

She'd left word with Dr Magnus's secretary for him to call her once he came in. Perhaps she should call there once again, just in case Dr Magnus had missed her message. Lisette couldn't think what good Dr Magnus could do, but he was such an understanding person, and she felt much better whenever she spoke with him.

She considered the bottle of pills in her bag. Perhaps it would be best to take a couple of them and sleep around the clock. She felt too drained just now to have energy enough to think.

The phone began to ring. Lisette stared at it for a moment without comprehension, then lunged up from the couch to answer it.

"Is this Lisette Seyrig?"

It was a woman's voice – one Lisette didn't recognize. "Yes. Who's calling, please?"

"This is Beth Garrington, Lisette. I hope I'm not disturbing you."

"That's quite all right."

"You poor dear! Maitland Redding phoned to tell me of the tragedy. I can't tell you how shocked I am. Danielle seemed such a dear from our brief contact, and she had such a great talent."

"Thank you. I'm sorry you weren't able to know her better." Lisette sensed guilt and embarrassment at the memory of that brief contact.

"Darling, you can't be thinking about staying in that flat alone. Is there someone there with you?"

"No, there isn't. That's all right. I'll be fine."

"Don't be silly. Listen, I have enough empty bedrooms in this old barn to open a hotel. Why don't you just pack a few things and come straight over?"

"That's very kind of you, but I really couldn't."

"Nonsense! It's no good for you to be there all by yourself. Strange as this may sound, but when I'm not throwing one of these invitational riots, this is a quiet little backwater and things are dull as church. I'd love the company, and it will do you a world of good to get away."

"You're really very kind to invite me, but I . . ."

"Please, Lisette – be reasonable. I have guest rooms here already made up, and I'll send the car around to pick you up. All you need do is say yes and toss a few things into your bag. After a good night's sleep, you'll feel much more like coping with things tomorrow."

When Lisette didn't immediately reply, Beth added carefully: "Besides, Lisette. I understand the police haven't ruled out the possibility of murder. In that event, unless poor Danielle simply forgot to lock up, there is a chance that whoever did this has a key to your flat."

"The police said they'd watch the house."

"He might also be someone you both know and trust, someone Danielle invited in."

Lisette stared wildly at the sinister shadows that lengthened about the flat. Her refuge had been violated. Even familiar objects seemed tainted and alien. She fought back tears. "I don't know what to think." She realized she'd been clutching the receiver for a long, silent interval.

"Poor dear! There's nothing you need think about! Now listen. I'm at my solicitor's tidying up some property matters for Aunt Julia. I'll phone right now to have my car sent around for you. It'll be there by the time you pack your toothbrush and pyjamas, and whisk you straight off to bucolic Maida Vale. The maids will plump up your pillows for you, and you can have a nice nap before I get home for dinner. Poor darling, I'll bet you haven't eaten a thing. Now, say you'll come."

"Thank you. It's awfully good of you. Of course I will."

"Then it's done. Don't worry about a thing, Lisette. I'll see you this evening."

XII

Dr Magnus hunched forward on the narrow seat of the taxi, wearily massaging his forehead and temples. It might not help his mental fatigue, but maybe the reduced muscle tension would ease his headache. He glanced at his watch. Getting on past ten. He'd had no sleep last night, and it didn't look as if he'd be getting much tonight. If only those girls would answer their phone!

It didn't help matters that his conscience plagued him. He had broken a sacred trust. He should never have made use of posthypnotic suggestion last night to persuade Lisette to return for a further session. It went against all principles, but there had been no other course: the girl was adamant, and he had to know – he was so close to establishing final proof. If only for one final session of regressive hypnosis . . .

Afterward he had spent a sleepless night, too excited for rest, at work in his study trying to reconcile the conflicting elements of Lisette's released memories with the historical data his research had so far compiled. By morning he had been able to pull together just enough facts to deepen the mystery. He had phoned his secretary at home to cancel all his appointments, and had spent the day at the tedious labor of delving through dusty municipal records and newspaper files, working feverishly as the past reluctantly yielded one bewildering clue after another.

By now Dr Magnus was exhausted, hungry and none too clean, but he had managed to establish proof of his theories. He was not elated. In doing so he had uncovered another secret, something undreamt of in his philosophies. He began to hope that his life work was in error.

"Here's the address, sir."

"Thank you, driver." Dr Magnus awoke from his grim revery and saw that he had reached his destination. Quickly, he paid the driver and hurried up the walk to Lisette's flat. Only a few lights were on, and he rang the bell urgently – a helpless sense of foreboding making his movements clumsy.

"Just one moment, sir!"

Dr Magnus jerked about at the voice. Two men in plain clothes approached him briskly from the pavement.

"Stand easy! We're police."

"Is something the matter, officers?" Obviously, something was.

"Might we ask what your business here is, sir?"

"Certainly. I'm a friend of Miss Borland and Miss Seyrig. I haven't been able to reach them by phone, and as I have some rather urgent matters to discuss with Miss Seyrig, I thought perhaps I might try reaching her here at her flat." He realized he was far too nervous.

"Might we see some identification, sir?"

"Is there anything wrong, officers?" Magnus repeated, producing his wallet.

"Dr Ingmar Magnus." The taller of the pair regarded him quizzically. "I take it you don't keep up with the news, Dr Magnus."

"Just what is this about!"

"I'm Inspector Bradley, Dr Magnus, and this is Detective Sergeant Wharton. CID. We've been wanting to ask you a few questions, sir, if you'll just come with us."

It was totally dark when Lisette awoke from troubled sleep. She stared wide-eyed into the darkness for a moment, wondering where she was. Slowly memory supplanted the vague images of her dream. Switching on a lamp beside her bed, Lisette frowned at her watch. It was close to midnight. She had overslept.

Beth's Rolls had come for her almost before she had had time hastily to pack her overnight bag. Once at the house in Maida Vale, a maid – wearing a more conventional uniform than those at her last visit – had shown her to a spacious guest room on the top floor. Lisette had taken a sedative pill and gratefully collapsed onto the bed. She'd planned to catch a short nap, then meet her hostess for dinner. Instead she had slept for almost ten solid hours. Beth must be convinced she was a hopeless twit after this.

As so often happens after an overextended nap, Lisette now felt restless. She wished she'd thought to bring a book. The house was completely silent. Surely it was too late to ring for a maid. No doubt Beth had meant to let her sleep through until morning, and by now would have retired herself. Perhaps she should take another pill and go back to sleep herself.

On the other hand, Beth Garrington hardly seemed the type to make it an early night. She might well still be awake, perhaps watching television where the noise wouldn't disturb her guest. In any event, Lisette didn't want to go back to sleep just yet.

She climbed out of bed, realizing that she'd only half undressed before falling asleep. Pulling off bra and panties, Lisette slipped into the antique nightdress of ribbons and lace she'd brought along. She hadn't thought to pack slippers or a robe, but it was a warm night, and the white cotton gown was modest enough for a peek into the hall.

There was a ribbon of light edging the door of the room at the far end of the hall. The rest of the hallway lay in darkness. Lisette stepped quietly from her room. Since Beth hadn't mentioned other guests, and the servants' quarters were elsewhere, presumably the light was coming from her hostess's bedroom and indicated she might still be awake. Lisette decided she really should make the effort to meet her hostess while in a conscious state.

She heard a faint sound of music as she tiptoed down the hallway. The door to the room was ajar, and the music came from within. She was in luck; Beth must still be up. At the doorway she knocked softly.

"Beth? Are you awake? It's Lisette."

There was no answer, but the door swung open at her touch.

Lisette started to call out again, but her voice froze in her throat. She recognized the tune she heard, and she knew this room. When she entered the bedroom, she could no more alter her actions than she could control the course of her dreams.

It was a large bedroom, entirely furnished in the mode of the late Victorian period. The windows were curtained, and the room's only light came from a candle upon a night table beside the huge four-poster bed. An antique gold pocket watch lay upon the night table also, and the watch was chiming an old music-box tune.

Lisette crossed the room, praying that this was no more than another vivid recurrence of her nightmare. She reached the night table and saw that the watch's hands pointed toward midnight. The chimes stopped. She picked up the watch and examined the picture that she knew would be inside the watchcase.

The picture was a photograph of herself.

Lisette let the watch clatter onto the table, stared in terror at the four-poster bed.

From within, a hand drew back the bed curtains.

Lisette wished she could scream, could awaken.

Sweeping aside the curtains, the occupant of the bed sat up and gazed at her.

And Lisette stared back at herself.

"Can't you drive a bit faster than this?"

Inspector Bradley resisted the urge to wink at Detective Sergeant

Wharton. "Sit back, Dr Magnus. We'll be there in good time. I trust you'll have rehearsed some apologies for when we disrupt a peaceful household in the middle of the night."

"I only pray such apologies will be necessary," Dr Magnus said, continuing to sit forward as if that would inspire the driver to go faster.

It hadn't been easy, Dr Magnus reflected. He dare not tell them the truth. He suspected that Bradley had agreed to making a late night call on Beth Garrington more to check out his alibi than from any credence he gave to Magnus's improvised tale.

Buried all day in frenzied research, Dr Magnus hadn't listened to the news, had ignored the tawdry London tabloids with their lurid headlines: "Naked Beauty Slashed in Tub" "Nude Model Slain in Bath" "Party Girl Suicide or Ripper's Victim?" The shock of learning of Danielle's death was seconded by the shock of discovering that he was one of the "important leads" police were following.

It had taken all his powers of persuasion to convince them to release him – or, at least, to accompany him to the house in Maida Vale. Ironically, he and Lisette were the only ones who could account for each other's presence elsewhere at the time of Danielle's death. While the CID might have been sceptical as to the nature of their late night session at Dr Magnus's office, there were a few corroborating details. A barman at the Catherine Wheel had remembered the distinguished gent with the beard leaving after his lady friend had dropped off of a sudden. The cleaning lady had heard voices and left his office undisturbed. This much they'd already checked, in verifying Lisette's whereabouts that night. Half a dozen harassed records clerks could testify as to Dr Magnus's presence for today.

Dr Magnus grimly reviewed the results of his research. There was an Elisabeth Beresford, born in London in 1879, of a well-to-do family who lived in Cheyne Row on the Chelsea Embankment. Elisabeth Beresford married a Captain Donald Stapledon in 1899 and moved to India with her husband. She returned to London, evidently suffering from consumption contracted while abroad, and died in 1900. She was buried in Highgate Cemetery. That much Dr Magnus had initially learned with some difficulty. From that basis he had pressed on for additional corroborating details, both from Lisette's released memories and from research into records of the period.

It had been particularly difficult to trace the subsequent branches of the family – something he must do in order to establish that Elisabeth Beresford could not have been an ancestress of Lisette Seyrig. And it disturbed him that he had been unable to locate Elisabeth Stapledon née Beresford's tomb in Highgate Cemetery.

Last night he had pushed Lisette as relentlessly as he dared. Out of her resurfacing visions of horror he finally found a clue. These were not images from nightmare, not symbolic representations of buried fears. They were literal memories.

Because of the sensation involved and the considerable station of the families concerned, public records had discreetly avoided reference to the tragedy, as had the better newspapers. The yellow journals were less reticent, and here Dr Magnus began to know fear.

Elisabeth Stapledon had been buried alive.

At her final wishes, the body had not been embalmed. The papers suggested that this was a clear premonition of her fate, and quoted passages from Edgar Allan Poe. Captain Stapledon paid an evening visit to his wife's tomb and discovered her wandering in a dazed condition about the graves. This was more than a month after her entombment.

The newspapers were full of pseudo-scientific theories, spiritualist explanations and long accounts of Indian mystics who had remained in a state of suspended animation for weeks on end. No one seems to have explained exactly how Elisabeth Stapledon escaped from both coffin and crypt, but it was supposed that desperate strength had wrenched loose the screws, while providentially the crypt had not been properly locked after a previous visit.

Husband and wife understandably went abroad immediately afterward, in order to escape publicity and for Elisabeth Stapledon to recover from her ordeal. This she very quickly did, but evidently the shock was more than Captain Stapledon could endure. He died in 1902, and his wife returned to London soon after, inheriting his extensive fortune and properties, including their house in Maida Vale. When she later inherited her own family's estate – her sole brother fell in the Boer War – she was a lady of great wealth.

Elisabeth Stapledon became one of the most notorious hostesses of the Edwardian era and on until the close of the First World War. Her beauty was considered remarkable, and men marvelled while her rivals bemoaned that she scarcely seemed to age with the passing years. After the War she left London to travel about the exotic East. In 1924 news came of her death in India.

Her estate passed to her daughter, Jane Stapledon, born abroad in 1901. While Elisabeth Stapledon made occasional references to her daughter, Jane was raised and educated in Europe and never seemed to have come to London until her arrival in 1925. Some had suggested that the mother had wished to keep her daughter pure from her own Bohemian life style, but when Jane Stapledon appeared, it seemed more likely that her mother's motives for her seclusion had been born of jealousy. Jane Stapledon had all her mother's beauty – indeed, her older admirers vowed she was the very image of Elisabeth in her youth. She also had inherited her mother's taste for wild living; with a new circle of friends from her own age group, she took up where her mother had left off. The newspapers were particularly scandalized by her association with Aleister Crowley and others of his circle. Although her dissipations bridged the years of Flaming Youth to the Lost Generation, even her enemies had to admit she carried her years extremely well. In 1943 Jane Stapledon was missing and presumed dead after an air raid levelled and burned a section of London where she had gone to dine with friends.

Papers in the hands of her solicitor left her estate to a daughter living in America, Julia Weatherford, born in Miami in 1934. Evidently her mother had enjoyed a typical whirlwind resort romance with an American millionaire while wintering in Florida. Their marriage was a secret one, annulled following Julia's birth, and her daughter had been left with her former husband. Julia Weatherford arrived from the States early in 1946. Any doubts as to the authenticity of her claim were instantly banished, for she was the very picture of her mother in her younger days. Julia again seemed to have the family's wild streak, and she carried on the tradition of wild parties and bizarre acquaintances through the Beat Generation to the Flower Children. Her older friends thought it amazing that Julia in a minidress might easily be mistaken as being of the same age group as her young, pot-smoking, hippie friends. But it may have been that at last her youth began to fade, because since 1967 Julia Weatherford had been living more or less in seclusion in Europe, occasionally visited by her niece.

Her niece, Beth Garrington, born in 1950, was the orphaned daughter of Julia's American half-sister and a wealthy young Englishman from Julia's collection. After her parents' death in a plane crash in 1970, Beth had become her aunt's *protégée*, and carried on the mad life in London. It was apparent that Beth Garrington would inherit her aunt's property as well. It was also apparent that she was the spitting image of her Aunt Julia when the latter was her age. It would be most interesting to see the two of them together. And that, of course, no one had ever done.

At first Dr Magnus had been unwilling to accept the truth of the dread secret he had uncovered. And yet, with the knowledge of Lisette's released memories, he knew there could be no other conclusion.

It was astonishing how thoroughly a woman who thrived on notoriety could avoid having her photographs published. After all, changing fashions and new hair styles, careful adjustments with cosmetics, could only do so much, and while the mind's eye had an inaccurate memory, a camera lens did not. Dr Magnus did succeed in finding a few photographs through persistent research. Given a good theatrical costume and makeup crew, they all might have been taken of the same woman on the same day.

They might also all have been taken of Lisette Seyrig.

However, Dr Magnus knew that it *would* be possible to see Beth Garrington and Lisette Seyrig together.

And he prayed he would be in time to prevent this.

With this knowledge tormenting his thoughts, it was a miracle that Dr Magnus had held onto sanity well enough to persuade New Scotland Yard to make this late night drive to Maida Vale – desperate, in view of what he knew to be true. He had suffered a shock as severe as any that night when they told him at last where Lisette had gone.

"She's quite all right. She's staying with a friend."

"Might I ask where?"

"A chauffered Rolls picked her up. We checked registration, and it belongs to a Miss Elisabeth Garrington in Maida Vale."

Dr Magnus had been frantic then, had demanded that they take him there instantly. A telephone call informed them that Miss Seyrig was sleeping under sedation and could not be disturbed; she would return his call in the morning.

Controlling his panic, Dr Magnus had managed to contrive a disjointed tangle of half-truths and plausible lies – anything to convince them to get over to the Garrington house as quickly as possible. They already knew he was one of those occult kooks. Very well, he assured them that Beth Garrington was involved in a secret society of drug fiends and satanists (all true enough), that Danielle and Lisette had been lured to their most recent orgy for unspeakable purposes. Lisette had been secretly drugged, but Danielle had escaped to carry her roommate home before they could be used for whatever depraved rites awaited them – perhaps ritual sacrifice. Danielle had been murdered – either to shut her up or as part of the ritual – and now they had Lisette in their clutches as well.

All very melodramatic, but enough of it was true. Inspector Bradley knew of the sex and drugs orgies that took place there, but there was firm pressure from higher up to look the other way. Further, he knew enough about some of the more bizzare cult groups in London to consider that ritual murder was quite feasible, given the proper combination of sick minds and illegal drugs. And while it hadn't been made public, the medical examiner was of the opinion that the slashes to the Borland girl's throat and wrists had been an attempt to disguise the fact that she had already bled to death from two deep punctures through the jugular vein.

A demented killer, obviously. A ritual murder? You couldn't discount it just yet. Inspector Bradley had ordered a car.

"Who are you, Lisette Seyrig, that you wear my face?"

Beth Garrington rose sinuously from her bed. She was dressed in an off-the-shoulder nightgown of antique lace, much the same as that which Lisette wore. Her green eyes – the eyes behind the mask that had so shaken Lisette when last they'd met – held her in their spell.

"When first faithful Adrian swore he'd seen my double, I thought his brain had begun to reel with final madness. But after he followed you to your little gallery and brought me there to see your portrait, I knew I had encountered something beyond even my experience."

Lisette stood frozen with dread fascination as her nightmare came to life. Her twin paced about her, appraising her coolly as a serpent considers its hypnotized victim.

"Who are you, Lisette Seyrig, that yours is the face I have seen in my dreams, the face that haunted my nightmares as I lay dying, the face that I thought was my own?"

Lisette forced her lips to speak. "*Who* are you?"

"My name? I change that whenever it becomes prudent for me to do so. Tonight I am Beth Garrington. Long ago I was Elisabeth Beresford."

"How can this be possible?" Lisette hoped she was dealing with a madwoman, but knew her hope was false.

"A spirit came to me in my dreams and slowly stole away my mortal life, in return giving me eternal life. You understand what I say, even though your reason insists that such things cannot be."

She unfastened Lisette's gown and let it fall to the floor, then did the same with her own. Standing face to face, their nude bodies seemed one a reflection of the other.

Elisabeth took Lisette's face in her hands and kissed her full on the lips. The kiss was a long one; her breath was cold in Lisette's mouth. When Elisabeth released her lips and gazed longingly into her eyes, Lisette saw the pointed fangs that now curved downward from her upper jaw.

"Will you cry out, I wonder? If so, let it be in ecstasy and not in fear. I shan't drain you and discard you as I did your silly friend. No, Lisette, my new-found sister. I shall take your life in tiny kisses from night to night – kisses that you will long for with your entire being. And in the end you shall pass over to serve me as my willing chattel – as have the few others I have chosen over the years."

Lisette trembled beneath her touch, powerless to break away. From the buried depths of her unconscious mind, understanding slowly emerged. She did not resist when Elisabeth led her to the bed and lay down beside her on the silken sheets. Lisette was past knowing fear.

Elisabeth stretched her naked body upon Lisette's warmer flesh, lying between her thighs as would a lover. Her cool fingers caressed Lisette; her kisses teased a path from her belly across her breasts and to the hollow of her throat.

Elisabeth paused and gazed into Lisette's eyes. Her fangs gleamed with a reflection of the inhuman lust in her expression.

"And now I give you a kiss sweeter than any passion your mortal brain dare imagine, Lisette Seyrig – even as once I first received such a kiss from a dream-spirit whose eyes stared into mine from my own face. Why have you haunted my dreams, Lisette Seyrig?"

Lisette returned her gaze silently, without emotion. Nor did she flinch when Elisabeth's lips closed tightly against her throat, and the only sound was a barely perceptible tearing, like the bursting of a maidenhead, and the soft movement of suctioning lips.

Elisabeth suddenly broke away with an inarticulate cry of pain. Her lips smeared with scarlet, she stared down at Lisette in bewildered fear. Lisette, blood streaming from the wound on her throat, stared back at her with a smile of unholy hatred.

"*What* are you, Lisette Seyrig?"

"I am Elisabeth Beresford." Lisette's tone was implacable. "In another lifetime you drove my soul from my body and stole my flesh for your own. Now I have come back to reclaim that which once was mine."

Elisabeth sought to leap away, but Lisette's arms embraced her with sudden, terrible strength – pulling their naked bodies together in a horrid imitation of two lovers at the moment of ecstasy.

The scream that echoed into the night was not one of ecstasy.

At the sound of the scream – afterward they never agreed whether it was two voices together or only one – Inspector Bradley ceased listening to the maid's outraged protests and burst past her into the house.

"Upstairs! On the double!" He ordered needlessly. Already Dr Magnus had lunged past him and was sprinting up the stairway.

"I think it came from the next floor up! Check inside all the rooms!" Later he cursed himself for not posting a man at the door, for by the time he was again able to think rationally, there was no trace of the servants.

In the master bedroom at the end of the third-floor hallway, they found two bodies behind the curtains of the big four-poster bed. One had only just been murdered; her nude body was drenched in the blood from her torn throat – seemingly far too much blood for one body. The other body was a desiccated corpse, obviously dead for a great many years. The dead girl's limbs obscenely embraced the mouldering cadaver that lay atop her, and her teeth, in final spasm, were locked in the lich's throat. As they gaped in horror, clumps of hair and bits of dried skin could be seen to drop away.

Detective Sergeant Wharton looked away and vomited on the floor.

"I owe you a sincere apology, Dr Magnus." Inspector Bradley's face was grim. "You were right. Ritual murder by a gang of sick degenerates. Detective Sergeant! Leave off that, and put out an all-points bulletin for Beth Garrington. And round up anyone else you find here! Move, man!"

"If only I'd understood in time," Dr Magnus muttered. He was obviously to the point of collapse.

"No, *I* should have listened to you sooner," Bradley growled. "We might have been in time to prevent this. The devils must have fled down some servants' stairway when they heard us burst in. I confess I've bungled this badly."

"She was a vampire, you see," Dr Magnus told him dully, groping to explain. "A vampire loses its soul when it becomes one of the undead. But the soul is deathless; it lives on even when its previous incarnation has become a soulless demon. Elisabeth Beresford's soul lived on, until Elisabeth Beresford found reincarnation, in Lisette Seyrig. Don't you see? Elisabeth Beresford met her own reincarnation, and that meant destruction for them both."

Inspector Bradley had been only half listening. "Dr Magnus, you've done all you can. I think you should go down to the car with Detective Sergeant Wharton now and rest until the ambulance arrives."

"But you must see that I was right!" Dr Magnus pleaded. Madness danced in his eyes. "If the soul is immortal and infinite, then time has no meaning for the soul. Elisabeth Beresford was haunting herself."

BASIL COPPER

Doctor Porthos

BASIL COPPER WORKED as a journalist and editor of a local newspaper before becoming a full-time writer in 1970.

His first story in the horror field, 'The Spider', was published in 1964 in *The Fifth Pan Book of Horror Stories*, since when his short fiction has appeared in numerous anthologies, been extensively adapted for radio, and collected in *Not After Nightfall, Here Be Daemons, From Evil's Pillow, And Afterward the Dark, Voices of Doom, When Footsteps Echo, Whispers in the Night* and, more recently, *Cold Hand on My Shoulder* from Sarob Press.

Along with two non-fiction studies of the vampire and werewolf legends, his other books include the novels *The Great White Space, The Curse of the Fleers, Necropolis, The Black Death* and *The House of the Wolf* (the latter reissued in 2003 in a 25th-anniversary edition by Sarob). Copper has also written more than fifty hard-boiled thrillers about Los Angeles private detective Mike Faraday, and has continued the adventures of August Derleth's Sherlock Holmes-like consulting detective Solar Pons in several volumes of short stories and the novel *The Devil's Claw* (actually written in 1980, but not published until recently).

'Doctor Porthos' is another vampire story with a surprising twist at the end. It was optioned by Universal in the early 1970s for the television series *Rod Serling's Night Gallery* but, unlike another Copper story, 'Camera Obscura', it was never filmed.

I

NERVOUS DEBILITY, THE DOCTOR says. And yet Angelina has never been ill in her life. Nervous debility! Something far more powerful is involved here; I am left wondering if I should not call in specialist advice. Yet we are so remote and Dr Porthos is well spoken of by the local people. Why on earth did we ever come to this house? Angelina was perfectly well until then. It is extraordinary to think that two months can have wrought such a change in my wife.

In the town she was lively and vivacious; yet now I can hardly bear to look at her without profound emotion. Her cheeks are sunken and pale, her eyes dark and tired, her bloom quite gone at twenty-five. Could it be something in the air of the house? It seems barely possible. But in that case Dr Porthos' ministrations should have proved effective. But so far all his skills have been powerless to produce any change for the better. If it had not been for the terms of my uncle's will we would never have come at all.

Friends may call it cupidity, the world may think what it chooses, but the plain truth is that I needed the money. My own health is far from robust and long hours in the family business – ours is an honoured and well-established counting house – had made it perfectly clear to me that I must seek some other mode of life. And yet I could not afford to retire; the terms of my uncle's will, as retailed to me by the family solicitor, afforded the perfect solution.

An annuity – a handsome annuity to put it bluntly – but with the proviso that my wife and I should reside in the old man's house for a period of not less than five years from the date the terms of the will became effective. I hesitated long; both my wife and I were fond of town life and my uncle's estate was in a remote area, where living for the country people was primitive and amenities few. As I had understood it from the solicitor, the house itself had not even the benefit of gas-lighting; in summer it was not so bad but the long months of winter would be melancholy indeed with only the glimmer of candles and the pale sheen of oil lamps to relieve the gloom of the lonely old place.

I debated with Angelina and then set off one week-end alone for a tour of the estate. I had cabled ahead and after a long and cold railway journey which itself occupied most of the day, I was met at my destination by a horse and chaise. The next part of my pilgrimage occupied nearly four hours and I was dismayed on seeing into what a wild and remote region my uncle had chosen to penetrate in order to select a dwelling.

The night was dark but the moon occasionally burst its veiling of cloud to reveal in feeble detail the contours of rock and hill and tree; the chaise jolted and lurched over an unmade road, which was deeply rutted by the wheels of the few vehicles which had torn up the surface in their passing over many months. My solicitor had wired to an old friend, Dr Porthos, to whose good offices I owed my mode of transport, and he had promised to greet me on arrival at the village nearest the estate.

Sure enough, he came out from under the great porch of the timbered hostelry as our carriage grated into the inn-yard. He was a tall, spare man, with square pince-nez which sat firmly on his thin nose; he wore a many-pleated cape like an ostler and the green top hat, worn rakishly over one eye gave him a somewhat dissipated look. He greeted me effusively but there was something about the man which did not endear him to me.

There was nothing that one could isolate. It was just his general manner; perhaps the coldness of his hand which struck my palm with the clamminess of a fish. Then too, his eyes had a most disconcerting way of looking over the tops of his glasses; they were a filmy grey and their piercing glance seemed to root one to the spot. To my dismay I learned that I was not yet at my destination. The estate was still some way off, said the doctor, and we would have to stay the night at the inn. My ill-temper at his remarks was soon dispelled by the roaring fire and the good food with which he plied me; there were few travellers at this time of year and we were the only ones taking dinner in the vast oak-panelled dining room.

The doctor had been my uncle's medical attendant and though it was many years since I had seen my relative I was curious to know what sort of person he had been.

"The Baron was a great man in these parts," said Porthos. His genial manner emboldened me to ask a question to which I had long been awaiting an answer.

"Of what did my uncle die?" I asked.

Firelight flickered through the gleaming redness of Dr Porthos' wineglass and tinged his face with amber as he replied simply, "Of a lacking of richness in the blood. A fatal quality in his immediate line, I might say."

I pondered for a moment. "Why do you think he chose me as his heir?" I added.

Dr Porthos' answer was straight and clear and given without hesitation.

"You were a different branch of the family," he said. "New blood, my dear sir. The Baron was most particular on that account. He wanted to carry on the great tradition."

He cut off any further questions by rising abruptly. "Those were the Baron's own words as he lay dying. And now we must retire as we still have a fair journey before us in the morning."

II

Dr Porthos' words come back to me in my present trouble. "Blood, new blood . . ." What if this be concerned with those dark legends the local people tell about the house? One hardly knows what to think in this atmosphere. My inspection of the house with Dr Porthos confirmed my worst fears; sagging lintels, mouldering cornices, worm-eaten panelling. The only servitors a middle-aged couple, husband and wife, who have been caretakers here since the Baron's death; the local people sullen and unco-operative, so Porthos says. Certainly, the small hamlet a mile or so from the mansion had every door and window shut as we clattered past and not a soul was stirring. The house has a Gothic beauty, I suppose, viewed from a distance; it is of no great age, being largely re-built on the remains of an older pile destroyed by fire. The restorer – whether he be my uncle or some older resident I have not bothered to discover – had the fancy of adding turrets, a draw-bridge with castellated towers and a moated surround. Our footsteps echoed mournfully over this as we turned to inspect the grounds.

I was surprised to see marble statuary and worn obelisks, all tumbled and awry, as though the uneasy dead were bursting from the soil, protruding over an ancient moss-grown wall adjoining the courtyard of the house.

Dr Porthos smiled sardonically.

"The old family burial ground," he explained. "Your uncle is interred here. He said he likes to be near the house."

III

Well, it is done; we came not two months since and then began the profound and melancholy change of which I have already spoken. Not just the atmosphere – though the very stones of the house seem steeped in evil whispers – but the surroundings, the dark, unmoving trees, even the furniture, seem to exude something inimical to life as we knew it; as it is still known to those fortunate enough to dwell in towns.

A poisonous mist rises from the moat at dusk; it seems to doubly emphasize our isolation. The presence of Angelina's own maid and a handyman who was in my father's employ before me, do little to dispel the ambiance of this place. Even their sturdy matter of factness seems affected by a miasma that wells from the pores of the building. It has become so manifest of late that I even welcome the daily visits of Dr Porthos, despite the fact that I suspect him to be the author of our troubles.

They began a week after our arrival when Angelina failed to awake by my side as usual; I shook her to arouse her and my screams must have awakened the maid. I think I fainted then and came to myself in the great morning room; the bed had been awash with blood, which stained the sheets and pillows around my dear wife's head; Porthos' curious grey eyes had a steely look in them which I had never seen before. He administered a powerful medicine and had then turned to attend to me.

Whatever had attacked Angelina had teeth like the sharpest canine, Porthos said; he had found two distinct punctures in Angelina's throat, sufficient to account for the quantities of blood. Indeed, there had been so much of it that my own hands and linen were stained with it where I had touched her; I think it was this which had made me cry so violently. Porthos had announced that he would sit up by the patient that night.

Angelina was still asleep, as I discovered when I tiptoed in later. Porthos had administered a sleeping draught and had advised me to take the same, to settle my nerves, but I declined. I said I would wait up with him. The doctor had some theory about rats or other nocturnal creatures and sat long in the library looking through some of the Baron's old books on natural history. The man's attitude puzzles me; what sort of creature would attack Angelina in her own bedroom? Looking at Porthos' strange eyes, my old fears are beginning to return, bringing with them new ones.

IV

There have been three more attacks, extending over a fortnight. My darling grows visibly weaker, though Porthos has been to the nearest town for more powerful drugs and other remedies. I am in purgatory; I have not known such dark hours in my life until now. Yet Angelina herself insists that we should stay to see this grotesque nightmare through. The first evening of our vigil both Porthos and I slept; and in the morning the result was as the night before. Considerable emissions of blood and the bandage covering the wound had been removed to allow the creature access to the punctures. I hardly dare conjecture what manner of beast could have done this.

I was quite worn out and on the evening of the next day I agreed to Porthos' suggestion that I should take a sleeping draught. Nothing happened for several nights and Angelina began to recover; then the terror struck again. And so it will go on, my reeling senses tell me. I daren't trust Porthos and on the other hand I cannot accuse him before the members of my household. We are isolated here and any mistake I make might be fatal.

On the last occasion I almost had him. I woke at dawn and found Porthos stretched on the bed, his long, dark form quivering, his hands at Angelina's throat. I struck at him, for I did not know who it was, being half asleep, and he turned, his grey eyes glowing in the dim room. He had a hypodermic syringe half full of blood in his hand. I am afraid I dashed it to the floor and shattered it beneath my heel.

In my own heart I am convinced I have caught this creature which has been plaguing us, but how to prove it? Dr Porthos is staying in the house now; I dare not sleep and continually refuse the potions he urgently presses upon me. How long before he destroys me as well as Angelina? Was man ever in such an appalling situation since the world began?

I sit and watch Porthos, who stares at me sideways with those curious eyes, his inexpressive face seeming to hint that he can afford to watch and wait and that his time is coming; my pale wife, in her few intervals of consciousness sits and fearfully watches both of us. Yet I cannot even confide in her for she would think me mad. I try to calm my racing brain. Sometimes I think I shall go insane altogether, the nights are so long. God help me.

V

It is over. The crisis has come and gone. I have laid the mad demon which has us in thrall. I caught him at it. Porthos writhed as I got my hands at his throat. I would have killed him at his foul work, the syringe glinted in his hand. Now he has slipped aside, eluded me for the moment. My cries brought in the servants who have my express instructions to hunt him down. He shall not escape me this time. I pace the corridors of this worm-eaten mansion and when I have cornered him I shall destroy him. Angelina shall live! And my hands will perform the healing work of his destruction . . . But now I must rest. Already it is dawn again. I will sit in this chair by the pillar, where I can watch the hall. I sleep.

VI

Later. I awake to pain and cold. I am lying on earth. Something slippery trickles over my hand. I open my eyes. I draw my hand across my mouth. It comes away scarlet. I can see more clearly now. Angelina is here too. She looks terrified but somehow sad and composed. She is holding the arm of Dr Porthos.

He is poised above me, his face looking satanic in the dim light of the crypt beneath the house. He whirls a mallet while shriek after shriek disturbs the silence of this place. Dear Christ, the stake is against *my breast!*

PAUL McAULEY

Straight to Hell

BEFORE HE BECAME a full-time writer, Paul McAuley worked as a research biologist in various universities, and for six years was a lecturer in botany at St Andrews University.

His books include *Whole Wide World*, *Four Hundred Billion Stars*, *Pasquale's Angel*, *Fairyland*, *The Secret of Life* and *The Eye of the Tyger*, the latter a *Doctor Who* novella from Telos. His acclaimed "The Book of Confluence" trilogy comprises *Child of the River*, *Ancients of Days* and *Shrine of Stars*, while his latest novel, *White Devils*, is a thriller set in a near-future Africa greatly changed by out-of-control biotechnology. A new short-story collection, *Little Machines*, is available from PS Publishing.

The author has won the Philip K. Dick, Arthur C. Clarke, John W. Campbell, Sidewise and British Fantasy awards for his novels and short stories.

"Whenever I was ill and laid up in bed in my childhood, my grandmother (who lived next door) would bring me Lucozade and samples from her stacks of *Reader's Digest*," remembers McAuley. "In one of those I read an article about Rasputin. The trouble his murderers had in finishing him off (he proved to be almost as hard to kill as any cartoon character) stuck with me, and some time later turned into this story."

Twenty years after he last saw them, the writer still thinks that The

Clash, from whom he borrowed the title for this symbiotic story, was one of the greatest rock 'n' roll bands ever.

THE BOTTLES CAME SAILING out of the roaring dark. One and then another and then too many to count. Beautiful for a moment as they tumbled lazily in the black air like so many spent rocket stages, catching glints and sparks of light from the spots as they fell towards us.

Then the first shattered on the stage, a yard from where Vor slumped under the black puddle of his cloak, breathing loudly into his antique microphone, the one that looked like a miniature robot head. Glass splinters flying everywhere, and Vor too far gone to notice as more bottles fell, hitting Toad's drum riser with percussive thumps, hitting everywhere amongst the cables that snaked across the stage, smashing against the speaker cabinets. One knocked a baby spot around, the light scything across upturned faces; another slammed into Davy's keyboards and spun away into the wings. Davy's ornamental arpeggios cut off as he stepped back, although the taped effects were still playing. I sidestepped a bottle, still strumming the lazy, circular riff we'd settled into when Vor had collapsed into his fugue a long five minutes ago, and felt a sharp bite in my calf where a shard cut through my leather jeans.

The crowd's blood was up, its roar like the ocean turning under a storm, and now more than bottles were flying through the air: plastic cups, programmes fluttering like wounded birds, shoes, a crutch. As if the crowd was tearing itself to bits in its fury. A cup heavy with greasy yellow liquid splashed at my feet: the sharp stink of piss.

Someone darted past me – it was Koshchei, dodging as I swung the body of my guitar at him, smiling right at me for a moment, ropes of hair swinging around the pale blade of his face. He plucked a bottle from the air and hurled it back, then knelt over Vor and tenderly cradled him.

I had stopped playing now; Toad had abandoned his riser.

For a moment all you could hear was the sound of Vor's wet, hoarse breathing, the birdsong on the tape loop, and the clatter and smash of breaking glass.

Then the crowd's roar rose up again as two bouncers came forward, big men bulging out of their T-shirts and jeans, hunched shyly under the barrage of noise and flying stuff, passes swinging from their necks as they got their hands under Vor's shoulders and dragged him backwards, the heels of his boots bumping over cables. Koshchei scampered beside him, for all the world like a dog by its master.

Davy stepped up to his mike, his black duster dripping beer, welder's goggles gleaming blankly, and said, "Fuck you and goodnight."

I pulled the plug from my guitar and ran.

Stockholm, 15 September 2001. The first and last gig of Liquid Television's second European tour.

It wasn't the first time Vor had pulled shit like that. Even before he'd fallen under Koshchei's spell, he'd played head games – with himself, with the crowd, with us. Turning away from the mike mid-song to watch us drive it home without him, arms folded and a little smile tucked into his face. Striding out at the opening of a concert and reading page after page of Shelley's *Prometheus Unbound*, ignoring the crowd's impatient heckling. Launching into a song only to suddenly bring it to a halt, starting another and stopping that too, as if searching for the perfect groove. Singing a chorus over and over until his voice gave out, then holding the mike out to the crowd and letting them take over. Davy and me, we put up with it, because although we'd brought the band together, this skinny little twenty-year-old kid, young enough to be my son, was the star.

I never wanted to be anything other than a musician. I spent the seventies in a squat in Camden, the caretaker's house of a disused school. I lived in one room with my guitar and a couple of reel-to-reel tape recorders, LPs in cardboard boxes, a bed made out of a couple of pallets. I was a sort of post-hippie hippie, doing a tab of acid every day, living on Mars bars and leftover fruit that I scrounged from the market. Drawing the dole, sometimes going down to Kent to make some easy cash apple- or hop-picking. And always playing, sometimes hooking up with one of the bands on the local pub circuit but mostly doing my own thing, using the two tape recorders to experiment with layering and splicing of sounds. In the mid-1980s I hooked up with Davy, a public-school drop-out and electronics genius whose best mate had started a record label, XYZ. Davy was tall, blond, and intensely serious, a perfect foil to my nervous unfocused energy. We made trance music before anyone knew what it was (we didn't know either – we thought we were a kind of Fripp and Eno deal). We sold enough twelve-inch mixes to DJs to make a living, even had a minor chart hit, its riff lifted from the opening of Rachmaninov's Piano Concerto No. 2. XYZ grew too fast, developed cash-flow problems and folded; Davy and I started our own label and set up a studio where we recorded our own stuff and mixed and re-mixed tracks for other people. We were famous in our own circle, but never hit it big until one day this scroungey kid who'd been hanging around the studio dumped a sheaf of papers on the mixing desk and said he'd just written twenty songs and we should quit fucking around and make him a star.

That was Vor. That was two years ago.

He got what he wanted in six months. Then he met Koshchei, and now he was tearing everything down.

I don't even remember when Koshchei appeared on the scene. Somewhere during our first European tour, between Berlin and Kiev. Vor always had people hanging around him, a gang within the gang that was our band. Davy and I tolerated it, but the heavy partying and the heavy-duty drugs were beginning to affect Vor's performance. We were scheduled to record the crucial second album as soon as the tour ended, and as yet Vor had no new songs.

"They'll come," Vor would say, whenever Davy pressed him. "They'll come when I'm ready for them." Once, he said, with the shy smile that girls fell for, "They're all around us. You can just pluck them out of the air, once you know how."

My first memory of Koshchei is of seeing him talk with the army captain in charge of a border crossing. Our two coaches and three pantechnicons head-to-tail on a steep mountain road with pines crowding the slope above them, concrete blockhouses beside the toll gates, everyone standing in the road, shivering in the fresh cold wind and thinking about all the illegal shit stashed in their belongings, watching the very young and very nervous soldiers armed with machine guns walk up and down. And this tall man in a fur coat, greasy ropes of hair tumbling down his back, drawing the army captain aside, talking to him in a low soothing voice. Koshchei and the captain talking for about two minutes, then Koshchei coming over to the tour manager, who was standing with Davy and me, and saying that all was fine, we could go through, nothing to pay, no inspection.

"I know that man's family of old," Koshchei said. His smile was as quick and sharp as an assassin's knife.

He looked about forty then. At other times he looked twice that; at others, he could have been Vor's younger brother. He was even taller than Davy, wire-thin but immensely strong, his skin like paper, very white and coarsely textured, his eyes blue, with veins like little red ropes, his nose hooked. Although he doused himself in perfume, his personal odour was strong: spoiled butter, foul mud, fresh meat. I smelt it then, tainting the clean mountain air.

After the border incident, I started to notice that Koshchei was always close to Vor. He was in Vor's dressing room before gigs, stood in the shadows at the side of the stage and hustled away with him while the last chords of the last encore hung in the air; stood beside him at parties, stooping down to whisper something in our singer's ear, or performing some conjuring trick for the amusement of Vor and his entourage. Card tricks, mind-reading stunts – Koshchei was good at them, and ate pebbles and light bulbs too, crunching the glass and letting people see the fragments on his red tongue before he swallowed them.

Vor looked like hell. He was mixing coke and 'ludes and, I think, experimenting with heroin. And he was drinking heavily too, a bottle of Jack Daniel's a day plus swigs from whatever the people around him were drinking. We bought a case of foul plum brandy in Albania; Vor got through it in a week. On stage he was still on fire, burning with messianic fervour.

Off stage he looked drawn and weary, and he often fell asleep in some corner, Koshchei covering him with a fur wrap and tenderly rubbing his wrists.

Towards the end of the tour, I learned from Normal Norman, one of Vor's entourage, that Vor had given up snorting coke and heroin, was into this stuff Koshchei made. "Really thick and evil-smelling, like bad yogurt. Vor says it takes him to very strange places," Normal Norman said, adjusting his thick glasses with a forefinger, "but I wouldn't know where, because Koshchei doesn't give it up for anyone but Vor."

Whatever it was, it didn't stop Vor drinking, and he still looked terrible. He had a flare-up of acne, and permanent circles inked under his eyes, which he disguised with make-up before going on stage. He was throwing up a lot, too, blaming bad food and refusing all offers of medical attention, saying stubbornly that Koshchei was taking care of him.

One time, in Bucharest, a roadie went into the backstage bathroom and saw Vor kneeling in front of Koshchei, who was pissing in his mouth.

"It really creeps me out," Davy said, after he had told me about it.

"Different strokes," I said, although I didn't like it either.

"If it was a sex thing I wouldn't mind so much," Davy said.

"Maybe that's all it is. An S&M deal."

"It's more than that," Davy said.

I shrugged. Although Davy was terrific with any kind of electronic gear and drove his mixing desk with a subtle yet alert touch, he didn't know shit about people. But just this once he was right.

Koshchei was still with us when we finished the tour and went straight into the studios with no idea of what we were going to do. That didn't worry us too much – Davy and I had been working together a long time, and we had a deep box of tricks to draw on. But while we developed a couple of basic tracks by noodling about, adding this, taking away that, Vor either nodded out on one of the couches of the control booth, with Koshchei beside him, or didn't turn up at all. We racked up a couple of weeks of studio time and spent about a hundred thousand pounds, and still didn't have a single lyric or hook from Vor, and that was when we went around to his house and told him to get his shit together, taking turns to talk while Vor looked at us with a kind of dazed bafflement.

We were in the cavernous master bedroom, and Vor was stretched out under the canopy of his eighteenth-century four-poster, which he'd bought because Mozart was supposed have slept in it. He was bare-chested, and his thin white frame was marked with livid scratches and the knots of old cigarette burns. Someone was asleep under the heavy red velvet throw, curled up so that only a cap of dirty blond hair showed. Candles burned in front of mirrors, a glass half-full of thick white liquid stood on the bedside table, and there was a stack of dirty plates on the Turkestan carpet.

"He is able to do what you want," Koshchei said, when we had run out of breath. "More than that, you will be amazed by what he does."

"This is business," Davy said sharply. He was exasperated by Vor's dumb stoner act. "You keep out of it."

"This boy *is* my business," Koshchei said. "I cannot keep out of it."

"Fuck you," Davy said, and made to grab Koshchei's wrist.

It was three in the morning. The air was grainy and stale, and I had a headache from too much dope and nicotine and coffee, so maybe I only thought that I saw Davy's hand pass right through the sleeve of Koshchei's fur coat. Maybe he misjudged his reach, or maybe the man leaned back. That's what I thought then.

Davy swore, and shook his hand as if it had been burned. Vor giggled, and said, "He's with me. I need him. You leave him alone."

"You need to get to work," Davy said.

"I don't know if I'm ready to go down that road."

"You are ready," Koshchei said.

Davy ignored this, and said to Vor, "What happened to just plucking them out of the air?"

Vor said quietly, "The stuff I did before isn't even bad. It's trivial. It's nothing. I want to go deeper than that. I *know* I can go deeper, but it's scary. Worse than scary."

Koshchei said, "You have it in you to do great things, Clint."

Clint was Vor's real name: Clint Kelly. A half-Irish kid who'd grown up ragged and strange amongst the tower blocks of Hackney, a naive genius who'd taken his stage name from some old sci-fi novel.

The boy looked at me, looked at Davy. He said, "You don't know what you're asking. Give me time."

"We have to get the album out before September," Davy said. "That's when the next tour starts, and we don't even have a single track yet."

I said, "Maybe you should go away for a week. Rest up somewhere warm, away from all the pressure. Then come back and get started."

Vor laughed. "You don't get it. It isn't the contract. It isn't the fucking rock-star thing. It's in here," he said, and pressed the heels of his hands against his eyes. "It's in here. I want to go deeper than anyone ever has. I'm on the brink. I can feel it. But I can't let go."

Koshchei said, "But you want to. I know that you do."

Vor looked at Koshchei, and something passed between them. He said, "Yes. Yes, I want it so much. But I'm so afraid."

"I will be with you," Koshchei said, with such tenderness and such hunger that I shivered.

Davy took off his glasses and knuckled his eyes and said, "Does this mean that we're going to get to work?"

Koshchei stood, very tall and very thin inside his black floor-length fur coat. His eyes seemed full of blood. "Leave now. He does not need you. I will help him. We will give him what you want."

Vor took his hands away from his eyes and looked up at Koshchei, and for the first time he seemed truly frightened of his strange friend.

Vor was away for five days. He did not come to the studio; he was not at his house. He vanished. Davy was ready to cancel everything, convinced that Vor had run away, when the boy came into the studio and dumped a DAT cassette and a folder full of paper on the mixing desk. He was wide awake for the first time in months, very engaged and very serious, hovering at our shoulders while Davy and I read through the lyrics and listened to the voice guides that he'd laid down over a basic keyboard accompaniment. "Test Meat." "Throw Me in the Fire." "Nest of Salt." "Spook Speak." You know them all.

"I want a heavy beat," Vor said. "Something very fundamental, like the heartbeat of the world."

We got to work. Vor was on fire, roaring and wailing those extraordinary lyrics into his favourite antique microphone as if the studio was a stage in front of an audience of millions. He hardly ate, drank only a kind of tea that Koshchei made from aromatic bark, yet he exhausted us as he listened to the mixes over and over, making intense and detailed criticisms and suggestions as we layered drums and keyboards, guitar and orchestral and ambient effects. We did forty takes of the basic rhythm track for "King of Illiterature", so many versions of "Close as Cancer" that even Davy lost count.

And Koshchei was always there, watching Vor with an avid tenderness as the boy went deeper than did ever plummet sound.

I ran straight through the backstage maze into a limo. I still had my guitar; its head bumped the roof every time the limo hit a pothole. I got to the hotel inside ten minutes and went up to the floor where we had our suites. Davy was already there, sucking on a Beck's as he paced up and down outside Vor's suite, stopping every third or fourth pass to slam the flat of his palm against the door. Dressed like me in a long black duster coat, leather jeans, leather vest, silver boots, his hair dyed white. It was our patent space-cowboy look.

He saw me and thumped the door and yelled, "Come out, you fucker!"

"Is he in there?"

"He's in there."

"And—"

"He's in there too, the piece of shit. Christ, he must have slipped Vor something bad this time."

"Vor didn't ever need anyone to find bad shit."

Davy looked at me. He was still pumped up from the gig, his hair soaked in sweat, his eyes wide and staring. He said, "He was on another planet, man. He couldn't even speak."

Roy Menthorn, our manager, came out of the adjoining suite – mine, as it happened. He was in shirtsleeves, his tie at half-mast. He saw us and said, "The promoter is going to sue us," and might have said more, but then his cellphone rang and he disappeared back into the suite.

Davy sucked down the last of his beer, and used the heel of the bottle to bang on the door of Vor's suite.

I said, because it had stuck in my mind, "Did you see when Koshchei came on stage?"

"I saw it."

"He caught a bottle and threw it back."

"I don't care if he's Vor's guardian angel, his lover, or his fucking muse. He has to go."

"Absolutely."

Our stares locked. We both knew then that we would do anything necessary to get rid of Koshchei.

I said, "I'll call the hotel manager."

"Get Roy to do it. That's what we pay him for."

Roy Menthorn made the call and told us that the manager would be up in ten minutes, then retreated to one of the bedrooms to play dykes and little Dutch boys with his cellphone. Davy and I paced up and down, making a serious inroad on the rider. Toad stumbled in with two girls, snagged a couple of bottles of the Polish vodka he liked – Terminator, half battery acid, half rocket fuel – and vanished. Toad had a Ph.D. in astronomy, a bad coke habit and a salary, just like Roy Menthorn. We were a very post-twentieth-century band. In the beginning, Vor was one of our employees too, but when the royalties started pouring in they made his salary seem beside the point.

"Remember those first songs," Davy said.

"Written in crayon."

"Yeah, all different colours."

"On newspaper."

"They're still around somewhere."

"He said it was the only paper he could find."

"I guess they're worth a fortune," Davy said. He shucked his beer-stained duster coat and dropped it on a sofa. "Christ, this is so fucked up."

"Yeah. I feel like throwing a TV out the window."

Davy looked at me. Sweat had left a kind of tidemark of white dye along his hairline. He said, "Has the significance of this reached you yet, man?"

I was working on my third or fourth beer. I said, "I mean it about the TV. If there was a swimming pool down there I'd do it."

Davy actually went to the curtains and parted them and looked down. "A car park," he said. "We probably couldn't get the windows open, anyway."

I said, "He was such a sweet kid. Crazy, but not insane."

"Do you think he is now? Insane, I mean."

"I don't know. Maybe. That stuff Koshchei feeds him . . ."

"The fucker offered it to me once," Davy said.

"Did you take it?" I was genuinely interested.

"Fuck no. You're the one who does drugs."

"That's why he offered it to you."

"Probably. He makes it himself. Boils up these roots, chews them and lets them ferment."

"*Chews* them?"

"He told me that saliva helps the fermentation."

"Some kind of Russian *Masato*," I said.

"*Masato*?"

"Amazonian Indians make it from boiled manioc."

"Well, I never did think he was Russian."

"Wherever he's from, I think he's some kind of shaman. Remember the time he was caught pissing in Vor's mouth? I read later that Siberian shamans get high by eating fly agaric mushrooms, and anyone who drinks their piss gets high too. Their bodies purify the drug, and it comes out in the piss."

Davy ignored this and said, "How much will it cost to get rid of him, do you think?"

"No more than cancelling the rest of the tour, I suppose. Roy would know."

"It'll be worth it."

The hotel manager came up with a couple of security people, and insisted on unlocking the door to Vor's suite himself. Davy pushed past, and I was right behind him. The room was very dark, and stank of sweat and incense. The only light came from a lamp covered in a skull-and-crossbones scarf, and a sliver shining at the bottom of the bathroom door.

Vor lay on a sofa under a heap of fur coats, naked and sweating. His eyes were rolled back, showing mostly white, but he was breathing normally. His face had lost all its baby fat and his skin was as bloodless as parchment – a skull with cheekbones by Dior. There was a glass half-full of a thick milky liquid on the floor; Davy picked it up between thumb and forefinger, sniffed, made a face. We both knew what it was, and what we had to do. Roy was still sweet-talking the manager as we closed and locked the door and went into the bathroom.

Koshchei was wallowing in the huge scallop-shell bath, dreadlocks spread amongst a snow of iridescent bubbles. Their lavender scent didn't do much to disguise his strong odour. He was watching a portable TV hooked up to an extension cable and tuned to CNN.

Davy shut the door, leaned against it and said, "Where are the others?"

"The others?"

"The twins. Normal Norman. The rest of Vor's . . . people."

"I have sent them away. They are gone back to the house, or they are gone to where they first came from. It does not matter to me."

"So now it's just you and him," Davy said. "Nice and cosy under those furs."

Koshchei said nothing, his narrow face still turned to the TV.

Davy said, "We want to know what happened tonight."

"The boy is resting. When he wakes you ask him."

"He was as high as the moon," Davy said. "He didn't sing a note. Just howled through two numbers and then collapsed."

Koshchei smiled.

"We want you to go," I said.

"I make him what he is," Koshchei said. "You know that. So you also know you must put up with me."

"Not any more," I said.

"I think very much so. We are barely begun."

"You're killing him with that shit," Davy said.

"You have what you want, and he does not yet die."

Davy started a rant about lawyers, restraining orders, illegal entry into the country. "We'll get Vor into rehab," he said. "We'll get him away from you any way we can."

"I think not."

"Quit watching the fucking TV and look at me!"

"I do not think you would like that."

Davy pushed away from the door and reached for the remote, which lay on the edge of the bath, but Koshchei snatched it and held it up for a moment before dropping it into the bubbles and smiling at us.

"Fucker," Davy said, and kicked the TV into the bath.

A fat blue spark filled the room, filled the inside of my head. All the lights went out. A fire alarm started somewhere and a moment later one of the security men burst through the door, his torch swinging wildly across white tiles and the smoke which hung over the bubble-filled bath.

Koshchei was gone. So was Vor.

"They're at the house," Davy said.

It was two weeks later. Vor had placed ads in the *NME* and *Rolling Stone*, a single line of tiny white type centred on an all-black page announcing the death of Liquid Television. Davy and I had a big fight about it – Davy wanted to sue for breach of contract, I wanted to let it go. I was in London, in my flat. It was the middle of the afternoon, and Davy's phone call had woken me.

I said, "I know. It's over, Davy."

"No. No way is it over. We have a number one album in five countries. We have a video in heavy rotation on MTV."

"I still feel bad about that video."

"It saved us, man."

I had known that Vor wouldn't or couldn't handle a video shoot, so I had surreptitiously filmed him at work in the studio, using a couple of cheap web cameras. The director of the video for "Spook Speak" – fresh from an award-winning ad campaign for some Belgian beer – had used computer trickery to patch footage of Vor's face over a Pinocchio-like puppet.

Davy said, "I need more of your foresight. I need your help to get him away from that creature."

"You tried to kill Koshchei. If he wanted, he could press charges."

"He won't, for the same reason Colonel Tom never let Elvis tour outside the States. Because he isn't supposed to be here."

My flat was a penthouse overlooking Tower Bridge. I looked down twenty floors at the Thames's brown waters and said into the phone, "We have a number one album. We had a number one single for two weeks, before that boy band knocked us out. We had a good run. We should leave it. Move on."

"So why have you been keeping tabs on him?"

"I don't want Vor to get hurt," I said. It was a confession.

"Neither do I. And he's going to die if we don't get rid of Koshchei. So what are we going to do?"

"I'm seeing Toad tomorrow. Come with me."

"What does Toad know?"

"He's been hired on for Vor's new project. And he's been hanging around the house."

Davy laughed. "You never cease to amaze me, man. When and where?"

We met in a restaurant at Chelsea Harbour. Davy gave Toad the third degree, and Toad answered every question with his usual amiability. He told us that being in the house was like being on the set of the remake of *Performance* as directed by Aleister Crowley, that the Twins were down in the basement and never came up, that Normal Norman had snuck a drink of the white stuff and thrown a fit and then disappeared.

"People come and go all the time, auditioning for this mysterious big project, and Vor just lies there on the bed. Stuff disappears. He buys more."

Davy said, "And Koshchei is there."

While Toad and I ate our steaks, he was working his way through a bottle of Chablis.

"He comes and goes," Toad said. "I think he got all he wanted from Vor."

"What did he get?" I said.

Toad shrugged. "I dunno. But he isn't as attentive any more. I know he doesn't think much of Vor's big project. They had a fight about it."

Davy said, "Call me when Koshchei is there. We need to talk."

"I don't think it'll help," Toad said. "Like I said, him and Vor aren't so close any more."

Vor's house was a big, white neo-Palladian pile in Belsize Park, screened from the road by tall chestnut trees. The gravel drive was covered in their wet, hand-shaped leaves; the house seemed dark and deserted. I parked the ancient Escort van (Davy had bought it that morning from a dealer in High Barnet, cash, no names, no pack drill) and, carrying the tool bag between us, Davy and I slouched through the front door, which stood wide open.

The entrance hall and its marble staircase went up three storeys. The huge chandelier lay in ruins on the floor; the air was dark and freezing, and stank foully. Something moved in the far corner, and Davy swung the beam of his torch around, spotlighting the Twins. They hunched together, naked, in a matted caul of their own hair. They were sucking each other's fingers down to the bones, and whimpered and mewed until Davy turned the light away from them.

I whispered, "I have a bad feeling about this."

"Just back me up," Davy said, and called out loudly, asking if anyone was home.

No sound came back except for the echo of his voice.

I said, "He isn't human. No one lives through having a TV dumped in their bath."

"It was a trick," Davy said.

"We should wait for Toad."

"It's all a trick. Sleight of hand. Come on."

We started up the stairs.

Toad was on the second-floor landing.

He lay on his back in a circle painted with his own blood. A drumstick protruded from each eye socket. When I saw him, I dropped my side of the tool bag, and things clattered noisily down the stairs. Davy grabbed what was left and went on. I took a deep breath, and followed.

Vor's bedroom was lit only by a big lava lamp shaped like a space rocket, bubbling redly in one corner. Vor was lying in the four-poster, under a sheet stained with urine and spilled food. He must have been there for days. Incense tapers were burning in bunches, layering the air with veils of acrid blue smoke, but the stink from the bed was overpowering.

The windows were tented with heavy black drapes, the glass painted with thick silver paint. When I tried to pry one open, I found that it had been nailed shut.

Perhaps the noise woke Vor. He giggled and said, "I'm dreaming. He wouldn't let you in here."

"He's gone," Davy said. "He took what he wanted and now he's gone."

"Not quite," Koshchei said.

He stood in the doorway to the bathroom, thin as a Live Aid extra, piss-elegant in an electric-blue *shaitung* silk suit and sequinned cowboy boots. Smoke eddied around him in the gloom as, with a conjuror's grace, he plucked a live chick from his tangle of dreadlocks. For a moment, he allowed it to stand on his open palm – a yellow ball of fluff that cheeped hopefully as it looked around with bright black eyes – then he stuffed it into his mouth and devoured it with a wet crunching noise. A thin rill of blood ran down his chin when he smiled.

He said, "I always come back. I always finish what I begin. I like to think of it as a duty."

Davy said, "We're taking him away from you."

Koshchei dabbed chick blood from his chin with a black handkerchief and shook it into nothingness – or into the dark, smoky air. He said, "I'll stay, I think. The boy deserves nothing less."

"We're taking him to hospital," I said. My mouth was dry, burning with the taste of the incense smoke, and I was getting a headache.

"Oh, I think not. You see, you have come at just the right moment."

Davy said, "You fuck people up, you drain them of everything they have – and then what? You walk away? Not this time. We saw what you did to Toad. You can't walk away from murder."

"The Twins killed him," Koshchei said calmly. "They have grown very protective. As for this boy, I admit that I used him – but then, so did you. You're not interested in the boy, only in what he can do for you. You're jealous of me because I went to the source directly. And without me, he would not have gone where he did. Without me, he would have been no more than one more silly, vainglorious child with a talent for delivering bad poetry with utter conviction. With me, he has been to a place few have even glimpsed."

"I could have got there by myself," Vor said.

His voice seemed to come from a pit far beneath the bed. The room was so full of smoke now that the walls were disappearing. My sight throbbed with headachy red.

"You could not have gone there without me," Koshchei told him. "And I could not have gone there without you. That's the deal. That's always the deal." He stared at Davy and me through the gathering murk. "I get so little, compared to what I give. Surely you two gentlemen do not begrudge me."

Vor said, "I chose to do it. I wanted it so much, and he showed me how. Fuck off, both of you. You don't know what he did for me."

"You're too stoned or ill to know what you want," Davy said.

"I don't want anything any more," Vor said, and closed his eyes and drew the sheet over his face. His bed was like a catafalque, receding through red-lit smoke.

"You see," Koshchei said. "There is nothing you two gentlemen can—"

Davy shot him. The muzzle flash lit up the room, made everything solid and distinct for a moment. Koshchei slammed into the door and Davy shot him again and he sat down, blood on his white face and blood on his hand when he took it away from his chest. He looked up at Davy, smiling, and Davy shot him five more times and threw the gun down. He'd bought it that morning, too, in a pub in Dalston.

Koshchei coughed a little spray of blood, brought his hand to his mouth and coughed again. Something moved in his white throat and he spat the bullets into his palm and held them up and dropped them to the floor and laughed.

We both went for him then, driven by anger and fear and

desperation. Davy stabbed him so hard that the blade of the hunting knife went through his shoulder and stuck in the door frame; I hit him a roundhouse blow with the lump hammer, and that laid him out.

We looked at each other, both of us breathing hard, both of us speckled and spattered with Koshchei's blood. Then I turned away and was sick.

"We should finish him off," Davy said, without conviction. "Cut his throat. Smash his skull."

"I'm not up for it," I said. "Besides, shooting him didn't work, so stabbing him probably won't work either."

"Yeah. So we'll try Plan B."

We worked the knife out of Koschei, got him onto the bed and wrapped him in a sodden red velvet throw, binding it tightly with electrical cable. Smoke swirled around us; we choked on its acrid fumes. Davy threaded the hose down Koschei's oesophagus and jammed the plastic funnel between his teeth; I poured in the mixture of weedkiller and bleach until it ran back out of his nose, mixed with bloody chyme. Then we finished wrapping him in black plastic sheeting and rolled the heavy bundle downstairs.

The damp cold air outside began to clear my head. As we were lifting our victim into the back of the van, I said, "We should go back for Vor."

"I'll call an ambulance," Davy said. He dialled 999 as I started the van, gave Vor's address as I tore out of the driveway, threw the mobile out of the window as we cut through the heavy traffic at Swiss Cottage. We kept the windows down as we drove, and my head began to clear as I navigated stop-go traffic along the Euston Road. "The ambulance men will find all the blood," I said. "And they'll find Toad. They'll find his body."

"A break-in. A struggle, the villains long gone."

"Vor saw us."

"Vor is out of his head. Nothing he says will be believed. When we get back I'll start damage control, get Roy on the case. But first we have to dump this sack of shit."

We headed east across Shoreditch, through the City (there was a horrible moment when a policeman on duty at one of the checkpoints stared hard at our van, but he let us past), and along the A13, the four-square tower of Canary Wharf pirouetting past tangles of slip roads and Georgian terraces, traffic heavy on the sodium-lit dual carriageway and roundabouts of Dagenham, growing lighter after we passed the Blackwall Tunnel and the blister of the Millennium Dome.

We talked, reliving the moment of the attack, joking about putting everything behind us, although we knew that Liquid Television was over, and knew that our partnership was probably over too. The man-sized bundle of black plastic sheeting rolled heavily back and forth behind us, like a punked-up Egyptian mummy. We drove through Hornchurch and turned down a service road that stretched across the heaths of Rainham Marshes, drove past grim depots fenced with tall wire to a lonely jetty at the inshore edge.

The river was flat and dark under low clouds still underlit by the dying glow of sunset. By the van's headlights we wrestled the heavy bundle to the end of the concrete jetty and let it drop into the water.

It splashed, sank, and floated back up, turning in the current. And then the trapped air that buoyed it blurted out, and the black plastic wrapping fell away from the corpse's face as it sank.

It was not Koshchei. He had played his final trick. The pale face that blurred and faded as it sank into the black water was Vor's.

Davy and I drove back in silence. We abandoned the van near Bow Tube station, the keys left in the ignition for the benefit of any teenage joyriders who might be about, rode into town in silence, parted in silence.

I have not seen Davy since.

I have been holed up in my flat for more than a month now, living on groceries and booze ordered over the Internet and delivered to my door. I ventured out only once, to a local corner where I bought every wrap of coke and heroin that the kiddie dealers were carrying.

I don't think I'll outlast my stash.

I've seen Koshchei twice.

Once while idly flicking through TV channels, on an MTV news segment about a hot new folk singer. He was standing to one side of the pub stage, solitary amongst the press of the girl's eager audience.

And once yesterday, on the terrace of my flat, the security lights shining on his white face as he smiled at me before stepping away into the darkness beyond the rail.

I know he'll be back. He always comes back to finish what he has begun.

DENNIS ETCHISON

It Only Comes Out at Night

WHEN DENNIS ETCHISON WAS A TEENAGER, Ray Bradbury told him to write a new short story every week for a year. He has been trying to do that since he was fifteen, but hasn't accomplished it yet.

The winner of two World Fantasy Awards and three British Fantasy Awards, Karl Edward Wagner described him as "The finest writer of psychological horror this genre has produced".

Born in California in 1943, Etchison's stories have appeared in numerous periodicals and anthologies since 1961, and some of his best work has been collected in *The Dark Country*, *Red Dreams*, *The Blood Kiss* and *The Death Artist*. *Talking in the Dark* was a massive retrospective volume from Stealth Press marking the fortieth anniversary of his first professional sale. More recently his e-collection *Fine Cuts*, a volume of stories about Hollywood, appeared in book form from PS Publishing.

Etchison is also well-known as a novelist (*The Fog*, *Darkside*, *Shadowman*, *California Gothic* and *Double Edge*) and has published the movie novelizations *Halloween II*, *Halloween III* and *Videodrome* under the pseudonym "Jack Martin".

As an acclaimed anthologist he has edited *Cutting Edge*, *Masters of Darkness I-III*, *MetaHorror*, *The Museum of Horrors* and *Gathering the*

Bones, the latter an international anthology of new dark fiction from Australia, America and the United Kingdom, co-edited with Jack Dann and Ramsey Campbell.

Over the past two years Etchison has written thousands of script pages for the *Twilight Zone Radio Dramas*, based on Rod Serling's original television series. The dramatic adaptations continue to be broadcast worldwide and are also available on audio cassette and CD.

As the author explains, " 'It Only Comes Out at Night' was written for Kirby McCauley's *Frights*, a classic anthology in the field and one that remains in print to this day. I'm proud to have been a part of it. I was also amazed when the story was nominated for a World Fantasy Award, since I had not thought of it as a fantasy. I suppose the oddness of the tone and the oblique, unresolved nature of the story suggested a deeper mystery beyond the sleep-deprived, hallucinatory details. I was living through a particularly stressful period at the time. You are what you write."

Etchison also admits that he's not sure that he has ever written a vampire story, and he may well be right. But the atmospheric tale that follows (as the title indicates) *could* be a vampire story, and as it is one of my favourite pieces of fiction by one of the genre's foremost short-story writers, I decided to include it here anyway.

IF YOU LEAVE L.A. by way of San Bernardino, headed for Route 66 and points east, you must cross the Mojave Desert.

Even after Needles and the border, however, there is no relief; the dry air only thins further as the long, relentless climb continues in earnest. Flagstaff is still almost two hundred miles, and Winslow, Gallup and Albuquerque are too many hours away to think of making without food, rest and, mercifully, sleep.

It is like this: the car runs hot, hotter than it ever has before, the plies of the tires expand and contract until the sidewalls begin to shimmy slightly as they spin on over the miserable Arizona roads, giving up a faint odor like burning hair from between the treads, as the windshield colors over with essence of honeybee, wasp, dragonfly, mayfly, June bug, ladybug and the like, and the radiator, clotted with the bodies of countless kamikaze insects, hisses like a moribund lizard in the sun. . . .

All of which means, of course, that if you are traveling that way between May and September, you move by night.

Only by night.

For there are, after all, dawn check-in motels, Do Not Disturb signs for bungalow doorknobs; there are diners for mid-afternoon break-fasts, coffee by the carton; there are 24-hour filling stations bright as dreams – Whiting Brothers, Conoco, Terrible Herbst – their flags as unfamiliar as their names, with ice machines, soda machines, candy machines; and there are the sudden, unexpected Rest Areas, just off the highway, with brick bathrooms and showers and electrical outlets, constructed especially for those who are weary, out of money, behind schedule. . . .

So McClay had had to learn, the hard way.

He slid his hands to the bottom of the steering wheel and peered ahead into the darkness, trying to relax. But the wheel stuck to his fingers like warm candy. Off somewhere to his left, the horizon flickered with pearly luminescence, then faded again to black. This time he did not bother to look. Sometimes, though, he wondered just how far away the lightning was striking; not once during the night had the sound of its thunder reached him here in the car.

In the back seat, his wife moaned.

The trip out had turned all but unbearable for her. Four days it had taken, instead of the expected two-and-a-half; he made a great effort not to think of it, but the memory hung over the car like a thunderhead.

It had been a blur, a fever dream. Once, on the second day, he had been passed by a churning bus, its silver sides blinding him until he noticed a Mexican woman in one of the window seats. She was not looking at him. She was holding a swooning infant to the glass, squeezing water onto its head from a plastic baby bottle to keep it from passing out.

McClay sighed and fingered the buttons on the car radio.

He knew he would get nothing from the AM or FM bands, not out here, but he clicked it on anyway. He left the volume and tone controls down, so as not to wake Evvie. Then he punched the seldom-used middle button, the shortwave band, and raised the gain carefully until he could barely hear the radio over the hum of the tires.

Static.

Slowly he swept the tuner across the bandwidth, but there was only white noise. It reminded him a little of the summer rain yesterday, starting back, the way it had sounded bouncing off the windows.

He was about to give up when he caught a voice, crackling, drifting in and out. He worked the knob like a safecracker, zeroing in on the signal.

A few bars of music. A tone, then the voice again. ". . . Greenwich Mean Time." Then the station ID.

It was the Voice of America Overseas Broadcast.

He grunted disconsolately and killed it.

His wife stirred.

"Why'd you turn it off" she murmured. "I was listening to that. Good. Program."

"Take it easy," he said, "easy, you're still asleep. We'll be stopping soon."

". . . Only comes out at night," he heard her say, and then she was lost again in the blankets.

He pressed the glove compartment, took out one of the Automobile Club guides. It was already clipped open. McClay flipped on the overhead light and drove with one hand, reading over – for the hundredth time? – the list of motels that lay ahead. He knew the list by heart, but seeing the names again reassured him somehow. Besides, it helped to break the monotony.

It was the kind of place you never expect to find in the middle of a long night, a bright place with buildings (a building, at least) and cars, other cars drawn off the highway to be together in the protective circle of light.

A Rest Area.

He would have spotted it without the sign. Elevated sodium vapor lighting bathed the scene in an almost peach-colored glow, strikingly different from the cold blue-white sentinels of the Interstate Highway. He had seen other Rest Area signs on the way out, probably even this one. But in daylight the signs had meant nothing more to him than FRONTAGE ROAD or BUSINESS DISTRICT NEXT RIGHT. He wondered if it was the peculiar warmth of light that made the small island of blacktop appear so inviting.

McClay decelerated, downshifted and left Interstate 40.

The car dipped and bumped, and he was aware of the new level of sound from the engine as it geared down for the first time in hours.

He eased in next to a Pontiac Firebird, toed the emergency brake and cut the ignition.

He allowed his eyes to close and his head to sink back into the headrest. At last.

The first thing he noticed was the quiet.

It was deafening. His ears literally began to ring, with the high-pitched whine of a late-night TV test pattern.

The second thing he noticed was a tingling at the tip of his tongue.

It brought to mind a picture of a snake's tongue. Picking up electricity from the air, he thought.

The third was the rustling awake of his wife, in back.

She pulled herself up. "Are we sleeping now? Why are the lights . . .?"

He saw the outline of her head in the mirror. "It's just a rest stop, hon. I – the car needs a break." Well, it was true, wasn't it? "You want the rest room? There's one back there, see it?"

"Oh my God."

"What's the matter now?"

"Leg's asleep. Listen, are we or are we not going to get a—"

"There's a motel coming up." He didn't say that they wouldn't hit the one he had marked in the book for another couple of hours; he didn't want to argue. He knew she needed the rest – he needed it too, didn't he? "Think I'll have some more of that coffee, though," he said.

"Isn't any more," she yawned.

The door slammed.

Now he was able to recognize the ringing in his ears for what it was: the sound of his own blood. It almost succeeded in replacing the steady drone of the car.

He twisted around, fishing over the back of the seat for the ice chest.

There should be a couple of Cokes left, at least.

His fingers brushed the basket next to the chest, riffling the edges of maps and tour books, by now reshuffled haphazardly over the first-aid kit he had packed himself (tourniquet, forceps, scissors, ammonia inhalants, Merthiolate, triangular bandage, compress, adhesive bandages, tannic acid) and the fire extinguisher, the extra carton of cigarettes, the remainder of a half-gallon of drinking water, the thermos (which Evvie said was empty, and why would she lie?).

He popped the top of a can.

Through the side window he saw Evvie disappearing around the corner of the building. She was wrapped to the gills in her blanket.

He opened the door and slid out, his back aching.

He stood there blankly, the unnatural light washing over him.

He took a long, sweet pull from the can. Then he started walking.

The Firebird was empty.

And the next car, and the next.

Each car he passed looked like the one before it, which seemed crazy until he realized that it must be the work of the light. It cast an even, eerie tan over the baked metal tops, like orange sunlight through air thick with suspended particles. Even the windshields appeared to be filmed over with a thin layer of settled dust. It made him think of country roads, sundowns.

He walked on.

He heard his footsteps echo with surprising clarity, resounding down the staggered line of parked vehicles. Finally it dawned on him (and now he knew how tired he really was) that the cars must actually have people in them – sleeping people. Of course. Well hell, he thought, watching his step, I wouldn't want to wake anyone. The poor devils.

Besides the sound of his footsteps, there was only the distant *swish* of an occasional, very occasional car on the highway; from here, even that was only a distant hush, growing and then subsiding like waves on a nearby shore.

He reached the end of the line, turned back.

Out of the corner of his eye he saw, or thought he saw, a movement by the building.

It would be Evvie, shuffling back.

He heard the car door slam.

He recalled something he had seen in one the tourist towns in New Mexico: circling the park – in Taos, that was where they had been – he had glimpsed an ageless Indian, wrapped in typical blanket, ducking out of sight into the doorway of a gift shop; with the blanket over his head that way, the Indian had somehow resembled an Arab, or so it had seemed to him at the time.

He heard another car door slam.

That was the same day – was it only last week? – that she had noticed the locals driving with their headlights on (in honor of something or other, some regional election, perhaps: "'My face speaks for itself,' drawled Herman J. 'Fashio' Trujillo, Candidate for Sheriff"); she had insisted at first that it must be a funeral procession, though for whom she could not guess.

McClay came to the car, stretched a last time, and crawled back in.

Evvie was bundled safely again in the back seat.

He lit a quick cigarette, expecting to hear her voice any second, complaining, demanding that he roll down the windows, at least, and so forth. But, as it turned out, he was able to sit undisturbed as he smoked it down almost to the filter.

Paguate. Bluewater. Thoreau.

He blinked.

Klagetoh. Joseph City. Ash Fork.

He blinked and tried to focus his eyes from the taillights a half-mile ahead to the bug-spattered glass, then back again.

Petrified Forest National Park.

He blinked, refocusing. But it did no good.

A twitch started on the side of his face, close by the corner of his eye.

Rehoboth.

He strained at a road sign, the names and mileages, but instead a seemingly endless list of past and future shops and detours shimmered before his mind's eye.

I've had it, he thought. Now, suddenly, it was catching up with him, the hours of repressed fatigue; he felt a rushing out of something from his chest. No way to make that motel – hell, I can't even remember the name of it now. Check the book. But it doesn't matter. The eyes. *Can't control my eyes anymore.*

(He had already begun to hallucinate things like tree trunks and cows and Mack trucks speeding toward him on the highway. The cow had been straddling the broken line; in the last few minutes its lowing, deep and regular, had become almost inviting.)

Well, he could try for *any* motel. Whatever turned up next.

But how much farther would that be?

He ground his teeth together, feeling the pulsing at his temples. He struggled to remember the last sign.

The next town. It might be a mile. Five miles. Fifty.

Think! He said it, he thought it, he didn't know which.

If he could just pull over, pull over right now and lie down for a few minutes—

He seemed to see clear ground ahead. No rocks, no ditch. The shoulder, just ahead.

Without thinking he dropped into neutral and coasted, aiming for it.

The car glided to a stop.

God, he thought.

He forced himself to turn, reach into the back seat.

The lid to the chest was already off. He dipped his fingers into the ice and retrieved two half-melted cubes, lifted them into the front seat and began rubbing them over his forehead.

He let his eyes close, seeing dull lights fire as he daubed at the lids, the rest of his face, the forehead again. As he slipped the ice into his mouth and chewed, it broke apart as easily as snow.

He took a deep breath. He opened his eyes again.

At that moment a huge tanker roared past, slamming an aftershock of air into the side of the car. The car rocked like a boat at sea.

No. It was no good.

So. So he could always turn back, couldn't he? And why not? The Rest Area was only twenty, twenty-five minutes behind him. (Was that all?) He could pull out and hang a U and turn back, just like that. And then sleep. It would be safer there. With luck, Evvie wouldn't even know. An hour's rest, maybe two; that was all he would need.

Unless – was there another Rest Area ahead?

How soon?

He knew that the second wind he felt now wouldn't last, not for more than a few minutes. No, it wasn't worth the chance.

He glanced in the rearview mirror.

Evvie was still down, a lumpen mound of blanket and hair.

Above her body, beyond the rear window, the raised headlights of another monstrous truck, closing ground fast.

He made the decision.

He slid into first and swung out in a wide arc, well ahead of the blast of the truck, and worked up to fourth gear. He was thinking about the warm, friendly lights he had left behind.

He angled in next to the Firebird and cut the lights.

He started to reach for a pillow from the back, but why bother? It would probably wake Evvie, anyway.

He wadded up his jacket, jammed it against the passenger armrest, and lay down.

First he crossed his arms over his chest. Then behind his head. Then he gripped his hands between his knees. Then he was on his back again, his hands at his sides, his feet cramped against the opposite door.

His eyes were wide open.

He lay there, watching chain lightning flash on the horizon.

Finally he let out a breath that sounded like all the breaths he had ever taken going out at once, and drew himself up.

He got out and walked over to the rest room.

Inside, white tiles and bare lights. His eyes felt raw, peeled. Finished, he washed his hands but not his face; that would only make sleep more difficult.

Outside again and feeling desperately out of synch, he listened to his shoes falling hollowly on the cement.

"Next week we've got to get organized . . ."

He said this, he was sure, because he heard his voice coming back to him, though with a peculiar empty resonance. Well, this time tomorrow night he would be home. As unlikely as that seemed now.

He stopped, bent for a drink from the water fountain.

The footsteps did not stop.

Now wait, he thought, I'm pretty far gone, but—

He swallowed, his ears popping.

The footsteps stopped.

Hell, he thought, I've been pushing too hard. We. She. No, it was my fault, my plan this time. To drive nights, sleep days. Just so. As long as you *can* sleep.

Easy, take it easy.

He started walking again, around the corner and back to the lot.

At the corner, he thought he saw something move at the edge of his vision.

He turned quickly to the right, in time for a fleeting glimpse of something – someone – hurrying out of sight into the shadows.

Well, the other side of the building housed the women's rest room. Maybe it was Evvie.

He glanced toward the car, but it was blocked from view.

He walked on.

Now the parking area resembled an oasis lit by firelight. Or a western camp, the cars rimming the lot on three sides in the manner of wagons gathered against the night.

Strength in numbers, he thought.

Again, each car he passed looked at first like every other. It was the flat light, of course. And of course they were the same cars he had seen a half-hour ago. And the light still gave them a dusty, abandoned look.

He touched a fender.

It *was* dusty.

But why shouldn't it be? His own car had probably taken on quite a layer of grime after so long on these roads.

He touched the next car, the next.

Each was so dirty that he could have carved his name without scratching the paint.

He had an image of himself passing this way again – God forbid – a year from now, say, and finding the same cars parked here. The *same* ones.

What if, he wondered tiredly, what if some of these cars had been abandoned? Overheated, exploded, broken down one fine midday and left here by owners who simply never returned? Who would ever know? Did the Highway Patrol, did anyone bother to check? Would an automobile be preserved here for months, years by the elements, like a snakeskin shed beside the highway?

It was a thought, anyway.

His head was buzzing.

He leaned back and inhaled deeply, as deeply as he could at this altitude.

But he did hear something. A faint tapping. It reminded him of running feet, until he noticed the lamp overhead:

There were hundreds of moths beating against the high fixture, their soft bodies tapping as they struck and circled and returned again and again to the lens; the light made their wings translucent.

He took another deep breath and went on to his car.

He could hear it ticking, cooling down, before he got there. Idly he rested a hand on the hood. Warm, of course. The tires? He touched the left front. It was taut, hot as a loaf from the oven. When he took his hand away, the color of the rubber came off on his palm like burned skin.

He reached for the door handle.

A moth fluttered down onto the fender. He flicked it off, his finger leaving a streak on the enamel.

He looked closer and saw a wavy, mottled pattern covering his unwashed car, and then he remembered. The rain, yesterday afternoon. The rain had left blotches in the dust, marking the finish as if with dirty fingerprints.

He glanced over at the next car.

It, too, had the imprint of dried raindrops – but, close up, he saw that the marks were superimposed in layers, over and over again.

The Firebird had been through a great many rains.

He touched the hood.

Cold.

He removed his hand, and a dead moth clung to his thumb. He tried to brush it off on the hood, but other moth bodies stuck in its place. Then he saw countless shriveled, mummified moths pasted over the hood and top like peeling chips of paint. His fingers were coated with the powder from their wings.

He looked up.

High above, backed by banks of roiling cumulous clouds, the swarm of moths vibrated about the bright, protective light.

So the Firebird had been here a very long time.

He wanted to forget it, to let it go. He wanted to get back in the car. He wanted to lie down, lock it out, everything. He wanted to go to sleep and wake up in Los Angeles.

He couldn't.

He inched around the Firebird until he was facing the line of cars. He hesitated a beat, then started moving.

A LeSabre.

A Cougar.

A Chevy van.

A Corvair.

A Ford.

A Mustang.

And every one was overlaid with grit.

He paused by the Mustang. Once – how long ago? – it had been a luminous candy-apple red; probably belonged to a teenager. Now the windshield was opaque, the body dulled to a peculiar shade he could not quite place.

Feeling like a voyeur at a drive-in movie theater, McClay crept to the driver's window.

Dimly he perceived two large outlines in the front seat.

He raised his hand.

Wait.

What if there were two people sitting there on the other side of the window, watching him?

He put it out of his mind. Using three fingers, he cut a swath through the scum on the glass and pressed close.

The shapes were there. Two headrests.

He started to pull away.

And happened to glance into the back seat.

He saw a long, uneven form.

A leg, the back of a thigh. Blonde hair, streaked with shadows. The collar of a coat.

And, delicate and silvery, a spider web, spun between the hair and collar.

He jumped back.

His leg struck the old Ford. He spun around, his arms straight. The blood was pounding in his ears.

He rubbed out a spot on the window of the Ford and scanned the inside.

The figure of a man, slumped on the front seat.

The man's head lay on a jacket. No, it was not a jacket. It was a large, formless stain. In the filtered light, McClay could see that it had dried to a dark brown.

It came from the man's mouth.

No, not from the mouth.

The throat had a long, thin slash across it, reaching nearly to the ear.

He stood there stiffly, his back almost arched, his eyes jerking, trying to close, trying not to close. The lot, the even light reflecting thinly from each windshield, the Corvair, the van, the Cougar, the LeSabre, the suggestion of a shape within each one.

The pulse in his ears muffled and finally blotted out the distant gearing of a truck up on the highway, the death-rattle of the moths against the seductive lights.

He reeled.

He seemed to be hearing again the breaking open of doors and the scurrying of padded feet across paved spaces.

He remembered the first time. He remembered the sound of a second door slamming in a place where no new car but his own had arrived.

Or – had it been the door to his car slamming a second time, after Evvie had gotten back in?

If so, how? Why?

And there had been the sight of someone moving, trying to slip away.

And for some reason now he remembered the Indian in the tourist town, slipping out of sight in the doorway of that gift shop. He held his eyelids down until he saw the shop again, the window full of kachinas and tin gods and tapestries woven in a secret language.

At last he remembered it clearly: the Indian had not been entering the store. *He had been stealing away.*

McClay did not understand what it meant, but he opened his eyes, as if for the first time in centuries, and began to run toward his car. *If I could only catch my goddamn breath,* he thought.

He tried to hold on. He tried not to think of her, of what might have happened the first time, of what he may have been carrying in the back seat ever since.

He had to find out.

He fought his way back to the car, against a rising tide of fear he could not stem.

He told himself to think of other things, of things he knew he could control: mileages and motel bills, time zones and weather reports, spare tires and flares and tubeless repair tools, hydraulic jack and Windex and paper towels and tire iron and socket wrench and waffle cushion and traveler's checks and credit cards and Dopp Kit (toothbrush and paste, deodorant, shaver, safety blade, brushless cream) and sunglasses and Sight Savers and tear-gas pen and fiber-tip pens and portable radio and alkaline batteries and fire extinguisher and desert water bag and tire gauge and motor oil and his moneybelt with identification sealed in plastic—

In the back of his car, under the quilt, nothing moved, not even when he finally lost his control and his mind in a thick, warm scream.

CHELSEA QUINN YARBRO

Investigating Jericho

AUTHOR AND PROFESSIONAL TAROT READER Chelsea Quinn Yarbro published her first story in 1969. A full-time writer since the following year, she has sold more than sixty books and as many short stories.

Her novels include the werewolf volumes *The Godforsaken* and *Beastnights*, the quasi-fictional occult series *Messages from Michael* and *More Messages from Michael*, and the movie novelizations *Dead & Buried* and *Nomads*. Yarbro's "Sisters of the Night" trilogy (*The Angry Angel*, *The Soul of an Angel* and *Zhameni: The Angel of Death*) is about Dracula's three undead wives. Unfortunately, it was substantially rewritten by the editor.

However, the author is best-known for her series of historical horror novels featuring the Byronic vampire Saint-Germain, loosely inspired by the real-life eighteenth-century French count of the same name. The first book in the cycle, *Hotel Transylvania: A Novel of Forbidden Love* appeared in 1978. To date it has been followed by more than a dozen sequels, including *The Palace*, *Blood Games*, *Path of the Eclipse*, *Tempting Fate*, *Out of the House of Life*, *Darker Jewels*, *Better in the Dark*, *Mansions of Darkness*, *Writ in Blood*, *Blood Roses*, *Communion Blood*, *Come Twilight* and *A Feast in Exile*.

A spin-off sequence featuring Saint-Germain's lover Atta Olivia Clemens comprises *A Flame in Byzantium*, *Crusader's Torch* and *A*

Candle for D'Artagnan, while Yarbro's short fiction has been collected in *The Saint-Germain Chronicles* and *The Vampire Stories of Chelsea Quinn Yarbro.* She received the Grand Master Award at the 2003 World Horror Convention.

As she recalls: "I was on a panel with Stephen King more than twenty years ago in Knoxville, Tennessee, on which panel Steve said that, regarding *'Salem's Lot,* he believed a small town in a remote part of Maine could vanish and no one would notice. I disagreed, but it took me until the plane ride home to decide who would notice first and do the most about it. And eight years later, those confluences of thought resulted in this story."

I'll leave the reader to decide who was right . . .

PAPER ROLLED FROM THE printer in waves, and Morton Symes gathered it up from the floor, scowling at the columns of figures printed there. It was exactly what he had feared. He dragged the material back to his office and began to separate the pages and arrange them.

William Brewster was waiting impatiently when Morton finally came into his office. He wasted no time with polite trivia. "Well?"

"I think it's a taxpayers' revolt, sir," said Morton, holding out his newly assembled file. "According to our records, no one in Jericho has filed income tax returns for the past two years. No one."

"Jericho," said Brewster, his eyes growing narrow behind his horn-rimmed glasses. "Where is this place?"

"North of Colebrook, in New Hampshire. Near the Canadian border."

He held out a photocopy of a Rand McNally map. "I've marked it for you in red."

"Is that a joke?" Brewster asked suspiciously.

"No," Morton said, horrified. "No, sir. Not at all."

Brewster nodded, satisfied; then he said, "It might have been a good one, though."

"Thank you, sir," Morton said promptly. He stood more or less at attention while Brewster opened the file and scanned through it, pausing from time to time to click his tongue.

"Not a very big place by the look of it," said Brewster as he put the file down some twenty minutes later.

"Population: 2,579," Morton said. "As of two years ago."

"When they stopped paying taxes," Brewster said with that cold disapproval that made his whim law in the office.

"Well, you see," Morton pointed out as diplomatically as possible, "last year there were still a few paying taxes, a few. For the last taxable year, not one citizen sent in W-2s or anything else. Not even those entitled to refunds filed. It has to be a tax-payers' revolt." He waited while Brewster considered the information.

"I wonder why it took so long to find it?" Brewster mused, his expression suggesting that anyone lax enough to have let this pass might expect a very unpleasant interview.

"Well, it took awhile for the random sampling to catch up with a place that small. With nine states filing in our office, the computer has an enormous number of returns to deal with. And tax reform made it all so complicated . . ." Morton smiled miserably. "I guess we weren't looking as closely as we should have. There were other things on our minds." It took the greatest self-control for him not to twiddle the ends of his tie.

"It's very small; as you say, it wouldn't turn up quickly in a random comparison." Brewster was letting him and the rest of the office off the hook, and his expression said he knew it. "So. What are your plans?"

This time, Morton did pull his tie, but just once. "I thought . . . I thought I ought to go look around, investigate the situation, see what's happening up there." When he received no response from Brewster, he opened the file and indicated one set of figures. "You see? There's a small lumber mill that provides employment for over two hundred men and about a dozen women; none of them have filed, and neither has the lumber mill. It might mean that the mill has shut down, in which case there could be a minor recession in the town. I have to check the courts to find out if there's been a bankruptcy hearing on the mill. And the other large income is from the Jericho Inn, which specializes in sportsmen. There is no indication that it's still in operation, so I thought . . . well, it might make sense to go there and see for myself . . ."

Brewster glowered as Morton's words faded. "How long were you planning to be away?"

"I don't know; a week, maybe two, if the situation warrants the time." Morton shifted his weight from one leg to the other. Brewster always made him feel about eight years old.

"What would make the situation warrant it?" Brewster asked sharply.

"If the town turns out to be prosperous and is actively refusing to cooperate with us, then I might not need as much as a week; a few days ought to be enough to get a full report. But if the town is having trouble with unemployment, then I might have to stick around, to see how deep the rot goes." Morton could not read the cold look in Brewster's magnified eyes. "We're supposed to be compassionate, aren't we, sir? Not make snap judgments or arbitrary rulings? With the reform and all the changes, we were told to be understanding, weren't we? If the town's out of money, it could account for what they've done."

"It might," Brewster allowed. He leaned back and regarded Morton down the length of his long Roman nose, a maneuver calculated to be intimidating. "Why should I send you? Why not Callisher or Brody?"

"Well, I found it, sir," said Morton, as if he were about to lose a favorite toy.

Brewster nodded once, but returned to the same dominating pose. "That you did. That you did." He drummed long, thick fingers on the immaculate surface of his desk. "That's a point." His next question was so unexpected that Morton was shocked almost to silence. "Where do you come from?"

"I live in Pittsford, just south of – ," Morton began.

"I know where you live," said Brewster in his best condescending manner. "Where do you come from?"

"Oh." Morton was afraid he was blushing. "I come from Portland. In Michigan. Between Grand Rapids and Lansing." He was afraid that if he said anything more, he would stutter.

"Family still there?" Brewster inquired.

"Dad's in Chicago; Mom's dead; my older sister lives in Montana, running some kind of tourist ranch – I forget what you call them—"

"Dude ranches," Brewster supplied.

Morton bobbed his head up and down several times. "Yeah. That's it. She works there. My younger sister is married to a colonel in the army. They're stationed in Texas. They were in Europe." He did his best to look confident. "No family in New England anywhere that I know of."

Brewster straightened up. "That's something." He looked down at the file once more, thumbing his way through the printouts. "I'll authorize you to travel for a maximum of ten days. I expect a phone report every two days, backed up by a written report when you complete the investigation." He handed the file back to Morton. "You better come up with something. We don't want the evening news saying the IRS is persecuting innocent citizens. Best go over that village name by name."

"Of course," Morton assured him, doing his best to contain the panic he felt. "I'll be very careful, Mr Brewster," he vowed, his ordinary face taking on as much purpose as it could. "I'll report each day if you like. Tell me when you want me to call."

"Mid-afternoon should do," Brewster said, suddenly sounding very bored.

"Mid-afternoon, every day," said Morton.

"Every other day," corrected Brewster. "If I'm not available, my secretary will record your report, and I'll review it later. I expect to have numbers where I can reach you while you're gone."

"Certainly. Of course," said Morton, daring to give the hint of a smile.

Brewster made sure that did not last. "I expect you to have an evaluation for me within the first twenty-four hours as to the general economic condition of the community and some observations on the political disposition of the citizens." He indicated the file. "You don't want to end up on Dan Rather's bad side, do you?" He made it very plain that if anything went wrong, Morton would take all the heat himself.

"No," said Morton, blanching.

"Keep that in mind, and you should do well," said Brewster as he leaned forward. "Be astute, Symes."

Morton had never been admonished to be astute before, and did not quite know what would be an appropriate response. "I'll do what I can, sir." He wanted to make his escape while Brewster still seemed disposed to give it to him.

"Carry on, Symes," said Brewster, and at once ignored Morton, not so much as if he had left the room but as if he had disappeared altogether.

Northern New Hampshire was quite beautiful, the worn mountains dozing in the early-autumn afternoon, their trees still green, though no longer the deep, heady color of summer. The drive was so pleasant that Morton Symes castigated himself for lack of purpose as he drove northward, into increasingly remote regions, his chocolate-colored BMW humming efficiently, the tape deck playing some of Symes's favorite soft-rock hits. The one delay, caused by a road-repair crew blocking traffic for the better part of forty minutes, brought Morton to North Poindexter, near Colebrook, at sunset. He flipped a mental coin and elected to find a motel for the night rather than press on to Jericho.

"Just the one night?" asked the clerk in the insufferably quaint inn Morton found off the main street.

"Just the one."

"On your way to the lakes?" asked the clerk, making small talk while Morton filled out the necessary forms.

"No; Jericho." Morton looked at him over the rims of his glasses, a move he thought might discourage conversation.

"Jericho?" said the clerk in some surprise. "Why there?"

"Business," said Morton, even more tersely.

"In Jericho?" The clerk laughed once in disbelief.

"Why not in Jericho?" asked Morton, in spite of himself.

The clerk hesitated a bit longer than he should have. "Oh, nothing. Just don't get many . . . flatlanders going there; that's all. People from North Poindexter don't go there." He handed a key to Morton. "Second door on the left, at the end of the walk-way."

"Thanks," Morton said automatically as he took the key. He was about to pick up his suitcase when he could not resist asking, "Why don't people from here go to Jericho?"

This time the clerk considered his answer very carefully. "Not that kind of place," he said, and turned away, unwilling to say anything more.

Morton pondered over what the clerk had said, and decided that he might have been right in his assumption that the town was in some form of depression. If it had little tourist trade and the lumber mill was not doing well, it could be that the whole village was hanging on by the proverbial shoestring. He made his first meticulous notes, with records of mileage and amounts spent on fuel and food, then went to the most promising restaurant in town, certain that he was off to a good start.

Over baked chicken in the North Poindexter restaurant, he decided that he would do his best to be helpful to the people of Jericho. If, like their biblical namesake, their walls were "tumblin' down", he would offer to help the citizens shore them back up. He remembered the seminar he had attended three months ago, a seminar that stressed learning to relate to the problems of the taxpayer and to be compassionate and sympathetic in regard to their needs and their problems. He rehearsed in his head the right way to say things, so that he would not sound too much like a cop or an inquisitor.

Morning found him out of North Poindexter and on the road to Jericho by nine. He had taken great care to dress less formally than usual, in a tweed jacket and grey slacks instead of his usual three-piece suit. One of the things he had learned in the seminar was that most people found casual attire less intimidating and Morton did not want to get off to a bad start with the citizens of Jericho. He listened to light classics – they seemed more appropriate to this warm, windy day – and admired the scenery. In another month, with the trees in their autumnal glory, the drive would be spectacular; now it was pleasant, even refreshing. Morton made a mental note to take a few pictures before he left, so that he could recapture his sense of enjoyment, which led him to think about his destination. A remote village like Jericho might easily become his secret vacation haunt, where he could spend a few days away from the pressure of his work in an unspoiled place. He permitted himself a flight of fancy: his work with the townspeople had earned him their respect and possibly the affection of some, and he was regarded as their welcome outsider on his annual returns. Returns. He chuckled at his own mental pun. Then he concentrated on his driving and the road, making special note of the few buildings he saw at a distance and then the ones that were nearer.

Two tall Victorian atrocities at the bend of the road were Morton's first sight of Jericho. The houses were run-down, with peeling paint and broken windows, but even in their heyday neither would have been a sterling example of the carpenter's Gothic style, in large part because both were so overdone, with turrets and cupolas and widow's walks and piazzas and fan windows in such frenzied abundance that the basic lines of the houses themselves seemed to be lost behind it all. Morton slowed as he went past the houses, and fancied that they were leaning together, whispering – two ancient crones bedecked in elaborate gowns no longer in fashion. He chided himself for his overactive imagination as he slowed the car just as the rest of the town came into view.

The main street was predominantly nineteenth century, but with a few older buildings at the far end of the town. Two churches, both austere white buildings, one with a spire and one with a turret, were on opposite sides of and at opposite ends of the street; the older of the two – with the turret at the far end on the left – had been unpainted so long that the wood beneath had weathered to a scaled grey. Next to that church was a Federal-style building with an ancient and faded sign that proclaimed it the Jericho Inn. Between Morton and the Inn were a town hall; a single-story building with an imposing Victorian façade (Morton learned later that it was the bank); a 1930s-vintage post office; a cafe of sorts, in a building that had once been a private home and was now given over to offices; a small, neglected park; a barnlike building advertising feed, fuel, and ice; a hardware store with a display of plumbing tools and supplies in the window; two small wooden houses, both dating from about 1850, one with a sign tacked by the door saying, KNITTING AND SEWING: REASON-ABLE RATES; and a more recent house with an art nouveau stained-glass window over the front door; then a 1950s ranch-style house, hideously out of place. Opposite that house was the steepled church; and next to it, an open block over-grown with weeds, identified as the JERICHO PARK by a sign near a rusty children's playground that ended at a fenced schoolyard; next to that, opposite the two houses, was a medium-sized grocery store, its windows dusty and its doors closed; beyond the store was another house that had been converted to office space that advertised the services of John H. Lawler, accountant; then a more recent building, in the concrete-slab style, with JERICHO LUMBER COMPANY over the entrance; across from the post office was the Wallace's Department Store, its window displays at least two years out of date, the mannequins looking like escapees from a 1940s film noir; after that two small shops, one selling candy, the other a bookstore; then a box of a building, opposite the town hall, which housed the two-man police force and the three-cell jail; the place across from the Jericho Inn was much larger, the whole of a block and a half given over to the gardens – now in riotous ruin – of a grotesque mansion, which had started out Federal and had been added to in two distinct layers of Victoriana. Along the street, there were five different vehicles parked: a twenty-year-old Chevy pickup by the hardware store, a muddy Edsel in front of the post office, a four-year-old Cadillac across from the bank, a step van by the department store, and a cherry 1956 Thunderbird sports car by the park.

Morton stared at the town, noting that most of the secondary streets were filled with single- and two-family residences, and that no one seemed to be up and about, though the morning was closer to lunch than breakfast. He started down the main street, looking for signs of life.

In the distance a school bell rang, but there was no change apparent on the street.

After a brief period of consideration, Morton pulled in across the street from the town mansion and settled down to watch Jericho, wondering why the school bell seemed to attract no response other than the occasional answer of hoots from the volunteer fire department, a block and a half away.

An hour passed; two. Morton was hard put to keep his eyes open, or to pay attention to the main street, and when he did, he could detect no change. No wonder the town was depressed; no one appeared to work in it. In fact, no one seemed to *live* in it. Over his greatest determination Morton began to doze.

He was awakened at sunset by a tap on his window and a face all but pressed against the glass. He straightened up and adjusted his glasses, trying not to appear startled.

"Something the matter?" asked the uniformed cop as Morton rolled down the window.

"No," said Morton at once, adding, "sir," as an afterthought. "The afternoon . . . I got drowsy."

"It happens," said the cop, standing up. "You're new in town."

"Yes," said Morton, reaching into his pocket for his wallet. He opened it to show his IRS identification and his driver's license. "Morton Symes."

The policeman inspected these two documents narrowly, then gave a grudging nod. "It appears you are."

"And you?"

"Wilson, Dexter Wilson," he said, not offering his hand. "You passing through or staying?"

This was not a very promising beginning, but Morton was not deterred. "I have some business to do here."

"Uh-huh." Wilson rocked back on his heels. "Well, lots of luck with it." He made a gesture that was not quite a salute, and then ambled away.

Watching him go, Morton noticed that there were a few other people on the street, strolling in the last fading light of day. They moved silently, in pairs or singly, making no effort to stop for conversation. When they met, there was scarcely so much as a nod exchanged, and never did anyone hail one of the others moving along the sidewalk. This puzzled Morton, though he supposed that people living together in the same small town might not have much to say to each other after a time. There was also the taciturn nature of New Englanders, he reminded himself, their disinclination to small talk. He rolled up his window and locked the passenger door before he got out of the car.

There was no one at the reception desk in the Jericho Inn, which had the same dusty look of neglect as the rest of the town. Morton hesitated, then gave his attention to the large, old-fashioned register, noticing that the most recent guest had stopped there fourteen months ago. He frowned, then took a pen and added his own name, address, and occupation to the required lines. Assuming the Inn had no guests at the moment, he wondered if it would be proper simply to inspect the rooms and choose the one he liked best. He was weighing the possibilities, when he heard a voice rusty with disuse behind him.

"Get anything for you?"

Morton turned and saw a man in late middle years, rather scrawny and rumpled, standing in the door to the dining room.

"Why, yes," he said when he had recovered from the shock of being discovered. Little as he wished to admit it, the silent arrival of the man had terrified him for an instant. "I'd like a room. With a bath."

The man did not move; he regarded Morton with a measuring look. "Fixing to stay long?"

"Probably a week," said Morton.

"Not much to do around here," said the man.

"I'm here on business, not pleasure," Morton informed him. "I will need a week to complete it."

"Business?" repeated the man. "In Jericho?" He laughed unpleasantly as he shambled closer. "Don't have much fancy here," he said.

"You mean in the Inn?" Morton asked with a significant raise to one eyebrow.

"That; Jericho, too." The man was now behind the reception desk. "Might take less time than you think, your business."

"I doubt it," said Morton, determined to assert his authority and establish a more reasonable level of communication between them.

"Suit yourself. You want a room, do you?" He read the signature Morton had just put in the register. "IRS. Well, well, well."

"We have some questions about Jericho." Morton once again offered his identification. "I trust you take MasterCard."

"Cash," said the man. "Don't hold with plastic here."

Morton shook his head, uncertain if he had brought enough cash to pay for the whole week. His head ached at the thought of reviewing cash transactions with their lack of supporting paper. He wondered if the rest of the town were as unorthodox. "How much for a week?"

"Two hundred forty dollars for seven days," said the man. "No meals included. Linen changed twice a week. Coffee available in the morning upon request, two dollars extra."

Sighing, Morton drew three hundred dollars from his wallet and hoped that the remaining hundred would be sufficient. He hoped that the bank would be prepared to honor one of his credit cards if none of the businesses were willing. "I'll want coffee every morning, so that means $254; $46 change."

"Fast with those numbers, aren't you?" The man opened a drawer under the counter and handed four worn bills to Morton.

"You want a receipt?"

Morton blinked. "Of course," he said, knowing that not getting one was inconceivable.

"Now or when you leave?"

"Now," said Morton.

The man shook his head, but brought out a receipt pad and scribbled the date and amount on it. "Need anything more than that?"

Morton grew irritated. "Please state what the money is for, including the length of the stay and morning coffee."

Grudgingly, the man did as Morton requested. He tore off the receipt and handed it to Morton. "You can have the front center room," he said, pointing toward the ceiling. "First floor. Bay window. It's the Ivy Room. All our rooms are named for plants." He handed over a key. "The hot water don't work real good."

This information, under the circumstances, did not surprise Morton. "I'll keep that in mind," he said, and picked up his suitcase. "Is there a phone in the room?"

"Payphone's by the restrooms. That's all we got." The man jerked his thumb toward a narrow hallway. "Down that way."

"Thanks," said Morton, aware that he was late in phoning in. Brewster would be displeased, but that could not be helped. Morton started up the stairs, watching the desk clerk covertly, noticing how pale the man was. Perhaps he was ill, which would explain his rudeness. Then the clerk returned the stare, and Morton, abashed, averted his eyes and continued to his room.

The Ivy Room had ancient wallpaper covered in ivy twines. Luckily, it was faded, or it would have been hideous; as it was, there was an air of decayed gentility about the room, and Morton, while not delighted, was not as upset as he had feared he might be. The bathroom had an old-fashioned stand sink and a legged bathtub as long and narrow and deep as a coffin. The medicine cabinet of the sink lacked a mirror, though from the look of it there had been one some time ago. Morton set out his shaving gear and took out the mirror he always carried when he traveled. When he was satisfied with the arrangement of his things, and that the enormous towels were clean and fresh, he went back into the bedroom and set about hanging his clothes in the antique armoire that dominated one side of the room. It was too late to call Brewster now, he knew. As he sat down to make his report for the day, he did his best to suppress a twinge of guilt. The next afternoon he would explain it all to Brewster – from the payphone.

By the time he finished his report, it was quite dark. The two forty-watt bulbs in the ceiling fixture barely got rid of the gloom, and the desk lamp was not much brighter. With concealed exasperation, Morton changed his shirt and tie in preparation for finding supper. "It *is* supper in this part of the world, isn't it?" he said to the walls. Perhaps tomorrow he would also invest in some stronger light bulbs. Then he hesitated. The wiring in many of these old buildings could not take bright lights. He could get one of those battery-powered reading lights at the hardware store; that would do it.

To Morton's surprise, there were a number of people on the street when he walked out of the Inn. He noticed the same odd silence about them. He could tell they were curious about him, but no one approached him, and when he got too near any of the pedestrians they moved away from him, avoiding him. He thought that perhaps the clerk from the Inn had mentioned his work. How sad that so many people mistrusted the IRS, Molton thought as he found a coffee shop on one of the side streets not far from the post office.

A single waitress was behind the counter, a middle-aged woman with her hair in an untidy bun. She squinted as if she needed glasses as Morton came up to the counter. "We don't have much tonight," she said, her voice unusually low and full of disturbing implications. It was a voice made of spices and madness, and it turned her from a frump to a *femme fatale* in disguise.

"That's fine," said Morton with his best sincere smile. "I guess the rest have eaten."

She gave him a quick look. "You might say that."

Morton was more puzzled than ever. "Well, I've heard that some of these remote towns roll the sidewalks up early. Though you have lots of people out still."

"Uh-huh," said the waitress as she got out some flatware and set it in front of him as if she were unfamiliar with the task. "It's lamb stew – that's with vegetables in the stew and biscuits with gravy on the side."

"Fine," said Morton, who hated lamb. "That's fine." He looked around for a menu to see what he might have the next day, but could find none.

The waitress saw this and said, "There's a chalkboard. Most of the time, I tell anyone who wants to know."

"I see," said Morton, baffled.

"It'll take a couple minutes." She went through the swinging doors to the kitchen, and Morton listened for conversation or the banging of pots, but there was only silence.

You know, he told himself in his best inner-jocular style, if I were more credulous than I am, this place would be downright eerie. He looked around for a clock, and saw that the only one, on the wall over the cash register, was stopped at the improbable hour of 2:13. He was becoming more and more convinced that the economy of the town had collapsed, and that those who remained were hanging on by the slimmest of threads. Perhaps that's why I saw no one, he went on to himself. It may be that much of the town's population has moved away. It could be that many of the houses are deserted, that the offices have no one in them. He resolved to find out more in the morning.

The waitress returned with a white ironstone dish with his dinner spread over it "Coffee?" she asked in that disturbing voice of hers as she put the plate down in front of him.

"Yes, please," said Morton, not looking directly at her. "Is there any salt?"

Once again the waitress shot him a quick dagger of a look, and then concealed it with a smile. "Sorry. We ran out."

"That's all right," said Morton, adding one more item to his mental shopping list. He took a too-hot forkful of the stew and burned the roof of his mouth with it. He tried not to look too dismayed, but he panted over the stuff until he was sure he could swallow it without disaster. It was the strangest thing, he thought, that this lamb stew should taste so . . . so characterless, more like a TV dinner that had been in the microwave than a New England supper.

Morning began with some minion of the Inn leaving a tray with a pot of coffee, a carton of cream, and a few packets of sugar on a tray with a cup and two pieces of desiccated toast. Morton was already dressed and tying his shoes when the knock came on his door and he found this spartan fare waiting for him. Over the coffee – which was strong without being tasty – he looked through his report of the night before. The first thing on his morning agenda was a visit to the lumber mill, to find out if it was in operation at all. After that, he supposed he would have to speak with the banker, not only to learn more about the town, but to shore up his dwindling supply of cash.

The day was glary, with thin, high clouds turning the sun to a bright patch in a white sky. Morton shaded his eyes as he looked down the street and debated whether he should drive or walk. In a town like this, he thought that walking might be the wiser choice, so that he would not appear to be as much a stranger as the townspeople seemed to think him. So he ambled along the main street toward the older church, then made a right turn along the rutted road toward the jumble of buildings that housed the mill. As he strolled toward the small parking lot, he saw there were only two cars there – an elderly Jeep and a seven-year-old Pontiac in need of new paint – and that the incinerator cone was dark. For some unknown reason, Morton began to whistle as he approached the mill.

The first place he looked was the millpond, where a couple dozen waterlogged trunks rode low. There was no one around. He went toward the nearest building, his whistling making the silence more immense. He stared at the gaping doors, standing open as if to receive the logs, but with all the machinery quiet. Morton decided not to venture inside. Still whistling, he made his way back to the parking lot, taking his notebook out of his pocket and scribbling down his impressions before they left him.

Wending his way back to the Inn, he detoured along side streets, seeing gardens overrun with weeds and berry vines. Most of the houses needed paint, and a few of them had broken windows that showed no sign of patching. Just as I thought, Morton observed to himself as he continued to whistle. This town is empty. That's what happened. The mill has closed, and most of the people have moved away.

But, said another part of his mind, they have not got new jobs or addresses, and they have not filed taxes.

When Morton reached the bank, a sign in the door said: CLOSED

FOR LUNCH. OPEN AGAIN AT 1:30. Now that, Morton decided, was a real case of banker's hours. He checked his watch, and noted that he had forty-five minutes before the bank would open again. After a brief hesitation, he decided to go back to the cafe where he had had supper and get himself a bite of lunch; his breakfast had not been enough to sustain him for long.

To his irritated surprise, the cafe was closed. A hand-lettered sign in the window indicated they would be open at six. How on earth could they get by, doing so little business in a town like Jericho? Shrugging, Morton started up the street to the grocery store he had seen. He would buy some sandwich makings and a little something to augment tomorrow's breakfast.

There were two clerks in the grocery store, both teenagers, both listless, as if they had wakened less than ten minutes ago. Morton wondered if they were on some kind of drug – they moved so lethargically and could offer so little.

"The freezers are—" Morton began to the taller boy.

"Empty. Yes, sir. Power failure." He folded his arms. "There's canned stuff, and like that."

"Yes," said Morton dubiously. "And no fresh produce, I see."

"We got a couple dozen eggs," the boy offered.

"All right," said Morton, thinking he would ask the waitress to boil them for him that night. "I'll take a dozen."

"Okay." The boy moved off sluggishly, his eyes slightly unfocused.

Morton shook his head. He had always associated drug abuse with urban kids and city pressure. But of course that was naive. In a depressed village like this one, no wonder the kids looked for solace in drugs. He supposed the cops were aware of it, but he decided he would have to remark on it in any case.

The boy returned with a carton of eggs. "They're okay. I checked them."

"Thank you," said Morton, handing over forty dollars.

The boy stared at the money, then gave a self-conscious shrug and made change. "Oh yeah," he said with a slight laugh, which was echoed nastily by the other boy in the market.

"Is the manager in the store?" Morton asked as he took his bagged purchases.

"Yeah," said the second boy. "But he's resting."

That, Morton surmised, could mean anything. "I'd like to speak to him. If not today, then tomorrow. Will you tell him?"

"Sure," said the first boy, leaning back against the cash register as if he were exhausted.

Morton thanked them and went back to the Inn to put his meager provisions away.

It was 1:45 before the sign in the bank door was removed and someone unlocked the door. Morton, waiting impatiently across the street, hurried over and flung the door open.

The cavernous room was empty. No tellers stood at their windows; no officers sat at the desks beyond the low railing of dusty turned wood. Morton looked around in amazement. Then he called out, "Is anyone here?"

A door at the back of the room opened, creaking on its hinges. "Please come in," said the sonorous voice of a gaunt figure standing in the opening.

"You're the president of the bank?" Morton faltered, looking around him and becoming more convinced than ever that he was seeing the final death throes of Jericho.

"Yes," said the man. "Please come in," he repeated.

"Thank you," Morton said, starting to sense some relief, for surely he would now have the answer to his puzzle. He hefted his case and drew out his identification and his business card. "I'm Morton Symes. I'm with the IRS, as you can see." He held his identification up so that the tall, lean man could read the documents and see the picture.

The bank president barely glanced at it. "Yes, of course. Please sit down." He directed Morton to a high wing-backed chair covered in dark green velvet that matched the (closed) draperies at the tall windows. The president took his seat in a leather-upholstered chair behind a desk that was at least two hundred years old. "Now, what is it you want here, Mr Symes?"

"Well," Morton said, gathering his thoughts together and launching into his explanation. "We were reviewing the tax returns for this area, as we do from time to time, and it came to our attention that in the past two years almost no one in this village has filed tax returns with the IRS. Our records show no indication of the cause, and given the economic situation in the country, there have been times that isolated communities such as this one have been subjected to more fluctuations in their fortunes than in other, more largely economically based urban areas; yet, because of the lack of information available, we were in an awkward position – don't you see? Naturally, we are curious as to the reason for your whole village not paying taxes, or even filing forms saying that they made insufficient income, and I have been sent to investigate."

"I see," said the bank president.

Morton waited for the man to go on, to extrapolate or obfuscate, but was met with silence. Awkwardly, he continued. "Since I've come here – only yesterday, I admit – I've noticed that most of the town seems . . . deserted. There don't appear to be pupils in the school—"

"The semester hasn't started yet," said the bank president smoothly.

"—And the mill has been shut down."

"Most regrettable," said the bank president.

"Is that a permanent situation, do you think?" Morton said, reaching for his notebook.

"I believe so," said the bank president, with a very smooth widening of his mouth that did not succeed as a smile.

"How unfortunate," said Morton automatically. He had listened to tales of economic disasters so often that he had become something like an undertaker offering sympathy.

"It creates problems," said the bank president.

"Too much competition from the big companies, I guess, like Georgia-Pacific." It was a safe guess, Morton told himself, and not bad for an off-the-cuff remark; it made him sound more knowledgeable than he actually was.

"That is a factor," said the bank president. "You understand that since this bank was founded by my family . . . oh, generations ago, and our principal is tied up in tax-free bonds, for the most part – as you undoubtedly know – we are in a position to be able to carry many of those who remain here for a considerable time more. We have an obligation to this village, and to the people in it." He gave a delicate cough. "You said almost no one has filed tax returns for the past two years. Am I the exception?"

"Uh . . . Yes." Morton had not found that particular return in his first check of the town because the return was so vast and complicated that he had overlooked the Jericho address. Now he was glad he had taken the time to review. "You have more money in North Poindexter right now than you do in this town. And all over New England, for that matter. Your Boston holdings alone could finance a dozen Jerichos." He did not want to fawn or to appear unduly impressed, though he was startled by what he had discovered. "You're very well connected."

"Yes. That's what old money does for you," said the bank president. "Still, I can see you'd better have an explanation, and I'm afraid I can't offer you one right now – I have other affairs to attend to."

Morton almost said, "In an empty bank?" but held his tongue.

"If you're not busy, let me have some of your time later today. You come to my house this evening for cocktails, say, about, oh, 7:30. Just sherry or bourbon or rum," he went on. "We're not fancy in this place." He leaned back in his chair. "My wife will be delighted for your company." There was a slight change in his expression, as if he were being amused at Morton's expense.

"Is something the matter?" Morton asked, trying to be polite but without success:

The bank president did not answer at once. "Mrs Wainwright is a trifle older than I am," said the bank president. "She comes from a very old and distinguished European family. You may find her reserved, what they used to call 'high in the instep'. But don't let this bother you. She's a product of her time and culture, as are we all."

"Yes, of course," said Morton. He paused. "I can obtain the necessary documents, if you insist, but if you're willing to let me examine your records while I'm here—"

The bank president – Hewlett Wainwright was his name – held up his hand. "I'm sorry, but for the sake of the depositors and their privacy and constitutional rights, I must insist that you obtain your warrants and subpoenas." This time he made no attempt at a smile. "You understand I would be lax in my duty and my responsibility if I permitted you to ransack the accounts without the required documents."

"I understand," said Morton, ducking his head. "Certainly that's the prudent thing to do. I was only thinking that with the town in such a . . . depressed state, the sooner the tax situation is cleared up, the sooner you might go about setting things right again."

"Setting things right?" asked the bank president as if Morton had suddenly started speaking in Albanian.

"You know," Morton persisted, though his ears were scarlet, "arranging for federal aid. No doubt some of your townspeople could use a little assistance, a little retrenching, some retraining, perhaps—"

"My dear Mr Symes," said the bank president, doing his best to contain his temper. "We are not sniveling, whining creatures, to throw ourselves on the dubious mercy of the federal government. As long as I can afford it – and I have every reason to believe I will be able to afford it for some considerable time to come – I will see that Jericho is tended to. There is no reason for the government – federal, state, or any other – to intrude." He held out his hand. "Until this evening, Mr Symes."

Not even Brewster had routed Morton so efficiently. Stammering an apology, Morton got to his feet and made his way to the door, all the while wondering what could be making such demands on the bank president in this echoing, empty building. He closed the door to the bank president's office and all but tiptoed across the main chamber, finding its vacant teller cages almost sinister. "Don't be absurd," he whispered to himself as he reached the door.

The afternoon air was sweet, and the deserted street intrigued him.

It was comforting to stroll toward the Inn, free to stop and stare when he wanted to, or to make notes without being embarrassed. He whistled a tune he had heard last week – he thought it came from *Phantom of the Opera* – and considered going to the little police station, then kept on toward the Inn. If he was going to have cocktails with Hewlett Wainwright and his wife, he wanted to be properly dressed. He also had to make his report to Brewster.

Luckily, he had change enough to place the collect call, but he had to accept the criticism of his boss in return for his taking the call. Morton opened his notebook. "Mr Brewster," he began in his most official voice, "I'm sorry I wasn't able to reach you yesterday. Things turned out to be a little more complicated than either of us had anticipated."

"Anticipated?" Brewster repeated, some of his bluster still in his voice. "What do you mean?"

"There are . . . difficulties here." Morton sensed that the desk clerk was listening, but he vowed to continue no matter what. "The mill is closed, and many of the houses appear to be deserted."

"What does that have to do with the delay in your call?" Brewster demanded.

"I needed time to gather some information," said Morton, his patience all but deserting him "I didn't want to waste your time with giving you simple descriptions. I thought you'd rather have a complete report, not a catalog of ills."

Brewster coughed once, and while not mollified he was not as overbearing. "That was my decision to make, Symes, not yours. But if you'd had to call collect then, too, I can see why you might wait. How come you didn't use the phone credit card we issued you?"

Morton sighed "They appear to refuse credit cards here in Jericho. That's another reason that made me assume that the town is . . . failing. They won't take checks or credit cards – nothing but cash. I'll have to get more by the end of the week, or I won't be able to get enough gas to drive out of here." He did not give Brewster time to comment, but hurried on. "I have to be prepared to work with these people on their terms, Mr Brewster. I don't want them to think that we have no sympathy for their plight, or that we're punitive in our methods. These people need our help, sir. They need social services and housing grants and emergency funds to keep the whole place from turning into a graveyard."

"As bad as all that?" Brewster asked, not quite bored.

"I think it could be," Morton said carefully. "With the mill closed and most of the businesses looking pretty bad . . . I went to the grocery store, and there was no one shopping but me. I don't think they've done much to restock the shelves." He cleared his throat delicately. "You told us all last month that we need to pay attention to the economic curves in a place before dealing with the tax impact."

"So I did," said Brewster heavily, as if he now considered that a bad idea.

"And I want to be certain that we don't make a bad situation worse. There's no point in running this place into the ground if we don't have to. It's better to have them working for a little pay than on the welfare rolls, isn't it?" Morton hoped that he could find a way to gain Brewster's support. "If we can work out some kind of program for the whole town, it might mean the difference between staying afloat and going under."

"Yes, yes," said Brewster impatiently. "Well, it's something to think about, isn't it? The last thing we want is another one of those pity-the-poor-taxpayer stories on *60 Minutes*. And this is exactly the kind of situation they'd love." He paused, and Morton did not dare to interrupt. "Give it a couple of days, Symes, and call me again. Collect. I'll see that some cash is transferred to the bank for you, but you'll have to work out the vouchers when you get back, and we'll do what we can to arrange—" He stopped abruptly. "Call me day after tomorrow, at this time. And in the meantime, don't talk to anyone else about this – do you understand?"

"Yes," said Morton, anticipating that Brewster would find a way to take any credit coming from this venture for himself, and attach any blame to be had to Morton Symes. "Sure, Mr Brewster."

"That's good," said Brewster, turning cordial. "You'll have that cash transfer tomorrow. I'll see that it's wired to the bank—"

"Pardon me, sir," Morton interrupted. "Would you make the transfer to the bank in North Poindexter? I'll drive over and pick it up; it won't take long. I don't know what kind of cash reserves are at this bank, or even if there are any. And there's almost no staff."

Once more Brewster considered. "All right, North Poindexter it is. I will tell them to expect you by noon: how's that?"

"Fine. That's great." Morton looked down at his notes. "I haven't seen many kids aside from the two clerks at the store. The school appears to be closed. I'm going to check that out tomorrow, but I'm afraid that it means several families have left town. I'll try to get some figures on that tonight."

"Do as you think best, of course," said Brewster at his smoothest.

"Yes, sir," said Morton, all but saluting. "I'd better get ready for this cocktail thing, and then try to arrange for dinner at the cafe. I'll call you in two days, when I know more."

"Make sure it's all in your daily reports." Brewster coughed. "Good luck, Symes."

"Thank you, sir," said Morton, and hung up as soon as he heard

Brewster put down his receiver. He stood by the phone for a few minutes, curious about the innkeeper: how much had he heard, and what had he made of it? There was no way to ask him, but Morton felt he ought to try at some point to learn more about the man. As he made his way to his room, he decided he had better have a bite or two to eat before going to the Wainwright house, for drink on an empty stomach always made him giddy.

By quarter after seven, Morton was ready, his three-piece navy-blue pinstripe suit and pale blue shirt nicely set off by his discreet medallion-patterned silk tie. It would pass muster for all but the dressiest dinners in Boston and Washington, and certainly ought to do for cocktails in Jericho. He felt awkward that he had nothing to bring his hostess, but decided that on such short notice, he could be excused for not bringing flowers or candy or a bottle of French wine.

He saw that there were about a dozen people on the street, including the two policemen who served the village. As he opened the gate to the once-lavish and now-neglected gardens of the Wainwright house, he noticed that several of the people on the street were watching him covertly, almost – he smiled at the image – hungrily.

Hewlett Wainwright himself opened the door. "Please come in," he said formally, standing aside for Morton. "Welcome to our home."

"Thank you," said Morton as he stepped into the dimness of the entry hall. He noticed the authentic Tiffany light fixtures and decided that the house had probably not been rewired since they were installed. No wonder the Wainwrights used low-power bulbs with them; anything stronger would be courting fire and disaster. Still, he thought, as he made his way toward the parlor Mr Wainwright indicated, it might be worth it; the place was positively gloomy, with all that heavy, dark wood and the low light.

"My wife will join us directly; she takes a nap in the afternoon, you know, so she will be fresh for the evening." He indicated the parlor, which was an Art Nouveau treasure. "Go on in, Mr Symes. Make yourself comfortable."

Morton said a few words by way of thanks, and stepped into the parlor, marveling at what he saw there. By anyone's standards, every piece in the room was a valuable antique, and all kept in beautiful condition but for a fine patina of dust, one that could not be more than one or two days old. Aside from the Tiffany lamps, there were small statues of superb design, three of them most certainly tarnished silver. As Morton stopped to look at the largest of these – two lovers with attenuated bodies entwined like vines in an arbor – he heard a step behind him.

"Ah, there you are, my dear," said Hewlett Wainwright.

The woman in the door was elegantly attired in heavy black damask silk topped with a bodice of heavy Venetian black lace. Her hair was abundant and of a glossy white, waved back from her face and caught in some sort of twist that emphasized her slender neck and high brow. Certainly she was not young, but she was magnificent enough to catch Morton's breath in his throat. She smiled faintly, her full red lips turning up; she extended her hand to be kissed, not shaken. "Welcome to our home," she said as Morton took her hand.

Though he felt incredibly awkward, Morton bent over and kissed her fingers, trying to appear more practiced at this courtesy than he was. "I'm pleased to meet you, Mrs Wainwright."

"I am Ilona," she said. "That is one of the Hungarian variants of Helen." It was an explanation she had made many times before, but she had a way of speaking that created a kind of intimacy with her guests such that each of them felt they were being offered a special secret: Morton was no exception.

"Mr Symes is concerned for our village," Mr Wainwright told his wife. "He is from the Internal Revenue Service. You recall my remarks earlier?"

"Oh yes," said Ilona, her dark gaze not leaving Morton's face. "Those are the tax people, aren't they?"

"Yes. They are worried because we are the only people in Jericho who still pay taxes." He went to a gorgeous cabinet opposite the fireplace. "What would you like to drink, Mr Symes? I ought to warn you: we have no ice."

"Oh," said Morton with an effort, "whatever you recommend. I'm afraid I'm not an expert on such things." He knew he should not be staring at his hostess, but there was something about her, and it was not her elegance or her beauty – not at all faded by age – that held him fascinated.

"Ah," said Mr. Wainwright. "Well, in that case, I can recommend a Canadian whiskey; it isn't much available in this country, but, living so close to the border, from time to time I pick up a bottle or two when I'm north on business." He had taken out a large, squat glass with a hint of etching on it. "I'll pour you a little, and if you like it, I'll be happy to fill you up again." He poured out the whiskey and brought the drink to his guest. "I see you're captivated by Ilona. She is so lovely, isn't she?"

"Yes," said Morton, blushing with the admission.

"I don't blame you for staring. I remember the first time I set eyes on her; I thought I'd die if I looked away. You were very sweet to me then, my darling," Mr Wainwright said, addressing this last to his wife.

She lifted her shoulder; on her, even so mundane an action as a shrug was graceful. "And you were sweet to me. You had such savor then."

Morton blinked, startled at her choice of words. Then he recalled that English was not her first language, and he supposed he ought to expect an occasional strange turn of phrase from her. He tasted the whiskey and tried hard not to cough. "Very . . . unusual."

Hewlett Wainwright took that as a compliment. "Thank you; let me give you some more. And in a short while, I'll have Maggie bring in something to sop up the alcohol." He winked at Morton. "Nothing special, just a little cheese and some crackers, but it'll tone down the whiskey. Not that you have to worry about it tonight. The Inn's close enough, and you're not driving anywhere." He chuckled. "Enjoy our hospitality."

"What about you?" asked Morton, noticing that only he had a glass in his hand.

"Oh, Ilona never developed a taste for whiskey, and I've had to give it up." Wainwright patted his stomach. "You know how it is: after a certain age, you must watch what you eat and drink, or your system takes revenge. You wouldn't know that yet, but one day it will happen to you, too."

"I feel awkward – ," Morton began, only to have Wainwright make a dismissing gesture.

"Don't bother, Mr Symes. It's a pleasure to be able to offer you our hospitality, and it would be very disappointing if you were not pleased with what we offer." He indicated one of the rosewood chairs near the fireplace. "Sit down. Be comfortable. Ilona, persuade him for me."

Mrs Wainwright looked directly into Morton's eyes. "Please. Sit down. Have your drink. Be comfortable."

A trifle nonplussed, Morton did as he was told, thinking that if the situation became too awkward, he could always make his excuses and leave. "Thank you."

"Now then," said Hewlett Wainwright, coming to stand in front of the hearth. "I told you I'd explain what has happened in this village to account for our change of fortune here. I imagine your superiors are going to wonder about it, no matter what you do here. In a way, that's too bad; I hate to think of Jericho drawing attention to itself in its present state. However, I suppose we must accept our predicament as unavoidable. Eventually someone would notice our . . . absence."

Morton was trying not to look at Ilona Wainwright, but was not succeeding. "Your absence," he repeated as if the words made no sense at all.

"Certainly we have to contend with . . . many problems here. Once the mill closed, there was so little to hold on to, you must see. The mill, directly or indirectly, accounted for more than half the employment in Jericho, which meant that a sort of domino effect resulted from the closing. There have been some businesses that have been able to hold out, but generally we do not have a wide enough economic base to keep the town going. Which is why I've been extending credit to so many of the villagers through my personal fortune, which is quite extensive."

"Hewlett is of the old school," said Ilona with a fond glance at her husband. "I sometimes think that was why he wanted to marry me."

"Oh dearest!" Hewlett Wainwright guffawed. "I didn't care what you were or who you were or anything else about you; I cared only that you wanted me as much as I wanted you." He paused and turned toward Morton. "It was a second marriage for me; my first wife died ten years ago. She – my first wife – was the daughter of my father's closest business associate. You might say that our marriage was set from birth, and you would not be far wrong."

"You're worse than the old aristocracy," said Ilona fondly.

"Be that as it may. The second time I married, Mr Symes, I married to please myself, and when I brought my wife back here to Jericho, I was the happiest man in the world." He indicated the parlor. "It's no Carpathian castle, but it's not a hovel, either."

"Carpathian castles are cold," said Ilona. "More than half of them are in ruins." She looked at Morton with a strange expression in her mesmerizing eyes. "You think this place has become lifeless – you know nothing of it. There are places in the mountains of my homeland that appear to be on the far side of the grave, so lost are they."

"Don't exaggerate, my dear," Hewlett Wainwright asked with a playful grin. "Every part of Europe has some village or ruin that makes Jericho seem lively."

"I suppose so," said Morton dubiously. He had another taste of the whiskey, and hoped he could keep his head clear. "It must have seemed strange, coming here after living in Europe. There is so much history in Europe."

Ilona smiled this time widely. "We make our own history, don't we?" She turned her head as a small, shapeless woman bustled into the room with a little tray. "Here's the cheese. I hope you enjoy it, Mr Symes."

Morton looked at the hard yellow cheese and did his best to appear interested. "It's fine." He was glad he had had a little to eat before coming to this meeting and at the same time felt so hungry and uncomfortable in this strange company that he hardly cared that the cheese looked almost inedible.

"I'll cut you a slice, if you like," offered Hewlett Wainwright, motioning the maid away. He picked up the cheese slicer and set to work sawing "You'll find this has a lot of character. Not many places you can get this kind of cheese today."

"I see," said Morton, accepting the long shard of cheese laid across a dry cracker "Thanks." It was quite a job getting through the cheese and cracker; in the process he consumed most of the whiskey only to make the food swallowable. His head rang, but he did his best to smile as he set his glass aside. "You're very gracious. Tell me more, will you, about how the town ran into financial difficulties? Wasn't that two years ago?"

Hewlett refilled his glass as he embarked on a complicated tale that would have been hard enough to follow if Morton had had all his wits about him. As it was, he discovered that he was not able to make sense out of most of it, though he had a general description of a mill unable to keep up with modern big business, and a town that lived on its bounty; it was theme and variation on what he had already learned, but told with more convolutions. Still, with or without the embellishments, the story was basically a simple one: when the mill was closed, jobs and money disappeared, and most of Jericho was lost.

"My husband has made it more cut-and-dried than it is," said Ilona when Hewlett at last paused. "He hasn't mentioned his own role in preserving the place. His personal concern for the village has provided a livelihood for many of those who have remained here."

"But . . . but they haven't filed their taxes," said Morton, doing his best not to slur this statement.

"They had no reason," said Hewlett. "Most of them had very little income. There was nothing to report."

"But you know better than that," protested Morton, striving to keep his thoughts clear enough to continue. "We have to know when there is nothing to report, just as when there is. It's the information that's crucial – don't you see? The government cannot provide needed assistance if there is no record of the need – don't you see?" His head hummed like a shell held against his ear, the sound that was supposed to be like the sea and was not. "We have to be able to show that the circumstances have changed, that you are not . . . taking advantage, or . . ." He swallowed hard and tried again. "If you have new problems, there are other consequences than . . . Don't you see: if you haven't made money, then there are fewer penalties for not filing. But you have to file – don't you see?" He knew he was repeating himself, but was unable to stop himself. That one phrase – *don't you see?* – was stuck in his thoughts, persistent as allergy sniffles, and he could not rid himself of it.

"No," said Hewlett. "Oh, I've read the publications, but I cannot see why it is essential for you to have paperwork for no reason, because we have no money to report. Why, even the police chief and his assistant are paid from my personal accounts, not from the village budget, because those coffers are empty. If you like, they're the village's private security force now, and as such are my employees." He looked at Morton. "Would you like a little more whiskey?"

"Not right now," said Morton, who was astonished when Hewlett nevertheless put a bit more in his glass.

"Just in case you change your mind," said Hewlett. "More cheese?"

The room grew darker as the three of them conversed. Morton soon began to lose track of what he was trying to say, and after a while that no longer bothered him. He noticed that his host and hostess hovered close to him, which he decided was flattering, since it was not typical of New Englanders. He could feel them bend over him, and he tried to think of an adequate apology for his bad manners, for he was more than pleasantly tipsy. He knew he ought to make an excuse for his behavior, but he could not string the words together sensibly. He was simply aware of stretching out on the sofa – unthinkable behavior! – and of Ilona Wainwright fussing with his tie to loosen it, her stare boring into him as she did.

"Not too much, my dearest," Morton heard Hewlett say. "Not all at once, remember."

Whatever Ilona answered was lost to Morton, who felt overcome by fatigue, unable to move or think. He tried to explain how sorry he was but, to his intense chagrin, he passed out.

He woke in the Ivy Room of the Jericho Inn, his clothes neatly put away and his pajamas on, the blankets tucked under his chin. It was mid-morning, to judge by the position of the square of light from the window. Morton rubbed his eyes, groaning as he moved. He started to sit up, but stopped as dizziness made the room swing; he lowered his head and sighed. He damned himself roundly for getting drunk, and he shuddered at what the Wainwrights must have thought. He moved again, more slowly and gingerly, and this time made it to his elbows before vertigo took hold of him "Damn it," he muttered. "Damn, damn, damn."

The few times he had drunk too much, he had been left with a thumping headache and a queasy stomach, but never before had he felt weak. As he made himself sit up, his arms trembled with the effort, and a cold sweat broke out on his chest and neck. "This is absurd," he said to the wallpaper, embarrassed at how little strength he had, and how much work it took merely to drag himself to his feet. With a concentrated effort, he got out of bed and, steadying himself against the wall, he went toward the little bathroom, breathing as if he had just run two miles.

His waxy pallor surprised him, as did the dark shadows under his eyes, as if he had been beaten. Morton stared in the mirror, appalled at his own wan features. His hands shook as he did his best to shave, though when he was through he had several minor nicks, including one on his neck that bled more persistently than the others. As he toweled his face dry, he inspected the cuts and dotted them with iodine. How was he going to explain this to Brewster? he wondered. How was he going to account for his failure to gain the needed information? What excuse could he offer for his conduct? He puzzled over this, his wits moving more slowly than his body, as he dressed. Belatedly, he remembered that he had to drive to the bank in North Poindexter to get his cash. The thought of such a journey left him troubled, but he knew he had to go there before he ran out of money, and he had to be there this morning or Brewster would be curious and critical.

There was no one in the lobby of the Inn when Morton made his way down the stairs, and the street, once again, appeared all but empty. A face appeared at the window of one of the offices near the general store, but aside from that there was no one to be seen. Morton got into his chocolate BMW and started it cautiously, wincing as the engine erupted into life. Ordinarily he would have taken pleasure in the sound, but not this morning. He drove off at a sedate pace, and once on the two-lane state highway he did not risk going faster than forty.

By the time he reached North Poindexter, the worst of his dizziness had gone. His hands still felt weak, his thoughts seemed disordered, and his eyes squinted against the sun, but he no longer felt as if he could not keep steady. The busy, narrow streets pleased him, and he almost enjoyed having to hunt for a parking space.

The senior teller had Morton's voucher for cash, and after checking his credentials and getting his signature on the necessary documents, gave him eight hundred dollars. "Odd, you needing cash," she remarked as she slipped the papers into the appropriate files.

"Yes, it is," said Morton, adding, "Can you recommend a good place for lunch?" Now that he had said the words, he decided he was ravenous. It was not just the drink, he realized, that had made him so much not himself, but the lack of food. Whiskey and no supper, and no breakfast. No wonder he had felt poorly. "I want something more than a sandwich," he went on.

"Well," the senior teller said, "I don't know what to tell you. There's Edna's down the block; they're quite good, but they're pretty much soup-and-sandwich. Then there's the Federal Restaurant.

That's expensive, but the food is good, and they have a large lunch."
She looked at him more closely. "We don't have much in the way of
fancy eating in North Poindexter."

"You have more here than in Jericho," said Morton in a tone that
he hoped was funny. "That place was—"

"Jericho," echoed the senior teller. "You mean you've been over
in Jericho?"

"Yes," said Morton, baffled at the peculiar expression in the senior
teller's eyes. Speaking the word carefully, he asked, "Why?"

"Oh," said the senior teller with a belated and unconvincing show
of indifference, "it's nothing – the place is so remote, and with the
mill closed and all . . ."

When she did not go on, Morton grew more intrigued. "Has there
been trouble in Jericho? Other than the mill closing and people
being out of work, I mean?"

The senior teller shrugged. "You know how people say things
about places like that. It's gossip and rumors; all these little places in
New England have some of it. They're glad to think the worst of
villages like Jericho, so their own place seems better." She lowered
her voice. "It's not as if I believe what they say about the place, but it
is spooky; you'll give me that."

"I wouldn't use that word, perhaps," said Morton with caution,
"but I can understand when someone might."

"Yes; well, you see why there are stories about the place. Most of
them sound like some kind of horror movie, you know; one of those
George Romero things. You hear about weird creatures, or worse
than that, roaming the streets preying on decent folk. It's silly. It's just
talk. It's because the place is so . . . empty." She made a dismissing
movement with her hands. "I probably shouldn't be saying this. It's
not at all responsible."

"I appreciate it," said Morton "It's always disconcerting to be in
deserted places. While I've been there, I don't think I've seen more
than a dozen people. During the day, there's almost no one around,
and in the evening, the people on the streets don't say much. I think
having the mill gone makes it all so precarious that they don't like to
talk about it."

"Probably," said the senior teller, and moved away from him. "I'm
sorry, but I got work to do."

After Morton ordered a generous lunch at the Federal Restaurant,
he caught up on his report, trying to gloss over his misbehavior the
night before. "I don't know," he muttered as he read what he had
put down, "how else to account for it."

"Did you say something?" asked the waiter as he brought calf's
liver and onions with a spinach salad on the side. "More coffee?"

"Yes, please," said Morton, adding, "And a glass of tomato juice, if you would."

"Naturally," said the waiter, departing at once.

When he had finished his lunch and indulged in an excellent carrot cake with extra raisins, Morton decided he was getting better. Food was what he had needed. He no longer felt as light-headed as before, and some of his strength was returning. "That'll teach me to skip dinner," he said softly as he paid the bill.

Before he drove back to Jericho, he stopped to get some protein snacks: jerky, a few slices of ham and turkey, and a box of crackers. He had his hard-boiled eggs, and this ought to make things easier for him.

The police chief, a bulky man everyone called Willy, regarded Morton's identification askance. "I wondered when you'd be getting around to me," he said, his accent ringing with the flat vowels of New England and the east coast of Britain. "I don't know what I can do for you, and that's a fact."

"It may be," said Morton, feeling restored and just guilty enough to persevere with his investigation. "I have to ask. I hope you appreciate that."

"Of course," said Willy with resignation. "What do you need to know?"

"First, I need to know how many people have moved out of Jericho in the past eighteen months." Morton drew out his notebook and made a show of getting ready to write down the information.

"Oh, four, maybe five," said Willy after giving his answer some thought. "No more than that."

Morton stared at him. "That's absurd."

"Preacher Stonecroft, he left; him and his wife, that is. They went, oh, more'n a year ago. Sad to lose them, but the way things are around here . . ." He indicated the window, as if the view of main street provided the explanation. "They weren't our sort, not them. So they left."

"I see," said Morton, trying to guess why this man was lying.

"Over a year ago. So did the minister; he took those two orphaned boys and went west. That was before the Stonecrofts left, by maybe a couple months." Willy looked at his three empty cells visible through the open door.

"Also not your sort," Morton ventured.

"That's right. And the two boys probably needed to get out, with their folks newly dead." Willy sighed. "Henry and Dinah Hill."

"They were the boys' parents?" Morton asked, finding the police chief remarks a bit hard to follow.

"Yeah. They died and Reverend Kingsly took them away. He said it was for the best. He might have been right," said Willy.

"Where did they go?" Morton wanted to know.

"West," Willy told him, with a wave of his hand in that direction.

"But where west? Don't you know?" He would have to tell Brewster about Reverend Kingsly; somehow it ought to be possible to trace the man and the two orphans.

"He didn't tell us. I don't think he knew." Willy sighed. "Not that we hold it against him, you understand. In a case like his, he had to leave."

Morton scowled. "How do you mean, in a case like his?"

"The way things were going. Churchmen have to have a congregation, don't they?" Willy sighed again, this time letting his breath out slowly.

"And because the mill closed, people stopped going to church?" Morton asked, and decided at once that what the chief of police was trying so politely to say was that there was no money to support the churches in town; with the Wainwrights paying the villagers out of their own pocket, there would not be much left for the two ministers.

"Well, it wasn't quite like that, but . . . ." Willy looked toward the window again. "This isn't a very big place; it's never been a very big place. Things get hard in a town like this. We know what it's like to be cut off."

"You mean your isolation is working against you?" Morton asked hoping he had interpreted Willy's remark accurately.

"Well, some of us think it works *for* us, but it's all in how you look at it." He nodded twice. "I can't give you much more, Mr Symes. You've seen Jericho for yourself; you know what it's like here. No matter what the government does, things aren't going to change here a whole hell of a lot, if you take my meaning."

"Yes," said Morton, not at all certain that he followed Willy's implications. "Do you think you'd have time to draw up a list of the names and addresses of those people still living in town?"

"Still living?" repeated Willy. "Sure, I can do that."

Morton gave him his best stern but sincere smile. "Thank you very much for your help, Willy. I know this can't be easy for you."

"We get by," said Willy as Morton let himself out of the police station.

At the diner, Morton made a point of having a second order of pot roast and a dish of ice cream for dessert. He noticed once again that no one else was in the place, and this time he said, "Is it always this slow?"

"Most folks around here like to eat in," said the waitress without looking at him. "You know how it is."

"Yes," said Morton, thinking that at last he did.

"We keep to ourselves around here, especially since the mill closed." She regarded him with taunting eyes, the rest of her apparently consumed with boredom.

"It has had serious repercussions for the town, hasn't it?" Morton looked at the waitress once, then gazed toward the window so that she would not feel he was questioning her too closely.

"It's one of the things," said the waitress. "There are others."

"Yes," Morton said at once. "Of course there are." He paid for his supper and left a 22 percent tip, more than was allowed, but he wanted to let the waitress know he appreciated all she had told him.

As Morton went out the door, the waitress called after him, "You've not found out everything yet."

Morton paused, his hand on the latch. "What did you say?"

"You heard me," she responded. "Think about it."

"Of course," said Morton, wondering what she intended to imply. He thought about it as he stepped out onto the street, feeling a peculiar exhilaration from the darkness that he had never experienced before. He strode back toward the Inn, but found himself reluctant to return to his room. Inadvertently, he was drawn to the Wainwright house, his thoughts disordered as he looked up at the faded grandeur of the mansion.

"Mr Symes," called Ilona from a second-story window. "How nice to see you again."

"Thank you," said Morton, overcome with a sudden and inexplicable rush of desire that left him all but breathless. His pulse thrummed; his flesh quivered; he seemed to be burning with fever and locked in ice all at the same time. It was most improper for him to stand staring up and with such naked longing in his face – at the aristocratic features of Ilona Wainwright.

"It was a pleasure to have you with us last evening," she said, her red lips widening in a smile.

"You're very kind," Morton faltered. What was it about this woman that aroused him so intensely? What fascination did she work on him, that he felt drawn to her in a way he had thought existed only in fantasy? And how could he ever account for his reprehensible behavior to Hewlett Wainwright?

"Not at all," Ilona said, her voice low and seductive. "I only wish to . . . to entertain you again." She stepped out onto the little balcony that fronted her window. "Will you come in?"

"I . . . I don't know . . ." Morton was almost certain that he was blushing, and that made his embarrassment more acute. "Is your husband at home?" He could hardly believe that he could be so callous, so impolite as to speak to her that way. He moved back a few steps. "I'm sorry."

"Why?" Ilona asked, and that single word was as thrilling as a symphony.

"It's . . . it's all very awkward," Morton began. "You see, Mrs Wainwright, I don't . . . that is, I ought not . . . It would not be right to take advantage of you." Be sensible, he told himself. This woman is older than you, and she is married. You have no right to want her; you have no right to speak to her. It is wrong for you to do this.

"Is something troubling you, Mr Symes?" she asked, and there was the faintest suggestion of haughty laughter in her question.

Morton squared his shoulders "I have an obligation as an investigator for the IRS not to abuse my position, which is what I would be probably be doing if . . . It would be unforgivable of me to use my . . . power to . . . compromise you." As he spoke, he moved closer to the house.

Ilona appeared not to have heard him. "It has been so long since there was someone new in the village; I have been beside myself, wanting to meet someone new. Will you come in?" She leaned down, one long, pale hand extended. "I would be so grateful to you, if you would come in, Mr Symes."

"But . . ." All the protests he had intended to make faded from his lips. "Certainly, if you would like that."

"Very good, Mr Symes," said Ilona, her smile growing more vivid. "You will find the side door, there by the conservatory, open." With that, she left the balcony.

Morton all but fell through the door in his eagerness to see Ilona. Though part of his mind still tried to reason with him, to make him resist the favor that Ilona appeared to offer, it was quickly stilled as Ilona herself came into the sitting room, her face alight with anticipation. Morton made one last attempt to break away from her. "It's wrong of me to be here. I owe you and your husband . . ."

"If you believe you owe us something, all the more reason for you to stay," she said, coming to his side and resting her head on his shoulder. "How vigorous you are. How the life courses through your veins."

That odd compliment puzzled Morton, but not for long; Ilona turned her face to his, and her carmined lips fastened on his as she seized him in a surprisingly powerful embrace. Morton stopped thinking and gave himself to delirious, erotic folly.

It was almost time to phone in his report when Morton woke in his bed once again. His dizziness had returned three-fold, and his weakness was far greater than it had been previously. Morton put an unsteady hand to his forehead and tried to organize his thoughts before he made his call to Brewster.

"You sound as if you're coming down with something," his superior observed critically after Morton commenced his report.

"I think I might be," Morton allowed. "I feel . . . drained." He sighed. "I wish I understood it."

"Have the doctor check you over before you come back to the office; I don't want you starting something with the other investigators."

"Of course not," said Morton, then got on with his report. "According to the chief of police, not very many people have left town, though I personally have seen few of the remaining townspeople. If they still live here, they must work somewhere else during the day."

"You said the town is empty?" Brewster demanded. "Make yourself plain, Symes."

"Yes, sir," said Morton, squinting to read his notes. "It might as well be a ghost town during the day."

"I see," said Brewster in his best significant voice. "And where do you think the people work?"

"I want to find that out," said Morton, stifling a yawn. "I don't think it's North Poindexter, if that's the issue. I'm fairly certain that they're not going there, judging from how people in North Poindexter regard Jericho."

"All right," said Brewster. "And how is that?"

"They seem to think that this is a very strange town, that the people here are odd and their ways are old-fashioned or something of the sort." He leaned on the wall beside the payphone. "That doesn't sound like a lot of people from Jericho work there, does it?"

"Probably not," was all the concession Brewster would make.

"From what I've seen, this place is . . . growing in on itself. It's caught – you know how some of these little places get when the main industry falls through? Remember that town in West Virginia that sort of dried up when the factory that made chairs went under?"

"You do not need to remind me," said Brewster stiffly. "And you think this is another Lambford, do you?"

"Well," said Morton uncertainly, "I'm not positive, no, but it looks likely. If you could send a formal request for records and the rest of it, the bank president will show me the accounts here, but he won't do it without the paperwork. Which is his right, of course. I need a few more days to get all my facts together, and to see what the bank president can offer me" – unbidden, the image of Ilona Wainwright came to his mind, a vision so intense that he was not able to speak for three or four seconds, and he covered this up with a cough – "and . . . take some time to . . . assess what I find."

"What's wrong?" You get yourself attended to before you get any worse," demanded Brewster.

"Allergies, I think. It's probably allergies," Morton improvised. "I guess I should take another pill."

"Don't neglect it. We don't want to have to pay hospital bills for you," said Brewster as if he were speaking to a fractious six-year-old.

"I don't want to be any trouble," Morton assured him at once. "Pollen does it, and there's pollen in the fall."

"Yes," said Brewster in a tone that indicated he had heard more than enough about all of Morton's problems. "I will see that the proper documents are sent to the bank by express, or courier if that's necessary. That should be sufficient for your purposes."

Morton nodded to himself. "I don't think that Mr Wainwright will refuse any request if it's made properly and officially, but he has the interests of his depositors to defend, and it's proper for him to do it."

"If that's all, Symes?" Brewster's tone implied that he did not need Morton Symes to teach him his job.

"For the time being," said Morton, one hand to his head. "I'll call again day after tomorrow. And you'll have my written reports when I get back." His head was ringing now, and every word he spoke crashed through his skull.

"Keep your medical records separate from the rest. We'll have to review them for reimbursement." Brewster paused, then bade Morton a stiff farewell and hung up without further ado.

After his phone call and sitting in the empty lobby for almost half an hour, Morton was barely able to walk the short distance from the Inn to the diner, and when he got there he sat for some time staring at the menu, its offerings of corned beef and cabbage so uninteresting to him that he actually felt slightly sick as he read it. Corned beef and cabbage, and doubtless it had been boiled to the point of falling apart, the cabbage nothing more than tasteless vegetable goo. Finally, when the waitress came to take his order, he turned bleary eyes on her. "Is there any chance you could get me a steak, a rare one?"

"Steak?" said the waitress, a fleeting, ferocious look at the back of her eyes.

"Yes; you know, a slice of cow, singed but bloody." Morton put his elbows on the table, astonished at his own dreadful manners. "I'd like it soon, if you can arrange that."

"What about hamburger, singed but bloody?" asked the waitress, not quite mocking him.

"Fine," said Morton, but with a touch of regret; he had anticipated the satisfaction of tearing into the meat; that was not possible with hamburger. He waited for nearly fifteen minutes before the waitress came back with a plate of raw chopped beef and all the makings of steak tartare.

"I thought you might like this a little better," said the waitress with an expression that just missed being a leer. "I'll bring you some French bread, too—"

"Never mind," said Morton, whose hunger grew painfully intense as he looked at the mound of raw beef. "I'll manage." It shocked him to listen to his harsh words; he never treated people the way he was treating the waitress. He could not imagine what had come over him, and decided that it had to be the effect of his allergies, or whatever was making him so abominably weak. "I don't suppose that you suffer from allergies."

"Allergies? Not me." The waitress laughed nastily. "So you got allergies?" She did not wait for him to answer her question, but turned on her heel and left him with his steak tartare.

By morning, Morton was feeling quite restored. His sight no longer blurred if he moved quickly, and his headache had decreased to bearable levels. He almost passed up the two hard-boiled eggs that were delivered to his room by the sullen clerk, then forced them down so that he would not have another episode like the last. He had decided today he would have to inspect the bank records; he hoped that Hewlett Wainwright would not be too difficult about his requests. At the memory of his illicit meeting with Ilona, Morton cringed and wondered how he would be able to face her husband. He tried to direct his concentration back to the job he was entrusted to do, but Ilona intruded on all of it, her elegant, sensuous presence insinuating into the world of figures. Finally Morton set his reports aside and decided to pay a visit to the post office. If the documents he requested were there, he could get on with the work: he wanted to believe that his infatuation would diminish as he gave himself over to his task. Romance and tax forms rarely mixed, he decided, and thought of the many times he had found his affections waning as his enthusiasm for tracking down tax inconsistencies waxed. How he longed for his computer screen and the safe haven of dependable, sensible, bloodless figures. The impression of Ilona Wainwright's curving mouth and brilliant eyes could be exorcized by columns of numbers.

There was a single, aged clerk at the post office, a man of a uniform grey color, from his hair and eyes and skin to the sweater and trousers he wore. He monosyllabically refused to say whether the documents had come from the IRS for Hewlett Wainwright, and when pressed, closed the shutter in front of his counter.

Reluctantly, Morton started toward the bank, his eagerness fading with each step. He did not know how, guilt-stricken as he was, he could face Hewlett Wainwright; Ilona was Wainwright's wife, his wife. Morton had never allowed himself to be drawn into associating with a married woman before, and the realization that in a town as small as Jericho secrets were impossible to keep gave him more dread than the possibility of Brewster's wrath.

"Good day, Mr Symes. Morton!" Hewlett Wainwright came out of his private office effusively. He gestured to the one teller on duty. "How good of you to have those letters sent. I can't tell you how it relieves me. This way I have not compromised my depositors, have I?" His voice boomed through the vaulted room. "Come back to my office, and we can go over the records."

Morton was nonplussed by this exuberance, and he hesitated as he took the bank president's hand. "Why, thank you."

"You're looking a trifle less robust today. You don't mind my mentioning it, do you?" He guided Morton into his office. "You're the only game in town, and so you—" He broke off as Morton stared at him.

"The only game in town?" Morton said, appalled at his conflicting emotions.

Hewlett folded his arms. "A joke, a kind of pun, Morton. You . . . you're in demand because of it."

To his chagrin, Morton blushed. "Mr Wainwright, I don't know what to say to you. I never intended to do anything incorrect, and you must believe that—"

Hewlett clapped Morton on the back. "We don't worry about 'incorrect' here, not now." He indicated his visitor's chair. "Do sit down. And let me get the records you want. They're very old-fashioned. We don't have many computers in town these days."

"Since the mill closed," Morton supplied.

"No, not that," Hewlett said, frowning. "What did you used to do on Saturday afternoons when you were young, Morton?"

This abrupt change of subject made Morton blink. "Uh . . . I was a Boy Scout. We did nature walks and things like that."

Hewlett cocked his head. "Around here we went to the movies. Our mothers would take us over to the theater in North Poindexter and leave us while they went shopping and out to lunch and to the hairdresser and all the rest of it." He folded his hands. "Didn't you ever go see *Godzilla* or *Firemaidens from Outer Space*? Or *Dracula*?"

"No," Morton admitted, wondering what Hewlett Wainwright was attempting to tell him. "Sometimes we went roller-skating, but my family believed that children should be outside, doing wholesome things when we weren't in school."

"A-ha," said Hewlett seriously. "And you never sneaked off on your own?"

"Not for that, no," said Morton, more puzzled than ever.

Hewlett drummed his fingers on the table. "What do you think of Ilona's . . . appetites?"

Morton felt his face grow hot. "I . . . I never meant to do anything that you—"

"It doesn't matter what you meant," said Hewlett grandly. "It matters what we want."

"I didn't intend for—" Morton stopped, staring at Hewlett and noticing for the first time that the bank president was really quite an impressive figure of a man. "I'll leave at once, if you find me an embarrassment. I'll arrange for another investigator to come."

"You'll do that in any case," said Hewlett with calm certainty. "Because it is what we want."

"And. . . ." Morton let the single word trail off. "I'll leave," he offered, starting to get to his feet.

"I'm not through with you yet, Morton, and neither is Ilona. We can still have something from you, and we intend to get it. We're so very hungry." Hewlett leaned forward over his desk.

"Hungry?" Morton repeated, having trouble following Hewlett once again.

For the first time, Hewlett became impatient. "Damn it, man, are you really as ignorant as you appear? Are you really unaware of what has happened to you?"

"I . . . don't know what you're talking about. And if," Morton went on, suddenly certain that all these peculiar sidesteps were intended to keep him from his investigation, "it's your plan to withhold the figures the IRS has requested, you're going to be very disappointed."

Hewlett shook his head. "There is no point to this investigation. It doesn't apply to us, not now."

"The rules of the IRS apply to everyone, Mr Wainwright," said Morton with a sudden assumption of dignity he had not been able to find until that moment. "You understand that even when a town is in difficulties, we cannot make an exception of the people. It's not to their benefit. Everyone has to file income tax. Those are the rules."

Hewlett laughed, and this time there was no trace of joviality in the tone. "Death and taxes, death and taxes. It appears we are not allowed to have the release of death."

"When you die, your heirs will have to file for you in order to let us know that you are dead. Until then, I'm afraid you're all in the same situation as the rest of the country." Morton rose unsteadily. "If you don't mind, I have records to examine. I'm willing to do it at the Inn, if you'd rather."

"Morton, come to your senses," Hewlett ordered, his manner

becoming very grand. "Don't you know what's happened to you? Haven't you guessed what you've stumbled upon?"

"I wish you'd stop these melodramatic ploys," said Morton, his face becoming set. If he had felt a little better, he might have taken some satisfaction in setting Hewlett straight. "Your town could be in a lot of trouble, and there's no way you can get out of the consequences now. You can't decide not to file income taxes, Wainwright. That's not your decision to make."

"Isn't it?" Hewlett rose to his feet, his face darkening. "We're vampires here, Morton."

Morton stared; he had never heard so bizarre an excuse for failure to file. "What? Nonsense!"

"At first," said Hewlett resonantly, "there was just Ilona and me, but here in Jericho, we had our pick, and those we chose, chose others. Recently we've had to get by on . . . windfalls. Like you, Morton."

"Like me?" Morton laughed nervously. "Don't make your case any worse than it is. Just give me the records, and let me do my job. And don't try that kind of a farrididdle on—"

Hewlett shook his head, anger changing his expression to something more distressing than it had been. "You think I am lying to you, Morton? You believe that I've made this up?"

"It's ridiculous," said Morton flatly. "You'll have to come up with something better than that. And if you persist with so absurd a story, you will not find the IRS at all sympathetic. We try to be responsive to the predicaments of those taxpayers who are experiencing financial setbacks, but you're mocking our policy, and that will not work to your benefit." He touched his forehead, wishing he did not have a headache.

"And what will you think when you start desiring blood?" Hewlett asked, his tone leering now. "How do you plan to explain that?"

"Your threats mean nothing to me," said Morton.

"Wait until the next full moon," said Hewlett. "You'll be in for a shock then." He smacked his desk with the flat of his hand once. "For your own benefit, Symes, don't be too hasty. You're at risk now, and once you join our number—"

"Oh, come off it!" Morton said, heading toward the door. "I am not going to indulge you in this travesty of yours, Wainwright. If you had been candid with me, I might have been willing to extend myself on behalf of this town, but under the circumstances – circumstances that you have created, Mr Wainwright – there is no reason for me to do anything more than file my report and let the law take its course." Without waiting for any response, he strode through the office door and across the lobby.

From his place behind the desk, Hewlett Wainwright called out, "Wait for Ilona tonight, Symes. There is still a little wine left in your veins. Then wait for the full moon."

Morton considered leaving Jericho that very afternoon, but his fatigue was so great that he did not trust himself to drive on the winding, narrow roads as daylight faded. He occupied himself for the remainder of the day updating his reports and adding his own observations to the facts he had discovered. For the most part, he dealt very indirectly with his discoveries, but when it came to Wainwright's ludicrous claims, Morton hesitated. Matters would go badly enough in Jericho without the additional condemnation of the bank president's sarcasm. Morton decided that it was not proper for the entire town to suffer because the bank president was making insults and outlandish claims. There would be other ways to deal with Hewlett Wainwright; the townspeople had more than enough to contend with.

Dusk turned the Ivy Room dark, and Morton finally set his work aside. He knew he ought to go out for a meal, but his headache was worse, and it appeared to have killed his appetite. He went down to the lobby and asked for a pot of tea to be sent up along with some rolls. Then he tottered back up the stairs and promptly collapsed on his bed. His thoughts began to drift, and soon he was in that strange half-dreaming, half-waking state where his perceptions were as pliant as Silly Putty.

In this state, it seemed to him that he got up once again and went down onto the street, where he saw dozens of townspeople waiting in silence as he went toward the Wainwright house. He recognized the chief of police and the waitress who had served him his supper, but the rest meant nothing to him, almost as if they had no faces. Morton sensed they were watching him, though only a few were bold enough to do it openly. There was a brazen hunger in their faces that might have petrified him had this not been a dream. He kept moving.

Ilona Wainwright was in the overrun garden, standing beside a shapeless bush that Morton did not recognize. There were a few long flowers hanging on its branches, giving off a sensuous, sickly smell, cloying as overly sweet candies. Ilona, in a trailing lavender dress, smiled and held out her arm to him – part of Morton's mind wanted to laugh at Ilona for not wearing black – beckoning to him.

With the townspeople so near, Morton could hardly bring himself to move. He was compromising himself, his investigation, and the IRS by this infatuation with a married woman. It was one thing when their relationship was a matter of conjecture, for then he had recourse to plausible deniability. Once their trysts were known and seen, there would be no such means to refute any accusations made against him. He trembled as he looked at her; when she called his name, he succumbed.

How cold her arms were, and how she held him! The only thing lacking in the passion of her embrace was warmth. By the time they broke apart, Morton was shivering.

"You must come inside; let me warm you," said Ilona in her lowest, most seductive tone.

"I . . ." Morton could not break away from her.

"Come inside," she coaxed, going toward the open door that led from the garden into what had once been called the morning room.

Morton went with her, and passed into deeper sleep, to wake in the morning pale and ill, feeling as if he had spent the whole night in an endless fistfight, which he had lost. It took more than five minutes for him to get up, and when at last he did, he was more disoriented than he had been previously. He blinked stupidly, and stared at the atrocious wallpaper as if it might be ancient undeciphered writing rather than a bad representation of ivy leaves. Gradually his thoughts began to piece themselves together, each one adding to the sensation of vertigo building in him, and making him feel queasy.

"Got to get up," he said to himself, then fell silent as he heard the thready noise he made. God! he thought. This is more than allergies. I must have some kind of flu.

That was it, he decided as he pulled himself out of bed and felt his way along the wall. He had picked up some kind of virus, and it had distoned his perceptions. Yes, that explained it. The town was in trouble, no doubt of that, but because of the disease he was making more out of their troubles than existed. In the bathroom he stared in the mirror at his haggard features, then opened his mouth very wide in the hope that he might be able to see if his throat was red. The angle was wrong, and he could see nothing, though his throat was sore, and his head was full of thunder. He started to shave, doing his best to handle the razor with his customary care.

This time he managed not to nick himself, but his hands were shaking visibly by the time he put the razor away. His bones seemed without form, as if they were made of Jell-O instead of bone. He lowered his head and reached for his toothbrush. Another hour, he said to himself. Another hour, and I'll be gone from here, gone away. I'll make an appointment to see the doctor tomorrow. He considered that, then decided that he had better choose a different doctor, one who was not connected to the Service, so that if he had anything seriously wrong it would not get back to Brewster. As he finished with his teeth, he began to feel the first stirrings of satisfaction.

The sour-faced clerk was not at the desk, and it took Morton some little time to find him.

"I have work to do," the clerk announced, holding up the handle of his broom to make the point.

"I'd like to check out." Morton held up the key. "My bags are in the lobby."

The clerk sighed as if he were being asked to undertake all the labors of Hercules. "So you're going," he said as he started toward the hallway.

"Yes," said Morton, doing his best to be pleasant.

"Going to tell them Infernal Revenues that Jericho's down the drain, is that it?" His rancor was more for show than any strong feeling. "What'll they do to us?"

"I don't know," said Morton seriously. "My job is to investigate. There are others who make those decisions." He wiped his hands on his handkerchief before he looked over the bill that the clerk presented to him, all entries in a crabbed little hand.

"But you got to make recommendations" said the clerk.

"I have to make reports. Others will do the evaluations." Morton nodded as he checked the math. "It looks fine. How much more do I owe you?"

The clerk named the figure, and Morton presented him with the appropriate amount, then looked around the lobby. "This could be such a pretty place. I can't understand why you don't do something with it. Towns like this one can be real tourist attractions if you go about development the right way." It was only a friendly observation, but the clerk looked at him, much struck.

"Mr Symes," he said as Morton struggled to lift his bags. "What did you mean by that?"

Morton was starting to sweat; it embarrassed him that he could not do so little a thing as lift his bag without coming near fainting. "I meant . . . this place . . . is authentic. The setting . . . is beautiful." He put the suitcase down. "If you handled it right, you could develop some seasonal income, anyway."

The clerk nodded several times. "And there'd be a lot of people through here, you say?"

"In time." Morton had another go at hoisting his suitcase, and did rather better now.

"I'll take your things out to your car," said the clerk in an off-handed way. "No need for you to be puffing like that. Though a young man like you—" He left the rest of his remark to speculation.

"Thanks," said Morton, and turned his luggage over to the clerk. "You know where my car is."

"Sure do," said the clerk. "Look, when you get back to wherever your office is, can you find out what they'd do to us, I mean the IRS, if we wanted to turn this village into a tourist place?''

'I'll try. Who knows,'' Morton added with more encouragement than sincerity, "I might want to come back myself one of these days." He winced as the bright sunlight stabbed at his eyes; his dark glasses were taken from their case at once and clapped over his face.

"Shows good sense," said the clerk, nodding toward the glasses. "Light can be hard on a fella."

As Morton opened the trunk, he observed, "I had the impression that . . . pardon me if I'm wrong . . . that the people in Jericho aren't interested in change, and they wouldn't like turning this place into a tourist town"

The clerk shrugged. "Well, the mill's gone, and we're pretty damn stuck. I can't say I want to make it all quaint, but we got to eat, like everyone else." He finished stowing the luggage and slammed the trunk closed for Morton.

Morton offered a five-dollar bill, which was refused. "You find a way to make sure we get some new blood in here – that'll be more than enough." He stood back as Morton got into the car.

Morton started the engine and felt a touch of satisfaction in the muffled roar. "Someone else from our office will be contacting you soon."

"We'll be waiting," said the clerk, and to Morton's amazement, the man licked his lips. "Make sure you save a few for yourself."

Because he could think of no appropriate reply, Morton put the car in gear and started away, waving once to the clerk before he rolled his window up. Perhaps, he thought, Jericho would not be as difficult a place as he had feared. Perhaps there were things that they would accept as necessary and reasonable change in order to continue their town. He tabbed the little raised welts on his neck as he swung into the first big bend in the road. At least he had broken the ice; he could provide some explanation of what had happened – other than the ridiculous tale Wainwright had told – that would make it possible for the townspeople not to be encumbered with an unpayable tax burden. On the whole, he was satisfied with his job, though the episodes, real and imagined, with Ilona Wainwright made his conscience smart. But with a beautiful woman like that, one so irresistible, he supposed many men had fallen under her spell at one time or another. How ludicrous to call her a vampire. If he had remained there much longer, he might have started to believe it. Hell, he might be persuaded that he was one, too. "Absurd," he said out loud. The welts continued to itch, and he scratched them without thinking as he started down the lazy decline toward North Poindexter.

PETER TREMAYNE

Dracula's Chair

PETER TREMAYNE IS THE PSEUDONYM of historian and Celtic scholar Peter Berresford Ellis, who has published numerous works on Celtic history and cultures including *A Dictionary of Irish Mythology* and its companion volume *A Dictionary of Celtic Mythology*.

As Tremayne, he has published many novels in the horror and heroic fantasy genres, often concentrating on tales based on themes from Celtic mythology. However, he is best known today for his series of historical murder mysteries featuring a 7th Century Irish *religieuse*, Sister Fidelma, as his sleuth, who has to work under the ancient Irish law system with her companion Brother Eadulf, an Irish-trained Saxon monk. *Whispers of the Dead*, the fourteenth book in the series, has recently been published, and the series sells in nine European languages. There is even an International Sister Fidelma Society based in the United States but with members in over twelve countries.

Although Tremayne has published nearly eighty short stories, 'Dracula's Chair' was only his third.

"It was originally written as an epilogue to my novel *The Revenge of Dracula*," he explains, "the second volume in my 'Dracula' trilogy which also includes *Dracula Unborn* (a.k.a. *Bloodright*) and *Dracula, My Love*. I decided to omit it on the grounds that it was 'artistic overkill' and it was first published in an anthology in the late 1970s."

Tremayne's *Dracula* novels were last published in paperback as an omnibus volume by Signet in 1993 and have recently been optioned again for filming.

MAYBE THIS IS AN hallucination. Perhaps I am mad. How else can this be explained?

I sit here alone and helpless! So utterly alone! Alone in an age which is not mine, in a body which is not mine. Oh God! I am slowly being killed – or worse! Yet what is worse than death? That terrifying limbo that is the borderland of Hell, that state that is neither the restful sleep of death nor the perplexities of life but is the nightmare of undeath.

He is draining me of life and yet, *yet is it me who is the victim*? How can I tell him that the person he thinks I am, the person whose body my mind inhabits, is no longer in that body? How can I tell him that *I* am in the body of his victim? *I* . . . a person from another time, another age, another place!

God help me! He is draining me of life and I cannot prevent him!

When did this nightmare begin? An age away. I suppose it began when my wife and I saw the chair.

We were driving back to London one hot July Sunday afternoon, having been picnicking in Essex. We were returning about mid-afternoon down the A11, through the village of Newport, when my wife suddenly called upon me to pull over and stop.

"I've just seen the most exquisite chair in the window of an antique shop."

I was somewhat annoyed because I wanted to get home early that evening to see a vintage Humphrey Bogart film on the television, one I'd never seen before even though I have been a Bogart fan for years.

"What's the point?" I muttered grumpily, getting out of the car and trailing after her. "The shop's shut anyway."

But the shop wasn't shut. Passing trade on a Sunday from Londoners was apparently very lucrative and most antique shops in the area opened during the afternoons.

The chair stood like a lone sentinel in the window. It was square in shape, a wooden straight-backed chair with sturdy arms. It was of a plain and simple design, dark oak wood yet with none of the ornate woodwork that is commonly associated with such items. The seat was upholstered in a faded tapestry work which was obviously the original. It was a very unattractive upholstery for it was in a faded black with a number of once white exotic dragon's heads. The same upholstery was reflected in a piece which provided a narrow back rest – a strip a foot deep thrust across the middle of the frame. My impression of the chair was hardly "exquisite" – it was a squat, ugly and aggressive piece. Certainly it did not seem worth the £100 price ticket which was attached by string to one arm.

My wife had contrary ideas. It was, she felt, exactly the right piece to fill a corner in my study and provide a spare chair for extra guests. It could, she assured me, easily be re-upholstered to fit in with our general colour scheme of greens and golds. What was wanted, she said, was a functional chair and this was it. She was adamant and so I resigned myself to a minimum of grumbling, one eye on my watch to ensure I would not miss the Bogart film. The transaction was concluded fairly quickly by comparison with my wife's usual standard of detailed questioning and examination. Perhaps the vendor was rather more loquacious than the average antique dealer.

"It's a very nice chair," said the dealer with summoned enthusiasm. "It's a Victorian piece of eastern European origin. Look, on the back you can actually see a date of manufacture and the place of origin." He pointed to the back of the chair where, carved into the wood with small letters was the word "Bistritz" and the date "1887." The dealer smiled in the surety of knowledge. "That makes it Romanian in origin. Actually, I purchased the piece from the old Purfleet Art Gallery."

"The Purfleet Art Gallery?" said I, thinking it time to make some contribution to the conservation. "Isn't that the old gallery and museum over which there were some protests a few months ago?"

"Yes, do you know the place? Purfleet in Essex? The gallery was housed in an ancient building, a manor house called Carfax, which was said to date back to medieval times. The old gallery had been there since the late Victorian period but had to close through lack of government subsidies, and the building is being carved up into apartments."

I nodded, feeling I had, perhaps, made too much of a contribution.

The antique dealer went on obliviously.

"When the gallery closed, a lot of its *objets d'art* were auctioned and I bought this chair. According to the auctioneer's catalogue it had been in the old house when the gallery first opened and had belonged to the previous owner. He was said to have been a foreign nobleman . . . probably a Romanian by the workmanship of the chair."

Finally, having had her fears assuaged over matters of woodworm, methods of upholstery and the like, the purchase was concluded by my wife. The chair was strapped to the roofrack of my car and we headed homewards.

The next day was Monday. My wife, who is in research, had gone to her office while I spent the morning in my study doodling on pieces of paper and vainly waiting for a new plot to mature for the television soap-opera that I was scripting at the time. At mid-day my wife telephoned to remind me to check around for some price quotations for re-upholstering our purchase. I had forgotten all about the chair, still strapped to the roofrack of my car. Feeling a little guilty, I went down to the garage and untied it, carrying it up to my study and placing it in the alloted corner with a critical eye. I confess, I did not like the thing; it was so square and seemed to somehow challenge me. It is hard to define what I mean but you have, I suppose, seen certain types of people with thrust out jaws, square and aggressive? Well, the chair gave the same impression.

After a while, perhaps in response to its challenge, I decided to sit down in the chair, and as I sat, a sudden coldness spread up my spine and a weird feeling of unease came over me. So strong was it that I immediately jumped up. I stood there looking down at the chair and feeling a trifle self-conscious. I laughed nervously. Ridiculous! What would my friend Philip, who was a psychiatrist, say to such behaviour? I did not like the chair but there was no need to create physical illusions around my distaste.

I sat down again and, as expected, the cold feelings of unease were gone – a mere shadow in my mind. In fact, I was surprised at the comfort of the chair. I sat well back, arms and hands resting on the wooden arm rests, head leaning against the back, legs spread out. It was extremely comfortable.

So comfortable was it that a feeling of deep relaxation came over me, and with the relaxation came the desire to have a cat-nap. I must confess, I tend to enjoy a ten minute nap just after lunch. It relaxes me and stimulates the mind. I sat back, closed my drooping eyelids and gently let myself drift, drift . . .

It was dark when I awoke.

For an instant I struggled with the remnants of my dreams. Then my mind cleared and I looked about me. My first thought was the question – how long had I slept? I could see the dark hue of early evening through the tall windows. Then I started *for there were no tall windows in my study nor anywhere in our house!*

Blinking my eyes rapidly to focus them in the darkened room, I abruptly perceived that I was not in my study, nor was I in any room that I had even seen before. I tried to rise in my surprise and found that I could not move – some sluggish feeling in my body prevented me from coordinating my limbs. My mind had clarity and will but below my neck my whole body seemed numb. And so I just sat there, staring wildly at the unfamiliar room in a cold sweat of fear and panic. I tried to blink away the nightmare, tried to rationalize.

I could move my head around and doing so I found that I was

sitting in the same chair – that accursed chair! Yet it seemed strangely newer than I remembered it. I thought, perhaps it was a trick of the light. But I discovered that around my legs was tucked a woolen blanket while the top half of me was clad in a pajama jacket over which was a velvet smoking jacket, a garment that I knew I had never owned. My eyes wandered around the room from object to unfamiliar object, each unfamiliar item causing the terror to mount in my veins, now surging with adrenalin. I was in a lounge filled with some fine pieces of Victoriana. The chair in which I sat now stood before an open hearth in which a few coals faintly glimmered. In one corner stood a lean, tall grandfather clock, whose steady tick-tock added to the oppressiveness of the scene. There was, so far as I could see, nothing modern in the room at all.

But for me the greatest horror was the strange paralysis which kept me anchored in that chair. I tried to move until the sweat poured from my face with the effort. I even tried to shout, opening my mouth wide to emit strange choking-like noises. What in God's name had happened to me?

Suddenly a door opened. Into the room came a young girl of about seventeen holding aloft one of those old brass oil lamps, the sort you see converted into electric lamps these days by "trendy" people. Yet this was no converted lamp but a lamp from which a flame spluttered and emitted the odour of burning paraffin. And the girl! She wore a long black dress with a high button collar, with a white linen apron over it. Her fair hair was tucked inside a small white cap set at a jaunty angle on her head. In fact, she looked like a serving maid straight out of those Victorian drama serials we get so often on the television these days. She came forward and placed the lamp on a table near me, and then started, seeing my eyes wide open and upon her. I tried to speak to her, to demand, to exhort some explanation, to ask what the meaning of this trickery was, but only a strangled gasp came from my throat.

The girl was clearly frightened and bobbed what was supposed to be a curtsy in my direction before turning to the door.

"Ma'am! Ma'am!" her strong Cockney accent made the word sound like "Mum!" "Master's awake, ma'am. What'll I do?"

Another figure moved into the room, tall, graceful, wearing an elegant Victorian dress hung low at the shoulders, and leaving very little of her bust to the imagination. A black ribbon with a cameo was fastened to her pale throat. Her raven black hair was done up in a bun at the back of her head. Her face was small, heart-shaped, and pretty. The lips were naturally red though a trifle sullen for her features. The eyes were deep green and seemed a little sad. She came towards me, bent over me and gave a wan smile. There was a strange, almost unnatural pallor to her complexion.

"That's all, Fanny," she said. "I'll see to him now."

"Yes, ma'am," the girl bobbed another curtsy and was gone through the door.

"Poor Upton," whispered the woman before me. "Poor Upton. I wish I knew whether you hurt at all? No one seems to know from what strange malady you suffer."

She stood back and sighed sorrowfully and deeply.

"It's time for your medication."

She picked up a bottle and a spoon, pouring a bitter smelling amber liquid which she forced down my throat. I felt a numbing bitterness searing down my gullet.

"Poor Upton," she sighed again. "It's bitter I know but the doctor says it will take away any pain."

I tried to speak; tried to tell her that I was not Upton, that I did not want her medicine, that I wanted this play-acting to cease. I succeeded only in gnashing my teeth and making inarticulate cries like some wild beast at bay. The woman took a step backwards, her eyes widening in fright. Then she seemed to regain her composure.

"Come, Upton," she chidded. "This won't do at all. Try to relax."

The girl, Fanny, reappeared.

"Doctor Seward is here, ma'am."

A stocky man in a brown tweed suit, looking like some character out of a Dickens novel, stepped into the room and bowed over the woman's proffered hand.

"John," smiled the woman. "I'm so glad you've come."

"How are you, Clara," smiled the man. "You look a trifle weary, a little pale."

"I'm alright, John. But I worry about Upton."

The man turned to me.

"Yes, how is the patient? I swear he looks a little more alert today."

The woman, Clara, spread her hands and shrugged.

"To me he seems little better, John. Even when he seems more alert physically he can only growl like a beast. I try my best but I fear . . . I fear that . . ."

The man called John patted her hand and gestured her to silence. Then he came and bent over me with a friendly smile.

"Strange," he murmured. "Indeed, a strange affliction. And yet . . . yet I do detect a more intelligent gleam in the eyes today. Hello, old friend, do you know me. It's John . . . John Seward? Do you recognise me?"

He leaned close to my face, so close I could smell the scent of oranges on his breath.

I struggled to break the paralysis which gripped me and only succeeded in issuing a number of snarls and grunts. The man drew back.

"Upon my word, Clara, has he been violent at all?"

"Not really, John. He does excite himself so with visitors. But perhaps it is his way of trying to communicate with us."

The man grunted and nodded.

"Well, the only remedy for pain is to keep dosing him with the laudanum as I prescribed it. I think he is a little better. However, I shall call again tomorrow to see if there is a significant improvement. If not, I will ask your permission to consult a specialist, perhaps a doctor from Harley Street. There are a number of factors that still puzzle me – the anaemia, the apparent lack of red blood corpuscles or hemoglobin. His paleness and languor. And these strange wounds on his neck do not seem to be healing at all."

The woman bit her lip and lowered her voice.

"You may be frank with me, John. You have known Upton and me for some years now. I am resigned to the fact that there can only be a worsening of his condition. I do fear for his life."

The man glanced at me nervously.

"Should you talk like this in front of him?"

The woman sighed. "He cannot understand, of that I am sure. Poor Upton. Just to think that a few short days ago he was so full of life, so active, and now this strange disease has cut him down . . ."

The man nodded.

"You have been a veritable goddess, Clara, charity herself, nursing him constantly day and night. I shall look in again tomorrow, but if there is no improvement I shall seek permission to call in a specialist."

Clara lowered her head as if in resignation.

The man turned to me and forced a smile.

"So long, old fellow . . ."

I tried to call, desperately tried to plead for help. Then he was gone.

The minutes dragged into hours as the woman, Clara, who was supposed to be my wife, sat gazing into the fire, while I sat pinioned in my accursed chair opposite to her. How long we sat thus I do not truly know. From time to time I felt her gaze, sad and thoughtful, upon me. Then I became aware, somewhere in the house, of a clock commencing to strike. A few seconds later it was followed by the resonant and hollow sounds of the grandfather clock. Without raising my head I counted slowly to twelve. Midnight.

The woman Clara abruptly sprung from her chair and stood upright before the fire.

As I looked up she seemed to change slightly – it is hard to explain.

Her face seemed to grow coarser, more bloated. Her tongue, a red glistening object, darted nervously over her lips making them moist and of a deeper red than before, contrasting starkly to the sharp whiteness of her teeth. A strange lustre began to sparkle in her eyes. She raised a languid hand and began to massage her neck slowly, sensually.

Then, abruptly, she laughed – a low voluptuous chuckle that made the hairs on my neck bristle.

She gazed down at me with a wanton expression, a lascivious smile. "Poor Upton," her tone was a gloating caress. "He'll be coming soon. You'll like that won't you? Yet why he takes you first, I cannot understand. Why *you*? Am I not full of the warmth of life – does not warm, rich young blood flow in my veins? Why *you*?"

She made an obscene, seductive gesture with her body.

The way she crooned, the saliva trickling from a corner of those red – oh, so red – lips, made my heart beat faster yet at the same time, the blood seemed to deny its very warmth and pump like some ice-cold liquid in my veins.

What new nightmare was this?

How *he* appeared I do not know.

One minute there was just the woman and myself in the room. Then he was standing there.

A tall man, apparently elderly although his pale face held no aging of the skin, only the long white moustache which drooped over his otherwise clean-shaven face gave the impression of age. His face was strong – extremely strong, aquiline with a high-bridged nose and peculiarly arched nostrils. His forehead was loftily domed and hair grew scantily round the temples but profusely elsewhere. The eyebrows were massive and nearly met across the bridge of the nose.

It was his mouth which captured my attention – a mouth set in the long pale face, fixed and cruel looking, with teeth that protruded over the remarkably ruddy lips whose redness had the effect of highlighting his white skin and giving the impression of an extraordinary pallor. And where the teeth protruded over the lips, they were white and sharp.

His eyes seemed a ghastly red in the glow of the flickering fire.

The woman, Clara, took a step toward him, hands out as if imploring, a glad cry on her red wanton lips, her breasts heaving as if with some wild ectasy.

"My Lord," she cried, "you have come!"

The tall man ignored her. His red eyes were upon mine, seeming to devour me.

The woman raised a hand to massage her throat.

"Lord, take me first! Take me now!"

The tall man took a stride towards me, drawing back an arm and pushing her roughly aside.

"It is he that I shall take first," he said sibilantly, with a strange accent to his English. "You shall wait your turn which shall be in a little while."

The woman made to protest but he stopped her with an upraised hand.

"Dare you question me?" he said mildly. "Have no fear. You shall be my bountiful wine press in a while. But first I shall slake my thirst with him."

He towered over me as I remained helpless in that chair, that accursed chair. A smile edged his face.

"Is it not just?" whispered the tall man. "Is it not just that having thwarted me, you Upton Welsford, now become everything that you abhorred and feared?"

And while part of my mind was witnessing this obscene hallucination, another part of it began to experience a strange excitement – almost a sexual excitement as the man lowered his face to mine . . . closer came those awful red eyes to gaze deep into my soul. His mouth was open slightly, I could smell a vile reek of corruption. There was a deliberate voluptuousness about his movements that was both thrilling and appalling – he licked his lips like some animal, the scarlet tongue flickering over the white sharp teeth.

Lower came his head, lower, until it passed from my sight and I could hear the churning sound of his tongue against his teeth and could feel his hot breath on my neck. The skin of my throat began to tingle. Then I felt the soft shivering touch of his cold lips on my throat, the hard indent of two sharp white teeth!

For a while, how long I could not measure, I seemed to fall into a languorous ectasy.

Then he was standing above me, smiling down sardonically, a trickle of blood on his chin. My blood!

"There is one more night to feast with him," he said softly. "One night more and then, Upton Welford, you shall be my brother."

The woman exclaimed in anger.

"But you promised! You promised! When am I to be called?"

The tall man turned and laughed.

"Aye, I promised, my slender vine. You already bear my mark. You belong to me. You shall be one with me, never fear. Immortality will soon be yours and we shall share in the drinking. You will provide me with the wine of life. Have patience, for the greatest wines are long in the savouring. I shall return."

Then to my horror the man was gone. Simply gone, as if he had dissolved into elemental dust.

For some time I sat in horror staring at the woman who seemed to have retreated into a strange trance. Then the grandfather clock began to chime and the woman started, as if waking from a deep sleep. She stared in amazement at the clock and then towards the window where the faint light of early dawn was beginning to show.

"Good Lord, Upton," she exclaimed, "we seemed to have been up all night. I must have fallen asleep, I'm sorry."

She shook herself.

"I've had a strange dream. Ah well, no matter. I'd better get you up to bed. I'll go and wake poor Fanny to help me."

She smiled softly at me as she left the room; there was no trace of the wanton seductress left on her delicate features.

She left me sitting alone, alone in my prison of a chair.

I sit here alone and helpless. So utterly alone! Alone in an age which is not mine, in a body which is not mine. Oh God! I am slowly being killed – or worse! Yet what is worse than death? That terrifying limbo that is the borderland of Hell, that state that is neither the restful sleep of death nor the perplexities of life but is the nightmare of undeath.

And where is this person . . . the Upton Welsford whose body I now inhabit? Where is he? Has he, by some great effort of will, exchanged his body with mine? Is he even now awakening from that cat-nap sometime in the future? Awakening in my body, in my study, to resume my life? Is he doing even as I have done? What does it all mean?

Maybe this is an hallucination. Perhaps I am mad. How else can all this be explained?

SYDNEY J. BOUNDS

A Taste for Blood

SYDNEY JAMES BOUNDS WAS BORN in 1920 in Brighton, Sussex. In the early 1930s he discovered the American pulp magazines and by the end of the following decade he was contributing "spicy" stories to the monthly periodicals produced by Utopia Press. He was also writing hard-boiled gangster novels for John Spencer under such pseudonyms and house names as "Brett Diamond" and "Ricky Madison", and contributed short stories to their line of SF magazines which included *Futuristic Science Stories, Tales of Tomorrow* and *Worlds of Fantasy*.

Along with writing five SF novels during the 1950s, Bounds soon became a regular contributor to such magazines as *New Worlds Science Fiction, Science Fantasy, Authentic Science Fiction, Nebula Science Fiction, Other Worlds Science Stories* and *Fantastic Universe*. However, as the science fiction magazine markets started to dry up during the 1960s, the author began to notice the growth of paperbacks. He quickly became a prolific and reliable contributor to such anthology series as *New Writings in SF, The Fontana Book of Great Ghost Stories, The Fontana Book of Great Horror Stories,* the *Armada Monster Book* and the *Armada Ghost Book*.

One of his best-known stories, 'The Circus', was scripted by George A. Romero for a 1986 episode of the syndicated television series *Tales of the Darkside.*

Bounds has also pursued parallel careers as a successful children's writer and a Western novelist. In the late 1970s he wrote a number of science fiction novels for an Italian publisher, together with some new supernatural and crime stories. More recently, his 1953 novel *Dimension of Horror* has been reprinted by Wildside Press.

That publisher's imprint, Cosmos Books, has also issued the first-ever collections of the author's work as two print-on-demand volumes. Both *The Best of Sydney J. Bounds: Strange Portrait and Other Stories* and *The Wayward Ship and Other Stories* were edited by Philip Harbottle.

"In the long-ago I planned to write a story about a vampire who made use of a blood bank," recalls Bounds, "but never got around to writing it, until I was asked for a new story for this anthology. The idea is no longer new, so this is a variation on the theme."

The following tale appears here for the first time . . .

DR GREGOR HAD AN accent that Vic Farrow couldn't place. For that matter, Gregor's face suggested an age that Farrow couldn't be sure of. His voice, however, held a contempt that was painfully obvious.

"Alcohol, Mr. Farrow? After a serious accident, major surgery and recovery from a life-threatening situation, you dare to complain because you have lost your taste for alcohol?"

"Vodka, doctor. I'm a crime reporter and run on a bottle a day. Now I can't face my favourite booze – worse, I seem to have a craving for blood."

Gregor sniffed. "So? Blood is life, nothing to worry about there – you will adapt sooner than you think. But alcohol is a poison and, quite likely, the cause of your accident. Relax and accept the fact that your life has changed for the better."

On the way out Farrow met Nurse Terry, one of the team who had helped him recover from the operation after a van collided with his motorcycle.

She was small with short blonde hair and a ready smile, and she was wearing starched whites.

He jerked a thumb at the closed door of the consulting room. "Is he for real?"

She chose to take the question seriously. "Yes, he knows the real world better than most. Try to understand, Vic, that Dr Gregor is older than he appears; he knows, but sometimes forgets how difficult it can be for a patient after a transfusion. What you are feeling is a side effect and it will pass. Take this—"

She scribbled figures on a notepad, tore off the sheet and handed it to him. "This is the number of a local group prepared to help people with your problem. If it gets too bad, give them a ring."

"Will you be there?"

"I sometimes call in to see if I can help."

Outside the small private hospital – and hadn't he been lucky that the accident had happened almost outside the front door? – Farrow headed like a homing pigeon for the nearest pub.

But the smell of stale beer as he pushed open the door turned his stomach and made him retch. He swung away with a shudder, swearing. A supermarket, he decided: buy a bottle to take home.

He walked to the bus stop because his machine had been totalled, passing an old-fashioned butcher's shop with joints of meat displayed on white enamel trays. The smell almost overwhelmed him,

He wanted the blood oozing from the meat and licked his lips in anticipation. Fresh blood. He swallowed hard, imagining a pint of the best going down. This new urge filled him with alarm and he hurried away.

After he got off the bus, Farrow bought a bottle and a newspaper at his local supermarket and walked home. The managing editor had granted him sick leave and agreed to cover the hospital bill. He had been, after all, their number-one crime reporter.

Still, he couldn't afford to get out of touch. He opened the bottle and settled into a comfortable chair with a glass, tipped vodka into it and raised the glass to his lips. He couldn't swallow. Vodka, everyone told him, didn't smell, but something was seriously wrong.

Farrow hurled the glass at the wall and picked up the newspaper. A headline screamed:

MONSTER STRIKES A THIRD TIME

The maniac who attacks lonely women after dark has claimed another victim. Her body, drained of . . .

Not only women, he remembered, men too had been attacked. He read critically; this was the story he'd been working on, and whoever had taken over wasn't up to the job.

. . . blood.

Just reading about it gave him a raging thirst.

He went into the kitchen and poured a glass of water. He could swallow the tasteless stuff; it helped, but didn't satisfy. He popped a frozen meal in the microwave and ate; again it didn't satisfy. What he needed was . . .

The hours dragged until the evening when he gave up and rang the number that Nurse Terry had given him.

"Clubhouse. Edgar Shaw speaking."

"I need help—"

"What kind of help? How did you get this number?"

"I have a thirst for blood. Nurse Terry."

"Wait, please." He heard a rustling of paper. "Are you Vic Farrow?"

"Yes."

"She has mentioned your name, Mr Farrow, and I believe we can help you. Take down these directions to—"

The address was a select mews off a busy High Street and Farrow whistled when he considered how much the conversion must have cost. The door opened promptly when he pressed the bell push.

"Mr. Farrow? My name is Edgar Shaw and I am the duty welcomer. Please don't call me Ed – I dislike that immensely. Through here."

There was a heavy drape sealing off the halls, but it was Shaw who intrigued Farrow.

The official welcomer was immaculately groomed and expensively dressed in charcoal grey, his hair touched by the subtlest of waves. He might have been ushering Farrow into the presence of royalty, and anyone less like an 'Ed' was difficult to visualize.

Farrow found himself in a long room with a bar at the far end and large leather armchairs scattered around. The place suggested a superior Conservative club; certainly it was impossible to imagine Edgar Shaw desperate for blood.

A lightning glance around the room did not put Farrow at ease. The men appeared well-to-do and professionally barbered; the few ladies would not have been out of place at a Covent Garden first night. He saw a couple playing chess, a young man intent over a computer screen, someone quietly reading.

These people were not part of Farrow's usual circle; each had an air of confidence, arrogance even. He wondered if he'd come to the right place.

"Is Nurse Terry here?" he asked.

"Not yet, but she's expected." Shaw smiled, and suddenly seemed much younger. "I suppose we're not quite what you expected but, by chance, the members here this evening long ago mastered their natural inclination. Now let me get you your first drink."

He led Farrow the length of the room, paused at the bar counter and clapped his hands.

"Fellow members, tonight we welcome another with the age-old thirst. A toast, please, for Mr Vic Farrow."

They paused in whatever they were doing and gathered as a barman lined up a row of cut-crystal glasses and carefully filled them. Farrow was given the smallest.

"Life everlasting," Shaw said, and raised his glass.

All the members echoed his words: "Life everlasting."

Farrow lifted his glass; it contained a red liquid, already beginning to darken. He sniffed, and the craving started. He put the glass to his lips and took the first sip; slightly salty, but satisfying . . . and then he couldn't stop. He emptied his glass in one greedy gulp.

They were watching him, amused. *They* took controlled sips.

Someone laid a hand on his arm. Nurse Terry, still in uniform, had arrived.

"Never mind, Vic, self-control comes gradually. I'm pleased to see you here."

The barman passed her a drink and she sipped slowly, obviously enjoying it.

"It is blood, isn't it?" Farrow asked.

"Yes, of course. You see the advantage of a private club?"

"I'll join."

"But you are already a member!"

He passed his empty to the barman. "I'll have—"

"Not tonight," Terry said. "You lost a lot of blood, Vic, and that can have strange and unexpected effects. Slow down, and you will bring yourself under control. So no more till this time tomorrow."

"Whatever you say, Nurse."

Farrow was discouraged when he found that she was only interested in him as a patient; that other members showed no inclination to include him in their conversation.

He heard quiet mention of "gradually slipping our people into positions of power", and registered a sly glance when someone murmured "the media". He decided to leave.

Outside, he found himself in an odd mood. He'd got the drink he wanted – and would go back, treat the club as a drinking place – and apparently had been selected as a member. But drinking blood? He felt shame, and a touch of fear, not at all sure what he was getting into.

Next evening, his craving was back, stronger than before. He set off early for the clubhouse, licking his lips in anticipation, but got into an argument at the bus stop.

A fat woman with a shopping basket was in his way and, as he tried to push past, she shoved him back. "Who d'you think you are? You'll wait till I've got my seat."

Farrow stared at her neck, his hands twitching, his teeth grating. He saw a vein just below the surface and it acted like a magnet, drawing him—

A hand took a firm grip on his arm. "This way, Vic. I can give you a lift."

He left with reluctance, staring back at the fat woman with desperate longing.

Nurse Terry had her car parked nearby. "It was lucky I had some local shopping to do. You could get into trouble like that, Vic. This is why we have a discreet drinking club."

He sat frozen beside her as the car purred along. He had wanted to sink his teeth into that woman's neck and siphon off her blood. He'd needed to do that and felt as if someone had stunned him with a mallet.

"You'll be all right again after a drink." Terry said. "This is something we all go through."

"You too?"

"Of course. There are more of us than you realize."

Farrow's head was still in a whirl when they reached the clubhouse, but after one drink, slightly larger this time, his nerves quieted down. Until he picked up a late edition that someone had left on the counter. The headline caused him to sweat in near-panic.

A SICK MONSTER?

A Home Office psychiatrist insists that this criminal, who takes blood from his victims, is suffering from a rare disease and must be found and treated for his addiction. The public, however, may, not agree . . .

He was still shaken by the memory of how he'd almost attacked the fat woman, and the report shocked him.

Edgar Shaw took the paper from him with an amused smile. "Tabloid rubbish, Mr Farrow. This sort of thing is nothing to do with us. Obviously. We shall expect you to do better on our behalf."

When Vic Farrow left, he decided that tomorrow he would visit the hospital and demand an explanation from Dr Gregor.

But in the morning, Gregor refused to see him, and Nurse Terry told him, "The doctor says there's no point in wasting his time. The truth is he's annoyed with the lies you were writing for your paper. That's why we arranged your accident – to give you a chance to help your fellow creatures."

Farrow almost stopped breathing as he struggled with disbelief.

"It wasn't just a transfusion you had, Vic, but a complete blood change. Surely immortality is worth a little inconvenience?"

Dazed, Vic Farrow left the hospital. Immortality? Would that account for the strangeness he felt? He wandered along a busy street, filled with people no longer quite like himself, and into a side alley.

He found the service entrance where bins of medical rubbish awaited collection, and rummaged until he found an empty carton. The labelling gave him a new understanding of his situation.

FROZEN WHOLE BLOOD
Produce of Buda-Pesth.
Supplied by Vlad-Drac Enterprise.

MELANIE TEM

The Better Half

MELANIE TEM IS AN ADOPTION SOCIAL WORKER who lives in Denver, Colorado, with her husband, the writer and editor Steve Rasnic Tem. They have four children and three grandchildren.

Her novels include *Prodigal*, which won the Bram Stoker Award for best first novel, *Revenant*, *Black River* and *The Tides*. Two more recent titles include *Slain in the Spirit* and *The Deceiver*. *The Ice Downstream* is a new short-story collection.

In 2003 Tem also had two plays produced – the one-act *The Society for Lost Positives*, and the full-length *Comfort Me with Peaches*.

"In college I had a good friend who was beautiful, complex, vivacious, intelligent," explains the author. "She was in love with a young man who to all appearances was dim-witted, bland, boring, shallow. Over the two years they dated, she did his papers for him, tutored him in all subjects, told him how to dress and bought his clothes for him, taught him manners and elocution and how to dance. They got married. I lost touch with them.

"Many years later she and I crossed paths again. She was wan, haggard, nervous. She had not had a career outside the home. Her husband had become an internationally known attorney and law professor and a high-ranking military officer.

"I found this very creepy. 'The Better Half' posits as plausible an explanation as any."

The story that follows is another of those vampire tales that takes an oblique view of the theme. It is no less disturbing a piece of fiction for that . . .

KELLY OPENED THE DOOR before I'd even come close to her house. The opening and closing of the red door in the white house startled me, like a mouth baring teeth. I stopped where I was, halfway down the block. Kelly was wearing a yellow dress and something white around her shoulders. She stepped farther out onto the porch and shaded her eyes against the high July sun.

For some reason, I didn't want her to see me just yet. I stepped behind a thick lilac bush dotted with the hard purplish nubs of spent flowers. A small brown dog in the yard across the street yapped twice at me, then gave it up and went back to its spot in the shade.

I hadn't seen Kelly in fifteen years. I'd thought I'd forgotten her, but I'd have known her anywhere. In college we'd been very close for awhile. Now that I was older and more careful, I'd have expected not to understand the ardor I'd felt for her then; it distressed me that I understood it perfectly, even felt a pulse of it again, like hot blood. Watching her from a distance and through the purple and green filtering of the lilac bush, I found myself a little afraid of her.

Later I learned that it was not Kelly I had reason to fear. But my father had died in the spring, and I was afraid of everything. Afraid of loving. Afraid of not loving. Afraid of coming home or rounding a corner and discovering something terrible that I, by my presence, could have stopped. I cowered behind the lilac bush and wished I could make myself invisible. I wondered why she'd called. I wondered savagely why I'd come. I thought about retreating along the hot bright sidewalk away from her house. I could hardly keep myself from rushing headlong to her.

Slowly I approached her. It was obvious that she still hadn't seen me; she was looking the other way. Looking for me. I was, purposely, a few minutes late. Then she turned, and I knew with a chill that something was terribly wrong.

It wasn't just that she looked alien, although she was elegantly dressed on a Saturday morning in a neighborhood where a business suit on a weekday was an oddity. It wasn't just that I felt invaded, although her house was around the corner from the diner where Daddy and I had often had breakfast, the park where we'd walked sometimes, the apartment where we'd lived. It was more than that. There was something wrong with *her*. I stopped again and stared.

It was mid-July and high noon. Hot green light through the porch awning flooded her face, the same heavy brows, high cheekbones, slightly aquiline nose. She looked sick. The spots of color high on her cheeks could have been paint or fever. She was breathing hard. Even from here I could see that she was shivering violently. And around her shoulders, in the noonday summer heat, was a white fur jacket.

I have told myself that at that point I nearly left, but I don't think that's true. I stood there looking at her across the neat green of the Kentucky bluegrass in her north Denver lawn. Sprinklers were on, making rainbows. I was drawn to her as I'd always been. Something was wrong, and I was about to be drenched in it, too.

She saw me and smiled, a weak and heart-wrenching grimace. I wished desperately that I'd never come but the impulse toward self-preservation, like others throughout my life, came too late.

"Brenda! Hello!"

I opened the waist-high, filigreed, wrought-iron gate, turned to latch it carefully behind me, turned again to walk between even rows of pinwheel petunias. "Kelly," I said, with an effort holding out my hand. "It's good to see you."

Her hand was icy cold. I still vividly recall the shock of touching it, the momentary disorientation of having to remind myself that the temperature was nearly a hundred degrees. She leaned toward me over the porch railing, and a tiny hot breeze stirred the half-dozen windchimes that hung from the eave, making a sweet cacophony. Healthy plants hung thick around her, almost obscuring her face. I could smell both her honeysuckle perfume and the faint sickly odor of her breath. She was smiling cordially; her lips were pale pink, almost colorless, against the yellow-white of her teeth. There were dark circles under her eyes. For a moment I had the terrifying fantasy that she would tumble off the porch into my arms, and that when she hit she would weigh no more than the truncated melodies from the sway of the chimes.

Her voice was much as I remembered it: husky, controlled, well-modulated. But I thought I'd heard it break, as though the two words she'd spoken had been almost too much for her. She took a deep breath, encircled my wrist with the thin icy fingers of her other hand, and said, "Come in."

I had last seen Kelly at her wedding. I'd watched the ceremony from a gauzy distance, wondering how she could bring herself to do such a thing and whether I'd ever get the chance; my father had already been sick and my mother, of course, long gone. Then I had passed through a long reception line to have her press my hand and kiss my cheek as though she'd never seen me before. Or never would again.

Ron, her new husband, had bent to kiss me, too, and I'd made a point to cough at the silly musk of his aftershave. He was tall and very fair, with baby-soft stubble on his cheeks and upper lip. His big pawlike hands cupped my shoulders as he gazed earnestly down at me. "I love her, Brenda." He could have been reciting the Boy Scout pledge. "Already she's my better half."

Later I repeated that comment to my friends; we all laughed and rolled our eyes. Ron was always terribly sincere. He could be making an offhand remark about the weather or the cafeteria food, and from his tone and delivery you'd think he was issuing a proclamation to limit worldwide nuclear arms proliferation.

Ron was *simple*. Often you could tell he'd missed the punchline of a joke, especially if it was off-color; he'd chuckle good-naturedly anyway. He had a hard time keeping up with our rapid Eastern chatter, but he'd look from one speaker to the next like an alert puppy, as if he were following right along. He was such an easy target that few of us resisted the temptation to make fun of him.

Kelly, who was brilliant, got him through school. At first she literally wrote his papers for him; he was a poli sci major and she took languages, so it meant double studying for her, but she didn't seem to pull any more all-nighters than the rest of us. Gradually he learned to write first drafts, which she then edited meticulously; you'd see them huddled at a table in the library, Kelly looking grim, Ron looking earnest and genial and bewildered.

She taught him everything. How to write a simple sentence. How to study for an exam. How to read a paragraph from beginning to end and catch the drift. How to eat without grossing everybody out. How to behave during fraternity rush. At a time when the entire Greek system was the object of much derision on our liberal little campus, Ron became a proud and busy Delt; senior year he was elected president, and Kelly, demure in gold chiffon, clung to his arm.

We gossiped that she taught him everything he knew about sex, too. That first year, before the mores and the rules loosened to allow men and women in each other's rooms, everybody made out in the courtyard of the freshman women's dorm. Because Kelly said they had too much work to do, they weren't there as often as some of the rest of us; for a while that winter and spring, I spent most of my waking hours, and a few asleep, in the courtyard with a handsome and knowledgeable young man from New Jersey named Jan.

But Ron and Kelly were there often enough for us to observe them and comment on their form. His back would be hard against the wall and his arms stiffly down around her waist. She'd be stretched up to nuzzle in his neck – or, we speculated unkindly, to whisper instructions. At first, if you said hello on your way past – and we would, just to be perverse – Ron's innate politeness would have him nodding and passing the time of day. Kelly didn't acknowledge anything but Ron; she was totally absorbed in him. Before long, he had also learned to ignore us, or to seem to.

Kelly was moody, intense, determined. Absolutely focused. I knew her before she met Ron; they assigned us as roommates freshman year. There was something about her – besides our age, the sense that we were standing on a frontier – that made me tell her things I hadn't told anybody, hadn't even thought of before. And made me listen to her self-revelations with bated breath, as though I were witness to the birth of fine music or ferreting out the inkling of a mystery.

In those days Kelly was already fascinated by women who had died for something they believed in, like Joan of Arc about whom she read in lyrical French, or for something they were and couldn't help, like Anne Frank whose diary she read in deceptively robust German. I didn't understand the words – I was a sociology major – but I knew the stories, and I loved the way Kelly looked and sounded when she read. When she stopped, there would be a rapturous silence, and then one or both of us would breathe, "Oh, that was *beautiful*!"

After she met Ron, things between Kelly and me changed. At first all she talked about was him, and I understood that; I talked about Jan a lot, too. But gradually she quit talking to me at all, and when she listened it was politely, her pen poised over the essay whose editing I had interrupted.

Ron seemed as open and expansive and featureless as the prairies of his native Nebraska. I was convinced she was wasting her life. He wasn't good enough for her. I could not imagine what she saw in him.

Unless it was the unlimited opportunity to play puppeteer, sculptor, inventor. I said that to her one night when we were both lying awake, trying not to be disturbed by the party down the hall. She was my best friend, and I thought I owed it to her to tell her what I thought.

"What is it between you and Ron anyway?" I demanded, somewhat abruptly. We'd been complaining desultorily to each other about the noise and making derogatory comments about *some people's* study habits, and in my own ears I sounded suddenly angry and hurt, which was not what I'd intended. But I went on anyway. "What is this, a role-reversed Pygmalion, or what?"

She was silent for such a long time that I thought either she'd fallen asleep or she was completely ignoring me this time. I was just about to pose my challenge again, maybe even get out of bed and cross the room and shake her by the shoulders until she paid attention to me, when she answered calmly. "There are worse things."

"Kelly, you're beautiful and brilliant. You could have any man on this campus. Ron is just so *ordinary*."

"Ron is good for me, Brenda. I don't expect you to understand." But then she assuaged my hurt feelings by trying to explain. "He takes me out of myself."

That was the last time Kelly and I talked about anything important. It was practically the last time we talked at all. For the rest of freshman year I might have had a single room, except for intimate, hurtful evidence of her – stockings hung like empty skin on the closet door-knob to dry, bottles of perfume and makeup like a string of amulets across her nightstand – all of it carefully on her side of the room. The next year she roomed with a sorority sister, somebody whom I didn't know and whom I didn't think Kelly knew very well, either.

I was surprised and a little offended to get a wedding invitation. I told myself I had no obligation to go. I went anyway, and cried, and pressed her hand. To this day I'm not sure she knew who I was when I went through the reception line. I spent most of the reception making conversation with Kelly's parents, a gaunt pale woman who looked very much like Kelly and a tall fair robust man. They were proud of their daughter; Ron was a fine young man who would go far in this world. Her father was jocular and verbose; he danced with all the young women, several times with me. Her mother barely said a word, seldom got out of her chair; her smile was like the winter sun.

At the time I didn't know that I'd noticed all that about Kelly's parents. I hadn't thought about them in years, probably had never thought about them directly. But the impressions were all there, ready for the taking. If I'd just paid attention, I might have been warned.

And then I don't know what I would have done.

Since college, Kelly and I had barely kept in touch. For a while I had kept approximate track of her through mutual friends and the alumni newsletter. I moved out West because the dry climate might be better for Daddy's health, got a graduate degree in planning and a job with the Aurora city government. Left Daddy alone too much, then hired a stranger to nurse him so I could live my own life. As if there was such a thing.

From sporadic Christmas cards, I knew that Kelly and her family had lived in various parts of Europe; Ron was an attorney specializing in international law and a high-ranking officer in the military, and his job had something to do with intelligence, maybe the CIA. I knew that they had two sons. In every communication, no matter how brief, Kelly mentioned that she had never worked a day outside the home, that when Ron was away she sometimes went for days without talking to an adult, that her languages were getting rusty except for the language of the country she happened to be living in at the time. It seemed to me that even her English was awkward, childlike, although it was hard to tell from the few sentences she wrote.

Last year I'd received a copy of a form Christmas letter, run off on pale green paper with wreaths along the margin, ostensibly composed by Ron. It was so eloquent and interesting and grammatically sophisticated that at first I was a little shocked. Then I decided – with distaste, but also with a measure of relief that should have been a clue if I'd been paying attention – that Kelly must still be ghost-writing.

For some reason, I'd kept that letter, though as far as I could remember I hadn't answered it. After Kelly's call, I'd pulled it out and re-read it. The letter described the family's travels in the Alps; though it read like a travel brochure, the prose was competent and there were vivid images. It outlined the boys' many activities and commented, "Without Kelly, of course, none of this would be possible." It mentioned that Kelly had been ill lately, tired: "The gray wet winters of northern Europe really don't agree with her. We're hoping that some of her sparkle will return when we move back home."

I'd thought there was nothing significant in that slick, chatty, green-edged letter. I'd been wrong.

Kelly's house was very orderly and close and clean. She led me down a short hallway lined with murky photographs of people I didn't think I knew, into a living room where a fire crackled in a plain brick fireplace and not a speck of ash marred the dappled marble surface of the hearth. Heavy maroon drapes were pulled shut floor to ceiling, and all the lights were on; the room was stifling.

Startled and confused, I paused in the arched doorway while Kelly went on ahead of me. I saw her pull the white fur jacket closer around her, as if she were cold.

"We haven't lived here very long," she said over her shoulder. She was apologizing, but I didn't know what for.

"It's nice," I said, and followed her into the nightlike, winterlike room.

She gestured toward a rocker-recliner. "Make yourself at home."

I sat down. Though the chair was across the room, the part of my body which faced the fire grew hot in a matter of seconds, and I had started to sweat. Kelly pulled an ottoman nearly onto the hearth and huddled onto it hugging her knees.

I was quickly discomfited by the silence between us, through which I could hear her labored breathing and the spitting of the fire. "How long have you lived here?" I asked, to have something to say.

"Just a few months. Since the first of April." So she knew it was summer.

"How long will you be here?" I knew it was sounding like an interrogation, but I desperately needed to ground myself in time and space. That was not a new impulse, though I hadn't been so acutely aware of it before. I was shaking, and the heat was making my head swim. It seemed to me that I had been floating for a long time.

I understand now, of course, how misguided it was to look to Kelly for ballast. She had almost no weight herself by that time, no substance of her own, so she couldn't have held anybody down.

Abruptly, as often happened to me when I was invaded by even a hint of strong emotion – fear, pleasure, grief – I could feel the slight weight of my father's body in my arms, the web of his baby-fine hair across my lips. I closed my eyes against the pain and curled my arms into my chest as though to keep from dropping him.

Almost tonelessly Kelly asked, "What's wrong, Brenda?" and I realized I'd covered my face with my empty hands.

"You remind me of somebody," I said. That surprised me. I wasn't even sure what it meant. Self-stimulating like an autistic child, I was rocking furiously in the cumbersome chair. I forced myself to press my palms flat against its nubby arms, stopping the motion. "Somebody else who left me," I added.

She didn't ask me what I meant. She didn't defend against my interpretation of what had happened between us. She just cocked her head in a quizzical gesture so familiar to me that I caught my breath, although I wouldn't have guessed that I remembered anything significant about her.

Absently she picked two bits of lint off the brown carpet, which had looked spotless to me, and deposited them into her other palm, closing her fingers protectively. I noticed her silver-pink nails. I noticed that her mauve stockings were opaque, thicker than standard nylons, and that the stylish high-heeled boots she wore were fur-lined. I wanted to go sit beside her, have her hug me to warm us both. I was sweating profusely.

I think I was on the verge of telling her about my father. I think I might have said things to her that I hadn't yet said to myself. I'm still haunted by the suspicion that, if I'd spoken up at that moment, subsequent events might have turned out very differently. The thought makes my blood run cold.

But I didn't say anything, for at that moment Kelly's sons came home. I flinched as I heard a screen door slam, heard children's voices laughing and squabbling. It was as if their liveliness tore at something.

Daddy died while I was out. He hadn't wanted me to go, though he would never have said so. He hadn't liked the man, any man, I was with. When I came home – earlier than I'd intended though not early enough, determined not to see that man again – I'd found my father dead on the floor. If I'd been there I could have saved him, or at least held him while he died. I owed him. He gave me life.

Struggling to stay in focus when the boys burst in, I kept my eyes on Kelly. The transformation was remarkable. Many times after that I saw it happen to her, and I was always astounded, but that first time was like witnessing a miracle, or the results of a spectacular compact with the devil.

She filled out like an inflatable doll. Color flooded into her cheeks. Her shoulders squared and she sat up straight. By the time her boys found us and rushed into the living room, bringing with them like sirens their light and fresh air and energy, she was holding out her arms to them and beaming and the white fur jacket had slipped from her shoulders onto the hearth behind her, where I thought it might burn.

I stayed at Kelly's house for a long time that first day, though I hadn't intended to. When Kelly introduced me as an old friend from college, Joshua, the younger child, stared at me solemn-eyed and demanded, "Do you know my daddy, too?" I admitted that I did, or used to. He nodded. He was very serious.

We had a picnic lunch outside on the patio. I watched the children splash in the sprinkler and bounce on the backyard trampoline, watched Kelly bask like a chameleon in the sunshine. She was a nervous hostess. She fluttered and fussed to make sure the boys and I were served, persistently inquired whether the lemonade was sweet enough and whether the sandwiches had too much mayonnaise, was visibly worried whenever any of us stopped eating. She herself didn't eat at all, as if she wasn't entitled to. She didn't swat at flies or fan herself or complain about the heat. She hardly talked to me; her interactions with the children were impatient. She watched us eat and play, and the look on her face was near-panic, as if she couldn't be sure she was getting it right.

I was restless. I wasn't used to sitting still for so long without something to occupy me – television, a newspaper, knitting. At one point I got up and went over to join the boys. I tossed the new yellow frisbee, spotted Clay on the tramp, squirted Joshua with the sprinkler. I was clumsy and they didn't like it; my intrusion altered the rhythms of their play. "Quit it!" Josh shrieked when the water hit him, and Clay simply slid off the end of the trampoline and stalked away when he discovered I'd taken up position at the side.

Somewhat aimlessly, I strolled around the yard. Red and salmon late roses climbed the privacy fence; I touched their petals and thorns, bent to sniff their fragrance. "Ron likes roses," Kelly said from behind me, and I jumped; I hadn't realized how close she was. "That's why we planted all those bushes. They're hard to take care of, though. I'm still learning. Ron buys me books."

"They're beautiful," I said.

"They're a lot of care. He's never here to do any of it. It's part of my job."

Clay appeared at my elbow. He was carrying a framed and glass-covered family portrait big enough that he had to hold it with both hands.

"Clay!" his mother remonstrated, much more sharply than I'd have expected from her. "Don't drop that!"

"I'll put it back," he said lightly, dismissing her. "See," he said earnestly to me. "That's my dad."

I didn't know what I was supposed to say, what acknowledgement would be satisfactory. I looked at him, at his brother across the yard, at the portrait. It had been taken several years ago; the boys looked much younger. Kelly was pale and lovely, clinging to her husband's arm even though the photographer had no doubt posed her standing up straight. The uniformed man at the hub of the family grouping was taller, ruddier, and possessed of much more presence than I remembered. "You look like him." I finally said to Clay. "You both do." He grinned and nodded and took the heavy picture back into the house.

I sat on the kids' swing and watched a gray bird sitting in the apple tree. It was the wrong time of the season, between blossom and fruit, to tell whether there would be a good crop; I wondered idly whether Kelly made applesauce, whether Ron and the boys liked apple pie. "My dad put up those swings for us!" Joshua shouted from the wading pool, sounding angry. I took the lemonade pitcher inside for more ice, although no one who lived there had suggested it.

Being alone in Kelly's kitchen gave me a sense of just-missed intimacy. I guessed that she spent a good deal of time here, cooking and cleaning, but there seemed to be nothing personal about her in the room. I looked around.

The pictures on the wall above the microwave were standard, square, factory-painted representations of vegetables, a tomato and a carrot and an ear of corn, pleasant enough. On the single-shelf spice rack above the dishwasher were two red-and-white cans and two undistinguished glass bottles: cinnamon, onion powder, salt, and pepper. Nothing idiosyncratic or identifying. No dishes soaked in the sink; no meat was thawing on the counter for dinner.

I remember thinking that, if I looked through the cupboards and drawers and into the back shelves of the refrigerator, I'd surely find something about Kelly, but I couldn't quite bring myself to make such a deliberate search. Now, of course, I know that there wouldn't have been anything anyway. No favorite snacks of hers secreted away. No dishes that meant anything special to her. No special recipes. In the freezer I'd probably have found fudgsicles for Clay and Eskimo Pies for Josh, and no doubt there was a six-pack of Coors Lite on the top shelf of the refrigerator for Ron. But, no matter how deeply I looked or how broadly I interpreted, I wouldn't have found anything personal about Kelly, except in what she'd made sure was there for the others.

I set the pitcher on the counter and moved so that I was standing in the middle of the floor with my hands at my sides and my eyes closed. I held my breath. It was like being trapped in a flotation tank. I could hear the boys squealing and shouting outside, the hum of a lawnmower farther away and the ticking of a clock nearby, but the sounds were outside of me, not touching. I could smell whiffs and layers of homey kitchen odors – coffee, cinnamon, onions – but I had never been fed in this room.

I opened my eyes and was dizzy. Without knowing it, I had turned, so that now I was facing a little alcove that opened off the main kitchen. A breakfast nook, maybe, or a pantry. I rounded the multicolored plexiglas partition and caught my breath.

The place was a shrine. On all three walls, from the waist-high wainscoting nearly to the ceiling, were photographs of Ron and Clay and Joshua. Black-and-white photos on a plain white background, unlike the busy kitchen wallpaper in the rest of the room. Pictures of them singly and in various combinations: Ron in uniform, looking stoic and sensible; Clay doing a flip on the trampoline; Joshua in his Cub Scout uniform; the three of them in a formal pose, each boy with his hand on his father's shoulder; the boys by a Christmas tree. I counted; there were forty-three photographs.

I couldn't bring myself to go into the alcove. I think I was afraid I'd hear voices. And there was not a single likeness of Kelly anywhere on the open white walls.

Later, a grim and wonderful thought occurred to me: it would have been virtually impossible for a detective to find out anything useful about Kelly. Or for a voodoo practitioner to fashion an efficacious doll. There was little essence of her left. There were few details. By the end, it would have been easy to say that she had no soul.

For the rest of that summer and into the fall, I spent a great deal of time at Kelly's house. It started with lunch on Saturdays, always a picnic lunch with the boys on the patio, sandwiches and lemonade and chips. She never let me bring anything; she seemed to take offense when I tried to insist.

"Why don't you and I go somewhere for lunch, Kelly? Get a sitter for the boys or take them to the pool or something."

"The pool isn't safe. I don't like the kind of kids who go there."

Kelly and I never seemed to be alone together. Her sons were always there, in the same room or within earshot or about to rush in and demand something of her. I chafed. I didn't much like the boys anyway; I found them mouthy and rude, to me but especially to their mother, and altogether too high-spirited for my taste.

"It's nice to see a mother spend as much time with her kids as you do," I said once, lying, trying to understand, trying to get her to talk to me about something.

"We've always been – close," she said, a little hesitantly. "They both nursed until they were almost two. Sometimes Josh will still try to nip my breast. In play, you know."

A little taken aback, I said, "You seem to enjoy their company." I didn't know whether that was true or not.

She shrugged and laughed a little. "I think I've inherited my father's attitudes toward children. They'd be fine if you could teach them and train them and mold them into what you want. Otherwise, they're mostly irritating." She laughed again and shivered, hugged herself, passed a hand over her eyes. "But I don't have to *like* my kids in order to be a good mother, do I?"

For a long time, I didn't see Ron. He was always at work when I was there, and, no matter how late I stayed, he worked later.

"Come with me to see this movie. I've been wanting to see it for a long time, and it's about to leave town, and I don't want to go alone."

"There's a movie that the boys want to see. One of those Kung fu things. I promised I'd take them this weekend."

Kelly's roses faded, and the marigolds and petunias and then chrysanthemums came into their own. The apple tree bore nicely, tiny fruit clustered all on the south side of the tree because, Kelly speculated, the blossoms on the north side had been frozen early in the spring. That distressed her enormously; her eyes shone with tears when she talked about it. The boys went back to school.

"Now you have lots of free time. Let's go to the art museum one morning next week. I can take a few hours off."

"Oh, Brenda, the work around here is endless. Really. I have fall housecleaning to do. I'm redecorating Clay's room. There must be a dozen layers of wallpaper on those walls. My first responsibility is to Ron and the children. You're welcome to come here, though. I could fix you lunch."

One crisp Wednesday in late September I had a meeting over on her side of town, and I didn't have to be back at the office until my two o'clock staff meeting. Impulsively, I turned off onto a side street toward her house.

I had never been to Kelly's house on a weekday before. I had never dropped in on her unexpectedly. I had seldom dropped in on anybody unexpectedly; I liked to have time to prepare, and was keenly aware of the differences between people in private and people when they met the world, even the small and confusd part of the world represented by me. My heart was skittering uneasily, and I felt a little feverish, chilled, though the sun was warm and the sky brilliant. The houses and trees and fence rows along these old blocks had taken on that sharp-edged quaility that autumn sometimes imparts to a city; every brick seemed outlined, every flower and leaf a jewel.

I parked by the side of her house, across the street. I opened and shut the gate as quietly as I could. I stood for a while on her porch, listening to the windchimes, catching stray rainbows from the lopsided paper leaf Josh had made in school and hung in the front window. She had moved the plants inside for the winter, and the porch seemed bare. Finally I pushed the button for the doorbell and waited. A few cars went by behind me. I touched the doorbell button again, listened for any sound inside the house, could hear none.

When I tried the door, it opened easily. I went in quickly and shut the door behind me, thinking to keep out the light and dust. I was nearly through the front hall and to the kitchen before I called her name.

"In here, Brenda," she answered, as though she'd been expecting me. I stopped for a moment, bewildered; maybe I'd somehow forgotten that I had called ahead, or maybe we'd had plans for today that I hadn't written in my appointment book.

"Where?"

"In here."

I found her, finally, in the master bedroom. She was in bed, under the covers; she wore a scarf and a stocking cap on her head, mittens on the hands that pulled the covers up to her chin.

Around her neck I could see the collar of the white fur jacket. Her teeth were chattering, and her skin was so pale that it was almost green. I stood in the doorway and stared. The shaft of light through the blinded window looked wintry. "Kelly, what's wrong? Are you sick?" It was a question I could have asked months before; now it seemed impossible to avoid.

"I'm *cold*," she said weakly. "I – don't seem to have any energy."

"Should I call somebody?"

"No, it's all right. Usually if I stay in bed all day I'm all right by the time the boys get home from school."

"How often does this happen?"

"Oh, I don't know. Every other day or so now, I guess."

I had advanced into the room, stood by the side of the bed. I was reluctant to touch her. I now know that the contagion had nothing to do with physical contact with Kelly, that I was safer alone in that house with her than I've been at any time since. But that morning all I knew was cold fear, and alarm for my friend, and an intense, exhilarating curiosity. "Where's Ron?" I demanded. "Is he still out of town? Does he know about this?"

"He came home late last night," she told me, and I had no way of appreciating the significance of what she'd said.

"What shall I do? Should I call him at work? Or call a doctor?"

"No." With a great sigh and much tremulous effort, she lifted her feet over the side of the bed and sat up. I could feel her dizziness; I put my hand flat against the wall and lowered my head to let it clear. Kelly stood up. "Take me out somewhere," she said. "I'm hungry. Let's go to lunch."

Without my help, she made it out of the house, down the walk, and into the car. The sun had been shining in the passenger window, so it would be warm for her there. There was definitely a fall chill in the air, I decided, as I found myself shivering a little. "Where do you want to go?" I asked her.

"Someplace fast."

In Denver I have always been delighted, personally and professionally, by contrasts, one of which is the proximity of quiet residential neighborhoods like Kelly's to bustling commercial strips. We were five minutes from half a dozen fast-food places. Kelly said she didn't care which one, so I drove somewhat randomly and found the one with the least-crowded parking lot. She wanted to go inside.

The place was bright, warm, cacophonous. I saw Kelly wrap herself more tightly in the fur jacket, saw people glance at her and then glance away. She went to find a seat, as far away from the windows and the doors as she could, and I ordered for both of us, not knowing what she wanted, taking a chance. There was a very long line. When I finally got to her, she was staring with a stricken look on her face at the middle-aged woman in the ridiculous uniform who was clearing the tables and sweeping the floor. "I talked to her," Kelly whispered as I set the laden tray down. "She has a master's degree."

"In what?" I asked, making conversation. It seemed important to keep her engaged, though I didn't know what she was talking about. "Here's your shake. I hope chocolate's all right. They were out of strawberry."

When she didn't answer right away I looked at her more closely. The expression of horror on her face made my stomach turn. Her eyes were bloodshot and bulging. She was breathing heavily through her mouth. Her gloved hands on the tabletop were clawed, as if trying to find in the formica something to cling to. "That could be me a few years from now," she said hoarsely. "Working in a fast-food place, for a little extra money and something to do. Alone. That could be me."

"Don't be silly," I snapped. "You have a lot more going for you than that woman does."

Suddenly she was shrieking at me. "How do you know that? How can you know? I've let everybody down! Everybody! All my teachers and professors who said I had so much potential! My father! Everybody! You don't know what you're talking about!" Then, to my own horror, she struggled to her feet and hobbled out the door. For a moment, I really thought she'd disappeared, vanished somehow into the air that wasn't much thinner than she was. I told myself that was crazy and followed her.

The lunchtime crowd had filled in behind Kelly and was all of a piece again. I pushed through it and through the door, which framed the busy street scene as though it were a poor photograph, flat and without meaning to me until I entered it. I looked around. Kelly had collapsed on the hot sidewalk against the building. Her knees were drawn up, her head was down so that the stringy dark hair fell over her face, the collar of the jacket stood up around her ears. Two women in shorts and halter tops crouched beside her. I hurried, as though to save her from them, although, of course, by then Kelly wasn't the one who needed protecting.

I met Ron at the hospital. From the ambulance stretcher, in a flat high voice that almost seemed part of the siren, Kelly had told me how to reach him. I hadn't wanted to; I hadn't wanted him with us. By the time I made it through all the layers and synapses of the bureaucracy he worked in and heard his official voice on the other end of the line, I was furious. But I hadn't missed anything; Kelly was still waiting in the emergency room, slumped in a chair. Ron did not sound especially alarmed; I told myself it was his training. He said he'd be there in fifteen minutes, and he was.

They had just taken Kelly to be examined when he got there. I was standing at the counter looking after her, feeling bereft; they wouldn't let me go back behind the curtain with her, and she was too weak to ask for me. When the tall blond uniformed man strode by me, I didn't try to speak to him, and no one else did either. I doubt that Kelly asked for him, or gave permission, or even recognized him when he came. None of that was necessary. He was her husband. She was part of him. He had the right.

My father and I had been bound like that, too. If I'd asserted the right to be part of him, welcomed and treasured it, I could have been. Instead, I'd thought it was necessary for me to grow up, to separate. And so I'd lost him. Lost us both, I thought then, for without him I had no idea who I was.

I felt Ron's presence approaching me before I opened my eyes and saw him. "She's unconscious," he said. "They don't know yet what's wrong. You don't look very good yourself. Come and sit down."

I didn't let him touch me then, but I preceded him to a pair of orange plastic bucket chairs attached to a metal bar against the wall.

We were then sitting squarely side-by-side, and the chairs didn't move; I didn't make the effort to face him. He was friendly and solemn, as befitted the occasion. He took my hand in both of his, swallowing it. "Brenda," he said; he made my name sound far more significant than I'd ever thought it was, and – despite myself, despite the circumstances, despite what I'd have mistakenly called my better judgment – something inside me stirred gratefully. "It's nice to see you again after all these years. I'm sorry our reunion turned out to be like this. Kelly has talked a great deal about you over the past few months."

I nodded. I didn't know what to say.

"What happened?" Ron asked. He let go of my hand and it was cold. I put both hands in my pockets.

"She – collapsed," I told him. The more I told him, the angrier I became, and the closer to the kind of emptying, wracking sobs I'd been so afraid of. Now I know there's nothing to fear in being emptied; Kelly simply hadn't taken it far enough. To the end, some part of her fought it. I don't fight at all anymore.

"What do you mean? Tell me what happened. The details." He was moving in, assuming command. It crossed my mind to resist him, but from the instant he'd walked into the room I'd felt exhausted.

"I dropped by to see her. I was in the neighbourhood. When I got there she was sick. She asked me to take her out to lunch. So we—"

"Out?" His blond eyebrows rose and then furrowed disapprovingly. "Out of the house? With you?"

I mustered a little indignation. "What's wrong with that?"

"It's – unusual, that's all. Go on."

I told him the rest of what I knew. It seemed to take an enormous amount of time to say it all, though I wouldn't have thought I had that much to say. I stumbled over words. There were long silences. Ron listened attentively. At one point he rested his hand on my shoulder in a comradely way, and I was too tired and disoriented to pull free. When I finished, he nodded, and then someone came for him from behind the curtains and lights, and I was left alone again, knowing I hadn't said enough.

Kelly never came home from the hospital. She died without regaining consciousness. Many times since then I've wondered what she would have said to me if she'd awakened, what advice she would have given, what warning, how she would have passed the torch.

I wasn't there when she died. Ron was. He called me early the next morning to tell me. He sounded drained; his voice was flat and thin. "Oh, Ron," I said, foolishly, and then waited for him to tell me what to do.

"I'd like you to come over," he said. "The boys are having a hard time."

I haven't left since. I haven't been back to my apartment even to pick up my things; none of my former possessions seems worth retrieval. I had no animals to feed, no plants to water, no books or clothes or furniture or photographs that mean anything to me now.

Kelly kept her house orderly. From the first day, I could find things. The boys' schedules were predictable, although very busy; names and phone numbers of their friends' parents, Scout leaders, piano teachers were on a laminated list on the kitchen bulletin board. In her half of the master bedroom closet, I found clothes of various sizes, and the larger ones, from before she lost so much weight, fit fine.

The first week I took personal leave from work. Since then I've been calling in sick, when I think of it; most recently I haven't called in at all and, of course, they don't know where I am.

Ron is away a good deal. The work he does is important and mysterious; I don't know exactly what it is, but I'm proud to be able to help him do it.

But he was home that first week, and we got used to each other. "You're very different from the man I knew in college," I told him. We were sitting in the darkened living room. We'd been talking about Kelly. We'd both been crying.

He was sitting beside me on the couch. I saw him nod and slightly smile. "Kelly used to say I'd developed my potential beyond her wildest dreams," he admitted, "and she'd lost hers."

I felt a flash of anger against her. She was dead. "She had a choice," I pointed out. "Nobody forced her to do anything. She could have done other things with her life."

"Don't be too sure of that," he said, sharply. His tone surprised and hurt me. I glanced at him through the shadows, saw him lean forward to set his drink on the coffee table. He took my empty glass from my hands and put it down, too, then swiftly lowered his face to my neck.

There was a small pain and, afterwards, a small stinging wound. When he was finished he stood up, wiped his mouth with his breast pocket handkerchief, and went upstairs to bed. I sat up for a long time, amazed, touched, frightened. No longer lonely. No longer having decisions to be made or protection to construct. That first night, that first time, I did not feel tired or cold; the sickness has since begun, but the exhilaration has heightened, too.

Ron says he loves me. He says he and the boys need me, couldn't get along without me. I like to hear that. I know what he means.

JOHN BURKE

The Devil's Tritone

JOHN BURKE HAS WRITTEN around 150 books in all genres. Born in Rye, Sussex, he grew up in Liverpool, where his father became a Chief Inspector of Police.

During the 1930s Burke and Charles Eric Maine started *The Satellite,* one of the first science fiction fan magazines in Britain. He won an Atlantic Award in Literature for his first novel, *Swift Summer* (1949), and worked in publishing and the oil business before joining 20th Century-Fox Productions in 1963 as European story editor.

During the early 1950s he wrote several short science fiction novels and contributed many stories to such British SF magazines as *New Worlds, Science Fantasy* and *Nebula.*

Burke has also written novelizations of numerous TV and film titles, including *A Hard Day's Night, Dr Terror's House of Horrors, The Hammer Horror Omnibus, The Second Hammer Horror Film Omnibus, Privilege* and *Moon Zero Two.* Two tie-ins to the *UFO* television series were published under the pseudonym "Robert Miall".

Burke also edited the anthology series *Tales of Unease, More Tales of Unease* and *New Tales of Unease,* while *We've Been Waiting for You* is a collection from Ash-Tree Press of his best weird fiction, edited by Nicholas Royle. The author's latest book is the mystery *Wrong Turnings,* featuring "The Laird of the Law" characters from earlier novels.

"I have always been convinced that music can work more directly and hypnotically on one's feelings than any other art form," reveals Burke, "and at one stage wrote a screenplay called *The Devil's Discord* which was bought but never produced.

"In it, as quoted in Benjamin Halligan's 2003 study of British film-maker Michael Reeves's films, I aimed at showing that '. . . a lot of the hysteria produced by so-called magic spells could be due to the musical content of the incantations . . . What cast the spell was the musical rhythm and melody and the cadences of the often non-sensical words.'

"It struck me that there could be a vampiric element in resonant echoes from the past restored to or maintained in evil life by, as it were, a contemporary tuned circuit."

An unusual variation on the theme, the following story was written especially for this volume.

THE ORKNEY WIND HAD caused the postponement of one concert during the St Magnus Festival because a small circular window had been sucked out of the cathedral by the force of the gale. A less exposed recital given by the Drysdale Trio on Shapinsay started late because of the ferry's slow struggle across the short but turbulent stretch between Kirkwall and the island. But the recital had been a success. People who had taken that much trouble to get there in such weather conditions were determined to enjoy the music, even when one banshee wail of a more ferocious gust howled in quite the wrong key.

This came in the middle of *Variations on a Theme by Calum of the Clachan*, which Robert Drysdale had composed for the three of them – himself on violin, his wife Deirdre on the clarsach, and their daughter Fiona on flute. Somehow, although it produced such a grinding discord, the cry of the wind seemed an integral part of the work, producing a shiver for which the strange convolutions of the melody had been preparing the listener.

The day after the final concert, the ferry to the mainland ran four hours late because of the fury of the wind along the Pentland Firth. The Drysdales had never been seasick, but by the time Robert drove off the ramp on to solid ground he was still dizzy from bracing himself against the lurching and plunging of the vessel. Half a mile clear of the ferry terminal, he drew in to the side of the road.

"We'll have to find somewhere else to spend the night. It's too late to make Pitlochry by this evening."

They were due to play another recital in Hexham in Northumberland two days from now. He had planned to break the journey a good way down central Scotland, and then have plenty of time next day for a leisurely drive south of the Border.

Deirdre reached for the map and opened it across her lap. "Dornoch?" she suggested.

"Or a bit further inland. We could make Bonar Bridge, or . . . just a minute." Robert's finger jabbed at a name. "Kirkshiel. Only a few miles off the direct route. And couldn't be more appropriate."

"Why's that?"

"Calum of the Clachan, that's why. That's where he came from, and where he went back to in the end."

"I didn't think there ever was a place with a real name," said Fiona from the back seat. "Didn't he call himself 'of the Clachan' because his home village was abandoned during the Clearances and never had a real name of its own?"

As the wind buffeted the side of the Volvo, Robert thought of the wind of cruelty that had swept across the Highlands when rapacious landlords and their factors drove men off the land to make room for sheep. Some emigrated, others were resettled into jobs on the bleak coast which was utterly alien to them. Others, like Calum of the Clachan, wandered – an itinerant fiddler, literally scraping a living as he travelled.

Robert glanced at his wife. "You ought to feel in tune with the man. Your own ancestors did enough stravaiging in their time."

Deirdre laughed gently, as if dissociating herself from those wandering clarsairs from Eriskay who had carried their harps and their music from one glen to another, one misty hill to another, across land and water, one island to another.

"And he did find his way home in the end," Robert added.

There must have been a few gradual resettlements when the railway came reasonably close on its way up through Lairg. Kirkshiel was one of them: still pretty small, but at least there was an inn marked on the map. It was worth a try.

Robert drove beside the twists and turns of a winding river. Passing places were marked with triangular signs. During the first hour, they met only one caravan bumping along the road towards some hidden caravan park or perhaps simply seeking a patch in the trees beside the road.

Fiona began humming to herself. Robert, usually relaxed when he was driving and rarely distracted by irritating sounds, human or mechanical, paid no attention at first. Then the sound became a nagging nuisance, plucking at his mind with thorny insistence.

"What on earth's that you're droning away at?"

"I don't know. It just came into my head."

Fiona fell silent; but as they approached Kirkshiel she said: "That tune. It's getting louder in my head."

At this time of year in the northern isles and on the northern mainland there were little more than a couple of hours of near-darkness. But although the sun was still coating the treetops with a burnished glow, the sky ahead was sullen and threatening thunder. The wind had dropped, leaving a muggy stillness. Robert drove round a sharp bend, and the road began dipping towards a small settlement with a few lights in windows here and there.

The inn was called The Crofter's Rest. One of its windows was brighter than any of its neighbours.

Robert left the women in the Volvo and went into the bar. It was a long, low room with four stools, a high-backed trestle against the window, and two tables at the far end. A fruit machine blinked with a migraine-inducing dazzle in an alcove near the door to the toilets.

The landlord, in shirtsleeves, was resting his bony elbows on the bar, his rheumy eyes sizing up the newcomer without bothering to offer any greeting. His forearms were mottled with purple blotches, and his greying hair looked dusty rather than potentially silver.

"You could manage accommodation for three of us?" asked Robert. "Just for one night?"

"Three of you?"

"My wife and myself, and a room for my daughter."

"Aye." The landlord seemed neither welcoming nor reluctant. "And you'd be wanting to eat?"

"If you can rustle something up, that would be great."

"We're well stocked. Ready for tomorrow evening."

"You've got a function on? A party?"

"An annual event, aye."

When Robert went out to tell the women that they could come indoors, the landlord followed, not offering help with the two cases but peering with shameless curiosity at the instruments in the back of the estate wagon.

"Ye'd be musicians, then?"

"Just been to the St Magnus Festival in Orkney. Oddly enough," said Robert as he heaved one of the cases out, "we recently played some variations on a tune by one of your local characters – Calum of the Clachan."

"Just the right folk for tomorrow evening, then."

"Sorry?"

"Calum's Night, we call it. Once a year. Just the once. And there's need of music. The right kind o' music."

"I'm afraid we won't be here tomorrow evening."

"Now, that would be a pity. A great pity, since you've been sent here."

"Hardly. We just happened to notice the name on the map, and—"

"Well, let's say you were drawn here, then."

They were shown up a narrow flight of stairs to a cramped landing with two bedrooms and a bathroom opening off it. The ceilings were low, and the rooms were dark, each with only one small dormer window, but they were spotlessly clean, and there was a fresh smell from the bed linen.

As they unpacked, Deirdre said abruptly: "I think perhaps we ought to have driven on."

"Whatever for? This looks comfortable enough. Nice and quiet."

"There's something . . . waiting."

Robert put his arm round her. "Come on, now. Don't go all fey on us."

She turned away and began hanging two dresses in the narrow wardrobe.

When they went down, the landlord this time came along the bar to greet them. "Ready for a drink, now, sir?" He sounded almost pleased that they were here. "I'm Hamish. Hamish McReay."

"Drysdale. My wife Deirdre, our daughter Fiona."

Hamish nodded as if to grant this his approval, and when he had poured a pint of rather gassy beer and two orange-and-lemonades for them, he said: "Would trout or steak be what you'd be wanting for your meal?"

"Trout," said Deirdre and Fiona almost in chorus.

"Steak," said Robert.

They perched on the bar stools while Hamish went through a door with their order. When he came back, he seemed to have mellowed a fraction further and was ready to play the talkative host.

"Tomorrow evening, now. We've been let down by one of our locals. He's been training up for it since last year. But he . . . och, he wasnae up to it. Ran off at the last minute."

"Stage fright?"

"Been put off by silly tales. And some of those so-called professionals have been no better. There was one of those pop groups came here, talking big. Called themselves The Sons of the Gael, or some such thing. Pop music and what they said was traditional folk music. Or folk rock, or whatever name they chose to put on it. Some o' the younger folk liked them. They played what they called a gig on Calum's Night. The fiddler took some holding back that night, I'll grant ye. Said he'd be back the next year, but he never came. Quite a few like that. Say they'll come back, but they don't. And then we hear, every now and then, of some of them dying."

"These folk-pop groups," Robert sympathized. "All the same. Get high on the music and on drugs at the same time, and kill themselves with it."

"Aye," said Hamish without seeming quite to accept this. "It could be that, maybe."

"But this annual do – what's it all about?"

"Calum's Night, as I told ye. Every year there's a celebration. Some music, some dancing."

"What a coincidence, us being here so close to it."

"Och, no. That'll no' be a coincidence. It was meant. You being here, that is."

"But I've told you, we've got to be on our way tomorrow. We can't help out."

Hamish smiled with the infuriating smugness of someone who thought he knew better, and went to serve two young men who had just come in and propped themselves against the far end of the bar. Dark and almost gypsyish, they muttered between themselves, grinned, and stared at the strangers. Particularly at Fiona, with her red hair, redder than her mother's, in a tight casque over her head, with a little stub at the back like a seaman's tobacco quid.

Looking away, Fiona reached for a leaflet from a plastic container propped against an upright beam. Robert leaned over her shoulder as she opened the creased, faded pages. As a tourist pamphlet it was far from inspiring, listing a few fishing rights, a two-mile walk, and remains of a prehistoric stone circle.

"And no mention of their prodigal son?"

"Not a word."

Hamish lifted a flap to allow an elderly woman through, carrying two large plates which she put down on one of the tables. As they settled themselves around the table, she was on her way back to fetch a tray bearing another plate and a bowl of vegetables.

Fiona slid the leaflet back onto the bar.

"You'd have expected at least some mention of Calum of the Clachan. At least a couple of lines. I wonder if there's a plaque or a sign somewhere in the village?"

"Those who know," said the woman at her left shoulder, leaning over to put servers in the vegetable bowl, "hae no need of it."

"And those who don't know?" laughed Fiona.

"Are gey better without it."

Hamish cleared his throat with a warning growl, and the woman scuttled away. The young men finished their drinks and left, with a last glance at Fiona. Hamish sauntered along to lean on the counter above the Drysdales.

"Quiet tonight," said Deirdre politely, between mouthfuls.

"Saving themselves for tomorrow," said Hamish, "as ye'll see."

Robert clattered his knife down on the plate. "Mr McReay, I've already told you, we'll be off in the morning. We definitely won't be here tomorrow evening."

"It'd be a great shame for you to miss it. Wouldnae be right at all."

Robert spent a restless night. He felt that he had still not got his land legs back. The bed was swaying as if he were still aboard the ferry. Beside him, Deirdre was quite still and said nothing; but he knew that she was awake most of the night.

In the morning they were offered a large breakfast.

"Should see us most of the way," said Fiona.

The old woman said not a word, but made an odd little chuckling sound with her tongue against her teeth.

When Robert went to pay the bill, Hamish McReay hummed and hawed, and regretted that he had no way of coping with a credit card. When Robert took out his chequebook, Hamish agreed that yes, that would be all right.

"But why not wait till tomorrow morning? I'm thinking that then we might offer ye the two nights free of charge."

"But that's ridiculous."

"We'd be greatly beholden to ye."

"I'm afraid we have to be on our way. Right now."

Hamish took the cheque but pushed it away from him along the bar as if not taking it seriously. He made no effort to help Robert and Fiona as they took their two cases out to the car, but stood in the doorway of the inn watching them sceptically.

They settled themselves into their usual positions in the car, and Robert put the key into the ignition automatically, as he had done a thousand times before.

There was no response. Not a whisper from the engine.

The car refused to start.

Robert swore, and tried again. At last he got out and lifted the bonnet. Oil, water, points, fuses: everything seemed normal. After twenty frustrating minutes, he dug his mobile phone out and brought up the breakdown service number.

There was no response from the phone, either. They must be in a dead spot.

Resentfully Robert strode back to the inn, where Hamish was still standing in the doorway.

"May I use your phone?"

Hamish stood aside and waved his hand towards a shelf within a cramped alcove.

A cheerful voice took Robert's policy number and said, even more cheerfully, that there might be a slight delay because of his distance from one of their contract garages, but somebody would be on his way as soon as possible.

Robert stormed back to the car. He was damned if they would go back and wait in the inn, with Hamish McReay smirking at their discomfiture. Rather than that, they could fill in time by going to see where Calum lay. A hundred yards down the hill Robert could see the little church, and it would obviously be possible from there to see when the breakdown man arrived at the inn.

"Since we've got to fill in the time," he snapped, "let's go and visit the bloody man who brought us here."

They walked down to the squat little building, with its one tiny bell in its small cage on the roof. It might have been a scaled-down replica of one of Telford's austere "Parliamentary" churches. There was a scattering of graves in the churchyard, with a few little pots of fresh flowers in front of the headstones, and grass which had been neatly trimmed. Robert checked that they could indeed see the Volvo from here, and then tried the church door. It squeaked open, and they went in.

The interior was cold in spite of the warmth of the morning outside. The walls were a plain, chill white, the backs of the pews stiffly upright. A board displayed lopsided numbers of last week's hymns. Against the north wall was what looked like a small stone coffin, with a child's name and date of death on it. Facing it from the south wall was a larger tomb, but this one was incongruously in heavy wood, pock-marked with knots.

The three of them stared down at the faded paint that formed a succession of red and green stripes across the lid, like a crude representation of straps holding a cabin trunk together.

Behind them a peevish, reedy voice said: "I suppose you've come for a cheap thrill?"

The minister was a short man with narrow shoulders and a narrow face. His pursed lips were tightening as if to deliver a bitter sermon right here and now.

"Our car has broken down," said Robert, "and we're stuck here until someone comes to fix it. We're simply filling in time."

"Hm. You know this accursed man's reputation?"

"We know his music. Actually, we've played some of it. Variations on one of his fiddle themes."

"May God forgive you." The minister's sallow cheeks were puckered with loathing as he stared at the strange wooden sarcophagus. "The creature should never have been laid to rest here. If he *does* rest." He drew a deep, shuddering breath. "Like his devilish master, he should have been forbidden the solace of a consecrated place."

"His master?" whispered Fiona, puzzled.

"The devil Paganini. A wanderer himself – a poisonous visitor to Scotland in the 1830s, making hideous discord in his music across the land and in the minds of his listeners."

"Paganini did develop some rather startling harmonics in his playing," Robert agreed, "but nowadays we take them for granted, and—"

"We take too many evils for granted. And allow too many disciples of the Devil to indulge in their wicked orgies."

"Even Paganini was forgiven in the end, and duly reburied in—"

"Forgiven by his acolytes, themselves the servants of evil. But Calum of the Clachan was never known even to *seek* forgiveness. He lived only for his music. Or one might say he lived *on* it. Wandering from shameless town to innocent village, indulging in his wild flights, urging people on to dance themselves into perdition. They speak of at least three women who danced themselves to death – and he fed on them. His music fed on them, and kept him alive."

"I take it," said Robert sardonically, "that you won't be having any performances in the church here, in connection with Calum's Night?"

"I'll have no such blasphemy in this place." The minister glanced apprehensively at the wooden tomb. "I would never risk letting them get so . . . so close. *You* ought not to be so close if you've come to take part in their obscenities."

"We came only out of curiosity, and to find a bed for the night." It must, thought Robert, be awkward for the minister of a parish as small and inbred as this to be at odds with the locals. "Look," he ventured, "if you disapprove so strongly of their little annual festivity, aren't you in a position to condemn it from your pulpit?"

"I have learned to turn a blind eye and a deaf ear to what goes on just this one night of the year." The reediness of the priest's voice became a shrill lament. "All the rest of the year, they come to church meekly enough. Just that there's the one night a year, one night in honour of . . ." He stopped, his breathing shaking his body . . . "Nay, in *dishonour* . . ." He held out shaking hands towards the woodwork, but did not touch it. "Something evil has for too long infested that box. Gone on living when it ought to have died long ago."

"You don't really believe in—"

"I pray to believe only in what is right." The minister was visibly trying to control himself. "You say you are musicians. And you will be playing for him tonight?"

"Certainly not. We've got bogged down for an hour or two, but—"

"You have let yourself be trapped." Walking away, the priest turned at the doorway. "I shall pray for you." He did not sound optimistic.

*   *   *

They walked back up the slope and reluctantly went back into the inn, where the old woman served them coffee and biscuits while Hamish McReay polished the bar counter and checked his pumps at a self-satisfied, leisurely pace.

"This isn't good enough. What do we pay these breakdown people for?" Robert drained his coffee and went to the phone again.

This time the response was less cheerful. There had been an unusual number of accidents that morning, and the garage nearest to Kirkshiel had had trouble with their breakdown vehicle. "And" – the voice grew wary and uncomfortable – "one of the men there says something about not fancying anything in Kirkshiel today. Tomorrow should be all right, but today . . . well, there's something about it that people round there don't fancy."

"This is ridiculous. The weather's perfectly reasonable. No problems. Can't you call somebody else in?"

"I've done my best. But there's just something odd about that place. I do assure you that we'll have organized something by tomorrow."

Fiona and Deirdre looked up at Robert as he came back. Even without uttering a single question their faces were as unoptimistic as the minister's had been.

"Tomorrow!" Robert raged. "Everthing can be fixed tomorrow, but for some bloody stupid reason not today."

"Your car will start in the morning." Hamish was beginning to polish an array of glasses. "Have nae fear. And now" – he puffed breath onto a glass and rubbed away – "ye'll have to stay another night. Now ye'll be playing for Calum's Night. Which is as it should be."

"I've a damn good mind to start walking. It can't be that many miles to—"

"Daddy," said Fiona very quietly, "I don't think they'd let us."

"What d'you mean? Who's to stop us?"

"In any case," said Deirdre, "we're not going to walk away and leave our instruments. Not even just to go for a stroll."

"Your car will start in the morning," said Hamish again.

There was nothing for it. With a bad grace Robert accepted that they would have to eat lunch here, and somehow pass away the hours of the afternoon. And then?

It was an excellent lunch, but he had difficulty in forcing down each mouthful. His wife and daughter ate slowly, but seemed to appreciate the food. As they were finishing, Deirdre said:

"We can't just sit here and sulk. And somehow I don't fancy an afternoon nap."

"I wouldn't sleep a wink," Robert agreed ruefully.

"So why don't we bring the instruments in, and rehearse? We're not going to have as much time as we'd like when we do reach Hexham, so why not practise now?"

In such surroundings, and in such a situation, Robert felt in no mood to tackle the music he loved. But Deirdre was right. Practising would soon draw them in, and would do them good.

They brought the violin, the clarsach and the flute in. Still wearing that infuriatingly complacent grin, Hamish McReay was holding open a door which led to the back of the inn. Here they found a room more spacious than the general layout of the inn would have led one to guess at. At one end was a small, shallow platform with three chairs already in place.

Deirdre had been right. Within fifteen minutes they were absorbed in the problems and nuances of the programme that they had planned for Hexham. With one exception. There was an instinctive, unspoken agreement between them that the *Variations on a Theme by Calum of the Clachan* should not be played this afternoon.

When they stopped, Hamish was ready with a beer and the orange-and-lemonade that the women fancied, and which they needed after their exertions.

"And ye'll be glad of a wee rest before the commemoration begins."

"Look, after all this, you don't imagine we're going to be forced into playing at this shindig of yours?"

"What else would ye be doing with your evening?"

"Dammit, I won't be pressured."

Deirdre was beside him, speaking close to his left ear. "Robert, my love, it's too late. We should never have come here. But now we're here, we have to go through with this."

People began gathering early in the evening. At first they might have been no more than regulars dropping in for a dram on their way home from work. But they were unusually silent, saving their energies, glancing now and then at the door to the back room. The younger folk looked much as you would expect teenagers at a disco to look. But older men and women who came shuffling awkwardly in had the glazed expressions of folk in a hypnotic trance.

At last Hamish McReay opened the door, and the three musicians took their places on the low platform. At the other end of the room, trestle tables were loaded with food.

Robert gave the lead, and the trio went into a slip-jig of Irish origins. Then a lilting strathspey. A young couple danced lightly, laughing. One elderly woman began quietly clapping in time.

It was going to be all right, after all. A chore, to be dealt with and dismissed. A dull little local hop, nothing more. Get it over with, have a good night's sleep, and tomorrow morning start out early for Hexham.

As they played on, the tempo quickened. Robert found he was playing in dance rhythms that he had never come across before. His fingers kept escaping from his control, indulging themselves in fiendish double-stopping and wild swoops down a scale which had never existed before. Over and over again in the middle of a whirling passage the bow would strike the same two harsh, mocking notes of the deadly augmented fourth – the forbidden tritone interval which in medieval times had been condemned as the creation of the Devil. Some spirit was working within his head and within his fingers, stabbing out weird harmonics, double-stopping, and savage *col legno* bouncing off the back of the bow across the strings. And Deirdre's cascades of accompanying chords became a whirlpool lashing all of them into a fury. The mellow tones of Fiona's flute were becoming an eldritch shriek.

The dancers swung more wildly and laughed more loudly. The older people, still seated, began stamping their feet, stamping faster and faster to urge the players on.

Suddenly the clarsach, almost drowned in the racket, gave up. Deirdre sat doubled up, shaking her head, refusing to go on.

Robert and Fiona flung aggressive arpeggios and devilish trills at each other, like jazz musicians in a cutting session, until a roar and clatter of applause brought them to a brief halt.

"He's back again," said an elderly man at the back of the room, "just the way he said he'd be. Coming back to life."

Robert started playing again, but after two exuberant reels he found himself alone. Fiona had stopped playing, to run out onto the floor and into the arms of one of the dancers, one of those boys as dark as a gypsy. They had made a dizzying three turns of the floor when Deirdre roused herself and ran out to pull them apart. Clinging to Fiona, she looked up at her husband.

"Robert, you must stop now."

Robert was aware of a mutter of discontent, but he finished a phrase with a sustained trill and then, putting his fiddle down and demonstrating to the audience how his damp fingers needed drying out, he began wiping them on a handkerchief as he marched off towards the bar.

Several men were offering him drink. With sweat dripping from his forehead, he desperately needed a couple of pints, yet even before he was halfway through the first one he felt the world floating around him in strange swathes of sound – sound that he could somehow see rather than hear. And behind it laughter, triumphant laughter: not reassuring laughter, but something foul and derisive.

Voices muttered close to him, some flattering, some suspicious. "Better than that feeble laddie we had to make do wi' last year . . . Would ye not be agreeing that's the true voice, truer this time? . . . Will he be cheatin' on us? . . ."

A middle-aged man to Robert's left said: "Ye'll be another who'll nae come back?"

"Well, we do have a pretty full programme, this year and next."

"But if ye dinna come back, there'll be something missing from that programme. Something . . . or somebody. He has no patience with those who won't keep him alive." The man leaned closer, in the manner of so many public-bar soaks determined to confide a cherished belief at length. "Just before his death, Calum of the Clachan said that he'd do no more moving on. But somebody must come each year to keep the tradition alive. Let them come, and he'd be here to guide their fingers. He'd be ready to wake and take part again."

Robert was engulfed in an overpowering weariness. Somebody – Deirdre and Fiona, or Hamish McReay? – must have carried him upstairs. He knew nothing further until the morning, when he turned over with a groan to find the space beside him empty. Gingerly he eased himself out of bed and peered out of the little window.

Deirdre was just lifting her clarsach into the back of the Volvo. She went round to slide into the driver's seat, and he heard the familiar purr of the car starting, without any trouble. Then she was driving slowly down towards the church.

Deirdre took the clarsach carefully out of the car and carried it into the church and along towards the resting place of Calum of the Clachan. For a moment she felt faint. The sagging woodwork and pallid colours had been rejuvenated. The wood shone as if newly polished. The bands of red and green were bright as if someone overnight had vigorously repainted them.

Still, she had to do what she had come to do. She settled herself on the end of a pew, bent over her clarsach, and began a keening, crooning lullaby from the far reaches of the Hebrides. The gentleness of the harp became slowly louder, the strings fighting against her fingers, while a draught whistling round the church interior became a mocking laugh. She fought down the fear, and went on singing and playing until an indignant voice attacked her from behind.

"Isn't it enough that you defile the ears of my flock with your abominations of yestereve? Now you bring those blasphemies into my church? You're playing that infernal thing a lullaby!"

"I was attempting an exorcism."

The minister's bitter laugh was as derisive as that other whistling laughter. The echoes of Calum of the Clachan refused to die, but would go on dancing, skittering in and out of the columns, through the dusty old organ pipes, vibrating in the windows. And the minister was staring hopelessly at the colours on the tomb. Would they fade over the coming year, until someone was forced to play the music of madness and bring them back to life?

"You've never thought," Deirdre said, "of . . . well, opening up the coffin? Just to see whether . . ." She faltered, unsure of what she was daring to suggest and what he, in the depths of his soul, was trying to believe or disbelieve.

"I'll not be the one to disturb it." That was all he had to say.

Now all Deirdre wanted to do was escape. Out into the open air, staggering under the weight of the harp, putting it back in the car, driving back to where Robert and Fiona were waiting for her.

"What on earth have you been doing?" Robert demanded.

"I was told to get out."

"By the minister? He wouldn't be best pleased by having heathen music played in his church."

"No, not him. It was . . . *something* . . . in the building itself. In that tomb. I was told to get out," she repeated. "I was *driven* out. And yet," she faltered, "one of us is wanted back."

As they were about to leave, Hamish McReay came out, persistently smiling. "I told you the car would start in the morning." And he took Robert's cheque from his pocket, tore it into shreds, and tossed them into the morning breeze. "Until next year, then."

"There's no way we're coming back here," Robert assured him.

But his voice was as shaky as his hands. He looked down at them and wondered how he could have played so vigorously last night, and how he would ever be able to play again. They were somehow no longer his hands. They were drained of all colour save for a pattern of blue veins bulging up through the pale skin. He was drained; utterly drained.

Deirdre said: "Robert, please. Let me drive. You don't look up to it."

He had no strength to argue.

As they drove away from Kirkshiel, Robert was silent for a long time, watching the road ahead just as closely as if he were driving. This must be the right road, yet it felt as if they were in an utterly alien land, not knowing what was waiting for them round the next corner.

The first time he spoke was to suggest that they stop for a breather on the edge of a tiny, weed-choked lochan. Deirdre took a bottle of spring water out of the cooler bag and some plastic cups out of the glove compartment. It was a routine they had gone through so many times before. Yet it was still alien, each movement an effort.

Behind them, Fiona had taken her flute out. She started playing something which caused Robert to spill some of his drink on to his right knee.

"Stop that! What on earth is it?"

"I don't know. It just came to me, the way it did the other day. Was given to me," she added suddenly.

Deirdre, very calm and self-controlled, said: "Fiona, do put it out of your mind."

"I'm not sure that I can."

At last they crossed the Cheviot Hills and headed for Hexham. Parking in front of their hotel, Deirdre looked up at the glowing façade of the abbey.

"We made it." Robert spoke as if they had been pursued by wild Highlanders and then Border reivers all the way. "Thank God we're away from that dreadful place." He was trying to wrench himself back to normality, even to make a wry joke of it. "At any rate that's one engagement we won't be playing again."

"True, they're not really expecting you back there, Daddy. But one of us has to go back next year."

He turned to look into Fiona's eyes, which somehow he could no longer recognize. Through their ivory opaqueness shone an eager, intense challenge.

"You're not suggesting—"

"I shall go back next year. I have to."

"That's crazy. There's no way I'd let you."

"It's no good, Daddy. Someone has to keep the music pulsating in his heart."

"This is obscene. You've let that place get on your nerves."

His wife touched his arm. "Robert, I don't think you'll be able to stop her."

"One of us has to go back," intoned Fiona. "And it has to be me."

"Over my dead body."

Deirdre smiled a smile of infinite love and yet of infinite sadness, a fateful knowledge coming like grey mist out of the western waters.

"Dearest Robert, I'm afraid that's how it may well be."

MANLY WADE WELLMAN

Chastel

MANLY WADE WELLMAN, who died in 1986, was born in the village of Kamundongo in Portuguese West Africa. Following several childhood visits to London, he settled in the United States where he worked as a reporter before quitting his job in 1930 to write fiction full-time.

He was one of the most prolific contributors to the pulp magazines of the 1930s and 1940s, and his tales of horror, fantasy, science fiction, crime and adventure graced the pages of such legendary titles as *Weird Tales, Strange Stories, Wonder Stories, Astounding Stories* and *Unknown*, to name only a few.

He wrote more than seventy-five books in all genres, including mainstream novels and works on the American Civil War. He twice won the World Fantasy Award, and some of his best stories are collected in *Who Fears the Devil?, Worse Things Waiting, Lonely Vigils* and *The Valley So Low*. More recently, Night Shade Books has collected all Wellman's short fantasy fiction in a series of five uniform hardcover editions published under the umbrella title *The Selected Stories of Manly Wade Wellman*.

In 'Chastel', two of Wellman's best-known characters, Lee Cobbett and Judge Keith Hilary Pursuivant, join forces to battle an age-old seductress. The author revealed that the novella was based on fact:

"The Connecticut setting for a vampire outbreak harks back to long-ago Connecticut papers, which told of such things apparently happening. It's in the books cited here. Incidentally, both the poems I quote are actual ones.

"I've puzzled over the one from Grant's odd book, have never seen it anywhere else, and have never found anyone who had heard of it. Like Pursuivant here, I give myself to wonder if it isn't a fake antique, like Clark Saunders's better-known vampire poem to be found in Montague Summers."

"THEN YOU WON'T LET Count Dracula rest in his tomb?" inquired Lee Cobbett, his square face creasing with a grin.

Five of them sat in the parlor of Judge Keith Hilary Pursuivant's hotel suite on Central Park West. The Judge lounged in an armchair, a wineglass in his big old hand. On this, his eighty-seventh birthday, his blue eyes were clear, penetrating. His once tawny hair and mustache had gone blizzard-white, but both grew thick, and his square face showed rosy. In his tailored blue leisure suit, he still looked powerfully deep-chested and broad-shouldered.

Blocky Lee Cobbett wore jacket and slacks almost as brown as his face. Next to him sat Laurel Parcher, small and young and cinnamon-haired. The others were natty Phil Drumm the summer theater producer, and Isobel Arrington from a wire press service. She was blond, expensively dressed, she smoked a dark cigarette with a white tip. Her pen scribbled swiftly.

"Dracula's as much alive as Sherlock Holmes," argued Drumm. "All the revivals of the play, all the films—"

"Your musical should wake the dead, anyway," said Cobbett, drinking. "What's your main number, Phil? 'Garlic Time?' 'Gory, Gory Hallelujah?'"

"Let's have Christian charity here, Lee," Pursuivant came to Drumm's rescue. "Anyway, Miss Arrington came to interview me. Pour her some wine and let me try to answer her questions."

"I'm interested in Mr Cobbett's remarks," said Isobel Arrington, her voice deliberately throaty. "He's an authority on the super-natural."

"Well, perhaps," admitted Cobbett, "and Miss Parcher has had some experiences. But Judge Pursuivant is the true authority, the author of *Vampiricon*."

"I've read it, in paperback," said Isobel Arrington. "Phil, it mentions a vampire belief up in Connecticut, where you're having your show. What's that town again?"

"Deslow," he told her. "We're making a wonderful old stone barn into a theater. I've invited Lee and Miss Parcher to visit."

She looked at Drumm. "Is Deslow a resort town?"

"Not yet, but maybe the show will bring tourists. In Deslow, up to now, peace and quiet is the chief business. If you drop your shoe, everybody in town will think somebody's blowing the safe."

"Deslow's not far from Jewett City," observed Pursuivant. "There were vampires there about a century and a quarter ago. A family named Ray was afflicted. And to the east, in Rhode Island, there was a lively vampire folklore in recent years."

"Let's leave Rhode Island to H. P. Lovecraft's imitators," suggested Cobbett. "What do you call your show, Phil?"

"*The Land Beyond the Forest*," said Drumm. "We're casting it now. Using locals in bit parts. But we have Gonda Chastel to play Dracula's countess."

"I never knew that Dracula had a countess," said Laurel Parcher.

"There was a stage star named Chastel, long ago when I was young," said Pursuivant. "Just the one name – Chastel."

"Gonda's her daughter, and a year or so ago Gonda came to live in Deslow," Drumm told them. "Her mother's buried there. Gonda has invested in our production."

"Is that why she has a part in it?" asked Isobel Arrington.

"She has a part in it because she's beautiful and gifted," replied Drumm, rather stuffily. "Old people say she's the very picture of her mother. Speaking of pictures, here are some to prove it."

He offered two glossy prints to Isobel Arrington, who murmured "Very sweet," and passed them to Laurel Parcher. Cobbett leaned to see.

One picture seemed copied from an older one. It showed a woman who stood with unconscious stateliness, in a gracefully draped robe with a tiara binding her rich flow of dark hair. The other picture was of a woman in fashionable evening dress, her hair ordered in modern fashion, with a face strikingly like that of the woman in the other photograph.

"Oh, she's lovely," said Laurel. "Isn't she, Lee?"

"Isn't she?" echoed Drumm.

"Magnificent," said Cobbett, handing the pictures to Pursuivant, who studied them gravely.

"Chastel was in Richmond, just after the First World War," he said slowly. "A dazzling Lady Macbeth. I was in love with her. Everyone was."

"Did you tell her you loved her?" asked Laurel.

"Yes. We had supper together, twice. Then she went ahead with her tour, and I sailed to England and studied at Oxford. I never saw her again, but she's more or less why I never married."

Silence a moment. Then: "*The Land Beyond the Forest*," Laurel repeated. "Isn't there a book called that?"

"There is indeed, my child," said the Judge. "By Emily de Laszowska Gerard. About Transylvania, where Dracula came from."

"That's why we use the title, that's what Transylvania means," put in Drumm. "It's all right, the book's out of copyright. But I'm surprised to find someone who's heard of it."

"I'll protect your guilty secret, Phil," promised Isobel Arrington. "What's over there in your window, Judge?"

Pursuivant turned to look. "Whatever it is," he said, "it's not Peter Pan."

Cobbett sprang up and ran toward the half-draped window. A silhouette with head and shoulders hung in the June night. He had a glimpse of a face, rich-mouthed, with bright eyes. Then it was gone. Laurel had hurried up behind him. He hoisted the window sash and leaned out.

Nothing. The street was fourteen stories down. The lights of moving cars crawled distantly. The wall below was course after course of dull brick, with recesses of other windows to right and left, below, above. Cobbett studied the wall, his hands braced on the sill.

"Be careful, Lee," Laurel's voice besought him.

He came back to face the others. "Nobody out there," he said evenly. "Nobody could have been. It's just a wall – nothing to hang to. Even that sill would be tricky to stand on."

"But I saw something, and so did Judge Pursuivant," said Isobel Arrington, the cigarette trembling in her fingers.

"So did I," said Cobbett. "Didn't you, Laurel?"

"Only a face."

Isobel Arrington was calm again. "If it's a trick, Phil, you played a good one. But don't expect me to put it in my story."

Drumm shook his head nervously. "I didn't play any trick, I swear."

"Don't try this on old friends," she jabbed at him. "First those pictures, then whatever was up against the glass. I'll use the pictures, but I won't write that a weird vision presided over this birthday party."

"How about a drink all around?" suggested Pursuivant.

He poured for them. Isobel Arrington wrote down answers to more questions, then said she must go. Drumm rose to escort her. "You'll be at Deslow tomorrow, Lee?" he asked.

"And Laurel, too. You said we could find quarters there."

"The Mapletree's a good auto court," said Drumm. "I've already reserved cabins for the two of you."

"On the spur of the moment," said Pursuivant suddenly, "I think I'll come along, if there's space for me."

"I'll check it out for you, Judge," said Drumm.

He departed with Isobel Arrington. Cobbett spoke to Pursuivant. "Isn't that rather offhand?" he asked. "Deciding to come with us?"

"I was thinking about Chastel." Pursuivant smiled gently. "About making a pilgrimage to her grave."

"We'll drive up about nine tomorrow morning."

"I'll be ready, Lee."

Cobbett and Laurel, too, went out. They walked down a flight of stairs to the floor below, where both their rooms were located. "Do you think Phil Drumm rigged up that illusion for us?" asked Cobbett.

"If he did, he used the face of that actress, Chastel."

He glanced keenly at her. "You saw that."

"I thought I did, and so did you."

They kissed goodnight at the door to her room.

Pursuivant was ready next morning when Cobbett knocked. He had only one suitcase and a thick, brown-blotched malacca cane, banded with silver below its curved handle.

"I'm taking only a few necessaries, I'll buy socks and such things in Deslow if we stay more than a couple of days," he said. "No, don't carry it for me, I'm quite capable."

When they reached the hotel garage, Laurel was putting her luggage in the trunk of Cobbett's black sedan. Judge Pursuivant declined the front seat beside Cobbett, held the door for Laurel to get in, and sat in the rear. They rolled out into bright June sunlight.

Cobbett drove them east on Interstate 95, mile after mile along the Connecticut shore, past service stations, markets, sandwich shops. Now and then they glimpsed Long Island Sound to the right. At toll gates, Cobbett threw quarters into hoppers and drove on.

"New Rochelle to Port Chester," Laurel half chanted, "Norwalk, Bridgeport, Stratford—"

"Where, in 1851, devils plagued a minister's home," put in Pursuivant.

"The names make a poem," said Laurel.

"You can get that effect by reading any timetable," said Cobbett. "We miss a couple of good names – Mystic and Giants Neck, though they aren't far off from our route. And Griswold – that means Gray Woods – where the Judge's book says Horace Ray was born."

"There's no Griswold on the Connecticut map anymore," said the Judge.

"Vanished?" said Laurel. "Maybe it appears at just a certain time of the day, along about sundown."

She laughed, but the Judge was grave.

"Here we'll pass by New Haven," he said. "I was at Yale here, seventy years ago."

They rolled across the Connecticut River between Old Saybrook

and Old Lyme. Outside New London, Cobbett turned them north on
State Highway 82 and, near Jewett City, took a two-lane road that
brought them into Deslow, not long after noon.

There were pleasant clapboard cottages among elm trees and
flower beds. Main Street had bright shops with, farther along, the
belfry of a sturdy old church. Cobbett drove them to a sign saying
MAPLETREE COURT. A row of cabins faced along a cement-floored
colonnade, their fronts painted white with blue doors and window
frames. In the office, Phil Drumm stood at the desk, talking to the
plump proprietress.

"Welcome home," he greeted them. "Judge, I was asking Mrs
Simpson here to reserve you a cabin."

"At the far end of the row, sir," the lady said. "I'd have put you
next to your two friends, but so many theater folks have already
moved in."

"Long ago I learned to be happy with any shelter," the Judge
assured her.

They saw Laurel to her cabin and put her suitcases inside, then
walked to the farthest cabin where Pursuivant would stay. Finally
Drumm followed Cobbett to the space next to Laurel's. Inside,
Cobbett produced a fifth of bourbon from his briefcase. Drumm
trotted away to fetch ice. Pursuivant came to join them.

"It's good of you to look after us," Cobbett said to Drumm above
his glass.

"Oh, I'll get my own back," Drumm assured him. "The Judge and
you, distinguished folklore experts – I'll have you in all the papers."

"Whatever you like," said Cobbett. "Let's have lunch, as soon as
Laurel is freshened up."

The four ate crab cakes and flounder at a little restaurant while
Drumm talked about *The Land Beyond the Forest*. He had signed the
minor film star Caspar Merrick to play Dracula. "He has a fine
baritone singing voice," said Drumm. "He'll be at afternoon rehearsal."

"And Gonda Chastel?" inquired Pursuivant, buttering a roll.

"She'll be there tonight." Drumm sounded happy about that.
"This afternoon's mostly for bits and chorus numbers. I'm directing
as well as producing." They finished their lunch, and Drumm rose.
"If you're not tired, come see our theater."

It was only a short walk through town to the converted barn.
Cobbett judged it had been built in Colonial times, with a recent roof
of composition tile, but with walls of stubborn, brown-gray New
England stone. Across a narrow side street stood the old white
church, with a hedge-bordered cemetery.

"Quaint, that old burying ground," commented Drumm. "Nobody's spaded under there now, there's a modern cemetery on the far side, but Chastel's tomb is there. Quite a picturesque one."

"I'd like to see it," said Pursuivant, leaning on his silver-banded cane.

The barn's interior was set with rows of folding chairs, enough for several hundred spectators. On a stage at the far end, workmen moved here and there under lights. Drumm led his guests up steps at the side.

High in the loft, catwalks zigzagged and a dark curtain hung like a broad guillotine blade. Drumm pointed out canvas flats, painted to resemble grim castle walls. Pursuivant nodded and questioned.

"I'm no authority on what you might find in Transylvania," he said, "but this looks convincing."

A man walked from the wings toward them. "Hello, Caspar," Drumm greeted him. "I want you to meet Judge Pursuivant and Lee Cobbett. And Miss Laurel Parcher, of course." He gestured the introductions. "This is Mr Caspar Merrick, our Count Dracula."

Merrick was elegantly tall, handsome, with carefully groomed black hair. Sweepingly he bowed above Laurel's hand and smiled at them all. "Judge Pursuivant's writings I know, of course," he said richly. "I read what I can about vampires, inasmuch as I'm to be one."

"Places for the Delusion number!" called a stage manager.

Cobbett, Pursuivant and Laurel went down the steps and sat on chairs. Eight men and eight girls hurried into view, dressed in knockabout summer clothes. Someone struck chords on a piano, Drumm gestured importantly, and the chorus sang. Merritt, coming downstage, took solo on a verse. All joined in the refrain. Then Drumm made them sing it over again.

After that, two comedians made much of confusing the words vampire and empire. Cobbett found it tedious. He excused himself to his companions and strolled out and across to the old, tree-crowded churchyard.

The gravestones bore interesting epitaphs: not only the familiar PAUSE O STRANGER PASSING BY/ AS YOU ARE NOW SO ONCE WAS I, and A BUD ON EARTH TO BLOOM IN HEAVEN, but several of more originality. One bewailed a man who, since he had been lost at sea, could hardly have been there at all. Another bore, beneath a bat-winged face, the declaration DEATH PAYS ALL DEBTS and the date 1907, which Cobbett associated with a financial panic.

Toward the center of the graveyard, under a drooping willow, stood a shedlike structure of heavy granite blocks. Cobbett picked his way to the door of heavy grillwork, which was fastened with a rusty padlock the size of a sardine can. On the lintel were strongly carved letters: CHASTEL.

Here, then, was the tomb of the stage beauty Pursuivant remembered so romantically. Cobbett peered through the bars.

It was murkily dusty in there. The floor was coarsely flagged, and among sooty shadows at the rear stood a sort of stone chest that must contain the body. Cobbett turned and went back to the theater. Inside, piano music rang wildly and the people of the chorus desperately rehearsed what must be meant for a folk dance.

"Oh, it's exciting," said Laurel as Cobbett sat down beside her. "Where have you been?"

"Visiting the tomb of Chastel."

"Chastel?" echoed Pursuivant. "I must see that tomb."

Songs and dance ensembles went on. In the midst of them, a brisk reporter from Hartford appeared, to interview Pursuivant and Cobbett. At last Drumm resoundingly dismissed the players on stage and joined his guests.

"Principals rehearse at eight o'clock," he announced. "Gonda Chastel will be here, she'll want to meet you. Could I count on you then?"

"Count on me, at least," said Pursuivant. "Just now, I feel like resting before dinner, and so, I think, does Laurel here."

"Yes, I'd like to lie down for a little," said Laurel.

"Why don't we all meet for dinner at the place where we had lunch?" said Cobbett. "You come too, Phil."

"Thanks, I have a date with some backers from New London."

It was half-past five when they went out.

Cobbett went to his quarters, stretched out on the bed, and gave himself to thought.

He hadn't come to Deslow because of this musical interpretation of the Dracula legend. Laurel had come because he was coming, and Pursuivant on a sudden impulse that might have been more than a wish to visit the grave of Chastel. But Cobbett was here because this, he knew, had been vampire country, maybe still was vampire country.

He remembered the story in Pursuivant's book about vampires at Jewett City, as reported in the Norwich *Courier* for 1854. Horace Ray, from the now vanished town of Griswold, had died of a "wasting disease." Thereafter his oldest son, then his second son had also gone to their graves. When a third son sickened, friends and relatives dug up Horace Ray and the two dead brothers and burned the bodies in a roaring fire. The surviving son got well. And something like that had happened in Exeter, near Providence in Rhode Island. Very well, why organize and present the Dracula musical here in Deslow, so near those places?

Cobbett had met Phil Drumm in the South the year before, knew him for a brilliant if erratic producer, who relished tales of devils and the dead who walk by night. Drumm might have known enough stage magic to have rigged that seeming appearance at Pursuivant's window in New York. That is, if indeed it was only a seeming appearance, not a real face. Might it have been real, a manifestation of the unreal? Cobbett had seen enough of what people dismissed as unreal, impossible, to wonder.

A soft knock came at the door. It was Laurel. She wore green slacks, a green jacket, and she smiled, as always, at sight of Cobbett's face. They sought Pursuivant's cabin. A note on the door said: MEET ME AT THE CAFÉ.

When they entered there, Pursuivant hailed them from the kitchen door. "Dinner's ready," he hailed them. "I've been supervising in person, and I paid well for the privilege."

A waiter brought a laden tray. He arranged platters of red-drenched spaghetti and bowls of salad on a table. Pursuivant himself sprinkled Parmesan cheese. "No salt or pepper," he warned. "I seasoned it myself, and you can take my word it's exactly right."

Cobbett poured red wine into glasses. Laurel took a forkful of spaghetti. "Delicious," she cried. "What's in it, Judge?"

"Not only ground beef and tomatoes and onions and garlic," replied Pursuivant. "I added marjoram and green pepper and chile and thyme and bay leaf and oregano and parsley and a couple of other important ingredients. And I also minced in some Italian sausage."

Cobbett, too, ate with enthusiastic appetite. "I won't order any dessert," he declared. "I want to keep the taste of this in my mouth."

"There's more in the kitchen for dessert if you want it," the Judge assured him. "But here, I have a couple of keepsakes for you."

He handed each of them a small, silvery object. Cobbett examined his. It was smoothly wrapped in foil. He wondered if it was a nutmeat.

"You have pockets, I perceive," the Judge said. "Put those into them. And don't open them, or my wish for you won't come true."

When they had finished eating, a full moon had begun to rise in the darkening sky. They headed for the theater.

A number of visitors sat in the chairs and the stage lights looked bright. Drumm stood beside the piano, talking to two plump men in summer business suits. As Pursuivant and the others came down the aisle, Drumm eagerly beckoned them and introduced them to his companions, the financial backers with whom he had taken dinner.

"We're very much interested," said one. "This vampire legend intrigues anyone, if you forget that a vampire's motivation is simply nourishment."

"No, something more than that," offered Pursuivant. "A social motivation."

"Social motivation," repeated the other backer.

"A vampire wants company of its own kind. A victim infected becomes a vampire, too, and an associate. Otherwise the original vampire would be a disconsolate loner."

"There's a lot in what you say," said Drumm, impressed.

After that there was financial talk, something in which Cobbett could not intelligently join. Then someone else approached, and both the backers stared.

It was a tall, supremely graceful woman with red-lighted black hair in a bun at her nape, a woman of impressive figure and assurance. She wore a sweeping blue dress, fitted to her slim waist, with a frill-edged neckline. Her arms were bare and white and sweetly turned, with jeweled bracelets on them. Drumm almost ran to bring her close to the group.

"Gonda Chastel," he said, half-prayerfully. "Gonda, you'll want to meet these people."

The two backers stuttered admiringly at her. Pursuivant bowed and Laurel smiled. Gonda Chastel gave Cobbett her slim, cool hand. "You know so much about this thing we're trying to do here," she said, in a voice like cream.

Drumm watched them. His face looked plaintive.

"Judge Pursuivant has taught me a lot, Miss Chastel," said Cobbett. "He'll tell you that once he knew your mother."

"I remember her, not very clearly," said Gonda Chastel. "She died when I was just a little thing, thirty years ago. And I followed her here, now I make my home here."

"You look very like her," said Pursuivant.

"I'm proud to be like my mother in any way," she smiled at them. She could be overwhelming, Cobbett told himself.

"And Miss Parcher," went on Gonda Chastel, turning toward Laurel. "What a little presence she is. She should be in our show – I don't know what part, but she should." She smiled dazzlingly. "Now then, Phil wants me on stage."

"Knock-at-the-door number, Gonda," said Drumm.

Gracefully she mounted the steps. The piano sounded, and she sang. It was the best song, felt Cobbett, that he had heard so far in the rehearsals. "Are they seeking for a shelter from the night?" Gonda Chastel sang richly. Caspar Merritt entered, to join in a recitative. Then the chorus streamed on, singing somewhat shrilly.

Pursuivant and Laurel had sat down. Cobbett strode back up the aisle and out under a moon that rained silver-blue light.

He found his way to the churchyard. The trees that had offered pleasant afternoon shade now made a dubious darkness. He walked underneath branches that seemed to lower like hovering wings as he approached the tomb structure at the center.

The barred door that had been massively locked now stood open. He peered into the gloom within. After a moment he stepped across the threshold upon the flagged floor.

He had to grope, with one hand upon the rough wall. At last he almost stumbled upon the great stone chest at the rear.

It, too, was flung open, its lid heaved back against the wall.

There was, of course, complete darkness within it. He flicked on his cigar lighter. The flame showed him the inside of the stone coffer, solidly made and about ten feet long. Its sides of gray marble were snugly fitted. Inside lay a coffin of rich dark wood with silver fittings and here, yet again, was an open lid.

Bending close to the smudged silk lining, Cobbett seemed to catch an odor of stuffy sharpness, like dried herbs. He snapped off his light and frowned in the dark. Then he groped back to the door, emerged into the open, and headed for the theater again.

"Mr Cobbett," said the beautiful voice of Gonda Chastel.

She stood at the graveyard's edge, beside a sagging willow. She was almost as tall as he. Her eyes glowed in the moonlight.

"You came to find the truth about my mother," she half-accused.

"I was bound to try," he replied. "Ever since I saw a certain face at a certain window of a certain New York hotel."

She stepped back from him. "You know that she's a—"

"A vampire," Cobbett finished for her. "Yes."

"I beg you to be helpful – merciful." But there was no supplication in her voice. "I already realized, long ago. That's why I live in little Deslow. I want to find a way to give her rest. Night after night, I wonder how."

"I understand that," said Cobbett.

Gonda Chastel breathed deeply. "You know all about these things. I think there's something about you that could daunt a vampire."

"If so, I don't know what it is," said Cobbett truthfully.

"Make me a solemn promise. That you won't return to her tomb, that you won't tell others what you and I know about her. I – I want to think how we two together can do something for her."

"If you wish, I'll say nothing," he promised.

Her hand clutched his.

"The cast took a five-minute break, it must be time to go to work again," she said, suddenly bright. "Let's go back and help the thing along."

They went.

Inside, the performers were gathering on stage. Drumm stared unhappily as Gonda Chastel and Cobbett came down the aisle.

Cobbett sat with Laurel and Pursuivant and listened to the rehearsal.

Adaptation from Bram Stoker's novel was free, to say the least. Dracula's eerie plottings were much hampered by his having a countess, a walking dead beauty who strove to become a spirit of good. There were some songs, in interesting minor keys. There was a dance, in which men and women leaped like kangaroos. Finally Drumm called a halt, and the performers trooped wearily to the wings.

Gonda Chastel lingered, talking to Laurel. "I wonder, my dear, if you haven't had acting experience," she said.

"Only in school entertainments down South, when I was little."

"Phil," said Gonda Chastel, "Miss Parcher is a good type, has good presence. There ought to be something for her in the show."

"You're very kind, but I'm afraid that's impossible," said Laurel, smiling.

"You may change your mind, Miss Parcher. Will you and your friends come to my house for a nightcap?"

"Thank you," said Pursuivant. "We have some notes to make, and we must make them together."

"Until tomorrow evening, then Mr Cobbett, we'll remember our agreement."

She went away toward the back of the stage. Pursuivant and Laurel walked out. Drumm hurried up the aisle and caught Cobbett's elbow.

"I saw you," he said harshly. "Saw you both as you came in."

"And we saw you, Phil. What's this about?"

"She likes you." It was half an accusation. "Fawns on you, almost."

Cobbett grinned and twitched his arm free. "What's the matter, Phil, are you in love with her?"

"Yes, God damn it, I am. I'm in love with her. She knows it but she won't let me come to her house. And you – the first time she meets you, she invites you."

"Easy does it, Phil," said Cobbett. "If it'll do you any good, I'm in love with someone else, and that takes just about all my spare time."

He hurried out to overtake his companions.

Pursuivant swung his cane almost jauntily as they returned through the moonlight to the auto court.

"What notes are you talking about, Judge?" asked Cobbett.

"I'll tell you at my quarters. What do you think of the show?"

"Perhaps I'll like it better after they've rehearsed more," said Laurel. "I don't follow it at present."

"Here and there, it strikes me as limp," added Cobbett.

They sat down in the Judge's cabin. He poured them drinks. "Now," he said, "there are certain things to recognize here. Things I more or less expected to find."

"A mystery, Judge?" asked Laurel.

"Not so much that, if I expected to find them. How far are we from Jewett City?"

"Twelve or fifteen miles as the crow flies," estimated Cobbett. "And Jewett City is where that vampire family, the Rays, lived and died."

"Died twice, you might say," nodded Pursuivant, stroking his white mustache. "Back about a century and a quarter ago. And here's what might be a matter of Ray family history. I've been thinking about Chastel, whom once I greatly admired. About her full name."

"But she had only one name, didn't she?" asked Laurel.

"On the stage she used one name, yes. So did Bernhardt, so did Duse, so later did Garbo. But all of them had full names. Now, before we went to dinner, I made two telephone calls to theatrical historians I know. To learn Chastel's full name."

"And she had a full name," prompted Cobbett.

"Indeed she did. Her full name was Chastel Ray."

Cobbett and Laurel looked at him in deep silence.

"Not apt to be just coincidence," elaborated Pursuivant. "Now then, I gave you some keepsakes today."

"Here's mine," said Cobbett, pulling the foil-wrapped bit from his shirt pocket.

"And I have mine here," said Laurel, her hand at her throat. "In a little locket I have on this chain."

"Keep it there," Pursuivant urged her. "Wear it around your neck at all times. Lee, have yours always on your person. Those are garlic cloves, and you know what they're good for. You can also guess why I cut up a lot of garlic in our spaghetti for dinner."

"You think there's a vampire here," offered Laurel.

"A specific vampire." The Judge took a deep breath into his broad chest. "Chastel. Chastel Ray."

"I believe it, too," declared Cobbett tonelessly, and Laurel nodded. Cobbett looked at the watch on his wrist.

"It's past one in the morning," he said. "Perhaps we'd all be better off if we had some sleep."

They said their good nights and Laurel and Cobbett walked to where their two doors stood side by side. Laurel put her key into the lock, but did not turn it at once. She peered across the moonlit street.

"Who's that over there?" she whispered. "Maybe I ought to say, what's that?"

Cobbett looked. "Nothing, you're just nervous. Good night, dear."

She went in and shut the door. Cobbett quickly crossed the street.

"Mr Cobbett," said the voice of Gonda Chastel.

"I wondered what you wanted, so late at night," he said, walking close to her.

She had undone her dark hair and let it flow to her shoulders. She was, Cobbett thought, as beautiful a woman as he had ever seen.

"I wanted to be sure about you," she said. "That you'd respect your promise to me, not to go into the churchyard."

"I keep my promises, Miss Chastel."

He felt a deep, hushed silence all around them. Not even the leaves rustled in the trees.

"I had hoped you wouldn't venture even this far," she went on. "You and your friends are new in town, you might tempt her specially." Her eyes burned at him. "You know I don't mean that as a compliment."

She turned to walk away. He fell into step beside her. "But you're not afraid of her," he said.

"Of my own mother?"

"She was a Ray," said Cobbett. "Each Ray sapped the blood of his kinsmen. Judge Pursuivant told me all about it."

Again the gaze of her dark, brilliant eyes. "Nothing like that has ever happened between my mother and me." She stopped, and so did he. Her slim, strong hand took him by the wrist.

"You're wise and brave," she said. "I think you may have come here for a good purpose, not just about the show."

"I try to have good purposes."

The light of the moon soaked through the overhead branches as they walked on. "Will you come to my house?" she invited.

"I'll walk to the churchyard," replied Cobbett. "I said I wouldn't go into it, but I can stand at the edge."

"Don't go in."

"I've promised that I wouldn't, Miss Chastel."

She walked back the way they had come. He followed the street on under silent elms until he reached the border of the churchyard. Moonlight flecked and spattered the tombstones. Deep shadows lay like pools. He had a sense of being watched from within.

As he gazed, he saw movement among the graves. He could not define it, but it was there. He glimpsed, or fancied he glimpsed, a head, indistinct in outline as though swathed in dark fabric. Then another. Another. They huddled in a group, as though to gaze at him.

"I wish you'd go back to your quarters," said Gonda Chastel beside him. She had drifted after him, silent as a shadow herself.

"Miss Chastel," he said, "tell me something if you can. Whatever happened to the town or village of Griswold?"

"Griswold?" she echoed. "What's Griswold? That means gray woods."

"Your ancestor, or your relative, Horace Ray, came from Griswold to die in Jewett City. And I've told you that I knew your mother was born a Ray."

Her shining eyes seemed to flood upon him. "I didn't know that," she said.

He gazed into the churchyard, at those hints of furtive movement.

"The hands of the dead reach out for the living," murmured Gonda Chastel.

"Reach out for me?" he asked.

"Perhaps for both of us. Just now, we may be the only living souls awake in Deslow." She gazed at him again. "But you're able to defend yourself, somehow."

"What makes you think that?" he inquired, aware of the clove of garlic in his shirt pocket.

"Because they – in the churchyard there – they watch, but they hold away from you. You don't invite them."

"Nor do you, apparently," said Cobbett.

"I hope you're not trying to make fun of me," she said, her voice barely audible.

"On my soul, I'm not."

"On your soul," she repeated. "Good night, Mr Cobbett."

Again she moved away, tall and proud and graceful. He watched her out of sight. Then he headed back toward the motor court.

Nothing moved in the empty street. Only one or two lights shone here and there in closed shops. He thought he heard a soft rustle behind him, but did not look back.

As he reached his own door, he heard Laurel scream behind hers.

Judge Pursuivant sat in his cubicle, his jacket off, studying a worn little brown book. Skinner, said letters on the spine, and *Myths and Legends of Our Own Land*. He had read the passage so often that he could almost repeat it from memory:

"To lay this monster he must be taken up and burned; at least his heart must be; and he must be disinterred in the daytime when he is asleep and unaware."

There were other ways, reflected Pursuivant.

It must be very late by now, rather it must be early. But he had no intention of going to sleep. Not when stirs of motion sounded outside, along the concrete walkway in front of his cabin. Did motion stand still, just beyond the door there? Pursuivant's great, veined hand touched the front of his shirt, beneath which a bag of garlic hung like an amulet. Garlic – was that enough? He himself was fond of garlic, judiciously employed in sauces and salads. But then, he could see himself in the mirror of the bureau yonder, could see his broad old face with its white sweep of mustache like a wreath of snow on a sill. It was a clear image of a face, not a calm face just then, but a determined one. Pursuivant smiled at it, with a glimpse of even teeth that were still his own.

He flicked up his shirt cuff and looked at his watch. Half past one, about. In June, even with daylight savings time, dawn would come early. Dawn sent vampires back to the tombs that were their melancholy refuges, "asleep and unaware," as Skinner had specified.

Putting the book aside, he poured himself a small drink of bourbon, dropped in cubes of ice and a trickle of water, and sipped. He had drunk several times during that day, when on most days he partook of only a single highball, by advice of his doctor; but just now he was grateful for the pungent, walnutty taste of the liquor. It was one of earth's natural things, a good companion when not abused. From the table he took a folder of scribbled notes. He looked at jottings from the works of Montague Summers.

These offered the proposition that a plague of vampires usually stemmed from a single source of infection, a king or queen vampire whose feasts of blood drove victims to their graves, to rise in their turn. If the original vampires were found and destroyed, the others relaxed to rest as normally dead bodies. Bram Stoker had followed the same gospel when he wrote *Dracula*, and doubtless Bram Stoker had known. Pursuivant looked at another page, this time a poem copied from James Grant's curious *Mysteries of All Nations*. It was a ballad in archaic language, that dealt with baleful happenings in "The Towne of Peste" – Budapest?

> It was the Corpses that our Churchyardes filled
> That did at midnight lumberr up our Stayres;
> They suck'd our Bloud, the gorie Banquet swilled,
> And harried everie Soule with hydeous Feares . . .

Several verses down:

> They barr'd with Boltes of Iron the Churchyard-pale
> To keep them out; but all this wold not doe;
> For when a Dead-Man has learn'd to draw a naile,
> He can also burst an iron Bolte in two.

Many times Pursuivant had tried to trace the author of that verse. He wondered if it was not something quaintly confected not long before 1880, when Grant published his work. At any rate, the Judge felt that he knew what it meant, the experience that it remembered.

He put aside the notes, too, and picked up his spotted walking stick. Clamping the balance of it firmly in his left hand, he twisted the handle with his right and pulled. Out of the hollow shank slid a pale, bright blade, keen and lean and edged on both front and back.

Pursuivant permitted himself a smile above it. This was one of his most cherished possessions, this silver weapon said to have been forged a thousand years ago by St Dunstan. Bending, he spelled out the runic writing upon it:

Sic pereant omnes inimici tui, Domine

That was the end of the fiercely triumphant song of Deborah in the Book of Judges: So perish all thine enemies, O Lord. Whether the work of St Dunstan or not, the metal was silver, the writing was a warrior's prayer. Silver and writing had proved their strength against evil in the past.

Then, outside, a loud, tremulous cry of mortal terror.

Pursuivant sprang out of his chair on the instant. Blade in hand, he fairly ripped his door open and ran out. He saw Cobbett in front of Laurel's door, wrenching at the knob, and hurried there like a man half his age.

"Open up, Laurel," he heard Cobbett call. "It's Lee out here!"

The door gave inward as Pursuivant reached it, and he and Cobbett pressed into the lighted room.

Laurel half-crouched in the middle of the floor. Her trembling hand pointed to a rear window. "She tried to come in," Laurel stammered.

"There's nothing at that window," said Cobbett, but even as he spoke, there was. A face, pale as tallow, crowded against the glass. They saw wide, staring eyes, a mouth that opened and squirmed. Teeth twinkled sharply.

Cobbett started forward, but Pursuivant caught him by the shoulder. "Let me," he said, advancing toward the window, the point of his blade lifted.

The face at the window writhed convulsively as the silver weapon came against the pane with a clink. The mouth opened as though to shout, but no sound came. The face fell back and vanished from their sight.

"I've seen that face before," said Cobbett hoarsely.

"Yes," said Pursuivant. "At my hotel window. And since."

He dropped the point of the blade to the floor. Outside came a whirring rush of sound, like feet, many of them.

"We ought to wake up the people at the office," said Cobbett.

"I doubt if anyone in this little town could be wakened," Pursuivant told him evenly. "I have it in mind that every living soul, except the three of us, is sound asleep. Entranced."

"But out there—" Laurel gestured at the door, where something seemed to be pressing.

"I said, every living soul," Pursuivant looked from her to Cobbett. "Living," he repeated.

He paced across the floor, and with his point scratched a perpendicular line upon it. Across this he carefully drove a horizontal line, making a cross. The pushing abruptly ceased.

"There it is, at the window again," breathed Laurel.

Pursuivant took long steps back to where the face hovered, with black hair streaming about it. He scraped the glass with his silver blade, up and down, then across, making lines upon it. The face drew away. He moved to mark similar crosses on the other windows.

"You see," he said, quietly triumphant, "the force of old, old charms."

He sat down in a chair, heavily. His face was weary, but he looked at Laurel and smiled.

"It might help if we managed to pity those poor things out there," he said.

"Pity?" she almost cried out.

"Yes," he said, and quoted:

> "'. . . Think how sad it must be
> To thirst always for a scorned elixir,
> The salt of quotidian blood.'"

"I know that," volunteered Cobbett. "It's from a poem by Richard Wilbur, a damned unhappy poet."

"Quotidian," repeated Laurel to herself.

"That means something that keeps coming back, that returns daily," Cobbett said.

"It's a term used to refer to a recurrent fever," added Pursuivant.

Laurel and Cobbett sat down together on the bed.

"I would say that for the time being we're safe here," declared Pursuivant. "Not at ease, but at least safe. At dawn, danger will go to sleep and we can open the door."

"But why are we safe, and nobody else?" Laurel cried out. "Why are we awake, with everyone else in this town asleep and helpless?"

"Apparently because we all of us wear garlic," replied Pursuivant patiently, "and because we ate garlic, plenty of it, at dinnertime. And because there are crosses – crude, but unmistakable – wherever something might try to come in. I won't ask you to be calm, but I'll ask you to be resolute."

"I'm resolute," said Cobbett between clenched teeth. "I'm ready to go out there and face them."

"If you did that, even with the garlic," said Pursuivant, "you'd last about as long as a pint of whiskey in a five-handed poker game. No, Lee, relax as much as you can, and let's talk."

They talked, while outside strange presences could be felt rather than heard. Their talk was of anything and everything but where they were and why. Cobbett remembered strange things he had encountered, in towns, among mountains, along desolate roads, and what he had been able to do about them. Pursuivant told of a vampire he had known and defeated in upstate New York, of a werewolf in his own Southern countryside. Laurel, at Cobbett's urging, sang songs, old songs, from her own rustic home place. Her voice was sweet. When she sang "Round is the Ring," faces came and hung like smudges outside the cross-scored windows. She saw, and sang again, an old Appalachian carol called "Mary She Heared a Knock in the Night." The faces drifted away again. And the hours, too, drifted away, one by one.

"There's a horde of vampires on the night street here, then." Cobbett at last brought up the subject of their problem.

"And they lull the people of Deslow to sleep, to be helpless victims," agreed Pursuivant. "About this show, *The Land Beyond the Forest,* mightn't it be welcomed as a chance to spread the infection? Even a townful of sleepers couldn't feed a growing community of blood drinkers."

"If we could deal with the source, the original infection—" began Cobbett.

"The mistress of them, the queen," said Pursuivant. "Yes. The one whose walking by night rouses them all. If she could be destroyed, they'd all die properly."

He glanced at the front window. The moonlight had a touch of slaty gray.

"Almost morning," he pronounced. "Time for a visit to her tomb."

"I gave my promise I wouldn't go there," said Cobbett.

"But I didn't promise," said Pursuivant, rising. "You stay here with Laurel."

His silver blade in hand, he stepped out into darkness from which the moon had all but dropped away. Overhead, stars were fading out. Dawn was at hand.

He sensed a flutter of movement on the far side of the street, an almost inaudible gibbering of sound. Steadily he walked across. He saw nothing along the sidewalk there, heard nothing. Resolutely he tramped to the churchyard, his weapon poised. More grayness had come to dilute the dark.

He pushed his way through the hedge of shrubs, stepped in upon the grass, and paused at the side of a grave. Above it hung an eddy of soft mist, no larger than the swirl of water draining from a sink. As Pursuivant watched, it seemed to soak into the earth and disappear. That, he said to himself, is what a soul looks like when it seeks to regain its coffin.

On he walked, step by weary, purposeful step, toward the central crypt. A ray of the early sun, stealing between heavily leafed boughs, made his way more visible. In this dawn, he would find what he would find. He knew that.

The crypt's door of open bars was held shut by its heavy padlock. He examined that lock closely. After a moment, he slid the point of his blade into the rusted keyhole and judiciously pressed this way, then that, and back again the first way. The spring creakily relaxed and he dragged the door open. Holding his breath, he entered.

The lid of the great stone vault was closed down. He took hold of the edge and heaved. The lid was heavy, but rose with a complaining grate of the hinges. Inside he saw a dark, closed coffin. He lifted the lid of that, too.

She lay there, calm-faced, the eyes half shut as though dozing.

"Chastel," said Pursuivant to her. "Not Gonda. Chastel."

The eyelids fluttered. That was all, but he knew that she heard what he said.

"Now you can rest," he said. "Rest in peace, really in peace."

He set the point of his silver blade at the swell of her left breast. Leaning both his broad hands upon the curved handle, he drove downward with all his strength.

She made a faint squeak of sound.

Blood sprang up as he cleared his weapon. More light shone in. He could see a dark moisture fading from the blade, like evaporating dew.

In the coffin, Chastel's proud shape shrivelled, darkened. Quickly he slammed the coffin shut, then lowered the lid of the vault into place and went quickly out. He pushed the door shut again and fastened the stubborn old lock. As he walked back through the churchyard among the graves, a bird twittered over his head. More distantly, he heard the hum of a car's motor. The town was waking up.

In the growing radiance, he walked back across the street. By now, his steps were the steps of an old man, old and very tired.

Inside Laurel's cabin, Laurel and Cobbett were stirring instant coffee into hot water in plastic cups. They questioned the Judge with their tired eyes.

"She's finished," he said shortly.

"What will you tell Gonda?" asked Cobbett.

"Chastel was Gonda."

"But—"

"She was Gonda," said Pursuivant again, sitting down. "Chastel died. The infection wakened her out of her tomb, and she told people she was Gonda, and naturally they believed her." He sagged wearily. "Now that she's finished and at rest, those others – the ones she had bled, who also rose at night – will rest, too."

Laurel took a sip of coffee. Above the cup, her face was pale.

"Why do you say Chastel was Gonda?" she asked the Judge. "How can you know that?"

"I wondered from the very beginning. I was utterly sure just now."

"Sure?" said Laurel. "How can you be sure?"

Pursuivant smiled at her, the very faintest of smiles.

"My dear, don't you think a man always recognizes a woman he has loved?"

He seemed to recover his characteristic defiant vigor. He rose and went to the door and put his hand on the knob. "Now, if you'll just excuse me for a while."

"Don't you think we'd better hurry and leave?" Cobbett asked him. "Before people miss her and ask questions?"

"Not at all," said Pursuivant, his voice strong again. "If we're gone, they'll ask questions about us, too, possibly embarrassing questions. No, we'll stay. We'll eat a good breakfast, or at least pretend to eat it. And we'll be as surprised as the rest of them about the disappearance of their leading lady."

"I'll do my best," vowed Laurel.

"I know you will, my child," said Pursuivant, and went out the door.

HOWARD WALDROP

Der Untergang Des Abendlandesmenschen

HOWARD WALDROP'S STORIES are filled with images from contemporary American culture – rock 'n' roll music, bad science fiction movies, cartoons, comic books and real-life characters have all found their way into his uniquely comic/tragic fiction.

Waldrop was born in 1946 in Houston, Mississipi, and has lived in Texas since he was four years old. He is consumed by fly-fishing. He is also a winner of the World Fantasy and Nebula Awards, and his novels include *Texas-Israeli War: 1999* (with Jake Saunders), *Them Bones, A Dozen Tough Jobs, You Could Go Home Again* and *The Search for Tom Purdue.*

His highly distinctive short fiction is collected in *Going Home Again, Howard, Who?: Twelve Outstanding Stories of Speculative Fiction, All About Strange Monsters of the Recent Past, Strange Things in Close-up: The Nearly Complete Howard Waldrop, Night of the Cooters: More Neat Stories, Dream Factories and Radio Pictures* and *Custer's Last Jump and Other Collaborations* (with A.A. Jackson, Leigh Kennedy, George R.R. Martin, Joseph F. Pumilia, Buddy Sanders, Bruce Sterling and Steven Utley).

The following story is typical Waldrop . . .

THEY RODE THROUGH THE flickering landscape to the tune of organ music.

Broncho Billy, short like an old sailor, and William S., tall and rangy as a windblown pine. Their faces, their horses, the landscape all darkened and became light; were at first indistinct then sharp and clear as they rode across one ridge and down into the valley beyond.

Ahead of them, in much darker shades, was the city of Bremen, Germany.

Except for organ and piano music, it was quiet in most of Europe.

In the vaults below the Opera, in the City of Lights, Erik the phantom played the *Toccata and Fugue* while the sewers ran blackly by.

In Berlin, Cesare the somnambulist slept. His mentor Caligari lectured at the University, and waited for his chance to send the monster through the streets.

Also in Berlin, Dr Mabuse was dead and could no longer control the underworld.

But in Bremen . . .

In Bremen, something walked the night.

To the cities of china eggs and dolls, in the time of sawdust bread and the price of six million marks for a postage stamp, came Broncho Billy and William S. They had ridden hard for two days and nights, and the horses were heavily lathered.

They reined in, and tied their mounts to a streetlamp on the Wilhelmstrasse.

"What say we get a drink, William S.?" asked the shorter cowboy. "All this damn flickering gives me a headache."

William S. struck a pose three feet away from him, turned his head left and right, and stepped up to the doors of the *gasthaus* before them.

With his high-pointed hat and checked shirt, William S. looked like a weatherbeaten scarecrow, or a child's version of Abraham Lincoln before the beard. His eyes were like shiny glass, through which some inner hellfires showed.

Broncho Billy hitched up his pants. He wore Levis, which on him looked too large, a dark vest, lighter shirt, big leather chaps with three tassles at hip, knee and calf. His hat seemed three sizes too big.

Inside the tavern, things were murky grey, black and stark white. And always, the flickering.

They sat down at a table and watched the clientele. Ex-soldiers, in the remnants of uniforms, seven years after the Great War had ended. The unemployed, spending their last few coins on beer. The air was thick with grey smoke from pipes and cheap cigarettes.

Not too many people had noticed the entrance of William S. and Broncho Billy.

Two had.

"Quirt!" said an American captain, his hand on his drinking buddy, a sergeant.

"What?" asked the sergeant, his hand on the barmaid.

"Look who's here!"

The sergeant peered toward the haze of flickering grey smoke where the cowboys sat.

"Damn!" he said.

"Want to go over and chat with 'em?" asked the captain.

"&%*$%@no!" cursed the sergeant. "This ain't our %&*!*$ing picture."

"I suppose you're right," said the captain, and returned to his wine.

"You must remember, my friend," said William S. after the waiter brought them beer, "that there can be no rest in the pursuit of evil."

"Yeah, but hell, William S., this is a long way from home."

William S. lit a match, put it to a briar pipe containing his favorite shag tobacco. He puffed on it a few moments, then regarded his companion across his tankard.

"My dear Broncho Billy," he said. "No place is too far to go in order to thwart the forces of darkness. This is something Dr Helioglabulus could not handle by himself, else he should not have summoned us."

"Yeah, but William S., my butt's sore as a rizen after two days in the saddle. I think we should bunk down before we see this doctor fellow."

"Ah, that's where you're wrong, my friend," said the tall, hawk-nosed cowboy. "Evil never sleeps. Men must."

"Well, I'm a man," said Broncho Billy. "I say, let's sleep."

Just then, Doctor Helioglabulus entered the tavern.

He was dressed as a Tyrolean mountain guide, in *lederhosen* and feathered cap, climbing boots and suspenders. He carried with him an alpenstock, which made a large *clunk* each time it touched the floor.

He walked through the flickering darkness and smoke and stood in front of the table with the two cowboys.

William S. had risen.

"Dr—" he began.

"Eulenspigel," said the other, an admonitory finger to his lips.

Broncho Billy rolled his eyes heavenward.

"Dr Eulenspigel, I'd like you to meet my associate and chronicler, Mr Broncho Billy."

The doctor clicked his heels together.

"Have a chair," said Broncho Billy, pushing one out from under the table with his boot. He tipped his hat up off his eyes.

The doctor, in his comic opera outfit, sat.

"Helioglabulus," whispered William S., "whatever are you up to?"

"I had to come incognito. There are . . . others who should not learn of my presence here."

Broncho Billy looked from one to the other and rolled his eyes again.

"Then the game is afoot?" asked William S., his eyes more alight than ever.

"Game such as man has never before seen," said the doctor.

"I see," said William S., his eyes narrowing as he drew on his pipe. "Moriarty?"

"Much more evil."

"More evil?" asked the cowboy, his fingertips pressed together. "I cannot imagine such."

"Neither could I, up until a week ago," said Helioglabulus. "Since then, the city has experienced wholesale terrors. Rats run the streets at night, invade houses. This tavern will be deserted by nightfall. The people lock their doors and say prayers, even in this age. They are reverting to the old superstitions."

"They have just cause?" asked William S.

"A week ago, a ship pulled into the pier. On board was – one man!" He paused for dramatic effect. Broncho Billy was unimpressed. The doctor continued. "The crew, the passengers were gone. Only the captain was aboard, lashed to the wheel. And he was – drained of blood!"

Broncho Billy became interested.

"You mean," asked William S., bending over his beer, "that we are dealing with – the undead?"

"I am afraid so," said Dr Helioglabulus, twisting his mustaches.

"Then we shall need the proper armaments," said the taller cowboy.

"I have them," said the doctor, taking cartridge boxes from his backpack.

"Good!" said William S. "Broncho Billy, you have your revolver?"

"What!? Whatta ya mean, 'do you have your revolver?' Just what do you mean? Have you ever seen me without my guns, William S.? Are you losing your mind?''

"Sorry, Billy," said William S., looking properly abashed.

"Take these," said Helioglabulus.

Broncho Billy broke open his two Peace-makers, dumped the .45 shells on the table. William S. unlimbered his two Navy .36s and pushed the recoil rod down in the cylinders. He punched each cartridge out onto the table-top.

Billy started to load up his pistols, then took a closer look at the shells; held one up and examined it.

"Goddam, William S.," he yelled. "Wooden bullets! Wooden bullets?"

Helioglabulus was trying to wave him to silence. The tall cowboy tried to put his hand on the other.

Everyone in the beer hall had heard him. There was a deafening silence, all the patrons turned toward their table.

"Damn," said Broncho Billy. "You can't shoot a wooden bullet fifteen feet and expect it to hit the broad side of a corncrib. What the hell we gonna shoot wooden bullets at?"

The tavern began to empty, people rushing from the place, looking back in terror. All except five men at a far table.

"I am afraid, my dear Broncho Billy," said William S., "that you have frightened the patrons, and warned the evil ones of our presence."

Broncho Billy looked around.

"You mean those guys over there?" he nodded toward the other table. "Hell, William S., we both took on twelve men one time."

Dr Helioglabulus sighed. "No, no, you don't understand. Those men over there are harmless; crackpot revolutionists. William and I are speaking of *nosferatu* . . ."

Broncho Billy continued to stare at him.

". . . the undead . . ."

No response.

". . . er, ah, vampires . . ."

"You mean," asked Billy, "like Theda Bara?"

"Not vamps, my dear friend," said the hawknosed wrangler. "Vampires. Those who rise from the dead and suck the blood of the living."

"Oh," said Broncho Billy. Then he looked at the cartridges. "These kill 'em?"

"Theoretically," said Helioglabulus.

"Meaning you don't know?"

The doctor nodded.

"In that case," said Broncho Bill, "we go halfies." He began to load his .45s with one regular bullet, then a wooden one, then another standard.

William S. had already filled his with wooden slugs.

"Excellent," said Helioglabulus. "Now, put these over your hatbands. I hope you never have to get close enough for them to be effective."

What he handed them were silver hatbands. Stamped on the shiny surface of the bands was a series of crosses. They slipped them on their heads, settling them on their hatbrims.

"What next?" asked Broncho Billy.

"Why, we wait for nightfall, for the *nosferatu* to strike!" said the doctor.

"Did you hear them, Hermann?" asked Joseph.

"Sure. You think we ought to do the same?"

"Where would we find someone to make wooden bullets for pistols such as ours?" asked Joseph.

The five men sitting at the table looked toward the doctor and the two cowboys. All five were dressed in the remnants of uniforms belonging to the War. The one addressed as Hermann still wore the Knight's Cross on the faded splendor of his dress jacket.

"Martin," said Hermann. "Do you know where we can get wooden bullets?"

"I'm sure we could find someone to make them for the automatics," he answered. "Ernst, go to Wartman's, see about them."

Ernst stood, then slapped the table. "Every time I hear the word vampire, I reach for my Browning!" he said.

They all laughed. Martin, Hermann, Joseph, Ernst most of all. Even Adolf laughed a little.

Soon after dark, someone ran into the place, white of face. "The vampire!" he yelled, pointing vaguely toward the street, and fell out.

Broncho Billy and William S. jumped up. Helioglabulus stopped them. "I'm too old, and will only hold you up," he said. "I shall try to catch up later. Remember . . . the crosses. The bullets in the heart!"

As they rushed out past the other table, Ernst, who had left an hour earlier, returned with two boxes.

"Quick, Joseph!" he said as the two cowboys went through the door. "Follow them! We'll be right behind. Your pistol!"

Joseph turned, threw a Browning automatic pistol back to Hermann, then went out the doors as hoofbeats clattered in the street.

The other four began to load their pistols from the boxes of cartridges.

The two cowboys rode toward the commotion.

"Yee-haw!" yelled Broncho Billy. They galloped down the well-paved streets, their horses' hooves striking sparks from the cobbles.

They passed the police and others running towards the sounds of screams and dying. Members of the Free Corps, ex-soldiers and students, swarmed the streets in their uniforms. Torches burned against the flickering black night skies.

The city was trying to overcome the *nosferatu* by force.

Broncho Billy and William S. charged toward the fighting. In the center of a square stood a coach, all covered in black crepe. The driver, a plump, cadaverous man, held the reins to four black horses. The four were rearing high in their traces, their hooves menacing the crowd.

But it was not the horses which kept the mob back.

Crawling out of a second story hotel window was a vision from a nightmare. Bald, with pointed ears, teeth like a rat, beady eyes bright in the flickering night, the vampire climbed from a bedroom to the balcony. The front of his frock coat was covered with blood, its face and arms were smeared. A man's hand stuck halfway out the window, and the curtains were spattered black.

The *nosferatu* jumped to the ground, and the crowd parted as he leaped from the hotel steps to the waiting carriage. Then the driver cracked his whip over the horses – there was no sound – and the team charged, tumbling people like leaves before the night wind.

The carriage seemed to float to the two cowboys who rode after it. There was no sound of hoofbeats ahead, no noise from the harness, no creak of axles. It was as if they followed the wind itself through the night-time streets of Bremen.

They sped down the flickering main roads. Once, when Broncho Billy glanced behind him, he thought he saw motorcycle headlights following. But he devoted most of his attention to the fleeing coach.

William S. rode beside him. They gained on the closed carriage.

Broncho Billy drew his left-handed pistol (he was ambidexterous) and fired at the broad back of the driver. He heard the splintery clatter of the wooden bullet as it ricocheted off the coach. Then the carriage turned ahead of them.

He was almost smashed against a garden wall by the headlong plunge of his mount, then he recovered, leaning far over in the saddle, as if his horse were a sailboat and he a sailor heeling against the wind.

Then he and William S. were closing with the hearse on a long broad stretch of the avenue. They pulled even with the driver.

And for the first time, the hackles rose on Broncho Billy's neck as he rode beside the black-crepe coach. There was no sound but him, his horse, their gallop. He saw the black-garbed driver crack the long whip, heard no *snap*, heard no horses, heard no wheels.

His heart in his throat, he watched William S. pull even on the other side. The driver turned that way, snapped his whip toward the taller cowboy. Broncho Billy saw his friend's hat fly away, cut in two.

Billy took careful aim and shot the lead horse in the head, twice. It dropped like a ton of cement, and the air was filled with a vicious, soundless image: four horses, the driver, the carriage, he, his mount and William S. all flying through the air in a tangle. Then the side of the coach caught him and the incessant flickering went out.

He must have awakened a few seconds later. His horse was atop him, but he didn't think anything was broken. He pushed himself out from under it.

The driver was staggering up from the flinders of the coach – strange, thought Broncho Billy, now I hear the sounds of the wheels turning, the screams of the dying horses. The driver pulled a knife. He started toward the cowboy.

Broncho Billy found his right-hand pistol, still in its holster. He pulled it, fired directly into the heart of the fat man. The driver folded from the recoil, then stood again.

Billy pulled the trigger.

The driver dropped as the wooden bullet turned his heart to giblets.

Broncho Billy took all the regular ammo out of his pistol and began to cram the wooden ones in.

As he did, motorcycles came screaming to a stop beside him, and the five men from the tavern climbed from them or their sidecars.

He looked around for William S. but could not see him. Then he heard the shooting from the rooftop above the street – twelve shots, quick as summer thunder.

One of William S.'s revolvers dropped four stories and hit the ground beside him.

The Germans were already up the stairs ahead of Broncho Billy as he ran.

When the carriage had crashed into them, William S. had been thrown clear. He jumped up in time to see the vampire run into the doorway of the residential block across the way. He tore after while the driver pulled himself from the wreckage and Broncho Billy was crawling from under his horse.

Up the stairs he ran. He could now hear the pounding feet of the living dead man ahead, unlike the silence before the wreck. A flickering murky hallway was before him, and he saw the door at the far end close.

William S. smashed into it, rolled. He heard the scrape of teeth behind him, and saw the rat-like face snap shut inches away. He came up, his pistols leveled at the vampire.

The bald-headed thing grabbed the open door, pulled it before him.

William S. stood, feet braced, a foot from the door and began to fire into it. His Colt .36s inches in front of his face, he fired again and again into the wooden door, watching chunks and splinters shear away. He heard the vampire squeal, like a rat trapped behind a trash can, but still he fired until both pistols clicked dry.

The door swung slowly awry, pieces of it hanging.

The *nosferatu* grinned, and carefully pushed the door closed. It hissed and crouched.

William S. reached up for his hat.

And remembered that the driver had knocked it off his head before the collision.

The thing leaped.

One of his pistols was knocked over the parapet.

Then he was fighting for his life.

The five Germans, yelling to each other, slammed into the doorway at the end of the hall. From beyond, they heard the sounds of scuffling, labored breathing, the rip and tear of cloth.

Broncho Billy charged up behind them.

"The door! It's jammed," said one.

"His hat!" yelled Broncho Billy. "He lost his hat!"

"Hat?" asked the one called Joseph in English. "Why his hat?"
The others shouldered against the gapped door. Through it, they saw flashes of movement and the flickering night sky.

"Crosses!" yelled Broncho Billy. "Like this!" He pointed to his hatband.

"Ah!" said Joseph. "Crosses."

He pulled something from the one called Adolf, who hung back a little, threw it through the hole in the door.

"*Cruzen!*" yelled Joseph.

"The cross!" screamed Broncho Billy. "William S.! The cross!"
The sound of scuffling stopped.

Joseph tossed his pistol through the opening.

They continued to bang on the door.

The thing had its talons on his throat when the yelling began. The vampire was strangling him. Little circles were swimming in his sight.

He was down beneath the monster. It smelled of old dirt, raw meat, of death. Its rat-eyes were bright with hate.

Then he heard the yell "A cross!" and something fluttered at the edge of his vision. He let go one hand from the vampire and grabbed it up.

It felt like cloth. He shoved it at the thing's face.

Hands let go.

William S. held the cloth before him as his breath came back in a rush. He staggered up, and the *nosferatu* put its hands over its face. He pushed toward it.

Then the Browning Automatic pistol landed beside his foot, and he heard noises at the door behind him.

Holding the cloth, he picked up the pistol.

The vampire hissed like a radiator.

William S. aimed and fired. The pistol was fully automatic.

The wooden bullets opened the vampire like a zipper coming off.

The door crashed outward, the five Germans and Broncho Billy rushed through.

William S. held to the doorframe and caught his breath. A crowd was gathering below, at the site of the wrecked hearse and the dead horses. Torchlights wobbled their reflections on the houses across the road. It looked like something from Dante.

Helioglabulus came onto the roof, took one look at the vampire and ran his alpenstock, handle first, into its ruined chest.

"Just to make sure," he said.

Broncho Billy was clapping him on the back. "Shore thought you'd gone to the last roundup," he said.

The five Germans were busy with the vampire's corpse.

William S. looked at the piece of cloth still clenched tightly in his own hand. He opened it. It was an armband.

On its red cloth was a white circle with a twisted black cross.

Like the decorations the Indians used on their blankets, only in reverse.

He looked at the Germans. Four of them wore the armbands; the fifth, wearing an old corporal's uniform, had a torn sleeve.

They were slipping a yellow armband over the arm of the vampire's coat. When they finished, they picked the thing up and carried it to the roof edge. It looked like a spitted pig.

The yellow armband had two interlocking triangles, like the device on the chest of the costumes William S. had worn when he played *Ben-Hur* on Broadway. The Star of David.

The crowd below screamed as the corpse fell toward them.

There were shouts, then.

The unemployed, the war-wounded, the young, the bitter, the

disillusioned. Then the shouting stopped ... and they began to chant.

The five Germans stood on the parapet, looking down at the milling people. They talked among themselves.

Broncho Billy held William S. until he caught his breath.

They heard the crowds disperse, fill in again, break, drift off, reform, reassemble, grow larger.

"Well, pard," said Broncho Billy. "Let's mosey over to a hotel and get some shut-eye."

"That would be nice," said William S.

Helioglabulus joined them.

"We should go by the back way," he said.

"I don't like the way this crowd is actin'," said Broncho Billy.

William S. walked to the parapet, looked out over the city.

Under the dark flickering sky, there were other lights. Here and there, synagogues began to flicker.

And then to burn.

TANITH LEE

Red as Blood

TANITH LEE BEGAN WRITING at the age of nine and became a
full-time writer in 1975, when DAW Books published her novel *The
Birthgrave.*

Since then she has written and published around sixty novels, nine
collections and over 200 short stories. She also had four radio plays
broadcast during the late 1970s and early 1980s, and scripted two
episodes of the cult BBC-TV series *Blake's 7.* She has twice won the
World Fantasy Award for short fiction and was awarded the British
Fantasy Society's August Derleth Award in 1980 for her novel *Death's
Master.* In 1998 she was shortlisted for the Guardian Award for
Children's Fiction for her novel *Law of the Wolf Tower,* the first volume
in the "Claidi Journal" series.

Tor Books has published *White as Snow,* the author's retelling of the
Snow White story, while Overlook Press has issued *A Bed of Earth* and
Venus Preserved, the third and fourth volumes, respectively, in the
"Secret Books of Paradys" series. More recent titles include *Cast a
Bright Shadow* and *Here in Cold Hell,* the first two books in the
"Lionwolf Trilogy", and *Piratica* is a novel for older children about
the exploits of a female pirate. She has also written a sequel to her
novel *The Silver Metal Lover* for Bantam Books, and rights to the 1981
original have been sold to Miramax Film Corp.

As the writer points out about the dark fairy tale that follows:

"There is a strong influence of the wonderful Oscar Wilde – especially his stories – and the Wildean elements also led me to assay a serious spiritual liberty in the last quarter.

"Meanwhile, I'd suspected that the character was a vampire for years. As was her mother – who didn't ask, we recall, for a pink-cheeked blonde daughter, with lips like roses or wine – but a snow-skinned, ebony-haired child, with a mouth red as fresh blood . . ."

THE BEAUTIFUL WITCH QUEEN flung open the ivory case of the magic mirror. Of dark gold the mirror was, dark gold like the hair of the Witch Queen that poured down her back. Dark gold the mirror was, and ancient as the seven stunted black trees growing beyond the pale blue glass of the window.

"*Speculum, speculum,*" said the Witch Queen to the magic mirror. "*Dei gratia.*"

"*Volente Deo. Audio.*"

"Mirror," said the Witch Queen. "Whom do you see?"

"I see you, mistress," replied the mirror. "And all in the land. But one."

"Mirror, mirror, who is it you do not see?"

"I do not see Bianca."

The Witch Queen crossed herself. She shut the case of the mirror and, walking slowly to the window, looked out at the old trees through the panes of pale blue glass.

Fourteen years ago, another woman had stood at this window, but she was not like the Witch Queen. The woman had black hair that fell to her ankles; she had a crimson gown, the girdle worn high beneath her breasts, for she was far gone with child. And this woman had thrust open the glass casement on the winter garden, where the old trees crouched in the snow. Then, taking a sharp bone needle, she had thrust it into her finger and shaken three bright drops on the ground. "Let my daughter have," said the woman, "hair as black as mine, black as the wood of these warped and arcane trees. Let her have skin like mine, white as this snow. And let her have my mouth, red as my blood." And the woman had smiled and licked at her finger. She had a crown on her head; it shone in the dusk like a star. She never came to the window before dusk: she did not like the day. She was the first Queen, and she did not possess a mirror.

The second Queen, the Witch Queen, knew all this. She knew how, in giving birth, the first Queen had died. Her coffin had been carried into the cathedral and masses had been said. There was an ugly rumour – that a splash of holy water had fallen on the corpse and the dead flesh had smoked. But the first Queen had been reckoned unlucky for the kingdom. There had been a plague in the land since she came there, a wasting disease for which there was no cure.

Seven years went by. The King married the second Queen, as unlike the first as frankincense to myrrh.

"And this is my daughter," said the King to his second Queen.

There stood a little girl child, nearly seven years of age. Her black hair hung to her ankles, her skin was white as snow. Her mouth was red as blood, and she smiled with it.

"Bianca," said the King, "you must love your new mother."

Bianca smiled radiantly. Her teeth were bright as sharp bone needles.

"Come," said the Witch Queen, "come, Bianca. I will show you my magic mirror."

"Please, Mamma," said Bianca softly. "I do not like mirrors."

"She is modest," said the King. "And delicate. She never goes out by day. The sun distresses her."

That night, the Witch Queen opened the case of her mirror.

"Mirror. Whom do you see?"

"I see you, mistress. And all in the land. But one."

"Mirror, mirror, who is it you do not see?"

"I do not see Bianca."

The second Queen gave Bianca a tiny crucifix of golden filigree. Bianca would not accept it. She ran to her father and whispered, "I am afraid. I do not like to think of Our Lord dying in agony on His cross. She means to frighten me. Tell her to take it away."

The second Queen grew wild white roses in her garden and invited Bianca to walk there after sundown. But Bianca shrank away. She whispered to her father, "The thorns will tear me. She means me to be hurt."

When Bianca was twelve years old, the Witch Queen said to the King, "Bianca should be confirmed so that she may take Communion with us."

"This may not be," said the King. "I will tell you, she has not been Christened, for the dying word of my first wife was against it. She begged me, for her religion was different from ours. The wishes of the dying must be respected."

"Should you not like to be blessed by the Church?" said the Witch Queen to Bianca. "To kneel at the golden rail before the marble altar? To sing to God, to taste the ritual Bread and sip the ritual Wine?"

"She means me to betray my true mother," said Bianca to the King. "When will she cease tormenting me?"

The day she was thirteen, Bianca rose from her bed, and there was a red stain there, like a red, red flower.

"Now you are a woman," said her nurse.

"Yes," said Bianca. And she went to her true mother's jewel box, and out of it she took her mother's crown and set it on her head.

When she walked under the old black trees in the dusk, the crown shone like a star.

The wasting sickness, which had left the land in peace for thirteen years, suddenly began again, and there was no cure.

The Witch Queen sat in a tall chair before a window of pale green and dark white glass, and in her hands she held a Bible bound in rosy silk.

"Majesty," said the huntsman, bowing very low.

He was a man, forty years old, strong and handsome, and wise in the hidden lore of the forests, the occult lore of the earth. He could kill too, for it was his trade, without faltering. The slender fragile deer he could kill, and the moon-winged birds, and the velvet hares with their sad, foreknowing eyes. He pitied them, but pitying, he killed them. Pity could not stop him. It was his trade.

"Look in the garden," said the Witch Queen.

The hunter looked through a dark white pane. The sun had sunk, and a maiden walked under a tree.

"The Princess Bianca," said the huntsman.

"What else?" asked the Witch Queen.

The huntsman crossed himself.

"By our Lord, Madam, I will not say."

"But you know."

"Who does not?"

"The King does not."

"Nor he does."

"Are you a brave man?" asked the Witch Queen.

"In the summer, I have hunted and slain boar. I have slaughtered wolves in winter."

"But are you brave enough?"

"If you command it, Lady," said the huntsman, "I will try my best."

The Witch Queen opened the Bible at a certain place, and out of it she drew a flat silver crucifix, which had been resting against the words: *Thou shalt not be afraid for the terror by night . . . Nor for the pestilence that walketh in darkness.*

The huntsman kissed the crucifix and put it about his neck beneath his shirt.

"Approach," said the Witch Queen, "and I will instruct you in what to say."

Presently, the huntsman entered the garden, as the stars were burning up in the sky. He strode to where Bianca stood under a stunted dwarf tree, and he kneeled down.

"Princess," he said, "pardon me, but I must give you ill tidings."

"Give them, then," said the girl, toying with the long stem of a wan, night-growing flower which she had plucked.

"Your stepmother, the accursed jealous witch, means to have you slain. There is no help for it but you must fly the palace this very night. If you permit, I will guide you to the forest. There are those who will care for you until it may be safe for you to return."

Bianca watched him, but gently, trustingly.

"I will go with you, then," she said.

They went by a secret way out of the garden, through a passage under the ground, through a tangled orchard, by a broken road between great overgrown hedges.

Night was a pulse of deep, flickering blue when they came to the forest. The branches of the forest overlapped and intertwined, like leading in a window, and the sky gleamed dimly through the panes of blue-coloured glass.

"I am weary," sighed Bianca. "May I rest a moment?"

"By all means," said the huntsman. "In the clearing there, foxes come to play by night. Look in that direction, and you will see them."

"How clever you are," said Bianca. "And how handsome." She sat on the turf and gazed at the clearing.

The huntsman drew his knife silently and concealed it in the folds of his cloak. He stooped above the maiden.

"What are you whispering?" demanded the huntsman, laying his hand on her wood-black hair.

"Only a rhyme my mother taught me."

The huntsman seized her by the hair and swung her about so her white throat was before him, stretched ready for the knife. But he did not strike, for there in his hand he held the dark golden locks of the Witch Queen, and her face laughed up at him, and she flung her arms about him, laughing.

"Good man, sweet man, it was only a test of you. Am I not a witch? And do you not love me?"

The huntsman trembled, for he did love her, and she was pressed so close that her heart seemed to beat within his own body.

"Put away the knife. Throw away the silly crucifix. We have no need of these things. The King is not one half the man you are."

And the huntsman obeyed her, throwing the knife and the crucifix far off among the roots of the trees. He gripped her to him and she buried her face in his neck, and the pain of her kiss was the last thing he felt in this world.

The sky was black now. The forest was blacker. No foxes played in the clearing. The moon rose and made white lace through the boughs, and through the backs of the huntsman's empty eyes. Bianca wiped her mouth on a dead flower.

"Seven asleep, seven awake," said Bianca. "Wood to wood. Blood to blood. Thee to me."

There came a sound like seven huge rendings, distant by the length of several trees, a broken road, an orchard, an underground passage. Then a sound like seven huge single footfalls. Nearer. And nearer.

Hop, hop, hop, hop. Hop, hop, hop.

In the orchard, seven black shudderings.

On the broken road, between the high hedges, seven black creepings.

Brush crackled, branches snapped.

Through the forest, into the clearing, pushed seven warped, misshapen, hunched-over, stunted things. Woody-black mossy fur, woody-black bald masks. Eyes like glittering cracks, mouths like moist caverns. Lichen bears. Fingers of twiggy gristle. Grinning. Kneeling. Faces pressed to the earth.

"Welcome," said Bianca.

The Witch Queen stood before a window of glass like diluted wine. She looked at the magic mirror.

"Mirror. Whom do you see?"

"I see you, mistress. I see a man in the forest. He went hunting, but not for deer. His eyes are open, but he is dead. I see all in the land. But one."

The Witch Queen pressed her palms to her ears.

Outside the window, the garden lay, empty of its seven black and stunted dwarf trees.

"Bianca," said the Queen.

The windows had been draped and gave no light. The light spilled from a shallow vessel, light in a sheaf, like pastel wheat. It glowed upon four swords that pointed east and west, that pointed north and south.

Four winds had burst through the chamber, and the grey-silver powders of Time.

The hands of the Witch Queen floated like folded leaves on the air, and through the dry lips the Witch Queen chanted:

"*Pater omnipotens, mittere digneris sanctum Angelum tuum de Infernis.*"

The light faded, and grew brighter.

There, between the hilts of the four swords, stood the Angel Lucefiel, sombrely gilded, his face in shadow, his golden wings spread and glazing at his back.

"Since you have called me, I know your desire. It is a comfortless wish. You ask for pain."

"You speak of pain, Lord Lucefiel, who suffer the most merciless pain of all. Worse than the nails in the feet and wrists. Worse than the thorns and the bitter cup and the blade in the side. To be called upon for evil's sake, which I do not, comprehending your true nature, son of God, brother of The Son."

"You recognize me, then. I will grant what you ask."

And Lucefiel (by some named Satan, Rex Mundi, but nevertheless the left hand, the sinister hand of God's design) wrenched lightning from the ether and cast it at the Witch Queen.

It caught her in the breast. She fell.

The sheaf of light towered and lit the golden eyes of the Angel, which were terrible, yet luminous with compassion, as the swords shattered and he vanished.

The Witch Queen pulled herself from the floor of the chamber, no longer beautiful, a withered, slobbering hag.

Into the core of the forest, even at noon, the sun never shone. Flowers propagated in the grass, but they were colourless. Above, the black-green roof hung down nets of thick green twilight through which albino butterflies and moths feverishly drizzled. The trunks of the trees were smooth as the stalks of underwater weeds. Bats flew in the daytime, and birds who believed themselves to be bats.

There was a sepulchre, dripped with moss. The bones had been rolled out, had rolled around the feet of seven twisted dwarf trees. They looked like trees. Sometimes they moved. Sometimes something like an eye glittered, or a tooth, in the wet shadows.

In the shade of the sepulchre door sat Bianca, combing her hair.

A lurch of motion disturbed the thick twilight.

The seven trees turned their heads.

A hag emerged from the forest. She was crook-backed, and her head was poked forward, predatory, withered and almost hairless, like a vulture's.

"Here we are at last," grated the hag, in a vulture's voice.

She came closer and cranked herself down on her knees and bowed her face into the turf and the colourless flowers.

Bianca sat and gazed at her. The hag lifted herself. Her teeth were yellow palings.

"I bring you the homage of witches, and three gifts," said the hag.

"Why should you do that?"

"Such a quick child, and only fourteen years. Why? Because we fear you. I bring you gifts to curry favour."

Bianca laughed. "Show me."

The hag made a pass in the green air. She held a silken cord worked curiously with plaited human hair.

"Here is a girdle that will protect you from the devices of priests, from crucifix and chalice and the accursed holy water. In it are knotted the tresses of a virgin, and of a woman no better than she should be, and of a woman dead. And here" – a second pass and a comb was in her hand, lacquered blue over green – "a comb from the deep sea, a mermaid's trinket, to charm and subdue. Part your locks with this, and the scent of ocean will fill men's nostrils and the rhythm of the tides their ears, the tides that bind men like chains. Last," added the hag, "that old symbol of wickedness, the scarlet fruit of Eve, the apple red as blood. Bite, and the understanding of Sin, which the serpent boasted of, will be made known to you." And the hag made her last pass in the air and extended the apple, with the girdle and the comb, towards Bianca.

Bianca glanced at the seven stunted trees.

"I like her gifts, but I do not quite trust her."

The bald masks peered from their shaggy beardings. Eyelets glinted. Twiggy claws clacked.

"All the same," said Bianca, "I will let her tie the girdle on me, and comb my hair herself."

The hag obeyed, simpering. Like a toad she waddled to Bianca. She tied on the girdle. She parted the ebony hair. Sparks sizzled, white from the girdle, peacock's eye from the comb.

"And now, hag, take a little bit bite of the apple."

"It will be my pride," said the hag, "to tell my sisters I shared this fruit with you." And the hag bit into the apple, and mumbled the bite noisily, and swallowed, smacking her lips.

Then Bianca took the apple and bit into it.

Bianca screamed – and choked.

She jumped to her feet. Her hair whirled about her like a storm cloud. Her face turned blue, then slate, then white again. She lay on the pallid flowers, neither stirring nor breathing.

The seven dwarf trees rattled their limbs and their bear-shaggy heads, to no avail. Without Bianca's art they could not hop. They strained their claws and ripped at the hag's sparse hair and her mantle. She fled between them. She fled into the sunlit acres of the forest, along the broken road, through the orchard, into a hidden passage.

The hag re-entered the palace by the hidden way, and the Queen's chamber by a hidden stair. She was bent almost double. She held her ribs. With one skinny hand she opened the ivory case of the magic mirror.

"*Speculum, speculum. Dei gratia.* Whom do you see?"

"I see you, mistress. And all in the land. And I see a coffin."

"Whose corpse lies in the coffin?"

"That I cannot see. It must be Bianca."

The hag, who had been the beautiful Witch Queen, sank into her tall chair before the window of pale cucumber-green and dark white glass. Her drugs and potions waited ready to reverse the dreadful conjuring of age that the Angel Lucefiel had placed on her, but she did not touch them yet.

The apple had contained a fragment of the flesh of Christ, the sacred wafer, the Eucharist.

The Witch Queen drew her Bible to her and opened it randomly. And read, with fear, the words: *Resurgat.*

It appeared like glass, the coffin, milky glass. It had formed this way. A thin white smoke had risen from the skin of Bianca. She smoked as a fire smokes when a drop of quenching water falls on it. The piece of Eucharist had stuck in her throat. The Eucharist, quenching water to her fire, caused her to smoke.

Then the cold dews of night gathered, and the colder atmospheres of midnight. The smoke of Bianca's quenching froze about her. Frost formed in exquisite silver scrollwork all over the block of misty ice that contained Bianca.

Bianca's frigid heart could not warm the ice. Nor the sunless green twilight of the day.

You could just see her, stretched in the coffin, through the glass. How lovely she looked, Bianca. Black as ebony, white as snow, red as blood.

The trees hung over the coffin. Years passed. The trees sprawled about the coffin, cradling it in their arms. Their eyes wept fungus and green resin. Green amber drops hardened like jewels in the coffin of glass.

"Who is that, lying under the trees?" the Prince asked, as he rode into the clearing.

He seemed to bring a golden moon with him, shining about his golden head, on the golden armour and the cloak of white satin blazoned with gold and blood and ink and sapphire. The white horse trod on the colourless flowers, but the flowers sprang up again when the hoofs had passed. A shield hung from the saddle bow, a strange shield. From one side it had a lion's face, but from the other, a lamb's face.

The trees groaned and their heads split on huge mouths.

"Is this Bianca's coffin?" said the Prince.

"Leave her with us," said the seven trees. They hauled at their roots. The ground shivered. The coffin of ice-glass gave a great jolt, and a crack bisected it.

Bianca coughed.

The jolt had precipitated the piece of Eucharist from her throat.

In a thousand shards the coffin shattered, and Bianca sat up. She stared at the Prince, and she smiled.

"Welcome, beloved," said Bianca.

She got to her feet and shook out her hair, and began to walk toward the Prince on the pale horse.

But she seemed to walk into a shadow, into a purple room; then into a crimson room whose emanations lanced her like knives. Next she walked into a yellow room where she heard the sound of crying, which tore her ears. All her body seemed stripped away; she was a beating heart. The beats of her heart became two wings. She flew. She was a raven, then an owl. She flew into a sparkling pane. It scorched her white. Snow white. She was a dove.

She settled on the shoulder of the Prince and hid her head under her wing. She had no longer anything black about her, and nothing red.

"Begin again now, Bianca," said the Prince. He raised her from his shoulder. On his wrist there was a mark. It was like a star. Once a nail had been driven in there.

Bianca flew away, up through the roof of the forest. She flew in at a delicate wine window. She was in the palace. She was seven years old.

The Witch Queen, her new mother, hung a filigree crucifix around her neck. "Mirror," said the Witch Queen. "Whom do you see?"

"I see you, mistress," replied the mirror. "And all in the land. I see Bianca."

GRAHAM MASTERTON

Laird of Dunain

GRAHAM MASTERTON HAS PUBLISHED a number of new horror novels over the past few years. These include *The Doorkeepers*, *Snowman*, *Swimmer*, *Trauma* (a.k.a. *Bonnie Winter*), *Unspeakable* and *A Terrible Beauty*. The latter is set in Cork, Ireland, where the author lived for four years before returning to England in 2002.

That same year also saw a special twenty-fifth anniversary edition of his debut horror novel, *The Manitou*, and the republication of much of his backlist, including *Flesh & Blood* and a double edition of *Ritual* and *Walkers*. *Spirit* and *The Chosen Child* were also recently both published in the United States for the first time.

"'The Laird of Dunain' was inspired by a holiday in Inverness," explains Masterton, who was born in Edinburgh, Scotland. "For some reason, the story has become very popular in Europe, and has been republished many times in many different languages. It was the first story of mine to appear in Poland in comic-book form, as 'Dziedzic Dunain'."

It was also especially written for this anthology . . .

"The tailor fell thro' the bed, thimbles an' a'
"The blankets were thin and the sheets they were sma'
"The tailor fell thro' the bed, thimbles an' a'

OUT ONTO THE LAWNS in the first gilded mists of morning came the
Laird of Dunain in kilt and sporran and thick oatmeal-coloured
sweater, his face pale and bony and aesthetic, his beard red as a
burning flame, his hair as wild as a thistle-patch.

Archetypal Scotsman; the kind of Scotsman you saw on tins of
shortbread or bottles of single malt whisky. Except that he looked so
drawn and gaunt. Except that he looked so spiritually hungry.

It was the first time that Claire had seen him since her arrival, and
she reached over and tapped Duncan's arm with the end of her
paintbrush and said, "Look, there he is! Doesn't he look *fantastic*?"

All nine members of the painting class turned to stare at the laird
as he fastidiously patrolled the shingle path that ran along the back of
Dunain Castle. At first, however, he appeared not to notice them,
keeping his hands behind his back and his head aloof, as if he were
breathing in the fine summer air, and surveying his lands, and
thinking the kind of things that Highland lairds were supposed to
think, like how many stags to cull, and how to persuade the Highlands Development Board to provide him with mains electricity.

"I wonder if he'd sit for us?" asked Margot, a rotund frizzy-haired
girl from Liverpool. Margot had confessed to Claire that she had
taken up painting because the smocks hid her hips.

"We could try asking him," Claire suggested – Claire with her
straight dark bob and her serious, well-structured face. Her husband,
her *former* husband, had always said that she looked "like a sensual
schoolmistress." Her painting smock and her Alice-band and her
moon-round spectacles only heightened the impression.

"He's so *romantic*," said Margot. "Like Rob Roy. Or Bonnie Prince
Charlie."

Duncan sorted through his box of watercolours until he found the
half-burned nip-end of a cigarette. He lit it with a plastic lighter with a
scratched transfer of a topless girl on it. "The trouble with painting in
Scotland," he said, "is that *everything* looks so fucking romantic. You
put your heart and your soul into painting Glenmoriston, and you
end up with something that looks like a Woolworth's dinner-mat."

"I'd still like him to sit for us," said Margot.

The painting class had arranged their easels on the sloping south
lawn of Dunain Castle, just above the stone-walled herb gardens.
Beyond the herb gardens the grounds sloped grassy and gentle to the
banks of the Caledonian Canal, where it cut its way between the
north-eastern end of Loch Ness and the city of Inverness itself, and
out to the Moray Firth. All through yesterday, the sailing-ships of the
Tall Ships Race had been gliding through the canal, and they had
appeared to be sailing surrealistically through fields and hedges, like
ships in a dream, or a nightmare.

Mr Morrissey called out, "Pay particular attention to the light; because it's golden and very even just now; but it'll change."

Mr Morrissey (bald, round-shouldered, speedy, fussy) was their course-instructor; the man who had greeted them when they first arrived at Dunain Castle, and who had showed them their rooms ("You'll *adore* this, Mrs Bright . . . such a view of the garden . . .") and who was now conducting their lessons in landscape-painting. In his way, he was very good. He sketched austerely; he painted monochromatically. He wouldn't tolerate sentimentality.

"You've not come to Scotland to reproduce The Monarch of the Glen," he had told them, when he had collected them from the station at Inverness. "You're here to paint life, and landscape, in light of unparalleled clarity."

Claire returned to her charcoal-sketching but she could see (out of the corner of her eye) that the Laird of Dunain was slowly making his way across the lawns. For some reason, she felt excited, and began to sketch more quickly and more erratically. Before she knew it, the Laird was standing only two or three feet away from her, his hands still clasped behind his back. His aura was prickly and electric, almost as if he were already running his thick ginger beard up her inner thighs.

"Well, well," he remarked, at last, in a strong Inverness accent. "You have all of the makings, I'd say. You're not one of Gordon's usual giglets."

Claire blushed, and found that she couldn't carry on sketching. Margot giggled.

"Hech," said the Laird, "I wasn't flethering. You're good."

"Not really," said Claire. "I've only been painting for seven months."

The Laird stood closer. Claire could smell tweed and tobacco and heather and something else, something cloying and sweet, which she had never smelled before.

"You're good," he repeated. "You can draw well; and I'll lay money that ye can paint well. Mr Morrissey!"

Mr Morrissey looked up and his face was very white.

"Mr Morrissey, do you have any objection if I fetch this unback'd filly away from the class?"

Mr Morrissey looked dubious. "It's supposed to be landscape, this morning."

"Aye, but a wee bit of portraiture won't harm her now, will it? And I'm dying to have my portrait painted."

Very reluctantly, Mr Morrissey said, "No, I suppose it won't harm."

"That's settled, then," the Laird declared; and immediately began to fold up Claire's easel and tidy up her box of watercolours.

"Just a minute—" said Claire, almost laughing at his impertinence.

The Laird of Dunain stared at her with eyes that were green like emeralds crushed with a pestle-and-mortar. "I'm sorry," he said. "You don't *object*, do you?"

Claire couldn't stop herself from smiling. "No," she said. "I don't object."

"Well, then," said the Laird of Dunain, and led the way back to the castle.

"Hmph," said Margot, indignantly.

He posed in a dim upper room with dark oak paneling all around, and a high ceiling. The principal light came from a leaded clerestory window, falling almost like a spotlight. The Laird of Dunain sat on a large iron-bound trunk, his head held high, and managed to remain completely motionless while Claire began to sketch.

"You'll have come here looking for something else, apart from painting and drawing," he said, after a while.

Claire's charcoal-twig was quickly outlining his left shoulder. "Oh, yes?" she said. She couldn't think what he meant.

"You'll have come here looking for peace of mind, won't you, and a way to sort everything out?"

She thought, briefly, of Alan, and of Susan, and of doors slamming. She thought of walking for miles through Shepherd's Bush, in the pouring April rain.

"That's what art's all about it, isn't it?" she retorted. "Sorting things out."

The Laird of Dunain smiled obliquely. "That's what my father used to say. In fact, my father believed it quite implicitly."

There was something about his tone of voice that stopped Claire from sketching for a moment. Something very serious; something *suggestive*, as if he were trying to tell her that his words had more than one meaning.

"I shall have to carry on with this tomorrow," she said.

The Laird of Dunain nodded. "That's all right. We have all the time in the world."

The next day, while the rest of the class took a minibus to Fort Augustus to paint the downstepping locks of the Caledonian Canal, Claire sat with the Laird of Dunain in his high gloomy room and started to paint his portrait. She used designer's colours, in preference to oils, because they were quicker; and she sensed that there was something mercurial in the Laird of Dunain which she wouldn't be capable of catching with oils.

"You're a very good sitter," she said, halfway through the morning.

"Don't you want to take a break? Perhaps I could make some coffee."

The Laird of Dunain didn't break his rigid pose, even by an inch. "I'd rather get it finished, if you don't mind."

She carried on painting, squeezing out a half a tube of red. She was finding it difficult to give his face any colour. Normally, for faces, she used little more than a palette of yellow ochre, terra verte, alizarin crimson and cobalt blue. But no matter how much red she mixed into her colours, his face always seemed anemic – almost deathly.

"I'm finding it hard to get your flesh-tones right," she confessed, as the clock in the downstairs hallway struck two.

The Laird of Dunain nodded. "They always said of the Dunains of Dunain that they were a bloodless family. Mind you, I think we proved them wrong at Culloden. That was the day that the Laird of Dunain was caught and cornered by half-a-dozen of the Duke of Cumberland's soldiers, and cut about so bad that he stained a quarter of an acre with his own blood."

"That sounds awful," said Claire, squeezing out more alizarin crimson.

"It was a long time ago," replied the Laird of Dunain. "The sixteenth day of April, 1746. Almost two hundred and fifty years ago; and whose memory can span such a time?"

"You make it sound like yesterday," said Claire, busily mixing.

The Laird of Dunain turned his head away for the very first time that day. "On that day, when he lay bleeding, the laird swore that he would have his revenge on the English for every drop of blood that he had let. He would have it back, he said, a thousandfold; and then a thousandfold more.

"They never discovered his body, you know, although there were plenty of tales in the glens that it was hurried away by Dunains and Macduffs. That was partly the reason that the Duke of Cumberland pursued the Highlanders with such savagery. He made his own promise that he would never return to England until he had seen for himself the body of Dunain of Dunain, and fed it to the dogs."

"Savage times," Claire remarked. She sat back. The laird's face was still appallingly white, even though she had mixed his skin-tones with almost two whole tubes of crimson. She couldn't understand it. She ran her hand back through her hair and said, "I'll have to come back to this tomorrow."

"Of course," said the Laird of Dunain.

On her way to supper, she met Margot in the oak-panelled corridor. Margot was unexpectedly bustling and fierce. "You didn't come with us yesterday and you didn't come with us today. Today we sketched sheep."

"I've been—" Claire began, inclining her head toward the Laird of Dunain's apartments.

"Oh, yes," said Margot. "I thought as much. We *all* thought as much." And then she went off, with wig-wagging bottom.

Claire was amazed. But then she suddenly thought: *she's jealous. She's really jealous.*

All the next day while the Laird of Dunain sat composed and motionless in front of her, Claire struggled with her portrait. She used six tubes of light red and eight tubes of alizarin crimson, and still his face appeared as starkly white as ever.

She began to grow more and more desperate, but she refused to give up. In a strange way that she couldn't really understand, her painting was like a battlefield on which she and the Laird of Dunain were fighting a silent, deadly struggle. Perhaps she was doing nothing more than struggling with Alan, and all of the men who had treated her with such contempt.

Halfway through the afternoon, the light in the clerestory window gradually died, and it began to rain. She could hear the raindrops pattering on the roof and the gutters quietly gurgling.

"Are you sure you can see well enough?" asked the laird.

"I can see," she replied, doggedly squeezing out another glistening fat worm of red gouache.

"You could always give up," he said. His voice sounded almost sly.

"I can *see*," Claire insisted. "And I'll finish this bloody portrait if it kills me."

She picked up her scalpel to open the cellophane wrapping around another box of designers' colours.

"I'm sorry I'm such an awkward subject," smiled the laird. He sounded as if it quite amused him, to be awkward.

"Art always has to be a challenge," Claire retorted. She was still struggling to open the new box of paints. Without warning, there was a devastating bellow of thunder, so close to the castle roof that Clair felt the rafters shake. Her hand slipped on the box and the scalpel sliced into the top of her finger.

"Ow!" she cried, dropping the box and squeezing her finger. Blood dripped onto the painting, one quick drop after another.

"Is anything wrong?" asked the laird, although he didn't make any attempt to move from his seat on the iron-bound trunk.

Claire winced, watching the blood well up. She was about to tell him that she had cut herself and that she wouldn't be able to continue painting when she saw that her blood had mingled with the wet paint on the laird's face *and had suffused it with an unnaturally healthy flush.*

"You've not hurt yourself, have you?" asked the laird.

"Oh, no," said Claire. She squeezed out more blood, and began to mix it with her paintbrush. Gradually the laird's face began to look rosier, and much more alive. "I'm fine, I'm absolutely fine." Thinking to herself: *now I've got you, you sly bastard. Now I'll show you how well I can paint. I'll catch you here for ever and ever, the way that I saw you, the way that I want you to be.*

The laird held his pose and said nothing, but watched her with a curious expression of satisfaction and contentedness, like a man who has tasted a particularly fine wine.

That night, in her room overlooking the grounds, Claire dreamed of men in ragged cloaks and feathered bonnets; men with gaunt faces and hollow eyes. She dreamed of smoke and blood and screaming. She heard a sharp, aggressive rattle of drums – drums that pursued her through one dream and into another.

When she woke up, it was still only five o'clock in the morning, and raining, and the window-catch was rattling and rattling in time to the drums in her dreams.

She dressed in jeans and a blue plaid blouse, and then she quiet-footedly climbed the stairs to the room where she was painting the laird's portrait. Somehow she knew what she was going to find, but she was still shocked.

The portrait was as white-faced as it had been before she had mixed the paint with her own blood. Whiter, if anything. His whole expression seemed to have changed, too, to a glare of silent emaciated fury.

Claire stared at the portrait in horror and fascination. Then, slowly, she sat down, and opened up her paintbox, and began to mix a flesh tone. Flake white, red and yellow ochre. When it was ready, she picked up her scalpel, and held her wrist over her palette. She hesitated for only a moment. The Laird of Dunain was glaring at her too angrily; too resentfully. She wasn't going to let a man like him get the better of her.

She slit her wrist in a long diagonal, and blood instantly pumped from her artery onto the palette, almost drowning the watercolours in rich and sticky red.

When the palette was flooded with blood, she bound her paint-rag around her wrist as tightly as she could, and gripped it with her teeth while she knotted it. Trembling, breathless, she began to mix blood and gouache, and then she began to paint.

She worked with her brush for almost an hour, but as fast as she applied the mixture of blood and paint, the faster it seemed to drain from the laird's chalk-white face.

At last – almost hysterical with frustration – she sat back and dropped her brush. The laird stared back at her – mocking, accusing, belittling her talent and her womanhood. Just like Alan. Just like every other man. You gave them everything and they still treated you with complete contempt.

But not this time. Not this time. She stood up, and unbuttoned her blouse, so that she confronted the portrait of the Laird of Dunain bare-breasted. Then she picked up her scalpel in her fist, so that the point pricked the plump pale flesh just below her navel.

"The sleepy bit lassie, she dreaded nae ill; the weather was cauld and the lassie lay still. She thought that the tailor could do her no ill."

She cut into her stomach. Her hand was shaking but she was calm and deliberate. She cut through skin and layers of white fat and deeper still, until her intestines exhaled a deep sweet breath. She was disappointed by the lack of blood. She had imagined that she would bleed like a pig. Instead, her wound simply glistened, and yellowish fluid flowed.

"There's somebody weary wi' lying her lane, there's some that are dowie, I trow wad be fain . . . to see that bit tailor come skippin' again."

Claire sliced upward, right up to her breastbone, and the scalpel was so sharp that it became lodged in her rib. She tugged it out, and the tugging sensation was worse than the pain. She wanted the blood, but she hadn't thought that it would hurt so much. The pain was as devastating as the thunderclap had been, overwhelming. She thought about screaming but she wasn't sure that it would do any good; and she had forgotten how.

With bloodied hands she reached inside her sliced-open stomach and grasped all the hot slippery heavy things she found there. She heaved them out, all over her painting of the Laird of Dunain, and wiped them around, and wiped them around, until the art-board was smothered in blood, and the portrait of the laird was almost completely obscured.

Then she pitched sideways, knocking her head against the oak-boarded floor. The light from the clerestory window brightened and faded, brightened and faded, and then faded away forever.

They took her to the Riverside Medical Centre but she was already dead. Massive trauma, loss of blood. Duncan stood in the car-park furiously smoking a cigarette and clutching himself. Margot sat on the leatherette seats in the waiting-room and wept.

They drove back to Dunain Castle. The laird was standing on the back lawn, watching the light play across the valley.

"She's dead, then?" he said, as Margot came marching up to him. "A grousome thing, no doubt about it."

Margot didn't know what to say to him. She could only stand in front of him and quake with anger. He seemed so self-satisfied, so calm, so pleased; his eyes green like emeralds, but flecked with red.

"Look," said the Laird of Dunain, pointing up to the birds that were circling overhead. "The hoodie-craws. They always know when there's a death."

Margot stormed up to the room where – only two hours ago – she had found Claire dying. It was bright as a church. And there on its board was the portrait of the Laird of Dunain, shining and clean, without a single smear of blood on it. The smiling, triumphant, rosy-cheeked Laird of Dunain.

"Self-opinionated chauvinist sod," she said, and she seized the art-board and ripped it in half, top to bottom. Out of temper. Out of enraged feminism. But, more than anything else, out of jealousy. Why had *she* never met a man that she would kill herself for?

And out in the garden, on the sloping lawns, the painting class heard a scream. It was a scream so echoing and terrible that they could scarcely believe that it had been uttered by one man.

In front of their eyes, the Laird of Dunain literally burst apart. His face exploded, his jawbone dropped out, his chest came bursting through his sweater in a crush of ribs and a bucketful of blood. There was so much blood that it sprayed up the walls of Dunain Castle, and ran down the windows.

They sat, open-mouthed, their paintbrushes poised, while he dropped onto the gravel path, and twitched, and lay still, while blood ran down everywhere, and the hoodie-craws circled and cried and cried again, because they always knew when there was a death.

"*Gie me the groat again, canny young man; the day it is short and the night it is lang; the dearest siller that ever I wan.*

"*The tailor fell thro' the bed, thimbles an' a'.*"

TINA RATH

A Trick of the Dark

TINA RATH SOLD HER FIRST dark fantasy story to *Catholic Fireside* in 1974. Since then her short fiction has appeared in both the small and mainstream press, including *Ghosts & Scholars*, *All Hallows*, *Women's Realm*, *Bella* and *The Magazine of Fantasy & Science Fiction*.

Her stories have been anthologized in *The Fontana Book of Great Ghost Stories*, *The Fontana Book of Horror Stories*, *Midnight Never Comes*, *Seriously Comic Fantasy*, Karl Edward Wagner's *The Year's Best Horror Stories: XV* and *The Mammoth Book of Vampire Stories by Women*.

With her husband, Tony, she has co-written stories for editor Mike Ashley's *Royal Whodunnits* and *Shakespearean Detectives*, and together they run Parlour Voices, a live reading/performance group.

More recently, Rath received a degree from London University for her thesis on 'The Vampire in Popular Fiction', and she edited *Conventional Vampires*, a thirtieth anniversary collection of vampire stories for The Dracula Society.

"The inspiration for this story was the cover of a paperback edition of *Dracula* ('The Most Famous Horror Story Ever Told')," reveals the author. "The illustration was obviously inspired by the Bela Lugosi *Dracula* film, and shows the Count in his vampire cloak bending menacingly over the sleeping Lucy. She is wearing a frilly nightie; there is a pretty coverlet on the bed, and a flowered lamp beside it.

"The contrast between the cosy bedroom and the dark, menacing (but erotic) figure of the vampire fascinated me and I tried to reproduce this atmosphere in my story. I hope I have succeeded."

'A Trick of the Dark' is published here for the first time.

"WHAT JOB FINISHES JUST at sunset?

Margaret jumped slightly. "What a weird question, darling. Park keeper, I suppose." Something made her turn to look at her daughter. She was propped up against her pillows, looking, Margaret thought guiltily, about ten years old. She must keep remembering, she told herself fiercely, that Maddie was nineteen. This silly heart-thing, as she called it, was keeping her in bed for much longer than they'd ever thought it would, but it couldn't stop her growing up . . . she must listen to her, and talk to her like a grown-up.

Intending to do just that, she went to sit on the edge of the bed. It was covered with a glossy pink eiderdown, embroidered with fat pink and mauve peonies. The lamp on Maddie's bedside table had a rosy shade. Maddie was wearing a pink bed-jacket, lovingly crocheted by her grandmother, and Maddie's pale blonde hair was tied back with a pink ribbon . . . but in the midst of this plethora of pink Maddie's face looked pale and peaky. The words of a story that Margaret had read to Maddie once – how many years ago? – came back to her: "Peak and pine, peak and pine." It was about a changeling child who never thrived, but lay in the cradle, crying and fretting, peaking and pining . . . in the end the creature had gone back to its own people, and she supposed that the healthy child had somehow got back to his mother, but she couldn't remember. Margaret shivered, wondering why people thought such horrid stories were suitable for children.

"What made you wonder who finishes work at sunset?" she asked.

"Oh – nothing," Maddie looked oddly shy, as she might have done if her mother had asked her about a boy who had partnered her at tennis, or asked her to a dance. If such a thing could ever have happened. She played with the pink ribbons at her neck and a little, a very little colour crept into that pale face. "It's just – well – I can't read all day, or—" She hesitated and Margaret mentally filled in the gap. She had her embroidery, her knitting, those huge complicated jigsaws that her friends were so good about finding for her, a notebook for jotting down those funny little verses that someone was going to ask someone's uncle about publishing . . . but all that couldn't keep her occupied all day.

"Sometimes I just look out of the window," Maddie said.

"Oh, darling . . ." Margaret couldn't bear to think of her daughter just lying there – just looking out of the window. "Why don't you call me when you get bored? We could have some lovely talks. Or I could telephone Bunty or Cissie or—''

It's getting quite autumnal after all, she thought, and Maddie's friends won't be out so much, playing tennis, or swimming or . . . You couldn't expect them to sit for hours in a sickroom. They dashed in, tanned and breathless from their games and bicycle rides, or wind-blown and glowing from a winter walk, and dropped off a jigsaw or a new novel . . . and went away.

"I don't mind, mummy," Maddie was saying. "It's amazing what you can see, even in a quiet street like this. I mean, that's why I like this room. Because you can see out."

Margaret looked out of the window. Yes. You could see a stretch of pavement, a bit of Mrs Creswell's hedge, a lamp-post, the postbox and Mrs Monkton's gate. It was not precisely an enticing view, and she exclaimed, "Oh, darling!" again.

"You'd be amazed who visits Mrs Monkton in the afternoons," Maddie said demurely.

"Good heavens, who—" Margaret exclaimed, but Maddie gave a reassuringly naughty giggle.

"That would be telling! You'll have to sit up here one afternoon and watch for yourself."

"I might," Margaret said. But how could she? There was always so much to do downstairs, letters to write, shopping to do, and cook to deal with. (Life to get on with?) She too, she realized, dropped in on Maddie, left her with things to sustain or amuse her. And went away.

"Perhaps we could move you downstairs, darling," she said. But that would be so difficult. The doctor had absolutely forbidden Maddie to use the stairs, so how on earth could they manage what Margaret could only, even in the privacy of her thoughts, call "the bathroom problem"? Too shame-making for Maddie to have to ask to be carried up the stairs every time she needed – and who was there to do it during the day? Maddie was very light – much too light – but her mother knew that she could not lift her, let alone carry her, by herself.

"But you can't see anything from the sitting-room," Maddie said.

"Oh darling—" Margaret realized she was going to have to leave Maddie alone again. Her husband would be home soon and she was beginning to have serious doubts about the advisability of reheating the fish pie . . . She must have a quick word with cook about cheese omelettes. If only cook wasn't so bad with eggs . . . "What's this about sunset anyway?" she said briskly.

"Sunset comes a bit earlier every day," Maddie said. "And just at sunset a man walks down the street."

"The same man, every night?" Margaret asked.

"The same man, always just after sunset," Maddie confirmed.

"Perhaps he's a postman?" Margaret suggested.

"Then he'd wear a uniform," Maddie said patiently. "And the same if he was a parkkeeper I suppose – they wear uniform too, don't they? Besides, he doesn't look like a postman."

"So – what does he look like?"

"It's hard to explain." Maddie struggled for the right words. "But – can you imagine a beautiful skull?"

"What! What a horrible idea!" Margaret stood up, clutching the grey foulard at her bosom. "Maddie, if you begin talking like this I shall call Dr Whiston. I don't care if he doesn't like coming out after dinner. Skull-headed men walking past the house every night indeed!"

Maddie pouted. "I didn't say that. It's just that his face is very – sculptured. You can see the bones under the skin, especially the cheekbones. It just made me think – he must even have a beautiful skull."

"And how is he dressed?" Margaret asked faintly.

"A white shirt and a sort of loose black coat," Maddie said. "And he has quite long curly black hair. I think he might be a student."

"No hat?" her mother asked, scandalized. "He sounds more like an anarchist! Really, Maddie, I wonder if I should go and have a word with the policeman on the corner and tell him that a suspicious character has been hanging about outside the house."

"No, mother!" Maddie sounded so anguished that her mother hastily laid a calming hand on her forehead.

"Now, darling, don't upset yourself. You must remember what the doctor said. Of course I won't call him if you don't want me to, or the policeman. That was a joke, darling! But you mustn't get yourself upset like this . . . Oh dear, your forehead feels quite clammy. Here, take one of your tablets. I'll get you a glass of water."

And in her very real anxiety for her daughter, worries about the fish pie and well-founded doubts about the substitute omelettes, Margaret almost forgot about the stranger. Almost, but not quite. A meeting with Mrs Monkton one evening when they had both hurried out to catch the last post and met in front of the postbox reminded her and she found herself asking if Mrs Monkton had noticed anyone "hanging about".

"A young man?" that lady exclaimed with a flash of what Margaret decided was rather indecent excitement. "But darling, there are no young men left." Margaret raised a hand in mute protest only to have it brushed aside by Mrs Monkton. "Well, not nearly enough to go round, anyway. I expect this one was waiting for Elsie."

Elsie worked for both Mrs Monkton and Margaret, coming in

several times a week to do "the rough", the cleaning that was beneath Margaret's cook and Mrs Monkton's extremely superior maid. She was a handsome girl with, it was rumoured, an obliging disposition, the sort who would never have been allowed across the threshold of a respectable household when Margaret was young. But nowadays . . . Mrs Monkton's suggestion did set Margaret's mind at rest. A hatless young man – yes, he must be waiting for Elsie. She might "have a word" with the girl about the propriety of encouraging young men to hang about the street for her; but, on the other hand, she might not . . . She hurried back home.

Bunty's mother came to tea, full of news. Bunty's elder sister was getting engaged to someone her mother described as "a bit n.q.o.s., but what can you do . . ." "N.q.o.s." was a rather transparent code for "not quite our sort". The young man's father was, it appeared, very, very rich, though no one was quite sure where he had made his money. He was going to give – to give outright! – (Bunty's mother had gasped) a big house in Surrey to the young couple. And he was going to furnish it too, unfortunately, according to his own somewhat . . . individual . . . taste.

"Chrome, my dear, chrome from floor to ceiling. The dining room looks like a milk bar. And as for the bedroom – Jack says" – she lowered her voice – "he says it looks like an avant-garde brothel in Berlin. Although how he knows anything about them I'm sure I'm not going to ask. But he's having nothing to do with the wedding," she added, sipping her tea as if it were hemlock. "I wonder my dear – would dear little Maddie be well enough to be a bridesmaid? It won't be until next June. I want to keep Pammy to myself for as long as I can . . ." She dabbed at her eyes.

"Of course," Margaret murmured doubtfully. And then, with more determination, "I'll ask the doctor."

And, rather surprising herself, she did. On Dr Whiston's next visit to Maddie, Margaret lured him into the sitting room with the offer of a glass of sherry and let him boom on for a while on how well Maddie was responding to his treatment. Then she asked the Question, the one she had, until that moment, not dared to ask.

"But when will Maddie be – quite well? Could she be a bridesmaid, say, in June next year?"

The doctor paused, sherry halfway to his lips. He was not used to being questioned. Margaret realized that he thought she had been intolerably frivolous. "Bridesmaid?" the doctor boomed. And then thawed, visibly. Women, he knew, cared about such things. "Bridesmaid! Well, why not? Provided she goes on as well as she has been.

And you don't let her get too excited. Not too many dress fittings, you know, and see you get her home early after the wedding. No dancing and only a tiny glass of champagne . . .''

"And will she ever we well enough . . . to . . . to . . . marry herself and to . . .'' But Margaret could not bring herself to finish that sentence to a man, not even a medical man.

"Marry – well, I wouldn't advise it. And babies? No. No. Still, that's the modern girl, isn't it? No use for husbands and children these days—'' and he boomed himself out of the house.

Margaret remembered that the doctor had married a much younger woman. Presumably the marriage was not a success . . . then she let herself think of Maddie. She wondered if Bunty's mother would like to exchange places with her. Margaret would never have to lose her daughter to the son of a nouveau riche war profiteer. Never . . . and she sat down in her pretty chintz-covered armchair and cried as quietly as she could, in case Maddie heard her. For some reason she never asked herself how far the doctor's confident boom might carry. Later she went up to her daughter, smiling gallantly.

"The doctor's so pleased with you, Maddie,'' she said. "He thinks you'll be well enough to be Pammy's bridesmaid! You'll have to be sure you finish her present in good time.''

Margaret had bought a tray cloth and six place mats stamped with the design of a figure in a poke bonnet and a crinoline, surrounded by flowers. Maddie was supposed to be embroidering them in tasteful naturalistic shades of pink, mauve and green, as a wedding gift for Pammy, but she seemed to have little enthusiasm for the task. Her mother stared at her, lying back in her nest of pillows. "Peak and pine! Peak and pine!'' said the voice in her head.

"Do you ever see your young man any more?'' she asked, more to distract herself than because she was really concerned.

"Oh, no,'' Maddie said, raising her shadowed eyes to her mother. "I don't think he was ever there at all. It was a trick of the dark.''

"Trick of the light, surely,'' Margaret said. And then, almost against her will, "Do you remember that story I used to read you? About the changeling child?''

"What, the one that lay in the cradle saying 'I'm old, I'm old, I'm ever so old'?'' Maddie said. "Whatever made you think of that?''

"I don't know,'' Margaret gasped. "But you know how you some-times get silly words going round and round your head – it's as if I can't stop repeating those words from the story. 'Peak and pine!' to myself over and over again.'' There, she had said it aloud. That must exorcize them, surely.

"But that's not from the changeling story,'' Maddie said. "It's from 'Christabel', – you know, Coleridge's poem about the weird Lady

Geraldine. She says it to the mother's ghost: 'Off wandering mother! Peak and pine!' We read it at school, but Miss Brownrigg made us miss out all that bit about Geraldine's breasts.''

"I should think so, too," Margaret said weakly.

Autumn became winter, although few people noticed by what tiny degrees the days grew shorter and shorter until sunset came at around four o'clock. Except perhaps Maddie, sitting propped up on her pillows, and watching every day for the young man who still walked down the street every evening, in spite of what she had told her mother. And even she could not have said just when he stopped walking directly past the window, and took to standing in that dark spot just between the lamp-post and the postbox, looking up at her . . .

"Where's your little silver cross, darling?" Margaret said suddenly, wondering vaguely when she had last seen Maddie wearing it.

"Oh, I don't know," Maddie said, too casually. "I think the clasp must have broken and it slipped off."

"Oh, but—" Margaret looked helplessly at her daughter. "I do hope Elsie hasn't picked it up. I sometimes think . . .''

"I expect it'll turn up," Maddie said. Her gaze slid away from her mother's face and returned to the window.

"How's Pammy's present coming along?" Margaret asked, speaking to that white reflection in the dark glass, trying to make her daughter turn back to her. She picked up Maddie's work-bag. And stared. One of the place mats had been completed. But the figure of the lady had been embroidered in shades of black and it was standing in the midst of scarlet roses and tall purple lilies. It was cleverly done: every fold and flounce was picked out . . . but Margaret found it rather disturbing. She was glad that the poke bonnet hid the figure's face . . . She looked up to realize that Maddie was looking at her almost slyly.

"Don't you like it?" her daughter asked.

"It's – it's quite modern isn't it?"

"What, lazy daisies and crinoline ladies, modern?" How long had Maddie's voice had that lazy mocking tone? She sounded like a world-weary adult talking to a very young and silly child.

Margaret put the work down.

"You will be all right, darling, won't you?" Margaret said, rushing into her daughter's room one cold December afternoon. "Only I must do some Christmas shopping, I really must . . ."

"Of course you must, mummy," Maddie said. "You've got my list, haven't you? Do try to find something really nice for Bunty, she's been so kind . . .''

And what I would really like to give her, Maddie thought, is a whole parcel of jigsaws . . . and all the time in the world to see how *she* likes them . . . She leaned against her pillows, watching her mother scurry down the street. Margaret would catch a bus at the corner by the church, and then an Underground train, and then face the crowded streets and shops of a near-Christmas West End London. Maddie would have plenty of time to herself. She knew (although her mother did not) that cook would be going out to have tea with her friend at Mrs Cresswell's at half-past three, and for at least one blessed hour Maddie would be entirely alone in the house.

She pulled herself further up in the bed, and fumbled in the drawer of her bedside table to find the contraband she had managed to persuade Elsie to bring in for her. Elsie had proved much more useful than Bunty or Cissie or any of her kind friends. She sorted through the scarlet lipstick, the eyeblack, the facepowder, and began to draw the kind of face she knew she had always wanted on the blank canvas of her pale skin. After twenty minutes of careful work she felt that she had succeeded rather well.

"I'm old, I'm old, I'm ever so old," Maddie crooned to herself. She freed her hair from its inevitable pink ribbon, and brushed it sleekly over her shoulders. Then she took off her lacy bed-jacket and the white winceyette nightie beneath it. Finally she slid into the garment that the invaluable Elsie had found for her (Heaven knew where, although Maddie had a shrewd suspicion it might have been stolen from another of Elsie's clients – perhaps the naughty Mrs Monkton). It was a nightdress made of layers of black and red chiffon, just a little too large for Maddie, but the way it tended to slide from her shoulders could have, she felt, its own attraction.

All these preparations had taken quite a long time, especially as Maddie had had to stop every so often to catch her breath and once to take one of her tablets . . . but she was ready just before sunset. She slipped out of bed, crossed the room, and sat in a chair beside the window. So. The trap was almost set. (But was she the trap or only the bait . . . ?) Only one thing remained to be done.

Maddie took out her embroidery scissors, and, clenching her teeth, ran the tiny sharp points into her wrist . . .

The bus was late and crowded. Margaret struggled off, trying to balance her load of packages and parcels and hurried down the road, past the churchyard wall, past Mrs Monkton's red-brick villa, past the post-box – and hesitated. For a moment she thought she had seen something – Maddie's strange man with the beautiful skull-like face?

But no, there were two white faces there in the shadows – no . . . there was nothing. A trick of the dark . . . She dropped her parcels in the hall and hurried up the stairs.

"Here I am, darling! I'm so sorry I'm late . . . Oh, Maddie . . . Maddie darling – whatever are you doing in the dark?"

She switched on the light.

"Maddie. Maddie, where are you?" she whispered. "What have you done?"

F. PAUL WILSON

Midnight Mass

OVER SEVEN MILLION COPIES of F. Paul Wilson's books are in print around the world and he is the author of such best-selling novels as *The Keep* (filmed in 1983) and *The Tomb*. In 1998 he resurrected his popular anti-hero Repairman Jack and recently published the seventh in the series, *Gateways*. Beacon Films is presently developing Jack into a franchise character.

In 2003 a micro-budget independent film adaptation of "Midnight Mass" (with a cameo by the author in the opening sequence) was released straight to video by Lions Gate. "Reviews were mixed, ranging from bad to just plain awful," reveals Wilson. More recently he combined the story with its two prequels, "The Lord's Work" and "Good Friday", and expanded them into an aggressive full-length novel that takes the battle to the undead.

In the following novella, which is a fast-moving thriller with echoes of Richard Matheson's *I Am Legend* and Stephen King's *'Salem's Lot*, Wilson comes up with a new twist on the theme while keeping his bloodsuckers strictly in the traditional vein . . .

I

IT HAD BEEN ALMOST a full minute since he'd slammed the brass knocker against the heavy oak door. That should have been proof enough. After all, wasn't the knocker in the shape of a cross? But no, they had to squint through their peephole and peer through the sidelights that framed the door.

Rabbi Zev Wolpin sighed and resigned himself to the scrutiny. He couldn't blame people for being cautious, but this seemed a bit overly so. The sun was in the west and shining full on his back; he was all but silhouetted in it. What more did they want?

I should maybe take off my clothes and dance naked?

He gave a mental shrug and savored the damp sea air. At least it was cool here. He'd bicycled from Lakewood, which was only ten miles inland from this same ocean but at least twenty degrees warmer. The bulk of the huge Tudor retreat house stood between him and the Atlantic, but the ocean's briny scent and rhythmic rumble were everywhere.

Spring Lake. An Irish Catholic seaside resort since before the turn of the century. He looked around at its carefully restored Victorian houses, the huge mansions arrayed here along the beach front, the smaller homes set in neat rows running straight back from the ocean. Many of them were still occupied. Not like Lakewood. Lakewood was an empty shell.

Not such a bad place for a retreat, he thought. He wondered how many houses like this the Catholic Church owned.

A series of clicks and clacks drew his attention back to the door as numerous bolts were pulled in rapid succession. The door swung inward revealing a nervous-looking young man in a long black cassock. As he looked at Zev his mouth twisted and he rubbed the back of his wrist across it to hide a smile.

"And what should be so funny?" Zev asked.

"I'm sorry. It's just—"

"I know," Zev said, waving off any explanation as he glanced down at the wooden cross slung on a cord around his neck. "I know."

A bearded Jew in a baggy black serge suit wearing a yarmulke and a cross. Hilarious, no?

So, *nu?* This was what the times demanded, this was what it had come to if he wanted to survive. And Zev did want to survive. Someone had to live to carry on the traditions of the Talmud and the Torah, even if there were hardly any Jews left alive in the world.

Zev stood on the sunny porch, waiting. The priest watched him in silence.

Finally Zev said, "Well, may a wandering Jew come in?"

"I won't stop you," the priest said, "but surely you don't expect me to invite you."

Ah, yes. Another precaution. The vampire couldn't cross the

threshold of a home unless he was invited in, so don't invite. A good habit to cultivate, he supposed.

He stepped inside and the priest immediately closed the door behind him, relatching all the locks one by one. When he turned around Zev held out his hand.

"Rabbi Zev Wolpin, Father. I thank you for allowing me in."

"Brother Christopher, sir," he said, smiling and shaking Zev's hand. His suspicions seemed to have been completely allayed. "I'm not a priest yet. We can't offer you much here, but—"

"Oh, I won't be staying long. I just came to talk to Father Joseph Cahill."

Brother Christopher frowned. "Father Cahill isn't here at the moment."

"When will he be back?"

"I – I'm not sure. You see—"

"Father Cahill is on another bender," said a stentorian voice behind Zev.

He turned to see an elderly priest facing him from the far end of the foyer. White-haired, heavy set, wearing a black cassock.

"I'm Rabbi Wolpin."

"Father Adams," the priest said, stepping forward and extending his hand.

As they shook Zev said, "Did you say he was on 'another' bender? I never knew Father Cahill to be much of a drinker."

"Apparently there was a lot we never knew about Father Cahill," the priest said stiffly.

"If you're referring to that nastiness last year," Zev said, feeling the old anger rise in him, "I for one never believed it for a minute. I'm surprised anyone gave it the slightest credence."

"The veracity of the accusation was irrelevant in the final analysis. The damage to Father Cahill's reputation was a *fait accompli.* Father Palmeri was forced to request his removal for the good of St Anthony's parish."

Zev was sure that sort of attitude had something to do with Father Joe being on "another bender."

"Where can I find Father Cahill?"

"He's in town somewhere, I suppose, making a spectacle of himself. If there's any way you can talk some sense into him, please do. Not only is he killing himself with drink but he's become quite an embarrassment to the priesthood and to the Church."

Which bothers you more? Zev wanted to ask but held his tongue.

"I'll try."

He waited for Brother Christopher to undo all the locks, then stepped toward the sunlight.

"Try Morton's down on Seventy-one," the younger man whispered as Zev passed.

Zev rode his bicycle south on 71. It was almost strange to see people on the streets. Not many, but more than he'd ever see in Lakewood again. Yet he knew that as the vampires consolidated their grip on the world and infiltrated the Catholic communities, there'd be fewer and fewer day people here as well.

He thought he remembered passing a place named Morton's on his way to Spring Lake. And then up ahead he saw it, by the railroad track crossing, a white stucco one-story box of a building with "Morton's Liquors" painted in big black letters along the side.

Father Adams' words echoed back to him: . . . *on another bender* . . .

Zev pushed his bicycle to the front door and tried the knob. Locked up tight. A look inside showed a litter of trash and empty shelves. The windows were barred; the back door was steel and locked as securely as the front. So where was Father Joe?

Then he spotted the basement window at ground level by the overflowing trash dumpster. It wasn't latched. Zev went down on his knees and pushed it open.

Cool, damp, musty air wafted against his face as he peered into the Stygian blackness. It occurred to him that he might be asking for trouble by sticking his head inside, but he had to give it a try. If Father Cahill wasn't here, Zev would begin the return trek to Lakewood and write this whole trip off as wasted effort.

"Father Joe?" he called. "Father Cahill?"

"That you again, Chris?" said a slightly slurred voice. "Go home, will you? I'll be all right. I'll be back later."

"It's me, Joe. Zev. From Lakewood."

He heard shoes scraping on the floor and then a familiar face appeared in the shaft of light from the window.

"Well I'll be damned. It *is* you! Thought you were Brother Chris come to drag me back to the retreat house. Gets scared I'm gonna get stuck out after dark. So how ya doin', Reb? Glad to see you're still alive. Come on in!"

Zev saw that Father Cahill's eyes were glassy and he swayed ever so slightly, like a skyscraper in the wind. He wore faded jeans and a black Bruce Springsteen *Tunnel of Love* Tour sweatshirt.

Zev's heart twisted at the sight of his friend in such condition. Such a mensch like Father Joe shouldn't be acting like a *shikker*. Maybe it was a mistake coming here. Zev didn't like seeing him like this.

"I don't have that much time, Joe. I came to tell you—"

"Get your bearded ass down here and have a drink or I'll come up and drag you down."

"All right," Zev said. "I'll come in but I won't have a drink."

He hid his bike behind the dumpster, then squeezed through the window. Father Joe helped him to the floor. They embraced, slapping each other on the back. Father Joe was a taller man, a giant from Zev's perspective. At six-four he was ten inches taller, at thirty-five he was a quarter-century younger; he had a muscular frame, thick brown hair, and – on better days – clear blue eyes.

"You're grayer, Zev, and you've lost weight."

"Kosher food is not so easily come by these days."

"All kinds of food is getting scarce." He touched the cross slung from Zev's neck and smiled. "Nice touch. Goes well with your zizith."

Zev fingered the fringe protruding from under his shirt. Old habits didn't die easily.

"Actually, I've grown rather fond of it."

"So what can I pour you?" the priest said, waving an arm at the crates of liquor stacked around him. "My own private reserve. Name your poison."

"I don't want a drink."

"Come on, Reb. I've got some nice hundred-proof Stoly here. You've got to have at least *one* drink—"

"Why? Because you think maybe you shouldn't drink alone?"

Father Joe smiled. "Touché."

"All right," Zev said. "*Bissel.* I'll have *one* drink on the condition that you *don't* have one. Because I wish to talk to you."

The priest considered that a moment, then reached for the vodka bottle.

"Deal."

He poured a generous amount into a paper cup and handed it over. Zev took a sip. He was not a drinker and when he did imbibe he preferred his vodka ice cold from a freezer. But this was tasty. Father Cahill sat back on a crate of Jack Daniel's and folded his arms.

"*Nu?*" the priest said with a Jackie Mason shrug.

Zev had to laugh. "Joe, I still say that somewhere in your family tree is Jewish blood."

For a moment he felt light, almost happy. When was the last time he had laughed? Probably more than a year now, probably at their table near the back of Horovitz's deli, shortly before the St Anthony's nastiness began, well before the vampires came.

Zev thought of the day they'd met. He'd been standing at the counter at Horovitz's waiting for Yussel to wrap up the stuffed derma he had ordered when this young giant walked in. He towered over the other rabbis in the place, looked as Irish as Paddy's pig, and wore a Roman collar. He said he'd heard this was the only place on the whole Jersey Shore where you could get a decent corned beef sandwich. He ordered one and cheerfully warned that it better be good. Yussel asked him what could he know about good corned beef and the priest replied that he grew up in Bensonhurst. Well, about half the people in Horovitz's on that day – and on any other day for that matter – grew up in Bensonhurst and before you knew it they were all asking him if he knew such-and-such a store and so-and-so's deli.

Zev then informed the priest – with all due respect to Yussel Horovitz behind the counter – that the best corned beef sandwich in the world was to be had at Shmuel Rosenberg's Jerusalem Deli in Bensonhurst. Father Cahill said he'd been there and agreed one hundred per cent.

Yussel served him his sandwich then. As he took a huge bite out of the corned beef on rye, the normal *tummel* of a deli at lunchtime died away until Horovitz's was as quiet as a *shoul* on Sunday morning. Everyone watched him chew, watched him swallow. Then they waited. Suddenly his face broke into this big Irish grin.

"I'm afraid I'm going to have to change my vote," he said. "Horovitz's of Lakewood makes the best corned beef sandwich in the world."

Amid cheers and warm laughter, Zev led Father Cahill to the rear table that would become theirs and sat with this canny and charming gentile who had so easily won over a roomful of strangers and provided such a *mechaieh* for Yussel. He learned that the young priest was the new assistant to Father Palmeri, the pastor at St Anthony's Catholic church at the northern end of Lakewood. Father Palmeri had been there for years but Zev had never so much as seen his face. He asked Father Cahill – who wanted to be called Joe – about life in Brooklyn these days and they talked for an hour.

During the following months they would run into each other so often at Horovitz's that they decided to meet regularly for lunch, on Mondays and Thursdays. They did so for years, discussing religion – Oy, the religious discussions! – politics, economics, philosophy, life in general. During those lunchtimes they solved most of the world's problems. Zev was sure they'd have solved them all if the scandal at St Anthony's hadn't resulted in Father Joe's removal from the parish.

But that was in another time, another world. The world before the vampires took over.

Zev shook his head as he considered the current state of Father Joe in the dusty basement of Morton's Liquors.

"It's about the vampires, Joe," he said, taking another sip of the Stoly. "They've taken over St Anthony's."

Father Joe snorted and shrugged.

"They're in the majority now, Zev, remember? They've taken over everything. Why should St Anthony's be different from any other parish in the world?"

"I didn't mean the parish. I meant the church."

The priest's eyes widened slightly. "The church? They've taken over the building itself?"

"Every night," Zev said. "Every night they are there."

"That's a holy place. How do they manage that?"

"They've desecrated the altar, destroyed all the crosses. St Anthony's is no longer a holy place."

"Too bad," Father Joe said, looking down and shaking his head sadly. "It was a fine old church." He looked up again, at Zev. "How do you know about what's going on at St Anthony's? It's not exactly in your neighborhood."

"A neighborhood I don't exactly have any more."

Father Joe reached over and gripped his shoulder with a huge hand.

"I'm sorry, Zev. I heard how your people got hit pretty hard over there. Sitting ducks, huh? I'm really sorry."

Sitting ducks. An appropriate description. Oh, they'd been smart, those bloodsuckers. They knew their easiest targets. Whenever they swooped into an area they singled out Jews as their first victims, and among Jews they picked the Orthodox first of the first. Smart. Where else would they be less likely to run up against a cross? It worked for them in Brooklyn, and so when they came south into New Jersey, spreading like a plague, they headed straight for the town with one of the largest collections of yeshivas in North America.

But after the Bensonhurst holocaust the people in the Lakewood communities did not take quite so long to figure out what was happening. The Reformed and Conservative synagogues started handing out crosses at Shabbes – too late for many but it saved a few. Did the Orthodox congregations follow suit? No. They hid in their homes and shules and yeshivas and read and prayed.

And were liquidated.

A cross, a crucifix – they held power over the vampires, drove them away. His fellow rabbis did not want to accept that simple fact because they could not face its devastating ramifications. To hold up a cross was to negate two thousand years of Jewish history, it was to say that the Messiah had come and they had missed him.

Did it say that? Zev didn't know. Argue about it later. Right now, people were dying. But the rabbis had to argue it now. And as they argued, their people were slaughtered like cattle.

How Zev railed at them, how he pleaded with them! Blind, stubborn fools! If a fire was consuming your house, would you refuse to throw water on it just because you'd always been taught not to believe in water? Zev had arrived at the rabbinical council wearing a cross and had been thrown out – literally sent hurtling through the front door. But at least he had managed to save a few of his own people. Too few.

He remembered his fellow Orthodox rabbis, though. All the ones who had refused to face the reality of the vampires' fear of crosses, who had forbidden their students and their congregations to wear crosses, who had watched those same students and congregations die en masse only to rise again and come for them. And soon those very same rabbis were roaming their own community, hunting the survivors, preying on other yeshivas, other congregations, until the entire community was liquidated and incorporated into the brotherhood of the vampire. The great fear had come to pass: they'd been assimilated.

The rabbis could have saved themselves, could have saved their people, but they would not bend to the reality of what was happening around them. Which, when Zev thought about it, was not at all out of character. Hadn't they spent generations learning to turn away from the rest of the world?

Those early days of anarchic slaughter were over. Now that the vampires held the ruling hand, the blood-letting had become more organized. But the damage to Zev's people had been done – and it was irreparable. Hitler would have been proud. His Nazi "final solution" was an afternoon picnic compared to the work of the vampires. They did in months what Hitler's Reich could not do in all the years of the Second World War.

There's only a few of us now. So few and so scattered. A final Diaspora. For a moment Zev was almost overwhelmed by grief, but he pushed it down, locked it back into that place where he kept his sorrows, and thought of how fortunate it was for his wife Chana that she died of natural causes before the horror began. Her soul had been too gentle to weather what had happened to their community.

"Not as sorry as I, Joe," Zev said, dragging himself back to the present. "But since my neighbourhood is gone, and since I have hardly any friends left, I use the daylight hours to wander. So call me the Wandering Jew. And in my wanderings I meet some of your old parishioners."

The priest's face hardened. His voice became acid.

"Do you, now? And how fares the remnant of my devoted flock?"

"They've lost all hope, Joe. They wish you were back."

He laughed. "Sure they do! Just like they rallied behind me when my name and honor were being dragged through the muck last year. Yeah, they want me back. I'll bet!"

"Such anger, Joe. It doesn't become you."

"Bullshit. That was the old Joe Cahill, the naive turkey who believed all his faithful parishioners would back him up. But no. Palmeri tells the bishop the heat is getting too much for him, the bishop removes me, and the people I dedicated my life to all stand by in silence as I'm railroaded out of my parish."

"It's hard for the commonfolk to buck a bishop."

"Maybe. But I can't forget how they stood quietly by while I was stripped of my position, my dignity, my integrity, of everything I wanted to be . . ."

Zev thought Joe's voice was going to break. He was about to reach out to him when the priest coughed and squared his shoulders.

"Meanwhile, I'm a pariah over here in the retreat house. A goddam leper. Some of them actually believe—" He broke off in a growl. "Ah, what's the use? It's over and done. Most of the parish is dead anyway, I suppose. And if I'd stayed there I'd probably be dead too. So maybe it worked out for the best. And who gives a shit anyway."

He reached for the bottle of Glenlivet next to him.

"No-no!" Zev said. "You promised!"

Father Joe drew his hand back and crossed his arms across his chest.

"Talk on, oh, bearded one. I'm listening."

Father Joe had certainly changed for the worse. Morose, bitter, apathetic, self-pitying. Zev was beginning to wonder how he could have called this man a friend.

"They've taken over your church, desecrated it. Each night they further defile it with butchery and blasphemy. Doesn't that mean anything to you?"

"It's Palmeri's parish. I've been benched. Let him take care of it."

"Father Palmeri is their leader."

"He should be. He's their pastor."

"No. He leads the vampires in the obscenities they perform in the church."

Father Joe stiffened and the glassiness cleared from his eyes.

"Palmeri? He's one of them?"

Zev nodded. "More than that. He's the local leader. He orchestrates their rituals."

Zev saw rage flare in the priest's eyes, saw his hands ball into fists, and for a moment he thought the old Father Joe was going to burst through.

Come on, Joe. Show me that old fire.

But then he slumped back onto the crate.

"Is that all you came to tell me?"

Zev hid his disappointment and nodded. "Yes."

"Good." He grabbed the scotch bottle. "Because I need a drink."

Zev wanted to leave, yet he had to stay, had to probe a little bit deeper and see how much of his old friend was left, and how much had been replaced by this new, bitter, alien Joe Cahill. Maybe there was still hope. So they talked on.

Suddenly he noticed it was dark.

"Gevalt!" Zev said. "I didn't notice the time!"

Father Joe seemed surprised too. He ran to the window and peered out.

"Damn! Sun's gone down!" He turned to Zev. "Lakewood's out of the question for you, Reb. Even the retreat house is too far to risk now. Looks like we're stuck here for the night."

"We'll be safe?"

He shrugged. "Why not? As far as I can tell I'm the only one who's been in here for months, and only in the daytime. Be pretty odd if one of those human leeches should decide to wander in here tonight."

"I hope so."

"Don't worry. We're okay if we don't attract attention. I've got a flashlight if we need it, but we're better off sitting here in the dark and shooting the breeze till sunrise." Father Joe smiled and picked up a huge silver cross, at least a foot in length, from atop one of the crates. "Besides, we're armed. And frankly, I can think of worse places to spend the night."

He stepped over to the case of Glenlivet and opened a fresh bottle. His capacity for alcohol was enormous.

Zev could think of worse places too. In fact he had spent a number of nights in much worse places since the holocaust. He decided to put the time to good use.

"So, Joe. Maybe I should tell you some more about what's happening in Lakewood."

After a few hours their talk died of fatigue. Father Joe gave Zev the flashlight to hold and stretched out across a couple of crates to sleep. Zev tried to get comfortable enough to doze but found sleep impossible. So he listened to his friend snore in the darkness of the cellar.

Poor Joe. Such anger in the man. But more than that – hurt. He felt betrayed, wronged. And with good reason. But with everything falling apart as it was, the wrong done to him would never be righted. He should forget about it already and go on with his life, but apparently he couldn't. Such a shame. He needed something to pull him out of his funk. Zev had thought news of what had happened to his old parish might rouse him, but it seemed only to make him want to drink more. Father Joe Cahill, he feared, was a hopeless case.

Zev closed his eyes and tried to rest. It was hard to get comfortable with the cross dangling in front of him so he took it off but laid it within easy reach. He was drifting toward a doze when he heard a noise outside. By the dumpster. Metal on metal.

My bicycle!

He slipped to the floor and tiptoed over to where Father Joe slept. He shook his shoulder and whispered.

"Someone's found my bicycle!"

The priest snorted but remained sleeping. A louder clatter outside made Zev turn, and as he moved his elbow struck a bottle. He grabbed for it in the darkness but missed. The sound of smashing glass echoed through the basement like a cannon shot. As the odor of scotch whiskey replaced the musty ambiance, Zev listened for further sounds from outside. None came.

Maybe it had been an animal. He remembered how raccoons used to raid his garbage at home . . . when he'd had a home . . . when he'd had garbage . . .

Zev stepped to the window and looked out. Probably an animal. He pulled the window open a few inches and felt cool night air wash across his face. He pulled the flashlight from his coat pocket and aimed it through the opening.

Zev almost dropped the light as the beam illuminated a pale, snarling demonic face, baring its fangs and hissing. He fell back as the thing's head and shoulders lunged through the window, its curved fingers clawing at him, missing. Then it launched itself the rest of the way through, hurtling toward Zev.

He tried to dodge but he was too slow. The impact knocked the flashlight from his grasp and it went rolling across the floor. Zev cried out as he went down under the snarling thing. Its ferocity was overpowering, irresistible. It straddled him and lashed at him, batting his fending arms aside, its clawed fingers tearing at his collar to free his throat, stretching his neck to expose the vulnerable flesh, its foul breath gagging him as it bent its fangs toward him. Zev screamed out his helplessness.

II

Father Joe awoke to the cries of a terrified voice.

He shook his head to clear it and instantly regretted the move. His head weighed at least two hundred pounds, and his mouth was stuffed with foul-tasting cotton. Why did he keep doing this to himself? Not only did it leave him feeling lousy, it gave him bad dreams. Like now.

Another terrified shout, only a few feet away.

He looked toward the sound. In the faint light from the flashlight rolling across the floor he saw Zev on his back, fighting for his life against—

Damn! This was no dream! One of those bloodsuckers had got in here!

He leaped over to where the creature was lowering its fangs toward Zev's throat. He grabbed it by the back of the neck and lifted it clear of the floor. It was surprisingly heavy but that didn't slow him. Joe could feel the anger rising in him, surging into his muscles.

"Rotten piece of filth!"

He swung the vampire by its neck and let it fly against the cinderblock wall. It impacted with what should have been bone-crushing force, but it bounced off, rolled on the floor, and regained its feet in one motion, ready to attack again. Strong as he was, Joe knew he was no match for a vampire's power. He turned, grabbed his big silver crucifix, and charged the creature.

"Hungry? Eat this!"

As the creature bared its fangs and hissed at him, Joe shoved the long lower end of the cross into its open mouth. Blue-white light flickered along the silver length of the crucifix, reflecting in the creature's startled, agonized eyes as its flesh sizzled and crackled. The vampire let out a strangled cry and tried to turn away but Joe wasn't through with it yet. He was literally seeing red as rage poured out of a hidden well and swirled through him. He rammed the cross deeper down the thing's gullet. Light flashed deep in its throat, illuminating the pale tissues from within. It tried to grab the cross and pull it out but the flesh of its fingers burned and smoked wherever they came in contact with the cross.

Finally Joe stepped back and let the thing squirm and scrabble up the wall and out the window into the night. Then he turned to Zev. If anything had happened—

"Hey, Reb!" he said, kneeling beside the older man. "You all right?"

"Yes," Zev said, struggling to his feet. "Thanks to you."

Joe slumped onto a crate, momentarily weak as his rage dissipated. *This is not what I'm about,* he thought. But it had felt so damn good to let it loose on that vampire. Too good. And that worried him.

I'm falling apart . . . like everything else in the world.

"That was too close," he said to Zev, giving the older man's shoulder a fond squeeze.

"Too close for that vampire for sure," Zev said, replacing his yarmulke. "And would you please remind me, Father Joe, that in the future if ever I should maybe get my blood sucked and become a vampire that I should stay far away from you.''

Joe laughed for the first time in too long. It felt good.

They climbed out at first light. Joe stretched his cramped muscles in the fresh air while Zev checked on his hidden bicycle.

"Oy," Zev said as he pulled it from behind the dumpster. The front wheel had been bent so far out of shape that half the spokes were broken. "Look what he did. Looks like I'll be walking back to Lakewood."

But Joe was less interested in the bike than in the whereabouts of their visitor from last night. He knew it couldn't have got far. And it hadn't. They found the vampire – or rather what was left of it – on the far side of the dumpster: a rotting, twisted corpse, blackened to a crisp and steaming in the morning sunlight. The silver crucifix still protruded from between its teeth.

Joe approached and gingerly yanked his cross free of the foul remains.

"Looks like you've sucked your last pint of blood," he said and immediately felt foolish.

Who was he putting on the macho act for? Zev certainly wasn't going to buy it. Too out of character. But then, what *was* his character these days? He used to be a parish priest. Now he was a nothing. A less than nothing.

He straightened up and turned to Zev.

"Come on back to the retreat house, Reb. I'll buy you breakfast."

But as Joe turned and began walking away, Zev stayed and stared down at the corpse.

"They say they don't wander far from where they spent their lives," Zev said. "Which means it's unlikely this fellow was Jewish if he lived around here. Probably Catholic. Irish Catholic, I'd imagine."

Joe stopped and turned. He stared at his long shadow. The hazy rising sun at his back cast a huge hulking shape before him, with a dark cross in one shadow hand and a smudge of amber light where it poured through the unopened bottle of Scotch in the other.

"What are you getting at?" he said.

"The Kaddish would probably not be so appropriate so I'm just wondering if maybe someone should give him the last rites or whatever it is you people do when one of you dies."

"He wasn't one of us," Joe said, feeling the bitterness rise in him. "He wasn't even human."

"Ah, but he used to be before he was killed and became one of them. So maybe now he could use a little help."

Joe didn't like the way this was going. He sensed he was being maneuvered.

"He doesn't deserve it," he said and knew in that instant he'd been trapped.

"I thought even the worst sinner deserved it," Zev said.

Joe knew when he was beaten. Zev was right. He shoved the cross and bottle into Zev's hands – a bit roughly, perhaps – then went and knelt by the twisted cadaver. He administered a form of the final sacrament. When he was through he returned to Zev and snatched back his belongings.

"You're a better man than I am, Gunga Din," he said as he passed.

"You act as if they're responsible for what they do after they become vampires," Zev said as he hurried along beside him, panting as he matched Joe's pace.

"Aren't they?"

"No."

"You're sure of that?"

"Well, not exactly. But they certainly aren't human anymore, so maybe we shouldn't hold them accountable on human terms."

Zev's reasoning tone flashed Joe back to the conversations they used to have in Horovitz's deli.

"But Zev, we know there's some of the old personality left. I mean, they stay in their home towns, usually in the basements of their old houses. They go after people they knew when they were alive. They're not just dumb predators, Zev. They've got the old consciousness they had when they were alive. Why can't they rise above it? Why can't they . . . resist?"

"I don't know. To tell the truth, the question has never occurred to me. A fascinating concept: an undead refusing to feed. Leave it to Father Joe to come up with something like that. We should discuss this on the trip back to Lakewood."

Joe had to smile. So *that* was what this was all about.

"I'm not going back to Lakewood."

"Fine. Then we'll discuss it now. Maybe the urge to feed is too strong to overcome."

"Maybe. And maybe they just don't try hard enough."

"This is a hard line you're taking, my friend."

"I'm a hard-line kind of guy."

"Well, you've become one."

Joe gave him a sharp look. "You don't know what I've become."

Zev shrugged. "Maybe true, maybe not. But do you truly think you'd be able to resist?"

"Damn straight."

Joe didn't know whether he was serious or not. Maybe he was just mentally preparing himself for the day when he might actually find himself in that situation.

"Interesting," Zev said as they climbed the front steps of the retreat house. "Well, I'd better be going. I've a long walk ahead of me. A long, *lonely* walk all the way back to Lakewood. A long, lonely, possibly *dangerous* walk back for a poor old man who—"

"All right, Zev! All *right*!" Joe said, biting back a laugh. "I get the point. You want me to go back to Lakewood. Why?"

"I just want the company," Zev said with pure innocence.

"No, really. What's going on in that Talmudic mind of yours? What are you cooking?"

"Nothing, Father Joe. Nothing at all."

Joe stared at him. Damn it all if his interest wasn't piqued. What was Zev up to? And what the hell? Why not go? He had nothing better to do.

"All right, Zev. You win. I'll come back to Lakewood with you. But just for today. Just to keep you company. And I'm not going anywhere near St Anthony's, okay? Understood?"

"Understood, Joe. Perfectly understood."

"Good. Now wipe that smile off your face and we'll get something to eat."

III

Under the climbing sun they walked south along the deserted beach, barefooting through the wet sand at the edge of the surf. Zev had never done this. He liked the feel of the sand between his toes, the coolness of the water as it sloshed over his ankles.

"Know what day it is?" Father Joe said. He had his sneakers slung over his shoulder. "Believe it or not, it's the Fourth of July."

"Oh, yes. Your Independence Day. We never made much of secular holidays. Too many religious ones to observe. Why should I not believe it's this date?"

Father Joe shook his head in dismay. "This is Manasquan Beach. You know what this place used to look like on the Fourth before the vampires took over? Wall-to-wall bodies."

"Really? I guess maybe sun-bathing is not the fad it used to be."

"Ah, Zev! Still the master of the understatement. I'll say one thing, though: the beach is cleaner than I've ever seen it. No beer cans or hypodermics." He pointed ahead. "But what's that up there?"

As they approached the spot, Zev saw a pair of naked bodies stretched out on the sand, one male, one female, both young and short-haired. Their skin was bronzed and glistened in the sun. The man lifted his head and stared at them. A blue crucifix was tattooed in the center of his forehead. He reached into the knapsack beside him and withdrew a huge, gleaming, nickel-plated revolver.

"Just keep walking," he said.

"Will do," Father Joe said. "Just passing through."

As they passed the couple, Zev noticed a similar tattoo on the girl's forehead. He noticed the rest of her too. He felt an almost-forgotten stirring deep inside him.

"A very popular tattoo," he said.

"Clever idea. That's one cross you can't drop or lose. Probably won't help you in the dark, but if there's a light on it might give you an edge."

They turned west and made their way inland, finding Route 70 and following it into Ocean County via the Brielle Bridge.

"I remember nightmare traffic jams right here every summer," Father Joe said as they trod the bridge's empty span. "Never thought I'd miss traffic jams."

They cut over to Route 88 and followed it all the way into Lakewood. Along the way they found a few people out and about in Bricktown and picking berries in Ocean County Park, but in the heart of Lakewood . . .

"A real ghost town," the priest said as they walked Forest Avenue's deserted length.

"Ghosts," Zev said, nodding sadly. It had been a long walk and he was tired. "Yes. Full of ghosts."

In his mind's eye he saw the shades of his fallen brother rabbis and all the yeshiva students, beards, black suits, black hats, crisscrossing back and forth at a determined pace on weekdays, strolling with their wives on Shabbes, their children trailing behind like ducklings.

Gone. All gone. Victims of the vampires. Vampires themselves now, most of them. It made him sick at heart to think of those good, gentle men, women, and children curled up in their basements now to avoid the light of day, venturing out in the dark to feed on others, spreading the disease . . .

He fingered the cross slung from his neck. *If only they had listened*!

"I know a place near St Anthony's where we can hide," he told the priest.

"You've traveled enough today, Reb. And I told you, I don't care about St Anthony's."

"Stay the night, Joe," Zev said, gripping the young priest's arm. He'd coaxed him this far; he couldn't let him get away now. "See what Father Palmeri's done."

"If he's one of them he's not a priest anymore. Don't call him Father."

"*They* still call him Father."

"Who?"

"The vampires."

Zev watched Father Joe's jaw muscles bunch.

Joe said, "Maybe I'll just take a quick trip over to St Anthony's myself—"

"No. It's different here. The area is thick with them – maybe twenty times as many as in Spring Lake. They'll get you if your timing isn't just right. I'll take you."

"You need rest, pal."

Father Joe's expression showed genuine concern. Zev was detecting increasingly softer emotions in the man since their reunion last night. A good sign perhaps?

"And rest I'll get when we get to where I'm taking you."

IV

Father Joe Cahill watched the moon rise over his old church and wondered at the wisdom of coming back. The casual decision made this morning in the full light of day seemed reckless and foolhardy now at the approach of midnight.

But there was no turning back. He'd followed Zev to the second floor of this two-story office building across the street from St Anthony's, and here they'd waited for dark. Must have been a law office once. The place had been vandalized, the windows broken, the furniture trashed, but there was an old Temple University Law School degree on the wall, and the couch was still in one piece. So while Zev caught some Z's, Joe sat and sipped a little of his scotch and did some heavy thinking.

Mostly he thought about his drinking. He'd done too much of that lately, he knew; so much so that he was afraid to stop cold. So he was taking just a touch now, barely enough to take the edge off. He'd finish the rest later, after he came back from that church over there.

He'd stared at St Anthony's since they'd arrived. It too had been extensively vandalized. Once it had been a beautiful little stone church, a miniature cathedral, really; very Gothic with all its pointed arches, steep roofs, crocketed spires, and multifoil stained glass windows. Now the windows were smashed, the crosses which had topped the steeple and each gable were gone, and anything resembling a cross in its granite exterior had been defaced beyond recognition.

As he'd known it would, the sight of St Anthony's brought back memories of Gloria Sullivan, the young, pretty church volunteer whose husband worked for United Chemical International in New York, commuting in every day and trekking off overseas a little too often. Joe and Gloria had seen a lot of each other around the church offices and had become good friends. But Gloria had somehow got the idea that what they had went beyond friendship, so she showed up at the rectory one night when Joe was there alone. He tried to explain that as attractive as she was, she was not for him. He had taken certain vows and meant to stick by them. He did his best to let her down easy but she'd been hurt. And angry.

That might have been that, but then her six-year-old son Kevin had come home from altar boy practice with a story about a priest making him pull down his pants and touching him. Kevin was never clear on who the priest had been, but Gloria Sullivan was. Obviously it had been Father Cahill – any man who could turn down the heartfelt offer of her love and her body had to be either a queer or worse. And a child molester was worse.

She took it to the police and to the papers.

Joe groaned softly at the memory of how swiftly his life had become hell. But he had been determined to weather the storm, sure that the real culprit eventually would be revealed. He had no proof – still didn't – but if one of the priests at St Anthony's was a pederast, he knew it wasn't him. That left Father Alberto Palmeri, St Anthony's fifty-five-year-old pastor. Before Joe could get to the truth, however, Father Palmeri requested that Father Cahill be removed from the parish, and the bishop complied. Joe had left under a cloud that had followed him to the retreat house in the next county and hovered over him till this day. The only place he'd found even brief respite from the impotent anger and bitterness that roiled under his skin and soured his gut every minute of every day was in the bottle – and that was sure as hell a dead end.

So why had he agreed to come back here? To torture himself? Or to get a look at Palmeri and see how low he had sunk?

Maybe that was it. Maybe seeing Palmeri wallowing in his true element would give him the impetus to put the whole St Anthony's incident behind him and rejoin what was left of the human race – which needed him now more than ever.

And maybe it wouldn't.

Getting back on track was a nice thought, but over the past few months Joe had found it increasingly difficult to give much of a damn about anyone or anything.

Except maybe Zev. He'd stuck by Joe through the worst of it, defending him to anyone who would listen. But an endorsement from an Orthodox rabbi had meant diddly in St Anthony's. And yesterday Zev had biked all the way to Spring Lake to see him. Old Zev was all right.

And he'd been right about the number of vampires here too. Lakewood was *crawling* with the things. Fascinated and repelled, Joe had watched the streets fill with them shortly after sundown.

But what had disturbed him more were the creatures who'd come out *before* sundown.

The humans. Live ones.

The collaborators.

If there was anything lower, anything that deserved true death more than the vampires themselves, it was the still-living humans who worked for them.

Someone touched his shoulder and he jumped. It was Zev. He was holding something out to him. Joe took it and held it up in the moonlight: a tiny crescent moon dangling from a chain on a ring.

"What's this?"

"An earring. The local Vichy wear them."

"Vichy? Like the Vichy French?"

"Yes. Very good. I'm glad to see that you're not as culturally illiterate as the rest of your generation. Vichy humans – that's what I call the collaborators. These earrings identify them to the local nest of vampires. They are spared."

"Where'd you get them?"

Zev's face was hidden in the shadows. "Their previous owners . . . lost them. Put it on."

"My ear's not pierced."

A gnarled hand moved into the moonlight. Joe saw a long needle clasped between the thumb and index finger.

"That I can fix," Zev said.

"Maybe you shouldn't see this," Zev whispered as they crouched in the deep shadows on St Anthony's western flank.

Joe squinted at him in the darkness, puzzled.

"You lay a guilt trip on me to get me here, now you're having second thoughts?"

"It is horrible like I can't tell you."

Joe thought about that. There was enough horror in the world outside St Anthony's. What purpose did it serve to see what was going on inside?

Because it used to be my church.

Even though he'd only been an associate pastor, never fully in charge, and even though he'd been unceremoniously yanked from the post, St Anthony's had been his first parish. He was here. He might as well know what they were doing inside.

"Show me."

Zev led him to a pile of rubble under a smashed stained glass window. He pointed up to where faint light flickered from inside.

"Look in there."

"You're not coming?"

"Once was enough, thank you."

Joe climbed as carefully, as quietly as he could, all the while becoming increasingly aware of a growing stench like putrid, rotting meat. It was coming from inside, wafting through the broken window. Steeling himself, he straightened up and peered over the sill.

For a moment he was disoriented, like someone peering out the window of a city apartment and seeing the rolling hills of a Kansas farm. This could not be the interior of St Anthony's.

In the flickering light of hundreds of sacramental candles he saw that the walls were bare, stripped of all their ornaments, of the plaques for the stations of the cross; the dark wood along the wall was scarred and gouged wherever there had been anything remotely resembling a cross. The floor too was mostly bare, the pews ripped from their neat rows and hacked to pieces, their splintered remains piled high at the rear under the choir balcony.

And the giant crucifix that had dominated the space behind the altar – only a portion of it remained. The cross-pieces on each side had been sawed off and so now an armless, life-size Christ hung upside down against the rear wall of the sanctuary.

Joe took in all that in a flash, then his attention was drawn to the unholy congregation that peopled St Anthony's this night. The collaborators – the Vichy humans, as Zev called them – made up the periphery of the group. They looked like normal, everyday people but each was wearing a crescent moon earring.

But the others, the group gathered in the sanctuary – Joe felt his hackles rise at the sight of them. They surrounded the altar in a tight knot. Their pale, bestial faces, bereft of the slightest trace of human warmth, compassion, or decency, were turned upward. His gorge rose when he saw the object of their rapt attention.

A naked teenage boy – his hands tied behind his back, was suspended over the altar by his ankles. He was sobbing and choking, his eyes wide and vacant with shock, his mind all but gone. The skin had been flayed from his forehead – apparently the Vichy had found an expedient solution to the cross tattoo – and blood ran in a slow stream down his abdomen and chest from his freshly truncated genitals. And beside him, standing atop the altar, a bloody-mouthed creature dressed in a long cassock. Joe recognized the thin shoulders, the graying hair trailing from the balding crown, but was shocked at the crimson vulpine grin he flashed to the things clustered below him.

"Now," said the creature in a lightly accented voice Joe had heard hundreds of times from St Anthony's pulpit.

Father Alberto Palmeri.

And from the group a hand reached up with a straight razor and drew it across the boy's throat. As the blood flowed down over his face, those below squeezed and struggled forward like hatchling vultures to catch the falling drops and scarlet trickles in their open mouths.

Joe fell away from the window and vomited. He felt Zev grab his arm and lead him away. He was vaguely aware of crossing the street and heading toward the ruined legal office.

V

"Why in God's name did you want me to see that?"

Zev looked across the office toward the source of the words. He could see a vague outline where Father Joe sat on the floor, his back against the wall, the open bottle of scotch in his hand. The priest had taken one drink since their return, no more.

"I thought you should know what they were doing to your church."

"So you've said. But what's the reason behind that one?"

Zev shrugged in the darkness. "I'd heard you weren't doing well, that even before everything else began falling apart, you had already fallen apart. So when I felt it safe to get away, I came to see you. Just as I expected, I found a man who was angry at everything and letting it eat up his *guderim*. I thought maybe it would be good to give that man something very specific to be angry at."

"You bastard!" Father Joe whispered. "Who gave you the right?"

"Friendship gave me the right, Joe. I should hear that you are rotting away and do nothing? I have no congregation of my own anymore so I turned my attention on you. Always I was a somewhat meddlesome rabbi."

"Still are. Out to save my soul, ay?"

"We rabbis don't save souls. Guide them maybe, hopefully give them direction. But only you can save your soul, Joe."

Silence hung in the air for awhile. Suddenly the crescent-moon earring Zev had given Father Joe landed in the puddle of moonlight on the floor between them.

"Why do they do it?" the priest said. "The Vichy – why do they collaborate?"

"The first were quite unwilling, believe me. They cooperated because their wives and children were held hostage by the vampires. But before too long the dregs of humanity began to slither out from under their rocks and offer their services in exchange for the immortality of vampirism."

"Why bother working for them? Why not just bare your throat to the nearest bloodsucker?"

"That's what I thought at first," Zev said. "But as I witnessed the Lakewood holocaust I detected the vampires' pattern. They can choose who joins their ranks, so after they've fully infiltrated a population, they change their tactics. You see, they don't want too many of their kind concentrated in one area. It's like too many carnivores in one forest – when the herds of prey are wiped out, the predators starve. So they start to employ a different style of killing. For only when the vampire draws the life's blood from the throat with its fangs does the victim become one of them. Anyone drained as in the manner of that boy in the church tonight dies a true death. He's as dead now as someone run over by a truck. He will not rise tomorrow night."

"I get it," Father Joe said. "The Vichy trade their daylight services and dirty work to the vampires now for immortality later on."

"Correct."

There was no humor in the soft laugh that echoed across the room from Father Joe.

"Swell. I never cease to be amazed at our fellow human beings. Their capacity for good is exceeded only by their ability to debase themselves."

"Hopelessness does strange things, Joe. The vampires know that. So they rob us of hope. That's how they beat us. They transform our friends and neighbors and leaders into their own, leaving us feeling alone, completely cut off. Some of us can't take the despair and kill ourselves."

"Hopelessness," Joe said. "A potent weapon."

After a long silence, Zev said, "So what are you going to do now, Father Joe?"

Another bitter laugh from across the room.

"I suppose this is the place where I declare that I've found new purpose in life and will now go forth into the world as a fearless vampire killer."

"Such a thing would be nice."

"Well screw that. I'm only going as far as across the street."

"To St Anthony's?"

Zev saw Father Joe take a swig from the Scotch bottle and then screw the cap on tight.

"Yeah. To see if there's anything I can do over there."

"Father Palmeri and his nest might not like that."

"I told you, don't call him Father. And screw *him*. Nobody can do what he's done and get away with it. I'm taking my church back."

In the dark, behind his beard, Zev smiled.

*   *   *

VI

Joe stayed up the rest of the night and let Zev sleep. The old guy needed his rest. Sleep would have been impossible for Joe anyway. He was too wired. He sat up and watched St Anthony's.

They left before first light, dark shapes drifting out the front doors and down the stone steps like parishioners leaving a predawn service. Joe felt his back teeth grind as he scanned the group for Palmeri, but he couldn't make him out in the dimness. By the time the sun began to peek over the rooftops and through the trees to the east, the street outside was deserted.

He woke Zev and together they approached the church. The heavy oak and iron front doors, each forming half of a pointed arch, were closed. He pulled them open and fastened the hooks to keep them open. Then he walked through the vestibule and into the nave.

Even though he was ready for it, the stench backed him up a few steps. When his stomach settled, he forced himself ahead, treading a path between the two piles of shattered and splintered pews. Zev walked beside him, a handkerchief pressed over his mouth.

Last night he had thought the place a shambles. He saw now that it was worse. The light of day poked into all the corners, revealing everything that had been hidden by the warm glow of the candles. Half a dozen rotting corpses hung from the ceiling – he hadn't noticed them last night – and others were sprawled on the floor against the walls. Some of the bodies were in pieces. Behind the chancel rail a headless female torso was draped over the front of the pulpit. To the left stood the statue of Mary. Someone had fitted her with foam rubber breasts and a huge dildo. And at the rear of the sanctuary was the armless Christ hanging head down on the upright of his cross.

"My church," he whispered as he moved along the path that had once been the center aisle, the aisle brides used to walk down with their fathers. "Look what they've done to my church!"

Joe approached the huge block of the altar. Once it had been backed against the far wall of the sanctuary, but he'd had it moved to the front so that he could celebrate Mass facing his parishioners. Solid Carrara marble, but you'd never know it now. So caked with dried blood, semen, and feces it could have been made of styrofoam.

His revulsion was fading, melting away in the growing heat of his rage, drawing the nausea with it. He had intended to clean up the place but there was so much to be done, too much for two men. It was hopeless.

"Fadda Joe?"

He spun at the sound of the strange voice. A thin figure stood uncertainly in the open doorway. A man of about fifty edged forward timidly.

"Fadda Joe, izat you?"

Joe recognized him now. Carl Edwards. A twitchy little man who used to help pass the collection basket at 10:30 Mass on Sundays. A transplantee from Jersey City – hardly anyone around here was originally from around here. His face was sunken, his eyes feverish as he stared at Joe.

"Yes, Carl. It's me."

"Oh, tank God!" He ran forward and dropped to his knees before Joe. He began to sob. "You come back! Tank God, you come back!"

Joe pulled him to his feet.

"Come on now, Carl. Get a grip."

"You come back ta save us, ain'tcha? God sent ya here to punish him, din't He?"

"Punish whom?"

"Fadda Palmeri! He's one a dem! He's da woist a alla dem! He—"

"I know," Joe said. "I know."

"Oh, it's so good to have ya back, Fadda Joe! We ain't knowed what to do since da suckers took ova. We been prayin fa someone like youse an now ya here. It's a freakin' miracle!"

Joe wanted to ask Carl where he and all these people who seemed to think they needed him now had been when he was being railroaded out of the parish. But that was ancient history.

"Not a miracle, Carl," Joe said, glancing at Zev. "Rabbi Wolpin brought me back." As Carl and Zev shook hands, Joe said, "And I'm just passing through."

"Passing t'rough? No. Dat can't be! Ya gotta stay!"

Joe saw the light of hope fading in the little man's eyes. Something twisted within him, tugging him.

"What can I do here, Carl? I'm just one man."

"I'll help! I'll do whatever ya want! Jes tell me!"

"Will you help me clean up?"

Carl looked around and seemed to see the cadavers for the first time. He cringed and turned a few shades paler.

"Yeah . . . sure. Anyting."

Joe looked at Zev. "Well? What do you think?"

Zev shrugged. "I should tell you what to do? My parish it's not."

"Not mine either."

Zev jutted his beard at Carl. "I think maybe he'd tell you differently."

Joe did a slow turn. The vaulted nave was utterly silent except for the buzzing of the flies around the cadavers.

A massive clean-up job. But if they worked all day they could make a decent dent in it. And then—

And then what?

Joe didn't know. He was playing this by ear. He'd wait and see what the night brought.

"Can you get us some food, Carl? I'd sell my soul for a cup of coffee."

Carl gave him a strange look.

"Just a figure of speech, Carl. We'll need some food if we're going to keep working."

The man's eyes lit again.

"Dat means ya staying?"

"For a while."

"I'll getcha some food," he said excitedly as he ran for the door. "An' coffee. I know someone who's still got coffee. She'll part wit' some of it for Fadda Joe." He stopped at the door and turned. "Ay, an' Fadda, I neva believed any a dem tings dat was said aboutcha. Neva."

Joe tried but he couldn't hold it back.

"It would have meant a lot to have heard that from you last year, Carl."

The man lowered his eyes. "Yeah. I guess it woulda. But I'll make it up to ya, Fadda. I will. You can take dat to da bank."

Then he was out the door and gone. Joe turned to Zev and saw the old man rolling up his sleeves.

"*Nu?*" Zev said. "The bodies. Before we do anything else, I think maybe we should move the bodies."

VII

By early afternoon, Zev was exhausted. The heat and the heavy work had taken their toll. He had to stop and rest. He sat on the chancel rail and looked around. Nearly eight hours work and they'd barely scratched the surface. But the place did look and smell better.

Removing the flyblown corpses and scattered body parts had been the worst of it. A foul, gut-roiling task that had taken most of the morning. They'd carried the corpses out to the small graveyard behind the church and left them there. Those people deserved a decent burial but there was no time for it today.

Once the corpses were gone, Father Joe had torn the defilements from the statue of Mary and then they'd turned their attention to the huge crucifix. It took a while but they finally found Christ's plaster arms in the pile of ruined pews. They were still nailed to the sawn-off cross-piece of the crucifix. While Zev and Father Joe worked at jury-rigging a series of braces to reattach the arms, Carl found a mop and bucket and began the long, slow process of washing the fouled floor of the nave.

Now the crucifix was intact again – the life-size plaster Jesus had his arms reattached and was once again nailed to his refurbished cross. Father Joe and Carl had restored him to his former position of dominance. The poor man was upright again, hanging over the center of the sanctuary in all his tortured splendor.

A grisly sight. Zev could never understand the Catholic attachment to these gruesome statues. But if the vampires loathed them, then Zev was for them all the way.

His stomach rumbled with hunger. At least they'd had a good breakfast. Carl had returned from his food run this morning with bread, cheese, and two thermoses of hot coffee. He wished now they'd saved some. Maybe there was a crust of bread left in the sack. He headed back to the vestibule to check and found an aluminium pot and a paper bag sitting by the door. The pot was full of beef stew and the sack contained three cans of Pepsi.

He poked his head out the doors but no one was in sight on the street outside. It had been that way all day – he'd spy a figure or two peeking in the front doors; they'd hover there for a moment as if to confirm that what they had heard was true, then they'd scurry away. He looked at the meal that had been left. A group of the locals must have donated from their hoard of canned stew and precious soft drinks to fix this. Zev was touched.

He called Father Joe and Carl.

"Tastes like Dinty Moore," Father Joe said around a mouthful of the stew.

"It is," Carl said. "I recognize da little potatoes. Da ladies of the parish must really be excited about youse comin' back to break inta deir canned goods like dis."

They were feasting in the sacristy, the small room off the sanctuary where the priests had kept their vestments – a clerical Green Room, so to speak. Zev found the stew palatable but much too salty. He wasn't about to complain, though.

"I don't believe I've ever had anything like this before."

"I'd be real surprised if you had," said Father Joe. "I doubt very much that something that calls itself Dinty Moore is kosher."

Zev smiled but inside he was suddenly filled with a great sadness. Kosher . . . how meaningless now seemed all the observances which he had allowed to rule and circumscribe his life. Such a fierce proponent of strict dietary laws he'd been in the days before the Lakewood holocaust. But those days were gone, just as the Lakewood community was gone. And Zev was a changed man. If he hadn't changed, if he were still observing, he couldn't sit here and sup with these two men. He'd have to be elsewhere, eating special classes of specially prepared foods off separate sets of dishes. But really, wasn't division what holding to the dietary laws in modern times was all about? They served a purpose beyond mere observance of tradition. They placed another wall between observant Jews and outsiders, keeping them separate even from other Jews who didn't observe.

Zev forced himself to take a big bite of the stew. Time to break down all the walls between people . . . while there was still enough time and people left alive to make it matter.

"You okay, Zev?" Father Joe asked.

Zev nodded silently, afraid to speak for fear of sobbing. Despite all its anachronisms, he missed his life in the good old days of last year. Gone. It was all gone. The rich traditions, the culture, the friends, the prayers. He felt adrift – in time and in space. Nowhere was home.

"You sure?" The young priest seemed genuinely concerned.

"Yes, I'm okay. As okay as you could expect me to feel after spending the better part of the day repairing a crucifix and eating non-kosher food. And let me tell you, that's not so okay."

He put his bowl aside and straightened from his chair.

"Come on, already. Let's get back to work. There's much yet to do."

VIII

"Sun's almost down," Carl said.

Joe straightened from scrubbing the altar and stared west through one of the smashed windows. The sun was out of sight behind the houses there.

"You can go now, Carl," he said to the little man. "Thanks for your help."

"Where youse gonna go, Fadda?"

"I'll be staying right here."

Carl's prominent Adam's apple bobbed convulsively as he swallowed.

"Yeah? Well den, I'm staying too. I tol' ya I'd make it up ta ya, din't I? An besides, I don't tink the suckas'll like da new, improved St Ant'ny's too much when dey come back tonight, d'you? I don't even tink dey'll get t'rough da doors."

Joe smiled at the man and looked around. Luckily it was July when the days were long. They'd had time to make a difference here. The floors were clean, the crucifix was restored and back in its proper position, as were most of the Stations of the Cross plaques. Zev had found them under the pews and had taken the ones not shattered beyond recognition and rehung them on the walls. Lots of new crosses littered those walls. Carl had found a hammer and nails and had made dozens of them from the remains of the pews.

"No. I don't think they'll like the new decor one bit. But there's something you can get us if you can, Carl. Guns. Pistols, rifles, shotguns, anything that shoots."

Carl nodded slowly. "I know a few guys who can help in dat department."

"And some wine. A little red wine if anybody's saved some."

"You got it."

He hurried off.

"You're planning Custer's last stand, maybe?" Zev said from where he was tacking the last of Carl's crude crosses to the east wall.

"More like the Alamo."

"Same result," Zev said with one of his shrugs.

Joe turned back to scrubbing the altar. He'd been at it for over an hour now. He was drenched with sweat and knew he smelled like a bear, but he couldn't stop until it was clean.

An hour later he was forced to give up. No use. It wouldn't come clean. The vampires must have done something to the blood and foulness to make the mixture seep into the surface of the marble like it had.

He sat on the floor with his back against the altar and rested. He didn't like resting because it gave him time to think. And when he started to think he realized that the odds were pretty high against his seeing tomorrow morning.

At least he'd die well fed. Their secret supplier had left them a dinner of fresh fried chicken by the front doors. Even the memory of it made his mouth water. Apparently someone was *really* glad he was back.

To tell the truth, though, as miserable as he'd been, he wasn't ready to die. Not tonight, not any night. He wasn't looking for an Alamo or a Little Big Horn. All he wanted to do was hold off the vampires till dawn. Keep them out of St Anthony's for one night. That was all. That would be a statement – *his* statement. If he found an opportunity to ram a stake through Palmeri's rotten heart, so much the better, but he wasn't counting on that. One night. Just to let them know they couldn't have their way everywhere with everybody whenever they felt like it. He had surprise on his side tonight, so maybe it would work. One night. Then he'd be on his way.

"What the fuck have you *done?*"

Joe looked up at the shout. A burly, long-haired man in jeans and a flannel shirt stood in the vestibule staring at the partially restored nave. As he approached, Joe noticed his crescent moon earring.

A Vichy.

Joe balled his fists but didn't move.

"Hey, I'm talking to you, mister. Are you responsible for this?"

When all he got from Joe was a cold stare, he turned to Zev.

"Hey, you! Jew! What the hell do you think *you're* doing?" He started toward Zev. "You get those fucking crosses off—"

"Touch him and I'll break you in half," Joe said in a low voice. The Vichy skidded to a halt and stared at him.

"Hey, asshole! Are you crazy? Do you know what Father Palmeri will do to you when he arrives?"

"*Father* Palmeri? Why do you still call him that?"

"It's what he wants to be called. And he's going to call you *dog meat* when he gets here!"

Joe pulled himself to his feet and looked down at the Vichy. The man took two steps back. Suddenly he didn't seem so sure of himself.

"Tell him I'll be waiting. Tell him Father Cahill is back."

"You're a priest? You don't look like one."

"Shut up and listen. Tell him Father Joe Cahill is back – and he's pissed. Tell him that. Now get out of here while you still can."

The man turned and hurried out into the growing darkness. Joe turned to Zev and found him grinning through his beard.

"'Father Joe Cahill is back – and he's pissed.' I like that."

"We'll make it into a bumper sticker. Meanwhile let's close those doors. The criminal element is starting to wander in. I'll see if we can find some more candles. It's getting dark in here."

IX

He wore the night like a tuxedo.

Dressed in a fresh cassock, Father Alberto Palmeri turned off County Line Road and strolled toward St Anthony's. The night was lovely, especially when you owned it. And he owned the night in this area of Lakewood now. He loved the night. He felt at one with it, attuned to its harmonies and its discords. The darkness made him feel so alive. Strange to have to lose your life before you could really feel alive. But this was it. He'd found his niche, his métier.

Such a shame it had taken him so long. All those years trying to deny his appetites, trying to be a member of the other side, cursing himself when he allowed his appetites to win, as he had with increasing frequency toward the end of his mortal life. He should have given in to them completely long ago.

It had taken undeath to free him.

And to think he had been afraid of undeath, had cowered in fear each night in the cellar of the church, surrounded by crosses. Fortunately he had not been as safe as he'd thought and one of the beings he now called brother was able to slip in on him in the dark while he dozed. He saw now that he had lost nothing but his blood by that encounter.

And in trade he'd gained a world.

For now it was his world, at least this little corner of it, one in which he was completely free to indulge himself in any way he wished. Except for the blood. He had no choice about the blood. That was a new appetite, stronger than all the rest, one that would not be denied. But he did not mind the new appetite in the least. He'd found interesting ways to sate it.

Up ahead he spotted dear, defiled St Anthony's. He wondered what his servants had prepared for him tonight. They were quite imaginative. They'd yet to bore him.

But as he drew nearer the church, Palmeri slowed. His skin prickled. The building had changed. Something was very wrong there, wrong inside. Something amiss with the light that beamed from the windows. This wasn't the old familiar candlelight, this was something else, something more. Something that made his insides tremble.

Figures raced up the street toward him. Live ones. His night vision picked out the earrings and familiar faces of some of his servants. As they neared he sensed the warmth of the blood coursing just beneath their skins. The hunger rose in him and he fought the urge to rip into one of their throats. He couldn't allow himself that pleasure. He had to keep the servants dangling, keep them working for him and the nest. They needed the services of the indentured living to remove whatever obstacles the cattle might put in their way.

"Father! Father!" they cried.

He loved it when they called him Father, loved being one of the undead and dressing like one of the enemy.

"Yes, my children. What sort of victim do you have for us tonight?"

"No victim, father – trouble!"

The edges of Palmeri's vision darkened with rage as he heard of the young priest and the Jew who had dared to try to turn St Anthony's into a holy place again. When he heard the name of the priest, he nearly exploded.

"Cahill? Joseph Cahill is back in my church?"

"He was cleaning the altar!" one of the servants said.

Palmeri strode toward the church with the servants trailing behind. He knew that neither Cahill nor the Pope himself could clean that altar. Palmeri had desecrated it himself; he had learned how to do that when he became nest leader. But what else had the young pup dared to do?

Whatever it was, it would be undone. *Now!*

Palmeri strode up the steps and pulled the right door open— and screamed in agony.

The light! The *light!* The LIGHT! White agony lanced through Palmeri's eyes and seared his brain like two hot pokers. He retched and threw his arms across his face as he staggered back into the cool, comforting darkness.

It took a few minutes for the pain to drain off, for the nausea to pass, for vision to return.

He'd never understand it. He'd spent his entire life in the presence of crosses and crucifixes, surrounded by them. And yet as soon as he'd become undead, he was unable to bear the sight of one. As a matter of fact, since he'd become undead, he'd never even *seen* one. A cross was no longer an object. It was a light, a light so excruciatingly bright, so blazingly white that it was sheer agony to look at it. As a child in Naples he'd been told by his mother not to look at the sun, but when there'd been talk of an eclipse, he'd stared directly into its eye. The pain of looking at a cross was a hundred, no, a thousand times worse than that. And the bigger the cross or crucifix, the worse the pain.

He'd experienced monumental pain upon looking into St Anthony's tonight. That could only mean that Joseph, that young bastard, had refurbished the giant crucifix. It was the only possible explanation.

He swung on his servants.

"Get in there! Get that crucifix down!"

"They've got guns!"

"Then get help. But get it *down*!"

"We'll get guns too! We can—"

"*No*! I want him! I want that priest alive! I want him for myself! Anyone who kills him will suffer a very painful, very long and lingering true death! Is that clear?"

It was clear. They scurried away without answering.

Palmeri went to gather the other members of the nest.

X

Dressed in a cassock and a surplice, Joe came out of the sacristy and approached the altar. He noticed Zev keeping watch at one of the windows. He didn't tell him how ridiculous he looked carrying the shotgun Carl had brought back. He held it so gingerly, like it was full of nitroglycerine and would explode if he jiggled it.

Zev turned, and smiled when he saw him.

"*Now* you look like the old Father Joe we all used to know."

Joe gave him a little bow and proceeded toward the altar.

All right: He had everything he needed. He had the Missal they'd found in among the pew debris earlier today. He had the wine; Carl had brought back about four ounces of sour red babarone. He'd found a smudged surplice and a dusty cassock on the floor of one of the closets in the sacristy, and he wore them now. No hosts, though. A crust of bread left over from breakfast would have to do. No chalice, either. If he'd known he was going to be saying Mass he'd have come prepared. As a last resort he'd used the can opener in the rectory to remove the top from one of the Pepsi cans from lunch. Quite a stretch from the gold chalice he'd used since his ordination, but probably more in line with what Jesus had used at that first Mass – the Last Supper.

He was uncomfortable with the idea of weapons in St Anthony's but he saw no alternative. He and Zev knew nothing about guns, and Carl knew little more; they'd probably do more damage to themselves than to the Vichy if they tried to use them. But maybe the sight of them would make the Vichy hesitate, slow them down. All he needed was a little time here, enough to get to the consecration.

This is going to be the most unusual Mass in history, he thought.

But he was going to get through it if it killed him. And that was a real possibility. This might well be his last Mass. But he wasn't afraid. He was too excited to be afraid. He'd had a slug of the Scotch – just enough to ward off the DTs – but it had done nothing to quell the buzz of the adrenalin humming along every nerve in his body.

He spread everything out on the white tablecloth he'd taken from the rectory and used to cover the filthy altar. He looked at Carl.

"Ready?"

Carl nodded and stuck the .38 caliber pistol he'd been examining in his belt.

"Been a while, Fadda. We did it in Latin when I was a kid but I tink I can swing it."

"Just do your best and don't worry about any mistakes."

Some Mass. A defiled altar, a crust for a host, a Pepsi can for a chalice, a fifty-year-old, pistol-packing altar boy, and a congregation consisting of a lone, shotgun-carrying Orthodox Jew.

Joe looked heavenward.

You do understand, don't you, Lord, that this was arranged on short notice?

Time to begin.

He read the Gospel but dispensed with the homily. He tried to remember the Mass as it used to be said, to fit in better with Carl's outdated responses. As he was starting the Offertory the front doors flew open and a group of men entered – ten of them, all with crescent moons dangling from their ears. Out of the corner of his eye he saw Zev move away from the window toward the altar, pointing his shotgun at them.

As soon as they entered the nave and got past the broken pews, the Vichy fanned out toward the sides. They began pulling down the Stations of the Cross, ripping Carl's makeshift crosses from the walls and tearing them apart. Carl looked up at Joe from where he knelt, his eyes questioning, his hand reaching for the pistol in his belt.

Joe shook his head and kept up with the Offertory.

When all the little crosses were down, the Vichy swarmed behind the altar. Joe chanced a quick glance over his shoulder and saw them begin their attack on the newly repaired crucifix.

"Zev!" Carl said in a low voice, cocking his head toward the Vichy. "Stop 'em!"

Zev worked the pump on the shotgun. The sound echoed through the church. Joe heard the activity behind him come to a sudden halt. He braced himself for the shot . . .

But it never came.

He looked at Zev. The old man met his gaze and sadly shook his head. He couldn't do it. To the accompaniment of the sound of renewed activity and derisive laughter behind him, Joe gave Zev a tiny nod of reassurance and understanding, then hurried the Mass toward the Consecration.

As he held the crust of bread aloft, he started at the sound of the life-sized crucifix crashing to the floor, cringed as he heard the freshly buttressed arms and crosspiece being torn away again.

As he held the wine aloft in the Pepsi can, the swaggering, grinning Vichy surrounded the altar and brazenly tore the cross from around his neck. Zev and Carl put up a struggle to keep theirs but were overpowered.

And then Joe's skin began to crawl as a new group entered the nave. There had to be at least forty of them, all of them vampires.

And Palmeri was leading them.

XI

Palmeri hid his hesitancy as he approached the altar. The crucifix and its intolerable whiteness were gone, yet something was not right. Something repellent here, something that urged him to flee. What?

Perhaps it was just the residual effect of the crucifix and all the crosses they had used to line the walls. That had to be it. The unsettling aftertaste would fade as the night wore on. Oh, yes. His nightbrothers and sisters from the nest would see to that.

He focused his attention on the man behind the altar and laughed when he realized what he held in his hands.

"Pepsi, Joseph? You're trying to consecrate Pepsi?" He turned to his nest siblings. "Do you see this, my brothers and sisters? Is this the man we are to fear? And look who he has with him! An old Jew and a parish hanger-on!"

He heard their hissing laughter as they fanned out around him, sweeping toward the altar in a wide phalanx. The Jew and Carl – he recognized Carl and wondered how he'd avoided capture for so long – retreated to the other side of the altar where they flanked Joseph. And Joseph . . . Joseph's handsome Irish face so pale and drawn, his mouth drawn into such a tight, grim line. He looked scared to death. And well he should be.

Palmeri put down his rage at Joseph's audacity. He was glad he had returned. He'd always hated the young priest for his easy manner with people, for the way the parishioners had flocked to him with their problems despite the fact that he had nowhere near the experience of their older and wiser pastor. But that was over now. That world was gone, replaced by a nightworld – Palmeri's world. And no one would be flocking to Father Joe for anything when Palmeri was through with him. "Father Joe" – how he'd hated it when way the parishioners had started calling him that. Well, their Father Joe would provide superior entertainment tonight. This was going to be *fun.*

"Joseph, Joseph, Joseph," he said as he stopped and smiled at the young priest across the altar. "This futile gesture is so typical of your arrogance."

But Joseph only stared back at him, his expression a mixture of defiance and repugnance. And that only fueled Palmeri's rage.

"Do I repel you, Joseph? Does my new form offend your precious shanty-Irish sensibilities? Does my undeath disgust you?"

"You managed to do all that while you were still alive, Alberto."

Palmeri allowed himself to smile. Joseph probably thought he was putting on a brave front, but the tremor in his voice betrayed his fear.

"Always good with the quick retort, weren't you, Joseph. Always thinking you were better than me, always putting yourself above me."

"Not much of a climb where a child molester is concerned."

Palmeri's anger mounted.

"So superior. So self-righteous. What about *your* appetites, Joseph? The secret ones? What are they? Do you always hold them in check? Are you so far above the rest of us that you never give in to an improper impulse? I'll bet you think that even if we made you one of us you could resist the blood hunger."

He saw by the startled look in Joseph's face that he had struck a nerve. He stepped closer, almost touching the altar.

"You do, don't you? You really think you could resist it! Well, we shall see about that, Joseph. By dawn you'll be drained – we'll each take a turn at you – and when the sun rises you'll have to hide from its light. When the night comes you'll be one of us. And then all the rules will be off. The night will be yours. You'll be able to do anything and everything you've ever wanted. But the blood hunger will be on you too. You won't be sipping your god's blood, as you've done so often, but *human* blood. You'll thirst for hot, human blood, Joseph. And you'll have to sate that thirst. There'll be no choice. And I want to be there when you do, Joseph. I want to be there to laugh in your face as you suck up the crimson nectar, and keep on laughing every night as the red hunger lures you into infinity.''

And it *would* happen. Palmeri knew it as sure as he felt his own thirst. He hungered for the moment when he could rub dear Joseph's face in the muck of his own despair.

"I was about to finish saying Mass," Joseph said coolly. "Do you mind if I finish?"

Palmeri couldn't help laughing this time.

"Did you really think this charade would work? Did you really think you could celebrate Mass on *this*?"

He reached out and snatched the tablecloth from the altar, sending the Missal and the piece of bread to the floor and exposing the fouled surface of the marble.

"Did you really think you could effect the Transubstantiation here? Do you really believe any of that garbage? That the bread and wine actually take on the substance of—" he tried to say the name but it wouldn't form "—the Son's body and blood?"

One of the nest brothers, Frederick, stepped forward and leaned over the altar, smiling.

"Transubstantiation?" he said in his most unctuous voice, pulling the Pepsi can from Joseph's hands. "Does that mean that this is the blood of the Son?"

A whisper of warning slithered through Palmeri's mind. Something about the can, something about the way he found it difficult to bring its outline into focus . . .

"Brother Frederick, maybe you should—"

Frederick's grin broadened. "I've always wanted to sup on the blood of a deity."

The nest members hissed their laughter as Frederick raised the can and drank.

Palmeri was jolted by the explosion of intolerable brightness that burst from Fredrick's mouth. The inside of his skull glowed beneath his scalp and shafts of pure white light shot from his ears, nose, eyes – every orifice in his head. The glow spread as it flowed down through his throat and chest and into his abdominal cavity, silhouetting his ribs before melting through his skin. Frederick was liquefying where he stood, his flesh steaming, softening, running like glowing molten lava.

No! This couldn't be happening! Not now when he had Joseph in his grasp!

Then the can fell from Frederick's dissolving fingers and landed on the altar top. Its contents splashed across the fouled surface, releasing another detonation of brilliance, this one more devastating than the first. The glare spread rapidly, extending over the upper surface and running down the sides, moving like a living thing, engulfing the entire altar, making it glow like a corpuscle of fire torn from the heart of the sun itself.

And with the light came blast-furnace heat that drove Palmeri back, back, back until he had to turn and follow the rest of his nest in a mad, headlong rush from St Anthony's into the cool, welcoming safety of the outer darkness.

XII

As the vampires fled into the night, their Vichy toadies behind them, Zev stared in horrid fascination at the puddle of putrescence that was all that remained of the vampire Palmeri had called Frederick. He glanced at Carl and caught the look of dazed wonderment on his face. Zev touched the top of the altar – clean, shiny, every whorl of the marble surface clearly visible.

There was fearsome power here. Incalculable power. But instead of elating him, the realization only depressed him. How long had this been going on? Did it happen at every Mass? Why had he spent his entire life ignorant of this?

He turned to Father Joe.

"What happened?"

"I – I don't know."

"A miracle!" Carl said, running his palm over the altar top.

"A miracle and a meltdown," Father Joe said. He picked up the empty Pepsi can and looked into it. "You know, you go through the seminary, through your ordination, through countless Masses *believing* in the Transubtantiation. But after all these years . . . to actually *know* . . ."

Zev saw him rub his finger along the inside of the can and taste it. He grimaced.

"What's wrong?" Zev asked.

"Still tastes like sour barbarone . . . with a hint of Pepsi."

"Doesn't matter what it tastes like. As far as Palmeri and his friends are concerned, it's the real thing."

"No," said the priest with a small smile. "That's Coke."

And then they started laughing. It wasn't that funny, but Zev found himself roaring along with other two. It was more a release of tension than anything else. His sides hurt. He had to lean against the altar to support himself.

It took the return of the Vichy to cure the laughter. They charged in carrying a heavy fire blanket. This time Father Joe did not stand by passively as they invaded his church. He stepped around the altar and met them head on.

He was great and terrible as he confronted them. His giant stature and raised fists cowed them for a few heartbeats. But then they must have remembered that they outnumbered him twelve to one and charged him. He swung a massive fist and caught the lead Vichy square on the jaw. The blow lifted him off his feet and he landed against another. Both went down.

Zev dropped to one knee and reached for the shotgun. He would use it this time, he would shoot these vermin, he swore it!

But then someone landed on his back and drove him to the floor. As he tried to get up he saw Father Joe, surrounded, swinging his fists, laying the Vichy out every time he connected. But there were too many. As the priest went down under the press of them, a heavy boot thudded against the side of Zev's head. He sank into darkness.

XIII

. . . a throbbing in his head, stinging pain in his cheek, and a voice, sibilant yet harsh . . .

". . . now, Joseph. Come on. Wake up. I don't want you to miss this!"

Palmeri's sallow features swam into view, hovering over him, grinning like a skull. Joe tried to move but found his wrists and arms tied. His right hand throbbed, felt twice its normal size; he must have broken it on a Vichy jaw. He lifted his head and saw that he was tied spread-eagle on the altar, and that the altar had been covered with the fire blanket.

"Melodramatic, I admit," Palmeri said, "but fitting, don't you think? I mean, you and I used to sacrifice our god symbolically here every weekday and multiple times on Sundays, so why shouldn't this serve as *your* sacrificial altar?"

Joe shut his eyes against a wave of nausea. This couldn't be happening.

"Thought you'd won, didn't you?" When Joe wouldn't answer him, Palmeri went on. "And even if you'd chased me out of here for good, what would you have accomplished? The world is ours now, Joseph. Feeders and cattle – that is the hierarchy. We are the feeders. And tonight you'll join us. But *he* won't. *Voila*!"

He stepped aside and made a flourish toward the balcony. Joe searched the dim, candlelit space of the nave, not sure what he was supposed to see. Then he picked out Zev's form and he groaned. The old man's feet were lashed to the balcony rail; he hung upside down, his reddened face and frightened eyes turned his way. Joe fell back and strained at the ropes but they wouldn't budge.

"Let him go!"

"What? And let all that good rich Jewish blood go to waste? Why, these people are the Chosen of God! They're a delicacy!"

"Bastard!"

If he could just get his hands on Palmeri, just for a minute.

"Tut-tut, Joseph. Not in the house of the Lord. The Jew should have been smart and run away like Carl."

Carl got away? Good. The poor guy would probably hate himself, call himself a coward the rest of his life, but he'd done what he could. Better to live on than get strung up like Zev.

We're even, Carl.

"But don't worry about your rabbi. None of us will lay a fang on him. He hasn't earned the right to join us. We'll use the razor to bleed him. And when he's dead, he'll be dead for keeps. But not you, Joseph. Oh no, not you." His smile broadened. "You're mine."

Joe wanted to spit in Palmeri's face – not so much as an act of defiance as to hide the waves of terror surging through him – but there was no saliva to be had in his parched mouth. The thought of being undead made him weak. To spend eternity like . . . he looked at the rapt faces of Palmeri's fellow vampires as they clustered under Zev's suspended form . . . like *them*?

He *wouldn't* be like them! He wouldn't allow it!

But what if there was no choice? What if becoming undead toppled a lifetime's worth of moral constraints, cut all the tethers on his human hungers, negated all his mortal concepts of how a life should be lived? Honor, justice, integrity, truth, decency, fairness, love – what if they became meaningless words instead of the footings for his life?

A thought struck him.

"A deal, Alberto," he said.

"You're hardly in a bargaining position, Joseph."

"I'm not? Answer me this: Do the undead ever kill each other? I mean, has one of them ever driven a stake through another's heart?"

"No. Of course not."

"Are you sure? You'd better be sure before you go through with your plans tonight. Because if I'm forced to become one of you, I'll be crossing over with just one thought in mind: to find you. And when I do I won't stake your heart, I'll stake your arms and legs to the pilings of the Point Pleasant boardwalk where you can watch the sun rise and feel it slowly crisp your skin to charcoal."

Palmeri's smile wavered. "Impossible. You'll be different. You'll want to thank me. You'll wonder why you ever resisted."

"You'd better sure of that, Alberto . . . for your sake. Because I'll have all eternity to track you down. And I'll find you, Alberto. I swear it on my own grave. Think on that."

"Do you think an empty threat is going to cow me?"

"We'll find out how empty it is, won't we? But here's the deal: Let Zev go and I'll let you be."

"You care that much for an old Jew?"

"He's something you never knew in life, and never will know: he's a friend." *And he gave me back my soul.*

Palmeri leaned closer. His foul, nauseous breath wafted against Joe's face.

"A friend? How can you be friends with a dead man?" With that he straightened and turned toward the balcony. "Do him! *Now!*"

As Joe shouted out frantic pleas and protests, one of the vampires climbed up the rubble toward Zev. Zev did not struggle. Joe saw him close his eyes, waiting. As the vampire reached out with the straight razor, Joe bit back a sob of grief and rage and helplessness. He was about to squeeze his own eyes shut when he saw a flame arc through the air from one of the windows. It struck the floor with a crash of glass and a *wooomp*! of exploding flame.

Joe had only heard of such things, but he immediately realized that he had just seen his first Molotov cocktail in action. The splattering gasoline caught the clothes of a nearby vampire who began running in circles, screaming as it beat at its flaming clothes. But its cries were drowned by the roar of other voices, a hundred or more. Joe looked around and saw people – men, women, teenagers – climbing in the windows, charging through the front doors. The women held crosses on high while the men wielded long wooden pikes – broom, rake, and shovel handles whittled to sharp points. Joe recognized most of the faces from the Sunday Masses he had said here for years.

St Anthony's parishioners were back to reclaim their church.

"Yes!" he shouted, not sure of whether to laugh or cry. But when he saw the rage in Palmeri's face, he laughed. "Too bad, Alberto!"

Palmeri made a lunge at his throat but cringed away as a woman with an upheld crucifix and a man with a pike charged the altar – Carl and a woman Joe recognized as Mary O'Hare.

"Told ya I wun't letcha down, din't I, Fadda?" Carl said, grinning and pulling out a red Swiss Army knife. He began sawing at the rope around Joe's right wrist. "Din't I?"

"That you did, Carl. I don't think I've ever been so glad to see anyone in my entire life. But how—?"

"I told 'em. I run t'rough da parish, goin' house ta house. I told 'em dat Fadda Joe was in trouble an' dat we let him down before but we shoun't let him down again. He come back fa us, now we gotta go back fa him. Simple as dat. And den *dey* started runnin' house ta house, an afore ya knowed it, we had ourselfs a little army. We come ta kick ass, Fadda, if you'll excuse da expression."

"Kick all the ass you can, Carl."

Joe glanced at Mary O'Hare's terror-glazed eyes as she swiveled around, looking this way and that; he saw how the crucifix trembled in her hand. She wasn't going to kick too much ass in her state, but she was *here*, dear God, she was here for him and for St Anthony's despite the terror that so obviously filled her. His heart swelled with love for these people and pride in their courage.

As soon as his arms were free, Joe sat up and took the knife from Carl. As he sawed at his leg ropes, he looked around the church.

The oldest and youngest members of the parishioner army were stationed at the windows and doors where they held crosses aloft, cutting off the vampires' escape, while all across the nave – chaos. Screams, cries, and an occasional shot echoed through St Anthony's. The vampires were outnumbered three to one and seemed blinded and confused by all the crosses around them. Despite their super-human strength, it appeared that some were indeed getting their asses kicked. A number were already writhing on the floor, impaled on pikes. As Joe watched, he saw a pair of the women, crucifixes held before them, backing a vampire into a corner. As it cowered there with its arms across its face, one of the men charged in with a sharpened rake handle held like a lance and ran it through.

But a number of parishioners lay in inert, bloody heaps on the floor, proof that the vampires and the Vichy were claiming their share of victims too.

Joe freed his feet and hopped off the altar. He looked around for Palmeri – he *wanted* Palmeri – but the vampire priest had lost himself in the melée. Joe glanced up at the balcony and saw that Zev was still hanging there, struggling to free himself. He started across the nave to help him.

XIV

Zev hated that he should be hung up here like a salami in a deli window. He tried again to pull his upper body up far enough to reach his leg ropes but he couldn't get close. He had never been one for exercise; doing a sit-up flat on the floor would have been difficult, so what made him think he could do the equivalent maneuver hanging upside down by his feet? He dropped back, exhausted, and felt the blood rush to his head again. His vision swam, his ears pounded, he felt like the skin of his face was going to burst open. Much more of this and he'd have a stroke or worse maybe.

He watched the upside-down battle below and was glad to see the vampires getting the worst of it. These people – seeing Carl among them, Zev assumed they were part of St Anthony's parish – were ferocious, almost savage in their attacks on the vampires. Months' worth of pent-up rage and fear was being released upon their tormentors in a single burst. It was almost frightening.

Suddenly he felt a hand on his foot. Someone was untying his knots. Thank you, Lord. Soon he would be on his feet again. As the cords came loose he decided he should at least attempt to participate in his own rescue.

Once more, Zev thought. *Once more I'll try.*

With a grunt he levered himself up, straining, stretching to grasp something, anything. A hand came out of the darkness and he reached for it. But Zev's relief turned to horror when he felt the cold clamminess of the thing that clutched him, that pulled him up and over the balcony rail with inhuman strength. His bowels threatened to evacuate when Palmeri's grinning face loomed not six inches from his own.

"It's not over yet, Jew," he said softly, his foul breath clogging Zev's nose and throat. "Not by a long shot!"

He felt Palmeri's free hand ram into his belly and grip his belt at the buckle, then the other hand grab a handful of his shirt at the neck. Before he could struggle or cry out, he was lifted free of the floor and hoisted over the balcony rail.

And the demon's voice was in his ear.

"Joseph called you a friend, Jew. Let's see if he really meant it."

XV

Joe was half way across the floor of the nave when he heard Palmeri's voice echo above the madness.

"Stop them, Joseph! Stop them now or I drop your friend!"

Joe looked up and froze. Palmeri stood at the balcony rail, leaning over it, his eyes averted from the nave and all its newly arrived crosses. At the end of his outstretched arms was Zev, suspended in mid-air over the splintered remains of the pews, over a particularly large and ragged spire of wood that pointed directly at the middle of Zev's back. Zev's frightened eyes were flashing between Joe and the giant spike below.

Around him Joe heard the sounds of the melée drop a notch, then drop another as all eyes were drawn to the tableau on the balcony.

"A human can die impaled on a wooden stake just as well as a vampire!" Palmeri cried. "And just as quickly if it goes through his heart. But it can take hours of agony if it rips through his gut."

St Anthony's grew silent as the fighting stopped and each faction backed away to a different side of the church, leaving Joe alone in the middle.

"What do you want, Alberto?"

"First I want all those crosses put away so that I can see!"

Joe looked to his right where his parishioners stood.

"Put them away," he told them. When a murmur of dissent arose, he added, "Don't put them down, just out of sight. Please."

Slowly, one by one at first, then in groups, the crosses and crucifixes were placed behind backs or tucked out of sight within coats.

To his left, the vampires hissed their relief and the Vichy cheered. The sound was like hot needles being forced under Joe's fingernails. Above, Palmeri turned his face to Joe and smiled.

"That's better."

"What do you want?" Joe asked, knowing with a sick crawling in his gut exactly what the answer would be.

"A trade," Palmeri said.

"Me for him, I suppose?" Joe said.

Palmeri's smile broadened. "Of course."

"No, Joe!" Zev cried.

Palmeri shook the old man roughly. Joe heard him say, "Quiet, Jew, or I'll snap your spine!" Then he looked down at Joe again. "The other thing is to tell your rabble to let my people go." He laughed and shook Zev again. "Hear that, Jew? A Biblical reference – Old Testament, no less!"

"All right," Joe said without hesitation.

The parishioners on his right gasped as one and cries of "No!" and "You can't!" filled St Anthony's. A particularly loud voice nearby shouted, "He's only a lousy kike!"

Joe wheeled on the man and recognized Gene Harrington, a carpenter. He jerked a thumb back over his shoulder at the vampires and their servants.

"You sound like you'd be more at home with them, Gene."

Harrington backed up a step and looked at his feet.

"Sorry, Father," he said in a voice that hovered on the verge of a sob. "But we just got you back!"

"I'll be all right," Joe said softly.

And he meant it. Deep inside he had a feeling that he would come through this, that if he could trade himself for Zev and face Palmeri one-on-one, he could come out the victor, or at least battle him to a draw. Now that he was no longer tied up like some sacrificial lamb, now that he was free, with full use of his arms and legs again, he could not imagine dying at the hands of the likes of Palmeri.

Besides, one of the parishioners had given him a tiny crucifix. He had it closed in the palm of his hand.

But he had to get Zev out of danger first. That above all else. He looked up at Palmeri.

"All right, Alberto. I'm on my way up."

"Wait!" Palmeri said. "Someone search him."

Joe gritted his teeth as one of the Vichy, a blubbery, unwashed slob, came forward and searched his pockets. Joe thought he might get away with the crucifix but at the last moment he was made to open his hands. The Vichy grinned in Joe's face as he snatched the tiny cross from his palm and shoved it into his pocket.

"He's clean now!" the slob said and gave Joe a shove toward the vestibule.

Joe hesitated. He was walking into the snake pit unarmed now. A glance at his parishioners told him he couldn't very well turn back now.

He continued on his way, clenching and unclenching his tense, sweaty fists as he walked. He still had a chance of coming out of this alive. He was too angry to die. He prayed that when he got within reach of the ex-priest the smoldering rage at how he had framed him when he'd been pastor, at what he'd done to St Anthony's since then would explode and give him the strength to tear Palmeri to pieces.

"No!" Zev shouted from above. "Forget about me! You've started something here and you've got to see it through!"

Joe ignored his friend.

"Coming, Alberto."

Father Joe's coming, Alberto. And he's pissed. Royally *pissed.*

XVI

Zev craned his neck around, watching Father Joe disappear beneath the balcony.

"Joe! Come back!"

Palmeri shook him again.

"Give it up, old Jew. Joseph never listened to anyone and he's not listening to you. He still believes in faith and virtue and honesty, in the power of goodness and truth over what he perceives as evil. He'll come up here ready to sacrifice himself for you, yet sure in his heart that he's going to win in the end. But he's wrong."

"No!" Zev said.

But in his heart he knew that Palmeri was right. How could Joe stand up against a creature with Palmeri's strength, who could hold Zev in the air like this for so long? Didn't his arms ever tire?

"Yes!" Palmeri hissed. "He's going to lose and we're going to win. We'll win for the same reason we'll always win. We don't let anything as silly and transient as sentiment stand in our way. If we'd been winning below and situations were reversed – if Joseph were holding one of my nest brothers over that wooden spike below – do you think I'd pause for a moment? For a second? Never! That's why this whole exercise by Joseph and these people is futile."

Futile . . . Zev thought. Like much of his life, it seemed. Like all of his future. Joe would die tonight and Zev would live on, a cross-wearing Jew, with the traditions of his past sacked and in flames, and nothing in his future but a vast, empty, limitless plain to wander alone.

There was a sound on the balcony stairs and Palmeri turned his head.

"Ah, Joseph," he said.

Zev couldn't see the priest but he shouted anyway.

"Go back Joe! Don't let him trick you!"

"Speaking of tricks," Palmeri said, leaning further over the balcony rail as an extra warning to Joe, "I hope you're not going to try anything foolish."

"No," said Joe's tired voice from somewhere behind Palmeri. "No tricks. Pull him in and let him go."

Zev could not let this happen. And suddenly he knew what he had to do. He twisted his body and grabbed the front of Palmeri's cassock while bringing his legs up and bracing his feet against one of the uprights of the brass balcony rail. As Palmeri turned his startled face toward him, Zev put all his strength into his legs for one convulsive backward push against the railing, pulling Palmeri with him. The vampire priest was overbalanced. Even his enormous strength could not help him once his feet came free of the floor. Zev saw his undead eyes widen with terror as his lower body slipped over the railing. As they fell free, Zev wrapped his arms around Palmeri and clutched his cold and surprisingly thin body tight against him.

"What goes through this old Jew goes through you!" he shouted into the vampire's ear.

For an instant he saw Joe's horrified face appear over the balcony's receding edge, heard Joe's faraway shout of "*No!*" mingle with Palmeri's nearer scream of the same word, then there was a spine-cracking jar and a tearing, wrenching pain beyond all comprehension in his chest. In an eyeblink he felt the sharp spire of wood rip through him and into Palmeri.

And then he felt no more.

As roaring blackness closed in he wondered if he'd done it, if this last desperate, foolish act had succeeded. He didn't want to die without finding out. He wanted to know—

But then he knew no more.

XVII

Joe shouted incoherently as he hung over the rail and watched Zev's fall, gagged as he saw the bloody point of the pew remnant burst through the back of Palmeri's cassock directly below him. He saw

Palmeri squirm and flop around like a speared fish, then go limp atop Zev's already inert form.

As cheers mixed with cries of horror and the sounds of renewed battle rose from the nave, Joe turned away from the balcony rail and dropped to his knees.

"Zev!" he cried aloud! "Good God, Zev!"

Forcing himself to his feet, he stumbled down the back stairs, through the vestibule, and into the nave. The vampires and the Vichy were on the run, as cowed and demoralized by their leader's death as the parishioners were buoyed by it. Slowly, steadily, they were falling before the relentless onslaught. But Joe paid them scant attention. He fought his way to where Zev lay impaled beneath Palmeri's already rotting corpse. He looked for a sign of life in his old friend's glazing eyes, a hint of a pulse in his throat under his beard, but there was nothing.

"Oh, Zev, you shouldn't have. You shouldn't have."

Suddenly he was surrounded by a cheering throng of St Anthony's parishioners.

"We did it, Fadda Joe!" Carl cried, his face and hands splattered with blood. "We killed 'em all! We got our church back!"

"Thanks to this man here," Joe said, pointing to Zev.

"No!" someone shouted. "Thanks to *you*!"

Amid the cheers, Joe shook his head and said nothing. Let them celebrate. They deserved it. They'd reclaimed a small piece of the planet as their own, a toe-hold and nothing more. A small victory of minimal significance in the war, but a victory nonetheless. They had their church back, at least for tonight. And they intended to keep it.

Good. But there would be one change. If they wanted their Father Joe to stick around they were going to have to agree to rename the church.

St Zev's.

Joe liked the sound of that.

NANCY HOLDER

Blood Gothic

NANCY HOLDER lives in San Diego with her seven-year-old daughter, Belle, who has just completed her own latest novel, *The Mistry of the Gost*.

Holder has sold around sixty novels and 200 short stories, essays and articles. She has received four Bram Stoker Awards, and has been nominated for a fifth.

Her work has appeared on the *Los Angeles Times*, *USA Today*, *Locus* and other best-seller lists, and she has been translated into over two dozen languages.

The author of many successful novelizations, her most recent books include *Buffy the Vampire Slayer/Angel: Heat* and the *Wicked* quartet about two feuding witch families: *Witch*, *Curse*, *Legacy* and *Spellbound*, all from Simon and Schuster. She also has a new novella in *Tales of the Slayer 3* about Buffy's predecessor, India Cohen.

"'Blood Gothic' was the very first horror short story I ever wrote," reveals the author. "I got a few rejections, one with a scrawled note of encouragement, and that kept me going for a couple of years.

"Then I met Charlie Grant and we had lunch at the Carnegie Deli in New York. He said he was looking for stories for his *Shadows* series of anthologies. I said, 'Oh, I have a story about a vampire!' and he looked as if he had just swallowed a cockroach. I was so embarrassed that I almost didn't send it to him. But he liked it, and he bought it. It was my first short-story sale.''

Holder's memorable debut can best be summed up as a dark romance . . .

SHE WANTED TO HAVE a vampire lover. She wanted it so badly that she kept waiting for it to happen. One night, soon, she would awaken to wings flapping against the window and then take to wearing velvet ribbons and cameo lockets around her delicate, pale neck. She knew it.

She immersed herself in the world of her vampire lover: she devoured Gothic romances, consumed late-night horror movies. Visions of satin capes and eyes of fire shielded her from the harshness of the daylight, from mortality and the vain and meaningless struggles of the world of the sun. Days as a kindergarten teacher and evenings with some overly eager, casual acquaintance could not pull her from her secret existence: always a ticking portion of her brain planned, proceeded, waited.

She spent her meager earnings on dark antiques and intricate clothes. Her wardrobe was crammed with white negligees and ruffled underthings. No crosses and no mirrors, particularly not in her bedroom. White tapered candles stood in pewter sconces, and she would read late into the night by their smoky flickerings, she scented and ruffled, hair combed loosely about her shoulders. She glanced at the window often.

She resented lovers – though she took them, thrilling to the fullness of life in them, the blood and the life – who insisted upon staying all night, burning their breakfast toast and making bitter coffee. Her kitchen, of course, held nothing but fresh ingredients and copper and ironware; to her chagrin, she could not do without ovens or stoves or refrigerators. Alone, she carried candles and bathed in cool water.

She waited, prepared. And at long last, her vampire lover began to come to her in dreams. They floated across the moors, glided through the fields of heather. He carried her to his crumbling castle, undressing her, pulling off her diaphanous gown, caressing her lovely body until, in the height of passion, he bit into her arched neck, drawing the life out of her and replacing it with eternal damnation and eternal love.

She awoke from these dreams drenched in sweat and feeling exhausted. The kindergarten children would find her unusually quiet and self-absorbed, and it frightened them when she rubbed her spotless neck and smiled wistfully. *Soon and soon and soon*, her veins chanted, in prayer and anticipation. *Soon.*

The children were her only regret. She would not miss her inquisitive relatives and friends, the ones who frowned and studied her as if she were a portrait of someone they knew they were supposed to recognize. Those, who urged her to drop by for an hour, to come with them to films, to accompany them to the seashore. Those, who were connected to her – or thought they were – by the mere gesturing of the long and milky hands of Fate. Who sought to distract her from her one true passion; who sought to discover the secret of that passion. For, true to the sacredness of her vigil for her vampire lover, she had never spoken of him to a single earthly, earthbound soul. It would be beyond them, she knew. They would not comprehend a bond of such intentioned sacrifice.

But she would regret the children. Never would a child of their love coo and murmur in the darkness; never would his proud and noble features soften at the sight of the mother and her child of his loins. It was her single sorrow.

Her vacation was coming. June hovered like the mist and the children squirmed in anticipation. Their own true lives would begin in June. She empathized with the shining eyes and smiling faces, knowing their wait was as agonizing as her own. Silently, as the days closed in, she bade each of them a tender farewell, holding them as they threw their little arms around her neck and pressed fervent summertime kisses on her cheeks.

She booked her passage to London on a ship. Then to Romania, Bulgaria, Transylvania. The hereditary seat of her beloved; the fierce, violent backdrop of her dreams. Her suitcases opened themselves to her long, full skirts and her brooches and lockets. She peered into her hand mirror as she packed it. "I am getting pale," she thought, and the idea both terrified and delighted her.

She became paler, thinner, more exhausted as her trip wore on. After recovering from the disappointment of the raucous, modern cruise ship, she raced across the Continent to find refuge in the creaky trains and taverns she had so yearned for. Her heart thrilled as she meandered past the black silhouettes of ruined fortresses and ancient manor houses. She sat for hours in the mists, praying for the howling wolf to find her, for the bat to come and join her.

She took to drinking wine in bed, deep, rich, blood-red burgundy that glowed in the candlelight. She melted into the landscape within days, and cringed as if from the crucifix itself when flickers of her past life, her American, false existence, invaded her serenity. She did not keep a diary; she did not count the days as her summer slipped away from her. She only rejoiced that she grew weaker.

It was when she was counting out the coins for a Gypsy shawl that she realized she had no time left. Tomorrow she must make for

Frankfurt and from there fly back to New York. The shopkeeper nudged her, inquiring if she were ill, and she left with her treasure, trembling.

She flung herself on her own rented bed. "This will not do. This will not do." She pleaded with the darkness. "You must come for me tonight. I have done everything for you, my beloved, loved you above all else. You must save me." She sobbed until she ached.

She skipped her last meal of veal and paprika and sat quietly in her room. The innkeeper brought her yet another bottle of burgundy and after she assured him that she was quite all right, just a little tired, he wished his guest a pleasant trip home.

The night wore on; though her book was open before her, her eyes were riveted to the windows, her hands clenched around the wineglass as she sipped steadily, like a creature feeding. Oh, to feel him against her veins, emptying her and filling her!

Soon and soon and soon . . .

Then, all at once, it happened. The windows rattled, flapped inward. A great shadow, a curtain of ebony, fell across the bed, and the room began to whirl, faster, faster still; and she was consumed with a bitter, deathly chill. She heard, rather than saw, the wineglass crash to the floor, and struggled to keep her eyes open as she was overwhelmed, engulfed, taken.

"Is it you?" she managed to whisper through teeth that rattled with delight and cold and terror. "Is it finally to be?"

Freezing hands touched her everywhere: her face, her breasts, the desperate offering of her arched neck. Frozen and strong and never-dying. Sinking, she smiled in a rictus of mortal dread and exultation. Eternal damnation, eternal love. Her vampire lover had come for her at last.

When her eyes opened again, she let out a howl and shrank against the searing brilliance of the sun. Hastily, they closed the curtains and quickly told her where she was: home again, where everything was warm and pleasant and she was safe from the disease that had nearly killed her.

She had been ill before she had left the States. By the time she had reached Transylvania, her anemia had been acute. Had she never noticed her own pallor, her lassitude?

Anemia. Her smile was a secret on her white lips. So they thought, but he *had* come for her, again and again. In her dreams. And on that night, he had meant to take her finally to his castle forever, to crown her the best-beloved one, his love of the moors and the mists.

She had but to wait, and he would finish the deed.

Soon and soon and soon.

She let them fret over her, wrapping her in blankets in the last days of summer. She endured the forced cheer of her relatives, allowed them to feed her rich food and drink in hopes of restoring her.

But her stomach could no longer hold the nourishment of their kind; they wrung their hands and talked of stronger measures when it became clear that she was wasting away.

At the urging of the doctor, she took walks. Small ones at first, on painfully thin feet. Swathed in wool, cowering behind sunglasses, she took tiny steps like an old woman. As she moved through the summer hours, her neck burned with an ungovernable pain that would not cease until she rested in the shadows. Her stomach lurched at the sight of grocery-store windows. But at the butcher's, she paused, and licked her lips at the sight of the raw, bloody meat.

But she did not go to him. She grew neither worse nor better.

"I am trapped," she whispered to the night as she stared into the flames of a candle by her bed. "I am disappearing between your world and mine, my beloved. Help me. Come for me." She rubbed her neck, which ached and throbbed but showed no outward signs of his devotion. Her throat was parched, bone-dry, but water did not quench her thirst.

At long last, she dreamed again. Her vampire lover came for her as before, joyous in their reunion. They soared above the crooked trees at the foothills, streamed like black banners above the mountain crags to his castle. He could not touch her enough, worship her enough, and they were wild in their abandon as he carried her in her diaphanous gown to the gates of his fortress.

But at the entrance, he shook his head with sorrow and could not let her pass into the black realm with him. His fiery tears seared her neck, and she thrilled to the touch of the mark even as she cried out for him as he left her, fading into the vapors with a look of entreaty in his dark, flashing eyes.

Something was missing; he required a boon of her before he could bind her against his heart. A thing that she must give to him . . .

She walked in the sunlight, enfeebled, cowering. She thirsted, hungered, yearned. Still she dreamed of him, and still he could not take the last of her unto himself.

Days and nights and days. Her steps took her finally to the schoolyard, where once, only months before, she had embraced and kissed the children, thinking never to see them again. They were all there, who had kissed her cheeks so eagerly. Their silvery laughter was like the tinkling of bells as dust motes from their games and antics whirled around their feet. How free they seemed to her who was so troubled, how content and at peace.

The children.

She shambled forward, eyes widening behind the shields of smoky glass.

He required something of her first.

Her one regret. Her only sorrow.

She thirsted. The burns on her neck pulsated with pain.

Tears of gratitude welled in her eyes for the revelation that had not come too late. Weeping, she pushed open the gate of the schoolyard and reached out a skeleton-limb to a child standing apart from the rest, engrossed in a solitary game of cat's cradle. Tawny-headed, ruddy-cheeked, filled with the blood and the life.

For him, as a token of their love.

"My little one, do you remember me?" she said softly.

The boy turned. And smiled back uncertainly in innocence and trust.

Then she came for him, swooped down on him like a great, winged thing, with eyes that burned through the glasses, teeth that flashed, once, twice . . .

soon and soon and soon.

LES DANIELS

Yellow Fog

LES DANIELS HAS BEEN a freelance writer, composer, film buff and musician. He has performed with such groups as Soop, Snake and The Snatch, The Swamp Steppers, and The Local Yokels. A CD of his 1960s group with actor Martin Mull, The Double Standard String Band, was recently released.

His first book was *Comix: A History of Comic Books in America*, since when he has written the non-fiction studies *Living in Fear: A History of Horror, Marvel: Five Fabulous Decades of the World's Greatest Comics* and *DC Comics: Sixty Years of the World's Favorite Comic Book Heroes*. More recently, he is the author of "The Complete History" volumes of *Superman: The Life and Times of The Man of Steel, Batman: The Life and Times of the Dark Knight* and *Wonder Woman: The Life and Times of the Amazon Princess*. Daniels is currently working on a new book about the early days of DC Comics.

His 1978 novel *The Black Castle* introduced his enigmatic vampire-hero Don Sebastian de Villanueva, whose exploits he continued in *The Silver Skull, Citizen Vampire, Yellow Fog* (an expanded version of the novella that appears here) and *No Blood Spilled*. His occasional short fiction has appeared in a number of anthologies, most recently *Dark Terrors 6*, and he has edited *Thirteen Tales of Terror* (with Diane Thompson) and *Dying of Fright: Masterpieces of the Macabre*.

"Like several other things I have written, this tale was inspired by a dream,'' explains Daniels. ''In this case I saw the startling image which climaxes chapter ten, 'The Wine Cellar'. Of course, this scene is a variation on a type of revelation which has appeared in several horror narratives. However, the changes which my subconscious had rung on the theme struck me as sufficiently startling to form the basis for a story. From there, it was merely a matter of working backwards toward the beginning.''

I. Black Plumes

THE BOY ON THE steps had been told to look unhappy, and he was doing his best, but he found it hard to mourn for a corpse he had never known, especially when the old man's death was making him money. Still, a job was a job, and Syd had no desire to lose this one. He stifled a smirk and glanced across the black-draped door toward his partner, but the sight of the old fellow with his fancy dress and his watery eyes was more than Syd could bear. He knew he must look just as foolish himself, wearing a top hat festooned with black crepe and carrying a long wand draped with more of the same, yet he felt a laugh rising in his chest that he barely succeeded in changing into a cough before it reached his lips. The crepe rustled, and Syd's partner altered his expression for an instant from dignified melancholy to threatening wrath. Mr Callender had paid Entwistle and Son a substantial sum for a proper funeral, and that meant that the mutes would remain mute.

Syd stiffened, hoping that the procession would arrive soon to relieve him of his post. His nose itched, and his left foot seemed to have gone numb. After a whole morning standing on duty in front of Callender's house, Syd was beginning to look to the long march to All Souls as a positive pleasure. It would at least mean a bit of exercise, and it would bring Syd closer to the time when he would finally be able to make a little profit out of the business. There was no pay in being apprenticed to an undertaker, even if it was Entwistle and Son. Just the Son now, actually, thought Syd, and it didn't look like he could expect to live much longer himself, except that he couldn't bear the thought of dying and letting anybody else bury him. Entwistle and Son was the best there was, and the hearse Syd saw turning the corner from Kensington High Street proved it.

Six matched black horses drew the hearse, their heads crowned with bobbing black plumes of dyed peacock feathers, their backs covered with hangings of black velvet. The low, black hearse, its glass sides etched in floral patterns, bore the oaken coffin upon a bed of lilies, under a canopy of more swaying black plumes. The driver proceeded at a measured pace to accommodate the mutes who trudged with downcast eyes beside the slowly rolling gilt-edged wheels. Behind them came the first mourning coach, and then the second; when the procession drew up before the house Syd was startled to see that there were no more. It seemed incredible that such an expensive funeral should have so few mourners; Syd could hardly believe that a man rich enough to afford Entwistle's best should have had so few friends.

The Son himself stepped from the second coach, the crepe on his hat fluttering across his face in the brisk autumn breeze. Syd snapped to attention like the soldiers he had seen outside Buckingham Palace guarding the Queen, and stared straight ahead as the undertaker glided up the steps with the black cloth alternately masking and unmasking his pale and furrowed face. Syd had learned long ago not to fear the dead, but he still feared the man who tended them, and he did not look to the side when he heard the sound of the brass door knocker. Shuffling steps approached the door, and the latch clicked.

"Mr Callender, please," said Mr Entwistle.

"Mr Callender asks that you wait for him outside," came the reply. The door closed quietly.

Syd stood so rigidly that he was starting to tremble as Mr Entwistle made his way stiffly down the steps and toward the second coach. Syd's feelings were a mixture of shock and delight; he saw that the expression on the face of his fellow mute was now genuinely grief-stricken. It was a revelation to discover a household too grand to receive Mr Entwistle, and Syd was far too impressed to do anything but stare when the door opened again to let the funeral party out.

There was a fat butler, a young gentleman with sandy side-whiskers, and a little lady with gray hair, but what Syd noticed was the one who stood behind them in the shadows. Her skin was fair, her eyes were of the lightest blue, and her hair was a blonde that was nearly white. There was next to no color in her, and she was as beautiful as a statue. All of them were dressed in black, and the little lady had the younger one by the arm.

"There's no need for you to come, Felicia," she said. "It's not the sort of thing a young lady ought to see."

"And yet you're going, Aunt Penelope."

"I'm no longer a young lady, and we can't send Mr Callender off alone on such a sad errand."

"But surely my place is with Reginald, Aunt Penelope."

"You've done more than enough for him already, and if he loves you he wouldn't dream of exposing you to such an ordeal. Beside, you're needed here to keep an eye on the servants, or there won't be much left of the feast by the time we return."

Neither the butler nor his master made any comment on this or anything else, but when the older woman said "I'll hear no more about it," the young gentleman took her arm and the butler closed the door behind them. Syd, whose only concern had been the pale angel who stayed behind, recollected himself and returned to his job, escorting Reginald Callender and the angel's Aunt Penelope to the first mourning coach. One of the horses stirred despite its blinders as they passed; everything else was still but Aunt Penelope's tongue.

"A gray day is just as well for a funeral, I think. It's appropriately solemn, but not really unpleasant. The day we buried poor Felicia's parents, the rain was so heavy it was almost a storm, and the child was crying so much on top of it, I don't think I've ever been so wet in all my born days. I really think it affected her, too. She's always been so delicate. A sunny day's not right, either, though. I remember burying a cousin when the day was so fine that it spoiled the whole occasion. It just wasn't fitting. No, I think a gray day is best."

She gestured decisively with her fan of black plumes and waited for Syd to open the carriage door.

"Uncle William chose the day, not I," said Reginald Callender as he helped Aunt Penelope up the step.

"Nonsense! If your Uncle William had his choice, this day never would have come at all. He would much rather have spent his fortune than left it all to you, Mr Callender. Not that you'll need it, with such a wealthy wife soon to be yours. It is a fine thing, though, is it not, to see two family fortunes joined along with their heirs?"

"No doubt," replied Callender as the door shut behind them and he took his seat beside his fiancee's aunt. His head throbbed already and he realized that burying his uncle would be more of an ordeal than whatever grief he felt would warrant. Last night he had taken too much whiskey, to calm his nerves and muffle his tactless conviction that he was, in his hour of bereavement, the luckiest man alive. What more could a man wish but riches and a beautiful wife, except to be free of the headache and a chattering woman who seemed to dote on death?

"It's a tragedy, the funeral party being so small, don't you think? Of course everything has been done in the very height of fashion, but it seems a shame that nobody's here to enjoy it."

"My uncle survived all his partners by some years, and I am his last living relative, as you know. The last of the Callenders. There is simply no one left to mourn him."

"And Felicia looked so lovely in that black silk! She can't keep wearing it, you know; she's not really in mourning, but it was so dear that it certainly should be seen. I took her to Jay's in Regent Street, you know. They make a specialty of mourning, and they furnished both of us for your uncle's funeral."

"Very handsomely, to be sure," murmured Callender, laying a hand beside his head in a gesture that he hoped would suggest intelligent interest while still providing him with the opportunity to massage an aching temple. The motion of the coach was beginning to make him slightly sick.

"Of course I've had dresses from Jay's before; so many of one's friends and family seem to die as the years pass. I think the widow's weeds are most attractive, but a woman can't be a widow before she's a wife, can she?"

Callender might have answered, but Aunt Penelope had turned from him to gaze out of the coach at the streets of London. "I see you have chosen to travel by way of the park," she said. "Very wise, I'm sure. I thought you might have chosen the shorter route instead, where we should hardly have been seen at all."

"It was my uncle's wish," said Callender. "He left instructions for his funeral with his solicitor, Mr Frobisher."

"What a clever man! I never thought of such a thing, but I must certainly make plans for my own passing at the first possible moment. Of course I have no fortune to compensate my heirs for the expense. . . ."

"I am sure that Felicia will be happy to accommodate you," sighed Callender.

"Do you think so? Yes, I suppose she will. Such a generous girl, and such a spiritual nature. Her thoughts are always with the angels."

Callender wished fervently that Aunt Penelope could be with the angels too. He closed his eyes and thought of Felicia. Just a moment's peace would be enough to bring him sleep.

"Then Kensal Green was your uncle's choice as well?"

"I beg your pardon?" said Callender, pulling himself back to consciousness.

"Kensal Green, I said. All Souls Cemetery. It's certainly where I would choose to rest in peace. I visit there sometimes, and I still think it's the loveliest cemetery in London, even if there are a few that have opened since. The first of anything is often the best, don't you think? And of course anything would be better than one of the old churchyards. You must have heard the stories about the pestilence bred in those awful places, and about the way the skeletons were dug up and stored in sheds to make way for more graves? It's enough to make a body shudder."

Callender looked up to see if she were shuddering, and almost thought he saw her waving at a passerby, but he could not be certain. Although thoroughly dismayed by her enjoyment of the proceedings, he decided to resign himself. He had little choice in any case, and a day of pleasure for his beloved's maiden aunt was a small enough additional tax on the life of happiness that lay before him. He settled back in his seat as the coach rolled on.

Felicia Lamb closed her book and sat for a moment staring into space. Critics had attacked the novel and its unknown author, Ellis Bell, and Felicia admitted to herself that she had sometimes been dismayed by the savagery of its setting and the brutishness of its characters. Yet something in the story had compelled her interest: the idea of an immortal love that transcended even death. Such a passion both fascinated and frightened her; half of her longed for something like it, but she realized that destiny had decided to provide her with a much more practical match. Reginald Callender had his virtues, as her Aunt Penelope was frequently at pain to point out, but she could hardly imagine anyone accusing him of a supernatural longing. Perhaps it was just as well, Felicia thought. She knew that she was inclined toward morbidity, as certainly her father's sister was, so it was possible that her fiance had been sent to help keep her feet firmly planted on the ground.

She sighed and placed the last volume of *Wuthering Heights* on the highly polished surface of a table in the center of the drawing room. What light from the afternoon sky pressed through the heavy curtains was weak and dismal; the pendulum of the clock in the corner seemed to push the hours on toward darkness. Surely it was late enough for Reginald and Aunt Penelope to have returned. Against her will Felicia pictured a terrible accident that might at one blow deprive her of the only two people whose lives touched her own. She realized it was a foolish fancy, yet she had lost both her parents at once a dozen years ago, and knew all too well that such things were possible. She had more faith in the next world than she had in her chances for happiness in this.

She gazed up at the portrait of Reginald's Uncle William that hung magisterially over the mantel, and she wondered where he was now. The round, ruddy face and the thick body were, of course, in a coffin under six feet of earth, but where was William Callender himself? And where were her mother and father? The spirits of the dead haunted her without ever appearing as phantoms; perhaps she would have been less troubled by them if they had. She longed for Reginald to return and pull her away from such brooding, even though she always half resented him when he did.

"Shall I light the fire, Miss?"

A ghost would have startled her less than the voice did, but she realized in an instant that it was only the butler. And while she doubted that flames could eliminate the chill she felt within her, a cheery fire would at least be welcome to anyone returning from a long funeral on a raw autumn day.

"Thank you, Booth. I think Mr Callender would appreciate it."
She heard his knees creak as he bent before the picture of his late
master, and she felt a twinge of regret that she had not tended to the
matter herself; it would have been much easier for her than it was for
the old man. Her guilt propelled her from the room to supervise the
preparations for the funeral feast, but she was not really needed for
that, either.

"Is everything ready, Alice?" she asked the pretty, dark-haired
maid. The girl, whose black uniform had lost its white ruffles to the
dignity of the day, gave Felicia a curtsey and a small smile.

"Oh yes, Miss, thank you. Mr Entwistle's people took care of
everything themselves, and it's very nice, I'm sure."

The sideboard was covered with food: a ham, a roast of beef, bread,
pies, cakes, and bottles of sherry and port. There was enough to feed
dozens of people, though only three were to be served.

"So much?" asked Felicia without stopping to consider the propriety of conversing with the servants on matters of form.

"Oh, yes, Miss. I asked them if there might be some mistake, but
the gentleman assured me it was all called for in Mr Callender's will.
May I serve you something, Miss?"

"Thank you, no," answered Felicia, who had never felt less hungry
in her life. "I'll wait for the others, Alice. Do I hear them coming in
now?"

"I'll go see, Miss," said the maid as she scurried off.

A moment later Felicia was joined by her Aunt Penelope, her eyes
bright beneath her black bonnet as she surveyed the lavish meal
spread out before her. "Well," she said, "this is very handsomely
done, Felicia. And so it should be, I say. Weddings and funerals are
important occasions. Will you pour me a glass of sherry, dear? Just a
small one."

Aunt Penelope popped a small cake into her mouth as Reginald
Callender strode into the room and reached for a bottle of port. He
filled a glass and swallowed it at once.

"A lovely funeral, Mr Callender," said Aunt Penelope. "And the
mausoleum was very splendid indeed. Did your uncle make provisions for you to join him there when you are called?"

Callender made no reply except to pour himself another drink. He
collected himself enough to offer a glass to Felicia, but she refused it
and seated herself on a small, straight-backed chair in a corner.

"I don't think I approve of closed coffins, however," said Aunt
Penelope.

Callender's face turned suddenly hard. "Surely you saw enough of
my uncle when he was lying in state, didn't you?"

"Oh, to be sure, Mr Callender. I meant no criticism. Sometimes, I suppose, the last look may be too painful to endure. Would you be kind enough to slice me some of that ham? Thank you. And how have you spent the day, Felicia?"

"In thinking of those who have gone before us, Aunt."

"Oh? And what were your conclusions, dear?"

"Only that there is much to know, and we know very little of it," said Felicia.

"Perhaps you will be wiser tomorrow evening, after our visit to Mr Newcastle."

Felicia's eyes widened, and she glanced anxiously back and forth between her aunt and her fiance.

"Newcastle? And who, pray tell, is Mr Newcastle, that you should visit him at night?" demanded Callender, brandishing the carving knife as he passed a plate of ham to Aunt Penelope.

"Why the spirit medium, of course," she said as she took the plate. "We passed his house on the way to Kensal Green."

Felicia sank back farther into her corner under Callender's accusing stare. "The spirit medium!" he roared, then turned to Aunt Penelope. "Is this some of your nonsense?"

"It is my own idea, Reginald," Felicia said quietly.

"I positively forbid it."

"You will forbid me nothing before I become your wife. You know how I long to know what lies behind this life. Why should you want to deny me?"

"Because it's all fraud and nonsense and superstition. How can an intelligent girl like you believe in such antiquated fancies in this day and age? This is 1847, and we are in an age of progress when such things should be cast aside once and for all."

"We progress in many things, Reginald; and why should not the knowledge of what lies beyond the veil be one of them? You must have heard of what Mr David Home has achieved, and I am told that Mr Newcastle's gifts are even more remarkable. I am certain that there are persons with the ability to see things that are invisible to us."

"What they see that's invisible to you is that you are a gullible woman with too much money. What's dead is dead, Felicia, and best forgotten."

She rose from her chair and clasped her hands together earnestly. "But the dead do live on, Reginald. How can you doubt it? Aren't you a Christian?"

Callender hacked viciously at the ham. "Yes, I'm a Christian. Church of England every Sunday, and money in the plate. But what do you think the Reverend Mr Fisher would say if he knew you were raising spooks? And what do you really know about this fellow

Newcastle? Must be a lunatic. It isn't safe, and I ask you again to forget this folly."

"I have promised to act as my niece's chaperone," volunteered Aunt Penelope as she helped herself to more sherry. "And in exchange she has agreed to accompany me to the Dead Room at Madame Tussaud's. Neither of us is quite brave enough to indulge her fancy alone, but we do intend to have our curiosity satisfied, Mr Callender."

"What? The place *Punch* calls The Chamber of Horrors? That's a fine place for a sensitive girl, I must say, but at least I suppose it's harmless. But this master of goblins is quite another matter. He's either a charlatan or a madman, and the fact that you are two helpless females instead of one does nothing to reassure me. I'll wager he wants more than a few shillings for admission too, eh?"

Aunt Penelope moved to her niece's side and put a hand on her shoulder which Felicia took gratefully.

"We shall not be dissuaded," said Aunt Penelope.

Callender smiled ruefully. "Then I suppose I must accompany you," he said.

"Oh, Reginald, will you?" Felicia asked eagerly. "Please come with us. I hope to speak with my mother and father again, and perhaps Mr Newcastle will let you commune with your Uncle William."

"I trust my Uncle William is happy where he is, Felicia, and I would not wish to drag him down again to the clay, even if I believed I could. Let him rest in peace, I say."

He put his arms around Felicia and led her across the room to a love seat as far removed as possible from the food that the dead man had ordered. "Can you not forget the dead?" he asked her. "We are among the living now, and whatever questions we have to ask of our forebears will be answered in due time. Until then, it is our duty to live our lives as best we can. Will you live for me instead of these idle dreams?"

Felicia's fingers stroked his face, but her eyes remained distant, "How can we know what we should do," she demanded, "when we do not know what lies ahead of us? How much pleasure can we take here, when we know it is only a school for the lessons we shall learn?"

"We may have been born to die," said Callender, "but that is only part of it. The pleasures offered to us here are not our enemies. We are young and wealthy, Felicia. We are blessed. Let us not spurn fate's favors."

"He's right, you know," said Aunt Penelope as she cut into a pie. "We shall be quit of this world soon enough without denying it. But still, Mr Callender, we shall make our visits."

"And if you must," he said, "I shall be with you."

He might have said more, but the butler interrupted him.

"Yes, Booth?" he murmured as the old man bent down to whisper in his ear. Callender rose, bowed to the ladies, and hurried out into the hall.

And there in the twilight stood the gaunt form of Mr Entwistle. "I know how these things are, sir," he said, "and I would not wish to keep you waiting." He handed Callender a few small objects tied in a handkerchief. "His rings, his pins, and his watch," he said.

Callender cringed, but thanked the undertaker nonetheless.

"I understand entirely," said Mr Entwistle. "It is not all uncommon for young gentlemen to experience a temporary embarrassment while waiting for the reading of the will. You may be sure that your uncle's estate will compensate us for our trouble." He bowed and slithered back into the gathering darkness.

Reginald Callender stood with his uncle's jewelry in his hand and a wave of disgust pouring over him. While Felicia worried about souls, he was forced to concern himself with the problem of raising enough money to keep the household in order. It was hardly gentlemanly behavior; in fact, it was almost like robbing the dead. Still, his uncle's adornments had been visible in the open coffin, yet had been rescued from the grave. Supported since childhood by the investments of his mother's brother, Callender truly had no notion of supporting himself except to sell what came to hand. It was only a temporary aberration, he told himself; soon the estate would make him rich.

Still, he was angry with himself, and more angry with Felicia for concerning herself with spirits when he was so desperate for material comfort. He saw the maid hurrying across the hallway and called out to her.

"Alice," he said. "come here for a moment."

The girl came slowly toward him.

"Are you happy with your position here?"

"Oh, yes sir," said Alice.

"And were you happy with my uncle?"

Alice blushed and nodded.

"Then we shall continue the same arrangement now that I am master?"

"Just as you say, sir," said Alice.

"Very well. My visitors will be leaving soon. I shall expect you later this evening, Alice. Everything will be as it was before. I will expect you at ten. And bring my uncle's riding crop."

II. The Resurrection Men

The boy with the crowbar strapped to his leg ordered another pint of beer. He rarely drank the stuff, because it cost too much and he had

no head for it anyway, but tonight he felt as jumpy as a cat, and
certain of enough money to buy a whole barrel if he liked. And
anyway, he told himself, it would be Syd's fault if he got drunk. They
had agreed to meet an hour ago in this pub, "The World Turned
Upside Down," and since Syd was so late, it became necessary to keep
buying beer. Henry could hardly expect to stay inside without
spending money, and even at that there had been a few jokes about
his age, but Henry Donahue was unconcerned. He was fifteen, after
all, and old enough to drink all he could hold, and old enough to rob
a grave. Still, he wished Syd would hurry.

Henry had picked the place himself, even though he had never
been inside before, partly for its proximity to Kensal Green and partly
because he had always liked its sign. Whether the globe on it was
really upside down he could not have said, but something in the idea
appealed to him. And things were quiet enough inside, which he
supposed was good, though he would have preferred enough of a
crowd to make him feel a bit less conspicuous. He was looking
around the dim room, convinced that all the other patrons were
watching him, when he saw the door open and Syd's sharp, pimply
face peer in. Henry gulped down the last of his drink and walked
briskly toward the door. Syd was half way inside, but Henry pushed
him out again.

"Let me come in for a minute, will you?" protested Syd.

"You're late enough without dawdling here any longer, don't you
think?"

"I know, I know, but I'm cold enough already, aren't I? Is it my
fault if I couldn't get away?"

"It'll be your fault if we're any later, Syd. I can't be out all night,
you know."

"You smell like you already have been, mate. A fine thing, drinking
on the job. You won't be much good for picking locks now, will you?"

Henry grabbed Syd's arm to quiet him. A lamplighter was shuffling
down the empty street toward them, the yellow fog of London
dimming the light of the small hand-lamp he carried. The two boys
leaned against the building with feigned unconcern, Henry gazing at
the sign while Syd read the words guaranteeing the availability of
Courage and Company's Entire and wondered how much of it Henry
had consumed. The old man climbed up his ladder, turned the gas
cock, applied his lamp, and scrambled down again, leaving the
entrance to the public house only a little brighter than it had been
before. The boys waited until his footsteps had died away.

"You were really scared of him, weren't you?" sneered Syd.
"Maybe you should run home now and forget all this, Henry."

"I'm not scared of anything. But there's no point in letting anyone know what we're up to, is there? Burke and Hare were hanged, weren't they?"

"They were murderers, you dunce, and we're not even stealing bodies. There's no market for 'em anymore, is there? All we're doing is relieving the old gent of some jewelry that he'll never miss. It would be a crime to let it rot with him, wouldn't it?"

"Not a crime you can be charged with," Henry said.

"Well, if you don't want the money, mate, you run along."

But Henry was already walking toward the cemetery, pulling his cap down over his shaggy red hair and turning his collar up against the cold and the eyes of passersby.

"You're sure he's got all this stuff on him, are you, Syd?"

"I saw it, didn't I? There's not much else to do when you work for an undertaker but look at the bodies. Just like there's not much for an apprentice locksmith to do but learn how to open things. I've just been waiting to meet a partner like you, Henry. We're in business now, you know, and we have splendid prospects."

The closer they got to Kensal Green the more unhappy Henry was. The houses were thinning out here, the lights were farther apart, and the fog filled the empty spaces. Henry began to feel as if he were lost somewhere out in the countryside, and would have happily turned back at once except for a certain reluctance to disgrace himself in front of Syd: it was easier to face corpses than to admit to a boy a year older than himself that he wanted nothing more out of life than to be back in his bed in a garret.

Henry watched his feet slip over the damp cobblestones; they were almost all he could see. The dark was bad enough, but the fog was worse. "We'll never find it," Henry said.

"What do you mean, we'll never find it? We're here!"

Henry looked up and saw something like a temple looming through the mist. There were columns and walls and fences, and it looked to him less like a churchyard than the Bank of England. The gigantic gates were clearly locked, and he could perceive nothing behind them but another wall of impenetrable fog.

"I don't want to open those gates," he said. "Someone might come along."

"Don't worry," Syd insisted. "We'll just climb the wall."

"What's the use?" said Henry. "We can't find anything in there. The fog."

"I know where it is, don't I? How many times have I been here, eh? It's my job. Just give me a leg up. Come on, over here."

Henry almost ran away, but he didn't. Instead he hurried toward the sound of Syd's voice, and was almost relieved to be touching someone else, even if it was his partner in a crime that he would have willingly abandoned. At least he was not alone. He squatted, close to the ground where the air was a little clearer, and made his hands into a cradle for Syd's foot.

Syd scrambled up, and Henry thought for an instant that he had broken a wrist. He grunted, and then lost Syd in the fog. "Where are you? Are you up?" A hand dropped down to him.

"Here. Grab it. Come on. Get off the street!"

Henry grabbed onto Syd's wrist and felt himself hauled up against the wall, scraping and squirming until he reached the top. "You're up?" said Syd. "Then drop down," and suddenly Henry was alone again.

He looked into the opaque night, shivered at the thought of an observer, and dropped into the darkness. He landed on Syd, and both of them tumbled on the wet grass of All Soul's Cemetery.

"That's fine. You'll kill us both."

"Are we in? Where are we, Syd?"

"Kensal Green, my boy. We're in. Follow me."

"Wait a minute, Syd! Where are you? You can't know where we're going."

"I tell you I know this place like I know my mother, even if I haven't seen her for years."

"Give us your hand then, will you? I'm lost."

"Take hold then. You'll hold a prettier hand than this one, once we're done."

Henry hung onto Syd, wandering through a sea of fog that might have been Heaven or Hell. From time to time a monument loomed up, a spire or an angel or a slab. Some of them were huge. He let Syd drag him through the clouds. It was so cold that his nose began to run, and all at once he was hungry. "We'll never find it, Syd. Let's go home."

"No. We'll never find it?"

Something loomed in the fog. Henry blinked twice and then sat down. "It's big enough," he said.

"The lock is small."

A gray box squatted in the yellow fog. A stone box, its roof pointed, with pillars beside the door. Two figures made of marble stood on either side of the door; they looked to Henry like women in nightshirts. He couldn't see much, but what he saw was enough.

Syd knocked on the door while Henry shuddered. "Mr Callender's residence?"

"Don't do that, Syd."

"No? Think he'll wake up, do you? Don't worry, I threw his guts away myself. If he did rise up, he'd fall right over."

"That's not funny."

"Don't laugh, then. Just open the door."

"I can't."

"You haven't even tried yet. You're terrified, that's what's wrong with you."

"I can't see, can I? How do you expect me to work?"

"I got a bunch of Lucifers, and I told you what the lock is like. Just work. The sooner you start, the sooner we'll be out of here."

Syd lit a match, and the way it colored his eyes was enough to send Henry toward the lock. He reached in his pocket and produced several instruments.

"I'd love to know how to work those."

"I'll teach you. Then you can do this by yourself."

"Don't be like that. Just a few more minutes, and we'll be rich men, Henry. You take care of the lock, and I'll take care of the body, all right?"

"Splendid," muttered Henry, his stiff fingers fumbling. He heard something snap, then wished he hadn't. Syd pushed him toward the metal door, and it fell away before them into hideous blackness. Henry twitched and looked toward the sky, but all he saw was the name "Callender" carved in the marble over his head. He lost his balance and sprawled against a wet wall as Syd shoved him into the house of the dead. The stink of dying flowers turned his stomach. He sat down in a corner and watched Syd strike another match and light a candle with it. The light flickered around stone walls like slabs. Henry looked outside and glimpsed a shadow. "There's something out there, Syd."

"Ghosts."

"Don't be smart, I saw a dog."

"Then shut the door and he won't see us."

"Too late for that," he said, but he pushed the iron door back.

Immediately he felt trapped. He hurriedly caught the edge of the door before it could swing shut, pulled the crowbar out from under the leg of his jagged trousers, and braced it against the jamb. The opening allayed his fear slightly, even when he saw wisps of fog drift through it, but Syd was not pleased with his handiwork.

"What do you think you're doing with that, then? Have you been walking stiff-legged all night so we could have a doorstop? Give it here."

Henry handed it over reluctantly, unhappy to be farther from the exit and closer to the sinister oblong of stone that brooded in the center of the small, dark room. Syd stuck the candle to the floor with its drippings, then turned to the sarcophagus and began to pry off its lid. Henry backed away at the hideous sound of scraping, grating stone and put one foot outside the tomb, relieved to find that they were not already imprisoned by some uncanny force. Syd pushed and grunted against the ponderous weight while Henry prayed that he would fail to move it.

"You could help," gasped Syd.

"A bargain's a bargain. The lock was my job, and the body's yours."

"It's only another box in there. It won't hurt you."

"I know it won't, since I'm not going near it."

"All right, then!" Syd threw himself furiously on the bar and the stone slab tilted ominously. For an instant he hung counterbalanced in the air; then the lid screeched and fell to the floor with a crash that sounded to Henry like the end of the world. And at the same instant Syd dropped on the other side and snuffed out the candle. The echoing tomb was black.

"Oh my God," whispered Henry.

"He's not likely to be much help to you when you're on a job like this one, is he, mate?"

Something shuffled in the dark, and another of Syd's matches burst into flame, making his face as red as a painted devil's, but no less reassuring to Henry for that. He was amazed to discover that he had not run away, then realized that he had been too startled to move. Syd lit the broken candle and handed it to him. "Hold this," he said.

"I don't want to look."

"Of course you do. I'll bet that's half of why you came."

Henry didn't answer, but neither did he turn away when Syd approached the oaken coffin in its bed of stone. The candle flame shimmered in his shaking hand, and he knew without a doubt that when the coffin opened a hideously mouldering corpse would rise from its depths and drag him straight to Hell. He thought he heard a dog howl somewhere outside. He closed his eyes. Wood croaked, and then he heard Syd groan. The groan rose into a wail.

"We've been robbed!"

"What?" Henry opened his eyes, and for an instant saw nothing but Syd's red, furious face.

"Look for yourself! It must have been old Entwistle, the grasping, bloody bastard. He's taken it all. The rings, the watch, the stickpin, too. There's nothing left but the damn body!"

Unwilling to believe his ears, Henry moved with the light until he could see into the coffin. He quickly checked the pale fingers and the black cravat. Nothing gleamed on them. He began to curse, then realized that he was staring into the face of a dead man.

It was not as bad as he had imagined. Just a plump old boy with rosy cheeks, really nothing to be afraid of; he looked as if he were taking a nap. It was only when Henry's nostrils caught the mingled odors of flowers, chemicals, and death that his stomach began to heave.

And then the iron door behind him crashed open.

Henry screamed, dropped the candle, and spun toward the sound. Silhouetted against the foggy night stood the gigantic figure of a man, his outstretched arms barring the way out of the tomb. Henry's mind went blank, his fanciful fear of the corpse forgotten in the sudden and very real conviction that he was doomed. The blood drained out of his face as he saw himself on the gallows, and he could hold on to only one idea: I'm caught, I'm caught, I'm caught. He hardly heard the low, calm voice of the figure at the door.

"Have you found what you seek?"

Henry was amazed to hear Syd's brassy answer.

"Nah, there's nothing here. Somebody's stripped him bare."

Another match flared. Syd's hand was steady, his expression insolent. "Bring that candle over here, will you, Henry?"

Henry was startled into action, almost believing that Syd's boldness might somehow set them free. Not even a second flame showed much of the dark intruder's face as he spoke again.

"These dead are mine."

"And welcome to 'em," answered Syd, moving back toward the doorway with the crowbar held behind his back. Henry followed him like a sonambulist, but stopped dead when he saw the tall man's face. The skin was pale under long, stringy black hair; the lips were hidden by a drooping black mustache; the eyes seemed no more than dark hollows, the left bisected by a scar that ran from brow to chin. The countenance was so expressionless that it might have been a mask.

"It's not the caretaker," Henry heard himself saying, "it's that spirit reader from across the way."

"That's torn it," said Syd, and he swung for the man's head with the crowbar. The blow never landed. Henry stood frozen and watched a long white hand shoot out to grasp Syd's wrist while another attached itself to its face, the fingers scrabbling like a pale spider. The man opened his arms in a gesture that seemed almost hospitable, and Syd's hand came off at the wrist in a shower of blood while the flesh of his face was ripped from the bones.

Henry dropped the candle again and dove for the darkness where the door had been.

He tumbled to the ground in a blind panic and crawled through the yellow fog. He thought about God. He ran.

A tree stopped him. It bloodied his nose and broke two fingers, but he got up and ran again.

A low tombstone caught him just below the kneecap. He rolled in the wet grass and whimpered. Then he arose and limped away.

He couldn't see where he was going, but he didn't stop until the agony of his broken leg compelled him to. He rested under a marble angel and waited for death to come.

It came on black wings.

III. The Spiritualist

The house near the cemetery where he had buried his Uncle William was so nondescript that Reginald Callender scarcely remembered having passed it twice before. He was almost disappointed. He had expected something either gaudy or else picturesquely dilapidated and sinister, but Mr Sebastian Newcastle's dwelling was an unpretentious house of good English brick, perhaps fifty years old. The tall cypresses surrounding it had a slightly funereal air, but that was all. Every window was dark but one, which glowed faintly through the fog.

Callender had accompanied Felicia and her Aunt Penelope despite his misgivings; he was not a man to tolerate argument from a woman, especially one he expected to have as his bride, and he was deeply suspicious of Felicia's interest in this spirit medium, who was certainly a charlatan and probably a criminal who prayed on the sentiments of bereaved ladies. And the fact that the man he already thought of as his enemy was so unpretentious in his tastes gave Callender pause. Subtlety always irritated him.

He helped Aunt Penelope out of the coach, and then Felicia, listening with approval when she told the driver to wait. Soon he would be giving orders to her servants himself, but until his uncle's estate could be settled he had so little cash on hand that he had been obliged to dismiss his own coachman, although he could hardly get along without the household servants, especially Alice. She would have to go soon enough, he told himself, but a glance at Felicia told him that the sacrifice would be worthwhile. Sometimes he wondered why it was necessary to wed a lady in order to bed her, but that was the way of the world, and meanwhile there were willing wenches in it.

A shapeless shadow flitted across the window as they approached the house, one of the ladies on each of his arms, and the look of it somehow sickened him, but they did not seem to have noticed. He opened his mouth to begin again his arguments about the foolish recklessness of the business they were embarked upon, but thought better of it. He had already decided to show them, and that was why he was here. The old woman was simply a sensation seeker, and would be just as happy to discover that the spiritualist was a fraud, but Felicia was something of a fanatic on the subject, and that would never do. Still, this night's work should settle that, and another night's work, after the wedding, would provide her with a new interest in life. Determined to take matters in his own hand, Callender rapped on the door with a gloved fist.

While he waited impatiently, Felicia reached past him and pulled on a narrow, rattling chain that he had never noticed. "The bell," she explained. "He may not hear you knocking from upstairs."

"No lights upstairs," said Callender. "Besides, I saw someone move down here, unless it was one of his confederates."

"Mr Newcastle has no need of confederates, nor has he any need of light."

Aunt Penelope, thrilled into temporary silence by her approach to the land that lies beyond death, gave a little squeal when the door in front of them abruptly opened.

A tall man stood on the threshold with a silver candlestick in his hand, a single flame illuminating a lean, pale face that was shadowed by black hair and a long mustache. Callender was startled for a moment by the scar, then dismissed it as an effective theatrical touch and spent most of the next few minutes trying to decide if it were real. The man, who was quite clearly Newcastle rather than a servant, stepped back silently and ushered them into an empty hall with a dusty carpet of no determinable pattern.

At the end of the hallway was a double door, and beyond that a room that seemed unnaturally dark even after their host had brightened it with his lone candle. Callender saw that both the floor and the ceiling had been painted black, and that black velvet draperies completely covered the walls. A small round table sat there surrounded by four high-backed wooden chairs; all of them appeared to have been made of ebony. The medium set his candlestick in the center of the table and stood quietly waiting for his visitors to follow him into the gloomy chamber. His clothing was a black as Callender's mourning, so that only his white face and hands were distinctly visible, apparently floating disembodied in the air. When the ladies entered with their dark cloaks and bonnets the effect was much the same, and Callender had no reason to believe that he looked any different. The illusion was disconcerting.

The two women sat down across from one another, but Mr Reginald Callender remained on his feet, squinting into the shadows where Sebastian Newcastle's eyes were hidden. He expected the spiritualist to flinch before his penetrating stare, but the fellow was imperturbable, and ultimately it was Callender who turned away in what he told himself was pure disdain. A mounting sense of irritation caused him to break the long silence at last.

"Well! Bring on your spooks sir, or must we pay you for them first?"

"Reginald!" Felicia's voice was harsher than he had ever heard it sound, and before he knew what had happened he was seated beside her, feeling very much like a chastened schoolboy and wondering for the first time if married life might be something less than pleasant. Aunt Penelope suppressed a nervous giggle. Callender had a deep desire to lash out at someone, but had difficulty deciding who it should be. Sebastian Newcastle sat down across the table from him.

"There will be no charge for your visit, Mr Callender, since I do not expect you to enjoy it."

"I don't know, I've always enjoyed conjuring tricks, but you won't find me as easy to fool as some of your visitors."

"Miss Lamb and her aunt are hardly fools, Mr Callender, even if they do seek to be still wiser than they are. And have you never wondered what waits beyond the grave?"

"We have churches to tell us that, and not for money."

"Your churches are far richer than I am, and likely to remain so."

"Well, Mr Newcastle, you'll have a chance to change that tonight. Here's ten guineas." Callender reached into his waistcoat pocket and placed the money on the table. He could ill afford to lose it. "If I see anything here that I cannot explain, that belongs to you." He pointed emphatically to the cash and noticed to his amazement that it was gone. "By God!" he said. "These are very materialistic spirits, sir."

"You will find that they have returned the money to your pocket, Mr Callender."

Callender felt for the money and almost forgot himself enough to curse.

"Is it there?" asked Aunt Penelope.

"I think Reginald's face answers that question for him," observed Felicia coldly. "Really, Reginald, we have not come here to insult our host, but to learn from him. Do be quiet, if only to please me. Mr Newcastle has promised to summon my parents tonight."

"Your parents were killed in a railway accident twelve years ago, Felicia, and if your father had not been one of the chief stockholders in that railway, this man would have no interest in him or in you."

"He will certainly have no interest if you will not give him the peace he needs to pierce the veil."

Callender reminded himself again that he had determined to hold his tongue, and realized ruefully that he should have done so. Even Aunt Penelope had said almost nothing.

"Silence is an aid to concentration," Newcastle said evenly.

Callender nodded almost imperceptibly, and was delighted to find himself rewarded at once when Felicia took his hand. He was more than a little startled, though, when Aunt Penelope did the same, and then he surmised that this was common behavior at a seance. Still, it took all his willpower to refrain from comment when he saw his fiancee's delicate fingers in the pale clutch of the man with the dark eyes.

The four of them sat quietly in the black room, Callender never taking his eyes from the medium who gradually sank back in his chair and allowed his head to slump forward. He looked like an old man dozing after a heavy dinner, reminding Callender of his Uncle William. After a few minutes the atmosphere grew chilly, and Callender was almost convinced that he could feel a damp breeze waft past him, although he could see no way it could have come into the room. Still, it was enough to make him look around uncomfortably, taking his eyes off the medium just long enough for something strange to happen.

For a moment Callender thought the man might be on fire. Vague tendrils of smoke seemed to be rising from his head, but they looked more like mist than smoke, and they wove patterns in the air that did not seem natural. Callender turned to his right and his left, but the two women holding his hands were not dismayed, and seemed to be regarding the display with intelligent approval. The medium groaned, and now his head was almost hidden by shifting fingers of mist. He seemed to be dissolving into the darkness. Callender started involuntarily and had half risen from his chair when a blast of frigid wind roared at him from across the table. The candle flame went out.

He felt Felicia's grip on his fingers increase till it was almost painful, and a certain unexpected weakness in his knees compelled him to sink down into his seat again. Nothing was visible except the writhing cloud of mist which seemed to glow with its own faint luminescence. He tried to convince himself that it was some sort of trick with chemicals, but he was not happy looking at it, especially when it began to coalesce into features which were not those of Sebastian Newcastle.

It was the face of a woman, its mouth working feebly as if it did not have the strength to speak. A sound came from somewhere that was like whispering, or the scurrying of rats. The face shifted and flickered, and sometimes it seemed to be a man with a full beard. Now there were two whispers, one lower than the other, and Callender began to believe that he could hear what they were saying. It was one word, repeated over and over again: "Felicia."

Callender knew that his hands were trembling, and hoped the women would not notice. The light of the glowing mist was gleaming in Felicia's eyes as she leaned forward across the table, and Callender was dismayed by the eagerness with which she seemed to welcome this horror, whether it was fraudulent or not. He hoped it was an illusion, for he had no wish to think it real, yet it infuriated him to realize that he could be frightened by a humbug. He closed his eyes, but the sound of the whispering, wavering voices was even more disturbing when he was blind to their source. He would have preferred to leave.

"Felicia," whispered the sibilant chorus. "Beware, daughter. Beware of false friends. There is one here whom you must not trust."

"Who is it?" asked Felicia breathlessly. She and her aunt stared into the shifting mist."

"It is the man," the voices cried.

"Which man?"

"The man who tells you these damned lies!" shouted Callender. He pushed back his chair and pulled his hands free while the floating faces burst into brilliant light and disappeared into impenetrable darkness. He fumbled for a match while Aunt Penelope screamed.

Callender struck a light on the side of the table and applied it at once to the candle. The two women stood behind him, clutched in one another's arms, and an indistinct figure sat slumped in the medium's chair. Callender waited for another trick, fearful that the flame would be extinguished again, but there was only silence in the black room. The body of Sebastian Newcastle was ominously still.

"Is he dead?" asked Aunt Penelope.

"I hope so," muttered Callender. He walked briskly to the figure in the chair and grasped it roughly by the hair to pull its hanging head up into the light. The features that rose up to meet him were those of his Uncle William.

The waxy eyelids were closed, but the full lips moved. "Dead," said Uncle William.

Aunt Penelope gasped and swayed into the arms of her niece, who hurried the fainting woman from the room with brisk efficiency, while Callender stood as if paralyzed and stared into the face of a familiar corpse. His fingers slipped slowly from its head, and its lips twisted themselves into a comfortable grin. When the eyes opened they were William Callender's: he might have been alive again.

"Surprised, are you my boy? Well, there will be more surprises in store for you soon. Wait till you talk to old Frobisher tomorrow about my will!"

Callender was hardly listening, although he would have cause to remember those words soon enough. Whatever it was in the chair seemed so relaxed and genial that it convinced him more than an army of phantoms could have done. "Is it really you?" he asked.

"Of course it's me!"

"Back from the dead?"

"Not so far to come, really. Takes time to travel on, you know.

Especially for someone like me, who's not what you could call spiritually advanced. But this Newcastle is a very clever fellow, and he's helping me along. Don't trifle with him, my boy."

Callender had almost forgotten that he was speaking to a ghost. Everything was very natural, and full of the ordinary irritations of talking with his uncle. "The man is a threat to Felicia," insisted the irate nephew. "Even the spirits of her parents told her so."

"Oh, no, my dear boy. They were talking about you."

"Me? Why should she beware of me?"

"You're not so spiritually advanced yourself, are you, Reginald? Much too interested in the pleasures of the flesh, of course, and very bad tempered on top of it. And possessive, of course. I'm sure you'd make the poor girl miserable. And I'm sorry to say you're really no more than a fortune hunter. You really should be more careful. Look."

Uncle William pointed to the door, and Reginald Callender turned to find Felicia standing there. Evidently she had heard everything. Callender felt a hot flush roar up his throat as he whirled to confront his uncle, but the figure in the chair was Sebastian Newcastle, smiling with his sharp teeth and holding a pack of cards in one hand. "Will you have your fortune told before you go, Mr Callender? No? Then I bid you a good evening." And with that the medium glided out of the chair and through the black velvet curtains that covered the walls.

Callender hurried to his fiancee's side. "Did you see him? Did you see Uncle William?"

Felicia nodded. "And so did Aunt Penelope. I had to help her out to the carriage, but she swears she never had such a stimulating evening in her life."

"And did you hear what he said?"

"Only what Mr Newcastle said to you. And since he has retired I believe we should follow his example."

Callender wondered for the first time but not the last if it was possible that she was mocking him. Yet he was confused enough to take her arm and walk halfway down the hall with her before he pulled away.

"He's a fraud, I tell you, and I can prove it." He hurried back into the black room, devoid of a strategy but determined to redeem himself. He glared around at emptiness and then rushed to a wall. "All tricks," he told himself. "The curtains!"

He grasped two fistfuls of midnight velvet and pulled them apart, peering fiercely through them, ready for almost any sight but the one that confronted him. There was no machinery, no hidden door. There was not even a wall. There was only the night, an ebony void where clouds of yellow fog obscured the stars. Callender swayed, keeping his feet only because he held onto the curtains. For a moment he felt like a man lying on his back and staring up at the sky. His head reeled.

Then he turned on his heel and walked stiffly out of the house to the carriage where the women waited.

IV. The Inheritance

Callender would have wasted no time in visiting his uncle's solicitor in any case, but the ghostly warning he had received was so alarming that he was awake and dressed and in the offices of Frobisher and Jarndyce long before the hour of noon. He tried to convince himself that what he had seen had been a dream, or a trick, or perhaps the result of mesmerism, which reportedly had the power to make a man see anything, but certainly the previous evening's entertainment was enough to make an heir curious about the terms of the will that would determine his future.

Rising early proved to be a fruitless gesture, however, since Callender was not expected until afternoon, and Clarence Frobisher had chosen to spend the morning in Chancery. A clerk had left the heir apparent to cool his heels in Frobisher's dusty chambers with no company and no entertainment except a shelf of leather bound law books. More than once Callender toyed with the idea of nipping out for a quick one, but missing his man would have been intolerable, and truth to tell, he had an almost superstitious conviction that fortune would favor him if he remained sober until the momentous meeting had been concluded.

Nothing prevented him from dozing, however, and his brain was as foggy as the streets of London when he opened one eye suspiciously and discovered the solicitor making his stately entrance, marred only by a cough which may have been intended to wake his client.

Clarence Frobisher, as Callender had had occasion to observe before, was a man with a very dry manner and an equally wet face. His voice was rasping and sandy; his attitude was distant and aloof; but his brow was perpetually dabbled with perspiration, his rheumy eyes seemed always on the verge of tears, and a soiled handkerchief was never far from his dripping nose. Callender had never liked Frobisher, but he was prepared to overlook the solicitor's personal shortcomings in exchange for the speedy delivery of Uncle William's estate.

Frobisher nodded and adjusted his rusty black suit as he lowered himself into an old horse-hair chair behind his heavy mahogany desk, its surface littered with papers and broken bits of sealing wax. He glanced at a document, reached for a quill pen, then seemed to recollect himself and peered at Callender over his gold eyeglasses.

"Mr Callender?"

"I've come about my Uncle William's estate."

"Well, sir. You are prompt. More than prompt, I might say."

"There is no difficulty with the will, I hope?"

"Difficulty?"

"No changes?"

"Changes? Certainly not."

Reginald Callender, now a man of property, allowed himself the luxury of a sigh. Yet something continued to nag at him. Perhaps it was the expression on Frobisher's moist lips. Had it been anyone else, he would have suspected the man was smiling.

"Then I am still the sole heir?"

"Sole heir? Yes, in a manner of speaking. There are other considerations. My fee, for one."

"Well," said Callender expansively, "I hope you will be handsomely paid."

"I have seen to that. Your uncle settled with me when the will was drawn."

"Nothing else, then?"

"The funeral arrangements were the first order of business, according to your uncle's orders. He wished no expense to be spared. There is a substantial bill from Entwistle and Son, but this is a pittance compared to the cost of the marble mausoleum."

Callender, who had not even considered this, felt thousands slipping through his fingers. "But of course the estate is large enough to pay for this," he suggested nervously.

"Precisely."

"And there is nothing else?"

"Nothing."

Something in this last exchange made Callender feel hollow inside. He could not shake off the feeling that Frobisher was toying with him. He watched the handkerchief working and wondered if the solicitor was laughing behind it.

"When I say nothing else," Callender began, "I mean no other claims against my uncle's fortune."

"Precisely."

"And when you say the estate is precisely large enough . . ."

"I am speaking as plainly as I can, Mr Callender."

Frobisher blew his nose and made a choking, wheezing sound.

"Then be plainer still, or be damned, sir! How much is left for me? Speak!"

Frobisher pocketed his handkerchief and picked up a sheet of paper. He glanced at it, blinked, and handed it to Callender. "What is left for you," he said, and paused to clear his throat, "is precisely nothing."

Callender looked at the desk, studying the grain of the wood. He found the pattern oddly intriguing; it held his attention totally for some time, long enough in fact for the solicitor to become somewhat alarmed.

"Mr Callender?"

"What?"

"A glass of port, perhaps?"

Callender laughed for an instant, and watched as the solicitor stepped to a sideboard and poured the wine. It struck him as really very decent of the old boy. He could hardly think of anything else except that he would be grateful for the drink, and when he gulped it down, it did restore him to a semblance of sanity. Then all at once his thoughts were racing so fast that he was almost dizzy.

"Nothing left?" he asked. "What became of it all?"

"He spent it."

"All of it? But he was worth a bloody fortune!"

"So he was, Mr Callender. Not even the bad investments he made in India could have made a pauper of him – or should I say of you? There's still some accounting to be made in regard to that, but I doubt if you will see enough from the colonies to stand you a good dinner."

"And the rest of it?"

"As I have said. It is more common than you might suppose for an elderly man of affairs to awake one day and realize that his hours with us are numbered, and that the money he has struggled to accumulate has brought him very little in the way of pleasure. Faced with the choices of delighting you or delighting himself, your uncle unhesitatingly decided on the latter course. You might say that he went out in a blaze of glory. Women, of course, and quite a bit of gambling as well. I suppose if he had won he would have been obliged to leave you something. . . ."

"But to have spent so much," Callender began.

"He became quite a generous man in his last days. Quite a bit was spent on diamonds, and I personally arranged the gift of a handsome residence to one of his favorite mistresses. He also gave substantial sums to some of the household servants, the only stipulation being that they remain in service until the day after he was laid to rest. There was a man named Booth, and a housemaid; I think her name was Alice. They should be gone by now."

Callender thought back to the empty house which he had hardly noticed in his eagerness to visit Frobisher and Jarndyce. "I should have whipped her harder," he muttered.

"I beg your pardon?"

"Nothing. At least there's still the house."

"Mortgaged to the hilt, I'm afraid. I think he meant for you to have it, but he surprised his doctors and himself by living longer than he anticipated, and his funds were very low. Still, you might realize something if you can sell it before the inevitable foreclosure. And there might be a bit left over from the Indian disaster; I believe your uncle's representative is on a ship bound for England now. A Mr Nigel Stone."

"Cousin Nigel! That idiot! No wonder everything was lost."

Frobisher consulted another document. "I understand that you were offered the post, but preferred to remain in London at your uncle's expense. Is my information incorrect?"

Callender pushed himself up from his chair and strode toward the door. He threw it open, then turned for a parting shot. "Of course I'll contest the will," he said.

"And I would be happy to represent you, but I do advise against it, since you are in fact the sole beneficiary. The problem is that the whole estate was spent before your turn came. To spend what little you have left on legal fees would be ill-advised."

"I suppose that advice is free, is it?" Callender looked around desperately. "I believe the old bastard did this just to spite me."

"I would hardly put it as bluntly as that," suggested Frobisher. "Mr Callender! You have forgotten your stick."

Callender whirled in the doorway and stormed back into the room to retrieve his ebony walking stick. He was tempted to smash it across Frobisher's desk, but managed to stop himself in time with the realization that he could hardly afford to replace it.

Reginald Callender retreated to the nearest public house and drank three glasses of neat gin in quick succession, but even that was not enough to keep his hand from trembling. He left the place and began to walk toward the house where Sally lived, trusting that the time the journey took would enable him to collect his thoughts.

In a sense Sally Wood was his mistress, though he was hardly fool enough to imagine that he was the only man who shared her favors. It was a considerable source of pride to him, however, to reflect that he was almost certainly the only one of her lovers who had never been obliged to pay her. She liked him, apparently; it pleased Callender to believe that was because he was more distinguished than most of the men she met at the music hall. Still, it was at least possible that his stature as the nephew of a wealthy and elderly gentleman had something to do with Sally's attitude; Callender wondered what she would say if she were to learn that he was destitute. Not that he would tell her, of course, but providing her with little presents or even the occasional meal might become a problem very soon. The real difficulty, though, lay with Felicia; the panic with which he contemplated keeping his poverty from her was what drove him on toward Sally's door.

Callender possessed a key to her lodging house, but after ascending the dark stairs he felt it advisable to pause at the door to her room before entering. He listened stealthily, always conscious of the occasion when he had intruded on a scene he would have chosen not to witness, yet there was no sound from inside but a woman's voice humming a snatch of song. Callender knocked. There was a rustling from within, and then the door opened to reveal Sally, undressed except for a black corset trimmed with red silk. A hairbrush backed with mother-of-pearl was in her hand.

"Reggie! Hello, dear."

Callender's brief touch of irritation at her use of the detested pet name was soon smothered in the warmth of her embrace. Enveloped in a cloud of perfume, he maneuvered Sally back across the threshold and shut the door behind him, then kissed her ravenously while his hands crawled over her exposed flesh. After a few moments she pushed him away, gasping and laughing at the same time. "A girl needs air, you know," she said, "and a lady likes to be spoken to first."

She sent him a smile over her shoulder, then sat down at a dressing table covered with pots of paint and powder. For the time Callender was content to lounge against the wall and watch as she brushed her gleaming chestnut hair. Sally was such a contrast to Felicia: ruddy rather than pale, voluptuous rather than slender, and distinctly physical rather than spiritual. It puzzled him that somehow he was not satisfied with Sally, who seemed to offer him everything he wanted, yet he was convinced with no proof to speak of that having his way with his fiancee would be a more stimulating experience than any that Sally could provide. It hardly mattered, though; Felicia's fortune in itself was sufficient to make her a much more suitable companion. A glance around the room was sufficient to convince Callender of that.

The cheerful disarray which might be charming in a mistress would be utterly unsuitable in a wife. The floor was dusty, the bed unmade, and every article of furniture was covered with piles of hastily discarded clothing. The general effect would have been the same, he thought, if there were an explosion in a dressmaker's shop.

A pamphlet half covered by a crumpled sheet caught his attention; he picked it up and straightened the wrinkled cover, embellished by a crude drawing of a cloaked, skeletal figure looming over a sleeping woman. Bats and gravestones decorated the lurid title: *Varney the Vampire, or The Feast of Blood.*

"Reading penny dreadfuls, Sally?"

"A girl gets bored sometimes. And it's a good story."

"It's rubbish."

"That's as may be, but it's exciting. It's about a gent who's dead, but he comes back at night and drinks people's blood. Sneaks right into their rooms, he does, and drains 'em dry while they sleep. He bites their throats." Sally touched her own throat to emphasize the point.

"Sounds deucedly unpleasant to me," observed Callender, flipping through the pages looking for more illustrations.

"And then they turn into vampires themselves, after he's done with them."

"He also seems to go about sticking logs into people," said Callender as he found a particularly lurid drawing.

"Oh, no Reggie. That's what they have to do to kill the vampires for good and all. Pound a stick of wood right into their hearts, they do." Sally laid a dramatic hand on her own substantial bosom.

"You don't believe this nonsense, do you?"

"I don't know about that, but it's something to think about, isn't it? Besides, I like the way it makes me feel. All goose pimply."

"Then I advise you to light a fire."

"Would you do it, Reggie dear? I've got my hands full."

"Getting ready to go out?"

"In a bit, dear. Why?"

"Because I know a better way to warm you up." Callender tossed the pamphlet back onto the bed and walked purposefully toward the dressing table. He buried his face in Sally's curly, perfumed hair and clutched one of her breasts in each of his hands. She arched her back, closed her eyes, and smiled as she felt his breath on her face.

"Go into a public for a drain of gin, did you?"

"Anything wrong with that?" asked Callender as he fumbled with her corset.

"You might have brought some with you."

"Aren't I intoxicating enough?"

"That you are, Reggie. It's wonderful to have a wealthy lover. Makes a girl feel special."

Callender tore at his cravat. "You'd love me without that, wouldn't you?"

"Of course I would. And I was sorry to hear about your uncle." She pushed his clumsy hands away and quickly undressed herself.

And before long they were on her bed, the forgotten copy of *Varney the Vampire* crushed beneath their thrashing bodies.

V. The Dead Room

The parade of kings stood still and a common man marched past. He was a guide, dressed in a uniform that made him look like a soldier, and he announced each crowned head of Europe in a hoarse voice that Callender found increasingly irritating. He was thoroughly sick of the officious little man and his apparently endless procession of wax effigies; his dislike of these soft statues and their false finery had begun before he had even entered Madame Tussaud's, when he had been informed that, due to the flammable nature of the exhibits, he would be obliged to throw away the last of his Uncle William's imported cigars.

And nothing before or after this affront to Callender had been calculated to soothe his temper. The expedition to Madame Tussaud's exhibition in Baker Street had begun disastrously when the cab Callender hired had arrived at Felicia Lamb's residence only to find her absent. Aunt Penelope, however, had been obtrusively present, coquettishly claiming Callender as her escort with the explanation that Mr Newcastle, the medium, had taken Felicia into his coach a quarter of an hour ago. Callender's initial indignation had rapidly given way to a feeling close to panic; he could not quite suppress the unreasonable fear that his fiancée had been abducted and he would never see her again. The journey to the wax museum, orchestrated by Aunt Penelope's incessant chatter, had been excruciating.

The upshot, which surprised him by irritating him, had been nothing at all. Felicia, eyes downcast demurely, had stood in the gaslit lobby of the Baker Street Bazaar, and she had been holding Sebastian Newcastle's long, thin arm. This apparent intimacy, combined with the anti-climax of it all, left Callender fuming, and as Aunt Penelope pulled him toward the exhibition, he thought he saw Felicia smile gratefully at her. Apparently Newcastle had paid for all their tickets, and there was nothing that Callender could reasonably be expected to do about that.

Callender's tour of the wax museum had become a nightmare long before he reached the chamber of horrors. He hardly noticed the exhibits, but he did not miss a single one of the glances exchanged by his fiancée and Sebastian Newcastle. They seemed to be hanging back deliberately, engaged in private conversation, while Callender was pushed forward by the press of the crowd and by Aunt Penelope, a woman he would willingly have strangled. Callender's face was hot, and his cravat was choking him: was it possible that Felicia was deliberately snubbing him? He was so intent on the couple behind him that he nearly knocked over the guide when the procession suddenly came to a halt in front of a door barred by a red velvet rope.

"This concludes the tour of the exhibition," announced the little man in the blue uniform. "The general exhibition, that is. But behind me, ladies and gentlemen, behind this rope, behind this door, there stands The Dead Room. Or, as some have been generous to call it, Madame Tussaud's Chamber of Horrors. Those of you who have purchased tickets for this special display may follow me now, but I caution you that this is a room filled with effigies of evil and engines of extermination. Here are the most notorious murderers and malefactors of history and of the present day, together with authentic devices of torture and execution, including the very guillotine that killed the King of France. In addition, you will see replicas of the severed heads of the King and his Queen Marie Antoinette, along with those of such notables as Mister Robespierre, all of them authentic impressions taken immediately after decapitation by the fair hands of Madame Tussaud when she was but a young girl, more than half a century ago. This is not an exhibit for the faint-hearted, ladies and gentlemen, but you have been warned, and those of you who are willing to brave The Dead Room will now please follow me."

Callender watched in some surprise as the crowd melted away; whether they were prudent or merely parsimonious, the British public did not seem inclined, at least on this night, to feast on horrors. In fact, there were finally only four customers, and they were all of Callender's party, although of course it was really Aunt Penelope's, a point she emphasized with a little cry of excitement as the portal to the Chamber of Horrors opened to admit her.

The room was dark, deliberately, thought Callender, and his first impression was of a crowd of men waiting in the shadows. As his eyes became accustomed to the lack of light, he realized that the figures had been grouped like prisoners waiting for sentence in the dock. And he noticed that there were women scattered among the men; an ancient woman in a gray gown particularly caught his eye. In general, though, they seemed to be a nondescript lot, and only statues anyway.

"So this is the celebrated Dead Room," boomed Callender, conscious that Felicia was following him. "It doesn't look that frightening. I'd gladly take the hundred guineas to spend the night among these frozen fiends."

"Sorry, sir," replied the smiling guide. "Dame Rumor offered that reward, not Madame Tussaud, who has no wish for visitors after we close our doors at night at ten o'clock. The only living human being allowed to spend the night among these figures is Madame Tussaud herself."

"Would you really have done it, Reginald?" gasped Aunt Penelope, and Callender was conscious of a certain satisfaction, even though he would have preferred to elicit a response from Felicia. He risked a glance backward, and was pleased to see her pale blue eyes upon him.

"Of course the story of the reward is a lie," he said. "There's nothing here to scare a school-boy. Who are those two fellows?'' He gestured with his stick at a pair of shaggy ruffians bedecked in caps and ragged scarves.

"Well, sir, you're taking them out of order, but since there are so few of you tonight I don't suppose it matters. Those are Burke and Hare. Ghouls, graverobbers and murderers, who stole bodies for a doctor's dissecting lessons, then turned to killing when the supply of fresh corpses ran short. Burke was executed in 1829, on his partner's evidence. They stole dignity from the dead and breath from the living. A most despicable pair, and one of our most popular groupings.''

The story, which reminded Callender of something in his own past, did not really amuse him. "Of course this sort of thing is far behind us," he observed, "now that we provide our medical schools with the specimens they need."

"Yet still there are vermin who would rob the dead," said Sebastian Newcastle. Callender's hand moved involuntarily toward the pocket of his waistcoat, and toward his Uncle William's watch. He wondered again how much power the medium might possess, then shook off his suspicions together with his memories of the seance. That vision had been the result of hypnotism, or fatigue, or perhaps of some drug, but it certainly had nothing to do with the supernatural.

"Surely no man could be so contemptible," murmured Felicia, and again Callender felt a flush of shame. Could they know? He remembered a line from an old play his uncle had dragged him to see, about conscience creating cowards, and he kept his peace. Yet it disturbed him to realize that neither Sebastian Newcastle nor Felicia Lamb had spoken a word to him, outside of perfunctory greetings, until the subject of rifling corpses had arisen. He looked desperately for a diversion, and found one he could hardly have hoped for, when Felicia's Aunt Penelope began to scream.

His eyes followed her pointing finger, then widened in shock when he saw what she had seen first. It was the old woman in gray, half hidden among the murderers. She rose. Her wrinkled face turned toward the dim gaslight, and her eyes gleamed as a small smile twisted her wizened features. A gigantic shadow rose behind her as she stood, and Callender stumbled backward as Aunt Penelope collapsed into his arms. They both would have fallen to the floor but for the cold, rigid bulk of Mr Newcastle. Callender felt Newcastle's hand close on his flailing wrist, and suddenly he was less afraid of a walking effigy than he was of the icy presence behind him. He saw in flashes the cold face of Newcastle, the rigid and contemptuous countenance of Felicia, and the wrinkled features of the old woman that glided toward him. All of them were pale.

"Madame Tussaud!" said the guide, scuttling back in a broad gesture that was equally composed of bowing and cringing. "I didn't expect you here!"

"You all but announced me, Joseph. And where else would a crone like me find her friends except among the dead? You may leave early tonight, Joseph; I shall be hostess to our guests. There is one among them who interests me."

Joseph virtually fled, and Callender whipped his head around from the disappearing form, expecting to find the eyes of the old waxworker focused on him, but he saw at once that Madame Tussaud was blinking intently at Sebastian Newcastle.

"Have we not met, sir?"

"I hardly think I could have encountered Madame without remembering her."

"You are gracious, but are you truthful?"

Madame Tussaud's English, however fluent, still betrayed her French upbringing, and there was something foreign in Newcastle's speech as well, but Callender could not identify it.

"You have a memorable face, I think," said the old woman.

"Now you flatter me," said Newcastle.

"That was hardly my intention, but your scar, if I may be so blunt, is all but unforgettable."

"I apologize if it affronts you."

"No, sir. It is I who should beg you pardon, but I think I remember you. One who has lived eighty-seven years, as I have, has seen much. And it seems to me that I recollect a man with a face like yours, or at least talk of him. But that was so many years ago that the man could hardly have been you."

Sebastian Newcastle contented himself with a bow. The Dead Room was so dark, and their faces so indistinct, that Callender could hardly tell what the two of them were thinking. More than anything, he was aware of the way Felicia's eyes shifted back and forth between the two. What really shocked him, though, was the sudden recovery of Aunt Penelope, who pulled herself out of his arms and demanded to know whether the two of them were acquainted or not.

"There were stories in Paris, when the Revolution raged," said Madame Tussaud, "about a magician, one who had found a way to keep himself alive forever."

"No doubt there were many such stories in a time of turmoil," said Newcastle.

"Of course," agreed Madame Tussaud. "And the man I speak of would have been older then than I am by now. This was more than fifty years ago. It can be no more than a coincidence."

"Men say that there are such things," said Newcastle.

"He was a Spaniard," said Madame Tussaud, "and I would have given much to model him in wax, but that is all behind us now. Will you look at my relics of the Revolution? I paid dearly for them."

"How so?" asked Felicia. Fascinated by the exchange between the others, Callender had almost forgotten her.

"With the blood on my hands, young lady, and with memories that will last as long as this old body holds them. I was apprenticed to my uncle, and the leaders of the Revolution ordered me to make impressions in wax of heads fresh from the basket of the executioner. Fresh from the blade of that!"

Madame Tussaud thrust her arm out dramatically. Her trembling finger pointed toward a looming silhouette of wooden beams and ropes. Even in the dim light, the slanted steel blade at the top gleamed dully.

"The guillotine," gasped Aunt Penelope.

She swayed toward it slowly, like a woman in a trance, and stared up at the sharp edge as if she expected it to shudder down and smash into its base at her approach. She lowered her eyes gradually, then bent over to examine the displays at the foot of the guillotine. She looked to Callender like a housekeeper examining the choice cuts in a butcher shop.

The waxy heads stared up reproachfully, their indignation three-fold: bad enough to have been cut off, worse yet to have been captured in wax, but unsupportable to be displayed to gawkers at a penny apiece. Aunt Penelope seemed to wilt under their gaze. She made a strange sound.

"I don't feel well at all," she said. "I think I should go home."

"We should all go," said Callender.

"No, no, my boy, I wouldn't think of it. Mr Newcastle is Madame Tussaud's old friend. You take me, and let the others stay." Aunt Penelope began to sway toward Callender's arms again, a habit which was becoming increasingly annoying.

"It's very good of you, Reginald," added Felicia with sweet finality. "I shall be quite safe here with Mr Newcastle."

Callender was sorely tempted to disagree, but he sensed the futility of argument. There was very little choice for anyone who wanted to look like a gentleman except to carry the old fool out and find her a cab. He tried to maintain his composure while he backed clumsily out of The Dead Room and the three who stayed behind smiled at him; he might not have succeeded if he had seen Aunt Penelope winking at her niece.

"Evidently age brings wisdom even to a woman such as she," Newcastle remarked.

"She's such a dear, really, even if she does rattle on sometimes. She knew how much I wanted to remain a little longer, and Reginald would have been bound to cause a scene of some sort."

"Then you wish to see more of my handiwork?" asked Madame Tussaud.

"No," Felicia replied at once. "I mean yes, of course, but, I really wanted to hear more about the gentleman you spoke of, the one who was so like Mr Newcastle."

"He might have been an ancestor, perhaps," suggested the man with the scar.

"And are such wounds as this passed on from father to son?" asked the old woman. She reached up and caressed Newcastle's cheek. "I could wish to make a model of such a face."

"For your Dead Room, Madame?" Newcastle asked.

"Mr Newcastle is no stranger to the dead," Felicia said. "He speaks to them. He is a spiritualist." She felt that she had to say something, even though a mixture of common courtesy and uncommon fear kept her from posing the question she longed to ask. There was some sort of understanding between these two, and she was impatient to share it. "This gentleman from Paris," she said at last. "Do you remember his name?"

"He was a Spanish nobleman . . . Don Sebastian . . . can you help me, Mr Newcastle?"

"I believe I can. Of course I have made a study of such things. His name was Don Sebastian de Villanueva, but I also recall that any claim he had to immortality was false. Was he not reported dead?"

The old woman thought for a moment. "A girl was found, driven quite out of her wits, who said she saw him shatter like glass, or vanish in a puff of smoke, or some such thing, so I suppose he is dead. Then again, a master of the black arts might be capable of such tricks, if he found it convenient to disappear for a time. . . ."

"Quite so," said Sebastian Newcastle, and Felicia Lamb shivered. From somewhere nearby she heard the tolling of a bell.

"The hour grows late," said Madame Tussaud, "and I am an old woman. I must ask you to leave me alone among my friends."

"Indeed, Miss Lamb," said Newcastle. He drew a silver watch from his waistcoat and glanced at its face. The watch was shaped like a skull. "The time is late, the museum is closed, and a man in my position must never be accused of keeping a young lady out till an indecent hour. We must take our leave. Goodnight, Madame."

The waxworker curtseyed, the medium bowed, and Felicia felt herself being hurried from The Dead Room, but as soon as she was through the door, Newcastle paused.

"Please wait here. I must return for a few seconds. I neglected to pay our guide for our tour."

Madame Tussaud was waiting for him in the shadows by the guillotine. "Don Sebastian," she said.

"Madame," he replied. "I trust you to keep my secret."

"You can hardly expect to keep it much longer from that girl, you know."

"It matters little. She will become a disciple. She wishes it."

"And has she said as much?"

"She need not speak for me to know."

"And have you many such disciples after half a century in London?"

"None," said Don Sebastian. He gazed at the wax figures around him. "But I have my dead, like you, and also those who will pay to see them. A small income, but my needs are simple."

"I think you need something that you cannot buy with gold, do you not?"

"Gold will buy more than than you think, sometimes. And when it will not, I feed as lightly as I can, so that my prey knows nothing more than a few days of weakness, soon forgotten. And I never drink from the same fountain twice. I rarely forget myself enough to dine too heavily, and if I do, well, there is a remedy for that."

"A physic made of wood, perhaps?"

"You are wise, Madame."

The old woman shuffled over to a rocking chair that sat in a corner. "If eighty-seven years have not made me wise, sir, then what can I hope for?"

"I had forgotten myself, Madame. Twice I have been driven back into the world of spirits, and so my years on earth have been scarcely more than yours."

"And did you never find peace?"

"Once, when an ancient world came to an end, its gods took me to their paradise, but after some centuries a spell of my own devising drew me back to earth again, to your Paris. And since I know how many less pleasant realms there are where spirits dwell, I am content to remain here."

The old woman settled back in her chair. "Then I wish you good night, sir, and bon voyage."

"I have forgotten one thing," said Don Sebastian. He raised his arm, and a shower of golden guineas streamed from his empty hand into the basket that contained the wax remains of Marie Antoinette.

"Very prettily done sir," said Madame Tussaud, "but I hope you have not damaged that head!"

"I would not dream of such a thing, Madame. You are an artist!"

*   *   *

VI. A Visitor from India

Reginald Callender sat in his uncle's study with the last bottle of his uncle's brandy on the desk in front of him. He still thought of what little was left here as his uncle's, since he himself had inherited nothing. And most of what remained in the house was gone now, sold to a furniture dealer to raise a bit of ready money. Callender had no head for business, just enough to know he had been cheated, but he hardly cared anymore. The laborers who came to loot the house had left him his bed, and the trappings of this one room where he had hidden while they gutted his birthright.

He had no idea what time it was. The thick velvet curtains kept out the sun, and he had already pawned his uncle's watch along with everything else pilfered from the coffin. His crime, if it was one, had brought him discouragingly little. He poured himself another drink. The glass was dirty, and the bottle was dusty from its sleep in the cellar. He wondered how such things could be cleaned. This, along with such mysteries as the cooking of food or the washing of clothes, were as enigmatic to him as the secret of what lay beyond the grave. He could only smoke and swear, drink and dream, but even two of these required money he did not possess.

And his dreams, infuriatingly enough, were of Sally Wood. He cursed himself for this. Now, if ever, his self interest demanded that he devote himself to dancing attendance upon Felicia Lamb, who clearly held his fate in her small hands. Yet it was Sally's heavy-lidded, full-lipped face that rose before him in the gloom, offering him not so much her beauty, and certainly not her love, but rather the sense of power that surged through him when he held her moaning in his arms. She could make him feel like a man again, and not the quivering, drink-soaked wretch he was becoming while he watched his fiancee and his fortune slip away. Still, to see her might be to risk everything: better to have another drink instead.

His trembling hand nearly dropped the bottle when he heard a heavy pounding from somewhere in the house. He sat frozen in his chair, baffled and suspicious, until the sound came again and he realized it was someone knocking loudly on the front door. He attempted to ignore it, but the visitor was so insistent that Callender finally dragged himself to his unsteady feet and went out into the hall. Stripped of its furnishings, the empty house reminded him of Sebastian Newcastle's, and it was the scarred and sinister medium that Callender half expected to greet on the doorstep.

Instead, it was a stranger, a beefy, red-faced man with graying hair and clothing that was not only a decade out of fashion, but seemed to have been cut to suit a man slimmer by several stone. He carried a small travelling bag in his left hand, and looked ready to knock again with his right when Callender pulled open the heavy oak door.

The two men peered at each other through a foggy gray that Callender dimly recognized as dusk, and at last the stranger spoke.

"Reggie?"

Callender, who was still at least sober enough to know his own name, did not find this an edifying remark.

"I know who I am, sir, damn your eyes, but who in blazes are you?"

"Don't you know me?"

"I've said as much, blast you! Go away!"

The man in the fog looked genuinely hurt. "But it's your cousin!" he said. "Nigel! Nigel Stone!"

Callender swayed in the doorway and blinked at his visitor. "Stone? From India?"

"That's right, and home at last. How's Uncle William?"

"Dead."

"Dead? Oh dear. Sorry."

"Yes," said Callender. "You'd better come in."

Callender swayed in the doorway and stepped unsteadily back inside. His cousin followed him into what Callender now realized was almost impenetrable blackness. Nigel Stone paused for a minute trying to get his bearings.

"My dear fellow! The place has been stripped bare!"

"Yes. Yes. It was the servants."

"Servants?"

"Yes. Servants. While I was at the funeral, they and their confederates stole all they could and carted it away."

"Good Lord. Beastly things, servants. Some of the brown fellows where I was would rob you blind if you didn't keep an eye on them. A blind eye, eh? Almost a joke."

"It's not funny to me, cousin."

"No. Of course not. Sorry."

"You'd better follow me into the study. This way."

The first thing Stone saw in the room was a brandy bottle flanked by two candles, stuck in their own grease to the surface of a massive desk. Callender sat down in a chair behind it and picked up his glass. In his haste to get his own seat, he neglected the courtesy of offering one to his cousin.

"Tell me, Cousin Nigel, how is business in India?"

"Not so good, I'm afraid. That's why Uncle William summoned me."

"Oh? Just how bad is it?"

"Bloody damned bad, if you want to know, my dear fellow. Haven't a farthing."

"Nothing left at all?" asked Callender. His eyes glistened in the candlelight as he drained his glass.

"Oh, there's a few boxes of textiles that I had shipped back with me. They should be here in the morning, but that was all I could save. It took the last penny to pay my passage home. No, I'm a liar. I still have half a crown. See?"

"You idiot!" Callender leaped out of his chair and lunged across the desk. He grasped Stone by the collar and hauled him forward, snuffing out a candle and sending the bottle smashing to the floor. Stone was too startled to do more than grunt at first, but when his cousin began to slam him against the desk, the older man broke free and pushed his drunken assailant across the room. Callender fell to the floor and lay there sobbing, both arms crossed over his face.

His cousin stood leaning on the desk, breathing heavily and wishing desperately for a drink from the broken bottle. "Empty anyway," he muttered. "Look here, Reggie! Are you all right?"

He moved hesitantly toward the quivering form on the carpet. "It wasn't my fault, really. It's conditions. You don't know what it's like there. Rebellion, robberies, and murder. The whole country's filled with madmen and fanatics. I was lucky to escape with my life!"

Callender sat up so suddenly that his cousin started back. "What is your life to me?" he wailed. "It's money that I need!"

"Really? What do you mean, old fellow? You must be rolling in the stuff. You're his heir, ain't you? I'm sure he didn't leave me anything, after all I've lost!"

Callender looked at Stone oddly. "What? His heir? Yes, of course I'm his heir." He laughed harshly. "But the money . . . the money isn't here yet. It's all tied up with those damned lawyers, and it may be weeks before I see any of it. You can see what a state I'm in."

"You really don't look well, my dear fellow," said Stone, helping Callender back to his chair. "I'm sorry to hear this, you know. Bit of trouble for both of us. I was really hoping, well, that I might be able to stay here for a while, just till I can get myself back on my feet, as it were. . . . I can lend you half a crown. . . ."

The two cousins laughed together, Stone with genuine mirth, Callender with a wheezing bitterness that ended with an offer of sorts. "I suppose you can stay, cousin, if you're willing to rough it."

"Rough it? I've done nothing else for ten years. We'll do fine together, eh? And buck up! It's only a matter of days."

"Days?" Callender asked sharply. "What day is this? What is the time?"

"Eh? It's Thursday, isn't it? And the last clock I passed said just after six, as near as I could see it through this damned fog."

"Thursday at six! Damn! I'm to dine with my fiancee in an hour."

"Your fiancee! Well, you are a fortunate fellow. And to think that I should find you in such a state." Stone paused and subjected his cousin to careful scrutiny. "You know, old fellow, you're really in no condition to meet a lady, or even a constable. You need a wash and a shave at least."

"Shave?" barked Callender. "With this hand? I might as well cut my throat and be done with it." The fingers he held before Stone's face were visibly trembling.

"I see. A case of the shakes. Well, we'll have to think of something else. I think I could do a bit of barbering, and I have a razor right here in my bag. You have some water? And a log for the fire. We must cheer you up, cuz. I mean to dance at your wedding."

"If there is a wedding."

"What? Something wrong?"

"Much. I'm half afraid I'm losing her. That damned spiritualist!"

"Eh? Someone out to lure her away from you? We can't have that."

"It hasn't come to that, I think," said Callender. "At least not yet. But he has some kind of hold on her, filling her head with stories of spooks, and spirits, and other worlds. I don't know how to fight it, but I feel he's changing her."

Nigel Stone's face was suddenly grimmer than Callender had imagined it could be. "That's a bad business," Stone said. "Very bad, fooling about with spirits."

"And what would you know about it?" sneered Callender.

"I didn't spend ten years in India for nothing, cuz. I may not have made any money, but at least I learned a thing or two. The whole country is rife with superstition, and what might be more than superstition. Men go mad believing in ghosts and demons there. They kill each other and they kill themselves, and some fall under spells that are unspeakable."

"Rubbish."

"And I tell you it's not rubbish! These things can happen, cuz, and even if they don't, just thinking about them can do the worst sort of harm to body and soul. We must do something for this girl before it's too late."

"You do it, then," said Callender. "She only laughs at me when I try." He paused, and contemplated Stone with new interest. "You look like you could do with a good dinner."

"I could indeed."

"Then come along with me tonight, will you? See if you can scare this nonsense out of Felicia before it injures her. I always end up trapped with her accursed aunt anyway."

"Has she an aunt?"

"Yes, a spinster, and about your age, cousin, but don't even think of it. No man could bear her. You stick to the niece. And as for now, do you remember where Uncle William's wine cellar is?''

"Downstairs somewhere, isn't it?''

"That's the idea. Fetch us a bottle of port, will you? Then it will be soon enough for the fire, and the water, and the razor, don't you think?''

"As you say.'' Nigel Stone hesitated for a moment at the thought of the wine, since Callender clearly had no need of it, but he decided he could stand a drop himself, and that this was justification enough for a descent into the cellar. With one backward glance he started out on his first task as the unpaid valet of the impoverished cousin he hoped would soon be a rich relative.

In the midst of what might have been a pleasant dinner, Stone tried to convince himself that the drop he had shared with his cousin really could not have made much difference. For Reginald Callender, helping himself to every decanter in sight, was as drunk as the lord he undoubtedly wished himself to be, and his increasingly erratic behavior interfered at least a bit with Stone's delight in the food, the drink, and the company.

Stone found the girl, Felicia Lamb, as pretty as a picture but not much more animated. Her aunt Penelope, however, was a lively, bird-like little woman who not only kept his plate and his glass filled, but had the courtesy if not the good taste to hang on his every word. For a man long cut off from polite society, such a dinner partner was a positive delight, and the luxury of her surroundings fulfilled the hopes that he had held for his Uncle William's house. Stone grew expansive, but he also remembered his promise to his cousin.

"I understand you take an interest in spiritualism,'' he said to Felicia.

"I do,'' she replied evenly.

"Did it never occur to you that it might be dangerous?''

"Dangerous? You betray your kinship with Mr Callender, sir. I refuse to accept the idea that my search for wisdom is a threat to me.''

"No? You could be right, I suppose. I wouldn't want to contradict a lady, but some of the things I saw in India would be enough to make a man cautious. Or even a woman.''

"Do tell us about it, Mr Stone,'' purred Aunt Penelope. "I'm sure it's fascinating.''

"Yes,'' interrupted Callender. "And informative, too. You listen to this, Felicia.'' His fiancee stiffened noticeably while he clumsily poured himself another brandy, spilling as much on the tablecloth as he did into his glass.

"Well,'' Stone began uncomfortably, "I don't want to make too much of this. Some of what goes on there is just tomfoolery, I reckon, like the fellows who send ropes into the air and then climb up 'em. No harm in that unless the rope breaks, eh?" He laughed, but only Aunt Penelope joined him. "I think it's just a trick anyway. What I mean to say is that some of 'em start out like that and then go on to do things that might hurt them badly. They think some of their gods or spirits are watching over them, so they feel free to walk on burning coals or lie down on beds of iron spikes. I've seen it! And they seem to be unharmed, too, but what if something went wrong, eh? What if the spirits weren't there when the fellow decided to take a nap? What then?"

"I'm sure I'm not interested in spikes, Mr Stone," Felicia said.

"No, my dear young lady, I'm sure you're not. But neither were these chaps, once upon a time. Do you see what I'm driving at? Nobody's born thinking of such things, but they're led into them by degrees."

"He's right, Felicia," said Callender. His speech was slurred, and she did not deign to reply.

"Then these things are really true?" asked Aunt Penelope.

"Damned if I know. Oh, pardon me. My point, though, is that it doesn't really matter if they're true or not, as long as people believe in 'em. Take the Thugs, for instance."

"Thugs?" asked Aunt Penelope. "Are they some sort of monster?"

"They're only men, but I suppose you could call 'em monsters too. They're a cult of murderers, men, women, and children. Whole families of 'em, whole villages, maybe even whole cities, all mad from believing in the spirits of the dead and some goddess of the dead that wants them to kill. They prey on travellers. Wiped out a whole caravan I would have been on if I hadn't been ill, just as if the earth had swallowed 'em up. Lord Bentinck hanged a lot of these Thugs, I've heard, but there are more, you may be sure of it. That's what thinking too much about the dead can do!"

"I only wish to learn of the secrets of the dead," said Felicia, "not to add to their number."

"The dead know nothing!" roared Callender. "Learn from me! Life!"

"Really, Reginald," said Felicia coolly. "And shall I learn by example?"

"Example? And what's the dead's example? Lie down and die yourself, I suppose?" Callender, drunk and angry, was half way up from his seat when Aunt Penelope tactfully interrupted.

"Please, Mr Callender. Let us hear Mr Stone out. And you be still, too, Felicia. It's not polite to argue with a guest, especially one who has travelled half way around the world to give us the benefit of his experience. Do tell us more, Mr Stone."

"Thank you, dear lady. What I mean to say is that if there are spirits, and you call them up, you can't tell what you'll get. If there are spirits, there must be wicked ones, don't you think? In India, they tell tales of an evil spirit. It's called a Baital, or a Vetala, or some such thing. It gets into corpses somehow, and makes them move about, and it draws the life out of every living thing it touches. Would you like to call up one of those? Could you put it down again?"

"It sounds like a vampire," Felicia suggested.

"Vampire? Oh, you mean that old book by Lord Byron. Read it when I was a lad. Quite made my hair stand on end. I suppose it's the same sort of thing."

"Please forgive me for contradicting you," said Felicia with excessive sweetness, "But *The Vampyre* was written by Lord Byron's physician, Dr Polidori. I know a gentleman who met them both."

"Really? No doubt you're right. Not much of a literary man myself."

"She reads too much," mumbled Callender, but he was ignored.

"And take the ghouls," continued Stone.

"What?" demanded Callender.

"Ghouls. Not the kind we have here, not grave robbers exactly. The Indian ghouls are creatures who tear open graves and, well, they feast on what they find there."

"How horrible." Aunt Penelope shuddered cheerfully.

"Isn't it? Of course, we eat dead things ourselves, don't we? I hope the sheep who provided this excellent mutton has gone to its reward, eh?"

"Oh, Mr Stone," laughed Aunt Penelope. "You're a wicked, wicked man."

"What's all this talk of robbing graves?" Reginald Callender was on his feet, a brimming glass of brandy in his hand. "You see what she does?" he shouted. "She turns us all into ghouls!" He whirled to face Felicia, and the brandy splashed over the front of her gown.

"Damn!" shouted Callender. He snatched up a napkin and applied it vigorously to her bodice.

"Your hands, sir!" cried Felicia.

"Mr Callender!" gasped Aunt Penelope.

"My word!" said Nigel Stone.

Felicia Lamb jumped up and gathered her skirts around her. "I believe it's time that we were all in bed," she announced. Her ordinarily pale face was flushed a hot pink.

"Fine!" roared Callender. "Let's all go together!"

Felicia, her head held high, swept from the room. Callender laughed harshly and sat back into his chair, barely conscious of his surroundings.

"Oh dear," said Aunt Penelope.

"Time to go home, old fellow," said Stone, pulling the comatose Callender to his feet. "My apologies, Miss Penelope. He took our uncle's death very hard."

"Goodnight, Mr Stone. I hope you will call on us again."

"Nothing would please me more," said Stone, grunting over the weight of his burden as he backed toward the door. "Good night."

Almost before he knew it, Nigel Stone was in the street. He might as well have been at sea. The thick, yellow fog made London look like a spirit world, one in which the misty glow of the street lamps revealed nothing but their own iridescence. His cousin was on his feet, but not much more. They had walked to dinner from Uncle William's house, and Stone knew that it could not be far away, but he was a bit worse for the wine himself, and not really sure of his bearings.

He longed for a cab, and he wondered how lost he was. Callender said "Sally" several times, but this only confused his cousin more.

Helping Callender across an intersection, Nigel Stone heard a horse snorting, and he dragged his burden back to a spot only a few feet from Felicia Lamb's house. Later, he convinced himself that he hadn't spoken to the driver because he realized they hadn't the money to hire a ride. What really decided him, though, before he even thought of his purse, was the sinister look of the driver. He was gaunt and pale, with dark hollows for eyes, and down the left side of his face ran a horrible scar.

VII. The Bride of Death

Felicia Lamb heard the old clock downstairs strike midnight before she thought it safe to rise from her curtained bed and begin to dress. It took her some time to prepare herself, but she was determined to do everything with exquisite care, for this was to be her ultimate rendezvous with the unknown.

She held neither lamp or candle when she slowly pulled open the door of her bed chamber and slipped out into the dark hall, but she had lived in this house all her life, and had no need of light to show her the way. Her only fear was that she might be detected, and that her aunt or even the servants might try to protect her from what could be considered danger, but which she knew she had desired from the day of her birth. So that she could be sure of silence, her feet were bare.

She tiptoed quickly down the carpeted staircase, her hand resting heavily on the bannister so that her tread would be light, then walked confidently through the hallway toward the door that led to the world beyond the home of her father and mother. She felt for the bolt, moved it with a practiced hand, and opened the door. Yellow fog drifted in to meet her and she stepped out into its embrace. She pulled the iron key from her bosom and locked the house behind her so that all within it might be safe. Then she stepped out into the shrouded street, wrapping her hooded cloak around her.

The coach was where she was told it would be waiting. Neither she nor the driver spoke a word, and the hooves of the horses had been muffled. There was hardly a sound to disturb the sleep of London as the coach rolled unerringly through the impenetrable mist.

Felicia still held the key clutched tightly in her fingers, but when her conveyance had rounded several corners, she threw her key into the gutter. It would never be recognized, and she did not intend to use it again.

She sat back quietly and waited to reach her destination, not even bothering to glance out the windows until the horses came to a smooth stop. She alighted without a moment's hesitation and stood almost blinded in thick clouds that might have been born in heaven or hell. A figure materialized beside her, almost as if it had drawn its substance from the fog; it guided her through a doorway and into darkness. Something shut behind her.

The two moved forward together, through a passageway which held at its end a globe of luminescence. Felicia felt that she was in a dream. The light resolved itself into a glowing ball of crystal, resting on an ebony table with chairs at either end, and casting its pale yellow light on an all-encompassing shroud of black velvet curtains. She was in the consulting room of Sebastian Newcastle, and he stood at her side.

He moved away from her and seated himself at the far end of the table, his face aglow in sickly light. "Will you not remove your cloak and sit with me, Miss Lamb?"

Felicia did neither. She was suddenly hesitant, suspicious. "Is this what you have promised me?" she said. "Only another seance?"

"Might it not be better so? There is much you could learn as you are, and much more that you may not wish to know."

"Then you have lied to me, sir?"

The light before Sebastian Newcastle's face flickered and dimmed. "Will you not wait, Felicia? What you seek comes soon enough, and lasts forever."

"Another seance, then? Will you call upon the dead for me? Will you call the shade of anyone I name?"

"I shall do what I can."

"Then call for me the spirit of a wizard. A master of the darkness, one who mastered death and reckoned not the price. Call for me the spirit of your double, Don Sebastian de Villanueva. Can you do it, Mr Sebastian Newcastle? Do you dare?"

"I can. But do you dare to let me?"

"Have I not asked it of you?"

"You have," he said. "You have asked too often to be denied. And yet the blame will be all mine."

"I absolve you," said Felicia Lamb.

"Spoken like the angel you so fervently desire to be," Sebastian said. His voice was almost brutal. "Will you do me the courtesy to sit down?"

"You can hardly hope to frighten me with gruff tones when we have come so far," Felicia said.

"No. Nothing will frighten you but what you cannot change. And when that terror comes, will you be brave enough to bear it, or brave enough to put an end to it?"

"Surely I shall be one or the other," she replied as she seated herself at the table. "Shall we begin?"

"I warn you because I care for you," Sebastian said.

"I believe it," she said. "Now show me who it is that cares for me so much."

She reached out for his cold hand, but he drew back. He did not speak. He crossed his arms before his face, and the light in the crystal was snuffed out in an instant. The black room was entombed in ebony.

Felicia stared ahead, her hand at her heart, more frightened than she would have admitted under torture. Something was about to happen, and she had longed for it, but she was half afraid that she would be ravished and murdered in the dark. Was that what she had demanded?

She hoped for a vision, but instead she heard a voice. It might have been human, indeed it must have been human, but the low, echoing, senseless syllables sounded more like an animal in agony. It ended in a note that was a hollow song of pain.

Sebastian's face appeared abruptly in the gloom. The flesh glowed with the pale blue light of putrescence, and the flame of decay grew brighter until the features burned away and left only a gleaming silver skull beneath. It spoke to her.

"What is worse than death, my love? Flee from it!"

The mouth that moved was full of unnaturally sharp teeth that gleamed like swords. The skull screamed, and then burst into flame. A dull and rusted blade dropped from the ceiling and sundered the skull from whatever held it erect. The flashes of fire turned cold blue as it rolled across the table toward Felicia; the hollow sockets where its eyes had been bubbled up with globes of glistening jelly, while locks of black and silky hair sprouted from the burnished surface of the silver skull.

The head fell upon her breast, and all at once Sebastian was in her arms. The black room was alive with silver.

"I am the one you seek," he said. "Turn away."

Felicia pulled away from him and stood, leaving him on his knees, his head bent over the arms of the ebony chair. He turned toward her, relieved to think that she would run from all that he could offer her. She took a deep breath, then pulled the dark hood from her face and the dark cloak from her body.

"I am the one you seek," she said. "Would you deny my desire, and your own?"

She wore a white wedding gown, its silk scarcely paler than her own ivory flesh.

The gown had been her mother's, forty years ago, when fashion was more graceful and less refined. Her arms were bare, her shoulders were bare, and her breasts were almost bare as well, the silk gathered beneath them and flowing down in delicate folds that brushed against the ebony floor. Felicia would never have dared to dress in such a manner if it had not been her wedding night, but now she exulted in her shamelessness. The glow around her turned the silk, her skin, her pale eyes, and her ashen hair to silver.

The black figure of Sebastian glided toward her.

"Destiny," he murmured.

He grasped her almost cruelly. She felt his cold breath upon her throat, his cold fingers in her flowing hair. She arched her back and exposed her white neck, but Sebastian pulled her forward and turned away from her.

He would not look at her as he spoke.

"I have become what I am, a creature of the night who feeds on blood, because I would not die. Why should you, a young woman with years of life before her, spurn the most precious gift in all creation?"

"Because I would know more of its creator." She reached out to touch his shoulder.

"If you care nothing for yourself, think of your friends. Think of your family."

"I have no friends," Felicia said. "As for my family, those I love most have gone before me. As for Aunt Penelope, I think she will be content with my fortune."

"And the young man?"

"You have seen what he is. I wish to God that I had seen it sooner."

"Then is there nothing for you in this world?"

"Nothing but to be rid of it."

"Then at least die a true death," Sebastian said, "and I will guide your spirit as I do those others you have seen, those who are lost. Take poison, cut your throat, jump from a tower, do anything but take this curse upon yourself. For many centuries I have carried it alone, and it is better so."

"You have not renounced your fate. In truth, I think you relish it. You love to be the lord of life and death, to stand between them and cast a cold eye on both. Is it because I am a woman that you think I do not know my own desires? Do you think that I am not as brave as you? Could it not be that I have been sent to end your loneliness forever?"

Sebastian whirled to confront her, his face a mask of fury. "Loneliness? Why need I be lonely when I have companions such as this to comfort me?"

The glowing curtains rippled in the black and silver room behind Sebastian. A shape appeared behind them: aimless, clumsy, menacing, and unutterably sad. A faltering white hand emerged through the drapes, and despite herself Felicia gasped. What shuffled into the room had been a boy. His shaggy hair was red, but his slack-jawed face was almost gray, and his eyes were those of an idiot. His lips were drooling, and his teeth were sharp. He limped toward Sebastian, one leg twisted and broken.

"Please, sir," he muttered.

"My God, Sebastian," Felicia said. "What is this?"

"A grave robber. He said his name was Henry Donahue. I found him and another at their work, and killed the first one outright, but by the time I caught young Donahue again, my fury and my bloodlust were so great that I slaked my thirst on him. And here he is, one of the living dead, and quite mad. I should have destroyed him, and surely I must, but now I am happy to have been delayed. Gaze on him. Is this what you wish to become?"

At the sound of her voice, the dead boy had turned toward Felicia. He dragged his shattered leg across the black carpet, his eyes fastened on her throat. Felicia felt suddenly naked and defenseless.

"Please, miss," said the boy.

He touched her.

Suddenly his hands were reaching for her throat, his dirty little teeth gnashing at the air as she tried to push him away. There was a strange strength in his small fingers. Felicia screamed.

The boy had her half sprawled on the ebony table when Sebastian yanked him back by his red hair and threw him across the room. Half of his scalp stayed in Sebastian's hand, and his head was a raw but bloodless wound as he implacably scuttled over the floor to reach the woman he wanted.

Sebastian pounced on him again, caught his twisted leg, and dragged the snarling creature through the velvet curtains and out of the room.

Felicia was alone, heart pounding, her breath coming in frantic gasps. She was terrified, and yet exhilarated too. She struggled down from the table top and collapsed into an ebony chair. From somewhere in the recesses of the house came a high pitched wail of agony that rose to a crescendo and then stopped abruptly. Felicia knew she would never see the boy again.

She waited.

When Sebastian returned to her, his hair hung over his face and his clothes were torn. His hands were spotted with blood. He looked at them and then at Felicia.

"There was little enough in him," Sebastian said. "He had been starved. Now you see what I would save you from."

Felicia trembled, but she remained where she was. "Between you and this boy is as much difference as there must have been in life," she said. "I will not be like him."

"Go!" shouted Sebastian, but even as he did he advanced upon her, his mouth twisting uncontrollably.

Felicia gritted her teeth and clutched the arms of the ebony chair with all her might. She held her head high, and felt the pulses throbbing in her long white neck as Sebastian overwhelmed her.

Then they were on the carpet, her carefully coiffed pale hair spilled upon its darkness, her gown in disarray, her body throbbing with delight and dread. She felt an ecstasy of fear, stunned more by the desires of her flesh than by the small, sweet sting she felt as he sank into her and life flowed between them. She rocked and moaned beneath the body of the man she loved. She took life and love and death and made them one.

And when it was over, Sebastian arose alone. She lay at ease, her limbs sprawled in graceful carelessness, her face marked by abandon hardly tinged by shock. She was pale as a marble statue, colored with a few drops of virgin's blood. She was at peace, but Sebastian knew that she would rise full of dark desire when the next sun set.

Even his tears, when they came, were tinged with her bright blood.

VIII. The Final Note

Nigel Stone paced through the empty rooms of the echoing house he shared with his cousin. He had been in the place for less than a day, but already its atmosphere oppressed him. He knew that Callender was upstairs somewhere sleeping off what must have been an appalling headache, yet somehow the mansion seemed utterly deserted, a fit abode for ghosts rather than men. Out of sheer desperation, Stone was tempted to drop off himself, on the settee in the study that had served him as a bed, but he fought the temptation, though there was little enough for a man to do in London when he had no money and no friends. It wasn't even a fit day for a stroll around the old town,

unfortunately; a heavy rain had been falling for most of the afternoon, interrupted from time to time by distant growls of thunder and
dim glimmerings of lightning.

Still, Stone decided that a storm would be more stimulating than
wandering through a house that seemed half haunted. He headed
for the door, threw it open, and stared out into the street. The rain
rattled down and splashed in the gutters; wind blew some of it into
Stone's face. Across the way a man scrambled for shelter, and his
antics made Stone feel very satisfied to be indoors after all. And yet
something in the power of the elements made him feel strong and
alive; he remembered how he had run shouting through storms
when he had been a boy.

As he looked out on nature's fury, Stone saw a coach round a
corner and pull up in front of the doorway that sheltered him. The
horses steamed and shivered in the downpour. Stone felt a trifle
foolish to be standing there, but would have been even more
ashamed to duck back inside like a frightened child, especially when
the coachman ducked down from his perch, his high hat dripping,
and scrambled up the steps to meet him. Stone did his best to act like
a prosperous householder.

"Mr Nigel Stone?" asked the coachman.

"What? Me?" stammered Stone. "Yes, of course it's me. What can I
do for you, my good man?"

"A message for you from a lady, sir. She said to wait for an answer."
He pulled a piece of paper from somewhere inside his soaking coat
and handed it to Stone. The wet ink was already beginning to blur.

> My Dear Mr Stone,
>   Please come at once, and if you can, come without
> Mr Callender. My niece Felicia vanished last night, and I fear
> for her safety. I believe I can rely on you, and no one else.

A drop of rain turned the signature to a gray smudge, but there could
be no doubt about the name. Stone felt pleasure at the summons,
and then a twinge of shame that he should take such delight in the
misfortune of a young woman.

"I'll come at once," he said.

"Then come with me, sir. I'll wait here while you get your great-
coat."

"No need for that," mumbled Stone. He was embarrassed to
confess that he owned no such garment, but not quite desperate
enough to pilfer his cousin's; he hoped the coachman would take his
scanty costume as a sign of dedication rather than desperation. A
blast of thunder ripped the sky apart as he hurried down the steps.

The same thunder woke Reginald Callender at last. He cursed, and sat up so quickly that he wrenched his back. His sheets were soaked with his own sweat, and they had begun to stink. He itched all over, and he started to tremble as soon as he awoke. And when he heard the rain, he was seized with a wild desire to run naked into London and wash himself clean, but he had just enough judgement left to realize this might not be wise.

Callender huddled under his quilts and pulled damp pillows over his head, trying without much success to shut out the world. Now that he was conscious again, he could not bear to lie awake alone with his own thoughts. Visions of doom hounded him in his own bed. He could not stay there.

He crawled out into the clammy air and began to shiver. He called for the servants, even though he knew that they were gone. Then he called for his cousin Nigel, but there was no reply. He felt utterly abandoned.

The house was too big for him. He had a sudden, unreasoning fear of being a small speck in a vast space. It was unbearable.

He pulled on such clothes as he could find, and took a pull from the bottle beside the bed. He thanked heaven for his uncle's cellar, which was still his even if the house would soon be sold for debts, and he dreaded the day when the wine would run dry. He drank again, and heard the rain battering against his window.

He hardly cared for the weather, though, when his mind was in such an uproar. There was a need in him to escape from these walls and from his memories. Compared to them, a thunderstorm was a small thing.

A song rang through his head, a tantalizing tune that meant nothing yet said much. Against it as a counterpoint rang heavy sounds of resentment and recrimination, memories of an evening when he had said and done much that might not be forgiven. Much wiser, he thought, to follow the notes of the sweeter, shallower song, and to forget the rest. He felt in his pockets, found a few shillings, then staggered down the staircase and out the door to stand under the streaming skies. He had no cash for a cab, but he knew the way to The Glass Slipper.

His journey was a vision. Water fell in curtains before him, and it rose in glistening fountains at every curb. Rainbows formed in every gaslight, and phantoms in the fog. His way was weary, but he was too tired to rest. From time to time the whirling wheels that passed him covered him in water, but it was no more to him than paint on lips that were already scarlet. Drenched and deranged, Reginald Callender made his way through forgotten streets until he reached his remembered goal.

The glass globes over the flickering flames at the entrance to The Glass Slipper seemed to Callender like stars in the heavens. He stepped over cigars, mud, and orange peels to reach the arch where a shilling brought him his way into the saloon bar.

"Buy us a bottle of fizz?" Callender pushed the drab out of his way and proceeded up into the balcony. This had always been a disorderly house, but now it struck him as the true home of chaos. Each face he saw was a twisted demon shape, and each voice a mockery. He was vaguely aware that some spurned him for the unshaven, sodden wretch he had become, but it mattered little when he knew he was so close to Sally Wood.

"Give your orders, gentlemen, please!" The harsh voice cut through the tobacco fumes, the smell of stale beer and cheap perfume. In another life Callender would have ignored the summons, but now that he was destitute he felt compelled to buy a glass of beer. A girl with plump arms and a vacant face offered to sell him sweets from a glass jar, but she backed away when she saw his expression. The orchestra struck up a tinny tune, and it was one Callender recognized. The gods were with him after all. It was Sally's song.

> Some girls place a price upon their maidenhood,
> Defend it, never spend it till the price is good.
> They wouldn't give a gent a tumble if they could.
> They couldn't if they would,
> They wouldn't if they could,
> But everybody knows Sally Wood.

And there she was, in a gaudy red dress, strutting saucily across the stage. She bawled out her litany, her skirts hiked up to her garters, and Callender dreamed of what lay beyond them. He wondered how many men shared the same dreams, perhaps even the same memories, and he hated them all.

Someone clapped him on the back and handed him a glass of brandy; he didn't even notice who it was. When Sally hit her final note and made a low curtsey in her low-cut dress, he stood stock still and stared while every other man in The Glass Slipper gave vent to boisterous shouts and applause. He did not move as Sally leaped from the stage, wove her way expertly through the orchestra, pushed through the crowd with a few playful slaps, and hurried up to the balcony bar. She passed within a few feet of Callender on her way to the spot where a man with a leathery face and gray sidewhiskers was standing. There was a bottle of champagne beside him on the bar, and he poured Sally a glass as she approached, her face flushed and her chestnut hair flowing.

Callender awoke from his paralysis and stumbled toward Sally. She turned when he grasped her arm.

"Reggie!" she said, and then she laughed. "You do look a sight!"

"It's the rain."

"You'd better go home, dear, or you'll catch your death. I'll talk to you another night."

She turned her back on him.

"Sally! You'll talk to me now!" He reached out for her again, but the stranger put himself between them.

"You can see that the lady is occupied," he said. His tone was the one that Callender had been accustomed to use when talking to servants. Callender tried to push him away, but the man was like an oak.

Callender took a swing at the man, who ducked back without hesitation and then put a bony fist in his opponent's face.

Callender was surprised to find himself sitting on the floor. His nose and mouth felt hot and wet. There was laughter all around him.

He was trying to decide what to do when he had another shock: he saw Sally slap her escort's face. This brought another roar from the crowd, which burst into wilder applause than it had ever granted one of her songs when Sally knelt down beside the stricken Callender and took him in her arms.

"Come on, Reggie," she said. "You're all right."

"Sally?" He didn't know what else to say.

"That's right, dear. You come along with me. Can't have my husband murdered, can I?"

Her words hardly registered as she helped him to his feet and out of The Glass Slipper.

The rain was still falling, and Callender lifted his face toward it to wash away the blood. He hardly looked where he was walking, but he was conscious enough to remember that her lodgings were just around the corner from the music hall. He dragged his boots through a puddle like a child, and he found a kind of pleasure in it. He had begun to love the storm. When the thunder rumbled, he made the same sort of noise himself. Sally just looked at him and smiled.

She led him up two flights of stairs and into her disordered room, as full of jumble as his own dwelling was barren, then sat him down on an unmade bed covered with clothes. He saw a pamphlet, half hidden by a dress, and picked it up.

"Still reading penny dreadfuls, Sal?"

"Oh, you mean the vampire. You should take that along, Reggie. I'm finished with that bit, and it's awfully good."

Callender shrugged and stuffed the thing into his pocket. His mind was fuddled, but somewhere in it was the glimmer of an idea. There was something else, too, something he wanted to remember.

"Look here. What was that you said to me back at the Slipper, eh?"

"What do you mean, dear? Take off your coat. It's wet."

"Leave me alone. I want to be wet."

"Have it your own way, then," said Sally, peeling off her gown and posing before him in her corset. "I just wanted to get you warm."

"Warm, is it? And what did you say to me back there about a husband?"

She sat beside him and ran her tongue across his lips. "Only that a girl has to take care of her intended, Reggie."

He looked at her blearily. "You must be mad," he said.

"Not half, I'm not. You promised to marry me, right here in this very bed, and I mean to hold you to it, Mr Reggie Callender."

"Dreaming," he said.

"What?"

"One of us is dreaming. Whatever made you think that I would marry you?"

"You did, dear. When your uncle died, you said, and you were wealthy in your own right, you said you'd make an honest woman of me. And now he's dead, ain't he? I can see you took it hard, with your kind heart, but that will pass, and then we'll be wed. You do love me, don't you dear? There's nobody else?"

He fumbled at her, more out of habit than passion. "Of course there's nobody else," he said.

"No?" Sally pushed him down on the bed and slapped him harder than she had the man in The Glass Slipper. "And what about Miss Felicia Lamb?"

Callender was too stunned to reply.

"You think I'm stupid, don't you? You thought I didn't know about her! What do you take me for?"

Callender just sat on the bed and looked across the room.

"Here," said Sally. "Have some gin." She pulled a bottle from a pile of dresses in a corner and gave it to Callender. He uncorked it and poured half of it down his throat.

"That's right," said Sally. "Get yourself used to the idea. You thought I was just a silly girl. That's what you think of all of us, ain't it? And that's why we do what we can to protect ourselves. You recollect a girl named Alice? Your uncle's maid. We were good friends, Alice and me. She told me all about you. Now I don't begrudge you your bit of fun, Reggie. I've had mine. We'll forget Alice, even if she has seen more of your uncle's money than ever I did. But I won't let you marry this Felicia Lamb."

Callender took another pull on the bottle and put his head in his hands. The liquor burned against his bleeding gums. This was hardly the evening he had planned.

"I saw her once, you know," Sally said. "A blueblood virgin with big eyes and a tiny mouth. She's no woman for a man like you. I'll bet she wouldn't even raise her skirt to piss!"

It was Callender's turn to slap Sally. Then he picked up his hat and his stick and shuffled toward the door. "She is the woman I love," he said.

"Love, is it?" shouted Sally. "See how much love you find there after today, Mr Callender! She'll have nothing to do with you now! You're mine! Do you think I spent two years on my back for the pure pleasure of it?" She rushed to follow him, shouting in his ear.

Callender summoned up a drunken dignity. "There is nothing you can do to prevent this marriage," he said. "You and I shall not meet again."

"I've stopped you already," Sally screamed. "I sent her a note, that's what I did. A letter telling her what you had been to me. She'll have read it by now, and that'll be an end to any love between you!"

Callender staggered back against the door. To have lost two fortunes in so short a time was more than he could bear. Without thinking, without even wishing to, he slammed his ebony walking stick into Sally's face.

She seemed bewildered, and she made a whimpering sound. He saw by the candlelight that he had turned her right eye into red pulp.

She put her hand to her face, and something came away in it. She dropped to her knees and began to wail.

Callender was horrified. He stooped to help her, but she pushed him away and crawled across the floor. She began to scream.

It was intolerable. He hit her again, this time on the top of her head, but it only made her screams louder.

He struck her twice more. The stick broke, and Sally slumped to the floor. The screaming stopped.

Callender ran down the stairs and into the street. In an alley, in the rain, he vomited again and again. At first he thought it would kill him, but when he was done his head began to clear. The storm was lifting, and the gleams of lightning seemed to come from miles away.

He was almost home when he realized that he was holding only half a stick. He gazed at the jagged stump in disbelief. He tried to convince himself that he had dropped the other half somewhere in the street, but he felt a sick certainty that it was lying beside Sally Wood. Could it be used to identify him? Callender had heard of the detective inspectors newly appointed to Scotland Yard, and of the tricks they could play in catching criminals of every kind. He could not take the chance of leaving anything behind.

The journey back was agonizing. He wanted nothing less than to visit Sally Wood again, yet speed seemed imperative since he knew her corpse would be discovered eventually. He had to be there and gone again before it was. He could not bear to think of what would happen if he were caught with her corpse, yet he could not think of anything else. He wanted a drink. He was half tempted to hurry home for one, yet all the while his feet were carrying him back to The Glass Slipper. His thoughts were so agitated that he found himself there before he was quite prepared.

Several loungers stood outside, and the faint sound of music came from within. It was as if nothing had happened. Could it be that they didn't know?

The thought froze Callender for an instant, and then he backed into the shadows of an alley. For the first time in his life he was afraid to be seen. Yet it was madness to remain here, a few feet from his crime but doing nothing to conceal it. He pulled down his hat and turned up his collar as if seeking protection from the rain, then stepped casually out into the street and walked briskly round the corner.

He looked up at Sally's solitary window, where a light still burned. There was no hue and cry, no sign of anything but sleep. He pushed the street door open cautiously, thanking whatever power might protect him that he had neglected to close anything behind him in his hurry to be gone. He crept up the stairs, his ear cocked for the slightest sound. The house was as still, he thought wryly, as a tomb.

And so it remained until he reached Sally's door. The sound he heard behind it gave him a chill the rain could not. He knew it must be his imagination, some symptom of a guilty conscience, but he would have sworn he recognized the melody of the song Sally had performed at The Glass Slipper not more than an hour ago. Someone seemed to be humming it.

Could this be a ghost? Another trick of that damned spiritualist? He didn't believe it. He couldn't. It had to be a trick of his own mind. A small thing, really, and he needed the rest of that stick.

He opened the door.

What he saw was worse than what he feared. It was Sally, her face awash with blood and her pretty hair matted down with it. She was crawling on her hands and knees around the room, singing her song as best she could through lips that dribbled blood. She had not died at all, but clearly she should have.

Sally knocked over a table, but still she sang her song. Callender realized that he had damaged her beyond repair. She had no idea that he was in the room.

His mouth twitched uncontrollably as he raised his boot and

brought it down with all his weight on the back of Sally's neck. He heard the spine snap.

He needed the last of the gin he took from her.

He picked up the second half of his walking stick and hurried home to his bed, where he spent the next three days attempting to convince himself that he had never left it.

IX. The Heiress

Three men dressed in blue gathered in front of a tall brick house near the gates of All Souls Cemetery. Their high hats held sturdy metal frames, and their knee-length coats had buttons made of brass. In each man's belt was a wooden staff; one of them used his to knock on the door.

They waited in the darkness and the damp. One of them shivered in the cold. "There's no one here," he said. "We should have come by day."

"And so we have, some of us, but we had no answer then, anymore than we have now."

"We could break down the door."

"We're only seeking information from a gentleman. The people have little enough use for Scotland Yard without us making a name for ourselves as housebreakers."

"Then knock again."

"I'll give the orders here," said the man with the staff, but he used it again anyway.

A light appeared in one of the windows.

"We've roused someone."

"Be still, will you?"

The door opened slowly and silently; a tall man with a black mustache appeared on the threshold, a black candle in his hand. Its flickering light gleamed unpleasantly on a long scar than ran down the left side of his face.

"Good evening, sir. I hope we have not disturbed you."

"I have been sleeping, constable. What brings you here?"

"A woman, sir. Miss Felicia Lamb."

"I do not see her with you."

"No sir. She's not to be seen anywhere, and that's what concerns us. Are you Mr Newcastle, sir?"

"I am."

"Well, sir, we've been informed that Miss Lamb was a frequent visitor here, and since she's vanished, we take it upon ourselves to make inquiries. We'd be most appreciative of any help."

"I see. Tell me, constable, how long has she been missing?"

"Just three days. It's Sunday, and she was last seen on Thursday night, at a dinner party."

"It has been longer than that since I have seen Miss Lamb, constable. Have you spoken to the people who dined with her?"

"Two of them sir. Her aunt, who mentioned you to us, and a friend of the family, a Mr Nigel Stone. The third would be her betrothed, a Mr Callender. We have visited him several times but found nobody home."

"Perhaps they have run away together."

"Yes. We thought of that. But why should they elope when they were already pledged?"

"From what I have seen of Mr Callender, he is a most headstrong young man."

"So we have been told. You know him, sir?"

"We have met twice. And even on such short acquaintance, I could not form a high opinion of his character."

"As you say, sir. We've had reports that he'd been drinking heavily."

"Just so. Is there more that I can do for you, constable? Would you care to search for Miss Lamb within?"

Sebastian Newcastle stepped aside and gestured into the black recesses of his home.

The three men from Scotland Yard looked into the darkness and then at each other.

"Well, sir," said their leader. "Since you've been good enough to offer, it follows that we needn't bother you tonight. Clearly you have nothing to hide."

"Then may I bid you goodnight, gentlemen? The hour is late."

"Just so, sir. Thanks for your trouble, and good night to you."

Sebastian shut the door and stood for a few moments with nothing to keep him company but the small flame of his candle. When he knew that the men had gone, he turned into the dark depths of the house and called for Felicia, but he knew before he spoke that there would be no answer. She could not be constrained at night; she wandered, ever weaker, through the valley of stones where the dead slept.

Sebastian went out into the night. He dissolved into an iridescent fog before the gates and drifted into All Souls, part of the thick mist that made the land look like a forgotten sea whose turbulence hid all but the wreckage of tortured trees and abandoned monuments. The landscape was more like a limbo for unhappy spirits than a part of the green earth.

He found Felicia sitting on a monument, her pale arms wrapped around the marble figure of an angel, her pale eyes staring off into the fog.

"Three men came to look for you," he said.

"And did three men leave?"

"Since they came from Scotland Yard, it seemed unwise to detain any of them."

"Police," Felicia said. "Have I destroyed your sanctuary here, Sebastian?"

"Perhaps, but that matters little when I see you as you are."

"I am as I wished to be."

"And was it worth it, then, to see life and death as two sides of the same coin, and to hold that coin in your own hand?"

"I have learned much," Felicia said.

"You have learned more than you bargained for. The price of that coin is blood."

Felicia hugged herself and looked down at the ground. "I cannot, Sebastian," she said.

"And yet you must," he said, "and most assuredly you will. The lives of others must become your life, and their blood your own. It is your fate, and none may resist it."

"I shall. I swear it. You know what I am now, better than any other could, but whatever I have become, I am still innocent of blood. I shall not stain my soul with it."

Sebastian turned away from her. She rose and took his arm. "I meant no reproach to you," she said.

"Then I must reproach myself. As you have said, I know what will become of you. You will grow weaker, and the thirst will grow stronger, until at length you will be transformed into the thirst. You saw how long I could resist you, for all my wish to do so."

"You did what I desired you to do," Felicia said.

"I would have done it anyway!"

Sebastian took her beautiful pale face into his cold hands. "You came to me as my bride," he said, "and I have been alone too long. Now I must see to it that you survive."

"Is there no other way?"

"If you can resist the thirst, then it will doom you. Your body will become too frail to move, but still it will contain your soul. Your spirit will never be free to seek the worlds beyond our own. It will be trapped in a lifeless husk, and you will be truly damned."

She gazed deeply into his dark eyes, then stiffened in his arms at the sound of a human voice nearby.

A lantern gleamed dully through the yellow fog.

"Three men," she said, long before she could see them.

"The constables," Sebastian said.

"Then let us greet them and be done with this." She laughed loudly and bitterly.

Three dark figures emerged from the mist, clustering around their light as if they feared to lose it.

"Mr Newcastle," one of them said.

Sebastian bowed slightly but made no reply.

"And Miss Felicia Lamb?"

"And what is that to you?" Felicia snapped.

"Your aunt said you were lost, Miss."

"And now I am found."

"Just so, Miss. But look where we've found you. In a graveyard, at night, and with nothing to cover you but a nightgown."

"This is my mother's wedding dress."

"Oh, I see. A wedding dress, is it? A runaway heiress and a foreign gentleman. You weren't quite honest with us, were you, Mr Newcastle?"

"Sometimes a gentleman must keep his tongue, constable," Felicia said. "Though you seem to know nothing of that."

"No, Miss, I'm no gentleman, right enough. Just a rough fellow trying to do his job. Still, I offer our protection if you ask for it. This is no fit place for a young lady, and no fit company if I'm any judge."

"You may never live to be a judge," Sebastian said. He cast his eye on the lantern in the constable's hand. At once its faint flame turned a blazing red; the metal was too hot to hold. The man screamed in anguish as he dropped the light; suddenly there was only blackness and the smell of burning flesh.

"There is danger in the dark," Sebastian said as he moved forward. He felt Felicia's grip on his shoulder and saw her pale eyes imploring him to stop. Together they watched the three men scramble away through the tombstones and the trees. At last there was silence.

"There will be danger from them," Sebastian finally said. "We might have feasted, and now we must flee. Was it wise for you to stop me?"

"I stopped you because I wanted nothing more than to let you go. To join you, in fact. The one on the right, the young one. I wanted him."

"He was yours, Felicia. He can be yours in a moment."

"No, Sebastian. It must not be. I cannot do what you have done. I never thought of it. I only dreamed of death, and peace, and freedom. I wanted knowledge, not the power to destroy."

"There is more to know," Sebastian said, "and time enough to know it, but only if you will take life."

She pulled back from him, and leaned against a marble slab engraved with the name of one long dead. She had never seemed more beautiful to him, and never more beloved, than when she renounced all that he could offer her.

"You have thrown away the mortal life that you were born to live," he said. "If you throw away this second chance, there will be nothing left for you but an eternity of emptiness."

"Would that be so different from what you endure?"

"At least I still exist. I walk the earth. What could be more precious?"

"Then this is all your magic offers you? The chance to walk the earth like other men?"

"Other men die," Sebastian said.

Felicia reached out to him, took one step forward, and then sank to her knees. "Help me," she murmured.

He looked down at her compassionately. "You must not kneel to me," he said, "or any man."

"I did not do it willingly," she said. "I cannot stand."

"You must have blood, and you must have it now."

"No," she said. "Too late. No blood. No life."

She sank into the damp grass. Sebastian hovered over her; he tried to raise her to her feet. He kissed her; he shouted at her.

Nothing mattered. She could not be awakened.

Sebastian swept her up in his arms and moved toward his house, but he realized at once that men would be waiting for him there. He turned back toward the stones, toward the tombs he had guarded for half a century, but there was no consolation in them. He searched her face for some faint flicker of life and saw nothing but cold perfection. Yet he knew that her soul was trapped within her corpse, and would remain there until time stopped.

He put her to rest in a tomb and raged through the night. Dogs howled, marble shattered like glass, and three men who trembled in the night fog came to the decision that their investigations might be best conducted in the light of day.

X. The Wine Cellar

Reginald Callender awoke to the sound of a distant and insistent banging. It came from far enough away so that it drifted slowly into his consciousness, becoming part of his dreams before it ended them. He was striking something again and again with his cane.

Then he was staring at the ceiling. His head throbbed with each repeated blow on the door downstairs, but Callender only cursed quietly and waited for the noise to stop. He wondered what day it was, and even if it were day at all. He raised one crusted eyelid and saw a stray shaft of sunlight break through the drawn curtains. Then he went back to sleep.

The next time he was disturbed, there was no putting it off. Someone had him by the shoulders, and was shaking him more savagely than the aftermath of drink could ever do. A splash of cold water hit him in the face. Callender shouted, sputtered, and looked up into the ruddy face of his cousin.

"God damn you, sir," Callender roared. "Have you gone completely mad?"

"You call me mad, do you? It's Monday morning. Where have you been for four days, eh? Do you know what's happened to the girl you're going to marry?"

"What? Sally?"

"Who's Sally? What are you talking about? I mean Miss Lamb!"

"Felicia. Of course. I went to see her . . . when was it? But the servants said that she was not at home to me."

"She wasn't at home to anyone, my dear fellow. She has been missing for the best part of a week."

Callender pulled himself into a sitting position. "How long has she been gone?"

"Since last Thursday. The night we had dinner at her house. The night I came to visit you."

"It's been a short enough visit, then, hasn't it? Where have you been ever since? And where's that bottle? My head!"

Callender felt under his bed and came up with what he sought.

"I thought you'd finished all the brandy," Stone said.

"So I did. But there's plenty of port. And now there's cause to celebrate as well. Felicia could never have read that letter, could she?"

"Letter? What letter?"

"A note from someone who wanted to drive us apart. Hasn't anyone seen it?"

"Who cares for letters at a time like this?" demanded Stone.

"No, of course not." Callender took a drink of wine. "And you say Felicia's gone?"

"Well, we did have some word of her."

"We?"

Stone's face turned a bit redder. "I've been with her aunt. Miss Penelope. She's terribly concerned, of course."

"Oh? You've been busy. The wealthy niece is missing, and all at once you're lodging in an elegant house with her spinster aunt."

"I'm doing what should have been done by you," Stone replied defensively. "Have you been locked in this empty house for all these days?"

"Of course I've been here," said Callender. "Where else would I have been?"

"That's what I decided, finally, even though those fellows from Scotland Yard were here more than once and said there wasn't a soul about."

Callender nearly dropped his bottle, and after he caught it he took a long drink. "Scotland Yard?"

"We naturally called them in when we couldn't find the girl, and they just as naturally sought to make inquiries of the man she's going to marry. I think they were a bit suspicious of you until they got some information."

"Thank God for that," said Callender. He sagged back on the bed. "Then I'm not suspected."

"Of course not! Look here, cousin, what's wrong with you? You don't seem to care what's happened to Felicia. Don't you want to hear what's become of her? She's been seen."

Stone paced indignantly across the room while Callender attempted to collect his thoughts. "Then she's safe?" he asked.

"I suppose you could say that, according to the law, but if you ask me I'd say she was in mortal danger. She was seen with that man Newcastle."

Callender leaped from the bed, still half dressed in trousers and a soiled shirt. "Newcastle!" he shouted. He grasped his cousin by the collar and stared wildly into his eyes. "What has he done with her?"

"I don't know, I'm sure," said Stone as he disengaged himself. "But the constables said she was wearing what she called a wedding gown."

"Didn't they stop her? Didn't they take her away with them? My God!"

"Well. They said there was no law against a girl getting married if she had a mind, or taking a walk with her husband in the night air, if it came to that. Even if it was in a graveyard. And I think he did something to frighten them."

Callender snatched up a coat that had been thrown over a chair and began to rummage through its pockets. Half of a broken walking stick rattled to the floor, but he ignored it. At last he found a bedraggled little book and waved it at his cousin with an air of triumph. He sat down heavily in the chair and began turning pages with intense concentration. "He's done for me," he muttered. "And now I'll do for him."

"Look here, Reggie," began Stone.

"Be quiet, you fool! Can't you see I'm reading?"

"I can see I'm no use here," said Stone, more baffled than ever when he saw his cousin reach down for the broken stick and clutch it triumphantly. "I'll let myself out. When you come to your senses, if you do, perhaps you'll do something to help us save Miss Lamb."

He strode from the room, and was halfway down the stairs when he heard Stone raving at him, or at the world.

"Save her? I'll save her! I'm the only one who can! I'm the only one who knows how!"

Nigel Stone never looked back. He locked the front door behind him and stepped out into the afternoon, the first he had seen with even a touch of sun since his arrival in London. He was content to take it as an omen. Elopements there might be, or even abductions, and madness certainly, but what did they matter? He was on his way to meet Miss Penelope Lamb, and for his own part he was happy.

A few minutes later, Reginald Callender came out of the same door and squinted into the same sunlight. His hair was disheveled, his cravat awry, his gait unsteady. He tried to hail a cab, but the first two drivers merely glanced at him and then passed by. A third pulled to a stop a few yards down the street, and Callender staggered after him. The cabman looked down from his perch.

"Let's see the color of your money before you climb aboard," he said.

Callender was obliged to go through his pockets once again. He pulled out Sally's penny dreadful, one half of a broken stick and then the other. A small flask completed the catalog of his possessions.

"Looks like you'll be walking," said the cabman as he trotted off.

Callender hurled *Varney the Vampire* after the retreating cab. "I don't need this anymore," he screamed. "And I don't need you!"

He was suddenly aware that he had attracted the attention of several passersby, and that he was standing in the middle of a tranquil street wailing like a fishwife. He recognized a neighbor who had been accustomed to tip his hat but now looked ostentatiously away. Callender saw the two sharp sticks and the flask that he had been waving in the air. He thrust them back into his coat and hurried away.

It was a long walk to All Souls Cemetery.

Callender's mind raced faster than his feet could carry him, but his thoughts ran in circles. He had lost everything: his fortune, his mistress, his bride, and her fortune too. The list ran through his mind like a litany, so that he began to suspect that he was losing his senses as well. In fact, he thought that he might welcome it if he could go completely mad, when his only alternative was to live in a world where he was besieged by devils.

At least he knew who was to blame. Newcastle had even produced his uncle's ghost, and by this time Callender was more than willing to believe that somehow the spiritualist had plundered his uncle's estate as well. But Newcastle wasn't a spiritualist, of course. He was a vampire.

The explanation seemed so simple to Callender now. Hadn't he heard Felicia holding forth on vampires just before she disappeared? Still, the one he really had to thank was Sally Wood, whose lurid little books on the subject had revealed not only the cause of his troubles, but a remedy for them. And if not a remedy, then at least revenge.

Callender felt a twinge of pity when he thought of Sally now; he wished he could have killed her quickly.

His next killing would have to be quick whether he wished it or not. As he approached Newcastle's house, he saw that the sun was low in the sky behind the trees of All Souls. Could it really be that the dead would rise soon?

He hurried toward Sebastian Newcastle's house, but what he saw there disturbed him even more than the setting sun. Before the entrance stood a man dressed in a long blue coat with brass buttons. Clearly the house was under the surveillance of Scotland Yard.

Callender hesitated. His plan had been to ransack the place, find Newcastle's undead corpse, and bury his broken cane in it, but this would hardly be possible under the circumstances. He might get some information from the constable on guard, but he hardly liked the idea of presenting himself to the law when he was a murderer himself. Should he risk it, or should he run?

His mouth was dry. He found the flask in his pocket and drained most of the port; the rest of it spilled down the front of his coat. The drink gave him courage enough to approach the house, and find out what he needed to know. He made an effort to regain his dignity, walking very carefully as he approached the lair of his nemesis. He decided as he took the last few steps that aggression might be more effective than supplication.

"What's going on here?" he said. "Where's Mr Newcastle?"

"That's what we'd like to know, sir. What's your business with him?"

"He's eloped with my fiancee. Is that business enough?"

"Are you Mr Callender? We've been wanting to talk to you. What do you know about all this?"

"Nothing but what I've been told. I quarreled with Miss Lamb, about nothing really, and now I hear this man has spirited her away. Have you any word of her?"

"No more than that, sir. She was seen with him once, in that graveyard yonder, but only then, and only for a moment."

"And have you searched the house?" demanded Callender.

"From top to bottom, sir."

"Are you certain? This is a strange house, you know," said Callender. "One night when I was here, the very walls seemed to dissolve into a fog."

"Indeed, sir! I've had nights like that myself. You seem to be having one now, if I may say so, and it ain't even night yet."

Callender ran the back of his hand over his dry lips. "How would you feel?" he asked. "What would you do? If I find this man Newcastle, I'll kill him."

"Well, sir, as to that, if a man ran off with my old woman, I'd buy him a drink! Eh? We mustn't take these things too serious." The constable paused, and squinted at Callender as if seeing him for the first time. "You wouldn't kill a lady, would you, sir?"

Callender swallowed hard. "Whatever do you mean?" he stammered. "Of course not!"

"Sometimes gentlemen lose their heads, in a manner of speaking. And Miss Lamb can't be found, you know."

"You're a fool," said Callender, turning on his heel.

"That's as may be, sir," the constable shouted at Callender's retreating back. "Will we find you at home, if something should turn up?"

Callender hurried off without bothering to reply. He could hardly have controlled himself for another second, especially when the talk of killing women started. The man seemed to be an ignorant commoner, but who could tell?

As he passed the cemetery once again, Callender noticed that the gates were open. He paused before them and peered in. This was where Felicia had been only a few hours before. If she and Newcastle were not in the house, might they not still be here? Callender entered All Souls.

The place was peaceful in the twilight, almost like a park with its green grass and gently rolling hills. Birds sang in the trees and perched on figures of white marble. This was like a city of the dead, and Callender hardly knew which way to turn in it. Rows of effigies and headstones stretched in every direction; in the distance lay clusters of white mausoleums.

Almost helplessly, he moved along the streets of marble toward his Uncle William's tomb. There his torment had started; perhaps it would end there, too. He had a vision, half inspired by Sally's cheap fiction, of rushing to that pale edifice and finding Felicia imprisoned there, the victim of a villain he could vanquish with one blow of his ebony stick. He longed to be a hero almost as much as he longed for another drink. He prayed to be free of his nightmare.

When he reached his goal, however, he found an avenging angel posed before it. Sitting in front of his uncle's final resting place was another man dressed in blue. His left hand was wrapped in bandages.

"Mr Callender," he said. "Paying your last respects?"

"I don't know you," said Callender as he backed away.

"We should be better acquainted, then. What brings you here this evening?"

It took Callender some time to find his tongue. "I'm told Miss Lamb was seen here," he finally said.

"At this very spot? Who told you that? None of my men, I'll warrant you."

"This is the only spot I know," said Callender. "My uncle is interred behind you."

"I see. And does he lie alone?"

"Is there someone else?" gasped Callender. "Felicia? Newcastle?"

"Neither of those, sir," said the chief constable.

"Then where are they?"

"We don't know yet." The chief constable stood up. "But we do know there are two bodies in that tomb that don't belong there, both of them horribly mutilated. The bodies of two young boys. What do you make of that, Mr Callender, sir?"

Callender backed away, almost convinced that this was another of his drunken dreams. The man from Scotland Yard just stared at him. Callender wheeled around and ran.

Running suited him, Callender decided. His lungs rasped, his heart thumped, and his stomach churned, but he was leaving everything behind him. When he glanced back, the immobile man in blue had dwindled to a tiny figure, no more threatening than a toy soldier.

Still, under darkening skies, Callender ran. He ran past monuments and mausoleums, through iron gates, then down streets where living men and women walked who scattered at the sight of him. He tumbled into the gutter once, and when he rose he was face to face with a lamplighter on his rounds. "So soon?" screamed Callender as he raced on.

He knew that he must be home before night fell.

He could hardly believe his good fortune when he reached the ugly, empty house that was his sanctuary. He fumbled for his key, and howled in agony when it was nowhere to be found. In panic, he pounded on the door, then to his amazement felt it open for him. Dimly he recalled that he had never had his key, and never locked the house. He slammed his door on the sunset and turned the bolt behind him. He was safe.

Callender sank to his knees in the dark hallway. He was ruined, and he acknowledged it. He wandered through the hollow rooms while the last rays of the day died outside. He was on the verge of tears, and he hated himself for that. The tears might have been for Felicia Lamb, or for Sally Wood, or even for his Uncle William, but all these had betrayed him. Callender wept for himself.

It made no difference.

He beat his hands against bare walls; he cursed the universe. It did not care.

At length his desolation brought him to himself, which was all that he had left to him. It was not enough. He could at least have a bottle to keep him company.

In the last week he had learned the way to the wine cellar. He thought he might take residence there, among the dusty bottles and the crates of cloth his cousin had brought back from India. He could make a bed for himself in the worthless textiles, and the wine would be close at hand. The idea pleased him. He made his way through the kitchen, and the pantry, where he found the stub of a candle to light his way.

The dark stairs were old friends to him, and the dark vault that he had reached was refuge. He found the shelves where the old port rested, and picked the best vintage left to him. He broke the top off the bottle and poured the rich, red liquid down his throat. He had to spit out a chip of glass, but at least it had only cut his lip.

He sat down in the dust and looked around. He drank again, but at the same time he noticed that something had been disturbed. One of the heavy boxes from India had been removed from the pile and set in the middle of the cellar. Its lid was loose.

Callender approached it cautiously. He left the candle on the floor, to keep both hands free. And as soon as he touched the top of the box, it clattered to the stones below.

There seemed to be nothing more inside than bolts of dyed cotton, but Callender was dissatisfied. He pulled the colored cloth aside. Beneath it was the face of Sebastian Newcastle.

Callender was too stunned to relish the sight, but only for a moment. He had found the lair of the vampire in the foundations of his own house. Felicia might be anywhere, in any state, but at least her betrayer had betrayed himself. Callender chuckled at a clever ruse that had gone awry. No doubt the vampire had imagined himself ingeniously concealed; he had not realized that Callender's thirst was as ravenous as his own. Callender tossed more cotton to the floor, and saw Sebastian Newcastle naked to the waist. The sight of this nude seducer drove him into a frenzy.

There were shadows all around him, and Callender knew that the sun had set. He knew the monster might leap up and devour him. He pulled half of the broken cane out of his coat; one end was needle sharp. He needed something to strike the fatal blow, and he needed it at once. The heavy butt end of the wine bottle would do.

Callender felt his own heart beating wildly, and this helped him to select the precise spot where he should strike. He placed the jagged point against the cold smooth skin. He smashed the shaft down with the heavy glass.

The ebony ripped through the yielding flesh, and a high pitched wail was forced from the corpse's lips, startling Callender into striking again and again. Each blow produced a delicate moan that made his skin crawl. The death agonies were uncanny. Something was wrong.

The vampire's body began to shake. It thrashed from side to side, then crumbled like a hollow shell. Pieces of flesh dropped away. A glass eye rolled across the cellar. The skin shattered. Something was breaking free.

Shards of Sebastian flew in all directions, and others settled into the box. Most of his face came to rest beside the other face beneath it.

Felicia Lamb lay among wax fragments, the sharp shaft of Callender's broken cane embedded in her breast.

Callender wondered why she didn't bleed. He had no way of knowing that there was not a drop of blood inside her. She was as white as a marble statue. Her golden hair, unleashed as he had never seen it, spread round her head like a halo. And all about her were parts of a waxen man, the remnants of Newcastle's last cruel joke.

Callender thought he saw Felicia's lashes flutter, her lips part, her fingers reaching toward her shattered heart. Then she was still, garbed in a gown of pure white silk. She looked like a sleeping angel.

His candle flared for an instant.

Callender laughed. He could hardly help himself. He picked up the bits of wax and smashed them underfoot. He found another bottle and broke its neck, drinking from sharp glass that sliced into his lips.

He heard footsteps overhead, and knowing that they came for him, he laughed again.

They found him there, his mouth dribbling blood, beside the punctured corpse of his beloved. The sound of his incoherent voice had drawn them to him.

There were three men in blue, one of them holding a lantern in his bandaged hand. Behind them came Nigel Stone, apologetically brandishing a key. The light sent shadows shimmering all over the wine cellar.

"Mr Callender," said the chief constable. "What have you been doing to Miss Lamb?"

XI. The Conscientious Cousin

Mr and Mrs Nigel Stone sat side by side on a horsehair settee and shared a bottle of fine old sherry.

Their wedding might have been a hasty one, but, as Mrs Stone observed, a hasty wedding was better than none at all. And furthermore, their union served to disperse the sadness that might have blighted both their lives.

"To think that I have married a hero!" chirped Mrs Stone.

"Not really," murmured Mr Stone. "I only let the fellows in to capture him."

"But you might have been killed!" she said.

"I suppose so. He did have another half of that stick in his coat."

"I have found a brave man and inherited a fortune in the same week," said Mrs Stone. "Was any woman ever so blessed?"

"Oh, I don't know," said Mr Stone. "I've come home from years in the wilderness, and right away I've found a charming bride. Surely I'm the lucky one."

The bride and groom exchanged chaste kisses.

"Did you hear that Madame Tussaud will be putting poor Felicia and your cousin on display?" asked Mrs Stone. "They will be part of a large addition to The Dead Room. It pleases me to think that the poor girl won't be forgotten."

"Indeed," said Mr Stone.

"Would it be in bad taste for us to visit the display?"

"Just as you think best, Penelope."

Mrs Stone took a thoughtful sip of sherry. "And what of Mr Newcastle?" she asked. "Has he been found?"

"Not a trace of him, I'm afraid." said Mr Stone. "The police think Reggie might have done away with him as well, and of course that's what the fool said he'd done when he shoved that stick into Felicia's heart."

"Yes," said Mrs Stone. "Was there much blood?"

"What? I really didn't like to look at her, to tell you the truth. She seemed quite clean, though, really, but poor old Reggie had blood all over his mouth."

"And had he really lost his mind?"

"What other explanation could there be for such unchivalrous behavior?" Mr Stone filled both their glasses. "I wonder if they'll keep him in the madhouse or just take him out and hang him. I wish there were more I could do for him somehow."

"I hardly think you need concern yourself, after his barbaric treatment of my niece."

"As you say, Penelope. At least I did him one good turn."

"And what was that?"

"A small thing, really. I went back to the house the day after all that happened, and I found a packing crate in the hallway."

"A packing crate?"

"Yes, and quite a large one. It was sealed, and the labels were on it, so I took it on myself to have it sent on, though heaven knows what business Reggie could have in India."

"India?"

"It was addressed to some fellow in Calcutta. I don't remember who it was, but it looked to me like some sort of Spanish name."

"A Spanish name?" said Mrs Stone. "Oh, dear!"

NEIL GAIMAN

Fifteen Cards from a Vampire Tarot

NEIL GAIMAN'S 2002 NOVEL *American Gods* won science fiction's Hugo Award and horror's Bram Stoker Award. His latest novel, *Coraline*, a dark fantasy for children which he had been writing for a decade, was a huge success on both sides of the Atlantic and even managed to beat its predecessor in the awards stakes.

On the illustrated front, his first *Sandman* graphic novel in seven years, entitled *Endless Nights*, is published by DC Comics and illustrated by seven different artists; *1602* is a new alternate-history mini-series from Marvel, and he has collaborated with artist Dave McKean on the children's picture book *The Wolves in the Walls*.

As well as all the above, *The New York Times* best-selling author has somehow also found the time to make a short vampire film entitled *A Short Film About John Bolton*, and he has recently started writing a new novel, with the working title of *Anansi Boys*.

Although the author only had a poem in the original edition of this book, we decided to replace it with the more unusual narrative that follows. "One day, perhaps, I'll finish the major arcana," confides Gaiman. "Seven cards, and seven little stories, still to go. And then there's the minor arcana."

Originally published in a volume showcasing the work of a number of different artists, "You can draw your own pictures," invites the author.

0. The Fool

"WHAT DO YOU WANT?"

The young man had come to the graveyard every night for a month now. He had watched the moon paint the cold granite and the fresh marble and the old moss-covered stones and statues in its cold light. He had started at shadows and at owls. He had watched courting couples, and drunks, and teenagers taking nervous short cuts: all the people who come through the graveyard at night.

He slept in the day. Nobody cared. He stood alone in the night and shivered, in the cold. It came to him then that he was standing on the edge of a precipice.

The voice came from the night all around him, in his head and out of it.

"What do you want?" it repeated.

He wondered if he dared to turn and look, realized that he did not.

"Well? You come here every night, in a place where the living are not welcome. I have seen you. Why?"

"I wanted to meet you," he said, without looking around. "I want to live for ever." His voice cracked as he said it.

He had stepped over the precipice. There was no going back. In his imagination, he could already feel the prick of needle-sharp fangs in his neck, a sharp prelude to eternal life.

The sound began. It was low and sad, like the rushing of an underground river. It took him several long seconds to recognize it as laughter.

"This is not life," said the voice.

It said nothing more, and after a while the young man knew he was alone in the graveyard.

I. The Magician

They asked St Germain's manservant if his master was truly a thousand years old, as it was rumoured he had claimed.

"How would I know?" the man replied. "I have only been in the master's employ for three hundred years."

II. The Priestess

Her skin was pale, and her eyes were dark and her hair was dyed a raven black. She went on a daytime talk show and proclaimed herself a vampire queen. She showed the cameras her dentally crafted fangs, and brought on ex-lovers who, in various stages of embarrassment, admitted that she had drawn their blood, and that she drank it.

"You can be seen in a mirror, though?" asked the talk-show hostess. She was the richest woman in America, and had got that way by bringing the freaks and the hurt and the lost out in front of her cameras, and showing their pain to the world.

The studio audience laughed.

The woman seemed slightly affronted. "Yes. Contrary to what people may think, vampires can be seen in mirrors and on television cameras."

"Well, that's one thing you finally got right, honey," said the hostess of the daytime talk show. But she put her hand over her microphone as she said it, and it was never broadcast.

V. The Pope

This is my body, he said, two thousand years ago. *This is my blood.*

It was the only religion that delivered exactly what it promised: life eternal, for its adherents.

There are some of us alive today who remember him. And some of us claim that he was a messiah, and some think that he was just a man with very special powers. But that misses the point. Whatever he was, he changed the world.

VI. The Lovers

After she was dead, she began to come to him, in the night. He grew pale, and there were deep circles under his eyes. At first, they thought he was mourning her. And then, one night, he was gone from the village.

It was hard for them to get permission to disinter her, but get it they did. They hauled up the coffin and they unscrewed it. Then they prised what they found out of the box. There was six inches of water in the bottom of the box: the iron had coloured it a deep, orange-ish red. There were two bodies in the coffin: hers, of course, and his. He was more decayed than she was. Later, someone wondered aloud how both of them had fitted in a coffin built for one. Especially given her condition, he said; for she was very obviously very pregnant.

This caused some confusion, for she had not been noticeably pregnant when she was buried.

Still later they dug her up for one last time, at the request of the church authorities, who had heard rumours of what had been found in the grave. Her stomach was flat. The local doctor told them all that it had just been gas and bloating as the stomach swelled. The townsfolk nodded sagely, almost as if they believed him.

VII. The Chariot

It was genetic engineering at its finest: they created a breed of humans to sail the stars: they needed to be possessed of impossibly long lifespans, for the distances between the stars were vast; space was

limited, and their food supplies needed to be compact; they needed
to be able to process local sustenance, and to colonize the worlds they
found with their own kind.

The homeworld wished the colonists well, and sent them on their
way. They removed all traces of their location from the ships'
computers first, however, to be on the safe side.

X. The Wheel of Fortune

What did you do with the doctor? she asked, and laughed. I thought
the doctor came in here ten minutes ago.

I'm sorry, I said. I was hungry. And we both laughed.

I'll go find her for you, she said.

I sat in the doctor's office, picking my teeth. After a while the
assistant came back.

I'm sorry, she said. The doctor must have stepped out for a while.
Can I make an appointment for you for next week?

I shook my head. I'll call, I said. But, for the first time that day, I was
lying.

XI. Justice

"It is not human," said the magistrate, "and it does not deserve the
trial of a human thing."

"Ah," said the advocate. "But we cannot execute without a trial:
there are the precedents. A pig that had eaten a child who had fallen
into its sty. It was found guilty and hanged. A swarm of bees, found
guilty of stinging an old man to death, was burned by the public
hangman. We owe the hellish creature no less."

The evidence against the baby was incontestable. It amounted to
this: a woman had brought the baby from the country. She said it was
hers, and that her husband was dead. She lodged at the house of a
coach maker and his wife. The old coach maker complained of
melancholia and lassitude, and was, with his wife and their lodger,
found dead by their servant. The baby was alive in its cradle, pale and
wide-eyed, and there was blood on its face and lips.

The jury found the little thing guilty, beyond all doubt, and
condemned it to death.

The executioner was the town butcher. In the sight of all the town
he cut the babe in two, and flung the pieces onto the fire.

His own baby had died earlier that same week. Infant mortality in
those days was a hard thing but common. The butcher's wife had
been brokenhearted.

She had already left the town, to see her sister in the city, and,
within the week, the butcher joined her. The three of them –
butcher, wife and babe – made the prettiest family you ever did see.

XIV. Temperance

She said she was a vampire. One thing I knew already, the woman was a liar. You could see it in her eyes. Black as coals they were, but she never quite looked at you, staring at invisibles over your shoulder, behind you, above you, two inches in front of your face.

"What does it taste like?" I asked her. This was in the parking lot, behind the bar. She worked the graveyard shift in the bar, mixed the finest drinks but never drank anything herself.

"V8 juice," she said. "Not the low-sodium kind, but the original. Or a salty gazpacho."

"What's gazpacho?"

"A sort of cold vegetable soup."

"You're shitting me."

"No."

"So you drink blood? Just like I drink V8?"

"Not exactly," she said. "If *you* get sick of drinking V8 you can drink something else."

"Yeah," I said. "Actually, I don't like V8 much."

"See?" she said. "In China it's not blood we drink, it's spinal fluid."

"What's that taste like?"

"Nothing much. Clear broth."

"You've tried it?"

"I know people."

I tried to figure out if I could see her reflection in the wing mirror of the truck we were leaning against, but it was dark, and I couldn't tell.

XV. The Devil

This is his portrait. Look at his flat, yellow teeth, his ruddy face. He has horns, and he carries a foot-long wooden stake in one hand, and his wooden mallet in the other.

Of course, there is no such thing as the devil.

XVI. The Tower

The tower's built of stone and spite,
Without a sound, without a sight,
– The biter bit, the bitter bite
(It's better to be out at night).

XVII. The Star

The older, richer, ones follow the winter, taking the long nights where they find them. Still, they prefer the northern hemisphere to the south.

"You see that star?" they say, pointing to one of the stars in the constellation of Draco, the Dragon. "We came from there. One day we shall return."

The younger ones sneer and jeer and laugh at this. Still, as the years become centuries, they find themselves becoming homesick for a place they have never been; and they find the northern climes reassuring, as long as Draco twines about the greater and lesser Bears, up near chill Polaris.

XIX. The Sun

"Imagine", she said, "that there was something in the sky that was going to hurt you, perhaps even kill you. A huge eagle or something. Imagine that if you went out in daylight the eagle would get you."

"Well," she said. "That's how it is for us. Only it's not a bird. It's bright, beautiful, dangerous daylight, and I haven't seen it now in a hundred years."

XX. Judgment

It's a way of talking about lust without talking about lust, he told them.

It is a way of talking about sex, and fear of sex, and death, and fear of death, and what else is there to talk about?

XXII. The World

"You know the saddest thing," she said. "The saddest thing is that we're you."

I said nothing.

"In your fantasies," she said, "my people are just like you. Only better. We don't die, or age, or suffer from pain or cold or thirst. We're snappier dressers. We possess the wisdom of the ages. And if we crave blood, well, it is no more than the way you people crave food, or affection, or sunlight – and besides, it gets us out of the house. Crypt. Coffin. Whatever. That's the fantasy."

"And the reality is?" I asked her.

"We're you," she said. "We're you, with all your fuck-ups and all the things that make you human – all your fears and lonelinesses and confusions . . . none of that gets better.

"But we're colder than you are. Deader. I miss daylight and food and knowing how it feels to touch someone and care. I remember life, and meeting people as people and not just as things to feed on or control, and I remember what it was to *feel* something, anything, happy or sad or *anything* . . ." And then she stopped.

"Are you crying?" I asked.

"We don't cry," she told me.

Like I said, the woman was a liar.

STEVE RASNIC TEM

Vintage Domestic

STEVE RASNIC TEM LIVES IN Denver, Colorado, with his wife, horror author Melanie Tem.

He has had more than 250 short stories published in such magazines and anthologies as *Weirdbook, Whispers, Fantasy Tales, Twilight Zone, Crimewave, The Magazine of Fantasy & Science Fiction, The Third Alternative, New Terrors 1, Shadows, Cutting Edge, MetaHorror, Dark Terrors, Horrors! 365 Scary Stories, White of the Moon, The Children of Cthulhu, Gathering the Bones, Great Ghost Stories, Dark Arts, Darkside 3* and various volumes of *The Year's Best Fantasy and Horror* and *The Mammoth Book of Best New Horror*.

He won the 1988 British Fantasy Award for his story 'Leaks', and his collection entitled *Ombres sur la Route* appeared in France several years ago. More recent collections have included the career-spanning *City Fishing* from Silver Salamander Press, which won The International Horror Guild Award, and *The Far Side of the Lake* from Ash-Tree Press. A chapbook entitled *The Man on the Ceiling*, written with Melanie and published by American Fantasy won both the Bram Stoker and World Fantasy awards, and his novella *In These Final Days of Sales* from Wormhole Books picked up another Bram Stoker Award.

The author's latest collaboration with his wife is the high-fantasy novel *Daughters*, and an experimental fantasy novel entitled *The Book of Days* recently appeared as a limited edition from Subterranean Press.

" 'Vintage Domestic' came out of my desire to put a familial face on the vampire legend," Tem reveals. "As an icon, the vampire is a glamorous figure. Those of us who are members of large families understand all too well how the nitty-gritty of everyday family relationships puts a spike to glamour."

The powerful story that follows is another that was originally written for this anthology . . .

SHE USED TO TELL him that they'd have the house forever. One day their children would live there. When Jack grew too old to walk, or to feed himself, she would take care of him in this house. She would feed him right from her own mouth, with a kiss. He'd always counted on her keeping this promise.

But as her condition worsened, as the changes accelerated, he realized that this was a promise she could not keep. The roles were to be reversed, and it was to be he who fed his lifetime lover with a kiss full of raw meat and blood. Sweet, domestic vintage.

Early in their marriage his wife had told him that there was this history of depression in her family. That's the way members of the family always talked about it: the sadness, the melancholy, the long slow condition. Before he understood what this meant he hadn't taken it that seriously, because at the time she never seemed depressed. Once their two oldest reached the teen years, however, she became sad, and slow to move, her eyes dark stones in the clay mask of her face, and she stopped telling him about her family's history of depression. When he asked her about the old story, she acted as if she didn't know what he was talking about.

At some point during her rapid deterioration someone had labeled his family "possibly dysfunctional." Follow-up visits from teachers and social workers had removed "possibly" from his family's thickening file. Studies and follow-up studies had been completed, detailed reports and addenda analyzing his children's behavior and the family dynamics. He had fought them all the way, and perhaps they had tired of the issue, because they finally gave up on their investigations. His family had weathered their accusations. He had protected his wife and children, fulfilled his obligations. Finally people left them alone, but they could not see that something sacred was occurring in this house.

The house grew old quickly. But not as quickly as his wife and children.

*   *   *

"You're so damned cheerful all the time," she said to him. "It makes me sick."

At one time that might have been a joke. Looking into her gray eyes at this moment, he knew it was not. "I'm maintaining," he said. "That's all." He thought maybe her vision was failing her. He was sure it had been months since he'd last smiled. He bent over her with the tea, then passed her a cracker. She stretched her neck and tried to catch his lips in her teeth. He expected a laugh but it didn't come.

"You love me?" she asked, her voice flat and dusty. He put the cracker in his mouth and let her take it from his lips. He could hear his teenage daughters in the next room moaning from the bed. They'd been there two months already, maybe more.

She reached up with a brittle touch across his cheek. "They take after me, you know?" And then she *did* smile, then opened her mouth around a dry cough of a laugh.

Downstairs their seven-year-old son made loud motorcycle noises with moist lips and tongue. Thank God he takes after his father, he thought, and would have laughed if he could. Beneath him his sweet wife moaned, her lips cracked and peeling. A white tongue flickered like the corner of a starched handkerchief.

He bit down hard into the tender scar on the inside of his mouth. He ground one tooth, two, through the tentative pain. When he tasted salt he began to suck, mixing the salt and iron taste with a saliva that had become remarkable in its quantity, until the frothy red cocktail was formed.

He bent over her lips with this beverage kiss and allowed her tongue to meet his, her razor teeth still held back in supplication. In this way he fed her when she could no longer feed herself, when she could not move, when she could not hunt, when in their house tall curtains of dust floated gently around them.

"The girls," she said, once her handkerchief tongue was soaked and her pale lips glistened pinkly.

But still he could not go into his daughters' bedroom, and had to listen to them moan their hunger like pale and hairless, motherless rats.

"Tell me again, Jack," his wife whispered wetly from the bed. "Tell me again how wonderful life is." These were among the last words she would ever use with him.

The young man at the front door wore the blue uniform of the delivery service. Overripe brown sacks filled each of his arms, blending into his fat cheeks as if part of them. He smiled all the time. Jack smiled a hungry smile back.

"Your groceries, sir." Behind him were the stirrings of dry skin against cloth, insect legs, pleadings too starved and faint to be heard clearly.

As the young man handed the sacks over to him, Jack's fingertips brushed the pale backs of the man's hands. He imagined he could feel the heat there, the youthful coursing through veins, feeding pale tissues, warming otherwise cold meat.

Sometimes he took his daughters hunting, if they were strong enough, but so far he had been able to limit them to slugs, worms, insects, small animals. He wondered how long he could hold them to that when the stores kept sending them tender young delivery boys. He wondered how long it would be before his daughters were as immobile as his wife, and begged him to bring them something more. Somewhere behind him there was a tiny gasp, the rising pressure of tears which could not fall.

Some evenings he would sit up talking to his family long into the night. They did not always respond precisely to his confessions of loneliness, of dreams which did not include them, and he wondered if it was because of the doors that separated them from him.

Sometimes he would go to the closet doors and open them. Where his wife stood, folded back against the wall with the coats and robes. Where his daughters leaned one against the other like ancient, lesbian mops. *Kiss us*, the dry whisper came from somewhere within the pale flaps of their faces. Jack still loved them desperately, but he could not do what they asked.

His youngest, his only son, had taken to his bed.

Jack brought his daughters mice and roaches he had killed himself. They sucked on them like sugar candy until most of the color was gone, and then they spat them out.

Months ago they had stopped having their periods. The last few times had been pale pink and runny. and Jack had cried for them, then cleaned them up with old burlap sacks.

His son disappeared from his bed one evening. Jack found him standing in the closet, his eyes full of moths, his hands stiffened into hooks.

Later his son would disappear from time to time, sometimes showing up in one of the other closets, clutching at mother or sisters, sometimes curled up inside the empty toy box (the boy had no more use for toys, having his own body to play with – sometimes he'd chew a finger into odd shapes).

Jack continued to feed his wife from his own mouth. Sometimes his mouth was so raw he could not tear any more skin off the insides.

Then he'd bite through a rat or a bird himself, holding its rank warmth in his cheeks until he could deliver the meal. She returned his kisses greedily, always wanting more than he could provide. But he had spoiled her. She would not feed any other way.

His son became a good hunter, and sometimes Jack would hear him feeding on the other side of the closet door. Pets began disappearing from the neighborhood, and Jack stopped answering the door even for delivery boys.

His daughters became despondent and refused to eat. When he opened their closet door they tried to disguise themselves as abandoned brooms. Finally Jack had to hold them one at a time, forcing his blood smeared tongue past their splintered lips into the dry cisterns of their mouths so that they might leech nourishment. Once he'd overcome their initial resistance they scraped his tongue clean, then threatened to carve it down to the root, but Jack always knew the exact moment to pull out.

Sometimes he wondered if they still considered him a good father, an adequate husband. He tried singing his children lullabies, reciting poetry to his wife. They nodded their full heads of dust in the gale of his breath, but said nothing.

When the food delivery boys no longer came he saved a portion of his kills for himself. And whenever possible he swallowed his own bloody wet kisses, and tried to remember the feel of his wife's hands on his face, back when her skin was soft and her breath was sweet.

In the houses around him, he knew a hundred hearts beat, desperately chasing life's apprehensions through a racecourse of veins. He tried to ignore the hunger brought on by such thinking. He tried to picture his neighbors' faces, but could not.

His family became so light he could carry them about the house without effort. If he hadn't heard their close whispers, he might have thought them a few old towels thrown across his shoulder. Sometimes he would set them down and forget them, later rushing around in panic to find where they'd been mislaid.

The lighter, the thinner they became, the more blood they seemed to require. When his mouth became too sore to chew he would apply razor blades to the scar tissue, slicing through new white skin into the thicker layers beneath, finally into muscle so that the blood would fill his mouth to spilling before he could get his mouth completely over theirs. Blood stained their thin chests with a rough crimson bib.

And still they grew thinner, their bones growing fibrous, pulpy before beginning to dissolve altogether. He made long rips in his forearms, his thighs, his calves, and held his wife and children up to drink there. The blood soaked through the tissues of their flesh, through the translucent fibres of their hair, washing through their skin until in the dusty shadows of the house they looked vaguely tanned.

But almost as quickly they were pale again, and thin as a distant memory.

He took to slicing off hunks of thigh muscle, severing fingertips, toes. His family ate for months off the bloody bits, their small rat teeth nibbling listlessly. They had ceased using words of any kind long ago, so they could not express their thanks. But Jack didn't mind. This was the family he'd always dreamed of. The look of appreciation in their colorless eyes was thanks enough.

At first he tore his clothes to rags to staunch the blood, but even the rags eventually fell apart. One day seeing his son sucking up the last bit of red from a torn twist of cloth he decided to forego the last vestiges of his modesty and throw the ragged clothes away. After that time he would walk about the dreary old house naked, wearing only the paperthin bodies of his family wrapped around him, their mouths fixed tightly to his oozing wounds.

This went on for months, wearing his family constantly, their feeding so regular and persistent it seemed to alter the very rhythm of his heart. He would wake up in the middle of the night to the soft sucking noise their lips and teeth made against his flesh. He would awaken a few hours later and the first thing he would see was the stupored look in their eyes as they gazed up at him in adoration. He was pleased to see that such constant nourishment fattened them and brought color to their skin so that eventually they fell off his body from the sheer weight of them.

Wriggling about his feet at first, they eventually decided to explore the house on their own. Obviously, they felt far healthier than before.

Again they did not thank him, but what did a good husband and father need of thanks?

They soon grew thin again, soft, transparent.

After a year he had not seen them again. Although occasionally he might swear to a face hidden within the upholstery, an eye rolling past a furniture leg, a dry mouth praying silently among the house plants filmed in a dark, furry dust.

After five years even the garbled whispering had stopped. He continued to watch over the house, intent on his obligation. And after preparing a blood kiss in the pale vacancy of his mouth, he was content to drink it himself.

HARLAN ELLISON

Try a Dull Knife

IN A CAREER THAT HAS spanned nearly fifty years, Harlan Ellison has won more awards for imaginative literature than any other living writer, including the Hugo, Nebula, Edgar, Writers Guild of America, Silver Pen, British Fantasy, Bram Stoker and World Fantasy. He has also received Lifetime Achievement Awards from the World Fantasy Convention and the Horror Writers Association.

He is the author or editor of more than seventy-five books and has written around 2,000 short stories, comic books, essays, articles and newspaper columns, plus two dozen teleplays and a dozen screen-plays. The *Washington Post* has described him as "one of the great living American short-story writers."

He made his professional debut in a 1956 edition of *Infinity Science Fiction,* since when he has published numerous acclaimed novels and such short-story collections as *Deathbird Stories, Strange Wine, Shatter-day, Stalking the Nightmare, Angry Candy, Slippage* and the *Edgeworks* series. He also edited the landmark science fiction anthologies *Dangerous Visions* and *Again, Dangerous Visions.*

Ellison is currently completing the editing of a collection of *The Thinking Machine,* detective stories by the late Jacques Futrelle, for The Modern Library. His own collection *Strange Wine* will be reissued (including a brand-new story, "The Final Experiment of the Son of Dr Moreau") under the author's own imprint, Edgeworks Abbey, in collaboration with i-books. From the same publishers, *Vic and Blood: The Continuing Adventures of A Boy and His Dog* recently appeared as a graphic novel, containing Ellison's post-apocalyptic short stories with illustrations by Richard Corben.

"Horror, as an identifiable sub-genre of literature, has been around at least since 1764 and *The Castle of Otranto*," the author explains, "notwithstanding that I like to think the first manifestation of it was in the earliest written record, the recounting of Gilgamesh cutting trail with Grendel, which has been the high-water mark for mind-numbing horror until Britney Spears came along.

"Neither here nor there. The point being: almost every single one of the common tropes in the horror canon has been written and rewritten, chewed and remasticated until they come festooned with familiarity and literary exhaustion. For me, the idea of the hoary cobwebbed vampire – sexually explicit or neutered – and the standard neck-suck, hold about as much scintillance as a plate of lima beans. (Speaking of horror. You show me someone who'll eat a lima bean without a cocked gun to his head, and I'll show you a child-molester, serial killer, or politician.)

"So I cannot bring myself to waste any fragment of what's left of my life, nor any smallest spark of my enormous talent, leavened only by my charming humility, writing a horror story that farts-again the tune told brilliantly by Stoker, Charnas, Matheson and the author of the screenplay for *Love at First Bite*.

"One day thirty or so years ago, I got an idea, though. It was during that brief, six-month interregnum when the madness of working in the film industry took me, and I 'went Hollywood'. I was surrounded by mooks, leaners, losers, schnorrers, leeches, time-wasters, blue-sky merchants, and scam artists of four or five sexual predilections. Having been a kid who was on the road at age thirteen, I was able to dog-paddle through them polluted waters, and came to landfall none the worse for having been assailed by human limpet mines. Left only with the idea for this story, which is – I hope – a new way of dealing with the neck-suck.

"Here is vampirism, though now thirty years' published, which nonetheless codifies the dossier of this rampant creature in *all* our lives. I had 'em; you got 'em; here's what they look like."

As you would expect from Harlan Ellison, the story that follows is about a very different kind of vampire . . .

IT WAS *pachanga* night at The Cave. Three spick bands all going at once, each with a fat momma shaking her meat and screaming *Vaya!* The sound was something visible, an assault in silver lamé and screamhorn. Sound hung dense as smog-cloud, redolent as skunk-scent from a thousand roaches of the best shit, no stems or seeds. Darkness shot through with the quicksilver flashes of mouths open to show gold bridgework and dirty words. Eddie Burma staggered in, leaned against a wall and felt the sickness as thick as cotton wool in his throat.

The deep scar-burn of pain was bleeding slowly down his right side. The blood had started coagulating, his shirt stuck to his flesh, but he dug it: it wasn't pumping any more. But he was in trouble, that was the righteous truth. Nobody can get cut the way Eddie Burma'd been cut and not be in deep trouble.

And somewhere back out there, in the night, they were moving toward him, coming for him. He had to get through to – who? Somebody. Somebody who could help him; because only now, after fifteen years of what had been happening to him, did Eddie Burma finally know what it was he had been through, what had been done to him . . . what was *being* done to him . . . what they would certainly do to him.

He stumbled down the short flight of steps into The Cave and was instantly lost in the smoke and smell and twisting shadows. Ethnic smoke, Puerto Rican smells, lush shadows from another land. He dug it; even with his strength ebbing, he dug it.

That was Eddie Burma's problem. He was an empath. He felt. Deep inside himself, on a level most people never even know exists, he felt for the world. Involvement was what motivated him. Even here, in this slum nightclub where intensity of enjoyment substituted for the shallow glamour and gaucherie of the uptown *boîtes*, here where no one knew him and therefore could not harm him, he felt the pulse of the world's life surging through him. And the blood started pumping again.

He pressed his way back through the crowd, looking for a phone booth, looking for a toilet, looking for an empty booth where he could hide, looking for the person or persons unknown who could save him from the dark night of the soul slipping toward him inexorably.

He caromed off a waiter, Pancho Villa moustache, dirty white apron, tray of draft beers. "Hey, where's the *gabinetto?*" He slurred the request. His words were slipping in their own blood.

The Puerto Rican waiter stared at him. Uncomprehending. "*Perdón?*"

"The toilet, the *pissoir*, the can, the head, the crapper. I'm bleeding to death, where's the potty?"

"Ohhh!" meaning dawned on the waiter. "*Excusados . . . atavio!*" He pointed. Eddie Burma patted him on the arm and slumped past, almost falling into a booth where a man and two women were groping one another darkly.

He found the door to the toilet and pushed it open. A reject from a Cuban superman film was slicking back his long, oiled hair in an elaborate pompadour before the foggy mirror. He gave Eddie Burma a passing glance and went back to the topography of his coiffure. Burma moved past him in the tiny room and slipped into the first stall.

Once inside, he bolted the door, and sat down heavily on the lidless toilet. He pulled his shirt up out of his pants, and unbuttoned it. It stuck to his skin. He pulled, gently, and it came away with the sound of mud squished underfoot. The knife wound ran from just below the right nipple to the middle of his waist. It was deep. He was in trouble.

He stood up, hanging the shirt on the hook behind the door, and pulled hanks of toilet paper from the grey, crackly roll. He dipped the paper in a wad, into the toilet bowl, and swabbed at the wound. Oh, God, *really* deep.

Then nausea washed over him, and he sat down again. Strange thoughts came to him, and he let them work him over:

This morning, when I stepped out the front door, there were yellow roses growing on the bushes. It surprised me; I'd neglected to cut them back last fall, and I was certain the gnarled, blighted knobs at the ends of the branches – still there, silently dead in reproach of my negligence – would stunt any further beauty. But when I stepped out to pick up the newspaper, there they were. Full and light yellow, barely a canary yellow. Breathing moistly, softly. It made me smile, and I went down the steps to the first landing, to get the paper. The parking lot had filled with leaves from the eucalyptus again, but somehow, particularly this morning, it gave the private little area surrounding and below my secluded house in the hills a more lived-in, festive look. For the second time, for no sensible reason, I found myself smiling. It was going to be a good day, and I had the feeling that all the problems I'd taken on – all the social cases I took unto myself – Alice and Burt and Linda down the hill – all the emotional cripples who came to me for succor – would shape up, and we'd all be smiling by end of day. And if not today, then certainly by Monday. Friday, the latest.

I picked up the paper and snapped the rubber band off it. I dropped the rubber band into the big metal trash basket at the foot of the stairs, and started climbing back up to the house, smelling the orange blossoms and the fine, chill morning air. I opened the paper as I climbed, and with all the suddenness of a freeway collision, the morning calm vanished from around me. I was stopped in mid-step, one leg raised for the next riser, and my eyes felt suddenly grainy, as though I hadn't had enough sleep the night before. But I had.

The headline read: EDWARD BURMA FOUND MURDERED.

But . . . I *was Eddie Burma.*

He came back from memories of yellow roses and twisted metal on freeways to find himself slumped against the side of the toilet stall, his head pressed to the wooden wall, his arms hanging down, the blood running into his pants top. His head throbbed, and the pain in his side shiver with fear. He could not sit there, and wait.

Wait to die, or wait for them to find him.

He knew they would find him. He knew it.

The phone. He could call . . .

He didn't know whom he could call. But there had to be someone. Someone out there who would understand, who would come quickly and save him. Someone who wouldn't take what was left of him, the way the others would.

They didn't need knives.

How strange that *that* one, the little blonde with the Raggedy Ann shoebutton eyes, had not known that. Or perhaps she had. But perhaps also the frenzy of the moment had overcome her, and she could not simply feed leisurely as the others did. She had cut him. Had done what they all did, but directly, without subtlety.

Her blade had been sharp. The others used much more devious weapons, subtler weapons. He wanted to say to her, "Try a dull knife." But she was too needing, too eager. She would not have heard him.

He struggled to his feet, and put on his shirt. It hurt to do it. The shirt was stained the color of teak with his blood. He could barely stand now.

Pulling foot after foot, he left the toilet, and wandered out into The Cave. The sound of "Mamacita Lisa" beat at him like gloved hands on a plate-glass window. He leaned against the wall, and saw only shapes moving moving moving in the darkness. Were they out there? No, not yet; they would never look here first. He wasn't known here. And his essence was weaker now, weaker as he died, so no one in the crowd would come to him with a quivering need. No one would feel it possible to drink from this weak man, lying up against a wall.

He saw a payphone, near the entrance to the kitchen, and he struggled toward it. A girl with long dark hair and haunted eyes stared at him as he passed, started to say something, then he summoned up strength to hurry past her before she could tell him she was pregnant and didn't know who the father was, or she was in pain from emphysema and didn't have doctor money, or she missed her mother who was still in San Juan. He could handle no more pains, could absorb no more anguish, could let no others drink from him. He didn't have that much left for his own survival.

My fingertips (he thought, moving) *are covered with the scars of people I've touched. The flesh remembers those touches. Sometimes I feel as though I am wearing heavy woolen gloves, so thick are the memories of all those touches. It seems to insulate me, to separate me from mankind. Not mankind from me, God knows, because they get through without pause or difficulty – but me, from mankind. I very often refrain from washing my hands for days and days, just to preserve whatever layers of touches might be washed away by the soap.*

Faces and voices and smells of people I've known have passed away. But still my hands carry the memories on them. Layer after layer of the laying-on of hands. Is that altogether sane? I don't know. I'll have to think about it for a very long time, when I have the time.

If I ever have the time.

He reached the payphone; after a very long time he was able to bring a coin up out of his pocket. It was a quarter. All he needed was a dime. He could not go back down there, he might not make it back again. He used the quarter, and dialed the number of a man he could trust, a man who could help him. He remembered the man now, knew the man was his only salvation.

He remembered seeing him in Georgia, at a revival meeting, a rural stump religion circus of screaming and Hallelujahs that sounded like !H!A!L!L!E!L!U!J!A!H! with dark black faces or red necks all straining toward the seat of God on the platform. He remembered the man in his white shirtsleeves, exhorting the crowd, and he heard again the man's spirit message.

"Get right with the Lord, before *he* gets right with *you*! Suffer your silent sins no longer! Take out your truth, carry it in your hands, give it to me, all the ugliness and cesspool filth of your souls! I'll wash you clean in the blood of the lamb, in the blood of the Lord, in the blood of the truth of the word! There's no other way, there's no great day coming without purging yourself, without cleansing your spirit! I can handle all the pain you've got boiling around down in the black lightless pit of your souls! Hear me, dear God hear me . . . I am your mouth, your tongue, your throat, the horn that will proclaim your deliverance to the Heavens above! Evil and good and worry and sorrow, all of it is mine, I can carry it, I can handle it, I can lift it from out of your mind and your soul and your body! The place is here, the place is me, give me your woe! Christ knew it, God knows it, *I* know it, and now *you* have to know it! Mortar and trowel and brick and cement make the wall of your need! Let me tear down that wall, let me hear all of it, let me into your mind and let me take your burdens! I'm the strength, I'm the watering place . . . come drink from my strength!"

And the people had rushed to him. All over him, like ants feeding on a dead beast. And then the memory dissolved. The image of the tent revival meeting dissolved into images of wild animals tearing at meat, of hordes of carrion birds descending on fallen meat, of small fish leaping with sharp teeth at helpless meat, of hands and more hands, and teeth that sank into meat.

The number was busy.

It was busy again.

He had been dialing the same number for nearly an hour, and the number was always busy. Dancers with sweating faces had wanted to use the phone, but Eddie Burma had snarled at them that it was a matter of life and death that he reach the number he was calling, and the dancers had gone back to their partners with curses for him. But the line was still busy. Then he looked at the number on the payphone, and knew he had been dialing himself all that time. That the line would always *always* be busy, and his furious hatred of the man on the other end who would not answer was hatred for the man who was calling. He was calling himself, and in that instant he remembered who the man had been at the revival meeting. He remembered leaping up out of the audience and taking the platform to beg all the stricken suffering ones to end their pain by drinking of his essence. He remembered, and the fear was greater than he could believe. He fled back to the toilet, to wait for them to find him.

Eddie Burma, hiding in the refuse room of a sightless dark spot in the netherworld of a universe that had singled him out for reality. Eddie Burma was an individual. He had substance. He had corporeality. In a world of walking shadows, of zombie breath and staring eyes like the cold dead flesh of the moon, Eddie Burma was a real person. He had been born with the ability to belong to his times; with the electricity of nature that some called charisma and others called warmth. He felt deeply; he moved through the world and touched; and was touched.

His was a doomed existence, because he was not only an extrovert and gregarious, but he was truly clever, vastly inventive, suffused with humor, and endowed with the power to listen. For these reasons he had passed through the stages of exhibitionism and praise-seeking to a state where his reality was assured. Was very much his own. When he came into a room, people knew it. He had a face. Not an image, or a substitute life that he could slip on when dealing with people, but a genuine reality. He was Eddie Burma, only Eddie Burma, and could not be confused with anyone else. He went his way, and he was identified as Eddie Burma in the eyes of anyone who ever met him. He was one of those memorable people. The kind other people who have no lives of their own talk about. He cropped up in conversations: "Do you know what Eddie said . . .?" or "Guess what happened to Eddie?" And there was never any confusion as to who was the subject under discussion.

Eddie Burma was a figure no larger than life, for life itself was large enough, in a world where most of those he met had no individuality, no personality, no reality, no existence of their own.

But the price he paid was the price of doom. For those who had nothing came to him and, like creatures of darkness, amorally fed off him. They drank from him. They were the succubi, draining his psychic energies. And Eddie Burma always had more to give. Seemingly a bottomless well, the bottom had been reached. Finally. All the people whose woes he handled, all the losers whose lives he tried to organize, all the preying crawlers who slinked in through the ashes of their non-existence to sup at his board, to slake the thirsts of their emptiness . . . all of them had taken their toll.

Now Eddie Burma stumbled through the last moments of his reality, with the wellsprings of himself almost totally drained. Waiting for them, for all his social cases, all his problem children, to come and finish him off.

I live in a hungry world, Eddie Burma now realized.

"Hey, man! C'mon outta th'crapper!" The booming voice and the pounding on the stall door came as one.

Eddie trembled to his feet and unbolted the door, expecting it to be one of them. But it was only a dancer from The Cave, wanting to rid himself of cheap wine and cheap beer. Eddie stumbled out of the stall, almost falling into the man's arms. When the beefy Puerto Rican saw the blood, saw the dead pale look of flesh and eyes, his manner softened.

"Hey . . . you okay, man?"

Eddie smiled at him, thanked him softly, and left the toilet. The nightclub was still high, still screaming, and Eddie suddenly knew he could not let *them* find this good place, where all these good people were plugged into life and living. Because for *them* it would be a godsend, and they would drain The Cave as they had drained him.

He found a rear exit, and emerged into the moonless city night, as alien as a cavern five miles down or the weird curvature of another dimension. This alley, this city, this night, could as easily have been Transylvania or the dark side of the moon or the bottom of the thrashing sea. He stumbled down the alley, thinking . . .

They have no lives of their own. Oh, this poisoned world I now see so clearly. They have only the shadowy images of other lives, and not even real other lives — the lives of movie stars, fictional heroes, cultural clichés. So they borrow from me, and never intend to pay back. They borrow, at the highest rate of interest. My life. They lap at me, and break off pieces of me. I'm the mushroom that Alice found with the words EAT ME *in blood-red on my id. They're succubi, draining at me, draining my soul. Sometimes I feel I should go to some mystical well and get poured full of personality again. I'm tired. So tired.*

There are people walking around this city who are running on Eddie Burma's drained energies, Eddie Burma's life-force. They're putt-putting around with smiles just like mine, with thoughts I've second-handed like old clothes passed on to poor relatives, with hand movements and expressions and little cute sayings that were mine, Scotch-taped over their own. I'm a jigsaw puzzle and they keep stealing little pieces. Now I make no scene at all, I'm incomplete, I'm unable to keep the picture coherent, they've taken so much already.

They had come to his party, all of the ones he knew. The ones he called his friends, and the ones who were merely acquaintances, and the ones who were using him as their wizard, as their guru, their psychiatrist, their wailing wall, their father confessor, their repository of personal ills and woes and inadequacies. Alice, who was afraid of men and found in Eddie Burma a last vestige of belief that males were not all beasts. Burt, the box-boy from the supermarket, who stuttered when he spoke, and felt rejected even before the rejection. Linda, from down the hill, who had seen in Eddie Burma an intellectual, one to whom she could relate all her theories of the universe. Sid, who was a failure, at fifty-three. Nancy, whose husband cheated on her. John, who wanted to be a lawyer, but would never make it because he thought too much about his club-foot. And all the others. And the new ones they always seemed to bring with them. There were always so many new ones he never knew. Particularly the pretty little blonde with the Raggedy Ann shoebutton eyes, who stared at him hungrily.

And from the first, earlier that night, he had known something was wrong. There were too many of them at the party. More than he could handle . . . and all listening to him tell a story of something that had happened to him when he had driven to New Orleans in 1960 with Tony in the Corvette and they'd both gotten pleurisy because the top hadn't been bolted down properly and they'd passed through a snow-storm in Illinois.

All of them hung to his words, like drying wash on a line, like festoons of ivy. They sucked at each word and every expression like hungry things pulling at the marrow in beef bones. They laughed, and they watched, and their eyes glittered . . .

Eddie Burma had slowly felt the strength ebbing from him. He grew weary even as he spoke. It had happened before, at other parties, other gatherings, when he had held the attention of the group, and gone home later, feeling drained. He had never known what it was.

But tonight the strength did not come back. They kept watching him, seemed to be *feeding* at him, and it went on and on, till finally he'd said he had to go to sleep, and they should go home. But they had pleaded for one more anecdote, one more joke told with perfect dialect and elaborate gesticulation. Eddie Burma had begun to cry, quietly. His eyes were red-rimmed, and his body felt as though the bones and musculature had been removed, leaving only a soft rubbery coating that might at any moment cave in on itself.

He had tried to get up; to go and lie down; but they'd gotten more insistent, had demanded, had ordered, had grown nasty. And then the blonde had come at him, and cut him, and the others were only a step behind. Somehow . . . in the thrashing tangle that had followed, with his friends and acquaintances now tearing at one another to get at him, he had escaped. He had fled, he did not know how, the pain of his knifed side crawling inside him. He had made it into the trees of the little glen where his house was hidden, and through the forest, over the watershed, down to the highway, where he had hailed a cab. Then into the city . . .

See me! See me, please! Just don't always come and take. Don't bathe in my reality and then go away feeling clean. Stay and let some of the dirt of you rub off on me. I feel like an invisible man, like a drinking trough, like a sideboard dripping with sweetmeats . . . Oh God, is this a play, and myself unwillingly the star? How the hell do I get off stage? When do they ring down the curtain? Is there, please God, a man with a hook . . . ?

I make my rounds, like a faith healer. Each day I spend a little time with each one of them. With Alice and with Burt and with Linda down the hill; and they take from me. They don't leave anything in exchange, though. It's not barter, it's theft. And the worst part of it is I always needed that, I always let them rob me. What sick need was it that gave them entrance to my soul? Even the pack rat leaves some worthless object when it steals a worthless object. I'd take anything from them: the smallest anecdote, the most used-up thought, the most stagnant concept, the puniest pun, the most obnoxious personal revelation . . . anything! But all they do is sit there and stare at me, their mouths open, their ears hearing me so completely they empty my words of color and scent . . . I feel as though they're crawling into me. I can't stand any more . . . really I can't.

The mouth of the alley was blocked.

Shadows moved there.

Burt, the box-boy. Nancy and Alice and Linda. Sid, the failure. John, who walked with a rolling motion. And the doctor, the juke-box repairman, the pizza cook, the used-car salesman, the swinging couple who swapped partners, the discothéque dancer . . . all of them.

They came for him.

And for the first time he noticed their teeth.

The moment before they reached him stretched out as silent and timeless as the decay that ate at his world. He had no time for self-pity. It was not merely that Eddie Burma had been cannibalized every day of the year, every hour of the day, every minute of every hour of every day of every year. The awareness dawned unhappily – in that moment of timeless time – that he had let them do it to him. That he was no better than they, only different. They were the feeders – and he was the food. But no nobility could be attached to one or the other. He needed to have people worship and admire him. He needed the love and attention of the masses, the worship of monkeys. And for Eddie Burma that was a kind of beginning to death. It was the death of his unselfconsciousness; the slaughter of his innocence. From that moment forward, he had been aware of the clever things he said and did, on a cellular level below consciousness. He was aware. Aware, aware, aware!

And awareness brought them to him, where they fed. It led to self-consciousness, petty pretensions, ostentation. And that was a thing devoid of substance, of reality. And if there was anything on which his acolytes could not nourish, it was a posturing, phony, *empty* human being.

They would drain him.

The moment came to a timeless climax, and they carried him down under their weight, and began to feed.

When it was over, they left him in the alley. They went to look elsewhere.

With the vessel drained, the vampires moved to other pulsing arteries.

– *Los Angeles, 1963, 1965, 1968*

KIM NEWMAN

Andy Warhol's Dracula
Anno Dracula 1978–79

KIM NEWMAN HAS WON the Bram Stoker Award, the British
Fantasy Award, the British Science Fiction Award, the Children of
the Night Award, the Fiction Award of the Lord Ruthven Assembly
and the International Horror Critics Guild Award.

His novels include *The Night Mayor, Bad Dreams, Jago, The Quorum,
Back in the USSR* (with Eugene Byrne), *Life's Lottery* and the acclaimed
Anno Dracula sequence – comprising the title novel, plus *The Bloody
Red Baron* and *Judgment of Tears* (a.k.a. *Dracula Cha Cha Cha*). *An
English Ghost Story* is currently being developed as a movie from a
script by the author, while *The Matter of Britain* is another collabora-
tion with Byrne.

As "Jack Yeovil" Newman has published a number novels loosely
inspired by the heroic fantasy "Warhammer" and Apocalyptic "Dark
Future" role-playing games. These include *Drachenfels, Beasts in Velvet*
and *Genevieve Undead. Silver Nails* is a recent collection of five stories
set in the Games Workshop universe and featuring the author's
recurrent character, vampire heroine Genevieve Dieudonné.

Under his own name, Newman's extremely clever short fiction,
which is often linked by recurring themes and characters, has been
collected in *The Original Dr Shade and Other Stories, Famous Monsters,*

Seven Stars, Unforgivable Stories and *Dead Travel Fast. Where the Bodies Are Buried* contains four interconnected novellas, and *Time and Relative* is a prequel to the BBC-TV series in Telos Publishing's "Doctor Who Novellas" series. Newman has also edited the alternate-history music anthology *In Dreams* with Paul J. McAuley.

His short story "Week Woman" was adapted for the Canadian TV series *The Hunger*, and in 2001 the author wrote and directed a 100-second short film, *Missing Girl*, for cable TV channel The Studio.

Newman's original contribution to this anthology was 'Red Reign' – the very first story in the acclaimed *Anno Dracula* sequence. As a treat for fans of the series, we decided to replace it in this volume with one of the most recent entries set in that same alternate history.

"Two editors – Ellen Datlow and Peter Crowther – asked for novellas at the same time," Newman recalls, "and I was planning another in the series that ought eventually to become *Johnny Alucard*. So I did a deal that they each get a bite at publishing it, read up a lot on Andy Warhol and wrote the thing.

"Readers interested in the cameo appearance characters, as strong a feature of this series as directors appearing as actors in John Landis films, are referred to

   <<www.pjfarmer.com/woldnewton/AnnoDracula.htm>>."

Designed to stand alone, 'Andy Warhol's Dracula' – along with seven more tales and other linking material – will eventually comprise the fourth and possibly final book in the *Anno Dracula* series.

For Sara and Randy

AS NANCY SNUFFED, HER blood curdled. The taste of vile scabs flooded his mouth. He pushed her away, detaching fangs from her worn wounds. Ropes of bloody spittle hung from her neck to his maw. He wiped his mouth on his wrist, breaking their liquid link. A last electric thrill shuddered, arcing between them. Her heart stopped.

He had pulled her backward onto the bed, holding her down to him as he worked at her throat, her hands feebly scrabbling his sides. Empty, she was dead weight on top of him. He was uncomfortably aware of the other garbage in the bed: magazines, bent spoons, hypodermic needles, used Kleenex, ripped and safety-pinned clothes, banknotes, congealed sandwiches, weeks of uneaten complimentary mints. A package of singles – Sid's 'My Way' – had broken under them, turning the much-stained mattress into a fakir's bed of nails. Vinyl shards stabbed his unbroken skin.

Johnny Pop was naked but for leopard-pattern briefs and socks, and the jewellery. Prizing his new clothes too much to get them gory, he had neatly folded and placed the suit and shirt on a chair well away from the bed. His face and chest were sticky with blood and other discharges.

As the red rush burst in his eyes and ears, his senses flared, more acute by a dozenfold. Outside, in iced velvet October night, police sirens sounded like the wailings of the bereaved mothers of Europe. Distant shots burst as if they were fired in the room, stabs of noise inside his skull. Blobby TV light painted a neon cityscape across ugly wallpaper, populated by psychedelic cockroaches.

He tasted the ghosts of the Chelsea Hotel: drag queens and vampire killers, junkies and pornographers, artists and freaks, visionaries and wasters. Pressing into his mind, they tried to make of his undead body a channel through which they could claw their way back to this plane of existence. Their voices shrieked, clamouring for attention. Cast out of Manhattan, they lusted for restoration to their paved paradise.

Though his throat protested, Johnny forced himself to swallow. Nancy's living blood had scarcely been of better quality than this dead filth. Americans fouled their bodies. Her habits would have killed her soon, even if she hadn't invited a vampire into Room 100. He didn't trouble himself with guilt. Some people were looking for their vampires, begging all their lives for death. His *nosferatu* hold upon the world was tenuous. He could only remain on sufferance. Without the willing warm, he would starve and die. They fed him. They were to blame for him.

Dead blood, heavy with Tuinol and Dilaudid, smote his brain, washing away the ghosts. He had to be careful; this city was thronged with the truly dead, loitering beyond the ken of the warm, desperate for attention from those who could perceive them. When he was feeding, they crowded around. Having been dead, however briefly, he was a beacon for them.

He yowled and threw the meat-sack off him. He sat up in the bed, nerves drawn taut, and looked at the dead girl. She was ghost-white flesh in black underwear. The flowering neck wound was the least of the marks on her. Scarifications criss-crossed her concave tummy. Pulsing slits opened like gills in her sides, leaking the last of her. The marks of his talons, they were dead mouths, beseeching more kisses from him.

Since arriving in America, he'd been careful to take only those who asked for it, who were already living like ghosts. They had few vampires here. Drained corpses attracted attention. Already, he knew, he'd been noticed. To prosper, he must practise the skills of his father-in-darkness. First, to hide; then, to master.

The Father was always with him, first among the ghosts. He watched over Johnny and kept him from real harm.

Sid, Belsen-thin but for his Biafra-bloat belly, was slumped in a ratty chair in front of blurry early early television. He looked at Johnny and at Nancy, incapable of focusing. Earlier, he'd shot up through his eyeball. Colours slid and flashed across his bare, scarred-and-scabbed chest and arms. His head was a skull in a spiky fright-wig, huge eyes swarming as *Josie and the Pussycats* reflected on the screen of his face. The boy tried to laugh but could only shake. A silly little knife, not even silver, was loosely held in his left hand.

Johnny pressed the heels of his fists to his forehead, and jammed his eyes shut. Blood-red light shone through the skin curtains of his eyelids. He had felt this before. It wouldn't last more than a few seconds. Hell raged in his brain. Then, as if a black fist had struck him in the gullet, peristaltic movement forced fluid up through his throat. He opened his mouth, and a thin squirt of black liquid spattered across the carpet and against the wall.

"Magic spew," said Sid, in amazement.

The impurities were gone. Johnny was on a pure blood-high now. He contained all of Nancy's short life. She had been an all-American girl. She had given him everything.

He considered the boy in the chair and the girl on the bed, the punks. Their tribes were at war, his and theirs. Clothes were their colours, Italian suits versus safety-pinned PVC pants. This session at the Chelsea had been a truce that turned into a betrayal, a rout, a massacre. The Father was proud of Johnny's strategy.

Sid looked at Nancy's face. Her eyes were open, showing only veined white. He gestured with his knife, realizing something had happened. At some point in the evening, Sid had stuck his knife into himself a few times. The tang of his rotten blood filled the room. Johnny's fangs slid from their gum-sheaths, but he had no more hunger yet. He was too full.

He thought of the punks as Americans, but Sid was English. A musician, though he couldn't really play his guitar. A singer, though he could only shout.

America was a strange new land. Stranger than Johnny had imagined in the Old Country, stranger than he could have imagined. If he drank more blood, he would soon be an American. Then he would be beyond fear, untouchable. It was what the Father wanted for him.

He rolled the corpse off his shins, and cleaned himself like a cat, contorting his supple back and neck, extending his foot-long tongue to lick off the last of the bloodstains. He unglued triangles of vinyl from his body and threw them away. Satisfied, he got off the bed and pulled on crusader white pants, immodestly tight around crotch and rump, loose as a sailor's below the knee. The dark purple shirt settled on his back and chest, sticking to him where his saliva was still wet. He rattled the cluster of gold chains and medallions – Transylvanian charms, badges of honour and conquest – that hung in the gap between his hand-sized collar-points.

With the white jacket, lined in blood-red silk, Johnny was a blinding apparition. He didn't need a strobe to shine in the dark. Sid raised his knifehand, to cover his eyes. The boy's reaction was better than any mirror.

'Punk sucks,' said Johnny, inviting a response.

'Disco's stupid,' Sid sneered back.

Sid was going to get in trouble. Johnny had to make a slave of the boy, to keep himself out of the story.

He found an unused needle on the bed. Pinching the nipple-like bulb, he stuck the needle into his wrist, spearing the vein perfectly. He let the bulb go and a measure of his blood – of Nancy's? – filled the glass phial. He unstuck himself. The tiny wound was invisibly healed by the time he'd smeared away the bead of blood and licked his thumbprint. He tossed the syrette to Sid, who knew exactly what to do with it, jabbing it into an old arm-track and squirting. Vampire blood slid into Sid's system, something between a virus and a drug. Johnny felt the hook going into Sid's brain, and fed him some line.

Sid stood, momentarily invincible, teeth sharpening, eyes reddened, ears bat-flared, movements swifter. Johnny shared his sense of power, almost paternally. The vampire buzz wouldn't last long, but Sid would be a slave as long as he lived, which was unlikely to be for ever. To become *nosferatu*, you had to give and receive blood; for centuries, most mortals had merely been giving; here, a fresh compact between the warm and the undead was being invented.

Johnny nodded towards the empty thing on the bed. Nobody's blood was any good to her now. He willed the command through the line, through the hook, into Sid's brain. The boy, briefly possessed, leaped across the room, landing on his knees on the bed, and stuck his knife into the already dead girl, messing up the wounds on her throat, tearing open her skin in dozens of places. As he slashed, Sid snarled, black fangs splitting his gums.

Johnny let himself out of the room.

They were calling him a vampire long before he turned.

At the Silver Dream Factory, the Mole People, amphetamine-swift dusk-til-dawners eternally out for blood, nicknamed him 'Drella': half-Dracula, half-Cinderella. The coven often talked of Andy's 'victims': first, cast-offs whose lives were appropriated for Art, rarely given money to go with their limited fame (a great number of them now truly dead); later, wealthy portrait subjects or Inter/VIEW advertisers, courted as assiduously as any Renaissance art patron (a great number of them ought to be truly dead). Andy leeched off them all, left them drained or transformed, using them without letting them touch him, never distinguishing between the commodities he could only coax from other people: money, love, blood, inspiration, devotion, death. Those who rated him a genius and those who ranked him a fraud reached eagerly, too eagerly, for the metaphor. It was so persistent, it must eventually become truth.

In Swimming Underground: My Years in the Warhol Factory *(1995), supervamp Mary Woronov (Hedy/The Shoplifter, 1965; The Chelsea Girls, 1966) writes: 'People were calling us the undead, vampires, me and my little brothers of the night, with our lips pressed against the neck of the city, sucking the energy out of scene after scene. We left each party behind like a wasted corpse, raped and carelessly tossed aside . . . Andy was the worst, taking on five and six parties a night. He even looked like a vampire: white, empty, waiting to be filled, incapable of satisfaction. He was the white worm – always hungry, always cold, never still, always twisting.' When told that the artist had actually turned vampire, Lou Reed arched a ragged eyebrow and quizzed, 'Andy was* alive?' *In the multitude of memoirs and word or song portraits that try to define Andy Warhol, there is no instance of anyone ever using the adjective 'warm' about him.*

Valerie Solanas, who prompted Andy's actual turning, took superstitious care to shoot him with home-made silver bullets. She tried wrapping .32 ammunition in foil, which clogged the chambers, before resorting to spray-paint in the style of Billy Name (Linich), the silver-happy decorator of the Factory who coffined himself in a tiny back room for two years, coming out only at dead of night to forage. The names are just consonants short of anagrams: Andy Warhola, Wlad Draculya; Valerie Solanas, Van Helsing. Valerie's statement, the slogan of a fearless vampire killer: 'he had too much control over my life.' On the operating table – 4:51 p.m., Monday, 3 June, 1968 – Andy Warhol's heart stopped. He was declared clinically dead but came back and lived on, his vision of death and disaster fulfilled and survived. The stringmeat ghost of the latter years was sometimes a parody of his living self, a walking Diane Arbus exhibit, belly scars like zippers, Ray-Ban eyes and dead skin.

Warhola the Vampyre sloped nosferatu-*taloned through the seventies, a fashion-setter as always, as – after nearly a century in the open in Europe – vampirism (of a sort) at last established itself in America. He had no get, but was the fountainhead of a bloodline. You can still see them, in galleries or* People, *on the streets after dark, in the clubs and cellars. Andy's kids: cloned creatures, like the endless replications of his silk-screen celebrity portraits, faces repeated until they become meaningless patterns of colour dots. When alive, Andy had said he wanted to become a machine and that everybody should be alike. How did he feel when his wishes were coming true? How did he feel about anything? Did he feel? Ever? If you spend any amount of time trying to understand the man and his work, you can't help but worry that he's reaching from beyond the grave and forcing you to become Valerie.*

Consider the signs, the symptoms, the symbols: that pale, almost-albino face, simultaneously babyish and ancient, shrinking like a bucket of salted slugs when exposed to the sun; the sharp or battered black clothes, stiff from the grave; the goggle-like dark glasses, hypnotic black holes where eyes should be; the Slavic monotone of the whispery voice and the pared-down, kindergarten vocabulary; the covert religiosity, the prizing of sacred or silver objects; the squirrelling-away of money and possessions in a centuried lair; even the artificial shocks of grey-white-silver hair. Are these not the attributes of a classical vampire, Dracula himself? Look at photographs taken before or after June 1968, and you can't tell whether he is or isn't. Like the murgatroyds of the 1890s, Andy was a disciple before he became a vampire. For him, turning was dropping the seventh veil, the last chitinous scrap of chrysalis, a final stage in becoming what he had always meant to be, an admission that this was indeed what was inside him.

His whole life had revolved around the dead.

– Kathleen Conklin, 'Destroying Drella', paper delivered at 'Warhol's Worlds', inaugural conference of The Andy Warhol Museum (April 21–23, 1995); revised for publication as 'Warhola the Vampyre' in *Who is Andy Warhol?*, edited by Colin MacCabe with Mark Francis and Peter Wollen (The British Film Institute and The Andy Warhol Museum, 1997).

He stepped out of the Chelsea Hotel onto the sidewalk of West 23rd Street, and tasted New York. It was the dead time, the thick hours before dawn, when all but the most committed night owls were home abed, or at least crashed out on a floor, blood sluggish with coffee, cigarettes or drugs. This was the vampire afternoon, and Johnny understood how alone he was. There were other vampires in this city, and he was almost ready to seek them out, but none like him, of his line.

America was vast, bloated with rich, fatty blood. The fresh country supported only a few ticks that tentatively poked probosces through thick hide, sampling without gorging. By comparison, Johnny was a hungry monster. Minutes after taking Nancy, he could have fed again, and again. He had to take more than he needed. He could handle dozens of warm bodies a night without bursting, without choking on the ghosts. Eventually, he would make children-in-darkness, slaves to serve him, to shield him. He must pass on the bloodline of the Father. But not yet.

He hadn't intended to come to this city of towers, with its moat of running water. His plan was to stick to the film people he had hooked up with in the Old Country, and go to fabled Hollywood on the Pacific. But there was a mix-up at JFK and he was detained in

Immigration while the rest of the company, American passports brandished like protective banners, were waved on to catch connecting flights to Los Angeles or San Francisco. He was stuck at the airport in a crowd of overeager petitioners, dark-skinned and warm, as dawn edged threateningly closer. The Father was with him then, as he slipped into a Men's Room and bled a Canadian flight attendant who gave him a come-on, invigorating himself with something new and wild. Buzzing with fresh blood, first catch of this new land, he concentrated his powers of fascination to face down the officials who barred his way. It was beneath him to bribe those who could be overpowered by force of will.

America was disorienting. To survive, he must adapt swiftly. The pace of change in this century was far more rapid than the glacial shifts of the long years the Father had in his Carpathian fastness. Johnny would have to surpass the Father to keep ahead, but bloodline would tell. Though of an ancient line, he was a twentieth-Century creature, turned only thirty-five years earlier, taken into the dark before he was formed as a living man. In Europe, he had been a boy, hiding in the shadows, waiting. Here, in this bright America, he could fulfil his potential. People took him for a young man, not a child.

Johnny Pop had arrived.

He knew that he had been noticed. He was working hard to fit in, but recognized how gauche he had been a few short weeks ago. On his first nights in New York, he had made mistakes. Blood in the water excited the sharks.

Someone stood on the corner, watching him. Two black men, in long leather coats. One wore dark glasses despite the hour, the other had a slim-brimmed hat with a tiny feather in the band. Not vampires, there was something of the predator about them. They were well armed. Silver shoe-buckles and buttons, coats loose over guns. And their bodies were weapons, a finished blade, an arrow shaft. From inside his coat, the black man in sunglasses produced a dark knife. Not silver, but polished hardwood.

Johnny tensed, ready to fight and kill. He had just fed. He was at his strongest.

The knifeman smiled. He balanced his weapon by its point, and tapped his forehead with its hilt, a warrior salute. He would not attack yet. His presence was an announcement, a warning. He was showing himself. This man had seen Johnny before he was seen. His night-skills were sharp.

Then, the knifeman and his partner were gone. They had seemed to disappear, to step into a shadow even Johnny's night eyes could not penetrate.

He suppressed a shudder. This city was not yet his jungle, and he was exposed here – out on the street in a white suit that shone like a beacon – as he had not been in the Old Country.

The black men should have destroyed him now. When they had a chance. Johnny would do his best to see that they did not get another.

It was time to move on, to join the crowd.

A mustard-yellow taxi cruised along the street, emerging like a dragon from an orange-pink groundswell of steam. Johnny hailed the cab, and slid into its cagelike interior. The seat was criss-crossed with duct tape, battlefield dressings on a fatal wound. The driver, a gaunt white man with a baggy military jacket, looked instinctively at the rear-view mirror, expecting to lock eyes with his fare. Johnny saw surprise in the young man's face as he took in the reflection of an empty hack. He twisted to look into the dark behind him and saw Johnny there, understanding at once what he had picked up.

'You have a problem?' Johnny asked.

After a moment, the taxi driver shrugged.

'Hell, no. A lot of guys won't even take spooks, but I'll take anyone. They all come out at night.'

Behind the driver's gunsight eyes, Johnny saw jungle twilight, purpled by napalm blossoms. He heard the reports of shots fired years ago. His nostrils stung with dead cordite.

Uncomfortable, he broke the connection.

Johnny told the driver to take him to Studio 54.

Even now, this late in the night, a desperate line lingered outside the club. Their breaths frosted in a cloud, and they stamped unfashion-ably shoed feet against the cold. Losers with no chance, they would cajole and plead with Burns and Stu, the hard-faced bouncers, but never see the velvet rope lifted. An invisible sign was on their foreheads. Worse than dead, they were boring.

Johnny paid off the cab with sticky bills lifted from Nancy's purse, and stood on the sidewalk, listening to the throb of the music from inside. 'Pretty Baby', Blondie. Debbie Harry's living-dead voice called to him.

The taxi did not move off. Was the driver hoping for another fare from among these damned? No, he was fixing Johnny in his mind. A man without a reflection should be remembered.

'See you again soon, Jack,' said the white man.

Like the black men outside the Chelsea, the taxi driver was a danger. Johnny had marked him. It was good to know who would come for you, to be prepared. The white man's name was written on his licence just as his purpose was stamped on his face. It was Travis. In Vietnam, he had learned to look monsters in the face, even in the mirror.

The cab snarled to life and prowled off.

Moving with the music, Johnny crossed the sidewalk towards the infernal doorway, reaching out with his mind to reconnect with the bouncers, muscular guys with Tom of Finland leather caps and jackets. Burns was a moonlighting cop with sad eyes and bruises, Stu a trust-fund kid with his own monster father in his head; Johnny's hooks were in both of them, played out on the thinnest of threads. They were not, would never be, his get, but they were his. First, he would have warm chattels; get would come later.

He enjoyed the wails and complaints from losers as he breezed past the line, radiating an 'open sesame' they could never manage. Stu clicked the studded heels of his motorcycle boots and saluted, fingers aligned with the peak of his black leather forage cap with Austro-Hungarian precision. Burns smartly lifted the rope, the little sound of the hook being detached from the eye exciting envious sighs, and stood aside. To savour the moment, Johnny paused in the doorway, knowing the spill of light from inside made his suit shine like an angelic raiment, and surveyed those who would never get in. Their eyes showed such desperation that he almost pitied them.

Two weeks ago, he had been among them, drawn to the light but kept away from the flame. Like some older creatures of his kind, he could not force his way into a place until he had been invited across the threshold. Then, his clothes – found in a suitcase chosen at random from the carousel at the airport – had not been good. Being *nosferatu* was unusual enough to get him attention. Steve Rubell was passing the door, and took note of Johnny's sharp, beautiful face. Possessed of the knack of seeing himself as others saw him, Johnny understood that the owner-manager was intrigued by the vampire boy on his doorstep. But Shining Lucifer himself couldn't get into 54 with a Bicentennial shirt, cowboy boots and black hair flattened like wet sealskin to his skull.

When he came back, the next night, he wore clothes that fit: a Halston suit – black outside in the dark, with a violet weave that showed under the lights – and a Ralph Lauren shirt with fresh bloodstains across the polo player. They still smelled faintly of their previous owner, Tony from Brooklyn. The bouncers didn't even need to check with Steve to let Johnny in, and he took the opportunity, later that night in the back rooms, to lay a tiny smear of his blood on them both, apparently a token of gratitude, actually a sigil of ownership. Johnny was saving them for later, knowing they would be needed.

As he ducked past the curtains and slid into 54, Johnny felt Tony's ghost in his limbs. He had taken much from Tony Manero, whom he had exsanguinated on the Brooklyn Bridge. From the boy, he had caught the blood rhythms that matched the music of the month. Tony had been a dancer; Johnny had inherited that from him, along with his fluffed-up but flared-back hairstyle and clothes that were not just a protective cover but a style, a display.

Tony was with him most nights now, a ghost. The kid had never made it to 54, but he'd been better than Brooklyn, good enough for Manhattan. Johnny thought Tony, whose empty carcass he had weighted and tossed off the Bridge, would be happy that some of him at least had made it in the real city. When the blood was still fresh in him, Johnny had followed its track, back to Tony's apartment, and slipped in – unnoticed by the kid's family, even the fallen priest – to take away his wardrobe, the night-clothes that were now his armour.

He let the music take him, responding to it with all his blood. Nancy's ghost protested, making puking motions at the sound of the disco despised by all true punks. By taking her, Johnny had won a great victory in the style wars. He liked killing punks. No one noticed when they were gone. They were all committing slow suicide anyway; that was the point, for there was no future. To love disco was to want to live for ever, to aspire to an immortality of consumption. Punks didn't believe in anything beyond death, and loved nothing, not even themselves.

He wondered what would happen to Sid.

A man-in-the-moon puppet, spooning coke up his nose, beamed down from the wall, blessing the throng with a 1978 benediction. As Johnny stepped onto the illuminated floor and strutted through the dancers, his suit shone like white flame. He had the beat with his every movement. Even his heart pulsed in time to the music. He smiled as he recognized the song, fangs bright as neons under the strobe, eyes red glitterballs. This was the music he had made his own, the song that meant the most of all the songs.

'Staying Alive', The Bee Gees.

In its chorus, he heard the wail of the warm as they died under his kisses, ah-ah-ah-ah, staying alive. In its lyric, he recognized himself, a woman's man with no time to talk.

His dancing cleared a circle.

It was like feeding. Without even taking blood, he drew in the blood of the crowd to himself, loosening the ghosts of those who danced with him from their bodies. Tulpa spirits stretched out through mouths and noses and attached to him like ectoplasmic straws. As he danced, he sucked with his whole body, tasting minds and hearts, outshining them all. No one came near, to challenge him. The Father was proud of him.

For the length of the song, he *was* alive.

*   *   *

Andrew Warhola was an American – born in Pittsburgh on 6 August 1928 – but his family were not. In The Life and Death of Andy Warhol *(1989), Victor Bockris quotes his statement 'I am from nowhere', but gives it the lie: 'The Warholas were Rusyns who had emigrated to America from the Ruthenian village of Mikova in the Carpathian Mountains near the borders of Russia and Poland in territory that was, at the turn of the century, part of the Austro-Hungarian Empire'. Bockris takes care, introducing early the theme that comes to dominate his biography, to note 'The Carpathian Mountains are popularly known as the home of Dracula, and the peasants in Jonathan Harker's description kneeling before roadside shrines, crossing themselves at the mention of Dracula's name, resemble Andy Warhol's distant relatives.'*

The third son of Ondrej and Julia Warhola grew up in Soho, an ethnic enclave that was almost a ghetto. From an early age, he seemed a changeling, paler and slighter than his family, laughably unfit for a future in the steel mills, displaying talent as soon as his hand could properly hold a pencil. Others in his situation might fantasize that they were orphaned princes, raised by peasant wood-cutters, but the Warholas had emigrated – escaped? – from the land of the vampires. Not fifty years before, Count Dracula had come out of Carpathia and established his short-lived empire in London. Dracula was still a powerful figure then, the most famous vampire in the world, and his name was spoken often in the Warhola household. Years later, in a film, Andy had an actress playing his mother claim to have been a victim, in childhood, of the Count, that Dracula's bloodline remained in her veins, passing in the womb to her last son. Like much else in Andy's evolving autobiography, there is no literal truth in this story but its hero spent years trying to wish it into reality and may even, at the last, have managed to pull off the trick. Before settling on 'Andy Warhol' as his eventual professional name, he experimented with the signature 'Andrew Alucard'.

Julia was horrified by her little Andrew's inclinations. For her, vampires were objects not of fascination but dread. A devout Byzantine Catholic, she would drag her children six miles to the wooden church of St John Chrystostom's on Saline Street and subject them to endless rituals of purification. Yet, among Andy's first drawings are bats and coffins. In the 1930s, as Dracula held court in one of his many exiles, the American illustrated press were as obsessed with vampires as movie stars. There were several successful periodicals – Weird Tales, Spicy Vampire Stories *– devoted almost entirely to their social activities. To look through these magazines, as the child Andy did, is to understand what it is to learn that a party, to which you cannot possibly secure an invitation, is going on after your bedtime. Literally, you had to die to get in. In Vienna, Budapest, Constantinople, Monte Carlo and private estates and castles scattered in a crescent across Europe, vampire kings and queens held court.*

Young Andrew clipped photographs and portraits from the magazines and hoarded them for the rest of his life. He preferred photographs, especially the blurred or distorted traces of those who barely registered on cameras or in mirrors. He understood at once that creatures denied the sight of their own faces must prize portrait painters. He wrote what might be called 'fan letters' to the leaders of vampire fashion: de Lioncourt of Paris, Andrew Bennett of London, the White Russian Rozokov. His especial favourites among the undead, understandably, were the child-vampires, those frozen infant immortals Noel Coward sings about in 'Poor Little Dead Girl'. His prize possession as a boy was an autographed portrait of the martyred Claudia, ward of the stylish de Lioncourt, considered a paragon and an archetype among her kind. He would later use this image – a subscription gift sent out by Night Life – *in his silk-screen,* Vampire Doll *(1963).*

In his fascination with the undead, Andy was in the avant-garde. There were still very few vampires in America, and those American-born or -made tended to flee to a more congenial Europe. There was a vampire panic in the wake of the First World War, as returning veterans brought back the tainted bloodline that burned out in the epidemic of 1919. The lost-generation newborns, who all incubated within their bodies a burning disease that ate them up from the inside within months, were ghastly proof that vampires would never 'take' in the New World. Congress passed acts against the spread of vampirism save under impossibly regulated circumstances. J. Edgar Hoover ranked vampires just below communists and well above organized crime as a threat to the American way of life. In the 1930s, New York District Attorney Thomas Dewey led a crusade against an influx of Italian vampires, successfully deporting coven-leader Niccolo Cavalanti and his acolytes. In the South, a resurgence of the Ku Klux Klan viciously curbed a potential renaissance of interlocked vampire hounforts in New Orleans and throughout the bayou country.

America, like Julia Warhola, considered all vampires loathsome monsters. Yet, as Andy understood, there was a dreadful glamour. During the Depression, glimpses of the high life lived in another continent and by another species seemed enticing. The Hungarian Paul Lukas was the first Hollywood actor to specialize in undead roles, from Scarface *(1932) to* The House of Ruthven *(1937). A few real vampires, even, made it in the movies: Garbo, Malakai, Chevalier Futaine. With the rise of fascism and the Second World War came a trickle of vampire refugees from the Old World. Laws were revised and certain practices tolerated 'for the duration', while Hoover's FBI – constantly nagged by America's witch-hunters Cardinal Spellman and Father Coughlin – compiled foot-thick dossiers on elders and newborns alike. As Nazi eugenicists strove to cleanse his bloodline from the Reich, Dracula himself aligned with the Allies, and a vampire underground in occupied Europe cooperated with the liberating forces.*

When the War was over, the climate changed again and a round of blacklistings, arrests and show trials – notably the prosecution for treason of American-born and -made vampire Benjamin Lathem by Robert F. Kennedy – drove all but those who could 'pass for warm' back to Europe. That was the era of the scare movies, with homburg-hatted government men taking crucifix and stake to swarthy, foreign infiltrators: I Married a Vampire *(1950),* I Was a Vampire for the FBI *(1951),* Blood of Dracula *(1958). Warhol was in New York by now, sketching shoes for ad layouts or arranging window displays for Bonwit Teller's, making a hundred thousand dollars a year but fretting that he wasn't taken seriously. Money wasn't enough for him; he needed to be famous too, as if under the curse described by Fritz Leiber in 'The Casket Demon' (1963) – unless known of and talked about, he would fade to nothingness. Like America, he had not outgrown his vampire craze, just learned to keep quiet about it.*

In 1956, the year Around the World in 80 Days *took the Best Picture Oscar, Andy took an extended trip with the frustratingly unforthcoming Charles Lisanby – Hawaii, Japan, India, Egypt, Rome, Paris, London. Throughout that itinerary, he saw vampires living openly, mingling with the warm, as adored as they were feared. Is it too much to suppose that, in a maharajah's palace or on a Nile paddle-wheeler, spurned by Charles and driven to abase himself before some exotic personage, he was bitten?*

– Conklin, ibid.

'Gee, who is that boy?' asked Andy, evenly. 'He is fantastic.'

Penelope was used to the expression. It was one of Andy's few adjectives. Everyone and everything was either 'fantastic' or 'a bore' or something similar, always with an elongated vowel early on. All television was 'fa-antastic'; World War II was 'a bo-ore'. Vintage cookie tins were 'si-imply wonderful'; income taxes were 'ra-ather old'. Famous people were 've-ery interesting'; living daylight was 'pra-actically forgotten'.

She turned to look down on the dance floor. They were sitting up on the balcony, above the churning masses, glasses of chilled blood on the table between them, at once shadowed enough to be mysterious and visible enough to be recognizable.

There was no point in coming to Studio 54 unless it was to be seen, to be noticed. At tomorrow's sunset, when they both rose from their day's sleep, it would be Penny's duty to go through the columns, reading out any mentions of their appearances, so that Andy could cluck and crow over what was said about him, and lament that so much was left out.

It took her a moment to spot the object of Andy's attention.

For once, he was right. The dancer in the white suit was fantastic. Fa-antastic, even. She knew at once that the boy was like her, *nosferatu.* His look, his style, was American, but she scented a whiff of European grave-mould. This was no newborn, no *nouveau,* but an experienced creature, practised in his dark-skills. Only a vampire with many nights behind him could seem so *young.*

It had to happen. She was not the first to come here. She had known that an invasion was inevitable. America could not hold out forever. She had not come here to be unique, but to be away from her kind, from her former lives. Though she had inevitably hooked up with Andy, she did not want to be sucked back into the world of the undead. But what she wanted meant very little any more, which was as it should be. Whatever came, she would accept. It was her duty, her burden.

She looked back at Andy. It took sharp senses indeed to distinguish his real enthusiasms from his feigned ones. He had worked hard – and it did not do to underestimate this languid scarecrow's capacity for hard work – to become as inexpressive as he was, to cultivate what passed in America for a lack of accent. His chalk-dusted cheeks and cold mouth gave nothing away. His wig was silver tonight, thick and stiff as a knot of foxtails. His suit was quiet, dark and Italian, worn with a plain tie.

They both wore goggle-like black glasses to shield their eyes from the club's frequent strobes. But, unlike some of his earlier familiars, Penny made no real attempt to look like him.

She watched the dancer spin, hip-cocked, arm raised in a disco *heil*, white jacket flaring to show scarlet lining, a snarl of concentration on his cold lovely face.

How could Andy not be interested in another of the undead? Especially one like this.

At least, the dancing boy meant the night wasn't a complete wash-out. It had been pretty standard, so far: two openings, three parties and a reception. One big disappointment: Andy had hoped to bring Miz Lillian, the President's mama, to the reception for Princess Ashraf, twin sister of the Shah of Iran, but the White House got wind and scuttled the plan. Andy's fall-back date, Lucie Arnaz, was hardly a substitute, and Penny was forced to make long conversation with the poor girl – whom she had never heard of – while Andy did the silent act most people thought of as deliberate mystification but which was actually simple sulking. The Princess, sharp ornament of one of the few surviving vampire ruling houses, was not exactly on her finest fettle, either – preoccupied by the troubles of her absolutist brother, who was currently back home surrounded by Mohammedan fanatics screaming for his impalement.

In the car between Bianca Jagger's party at the Tea Rooms and L.B. Jeffries's opening at the Photographers' Gallery, Paloma Picasso rather boringly went on about the tonic properties of human blood as face cream. Penny would have told the warm twit how stupid she was being about matters of which she plainly knew nothing, but Andy was frozen enough already without his faithful vampire companion teeing off someone so famous – Penny wasn't sure what exactly the painter's daughter was famous *for* – who was sure to get his name in *Vanity Fair*.

At Bianca's, Andy thought he'd spotted David Bowie with Catherine Deneuve, but it turned out to be a far less interesting couple. Another disappointment.

Bob Colacello, editor of *Inter/VIEW* and Andy's connection with the Pahlavis, wittered on about how well the Princess was bearing up, and was trying to sell him on committing to an exhibition in the new museum of modern art that the Shah had endowed in Teheran. Penny could tell that Andy was chilling on the idea, sensing – quite rightly – that it would not do well to throw in with someone on the point of losing everything. Andy elaborately ignored Bob, and that meant everyone else did too. He had been delighted to learn from her what 'being sent to Coventry' meant and redoubled his use of that ancient schoolboy torture. There was a hurt desperation in Bob's chatter, but it was all his own fault and she didn't feel a bit sorry for him.

At the Photographers', surrounded by huge blow-ups of war orphans and devastated Asian villages, Andy got on one of his curiosity jags and started quizzing her, Penny, about Oscar Wilde. What had he been like, had he really been amusing all the time, had he been frightened when the wolves gathered, how much had he earned, how famous had he really been, would he have been recognized everywhere he went? After nearly a hundred years, she remembered Wilde less well than many others she had known in the 1880s. Like her, the poet was one of the first modern generation of newborn vampires. He was one of those who turned but didn't last more than a decade, eaten up by disease carried over from warm life. She didn't like to think of contemporaries she had outlived. But Andy insisted, nagging, and she dutifully coughed up anecdotes and aphorisms to keep him contented. She told Andy that he reminded her of Oscar, which was certainly true in some ways. Penny dreaded being recategorized from 'fascinating' to 'a bore', with the consequent casting into the outer darkness.

All her life, all her afterlife, had been spent by her own choice in the shadows cast by a succession of tyrants. She supposed she was punishing herself for her sins. Even Andy had noticed; in the Factory, she was called "Penny Penance' or 'Penny Penitent'. However, besotted with titles and honours, he usually introduced her to outsiders as 'Penelope Churchward, Lady Godalming'. She had never been married to Lord Godalming (or, indeed, anyone), but Arthur Holmwood had been her father-in-darkness, and some vampire aristos did indeed pass on titles to their get.

She was not the first English rose in Andy's entourage. She had been told she looked like the model Jane Forth, who had been in Andy's movies. Penny knew she had only become Andy's Girl of the Year after Catherine Guinness left the Factory to become Lady Neidpath. She had an advantage over Andy's earlier debs, though: she was never going to get old. As Girl of the Year, it was her duty to be Andy's companion of the night and to handle much of the organizational and social business of the Factory, of Andy Warhol Enterprises, Incorporated. It was something she was used to, from her Victorian years as an 'Angel in the Home' to her nights as last governess of the House of Dracula. She could even keep track of the money.

She sipped her blood, decanted from some bar worker who was 'really' an actor or a model. Andy left his drink untouched, as usual. He didn't trust blood that showed up in a glass, and nobody ever saw him feeding. Penny wondered if he were an abstainer. Just now, the red pinpoints in his dark glasses were fixed. He was still watching the dancer.

The vampire in the white suit hooked her attention too.

For a moment, she was sure it was *him*, come back yet again, young and lethal, intent on murderous revenge.

She breathed the name, 'Dracula.'

Andy's sharp ears picked it up, even through the dreadful guff that passed for music these days. It was one of the few names guaranteed to provoke his interest.

Andy prized her for her connection to the late King Vampire. Penny had been at the Palazzo Otranto at the end. She was one of the few who knew the truth about the last hours of *il principe*, though she jealously kept that anecdote to herself. It was bad enough that the memories lingered.

'The boy looks like him,' she said. 'He might be the Count's get, or of his bloodline. Most vampires that Dracula made came to look like him. He spread his doppelgangers throughout the world.'

Andy nodded, liking the idea.

The dancer had Dracula's red eyes, his aquiline nose, his full mouth. But he was clean-shaven and had a bouffant of teased black hair, like a Broadway actor or a teenage idol. His look was as much Roman as Romanian.

Penny had understood on their first meeting that Andy Warhol didn't want to be just a vampire. He wanted to be *the* vampire, Dracula. Even before his death and resurrection, his coven had called him 'Drella'. It was meant to be cruel: he was the Count of the night hours, but at dawn he changed back into the girl who cleared away the ashes.

'Find out who he is, Penny,' Andy said. 'We should meet him. He's going to be famous.'

She had no doubt of that.

*   *   *

Flushed from dancing and still buzzed with Nancy's blood, Johnny moved on to the commerce of the night. The first few times, he had set up his shop in men's rooms, like the dealers he was rapidly putting out of business. Spooked by all the mirrors, he shifted from strip-lit johns to the curtained back rooms where the other action was. All the clubs had such places.

In the dark room, he felt the heat of the busy bodies and tasted ghosts, expelled on yo-yo strings of ectoplasm during orgasm. He threaded his way through writhing limbs to take up his habitual spot in a leather armchair. He slipped off his jacket, draping it carefully over the back of the chair, and popped his cufflinks, rolling his sleeves up to his elbows. His white lower arms and hands shone in the dark.

Burns, on a break, came to him first. The hook throbbed in his brain, jones throbbing in his bones like a slow drumbeat. The first shot of drac had been free, but now it was a hundred dollars a pop. The bouncer handed Johnny a crisp C-note. With the nail of his little finger, Johnny jabbed a centimetre-long cut in the skin of his left arm. Burns knelt down in front of the chair and licked away the welling blood. He began to suckle the wound, and Johnny pushed him away.

There was a plea in the man's eyes. The drac jolt was in him, but it wasn't enough. He had the strength and the senses, but also the hunger.

'Go bite someone,' Johnny said, laughing.

The bouncer's hook was in deep. He loved Johnny and hated him, but he'd do what he said. For Burns, hell would be to be expelled, to be denied for ever the taste.

A girl, in a shimmering fringed dress, replaced the bouncer. She had violent orange hair.

'Is it true?' she asked.

'Is what true?'

'That you can make people like you?'

He smiled, sharply. He could make people *love* him.

'A hundred dollars and you can find out,' he said.

'I'm game.'

She was very young, a child. She had to scrape together the notes, in singles and twenties. Usually, he had no patience for that, and pushed such small-timers out of the way to find someone with the right money, as curt as a bus driver. But he needed small bills too, for cab fare and tips.

As her mouth fixed on his fresh wound, he felt his barb sink into her. She was a virgin, in everything. Within seconds, she was his slave. Her eyes widened as she found she was able to see in the dark. She touched fingertips to her suddenly sharp teeth.

It would last such a pathetically short time, but for now she was a princess of the shadows. He named her Nocturna, and made her his daughter until dawn. She floated out of the room, to hunt.

He drew more cuts across his arm, accepted more money, gave more drac. A procession of strangers, all his slaves, passed through. Every night there were more.

After an hour, he had $8,500 in bills. Nancy's ghost was gone, stripped away from him in dribs and drabs, distributed among his children of the night. His veins were sunken and tingling. His mind was crowded with impressions that faded to nothing as fast as the scars on his milky skin. All around, in the dark, his temporary get bit each other. He relished the musical yelps of pain and pleasure.

Now, he thirsted again.

Vampires show up in the 1950s fashion drawings, if only through coded symbols: ragged-edged batwing cloaks, draped over angular figures; red lipstick mouths on sharp-cheeked black and white faces; tiny, almost unnoticeable, fangs peeping from stretched smiles. These in-jokes are self-criticism, a nervous admission of what had to happen next. To become 'Andy Warhol', the illustrator and window-dresser must die and be reborn as an Artist. Those who accuse him of being concerned only with his earnings – which, to be fair, is what he told anyone who would listen – forget that he abandoned a considerable income to devote all his energies to work which initially lost a lot of money.

Shortly before the Coca-Cola Bottle and Campbell's Soup Can series made him famous, and in a period when he feared he had recovered from one 'nervous breakdown' only to be slipping into another, Warhol did a painting – synthetic polymer and crayon on canvas – of Batman *(1960), the only vampire ever really to be embraced by America. Though justifiably eclipsed by Lichtenstein's appropriations from comic-strip panels,* Batman *is an important work in its own right, an idea seized but abandoned half-finished, the first flash of what would soon come to be called Pop Art. Like much from the period before Warhol hit upon repetition and manufacture as modes of expression, it seems incomplete, childish crayon scribbles across the cowled Bob Kane outline of the classic vampire vigilante. Exhibited at the Castelli Gallery, the work was the first Warhol piece to command a serious price from a private collector – an anonymous buyer on behalf of the Wayne Foundation – which may have encouraged the artist to continue with his personal work.*

During an explosion of creativity that began in 1962 and lasted at least until he was shot, Warhol took a lease on a former hat works at 231 East 47th Street and turned the loft space into the Factory, with the intention of producing Art on a production line. At the suggestion of assistant Nathan Gluck, Warhol seized upon the silk-screen process and ('like a forger'), turned out series of dollar bills, soup cans and Marilyn Monroes. It seemed that he didn't care what his subjects were, so long as they were famous. When Henry Geldzahler, Assistant Curator for 20th Century American Art at the Metropolitan Museum, told him that he should apply himself to more 'serious' subjects, Warhol began his 'death and disaster' series, images of car crashes, suicides and the electric chair. Straddling the trivial and the serious are his vampire portraits: Carmilla Karnstein *(1962),* Vampire Doll *(1963),* Lucy Westenra *(1963). Red-eyed and jagged-mouthed undead faces, reproduced in sheets like unperforated stamps, vivid greens and oranges for skin tones, the series reinvents the nineteenth-century genre of vampire portraiture. The vampire subjects Andy chose shared one thing: all had been famously destroyed. He produced parallel silk-screens of their true deaths: impalements, decapitations, disintegrations. These are perhaps the first great works, ruined corpses swimming in scarlet blood, untenanted bodies torn apart by grim puritans.*

In 1964, Andy delivered a twenty-by-twenty black and white mural called Thirteen Vampires *to the American pavilion at the New York World's Fair, where it was to be exhibited beside work by Robert Rauschenberg and Roy Lichtenstein. Among the thirteen, naturally, was Warhol's first Dracula portrait, though all the other undead notables represented were women. The architect Philip Johnson, who had commissioned the piece, informed Warhol that word had come from the Governor that it was to be removed because there was concern that it was offensive to the God-fearing. When Warhol's suggestion that the portraits all be defaced with burning crosses to symbolize the triumph of the godly was vetoed, he went out to the fair with Geldzahler and another of his assistants, Gerard Malanga, and painted the mural over with a thick layer of undead-banishing silver paint, declaring 'And that'll be my art.' We can only speculate about that lost Dracula portrait, which none of the few who saw it can describe in detail. Which of the many, many images of the King of the Vampires – then, truly dead for only five years – did Warhol reproduce? The most tantalizing suggestion, based on Malanga's later-retracted version, is that for the only time in his entire career as an Artist, Warhol drew on his own imagination rather than copied or reproduced from life. Andy lied constantly, but this is the only occasion when anyone has ever accused him of* making something up.

Warhol's first experiments with film, conducted in real time with the co-opted collaboration of whoever happened to be hanging about in the Factory, are steeped in the atmosphere of vampirism. The camera hovers over the exposed throat of John Giorno in Sleep *(1963) as if ready to pounce. The projection of film shot at twenty-four frames per second at the silent speed of sixteen frames per second gives Giorno's six-hour night a suggestion of vampire lassitude. The flashes of white leader that mark the change of shots turn dirty sheets into white coffin plush, and the death rattle of the projector is the only soundtrack (aside from the comical yawns and angry ticket-money-back demands of any audience members happening upon the film in a real theatre).*

That same year, Warhol shot more explicit studies of vampirism: in Kiss, *a succession of couples osculate like insects unable to uncouple their complex mouth-parts; in* Eat, *Robert Indiana crams his mouth with unidentifiable meats; and* Suck-Job *is an extended (thirty minutes) close-up of the face of a young man who is being nibbled by beings who never intrude into the frame or register on film. For* Suck-Job, *Warhol had arranged with Alex Ford, a real vampire, to 'appear' but Ford didn't take him seriously and failed to show up at the Factory for the shoot, forcing the artist to substitute pasty-faced but warm hustlers dragged off the street.*

When Warhol turned his camera on the Empire State Building in Empire *(1964), it saw the edifice first as the largest coffin in the world, jutting out of the ground as if dislodged by some seismic activity. As night slowly falls and the floodlights come on, the building becomes a cloaked predator standing colossal over New York City, shoulders sloped by the years, head sprouting a dirigible-mast horn. After that, Warhol had fellow underground film-maker Jack Smith swish a cape over Baby Jane Hudson in the now-lost* Batman Dracula *(1964). Only tantalizing stills, of Smith with a mouthful of plastic teeth and staring Lon Chaney eyes, remain of this film, which – as with the silver-coated* Thirteen Vampires *– is perhaps as Andy wanted it. As with* Sleep *and* Empire, *the idea is more important than the artefact. It is enough that the films exist; they are not meant actually to be seen all the way through. When Jonas Mekas scheduled* Empire *at the Film-makers' Co-Op in 1965, he lured Warhol into the screening room and tied him securely to one of the seats with stout rope, intent on forcing the creator to sit through his creation. When he came back two hours later to check up, he found Warhol had chewed through his bonds – briefly, an incarnation of Batman Dracula – and escaped into the night. In the early sixties, Warhol had begun to file his teeth, sharpening them to piranha-like needle-points.*

– Conklin, ibid.

A red-headed vampire girl bumped into her and hissed, displaying pearly fangs. Penelope lowered her dark glasses and gave the chit a neon glare. Cowed, the creature backed away. Intrigued, Penny took the girl by the bare upper arm, and looked into her mouth, like a dentist. Her fangs were real, but shrank as she quivered in Penny's *nosferatu* grip. Red swirls dwindled in her eyes, and she was warm again, a frail thing.

Penny understood what the vampire boy was doing in the back room. At once, she was aghast and struck with admiration. She had heard of the warm temporarily taking on vampire attributes by drinking vampire blood without themselves being bitten. There was a story about Katie Reed and a flier in the First World War. But it was rare, and dangerous.

Well, it used to be rare.

All around her, mayfly vampires darted. A youth blundered into her arms and tried to bite her. She firmly pushed him away, breaking the fingers of his right hand to make a point. They would heal instantly, but ache like the Devil when he turned back into a real boy.

A worm of terror curled in her heart. To do such a thing meant having a vision. Vampires, made conservative by centuries, were rarely innovators. She was reminded, again, of Dracula, who had risen among the *nosferatu* by virtue of his willingness to venture into new, large-scale fields of conquest. Such vampires were always frightening.

Would it really be a good thing for Andy to meet this boy?

She saw the white jacket shining in the darkness. The vampire stood at the bar, with Steve Rubell, ringmaster of 54, and the movie actress Isabelle Adjani. Steve, as usual, was flying, hairstyle falling apart above his bald spot. His pockets bulged with petty cash, taken from the overstuffed tills.

Steve spotted her, understood her nod of interest, and signalled her to come over.

'Penny darling,' he said, 'look at me. I'm like you.'

He had fangs too. And red-smeared lips.

'I . . . am . . . a vampiah!'

For Steve, it was just a joke. There was a bitemark on Adjani's neck, which she dabbed with a bar napkin.

'This is just the biggest thing evah,' Steve said.

'Fabulous,' she agreed.

Her eyes fixed the vampire newcomer. He withstood her gaze. She judged him no longer a newborn but not yet an elder. He was definitely of the Dracula line.

'Introduce me,' she demanded, delicately.

Steve's red eyes focused.

'Andy is interested?'

Penny nodded. Whatever was swarming in his brain, Steve was sharp.

'Penelope, this is Johnny Pop. He's from Transylvania.'

'I am an American, now,' he said, with just a hint of accent.

'Johnny, my boy, this is the witch Penny Churchward.'

Penny extended her knuckles to be kissed. Johnny Pop took her fingers and bowed slightly, an Old World habit.

'You cut quite a figure,' she said.

'You are an elder?'

'Good grief, no. I'm from the class of eighty-eight. One of the few survivors.'

'My compliments.'

He let her hand go. He had a tall drink on the bar, blood concentrate. He would need to get his blood count up, to judge by all his fluttering get.

Some fellow rose off the dance floor on ungainly, short-lived leather wings. He made it a few feet into the air, flapping furiously. Then there was a ripping and he collapsed onto the rest of the crowd, yelling and bleeding.

Johnny smiled and raised his glass to her.

She would have to think about this development.

'My friend Andy would like to meet you, Johnny.'

Steve was delighted, and slapped Johnny on the arm.

'Andy Warhol is the Vampire Queen of New York City,' he said. 'You have arrived, my deah!'

Johnny wasn't impressed. Or was trying hard not to be.

Politely, he said 'Miss Churchward, I should like to meet your friend Mr Warhol.'

So, this ash-faced creature was coven master of New York. Johnny had seen Andy Warhol before, here and at the Mudd Club, and knew who he was, the man who painted soup cans and made the dirty movies. He hadn't known Warhol was a vampire, but now it was pointed out, it seemed obvious. What else could such a person be?

Warhol was not an elder but he was unreadable, beyond Johnny's experience. He would have to be careful, to pay proper homage to this master. It would not do to excite the enmity of the city's few other vampires; at least, not yet. Warhol's woman – consort? mistress? slave? – was intriguing, too. She danced on the edge of hostility, radiating prickly suspicion, but he had a hook of a kind in her too. Born to follow, she would trot after him as faithfully as she followed her artist master. He had met her kind before, stranded out of their time, trying to make a way in the world rather than reshape it to suit themselves. It would not do to underestimate her.

'Gee,' Warhol said, 'you must come to the Factory. There are things you could do.'

Johnny didn't doubt it.

Steve made a sign and a photographer appeared. Johnny noticed Penelope edging out of shot just before the flash went off. Andy, Steve and Johnny were caught in the bleached corner. Steve, grinning with his fresh teeth.

'Say, Johnny,' Steve said, 'we will show up, won't we? I mean, I've still got my image.'

Johnny shrugged. He had no idea whether the drac suck Steve had taken earlier would affect his reflection. That had as much to do with Nancy as him.

'Wait and see what develops,' Johnny said.

'If that's the way it has to be, that's the way it is.'

It didn't do to think too hard about what Americans said.

'Gee,' mused Andy, 'that's, uh, fa-antastic, that's a thought.'
Within months, Johnny would rule this city.

From 1964 to 1968, Andy abandoned painting – if silk-screen can be called that – in favour of film. Some have suggested that works like Couch *(1964) or* The Thirteen Most Beautiful Boys *(1965) are just portraits that move; certainly, more people caught them as an ambient backdrop to the Exploding Plastic Inevitable than endured them reverentially at the Co-Op. Movies, not films, they were supposed to play to audiences too busy dancing or speeding or covering their bleeding ears to pay the sort of attention required by Hollywood narrative.*

By now, 'Andy's vampire movies' had gone beyond a standing joke – eight hours of the Empire State Building!! *– and were taken seriously by genuine underground film-makers like Stan Brakhage (who considered silent speed the stroke of genius). The Film-makers' Co-Op regularly scheduled 'Warhol Festivals' and word got out that the films were, well,* dirty, *which – of course – pulled in audiences.* Suck-Job *was about as close to vampirism as even the most extreme New York audiences had seen, even if it was silent, black-and-white and slightly out of focus. Isabelle Dufresne, later the supervamp Ultra Violet, saw* Suck-Job *projected on a sheet at the Factory, and understood at once the strategy of incompletion, whereby the meat of the matter was beyond the frame. In* Dead for Fifteen Minutes: My Years With Andy Warhol *(1988), Ultra Violet writes: 'Although my eyes remain focused on the face of the young man receiving the suck job, my attention is constantly drawn to the empty space on the sheet below the screen. I am being visually assaulted and insulted at the same time. It is unnerving: I want to get up and seize the camera and focus it downward to capture the action. But I can't, and that's where the frustration comes in.'*

Ultra Violet also reports that, during that screening, some Factory hangers-on present relieved the frustration by nibbling each other, drawing squeals of pain and streaks of quick-drying blood. Such tentative pretend-vampirism was common among the Mole People, the night-time characters Andy gathered to help make 'his' movies and turned into his private coven in the back room of Max's Kansas City. With no genuine undead available, Andy made do with self-made supervamps, who showed up on film if not at rehearsals: Pope Ondine (who drew real blood), Brigid (Berlin) Polk, Baby Jane Hudson (who had once been a real live movie star), Malanga's muse Mary Woronov, Carmillo Karnstein, Ingrid Supervamp. Brian Stableford would later coin the term 'lifestyle fantasists' for these people and their modern avatars, the goth murgatroyds. Like Andy, the Mole People already lived like vampires: shunning daylight, speeding all night, filing their teeth, developing pasty complexions, sampling each other's drug-laced blood.

The butcher's bill came in early. The dancer Freddie Herko, who appears in Kiss *(1963) and* Dance Movie/Roller Skates *(1963), read in Montague*

Summers's The Vampire: His Kith and Kin *(1928) that those who committed suicide spectacularly enough 'without fear' were reborn as 'powerful vampires'. Just before Hallowe'en 1964, Herko danced across a friend's Greenwich Village apartment, trailing a ten-foot Batman/Dracula cloak, and sailed elegantly out of a fifth-floor window. Having skim-read the Summers and not bothered to form a Pact with the Devil, an essential part of the immortality-through-self-slaughter gambit, Herko did not rise from the dead. When he heard of Herko's defenestration, Warhol was almost irritated. 'Gee,' he sighed, 'why didn't he tell me he was going to do it? We could have gone down there and filmed it.' Herko was just the first of the Warhol death cluster, his personal disaster series: Edie Sedgwick (1971), Tiger Morse (1972), Andrea Feldman (1972), Candy Darling (1974), Eric Emerson (1975), Gregory Battcock (1980), Tom Baker (1982), Jackie Curtis (1985), Valerie Solanas (1989), Ondine (1989). And Warhol himself (1968?). Only Andy made it back, of course. He had to be the vampire they all would have been, even Valerie.*

In 1965, the term 'vampire movies' took on another layer of meaning at the Factory, with the arrivals of Ronald Tavel, a playwright hired to contribute situations (if not scripts) for the films, and Edie Sedgwick, a blue-blood blonde who was, in many ways, Andy's ultimate supervamp. Movies like The Death of Radu the Handsome *(1965), with Ondine as Vlad the Impaler's gay brother, and* Poor Little Dead Girl *(1965), with Edie as the Vampire Claudia, run seventy minutes (two uninterrupted thirty-five minute takes, the length of a film magazine, stuck together), have intermittently audible soundtracks and mimic Hollywood to the extent of having something approaching narrative. Were it not for the incandescent personalities of the supervamps, the beautiful and the damned, these efforts would be more like 'zombie movies', shambling gestures of mimesis, constantly tripping up as the immobile image (Andy had the most stoned Mole Person handle the camera) goes in and out of focus or the walk-on 'victims' run out of things to do and say. Ondine, Edie and a few others understand that the films are their own shot at vampire immortality. With dime-store plastic fangs and shrouds from the dress-up chest, these living beings cavort, preserved on film while their bodies are long in the grave, flickering in undeath. For Andy, the film camera, like the silk-screen or the Polaroid, was a vampire machine, a process for turning life into frozen death, perfect and reproducible. Hurting people was always so interesting, and left the most fabulous Rorschach stain patterns on the sheets.*

Edie cut her hair to match Andy's wigs and took to wearing imitations of his outfits, especially for photographs and openings. They looked like asexual twins or clones, but were really trying to model themselves on that most terrifying denizen of the world of darkness, the old vampire couple. R.D. Laing's study Helga and Heinrich *(1970) suggests that, after centuries together, vampire couples mingle identities, sharing a consciousness between*

two frail-seeming bodies, finishing each other's sentences as the mind flickers between two skulls, moving in on their victims in an instinctive pincer movement. If one partner is destroyed, the other rots in sympathy. Edie would probably have gone that far – she did eventually commit suicide – but Andy was too self-contained to commit anything or commit to anything. He saw her as the mirror he didn't like to look in – his reflection reminded him that he was alive, after all – and would often play the mimic game, patterned after Harpo Marx, with her, triumphantly squirting milk from his mouth or producing a walnut from a fist to show that he was the original and she the copy. When he said he wanted everyone to be alike, he was expressing a solipsist not an egalitarian ideal: everyone was to be like him, but he was still to be the mould.
– Conklin, ibid.

He fed often now, less for sustenance than for business. This one, seized just before sunrise, was the last of three taken throughout a single April night. He had waylaid the Greek girl, a seamstress in the garment district, on her way to a long day's work. She was too terrified to make a sound as Johnny ripped into her throat. Blood poured into his gaping mouth, and he swallowed. He fed his lust, his need. It wasn't just blood, it was money.

The girl, dragged off the street into an alley, had huge, startled eyes. Her ghost was in him as he bled her. She was called Thana, Death. The name stuck in his craw, clogging the lizard stem of his brain that always came alive as he fed. She should have been called Zoë, Life. Was something wrong with her blood? She had no drugs, no disease, no madness. She started to fight him, mentally. The girl knew about her ghost, could struggle with him on a plane beyond the physical. Her unexpected skill shocked him.

He broke the bloody communion and dropped her onto some cardboard boxes. He was exhilarated and terrified. Thana's ghost snapped out of his mind and fell back into her. She sobbed soundlessly, mouth agape.

'Death,' he said, exorcizing her.

Her blood made him full to the point of bursting. The swollen veins around his mouth and neck throbbed like painful erections. Just after a big feed, he was unattractively jowly, turgid sacs under his jawline, purplish flush to his cheeks and chest. He couldn't completely close his mouth, crowded as it was with blocky, jagged fangs.

He thought about wasting Thana, fulfilling the prophecy of her name.

No. He must not kill while feeding. Johnny was taking more victims but drinking less from each, holding back from killing. If people had to be killed, he'd do it without taking blood, much as it went against the Father's warrior instinct that subjugation of the vanquished should be commemorated at least by a mouthful of hot blood. This was America and things were different.

Who'd have thought that there'd be such a fuss about Nancy and Sid? He was surprised by the extensive news coverage of another drab death at the Chelsea. Sid, a slave who could never finger Johnny without burning out his brain completely, was charged with murder. Out on bail, he was remanded back to jail for bottling Patti Smith's brother. On Riker's Island, he found out 'punk' had another meaning in prison. Kicked loose again, he had turned up dead of an overdose, with a suntan that struck witnesses as being unusual for February. It was either down to the political situation in Iran or Johnny's own enterprise: in the weeks when Sid was locked up and kicking, heroin had become infinitely purer, perhaps thanks to Persians getting their money out in drugs, perhaps dealers competing with drac. Because Sid was well-known, the ragged end of his life was picked apart by a continuing police investigation. Loose ends could turn up; someone like Rockets Redglare, who had dealt in Room 100, might remember seeing Sid and Nancy with a vampire on the night of the killing. Johnny had no idea that a singer who couldn't sing would be so famous. Even Andy was impressed by the headlines, and wondered whether he should do a Sid picture to catch the moment.

Johnny knelt by Thana, holding her scarf to her throat wound. He took her hand and put it up to the makeshift dressing, indicating where she should press. In her hating eyes, he had no reflection. To her, he was nothing.

Fine.

Johnny left the girl and looked for a cab.

He had a penthouse apartment now, rent paid in cash every month, at the Bramford, a Victorian brownstone of some reputation. A good address was important. He needed somewhere to keep his clothes, and a coffin lined with Transylvanian dirt. At heart, Johnny was a traditionalist. Andy was the same, prizing American antique furniture – American antique, hah! – and art deco bric-a-brac, filling his town house with the prizes of the past while throwing out the art of the future in his Factory.

Johnny had over $11,500,000 in several accounts, and cash stashes in safe-deposit boxes all over the city. He intended to pay income taxes on some of it, quite soon. In a moment of candour, he had discussed his business with the Churchward woman. She was the only vampire of real experience in the city, besides Andy – who clammed up when asked about feeding, though Johnny knew that he took nips from all his assistants. Johnny and Penelope couldn't decide whether what he did was against the law or not, but judged it best to keep quiet. Selling his own blood was a legal grey area, but assault and murder weren't. He was reluctant to relinquish those tools entirely, but accepted that standards of behaviour in America were ostensibly different from those of his European backwater homeland. It wasn't that assault and murder were less common here than in Romania, but the authorities made more noise about it.

Those like Thana, left alive after his caresses, might argue that his powers of fascination constituted coercion, that he had perpetrated upon them a form of rape or robbery. Statutes against organ-snatching might even be applicable. Penelope said that soon it wouldn't be safe to pick up a Mr Goodbar and suck him silly without getting a signature on a consent form.

The first real attempt to destroy Johnny had come not from the church or the law, but from criminals. He was cutting into their smack and coke action. A couple of oddly dressed black men came for him with silver razors. The iron of the Father rose up within him and he killed them both, shredding their clothes and faces to make a point. He found out their names from the *Daily Bugle*: Youngblood Priest and Tommy Gibbs. He wondered if the black men he had seen outside the Chelsea on the night he met Andy were in with that Harlem crowd. He had glimpsed them again, several times, singly and as a pair. They were virtual twins, though one was further into the dark than the other. The knifeman's partner packed a crossbow under his coat. They would not be so easy to face down.

The Mott Street Triads had found a vampire of their own – one of those hopping Mandarins, bound by prayers pasted to his forehead – and tried feeding and milking him, cooking their own drac. Markedly inferior, their product was exhausted within a month, an entire body gone to dust and sold on the street. Soon, such *nosferatu* slaves, captured and used up fast, would be common. Other vampires would sell their own drac, in America or their homelands. If the craze could take off in New York, then it would eventually trickle down to everywhere.

Johnny had repeatedly turned down offers of 'partnership' from the established suppliers of drugs. A cash payment of $6,000,000 to the Prizzi Family eliminated most of the hassle that his people had been getting on the street. The Harlem rogues were off his case. He could pass for Italian, which meant he was to be respected for the moment. Mafia elders like Corrado Prizzi and Michael Corleone were men of rough honour; younger wiseguys like John Gotti and Frank White, on the rise even as the dons were fading, were of a different stripe. Gotti, or someone like him, would eventually move into drac. By then, Johnny intended to be retired and in another city.

The cops were interested. He had spotted them at once, casually loitering around crime scenes, chatting with dazed witnesses, giving penetrating stares. He had them marked down: the bogus hippie with the woolly vest, the completely bald man with the good suit, the maniac driver in the battered porkpie hat. Like the Father, he knew when to be careful, when to be daring. The police meant nothing in this land. They didn't even have silver bullets like *Securitate* did in the Old Country.

His own children – the dhampires – were busy. With his blood in them, they changed for a while. The first few times, they just relished the new senses, the feel of fangs in their mouths, the quickening of reflexes. Then, red thirst pricked. They needed to assuage it, before the suck wore off.

Apparently, the biting had started in the semi-underground gay clubs, among the leather-and-chains community. Johnny guessed one of the Studio 54 bouncers was the fountainhead. Both Burns and Stu were denizens of those cruising places. Within a few months, the biting had got out of hand. Every week, there were deaths, as dhampires lost control during the red rush, took too much from their lovers of the moment.

The money, however, kept coming in.

In the lobby, already brightening with dawnlight, an unnerving twelve-year-old clacked together two pink Perspex eggs on a string. Johnny understood he was trying to get into the *Guinness Book of Records*. The child was a holy terror, allowed to run loose by his indulgent parents and their adoring circle. More than one resident of the Bramford had expressed a desire to be around when little Adrian Woodhouse 'got his comeuppance', but Johnny knew it would not do to cross the boy. If you intend to live for ever, do not make enemies of children.

He hurried towards the cage elevator, intent on getting out of ear range of the aural water torture.

'Johnny, Johnny . . .'

As he spun around, excess blood dizzied him. He felt it sloshing around inside. Everything was full: his stomach, his heart, his veins, his bladder, his lungs. It was practically backing up to his eyeballs.

The dhampire was cringing in a shrinking shadow.

'Johnny,' she said, stepping into the light.

Her skin darkened and creased, but she ignored it. She had crumpled bills in her hand, dirty money. He could imagine what she had done to get it.

It was the girl he had once called Nocturna. The Virgin of 54. She wasn't fresh any more, in any way.

'Please,' she begged, mouth open and raw.

'Things have changed,' he said, stepping into the elevator, drawing the mesh across between them. He saw her red-rimmed eyes.

'Take it,' she said, rolling the bills into tubes and shoving them through the grille. They fell at his feet.

'Talk to Rudy or Elvira,' he said. 'They'll fix you up with a suck.'

She shook her head, desperately. Her hair was a mess, singed white in patches. She grabbed the grille, fingers sticking through like worms.

'I don't want a suck, I want *you*.'

'You don't want me, darling. You can't afford me. Now, pull in your claws or you'll lose them.'

She was crying rusty tears.

He wrenched the lever and the elevator began to rise. The girl pulled her hands free. Her face sank and disappeared. She had pestered him before. He would have to do something about her.

It wasn't that he didn't do business that way any more, but that he had to be more selective about the clientele. For the briefest of suckles from the vein, the price was now $10,000. He was choosy about the mouths he spurted into.

Everyone else could just buy a suck.

Rudy and Elvira were waiting in the foyer of the apartment, red-eyed from the night, coming down slowly. They were dhampires themselves, of course. The Father had known the worth of warm slaves, his gypsies and madmen, and Johnny had taken some care in selecting the vassals he needed. As Johnny entered the apartment, peeling off his floor-length turquoise suede coat and tossing away his black-feathered white Stetson hat, Rudy leaped up from the couch, almost to attention. Elvira, constricted inside a black sheath dress low-necked enough to show her navel, raised a welcoming eyebrow and tossed aside *The Sensuous Woman*. Rudy took his coat and hat and hung them up. Elvira rose like a snake from a basket and air-kissed his cheeks. She touched black nails to his face, feeling the bloat of the blood.

They proceeded to the dining room.

Rudy Pasko, a hustler Johnny had picked up on the A-train, dreamed of turning, becoming like his master. Jittery, nakedly ambitious, *American*, he would be a real monster, paying everybody back for ignoring him in life. Johnny wasn't comfortable with Rudy's focused needs, but, for the moment, he had his uses.

Elvira, this year's complete Drac Hag, was a better bet for immortality. She knew when to run cool or hot, and took care to keep a part of herself back, even while snuffing mountains of drac and chewing on any youth who happened to be passing. She liked to snack on gay men, claiming – with her usual dreadful wordplay – that they had better taste than straights did. Andy had passed her on, from the Factory.

The money was on the polished oak dining table, in attaché cases. It had already been counted, but Johnny sat down and did it again. Rudy called him 'the Count', almost mockingly. The boy didn't understand; the money wasn't Johnny's until it was counted. The obsessive-compulsive thing was a trick of the Dracula bloodline. Some degenerate, mountain-dwelling distant cousins could be distracted from their prey by a handful of pumpkin seeds, unable to pass by without counting every one. That was absurd, this was important. Andy understood about money, why it was essential not for what it could buy but in itself. Numbers were beautiful.

Johnny's fingers were so sensitive that he could make the count just by riffling the bundles, by caressing the cash. He picked out the dirty bills, the torn or taped or stained notes, and tossed them to Rudy.

There was $158,591 on the table, a fair night's takings. His personal rake would be an even $100,000.

'Where does the ninety-one dollars come from, Rudy?'

The boy shrugged. The non-negotiable price of a suck was $500. There shouldn't be looser change floating around.

'Boys and girls have expenses,' Rudy said.

'They are not to dip into the till,' Johnny said, using an expression he had recently learned. 'They are to hand over the takings. If they have expenses, they must ask you to cover them. You have enough for all eventualities, have you not?'

Rudy looked at the heap of messy bills and nodded. He had to be reminded of his hook sometimes.

'Now, things must be taken care of.'

Rudy followed him into the reception room. The heart of the penthouse, the reception room was windowless but with an expanse of glass ceiling. Just now, with the sun rising, the skylight was curtained by a rolling metal blind drawn by a hand-cranked winch.

There was no furniture, and the hardwood floor was protected by a plastic sheet. It was Rudy's duty to get the room ready for Johnny by dawn. He had laid out shallow metal trays in rows, like seedbeds in a nursery.

Johnny undid his fly and carefully pissed blood onto the first tray. The pool spread, until it lapped against the sides. He paused his flow, and proceeded to the next tray, and the next. In all, he filled thirty-seven trays, each to a depth of about a quarter of an inch. He lost his bloat, face smoothing and tightening, clothes hanging properly again.

Johnny watched from the doorway as Rudy worked the winch,

rolling the blind. Rays of light speared down through the glass ceiling, falling heavily on the trays. Morning sun was the best, the purest. The trays smoked slightly, like vats of tomato soup on griddles. There was a smell that he found offensive, but which the warm – even dhampires – could not distinguish. Like an elder exposed to merciless daylight, the blood was turning to granulated material. Within a few hours, it would all be red dust, like the sands of Mars. Drac.

In the afternoon, as he slept in his white satin-lined coffin, a troop of good Catholic boys whose fear of Johnny was stronger than the bloodhooks in their brains came to the apartment and, under Elvira's supervision, worked on the trays, scooping up and measuring out the powdered blood into foil twists ('sucks' or 'jabs') that retailed for $500 each. After sunset, the boys (and a few girls) took care of the distribution, spreading out to the clubs and parties and street corners and park nooks where the dhampires hung out.

Known on the street as drac or bat's blood, the powder could be snuffed, swallowed, smoked or heated to liquid and injected. With a fresh user, the effect lasted the hours of the night and was burned out of the system at sunrise. After a few weeks, the customer was properly hooked, a dhampire, and needed three or four sucks a night to keep sharp. No one knew about long-term effects yet, though serious dhampires like Nocturna were prone to severe sunburn and even showed signs of being susceptible to spontaneous combustion. Besides a red thirst for a gulp or two of blood, the dhampire also had a need, of course, to raise cash to feel the habit. Johnny didn't care much about that side of the business, but the *Daily Bugle* had run editorials about the rise in mugging, minor burglary, car crime and other petty fund-raising activities.

Thus far, Johnny was sole supplier of the quality stuff. During their short-lived venture, the Triads had cut their dwindling drac with cayenne pepper, tomato paste and powdered catshit. The Good Catholics were all dhampires themselves, though he kicked them out and cut them off if they exceeded their prescribed dosage – which kept them scrupulously honest about cash. His major expenses were kickbacks to the Families, club owners, bouncers, street cops and other mildly interested parties.

Johnny Pop would be out of the business soon. He was greedy for more than money. Andy had impressed on him the importance of being famous.

Warhol and Tavel made Veneer *(1965), the first film version of Bram Stoker's* Dracula *(1897). In* Stargazer: Andy Warhol's World and His

Films *(1973)*, *Stephen Koch reports:* 'Warhol handed Tavel a copy of the novel with the remark that it might be easier to compose a scenario based on fiction than one spun out of pure fantasy. He had acquired the rights to the Stoker book for $3,000, he said; it ought to make a good movie. And so it did. It's not hard to guess why Warhol was impressed by Dracula. (I should mention in passing that, contrary to the myth he propagates, Warhol is quite widely read.) The book is filled with the sexuality of violence; it features a tough, erotic vampire dandy joyously dominating a gang of freaks; its theme is humiliation within a world that is simultaneously sordid and unreal; it is a history which at once did and did not happen, a purposeful lie. Finally, there is the question of class . . . I think Warhol participates very deeply in America's best-kept secret – the painful, deeply denied intensity with which we experience our class structure. We should not forget that we are speaking of the son of semi-literate immigrants, whose father was a steelworker in Pittsburgh. Within the terms of his own intensely specialized mentality, Warhol has lived through American class humiliation and American poverty. And Dracula, although British, is very much about the sexuality of social class as it merges with spiritual domination.'

Casting Edie as an ephebic silver-haired Dracula (Drella, indeed), Gerard Malanga as a whip-wielding but humiliated Harker and Ondine as a sly Van Helsing, Warhol populated the Factory's Transylvania and Carfax Abbey (the same 'set', black sheets hung with silver cobwebs) with lost souls. Well before Francis Ford Coppola, Warhol saw that the problems in filming the novel could be sidestepped by force of will. Indeed, he approached the enterprise with a deliberate diffidence that all but ensured this would not be a 'proper' film. Ronnie Tavel at least read half the book before getting bored and typing out a script in his usual three days. Since shooting consisted of a complete run-through of the script as a performance, with breaks only when the magazine ran out, Tavel considered that there ought to be actual rehearsals and that the actors should stoop to learning their lines. Too fearful of confrontation to disagree, Warhol simply sabotaged the rehearsals that Tavel organized and even the shooting of the film by inviting the Press and various parasites to the Factory to observe and interfere, and sending Malanga off on trivial errands or keeping him up until dawn at parties to prevent him from even reading the script (as in the book, Harker has the most to say). Koch, again: 'The sense that making a film was work – that it should involve the concentrated attention of work – was utterly banished, and on shooting day the Factory merely played host to another "Scene"', another party.'

Stoker's intricate plot is reduced to situations. Harker, in black leather pants and Victorian deerstalker, visits Castle Dracula, carrying a crucifix loaned to the production by Andy's mother, and is entertained, seduced and assaulted by the Count (Edie's enormous fangs keep slipping out of her mouth) and his three gesticulating vampire brides (Marie Mencken, Carmillo Karnstein, International Velvet). Later, in Carfax Abbey, Harker – roped to the Factory

Couch – watches as Dracula fascinates and vampirizes Mina (Mary Woronov) in a tango that climaxes with Mina drinking Campbell's Tomato Soup from a can that Dracula has opened with a thumb-talon and which he declares is his vampire blood. Van Helsing appears, with his fearless vampire hunters – Lord Godalming (Chuck Wein), Quincey Morris (Joe Dallesandro), Dr Seward (Paul America) – dragged by Renfield (a young, ravaged Lou Reed), who is leashed like a bloodhound.

Crucifixes, stakes, whips and communion wafers are tossed back and forth in a bit of knockabout that makes some of the cast giggle uncontrollably and drives others – notably, the still-tethered Malanga – to furious distraction. In Tavel's script, as in Stoker's novel, Van Helsing's band corner and destroy Dracula, who was to be spray-painted silver and suffocate, but Ondine is distracted when a girl who happens to be on the couch for no real reason – she seems to be a set-visitor straying into frame – calls him a 'phoney', and Ondine ignores the King Vampire to lash out at this impertinent chit, going for her face with his false fingernails. Ondine's methadrine rant rises in a crescendo, peaks and fades: 'May God forgive you, you're a phoney, Little Miss Phoney, you're a disgusting phoney, get off this set, you're a disgrace to humanity, you're a disgrace to yourself, you're a loathsome fool, your husband's a loathsome fool . . . I'm sorry, I just can't go on, this is just too much, I don't want to go on.' The camera, handled this time by Bud Wirtschafter, tries to follow the unexpected action, and for a few brief frames caught the ghost-white face of Andy himself hanging shocked in the gloom; the removal of this slip is perhaps the only proper edit in any Warhol film made before the arrival of Paul Morrissey. Van Helsing, inconsolable, stands alone and the film runs on and on as he reassembles himself.

Edie, fangs spat out but still regally and perfectly Dracula, gets Wirtschafter's attention by tossing the soup can at him, spattering the lens, and commands the frame, hands on hips, for a few seconds before the film runs out. 'I am Dracula,' she insists, the only line of dialogue taken directly (if unintentionally) from the book. 'I am Dracula,' she repeats, sure of herself for the last time in her life. Stoker had intended to inflict upon Dracula the defeat he eluded in reality, but Edie has dragged Warhol's Dracula movie back to the truth. In the Factory, Drella bests the squabbling Vampire Slayers and reigns for ever.

– Conklin, ibid.

Johnny Pop was certainly the social success of the Summer. He had just showed up at Trader Vic's with *Margaret Trudeau* on his elegant arm. Penelope was not surprised, and Andy was silently ecstatic. An inveterate collector of people, he delighted in the idea of the Transylvanian hustler and the Prime Minister's ex getting together. Margaux Hemingway would be furious; she had confided in Andy and Penny that she thought it was serious with Johnny. Penny could have told her what was serious with Johnny, but she didn't think any warm woman would understand.

From across the room, as everyone turned to look at the couple, Penny observed Johnny, realizing again why no one else saw him as she did. He had Olde Worlde charm by the bucketful, and that thirsty edge that had made him seem a rough beast was gone. His hair was an improbable construction, teased and puffed every which way, and his lips were a girl's. But his eyes were Dracula's. It had taken her a while to notice, for she had really known *il principe* only after his fire had dwindled. This was what the *young* Dracula, freshly *nosferatu*, must have been like. This was the bat-cloaked creature of velvet night who with sheer smoking magnetism had overwhelmed flighty Lucy, virtuous Mina and stately Victoria, who had bested Van Helsing and stolen an empire. He didn't dance so often now that he had the city's attention, but all his moves were like dancing, his gestures so considered, his looks so perfect.

He had told several versions of the story, but always insisted that he was Dracula's get, perhaps the last to be turned personally by the King Vampire in his five-hundred-year reign. Johnny didn't like to give dates, but Penny put his conversion at somewhere before the Last War. Who he had been when warm was another matter. He claimed to be a lineal descendant as well as get, the last modern son of some bye-blow of the Impaler, which was why the dying bloodline had fired in him, making him the true Son of Dracula. She could almost believe it. Though he was proud to name his Father-in-Darkness, he didn't like to talk about the Old Country and what had brought him to America. There were stories there, she would wager. Eventually, it would all come out. He had probably drained a commissar's daughter and got out one step ahead of Red vampire killers.

There was trouble in the Carpathians now. The Transylvania Movement, wanting to claim Dracula's ancient fiefdom as a homeland for all the displaced vampires of the world, were in open conflict with Ceauşescu's army. The only thing Johnny had said about that mess was that he would prefer to be in America than Romania. After all, the modern history of vampirism – so despised by the Transylvanians – had begun when Dracula left his homelands for what was in 1885 the most exciting, modern city in the world. She conceded the point: Johnny Pop was displaying the real Dracula spirit, not TM reactionaries like Baron Meinster and Anton Crainic who wanted to retreat to their castles and pretend it was still the Middle Ages.

Andy got fidgety as Johnny worked the room, greeting poor Truman Capote or venerable Paulette Goddard, sharp Ivan Boesky or needy Liza Minnelli. He was deliberately delaying his inevitable path to Andy's table. It was like a Renaissance court, Penny realized.

Eternal shifts of power and privilege, of favour and slight. Three months ago, Johnny had needed to be in with Andy; now, Johnny had risen to such a position that he could afford to hold himself apart, to declare independence. She had never seen Andy on the hook this badly, and was willing to admit that she took some delight in it. At last, the master was mastered.

Eventually, Johnny arrived and displayed his prize.

Penny shook Mrs Trudeau's hand and felt the chill coming from her. Her scarlet choker didn't quite match her crimson evening dress. Penny could smell the musk of her scabs.

Johnny was drinking well, these nights.

Andy and Johnny sat together, close. Neither had anything interesting to say, which was perhaps why they needed so many people around them.

Mrs Trudeau frowned, showing her own streak of jealousy. Penny wouldn't be able to explain to her what Andy and Johnny had, why everyone else was superfluous when they were together. Despite the fluctuations in their relationship, they were one being with two bodies. Without saying much, Johnny made Andy choke with laughter that he could never let out. There was a reddish flush to Andy's albino face.

'Don't mind them,' Penny told Mrs Trudeau. 'They're bats.'

'I don't suppose this'd do anything for you,' said the girl from *Star Wars* whose real name Penny had forgotten, cutting a line of red powder on the coffee table with a silver razor blade.

Penny shrugged.

Vampires did bite each other. If one were wounded almost to death, an infusion of another's *nosferatu* blood could have restorative powers. Blood would be offered by an inferior undead to a coven master to demonstrate loyalty. Penny had no idea what, if any, effect drac would have on her and wasn't especially keen on finding out. The scene was pretty much a bore.

Princess Leia was evidently a practised dhampire. She snorted through a tubed $100 bill and held her head back. Her eyes reddened and her teeth grew points.

'Arm wrestle?' she asked.

Penny wasn't interested. Dhampires all had this rush of vampire power but no real idea of what to do with it. Except nibble. They didn't even feed properly.

Most of the people at this party were drac addicts. They went for the whole bit, black capes and fingerless black widow web gloves, Victorian cameos at the throat, lots of velvet and leather, puffy minidresses over thighboots.

Half this lot had dracced themselves up completely for a midnight screening of *The Rocky Horror Picture Show* at the Waverly, and were just coming down, which meant they were going around the room, pestering anyone they thought might be holding out on a stash, desperate to get back up there. There was a miasma of free-floating paranoia, which Penny couldn't keep out of her head.

'Wait till this gets to the Coast,' said Princess Leia. 'It'll be monstrous.'

Penny had to agree.

She had lost Andy and Johnny at CBGB's, and fallen in with this crowd. The penthouse apartment apparently belonged to some political bigwig she had never heard of, Hal Philip Walker, but he was out of town and Brooke Hayward was staying here with Dennis Hopper. Penny had the idea that Johnny knew Hopper from some foreign debauch, and wanted to avoid him – which, if true, was unusual.

She was welcome here, she realized, because she was a vampire.

It hit her that if the drac ran out, there was a direct source in the room. She was stronger than any warm person, but it was a long time since she had fought anyone. The sheer press of dhampires would tell. They could hold her down and cut her open, then suck her dry, leaving her like crushed orange pulp. For the first time since turning, she understood the fear that the warm had of her kind. Johnny had changed things permanently.

Princess Leia, fanged and clawed, eyed her neck slyly, and reached out to touch her.

'Excuse me,' said Penny, slipping away.

Voices burbled in her mind. She was on a wavelength with all these dhampires, who didn't know how to communicate. It was just background chatter, amplified to skull-cracking levels.

In the bedroom where she had left her coat, a Playmate of the Month and some rock 'n' roll guy were messily performing dhampire 69, gulping from wounds in each other's wrists. She had fed earlier, and the blood did nothing for her.

A Broadway director tried to talk to her.

Yes, she had seen *Pacific Overtures.* No, she didn't want to invest in *Sweeney Todd.*

Where had anybody got the idea that she was rich?

That fat Albanian from *Animal House*, fangs like sharpened cashew nuts, claimed that new-found vampire skills had helped him solve Rubik's cube. He wore a black Inverness cape over baggy Y-fronts. His eyes flashed red and gold like a cat's in headlights.

Penny had a headache.

She took the elevator down to the street.

*   *   *

While looking for a cab, she was accosted by some dreadful drac hag. It was the girl that Johnny called Nocturna, now a snowy-haired fright with yellow eyes and rotten teeth.

The creature pressed money on her, a crumpled mess of notes.

'Just a suck, precious,' she begged.

Penny was sickened.

The money fell from the dhampire's hands, and was swept into the gutter.

'I think you'd better go home, dear,' advised Penny.

'Just a suck.'

Nocturna laid a hand on her shoulder, surprisingly strong. She retained some *nosferatu* attributes.

'Johnny still loves me,' she said, 'but he has business to take care of. He can't fit me in, you see. But I need a suck, just a little kiss, nothing serious.'

Penny took Nocturna's wrist but couldn't break the hold.

The dhampire's eyes were yolk yellow, with shots of blood. Her breath was foul. Her clothes, once fashionable, were ragged and gamy.

Penny glanced up and down the street. She could use a cop, or Spider-Man. People were passing, but in the distance. No one noticed this little scene.

Nocturna brought out something from her reticule. A Stanley knife. Penny felt a cold chill as the blade touched her cheek, then a venomous sting. The tool was silvered. She gasped in pain, and the dhampire stuck her mouth over the cut.

Penny struggled, but the dhampire was suddenly strong, juiced up by pure drac. She would make more cuts and take more sucks.

'You're his friend,' Nocturna said, lips red. 'He won't mind. I'm not being unfaithful.'

Penny supposed she deserved this.

But, as the red rush dazed Nocturna, Penny broke free of the dhampire. She dabbed her cheek. Because of the silver, the cut would stay open, perhaps even leave a scar. Penny had too many of those, but this one would be where it showed.

There were people nearby, watching. Penny saw their red eyes. More dhampires, out for drac, out for her blood. She backed towards the lobby, cursing Johnny Pop.

Nocturna staggered after her.

A taxi cab stormed down the street, scattering dhampires. Penny stuck out her hand and flagged it down. Nocturna howled, and flew at her. Penny wrenched open the cab door and threw herself in. She told the driver to drive off, anywhere, fast.

Nocturna and the others hissed at the window, nails scratching the glass.

The cab sped up and left them behind.

Penny was resolved. Penance was one thing, but enough was enough. She would get out of this city. The Factory could run itself. She would leave Andy to Johnny, and hope that they were satisfied with each other.

'Someday a rain's gonna come,' said the taxi driver. 'And wash the scum off the streets.'

She wished she could agree with him.

It is easy to overstate the importance of Nico to Warhol's late sixties work. She was, after all, his first 'real' vampire. Croaking, German and blonde, she was the dead image of Edie, and thus of Andy. Nico Otzak, turned some time in the fifties, arrived in New York in 1965, with her doll-like get Ari, and presented her card at the Factory.

She trailed the very faintest of associations with Dracula himself, having been a fringe member of that last party, in Rome 1959, which climaxed in the true death of the Vampire King. 'She was mysterious and European,' Andy said, abstaining from any mention of the 'v' word, 'a real moon-goddess type.' Like Dracula, she gave the impression of having used up the Old World and moved on, searching for 'a young country, full of blood.'

In Edie: An American Biography *(1982), Jean Stein definitively refutes the popular version, in which the naive, warm American is supplanted by the cold, dead European. Edie Sedgwick was on the point of turning from vampire to victim before Nico's arrival; she had made the cardinal error of thinking herself indispensable, a real star, and Andy was silently irked by her increasing need for publicity as herself rather than as his mirror. She had already strayed from the Factory and towards the circle of Bob Dylan, tempted by more serious drug habits and heterosexuality. Edie was justifiably miffed that the limited financial success of the films benefited only Andy; his position was that she was rich anyway – 'an heiress', one of his favourite words – and didn't need the money, though far-less well-off folk did as much or more work on the films and silk-screens for similarly derisory pay. Edie's self-destruction cannot be laid entirely on Andy and Nico – the Dylan crowd hardly helped, moving her up from amphetamines to heroin – but it is undeniably true that without Warhol, Edie would never have become, in the English expression, 'dead famous'.*

With Nico, Andy finally had his vampire. At the back of their association must have been the possibility – the promise? – that she would turn him, but for the moment, Andy held back. To become someone's get would have displaced him from the centre of his life, and that was insupportable. When he turned, a circumstance that remains mysterious, he would do so through anonymous blood donation, making himself – as usual – his own get, his own creature. Besides, no one could seriously want Nico for a mother-in-darkness; for the rest of her nights, she drew blood from Ari, her own get, and this vampire incest contributed to the rot that would destroy them both.

Andy was especially fascinated by Nico's relationship with mirrors and film. She was one of those vampires who have no reflection, though he did his best to turn her into a creature who was all reflection with no self. He had her sing 'I'll Be Your Mirror', for instance. 'High Ashbury', the oddest segment of *****/* Twenty-Four-Hour Movie *(1966), places Ondine and Ultra Violet either side of an absence, engaged in conversation with what seems to be a disembodied voice. There are signs of Nico's physical presence during the shoot: the displacement of cushions, a cigarette that darts like a hovering dragonfly, a puff of smoke outlining an oesophagus. But the vampire woman just isn't there. That may be the point. Andy took photographs of silver-foiled walls and untenanted chairs and passed them off as portraits of Nico. He even silk-screened an empty coffin for an album cover.*

Having found his vampire muse, Andy had to do something with her, so he stuck her together with the Velvet Underground – a band who certainly weren't that interested in having a girl singer who drank human blood – as part of the Exploding Plastic Inevitable, the club events he staged at the Dom on St Mark's Place in 1966. Amid so much black leather, he dressed Nico in bone white and put an angelic spotlight on her, especially when she wasn't singing. Lou Reed bought a crucifix, and started looking for a way out. The success of the EPI may well have been partially down to a wide cross-section of New Yorkers who were intrigued by Nico; most Americans in 1966 had never been in a room with a vampire, a real vampire. Andy knew that and made sure that, no matter how conveniently dark the rest of the packed club was, Nico was always visible, always the red-eyed wraith murmuring her way through 'Femme Fatale' without taking a breath. That song, of course, is a promise and a threat: 'Think of her at nights, feel the way she bites . . .'

As the Velvets performed, Warhol hid in the rafters like the Phantom of the Opera, working the lights and the projectors, cranking up the sound. Like Ulysses, he filled his ears with wax to get through the night. Behind the band, he screened his films. Often, as his real vampire paraded herself, he would show Veneer, *trying to project Edie onto Nico as he projected himself upon them both.*

Everybody agrees: between 1966 and 1968, Andy Warhol was a monster.
                                                                    – Conklin, ibid.

Johnny was one of the privileged few allowed into Andy's town house to witness the artist's levée. At high summer, it was impractical to wait for sundown before venturing out – so Johnny had to be ferried the short distance from the Bramford to East 66th St in a sleek limo with Polaroid windows and hustle under a parasol up to the door of Number 57.

With the Churchward woman's desertion, there was a blip in the smooth running of Andy's social life and he was casting around for a replacement Girl of the Year. Johnny was wary of being impressed into taking on too many of Penny Penitent's duties. There were already so many demands on his time, especially with that mad Bella Abzug whipping the NYPD into a frenzy about 'the drac problem'. It wasn't even illegal yet, but his dealers were rousted every night, and his pay-offs to the Families and the cops ratcheted up every week, which pushed him to raise the price of a suck, which meant the dhamps had to peddle more ass or bust more head to scrape together the cash they needed. The papers were full of vampire murders, and real vampires weren't even suspects.

The two-storey lobby of Number 57 was dominated by imperial busts – Napoleon, Caesar, Dracula – and still-packed crates of sculptures and paintings. Things were everywhere, collected but uncatalogued, most still in the original wrapping.

Johnny sat on an upholstered *chaise longue* and leafed through a male pornographic magazine that was on top of a pile of periodicals that stretched from *The New York Review of Books* to *The Fantastic Four*. He heard Andy moving about upstairs, and glanced at the top of the wide staircase. Andy made an entrance, a skull-faced spook-mask atop a floor-length red velvet dressing gown which dragged behind him as he descended, like Scarlett O'Hara's train.

In this small, private moment – with no one else around to see – Andy allowed himself to smile, a terminally ill little boy indulging his love of dressing-up. It wasn't just that Andy was a poseur, but that he let everyone know it and still found the reality in the fakery, making the posing the point. When Andy pretended, he just showed up the half-hearted way everyone else did the same thing. In the months he had been in New York, Johnny had learned that being an American was just like being a vampire, to feed off the dead and to go on and on and on, making a virtue of unoriginality, waxing a corpse-face to beauty. In a country of surfaces, no one cared about the rot that lay beneath the smile, the shine and the dollar. After the persecutions of Europe, it was an enormous relief.

Andy extended a long-nailed hand at an occasional table beside the *chaise longue*. It was heaped with the night's invitations, more parties and openings and galas than even Andy could hit before dawn.

'Choose,' he said.

Johnny took a handful of cards, and summarized them for Andy's approval or rejection. Shakespeare in the Park, Paul Toombs in *Timon of Athens* ('Gee, misa-anthropy'). A charity ball for some new wasting disease ('Gee, sa-ad'). An Anders Wolleck exhibit of metal sculptures ('Gee, fa-abulous'). A premiere for the latest Steven Spielberg film, *1941* ('Gee, wo-onderful'). A screening at Max's Kansas City of a work in progress by Scott and Beth B, starring Lydia

Lunch and Teenage Jesus ('Gee, u-underground'). A nightclub act by Divine ('Gee, na-aughty'). Parties by and for John Lennon, Tony Perkins ('Ugh, *Psycho*'), Richard Hell and Tom Verlaine, Jonathan and Jennifer Hart ('Ick!'), Blondie ('The cartoon character or the band?'), Malcolm McLaren ('Be-est not'), David JoHansen, Edgar Allan Poe ('Ne-evermore'), Frank Sinatra ('Old Hat Rat Pack Hack!')

The night had some possibilities.

Andy was in a sulk. Truman Capote, lisping through silly fangs, had spitefully told him about an Alexander Cockburn parody, modelled on the lunch chatter of Warhol and Colacello with Imelda Marcos as transcribed in *Inter/VIEW*. Andy, of course, had to sit down in the middle of the party and pore through the piece. In Cockburn's version, Bob and Andy took Count Dracula to supper at Mortimer's Restaurant on the Upper East Side and prodded him with questions like 'Don't you wish you'd been able to spend Christmas in Transylvania?' and 'Is there still pressure on you to think of your image and act a certain way?'

Johnny understood that the real reason why the supposedly un-flappable artist was upset was that he had been scooped. After this, Andy wouldn't be able to run an interview with Dracula. He'd been hoping that Johnny would channel the Father's ghost, as others had channelled such *Inter/VIEW* subjects as the Assyrian wind-demon Pazuzu and Houdini. Andy didn't prize Johnny just because he was a vampire; it was important that he was of the direct Dracula line.

He didn't feel the Father with him so much, though he knew he was always there. It was as if he had absorbed the great ghost almost completely, learning the lessons of the Count, carrying on his mission on Earth. The past was fog now. His European life and death were faint, and he told varying stories because he remembered differently each time. But in the fog stood the red-eyed, black-caped figure of Dracula, reaching out to him, reaching out through him.

Sometimes, Johnny Pop thought he *was* Dracula. The Churchward woman had almost believed it, once. And Andy would be so delighted if it were true. But Johnny wasn't *just* Dracula.

He was no longer unique. There were other vampires in the country, the city, at this party. They weren't the Olde Worlde seigneurs of the Transylvania Movement, at once arrogant and pitiful, but Americans, if not by birth then by inclination. Their extravagant names had a copy-of-a-copy paleness, suggesting hissy impermanence: Sonja Blue, Satanico Pandemonium, Skeeter, Scumbalina. Metaphorical (or actual?) children-in-darkness of Andy Warhol, the first thing they did upon rising from the dead was – like an actor landing a first audition – change their names. Then, with golden drac running in their veins, they sold themselves to the dhamps, flooding to New York where the most suckheads were. In cash, they were richer than most castle-bound TM elders, but they coffined in camper vans or at the Y, and wore stinking rags.

Andy snapped out of his sulk. A vampire youth who called himself Nothing paid homage to him as the Master, offering him a criss-crossed arm. Andy stroked the kid's wounds, but held back from sampling the blood.

Johnny wondered if the hook he felt was jealousy.

Johnny and Andy lolled on the back seat of the limo with the sunroof open, playing chicken with the dawn.

The chatter of the night's parties still ran around Johnny's head, as did the semi-ghosts he had swallowed with his victims' blood. He willed a calm cloud to descend upon the clamour of voices and stilled his brain. For once, the city was quiet.

He was bloated with multiple feedings – at every party, boys and girls offered their necks to him – and Andy seemed flushed enough to suggest that he had accepted a few discreet nips somewhere along the course of the night. Johnny felt lassitude growing in him, and knew that after relieving himself and letting the Good Catholics go to work he would need to hide for a full day in the refrigerated coffin unit that was his New York summer luxury.

The rectangle of sky above was starless pre-dawn blue-grey. Red tendrils were filtering through, reflected off the glass frontages of Madison Avenue. The almost-chill haze of four a.m. had been burned away in an instant, like an ancient elder, and it would be another murderously hot day, confining them both to their lairs for a full twelve hours.

They said nothing, needed to say nothing.

Valerie Solanas was the founder and sole member of the Society for Killing All Vampires, authoress of the self-published SKAV Manifesto. *In bite-sized quotes, the* Manifesto *is quite amusing – 'enlightened vampires who wish to demonstrate solidarity with the Movement may do so by killing themselves' – but it remains a wearisome read, not least because Valerie never quite sorted out what she meant by the term 'vampire'. Of course, as an academic I understand entirely the impatience she must have felt with what she considered irrelevancies like agenda-setting and precise definitions of abstruse language. In the end, Valerie was a paranoid sociopath, and the vampires were her enemies, all of whom were out to get her, to stand in her way. At first, she didn't even mean* nosferatu *when she referred to vampires, but a certain type of patriarchal oppressor. At the end, she meant everyone else in the world.*

She is in one of the little-known films, I, Vampire *(1967) – mingling briefly with Tom Baker as the vampire Lord Andrew Bennett, and Ultra Violet, the wonderfully-named Bettina Coffin and a Nico-shaped patch of empty screen. She had various grudges against Andy Warhol – he had lost a playscript she'd sent him, he wouldn't publish her book, he didn't make her famous – but no more than any one of a dozen other Mole People. Billy Name has said that he was never sure whether he should kill himself or Andy, and kept putting off the decision.*

 Oliver Stone's Who Shot Andy Warhol? *is merely the culmination of thirty years of myth and fantasy. It bears repeating that the conspiracy theories Stone and others have espoused have little or no basis in fact, and Valerie Solanas acted entirely on her own, conspiring or colluding with no one. Stone's point, which is well taken, is that in June 1968, someone had to shoot Andy Warhol; if Valerie hadn't stepped up to the firing line, any one of a dozen others could as easily have melted down the family silver for bullets. But it was Valerie.*

 By 1968, the Factory had changed. It was at a new location, and Warhol had new associates – Fred Hughes, Paul Morrissey, Bob Colacello – who tried to impose a more businesslike atmosphere. The Mole People were discouraged from hanging about, and poured out their bile on Andy's intermediaries, unable to accept that they had been banished on the passive dictate of Warhol himself. Valerie turned up while Andy was in a meeting with art critic Mario Amaya and on the phone with yet another supervamp – Viva – and put two bullets into him, and one incidentally into Amaya. Fred Hughes, born negotiator, apparently talked her out of killing him and she left by the freight elevator.

 It was a big story for fifteen minutes, but just as Andy was declared clinically dead at Columbus Hospital news came in from Chicago that Robert Kennedy had been assassinated. Every newspaper in America remade their front pages, bumping the artist to 'and in other news . . .'

 Kennedy stayed dead. Andy didn't.

– Conklin, ibid.

The Halloween party at 54 was desperately lavish, and Steve made him Guest of Honour, naming him the Official Spectre at the Feast.

 In a brief year, Johnny had become this town's favourite monster. Andy was Vampire Master of New York, but Johnny Pop was Prince of Darkness, father and furtherer of a generation of dhamps, scamps and vamps. There were songs about him ('Fame, I'm Gonna Live Forever'), he had been in a movie (at least his smudge had) with Andy (Ulli Lommel's *Drac Queens*), he got more neck than a giraffe, and there was a great deal of interest in him from the Coast.

 Cakes shaped like coffins and castles were wheeled into 54, and the Man in the Moon sign was red-eyed and fang-toothed in homage. Liberace and Elton John played duelling pianos, while the monster-disguised Village People – the Indian as the Wolf Man, the Cowboy as the Creature From the Black Lagoon, the Construction Worker as the Frankenstein Monster, the Biker as Dracula, the Cop as the Thing From Another World, the Soldier as the Hunchback of Notre Dame – belted out a cover of Bobby 'Boris' Pickett's 'The Monster Mash'.

The day drac became a proscribed drug by Act of Congress, Johnny stopped manufacturing it personally and impressed a series of down-on-their-luck *nosferatu* to be undead factories.

The price of the product shot up again, as did the expense of paying off the cops and the Mob, but his personal profits towered almost beyond his mind's capacity to count. He knew the bubble would burst soon, but he was ready to diversify, to survive into another era. It would be the eighties soon. That was going to be a different time. The important thing was going to be not drac or fame or party invites, but money. Numbers would be his shield and his castle, his spells of protection, invisibility and fascination.

He didn't dance so much now. He had made his point. But he was called onto the floor. Steve set up a chant of 'Johnny Pop, Johnny Pop' that went around the crowd. Valerie Perrine and Steve Guttenberg gave him a push. Nastassja Kinski and George Burns slapped his back. Peter Bogdanovich and Dorothy Stratten kissed his cheeks. He slipped his half-caped Versace jacket off and tossed it away, cleared a space, and performed, not to impress or awe others as before, but for himself, perhaps for the last time. He had never had such a sense of his own power. He no longer heard the Father's voice, for he *was* the Father. All the ghosts of this city, of this virgin continent, were his to command and consume.

Here ended the American Century. Here began, again, the Anni Draculae.

Huge, lovely eyes fixed him from the crowd. A nun in full penguin suit. Red, red heart-shaped lips and ice-white polished cheeks. Her pectoral cross, stark silver against a white collar, smote him with a force that made him stagger. She wasn't a real nun, of course, just as the Village People weren't real monsters. This was a party girl, dressed up in a costume, trying to probe the outer reaches of bad taste.

She touched his mind, and an electricity sparked.

He remembered her. The girl whose name was Death, whom he had bitten and left holding a scarf to a leaking neck-wound. He had taken from her but now, he realized, she had taken from him. She was not a vampire, but he had turned her, changed her, made her a huntress.

She lifted her crucifix daintily and held it up. Her face was a gorgeous blank.

Her belief gave the symbol power and he was smitten, driven back across the flashing dance floor, between stumbling dancers. Death glided after him like a ballet dancer, instinctively avoiding people, face red and green and purple and yellow with the changing light. At the dead centre of the dance floor, she held her cross up high above her head. It was reflected in the glitterball, a million shining cruciforms dancing over the crowds and the walls.

Johnny felt each reflected cross as a whiplash. He looked around for help.

All his friends were here. Andy was up there on a balcony, somewhere, looking down with pride. And Steve had planned this whole evening for him. This was where his rise had truly begun, where he had sold his first suck, made his first dollars. But he was not safe here. Death had consecrated Studio 54 against him.

Other vampires in the crowd writhed in pain. Johnny saw the shredded-lace punk princess who called herself Scumbalina holding her face, smoking crosses etched on her cheeks and chin. Even the dhampires were uncomfortable, haemorrhaging from noses and mouths, spattering the floor and everyone around with their tainted blood.

Death was here for him, not the others.

He barged through the throng, and made it to the street. Dawn was not far off. Death was at his heels.

A taxi was waiting for him.

Inside the hack, he told the driver to take him to the Bramford.

He saw the nun step out of 54 as the vehicle moved off. He searched inside himself for the Father, willing the panic he had felt to subside. His flight from the party would be remembered. It did not do to show such weakness.

Something was still wrong. What was it?

The nun had shaken him. Had the girl become a real nun? Was she dispatched by some Vatican bureau, to put an end to him? The Church had always had its vampire killers. Or was she working with the Mafia? To evict him from the business he had created, so that the established crime families could claim drac fortunes for their own. Perhaps she was a minion of one of his own kind, a cat's-paw of the Transylvania Movement. At the moment, Baron Meinster was petitioning the UN for support, and TM elders considered Johnny an upstart who was bringing vampirism into disrepute by sharing it so widely.

Throughout the centuries, Dracula had faced and bested enemies almost without number. To be a visionary was always to excite the enmity of inferiors. Johnny felt the Father in him, and sat back in the cab, planning.

He needed soldiers. Vampires. Dhampires. Get. An army, to protect him. Intelligence, to foresee new threats. He would start with Rudy and Elvira. It was time that he gave them what they wanted, and turned them. Patrick Bateman, his young investment adviser, was another strong prospect. Men like Bateman, made vampires, would be perfect for the coming era. The Age of Money.

The taxi parked, outside the Bramford. It was full night, and a thin frost of snow lay on the sidewalks, slushing in the gutters.

Johnny got out and paid off the taxi driver.

Familiar mad eyes. This was someone else he had encountered in the past year. Travis. The man had changed: the sides of his head were shaved and a Huron ridge stood up like a thicket on top of his skull.

The cabbie got out of the taxi.

Johnny could tear this warm fool apart if he tried anything. He could not be surprised.

Travis extended his arm, as if to shake hands. Johnny looked down at Travis's hand, and suddenly there was a pistol – shot out on a spring device – in it.

'Suck on this,' said Travis, jamming the gun into Johnny's stomach and pulling the trigger.

The first slug passed painlessly through him as if he were made of water. There was an icy shock, but no hurt, no damage. An old-fashioned lead bullet. Johnny laughed out loud. Travis pulled the trigger again.

This time, it was silver.

The bullet punched into Johnny's side, under his ribs, and burst through his back, tearing meat and liver. A hurricane of fire raged in the tunnel carved through him. The worst pain of his *nosferatu* life brought him to his knees, and he could *feel* the cold suddenly – his jacket was back at 54 – as the wet chill of the snow bit through his pants and at the palm of his outstretched hand.

Another silver bullet, through the head or the heart, and he would be finished.

The taxi driver stood over him. There were others, in a circle. A crowd of Fearless Vampire Killers. The silent nun. The black man with wooden knives. The black man with the crossbow. The cop who'd sworn to break the Transylvania Connection. An architect, on his own crusade to avenge a family bled dead by dhamps. The ageing beatnik from the psychedelic van, with his smelly tracking dog. A red-skinned turncoat devil boy with the tail and sawn-off horns. The exterminator with the skull on his chest and a flame-thrower in his hands.

This company of stone loners was brought together by a single mission, to put an end to Johnny Pop. He had known about them all, but never guessed that they might connect with each other. This city was so complicated.

The cop, Doyle, took Johnny's head and made him look at the Bramford.

Elvira was dead on the front steps, stake jutting from her cleavage, strewn limbs like the arms of a swastika. Rudy scuttled out of the shadows, avoiding Johnny's eyes. He hopped from one foot to another, a heavy briefcase in his hands. The arrow man made a dismissive gesture, and Rudy darted off, hauling what cash he could take. The Vampire Killers hadn't even needed to bribe him with their own money.

There was a huge crump, a rush of hot air, and the top floor windows all exploded in a burst of flame. Glass and burning fragments rained all around. Johnny's lair, his lieutenants, his factory, a significant amount of money, his coffin of earth. All gone in a moment.

The Vampire Killers were grimly satisfied.

Johnny saw people filling the lobby, rushing out onto the streets. Again, he would have an audience.

The Father was strong in him, his ghost swollen, stiffening his spine, deadening his pain. His fang-teeth were three inches long, distending his jaw. All his other teeth were razor-edged lumps. Fresh rows of piranha-like fangs sprouted from buds he had never before suspected. His nails were poison daggers. His shirt tore at the back as his shoulders swelled, loosing the beginnings of black wings. His shoes burst and rips ran up the sides of his pants.

He stood up, slowly. The hole in his side was healed over, scabbed with dragon scales. A wooden knife lanced at him, and he batted it out of the air. Flame washed against his legs, melting the snow on the sidewalk, burning away his ragged clothes, hurting him not a bit.

Even the resolute Killers were given pause.

He fixed all their faces in his mind.

'Let's dance,' Johnny hissed.

Now Andy was really a vampire, we would all see finally, doubters and admirers, what he had meant all along.

It has been a tenet of Western culture that a vampire cannot be an artist. For a hundred years, there has been fierce debate on the question. The general consensus on many careers is that many a poet or a painter was never the same man after death, that posthumous work was always derivative self-parody, never a true reaction to the wondrous new nightlife opened up by the turning. It is even suggested that this symptom is not a drawback of vampirism but proof of its superiority over life; vampires are too busy being to pass comment, too concerned with their interior voyages to bother issuing travel reports for the rest of the world to pore over.

The tragedies are too well known to recap in detail. Poe reborn, struggling with verses that refuse to soar; Dali, growing ever richer by forging his own work (or paying others to); Garbo, beautiful for ever in the body but showing up on film as a rotting corpse; Dylan, born-again and boring as hell; de Lioncourt, embarrassing all nosferatu with his MOR goth rocker act. But Andy was the Ultimate Vampire before turning. Surely, for him, things would be different.

Alas, no.

Between his deaths, Andy worked continuously. Portraits of Queens and inverted Tijuana crucifixes. Numberless commissioned silk-screens of anyone rich enough to hire him, at $25,000 a throw. Portraits of world-famous boxers (Mohammed Ali, Apollo Creed) and football players (O.J. Simpson, Roy Race) he had never heard of. Those embarrassingly flattering likenesses, impossible to read as irony, of the Shah, Ferdinand and Imelda, Countess Elisabeth Bathory, Victor Von Doom, Ronnie and Nancy. And he went to a lot of parties, at the White House or in the darkest dhampire clubs.

There's nothing there.

Believe me, I've looked. As an academic, I understand exactly Andy's dilemma. I too was considered a vampire long before I turned. My entire discipline is reputed to be nothing more than a canny way of feeding off the dead, prolonging a useless existence from one grant application to the next. And no one has ever criticized elder vampires for their lack of learning. To pass the centuries, one has to pick up dozens of languages and, in all probability, read every book in your national library. We may rarely have been artists, but we have always been patrons of the arts.

Among ourselves, the search has always been on for a real vampire artist, preferably a creature turned in infancy, before any warm sensibility could be formed. I was tempted in my reassessment of Andy's lifelong dance with Dracula to put forward a thesis that he was such a discovery, that he turned not in 1968 but, say, 1938, and exposed himself by degrees to sunlight, to let him age. That would explain the skin problems. And no one has ever stepped forth to say that they turned Andy. He went into hospital a living man and came out a vampire, having been declared dead. Most commentators have suggested that he was transfused with vampire blood, deliberately or by accident, but the hospital authorities strenuously insist this is not so. Sadly, it won't wash. We have to admit it; Andy's best work was done when he was alive; the rest is just the black blood of the dead.

– Conklin, ibid.

Johnny lay broken on the sidewalk, a snow angel with cloaklike wings of pooled, scarlet-satin blood. He was shot through with silver and wood, and smoking from a dousing in flame. He was a ghost, locked in useless, fast-spoiling meat. The Father was loosed from him, standing over his ruin, eyes dark with sorrow and shame, a pre-dawn penumbra around his shoulders.

The Vampire Killers were dead or wounded or gone. They had not bought his true death easily. They were like him in one way; they had learned the lesson of *Dracula*, that only a family could take him down. He had known there were hunters on his track; he should have foreseen they would band together, and taken steps to break them apart as the Father would have done, had done with his own persecutors.

With the New York sunrise, he would crumble to nothing, to a scatter of drac on the snow.

Bodies moved nearby, on hands and knees, faces to the wet stone, tongues lapping. Dhampires. Johnny would have laughed. As he died, he was being sucked up, his ghost snorted by addicts.

The Father told him to reach out, to take a hold.

He could not. He was surrendering to the cold. He was leaving the Father, and letting himself be taken by Death. She was a huge-eyed fake nun.

The Father insisted.

It wasn't just Johnny dying. He was the last link with the Father. When Johnny was gone, it would be the end of Dracula too.

Johnny's right hand twitched, fingers clacking like crabclaws. It had almost been cut through at the wrist, and even his rapid healing couldn't undo the damage.

The Father instructed.

Johnny reached out, fingers brushing a collar, sliding around a throat, thumbnail resting against a pumping jugular. He turned his head, and focused his unburst eye.

Rudy Pasko, the betrayer, the dhampire.

He would kill him and leave the world with an act of vengeance.

No, the Father told him.

Rudy's red eyes were balls of fear. He was swollen with Johnny's blood, overdosing on drac, face shifting as muscles under the skin writhed like snakes.

'Help me,' Johnny said, 'and I'll kill you.'

Rudy had boosted a car, and gathered Johnny together to pour him into the passenger seat. The dhampire was on a major drac trip, and saw the light at the end of his tunnel. If he were to be bitten by Johnny in his current state, he would die, would turn, would be a dhampire no longer. Like all the dhamps, his dearest wish was to be more, to be a full vampire.

It wasn't as easy as some thought. They had to be bitten by the vampire whose blood they had ingested. Most street drac was cut so severely that the process was scrambled. Dhampires had died. But Rudy knew where the blood in him had come from. Johnny realized that his Judas had betrayed him not just for silver, but because Rudy thought that if he spilled enough of Johnny's blood, he could work the magic on his own. In the British idiom that he had learned from Sid, Rudy was a wanker.

They arrived at Andy's town house just before dawn.

If Johnny could get inside, he could survive. It wasn't easy, even with Rudy's help. During the fight, he had shape-shifted too many times, sustained too many terrible wounds, even lost body parts. He had grown wings, and they'd been shredded by silver bullets, then ripped out by the roots. Important bones were gone from his back. One of his feet was lopped off and lost in the street. He hoped it was hopping after one of his enemies.

He had tasted some of them, the Vampire Killers. In Doyle's blood, he found a surprise: the drac-busting cop was a secret dhampire, and had dosed himself up to face Johnny. The knifeman, who had vampire blood in him from a strange birth, had stuffed himself with garlic, to make his blood repulsive.

The blood was something. He was fighting now.

Rudy hammered on Andy's door, shouting. Johnny had last seen Andy at 54, at the party he had left. He should be home by now, or would be home soon. As dawn approached, Johnny felt himself smoking. It was a frosty All Hallows' morn, but the heat building up like a fever inside him was monsoon-oppressive and threatened to explode in flames.

Johnny's continued life depended on Andy having made it home.

The door was opened. It was Andy himself, not yet out of his party clothes, dazzled by the pinking end of night. Johnny felt waves of horror pouring off the artist, and understood exactly how he must look.

'It's just red, Andy. You use a lot of red.'

Rudy helped him into Andy's hallway. The gloom was like a welcoming cool in midsummer. Johnny collapsed on the *chaise longue*, and looked at Andy, begging.

Only one thing could cure him. Vampire blood.

His first choice would have been the Churchward woman, who was almost an elder. She had survived a century and was of a fresh bloodline. But Penny was gone, fleeing the city and leaving them all in the bloody lurch.

It would have to be Andy. He understood, and backed away, eyes wide.

Johnny realized he didn't even know what Andy's bloodline was. Who had made him?

Andy was horrified. He hated to be touched. He hated to give anything, much less himself.

Johnny had no choice. He reached out with what was left of his mind and took hold of the willing Rudy. He made the dhamp, still hopped up on prime drac, grab Andy by the arms and force him across the lobby, bringing him to the *chaise longue* as an offering for his Master.

'I'm sorry, Andy,' said Johnny.

He didn't prolong the moment. Rudy exposed Andy's neck, stringy and chalky, and Johnny pounced like a cobra, sinking his teeth into the vein, opening his throat for the expected gush of life-giving, mind-blasting vampire blood. He didn't just need to take blood, he needed a whole ghost, to replace the tatters he had lost.

Johnny nearly choked.

He couldn't keep Andy's blood down. His stomach heaved, and gouts poured from his mouth and nose.

How had Andy done it? For all these years?

Rudy looked down on them both, wondering why Johnny was trying to laugh, why Andy was squealing and holding his neck, what the frig was going down in the big city?

Andy wasn't, had never been, a vampire.

He was still alive.

Johnny at last understood just how much Andy Warhol was his own invention.

Andy was dying now, and so was Johnny.

Andy's blood did Johnny some good. He could stand up. He could take hold of Rudy, lifting him off his feet. He could rip open Rudy's throat with his teeth and gulp down pints of the dhamp's drac-laced blood. He could toss Rudy's corpse across the lobby.

That taken care of, he cradled Andy, trying to get the dying man's attention. His eyes were still moving, barely. His neck-wound was a gouting hole, glistening with Johnny's vampire spittle. The light was going out.

Johnny stuck a thumbnail into his own wrist and poured his blood into Andy's mouth, giving back what he had taken. Andy's lips were as red as Rita Hayworth's. Johnny coaxed him and finally, after minutes, Andy swallowed, then relaxed and let go, taking his first and final drac trip.

In an instant, as it happens sometimes, Andy Warhol died and came back. It was too late, though. Valerie Solanas had hurt him very badly, and there were other problems. The turning would not take.

Johnny was too weak to do anything more.

Andy, Warhola the Vampyre at last, floated around his hallway, relishing the new sensations. Did he miss being a magnificent fake?

Then the seizures took him and he began to crumble. Shafts of light from the glass around the door pierced him, and he melted away like the Wicked Witch of the West.

Andy Warhol was a vampire for only fifteen minutes.

Johnny would miss him. He had taken some of the man's ghost, but it was a quiet spirit. It would never compete with the Father for mastery.

Johnny waited. In a far corner, something stirred.

He had written his own epitaph, of course. 'In the future, everyone will live for ever, for fifteen minutes.'

Goodbye, Drella. At the end, he gave up Dracula and was left with only Cinderella, the girl of ashes.

The rest, his legacy, is up to us.

– Conklin, ibid.

Rudy could have been a powerful vampire. He rose, turned, full of *nosferatu* vigour, eager for his first feeding, brain a-buzz with plans of establishing a coven, a drac empire, a place in the night.

Johnny was waiting for him.

With the last of his strength, he took Rudy down and ripped him open in a dozen places, drinking his vampire blood. Finally, he ate the American boy's heart. Rudy hadn't thought it through. Johnny spat out his used-up ghost. Sad little man.

He exposed Rudy's twice-dead corpse to sunlight, and it powdered. The remains of two vampires would be found in Andy's house, the artist and the drac dealer. Johnny Pop would be officially dead. He had been just another stage in his constant turning.

It was time to quit this city. Hollywood beckoned. Andy would have liked that.

At nightfall, bones knit and face reforming, he left the house. He went to Grand Central Station. There was a cash stash in a locker there, enough to get him out of the city and set him up on the Coast.

The Father was proud of him. Now, he could acknowledge his bloodline in his name. He was no longer Ion Popescu, no longer Johnny Pop; he was Johnny Alucard.

And he had an empire to inherit.

About the Editor

STEPHEN JONES lives in London. He is the winner of three World Fantasy Awards, three Horror Writers Association Bram Stoker Awards and three International Horror Guild Awards as well as being a fifteen-time recipient of the British Fantasy Award and a Hugo Award nominee. A former television producer/director and genre movie publicist and consultant (the first three *Hellraiser* movies, *Night Life*, *Nightbreed*, *Split Second*, *Mind Ripper*, *Last Gasp* etc.), he is the co-editor of *Horror: 100 Best Books*, *The Best Horror from Fantasy Tales*, *Gaslight & Ghosts*, *Now We Are Sick*, *H.P. Lovecraft's Book of Horror*, *The Anthology of Fantasy & the Supernatural*, *Secret City: Strange Tales of London*, *Great Ghost Stories* and *The Mammoth Book of Best New Horror*, *Dark Terrors*, *Dark Voices* and *Fantasy Tales* series. He has written *Creepshows: The Illustrated Stephen King Movie Guide*, *The Essential Monster Movie Guide*, *The Illustrated Vampire Movie Guide*, *The Illustrated Dinosaur Movie Guide*, *The Illustrated Frankenstein Movie Guide* and *The Illustrated Werewolf Movie Guide*, and compiled *The Mammoth Book of Terror*, *The Mammoth Book of Vampires*, *The Mammoth Book of Zombies*, *The Mammoth Book of Werewolves*, *The Mammoth Book of Frankenstein*, *The Mammoth Book of Dracula*, *The Mammoth Book of Vampire Stories By Women*, *Shadows Over Innsmouth*, *Weird Shadows Over Innsmouth*, *Dancing With the Dark*, *Dark of the Night*, *Dark Detectives*, *White of the Moon*, *Keep Out the Night*, *By Moonlight Only*, *Don't Turn Out the Light*, *Exorcisms and Ecstasies* by Karl Edward Wagner, *The Vampire Stories of R. Chetwynd-Hayes*, *Phantoms and Fiends* and *Frights and Fancies* by R. Chetwynd-Hayes, *James Herbert: By Horror Haunted*, *The Conan Chronicles* by Robert E. Howard (two volumes), *The Emperor of Dreams: The Lost Worlds of Clark Ashton Smith*, *Clive Barker's A-Z of Horror*, *Clive Barker's Shadows in Eden*, *Clive Barker's The Nightbreed Chronicles* and the *Hellraiser Chronicles*. You can visit his website at www.herebedragons.co.uk/jones